The Bells of Bow

Dream On

Gilda O'Neill

arrow books

This edition published by Arrow Books in 2005

Arrow Books
The Random House Group Limited
20 Vauxhall Bridge Road, London SW1V 2SA

Random House Australia (Pty) Limited
20 Alfred Street, Milsons Point, Sydney
New South Wales 2061, Australia

Random House New Zealand Limited
18 Poland Road, Glenfield
Auckland 10, New Zealand

Random House (Pty) Limited
Isle of Houghton, Corner Boundary Road & Carse O'Gowrie,
Houghton, 2198, South Africa

The Random House Group Limited Reg. No. 954009

www.randomhouse.co.uk

A CIP catalogue record for this book
is available from the British Library

Papers used by Random House are natural, recyclable
products made from wood grown in sustainable forests.
The manufacturing processes conform to the environmental
regulations of the country of origin

ISBN 0 09 191101 X

Printed and bound in Great Britain by
Cox & Wyman Ltd, Reading, Berkshire

The Bells
of Bow

For all those London families,
including my own, who put up
with so much, so bravely and
with such good humour.

1

'Shove over then, Babs. Let the dog see the rabbit.'

Babs shuffled sideways on her bottom across the faded brocade of the dressing table stool and perched herself on its very edge, making room for her twin sister Evie to sit down beside her.

Evie took a slow, deep breath. 'Here goes,' she said and, with her eyes tightly closed, she pulled off the knotted turban that had been covering her hair.

'You're mad,' gasped Babs, staring at the reflected multiple images of her twin which were now grinning back at her from the triple-framed looking glass. 'Why d'yer do it? You wait and see, when yer unwind them pipe cleaners, it'll all fall out. Then what'll yer do?'

'Leave off, Babs, don't spoil it for me,' Evie snapped. She studied her image carefully as she began to unwind the make-do curlers from her newly platinum-blonde hair. She tossed a bleach-covered pipe cleaner carelessly into the pink glass tray of the dressing table set. 'It's only a bit of Hiltone,' she said dismissively and ducked her chin to get a better look at the effects of the peroxide on her previously dark brown hair. 'I think it looks great. Why don't you do yours?'

Babs shook her head and blew noisily through her pursed lips. 'No fear,' she said, opening up her mascara compact and then spitting daintily into it. As she pretended to be engrossed with the task of rubbing the little

1

brush back and forth across the gradually softening block of eye make-up, she looked sideways through her lashes at her sister. She couldn't keep quiet any longer. 'I don't think it's me, and anyway,' she added solemnly, 'I'm far too sensible to ruin *my* hair.' Then she spoilt the effect of what she was saying by bursting into laughter. She shoved Evie playfully in the ribs. 'And I think one nutcase in the family's quite enough, thank you very much.'

Evie joined in easily with her sister's laughter. 'Yer not worried about yer hair, Babs,' she said, shoving her back, 'yer just a rotten scaredy-cat.' Then she paused and considered her profile in the mirror. Turning to Babs, she put her hands behind her head and pouted, practising the seductive, glamour-girl pose that she had kept stored in her memory from one of their many visits to the pictures. 'What d'yer think – good, eh?'

'Yer barmy, I told yer.'

'Why don't yer just relax for once? Do something wild.' Evie twisted round and peered at Babs over her shoulder through sultry, narrowed eyes. ''Ere, what d'yer reckon to this one? Betty Grable, eh?'

'Shut up, Evie,' Babs giggled, 'yer'll have me poking the brush in me eye.'

'Mouse,' hissed Evie and got on with unwinding the rest of the pipe cleaners from her shining, shoulder-length hair.

Used to her sister's taunts, Babs ignored the comment and leaning forward, got on with carefully stroking the thick black paste onto her already darkly luxuriant lashes.

'Plug that lamp in, Babs,' Evie demanded, squinting sideways at her reflection.

'What did your last servant die of,' Babs answered almost automatically. 'Overwork?'

'Go on, Babs, don't be mean. I wanna see what it looks like.'

'Yer can see already. And it won't be dark for ages

yet.' She glanced down at the face of her marcasite wrist watch. 'It ain't even half past seven.'

'Babs . . .' Evie whined, and dragged the pale blue lamp, with its chalk base shaped like a sleeping cat, towards her side of the dressing table.

'Aw, all right,' said Babs grudgingly, and bent down to push in the plug. 'Yer've always got to have yer own way,' she mumbled from under the dressing table.

Evie dragged the lamp even closer, as near as the already stretched flex would allow.

'Mind,' Babs warned her. 'Yer'll have the plug out.'

Satisfied that the lamp was close enough to give sufficient light for her inspection, Evie tossed the last pipe cleaner down in front of her and then ran her fingers through her bright blonde halo, smoothing it down into a sleek, bouncy page boy. Looking from her own reflection to that of her sister sitting by her side, she shook her head slowly and said, 'Yer know, Babs, after all this time of looking exactly the same . . . look at us now, chalk and cheese.' She paused. 'Just look at us – completely different.'

Babs put her mascara block down beside the pipe cleaners and, with a frown, compared their reflected images. After a moment's pause she spoke; she sounded confused. 'But we'll always have the same face.' She paused again. 'I reckon it'll take a bit of getting used to, you being blonde. And, d'yer know what, Eve?' she asked, her expression softening into a smile. 'That's the best reason I can think of for me to leave me hair exactly as it is. For the first time in seventeen years, I'm gonna be just me.'

'What you on about?'

'You know, not "twin" or "which one are you?" But just *me*, Babs Bell. I'll probably get called the "dark one" or the "brunette", but at least I won't be just "twin" any more.'

3

A slow smile spread over Evie's face, making a deep dimple appear in the creamy pale skin of her cheek. 'Yer know, Babs, yer've got something there.' She turned her head from side to side, staring into the looking glass. 'It's strange though, innit?'

Babs's likeness gazed back at her sister from the mirror. 'Yeah,' she said. 'But I really like the idea. I think. Mind you, we won't be able to kid the fellers along any more.'

Evie's smile widened into a broad, mischievous grin. 'We've had some laughs doing that though, ain't we?'

'How about when we got caught out that time?' Babs said, her eyes wide at the thought of it. She drew her bottom lip into her mouth, suppressing a giggle. 'When them two blokes realised our dimples was on different sides. Remember? They went crackers.'

Evie laughed out loud. 'Yeah, I remember. What a pair they were. And how about them horrible green trousers that one had on? What a nit. I dunno why they got so upset though. We was only having a laugh.'

'They reckoned we'd made fools out of 'em, I suppose,' said Babs, turning to her sister for a better look at her hair. 'They didn't need much help with that though, did they? Right pair of idiots.' She lifted a lock of Evie's thick, blonded hair and examined it closely. 'Yer'll have to watch it don't break off, yer know, Eve. It's gone a bit dry on the ends here.'

Evie pulled away from her sister. 'Don't start with yer fussing again, Babs. It's what it looks like what matters, and that's the only reason I did it – to look good. When this war starts I mean to look me very best, 'cos I'm really gonna enjoy meself, no matter what.'

Babs's infectious laughter burst out again. 'You enjoy yerself? Well, won't that make a change – I don't think.'

Evie stood up and stretched her arms wide. 'I'm gonna live for today and sod tomorrow. Who knows what might happen – today, tomorrow, next week . . .' Then she sat down again, shoving Babs to the very edge of the seat, and began applying a thick coat of glossy red lipstick to her full, wide mouth. ''Cos the way things are going,' she said through stretched lips, 'it won't be long before the rest of the fellers from round here disappear off into the forces. Then who are we gonna get to take us out, eh? Tell me that.' Evie smacked her lips together and examined the results of her efforts in the mirror. 'I mean to have a few laughs while there's still some blokes left to have a few laughs with.'

Babs pulled out her hankie from the cap sleeve of her dress and wrapped a corner of it round her index finger. 'Hold still,' she said, and dabbed at the edge of her sister's mouth. 'Yer've got a smudge.' Babs leant back and checked Evie's lips. Satisfied that they looked OK, she continued, 'I dunno what yer so worried about, there's plenty of soldiers around. The streets are full of 'em. Yer practically trip over the buggers on the way to work.'

'But for how long?' Evie answered with a sigh as she handed Babs the lipstick. She picked up her gold and black compact and dusted her face with the pale pink powder. 'I don't wanna wind up an old maid like Minnie or Clara, do I? Mind you, at least them two have got each other for company. Say I wound up like Miss Peters, all by meself? I couldn't stand that, Babs, I'd go mad, I just know I would.'

Babs paused with the lipstick inches from her mouth. 'You? An old maid? Yer barmy, you are, Evie Bell. I told yer, yer stone-bonking barmy.'

'Good, though, innit?' chuckled Evie and went cross-eyed, making her twin erupt into another fit of laughter. 'Come on now, girl,' Evie said with mock severity, 'no time for all this mucking about.' She stood up, straight-faced, and smoothed down her brown and cream spotted crepe dress – identical to the one Babs was wearing – over her slim but curvaceous hips. 'If we wanna find ourselves a couple of chaps in the queue to take us in tonight and show us a good time after, we'd better get a move on, or they'll all be spoken for.'

'If it hadn't been for you, I'd have been ready ages ago.' Babs hurriedly applied her lipstick, clicked the cap back onto the tube and stretched across to the bed to pick up her jacket and hat.

She had no need to stand up to reach her things; the front bedroom of number six Darnfield Street was small, exactly like those in all the other houses in Darnfield Street and most of the houses in the other little turnings which led off Grove Road in Bow. Grove Road itself was lined with tall, three-storey houses with spacious basements, which had once been the homes of comfortably off City clerks and artisans. They were now mostly divided into high-ceilinged flats occupied by working-class families who made whatever, often unreliable, living they could from the docks, the local street markets and a variety of struggling factories in the surrounding area. But number six was typical of many of the side streets off Grove Road in having only two small rooms upstairs and two rooms down – the front parlour and the kitchen – plus a stone-floored scullery and a wooden shack of a lavatory out the back. The front bedroom was only just big enough to hold the walnut veneered furniture that their father had bought secondhand the week he and Violet had got married. In the room was crammed a narrow wardrobe, a matching dressing table and stool and a double bed with a salmon pink satin eiderdown that once had been shared by the twins' parents. But their parents no longer slept in the little front bedroom of number six. Ten years ago, Violet, the twins' mum, had left to go down the market and had never returned, preferring to leave her family and spend the rest of her

6

life with a stall holder with a great fat belly but a pocketful of money. The girls now slept in the front bedroom while their dad, Georgie 'Ringer' Bell, slept alone in the back bedroom that the twins had once occupied. And since then, Ringer had been a changed man, everyone said it. The politer neighbours whispered that he was a 'shadow of the fine man he used to be', while the less delicate ones said outright that he had turned into a morose, self-pitying boozer, and that it was his own fault he'd lost his decent, regular job as a driver with the Union Cartage.

'Now don't make no noise,' whispered Eve, creeping out from the bedroom onto the landing. 'We don't wanna wake him. He'll only try and tap us for a few bob.'

'But he's been asleep since this afternoon,' Babs replied, muttering the words under her breath as they stepped gingerly onto the uncarpeted wooden stairway. 'He's bound to be awake by now.'

'Don't bet on it, Babs. From the stench of beer on him when he got back from the pub at dinner time he's sunk enough pints to keep him asleep in that armchair till tomorrow morning.'

'But he'll be sure to wanna know where we're going,' protested Babs.

'D'yer reckon?' asked Evie cynically. 'Won't you ever learn?'

Babs shrugged. 'Well, he might do.'

'If he was interested, which I doubt,' Evie answered her wearily and far more loudly than she'd intended, 'surely even *he* can work out that it's Saturday night. So where'd he think we'd be going?'

'Who's that?' a thick, slurred voice asked from the back kitchen.

'Only us, Dad,' Evie soothed him, all the time moving carefully along the narrow passage which led towards the street door. 'You go back to sleep.'

Just as she reached out to put her hand on the latch, Georgie mumbled something else, this time unintelligible. Evie stopped in her tracks and waited a moment. When there was no more noise from the kitchen, she hissed at Babs, 'Go and see if he's gone back to sleep.'

Babs opened her mouth to object but Evie urged her on with a quick sideways nod of her head. 'Go on, hurry up.'

Babs tutted and crept back down the dim passage, past the closed door to the front room, and stopped by the open doorway of the kitchen. She looked into the little room and saw her father slumped, as usual, in the high-backed carver chair that stood by the gas stove which had been fitted into the old fireplace. His chest rose and fell in time with his coarse, drunken breathing.

Babs went over to him and touched him gently on the hand. 'You all right, Dad?' she asked softly.

Ringer groaned and shifted his large, although no longer muscular frame in the hard wooden seat, but he didn't wake.

'See yer later,' she whispered gently. 'Me and Evie's going to the Troxy. We won't be late.' She bent forward and kissed the sleeping man's forehead.

'Babs.'

On hearing Evie whisper her name, Babs turned round; she gasped and drew back in alarm, taken aback by the sight of her still unfamiliarly blonde sister standing tight-lipped in the kitchen doorway. 'Yer made me jump.'

'Come on,' Evie commanded as she walked back down the passage. 'Leave him. Or we'll never get to the bloody picture palace.'

She stood impatiently by the street door, waiting for Babs to join her. 'And yes, I've got it,' she said, before Babs could ask, holding up the latch key and then dropping it into her handbag which she closed with a snap

8

of the clasp before pulling the door open wide. 'Least it's not raining again tonight.'

'No,' said Babs, looking up at the clear, deepening blue of the late evening sky. 'Thank gawd for that and all. All that rotten rain was really beginning to get me down.'

The twins stepped out from the gloomy passageway of number six into the bright warmth of the August evening and the lively, tight-knit community of Darnfield Street. Next door, at number eight, down towards the blocked canal end of the street, Maudie Peters was using a wet rag to wipe down the stone ledge of her front window.

'Evening, Miss Peters,' they called out, as though they were speaking with a single voice.

'Evening, girls,' she answered, wringing out her cloth into the pail that stood by her side. 'This sun makes everything look so dusty. Still, mustn't complain, it's lovely to have some nice weather for a change.' She looked up at the twins and a smile spread across her face. 'You're looking very glamorous,' she said, wiping her cheek with the back of her hand. 'A new look?'

'Yeah, good, innit?' grinned Evie in reply.

'And you're . . .'

'Evie,' said Babs, then added hurriedly, 'No, I mean *she's* Evie.'

Maudie chuckled. 'It'll make it easier to tell you apart.'

'Like it, do yer, Miss Peters?' Evie asked, turning her head from side to side to give her a better look.

'Very much, Evie. In fact, as always, you both look a picture.'

'Ta,' the twins said in happy unison.

'Have a nice time, girls, must get on.' Maudie Peters returned her attention to her window ledge and her wiping down.

'She ain't bad when she smiles,' said Babs under her breath as she and her twin walked towards the open end of Darnfield Street where it joined Grove Road, the main

9

thoroughfare that stretched from Victoria Park to Mile End.

'Yeah, she's a funny one though,' Evie said, glancing back over her shoulder at Maudie. 'Never seemed like she fitted in round here somehow.' She shook her head in puzzlement. 'Bit of a frump really but still knows when someone looks good. I reckon she could be a bit of a looker herself if she made an effort. Nice though, in her way.'

'Yeah, I like her. How old d'yer reckon she is?'

'Dunno,' said Evie, screwing up her face as she tried to work it out. 'Late thirties? Forty maybe?'

'Don't,' protested the seventeen-year-old Babs, a look of dread in her eyes. 'I hate the thought of getting as old as that.'

'I'm never gonna get old,' Evie said firmly.

'Dozy mare.'

'No, I mean it. I'll always be young at heart, me, no matter how old I am in years. You just wait and see.'

'Prove it then,' Babs dared her, and dragged her sister over to a group of chanting girls who were playing skipping games in the middle of the street with a length of old washing line.

'Give us a go, kids,' said Babs, rubbing her hands eagerly together.

'Here y'are then,' chirped one of the youngsters, pushing a smaller girl out of the way to make room for the twins.

Without another word, Evie and Babs dropped their handbags onto the kerbside and ran and jumped straight into the path of the turning rope. Holding their skirts down with one hand and their hats on with the other, they both skipped while the kids sang out at the tops of their voices:

Underneath the spreading Chestnut Tree
Neville Chamberlain said to me

10

If yer want to get your gas mask free
Then join the bleeding ARP!

Across the road from the Bells' house, Minnie Watts and Clara Thomas, two fine, large late-middle-aged women who lived in the upstairs rooms of number five, stood on their street doorstep enjoying the warmth of the late evening sun, laughing with pleasure at the sight of the twins skipping so enthusiastically.

'Wish we was still young enough,' one of the women called to the twins, tucking her meat-plate sized hands under the front of her enormous cross-over apron.

'And who said yer wasn't, Min?' Evie called back to her as she bounced up and down on the spot in time to the twirling rope. 'Come on. Come over and have a go.'

Minnie and Clara looked at each other. Clara shrugged then nodded. With a chuckle, the two big women waddled over to the laughing youngsters.

Babs and Evie ducked neatly out from the path of the turning rope, making room for Minnie and Clara.

'Yer'll have to slow down while we get in,' instructed Minnie, positioning herself at the ready, her fat, pink tongue stuck between her lips. 'We ain't as young as we used to be.'

Then, laughing and puffing, she and Clara threw themselves into the game.

Babs and Evie clapped and cheered as the two women, huge bosoms bouncing, heaved themselves over the slowly turning rope while the kids recited 'Salt, mustard, vinegar, pepper'.

'We've gotta go now, see yer,' Babs yelled over the shrill children's voices. 'Enjoy yerselves.'

'Yeah, see yer, gels,' gasped Minnie, staggering away from the rope. 'Have a good time.'

Clara, whose tightly waved steel-grey hair hadn't shifted an inch, raised her hand to wave goodbye to the twins. 'Come on, kids,' she wheezed as she joined her friend. 'Me and Min'll turn the rope for you young'uns while you have a go. We've done all the jumping about we can manage for one day.'

Evie and Babs waved back and bent down to pick up their bags from the kerb. As they stood up they were nearly knocked over by two scruffy little boys who darted out from behind the baker's shop and raced past them before disappearing over the wall of the Drum and Monkey, the pub which stood on the opposite corner.

'Jenners?' asked Evie, looking towards the pub wall behind which the boys had vanished.

'Yeah,' Babs nodded. 'Another two. Seem to breed overnight, that family.'

'How many they got now?' Evie pondered as she repositioned her hat and fastened it securely with the long, pearl-topped pin.

'Dunno,' Babs said, shaking her head in wonder. 'I've lost count and yer hardly ever see her to get the chance to ask. Probably too busy with all them kids.'

'I think it'd be funny having more than the two of us, don't you?' Evie mused, linking arms with Babs. 'I never wanted any more brothers or sisters.'

Before the girls had moved more than a couple of steps, the heads of the two tousled-haired boys reappeared over the wall. 'Guess what, gels?' one of them whined pathetically. 'There ain't no empties to nick over here, not a single one.'

'Nellie's probably got 'em all hidden away from thieving little toerags like you two, that's why,' laughed Babs, turning round to face them.

'We was gonna get ourselves fish and taters with the money and all,' snivelled the other boy. 'We're really starving.'

'Yeah, yer look hungry,' said Evie, staring at the rosy-cheeked, chubby-faced child.

12

'Chuck out yer mouldies for us, twins,' he pleaded. 'Go on. Please.'

'Take this for yer cheek, yer pair of villains,' laughed Evie. Taking a couple of coppers from her bag she flipped them towards the boys.

The boys scrambled back over the wall to retrieve the shiny treasure. 'Cor, ta, twin!'

Now Babs was laughing too. 'Twin! I dunno. We'll have to wear labels round our necks till everyone knows which of us is the blonde one.'

'I'd have thought that was quite obvious,' snapped a short and bony elderly woman. Her narrow lips pursed, she moved towards them like a pint-sized sergeant major leading the troops on a parade ground. Trailing several yards behind the woman was an even shorter thin-faced ferret of a man who, apart from his wrinkled old man's face, looked for all the world like a reluctant child being dragged back to school after the summer holidays by his bullying mother. The two were husband and wife, Nobby and Alice Clarke, the couple who lived downstairs from Minnie and Clara at number five.

'Obvious, is it?' asked Babs, hands on hips. 'All right then, which one am I?'

'Don't yer start yer old nonsense with me, my girl,' snapped Alice.

'Bloody hell, twin,' beamed Nobby, as he caught up with his wife. 'What yer gone and done to yerself now?'

Evie flashed him a dazzling, dimpled-pierced smile. 'Like it, do yer, Nobby?'

'Yeah, not half.'

'She's had them crackers in her hair again, Nobby. And bleach this time. Just look at her,' fumed Alice.

'I am, Alice, I am.' Nobby was too busy gawking at Evie to notice Alice's hand come round with a sharp wallop on his ear.

'Oi!' he complained, his face screwed up with pain.

13

Alice's response was to tut loudly and to grab the unfortunate Nobby roughly by the arm. 'I dunno,' she spluttered as she propelled him towards number five. 'Throwing money away on them Jenner kids like it comes off trees and then blonding and waving their hair. Whatever next, eh? Tell me that. That Georgie Bell had better keep an eye on them girls of his or they'll turn out just like their no-good mother. You mark my words if they don't. What a family.' Then she turned back towards the end of the street and, letting go of her husband, she tucked her fists into her waist and bellowed, 'And now where's that Micky got to?'

As if on cue, Micky Clarke, Alice and Nobby's fifteen-year-old grandson, turned into the street at a fast trot. But at the sight of Evie, he pulled up dead and let out a long low whistle.

'Cor!' he said with an enthusiasm as unwisely undisguised as his grandad's had been. 'What a sight for sore eyes.'

Evie winked at him and blew him a kiss. 'Like it?' she asked, flicking her thick bobbed hair back over her shoulder.

With his mouth wide open and his eyes fixed on Evie, Micky stumbled forward, tripped down the pavement and went careering into his nan's arms. 'Blimey, twin,' he breathed, 'you ain't kidding I like it. I thought it was Veronica Lake standing there.'

Evie glowed while Babs sighed, 'We ain't never gonna get to see no film at this rate.'

'Right bloody smashing,' said Micky, still transfixed by the glorious sight of Evie posing before him. 'Bloody smashing.'

'And that's enough of that talk, thank you very much,' Alice snarled and cuffed her grandson round the back of his head even more soundly than she'd walloped her husband.

'Oi, Nan,' Micky complained, rubbing the sting away, 'that bloody hurt, that did.'

'Good, it was meant to. And I mean it, any more of that talk and I'll wash yer mouth out with soap and water, you just see if I don't. And I'll tell yer mother of yer, just for luck.'

'Nan,' whinged Micky, his cheeks flaming from the embarrassment of knowing that the twins were standing there watching the whole shameful pantomime. 'Leave off, Nan. Let go of us.'

With a little lift of his chin, Nobby smiled grimly at the twins. 'Kids, eh?' he sighed for want of something better to say.

'D'yer want a bit of tea?' Alice growled at her grand-son.

'No thanks, Nan, not till I've seen Terry,' Micky answered quietly, still squirming as he tried to release himself from his grandmother's humiliating clutches. But his efforts were in vain; little and old she might have been, but Alice Clarke's grip wouldn't have disgraced an eighteen-stone stevedore.

'And yer can keep away from that sister of his and all,' she snapped.

'Blimey, Nan, what's wrong with Mary Simpkins all of a sudden?'

'Never you mind, me lad. And what did I just tell yer about that mouth o' your'n?'

'Sorry, Nan.' Knowing he was unlikely to get the better of his grandmother, Micky gave in without another word.

'I don't know,' Alice tutted and, shaking her head, pushed Micky away from her in the direction of number four, the Simpkins's house which was across the street next to the baker's. 'Honestly, the way the world is nowadays. It wasn't like this when I was a girl, I'm telling yer. We had a bit of respect for our elders and betters. *And*, when I was thirteen, I didn't have a chest on me like

15

that Mary Simpkins has got on her. Disgusting, I call it, bosoms all over the place.'

Micky tried to muster a little dignity as he crossed the street, but he couldn't resist looking back over his shoulder at his grandad. Micky and Nobby bravely chanced rolling their eyes at one another, and then Micky really took his life in his hands by flashing a crafty wink and a wave at the twins as they turned out of Darnfield Street and into Grove Road.

'I can see yer, Micky,' the twins heard Alice bark at her grandson. 'I won't let this drop, yer know. I'll be telling yer mother on yer, you just see if I don't.'

'Poor kid,' Evie said with a chuckle as they headed towards the Mile End Road. 'Fancy having yer nan showing you up like that.'

'It's your fault, Evie. Yer should know better. Yer shouldn't encourage him.'

'What, me encourage young Micky?' Evie grinned to herself.

'Yes,' replied Babs flatly. 'You. You should leave him alone. He's a good little kid, despite his nan.'

'Yeah, he's all right. So might as well let him dream, eh? Dreaming never hurt no one.'

'No? Well, how about young Mary? It might hurt her all right.'

'What yer on about?'

'Mary Simpkins. She's another good kid, and yer know she's keen on Micky. But how can she hope to compete with you, the bloody blonde bombshell, flirting with her sweetheart?'

'Blimey, Babs, it was just a bit of fun. Why'd yer always have to take things so seriously?'

'And why do *you* always have to think everything's just one big lark?'

Evie pouted at her sister's reprimand. 'I don't.'

'Aw, come on, Evie, don't get a gob on yer.' Babs

affectionately linked her arm through her sister's. 'We've wasted enough time without you showing off. All the blokes'll have gone in as it is. And I bet we've missed the first film. And if we don't get a move on, we won't even get a seat, let alone see the main feature.'

As they dodged across Grove Road through the sparse Saturday evening traffic, Evie tossed back her hair as it tumbled from beneath her little brown felt hat, making it bounce around the wide shoulders of her matching linen swagger jacket. 'It looks all right, don't it, Babs,' she stated more than asked. 'Really suits me.'

'They seem to think so,' her sister answered, nodding back across to the other side of the road.

'Who? Who yer talking about?'

'Them two blokes over there.'

Evie turned and looked over to where Babs was now pointing discreetly, towards the high brick arch that carried the railway line over Grove Road. Two young men, nattily turned out in dark grey suits, white shirts and nifty black trilby hats, were waving at them.

'Don't do that, Eve. Don't wave back,' Babs hissed, horrified by her twin's uninhibited reaction. 'Yer do know who that tall one is, don't yer?'

The taller of the two men took out a cigarette case from his inside pocket and offered it to his companion, all the while keeping his gaze firmly fixed on the twins.

'Course I do,' Evie answered her sister, but she was concentrating her smile on the one with the cigarette case. 'It's that Albie Denham. Come on.'

'Evie!' protested Babs. 'Don't be so stupid. We don't wanna get hiked up with the likes of him. And just look at his mate. From the size of them shoulders, he should be in a cage. Built like a bloody gorilla, he is.'

'Suit yerself,' said Eve with a shrug. 'If yer don't wanna come, I'll catch up with yer later.'

Reluctantly, Babs, as they both knew she would,

17

followed her twin back across the road.

'Hello, girls,' said Albie casually. He drew hard on his cigarette and slowly released a cloud of blue-grey smoke into the still warm evening air. 'Me and Chas here was just going off to maybe have a bit of a dance.'

Evie swung her shoulders from side to side and stared up at him. 'Aw yeah?' she said. 'Hear that, Babs? The boys here're going dancing.'

Babs took a deep breath and said quietly but very deliberately through her teeth, 'We'll miss the film, Eve.'

Evie either didn't hear her sister or else she chose to ignore her. 'Dancing, eh?'

'That's right,' Albie said, grinding out the barely smoked cigarette under the heel of his highly polished black shoe. 'So. D'yer fancy it, then?'

'Fancy what?' asked Eve, all wide-eyed innocence.

'Dancing, of course,' he said, and grinned at his mate. 'Or did yer have something else in mind?'

'Yer out o' luck, I'm afraid,' Evie sighed with a sad little smile. 'Yer see, me and me sister here are going to the Troxy. We love going to the pictures, don't we, Babs?'

'Yeah,' Babs readily agreed. 'We do. We love it. That's why we're going tonight.'

'See?' Evie's voice was full of mock remorse. 'Can't be helped, but I'm sorry, no. Anyway, I don't think some crummy little dance'd interest us, do you, Babs?' She turned to face her sister and they both giggled.

'No, I don't think some crummy little dance'd interest us at all. Thanks all the same.' Babs lifted her chin and smiled triumphantly at Albie Denham. 'Seems like yer gonna have to dance with yer mate. Shame, innit?'

'Yer right, that really is a shame, ain't it, Chas?' Albie turned to his friend and tutted with disappointment, his arms held wide to show his deep regret. 'Yer see, me and Chas wasn't planning to go to no bug house, was we? We

18

was going up West to a little supper club. Have a dance, a nice little bit to eat. Something a bit fancy. Aw, yeah, and we're going in the Riley. Ain't that right, Chas?'

'Yeah,' answered Chas in a gruff, toneless voice. 'In the Riley.'

'Riley, eh?' Evie said slowly, then flashed a sly look at Babs who, in silent reply, raised her eyebrows just enough to show that she had cottoned on to her sister's meaning.

'Yeah, it's a Riley Kestrel, if yer must know.' Chas said it proudly as though the vehicle belonged to him.

'That's a motor car, ain't it?' Evie asked carelessly.

'Certainly is, darling.' Albie curled his fingers over and studied his nails. 'Parked just round the corner in Cordova Road, as a matter o' fact. Not twenty-five yards from this very spot.'

'What yer doing round here then?' Babs asked with her most charming, dimpled smile; the idea of a ride in a motor car suddenly made Albie and his goon of a mate seem worth at least a little bit of effort.

'Apart from looking for pretty gels like you two, yer mean?' Albie said with a wink. 'Me and Chas here have been making calls on one or two of me mum's customers, some people what had a few debts to settle.' Albie reached into his trousers pocket and produced a fat roll of money. 'So I got plenty of loose change for a night out.'

Without another word, Evie let Albie put his arm round her shoulders and guide her towards where the car was parked. Babs walked behind them, with Albie's dim mate, Chas, at her side.

'Been in a motor before, sweetheart?' Chas asked Babs.

'Once or twice,' lied Babs.

'I'm Chas,' he said as they turned off Grove Road into Cordova Road.

'I know,' said Babs, with a disbelieving roll of her eyes.

19

'So Albie said. Several times.'

When they reached the gleaming black motor, Albie opened the front passenger door and gestured for Evie to climb into the expensive smelling interior. 'There y'are, Evie,' he said. 'In yer get, gel.'

'Yer know me name,' Evie said, sounding impressed, despite promising herself to appear nonchalant even if she felt far from it.

'Course I know yer name.'

'How?'

'Well, I'd hardly *not* know the names of two lookers like the Bell twins, now would I?'

Just as Babs had done earlier, Evie treated Albie to the full dimple treatment. 'Yer very kind,' she beamed up at him. 'A right gentleman, but, if yer don't mind, I'll sit in the back with Babs.'

Albie smiled down at her as he pulled open the back door. 'Whatever you say, sweetheart.'

Evie sat down on the soft, leather-covered seat and swung her legs in after her as though to the manner born. Nobody could have guessed as much, but it was a manoeuvre that she had never actually done before; she was just copying the way the film stars did it on the newsreels.

Babs looked questioningly at her sister as she settled down beside her. 'Why ain't yer going in the front?'

'Don't wanna spoil him too soon, now do I?' Evie said.

By the time Albie drew the Riley to a halt outside the canopied doorway of the supper club, the twins were in such a state of excitement that they were finding it increasingly hard to disguise their feelings: not only was it the first time that they had ever been to a West End club but, regardless of what Babs had claimed earlier, it was the first time that either of them had been in a car, let alone in one as flash as a Riley Kestrel.

20

As Albie engaged the handbrake, Evie grasped Babs's hand and whispered, 'Don't let on we've never done none of this before, right?'

'I ain't silly,' Babs answered her, although in fact hardly able to contain herself. 'I ain't gonna muck up a chance like this to enjoy meself, now am I?'

'Bit better than the Troxy, eh, Babs?' Eve said to her sister out of the side of her mouth as Albie reached down to help her from the car.

'You ain't kidding,' Babs whispered back as she held out her hand to Chas and stepped out of the other side of the car.

'Mr Denham, good to see you again, sir.' The grey-haired, scarlet-liveried doorman saluted with military sharpness in response to Albie handing him half a crown. As far as the astonished twins could see, he had given it to the man just for standing there. 'Straight through, sir,' the man added smartly. 'Enjoy your evening.'

The man set the brass and mahogany framed revolving door into motion and waved Albie and his party through into a lobby which led to a subtly lit room humming with the buzz of discreet conversation. A band on a little stage at the far end of the room played the latest swing tunes. The moment the twins' eyes became accustomed to the subdued lighting, they instinctively turned to one another.

'Blimey,' gasped Babs, unable to stop herself gawping. 'Will yer look at this, Eve.'

'Smart, eh?' Albie said with a smug grin which immediately put Babs back on her guard.

'Very nice,' answered Evie, hoping she sounded more relaxed than she felt.

'Glad yer like it,' Albie stated just as nonchalantly.

Babs opened and closed her mouth, frantically trying – and failing – to think of some sophisticated or witty remark. To her relief Albie was distracted by a black-suited waiter appearing at their side. Albie took the wad of money he had flaunted at the girls earlier and, with ostentatious slowness, peeled off one of the notes. 'Make sure yer look after us,' he said without looking at the man. 'I want me guests to enjoy 'emselves.'

The waiter took the money, inclined his head and snapped his fingers at an unseen colleague.

'Here we go, gels,' Albie announced and moved through the crowded room towards the table from which another waiter was removing a disgruntled looking party of six.

The waiter whispered to the man who was objecting the most strongly and pointed to Albie. The man swallowed hard and, after a momentary pause, appeared happy to allow his party to be relocated to another table stuck in a corner by the kitchen, much further away from the little stage where the band was performing.

'Right,' said Albie, seemingly oblivious of the previous occupant of the plush and gilt chair in which he was settling himself. 'Drinks.'

'Gin and orange for us, right, Babs?' suggested Evie, flashing a signal with her eyes for her sister to agree with her.

'Lovely,' Babs responded. She'd have preferred a port and lemon but her sister's message about what she thought they should order was clear.

'Pint for me,' growled Chas.

The waiter shook his head apologetically. 'Sorry, sir. The club doesn't serve beer.'

'Two Scotches,' snapped Albie with a glare at Chas. 'And no water.'

After they had rapidly downed the first round of drinks – the girls from nerves and the men from habit – and had a second lot set up before them, Albie stood up. 'Dance,' he commanded rather than asked.

'Don't mind if I do,' Evie replied as though she had a choice in the matter, and pushing back her chair she held out her hand for him to lead her onto the floor.

'You?' asked Chas less confidently after his mistake about the beer.

'If yer like,' Babs answered him warily. Like her sister, she loved music and dancing, but she had already compared the size of Chas's enormous feet with her own petite size fours and was not a little concerned for their safety. But, as the band began playing, she soon forgot her worries, drawn in by the rhythm of the samba, she was delighted, not to mention amazed, when Chas turned out to be surprisingly light on his huge feet.

As the couples danced past one another, Babs leant close to Evie. 'Look at them frocks, Eve, even better than the ones we do at work.'

'Gorgeous,' Evie mouthed back at her as Albie whirled her past. She closed her eyes blissfully, letting the music wash over her and, just as she did at home when she listened to the wireless, she began singing along with the band.

'D'yer mean that?' Albie asked.

'What?' Evie murmured.

'That I'm the one?'

Evie's eyes flicked open and she looked up at him with a grin. 'I was singing along with the band, yer great daft hap'orth. It's "Night and Day", innit? It's just a song. Don't mean nothing.'

'Don't it?' Albie inclined his head then gave a slow, proprietorial nod. 'Well, ne'mind, but I'm telling yer, yer've got quite a voice.'

'I know I have,' she said, her grin becoming even saucier. 'And so's our Babs. We're a pair of very gifted girls. Everyone says so.'

'I can see that for meself,' Albie answered, looking down at her appreciatively. Then, much to Evie's

23

surprise, he suddenly stopped dancing, took her by the wrist, and led her through the crowd towards the stage. 'Matter o' fact . . .' he said. 'Come on, come with me.'

Evie let herself be led through the packed dance floor. Babs caught her eye as Albie swept past her and Chas. 'Don't ask me,' Evie called over her shoulder and shrugged.

When they reached the stage, Albie tapped the pianist, who was also the band leader, on the back and, leaning forward, said something to him that Evie couldn't make out. The piano player raised his hand and the music stopped. Everyone in the club turned to look towards the stage to see what was going on.

'What's it to be?' the band leader asked Evie with a questioning raising of his eyebrows.

Evie frowned. 'Sorry?'

'What are you going to sing for us?'

'What, me?'

He nodded.

Evie's already big blue eyes widened and she held out her hand to him and stepped up onto the stage. 'D'yer know "Somewhere Over The Rainbow"? It's the latest. From that new American film. I learnt it off the wireless.'

The band leader nodded again. 'Sure, I know it.'

A single spotlight was turned on her, the music began and, with her lovely, clear, strong voice, Evie began singing. After only a few bars there was no other sound in the club save for Evie and the piano. All conversation had stopped, the audience was enchanted.

Before the final note had died away, the clapping began. Her face glowing with success, Evie reached down to her sister who was standing by the stage between Albie and Chas. 'Come on, Babs,' she encouraged her, shouting over the applause. 'Let's give 'em a treat.'

Babs shook her head. 'No fear! You ain't getting me up there.'

24

'Go on,' Albie insisted, and, before Babs knew what was happening, he had lifted her right off her feet and onto the stage.

'Yer rotten cow,' Babs hissed but, as she knew she would, she was soon joining in with her twin's irresistible giggles. 'Right then,' she said, shading her eyes from the bright spotlight. 'Let's get this over with. What we gonna give 'em?'

'"Cheek to Cheek?"' suggested Evie, looking across to the piano player.

'What else?' he replied, gazing with wonder at the sight of the two beautiful girls standing before him who, apart from their contrasting hair colours, were identical.

By the time the audience eventually let the girls get down from the stage and return to their seats for a much-needed drink, Babs was as excited as Evie and the Bell twins knew that they had scored a hit. They also knew that, as usual, they had made a particular impression on all the men present.

Albie and Chas beamed with pleasure as they swaggered back to their table, guiding 'their' girls before them.

'I love it,' smirked Chas as he sat down without pulling Babs's chair out for her. 'Everyone's looking at me,' and he straightened the lapels of his already immaculate jacket. 'Makes yer feel great, don't it, being so popular?'

On hearing Chas's totally misplaced boast, Evie and Babs both spluttered into their drinks, nearly choking themselves.

The rest of the night passed in a blur of music, drinking and dancing, and after what seemed like only a few more turns round the dance floor, it was getting on for three o'clock, way past the time that the club should have closed.

'Time we was off,' said Albie and nodded to one of the waiting staff to fetch their things. 'If it's still not raining out, I think we'll have a little walk in the fresh air,' he announced as he stood up. 'Before we get back in the car.'

The four of them walked through the pre-dawn chill of the West End streets still busy despite the late hour. Albie, with Evie clinging to him, led the way, and Babs, her shoulder roughly encircled by Chas's huge tree trunk of an arm, followed along behind them.

'Where we going?' asked Evie coquettishly, glancing up at Albie through her lashes as she tottered along beside him on her high heels.

'Nowhere, I just like to get a bit of air in me lungs, that's all, like to look after meself,' he answered.

'In that case,' Evie quipped back, quick as a flash, 'yer won't mind if we have a little breather then.' And with that she pulled Albie into a shop doorway, threw her arms round his neck and kissed him smartly on the mouth.

Before Babs had a chance to protest, Chas followed suit and bent his head down and hurriedly planted a smacker right on her tightly shut lips, almost knocking her hat over her eyes in his haste. He might have been a fast mover, but he wasn't quick enough to avoid the flat of Babs's hand as she slapped him firmly round the face.

'Ow,' he winced, rubbing his stinging cheek with his great wide paw of a hand. 'That bloody hurt.'

'Good,' Babs snapped at him, straightening her hat and patting her hair into place. 'It was meant to. Yer might be twice as big as me, but don't push yer luck, moosh.'

Babs sounded brave but it was only when she heard the sound of Albie's laughter and him saying, 'Ne'mind, Chas,' that she felt *she* hadn't pushed her luck too far.

'Yer ready, gels?' Albie asked and held out his cigarette case to Chas by way of compensation. 'I think it's time we was getting you two home.'

For the journey back to Bow, Evie consented to get in

the front seat with Albie, but Babs wasn't so amenable. She made Chas promise to keep his hands to himself before she would agree to sit alongside him in the back. The pathetic expression which spread across his face was like a cross between that of a naughty pup that had been caught weeing on the front parlour carpet and a little boy who'd just broken his new toy train. It was enough to have both girls laughing out loud and Babs chummily shifting over right next to Chas and linking her arm through his. She even let him have a little bit of a kiss and cuddle to cheer him up.

Chas was just getting into his stride when Babs suddenly pushed him away and sat up straight. 'Right,' she announced determinedly. 'The Aberdeen, this'll do us. Thanks, Albie.'

'But we're only at the top of the Roman.' Chas sounded very disappointed.

'I know, but, like I said, we're getting out here by the pub.'

Evie turned round in her seat. 'Babs?'

'It's nearly daylight, Eve, we don't wanna get Dad all worked up, hearing a car outside.'

Evie reluctantly agreed and, with a shrug at Albie, she reached for the door handle.

'Not so fast,' Albie said and grabbed her into his arms. They were soon locked in a passionate and very noisy embrace.

Chas took the action in the front seat to be a signal for him to do the same, and almost smothered Babs in his enthusiastic determination to have another kiss.

'We really had better be going,' croaked Babs hoarsely when she'd finally manage to extricate herself from his grip. 'Come on, Evie.'

The girls stood on the pavement outside the Earl of Aberdeen, watching the Riley draw away in the early morning light.

Evie blew a kiss in the direction of the departing car. 'What a feller,' she sighed and, taking her sister's arm, began to walk along Grove Road, back to Darnfield Street. 'And you was getting on all right with that Chas and all,' she added with a sideways glance at Babs.

'Huh!' sniffed Babs. 'What a cheek. Thinks he's God's gift, that one.'

'Good-looking.'

'Yeah, I suppose so,' Babs agreed grudgingly. 'Ain't a bad kisser neither, but he's a right cloth head. He ain't got a thing between his ears.'

Evie widened her eyes in mock disapproval. 'Do what? Well, that's a new one on me. I've never seen a bloke what *did* have a thing between his ears.'

'Dirty mare!' laughed Babs.

As they turned into Darnfield Street, the twins were shaking with laughter.

'Ssshhh,' gasped Babs, trying desperately to control herself. 'Yer'll wake everyone up.' She jerked her head in the direction of number five, the Clarkes's house. 'The old curtain twitcher's at it.'

'Good,' Evie shouted. 'Let 'em all wake up. I don't care. I want everyone to know I'm happy.'

By the time they'd reached their front door, Babs no longer had any trouble with sounding serious. She was in deadly earnest as she warned her sister, 'Be careful, Evie, we've had a laugh but he's still Albie Denham, yer know.'

'Yeah, I know,' Evie answered her wearily as she rooted round in her handbag for the latch key.

'You ain't thinking of seeing him again, are yer?'

'Matter o' fact I am,' she said, echoing one of Albie's phrases. She turned her bag towards the dim glow of the street light. 'When you was busy with old Charlie boy in the back seat, Albie asked me to go flapping with him.'

'Flapping?'

'Yeah, yer know,' Evie said, with a satisfied grin as she

at last produced the door key from the messy depths of her bag. 'Dog racing, over the Hackney Marshes.'

'I do know, Evie. And *you* know it ain't legal, don't yer?'

'Course I know.'

'So. Are yer going?'

'Yer kidding, ain't yer? Him and Chas was going over there right now. I told him. I said, what, on a Sunday morning? I have to have me lay-in of a Sunday. I like to get me beauty sleep.'

'Yeah, yer need it and all, you ugly cow.' Babs's tone sounded light and easy, but her expression was worried, strained even.

'Talking about yerself again?' Evie cracked back, elbowing Babs out of the way so she could open the door.

'No, I was talking about *you*. I said ugly cow, not gorgeous creature. You ain't gone mutton as well as stupid have yer?' Babs still spoke with a straight face, but as soon as Evie turned to look at her, it was hopeless and the pair of them were almost helpless with laughter as they tried to push one another out of the way, fighting to be the first to get inside the narrow doorway of number six. Evie got inside first and, like a stubborn cork being released from a bottle, Babs went tumbling in after her along the passage. When she'd managed to steady herself, she turned round to shut the street door, but Evie reached out and stopped her.

'Hold up, Babs,' she said, slipping past her sister. 'If Dad ain't awake after all that, nothing'll wake him.'

'What?'

'You listen.' Evie stepped outside onto the pavement, put her hands either side of her mouth to concentrate the sound, and called out loudly across the street, 'Oi, Alice. Yer wanna get Nobby to get his cloth and pail out for yer. Yer dunno what yer might be missing with all that muck on yer windows.' Then, with a haughty flick of her blonde

29

hair and a wink at her sister, Evie strutted back inside number six. But this time it was she who wasn't allowed to shut the street door behind her.

Babs stood on tiptoes and called out over her sister's shoulder, 'Yer can go off duty now, Alice, we're home. Night night, sleep tight!'

2

Albie got out of the Riley and shivered. Although it was
not even the end of August yet, an early morning mist lay
over the Hackney Marshes bringing an autumn chill to
the air. Albie sank his hands deep into his pockets.

'Could do with them two twins to come and keep us
warm,' smirked Chas, shrugging his huge shoulders down
into his jacket as they set off across the damp grass. 'I
reckon we're well in there, Albie. I tell yer what, yer
should have asked 'em to come over here with us.'

'Yer a daft sod. Don't you know nothing? I couldn't
have asked 'em to come over here,' lied Albie. 'This
flapping lark don't do for girls. Yer know what they're
like. They don't like getting their little shoes dirty or
nothing, do they? And they have to get their heads down
after a night out. Need their beauty kip, see. Not like us.'

'Aw, yeah, course,' agreed Chas. He spoke with a
confidence that implied that the female psyche held no
secrets for him. 'I wasn't thinking.'

Albie suppressed a smile as he and Chas walked over
the dew-covered ground towards a group of half a dozen
men who were standing around stamping their feet and
sharing the contents of a leather-covered hip flask.

'All right, Dad?' Albie called out as they got near
them.

The man who had just had his turn at taking a swig
wiped his mouth with the back of his hand and gave the

hip flask to one of the others in the circle. 'Where you two been?' he growled, swaggering over to Albie and Chas. 'I expected you here over half an hour ago.' He was in his late fifties, not quite as tall as Albie, but still a big man and still more than handsome for his age.

'Morning, Bernie,' said Chas respectfully.

'I asked you a question, boy,' Bernie said coldly, jabbing a finger towards Albie's chest and ignoring Chas's attempts to be polite. 'Been birding it again, I suppose,' he sneered.

'Hark who's talking,' muttered Albie indignantly. His jaw was rigid from the effort of keeping his temper.

'What did you say?' Bernie demanded. His tone and expression were menacing.

Chas shifted uncomfortably from foot to foot.

Albie stared at his father for what was nearly a moment too long, but then said flatly, 'Nothing, Dad. I never said nothing.'

'Well, yer better not have,' snapped Bernie. 'And yer'd better not have spent all that dough yer collected last night neither, 'cos yer know I'm meant to be running the book here this morning. Or did yer get too pissed last night to remember?' He leant forward and said in an ominously quiet voice, 'I've got some big players here, over from Bermondsey way they are, and if you muck it up, boy . . .'

Albie's reply was to reach inside his jacket and produce the still fat roll of banknotes; it was only slightly depleted by the cost of entertaining the Bell sisters. He handed the money over.

Bernie snatched the roll from his son, licked his thumb and began counting. Next he made rapid calculations about how much his son had actually given him, how much of it he could use to stand for bets and how much of it he would have to account for to his wife, Queenie.

Albie watched, knowing full well what his dad was up

to – calculating how to con his wife out of as much as possible.

'As if I'd ever spend Mum's money,' Albie said with a sad shake of his head. His face was a picture of hurt innocence, but it didn't last long; he could never resist saying what was in his head or needling anyone when he had the opportunity. 'I leave you to do that, you greedy old bastard,' he added under his breath.

'What you mumbling about now?' demanded Bernie, looking up from his calculations.

'Nothing, Dad. What d'you take me for?'

'Stupid, that's what.' Bernie tapped the side of his head with the tip of his index finger. 'Yer don't use yer brain, that's your trouble.' He shoved the money deep into his trouser pocket and then, putting on a broad smile, strode back to his companions. 'Right, chaps,' he said to them, rubbing his hands together enthusiastically. 'We're in business. Who wants how much on what dog?'

As Bernie noted down the wagers being thrust at him by the group of gamblers, all only too eager to part with their wages, the dog owners, the men who earlier had been drinking with Bernie, went over to their cars and vans to fetch the dogs. Albie and Chas got on with their job of setting up the lure.

'Mind out, Chas, for gawd's sake,' yelled Albie. 'Yer'll get oil all over me suit.'

'Sorry, Albie,' Chas apologised, and flicked the rope he was clumsily attempting to tie clear of Albie's trousers. 'I can't get this end to hold right.'

'Give it here.' Albie snatched the rope from Chas and wound one end round the metal drum of an old car wheel mounted on a wooden frame. 'I dunno why I didn't do it meself in the first place,' he complained. 'Bloody useless, you are, Chas. Completely hopeless.' Being reprimanded by his father in front of Chas had made Albie really tense. 'Yer don't use yer brain, that's your trouble,' he added in

33

spiteful imitation of his dad. He fastened the rope with a firm double knot, pulling it much tighter than he needed to. The effect was not just to make the rope secure, it also made the rabbit fur lure on the end bounce jerkily across the grass. The six highly-strung greyhounds yelped with excitement and strained at their leashes in the struggle to get at the furry prize.

'Now see what yer've done,' Albie snapped at the totally baffled Chas. 'Yer'll wear 'em out before the first race. And me dad'll just love that.'

'But I—'

'Shut it, Chas.'

Chas shut up and stood watching Albie check his handiwork. The wheel drum to which Albie had attached the end of the rope was itself attached by a belt to a little petrol-driven engine which, when it was set in motion, would wind up the rope and drag the artificial hare along to get the dogs moving at full stretch.

Satisfied that he had set up the contraption properly, Albie straightened up. He went to brush down the knees of his trousers but looked with disgust at his oil covered hands. 'Get us a rag,' he commanded Chas. Chas opened his mouth to speak but Albie interrupted him, 'No, I don't know where from, Chas. Just find one.'

While Chas went round asking anybody and everybody if they had a cloth he could borrow, Albie went over to Bernie. 'Ready when you are, Dad,' he said flatly, still preoccupied with the state of his hands.

'With you in a mo, son,' Bernie answered him pleasantly – he was always pleasant when he was with punters who were handing over their money, especially when the bets were as big as the ones he was taking.

'Might as well blow the lot,' one man said, and laughed sardonically to his pal as he emptied his wallet and handed the contents to Bernie. 'If this war breaks out and we all get gassed to death, what'll be the use of money then, eh?'

Bernie joined in with the laughter as he pocketed the cash. Finally satisfied that he had taken all he could from the punters, he closed his notebook and pointed at the dog owners. 'Line 'em up, lads.'

The men grasped the greyhounds' collars, doing their best to steady the dogs before the off, while keeping one eye on the handkerchief which Bernie held high above his head.

Bernie dropped the handkerchief and nodded at Albie – the signal for him to start the machine and get the hare moving. But Albie didn't see his father's signal. Chas had moved in front of him, blocking his view.

'Here y'are, Albie,' he said. 'I got yer cloth for yer hands.'

'You stupid great bastard!' screamed Bernie from the starting line but Albie couldn't hear him; the noise of the punters, the dog owners and the dogs themselves, almost hysterical at not being released, drowned Bernie's furious hollering.

'What's going on?' demanded one of the South London punters. 'We come all the way over the river for this? It's a bloody joke innit?'

Albie threw the rag to the ground, shoved Chas out of the way and ran over to Bernie to try and explain.

'Look, Dad, I'd asked Chas to get me a cloth to wipe me hands, that's all. I had grease on 'em.'

'You what?' The man who had emptied his wallet sneered incredulously at Albie and looked round at the other punters for confirmation that he hadn't heard wrongly. 'You was worried about a bit o' grease on yer hands? What are yer, a bleed'n Mary Ann or something?'

'It's a new suit,' said Albie drawing himself up to his full height. 'Some of us don't like walking about like bloody tramps.'

35

'New suit?' the man said scornfully, turning to speak to the man at his side. 'I'll show him new suit.' With that he spun round, his fist drawn well back, ready to let Albie have it full on the chin.

But Albie was too quick for him. He grabbed the man's arm and stopped his swing dead. 'Don't make me laugh.' This time it was Albie who sounded disdainful.

'I don't wanna be difficult or nothing,' said one of the dog owners sarcastically, 'but are we gonna have this race or are we gonna stand about chatting like a load of old women?'

'All right, all right.' Bernie was wild, but he was doing his best to keep his voice calm in front of the punters. 'Just give me a minute.' He took Albie by the arm and led him a few feet away from the others. 'Yer don't wanna start nothing with that mob, do you hear me?'

'Them? They couldn't knock the skin off a rice pudden. None of 'em. They won't hurt me.'

'I didn't meant that, yer stupid great sod.' Bernie spat the words at his son. 'Now just shut up. There's a lot of money riding on this race and I don't wanna have to go giving it all back, now do I?' Bernie poked his finger hard into Albie's chest. 'You mess it up again, boy . . .'

'I'll give him mess it up.'

'Shut up, I said.'

'No one talks to me like that. No one.'

'He's right, Bern.'

Bernie turned round to see Chas standing behind him.

'That bloke's a right mouthy bastard. You ought to hear what he's saying about Albie over there now.'

Chas was nearly twice as broad as Bernie but it didn't matter, Bernie grabbed hold of his lapels and started hollering at him to keep his nose out of it.

Albie took his chance and, pulling off his jacket as he ran, he sprinted over to confront the man who'd dared question his masculinity. He had surprise on his side and

36

his first punch hit the mark, catching his opponent squarely on the side of his face, sending him reeling backwards, blood spurting from his mouth.

'I'll show you who's a Mary Ann.' Albie's breathing was rapid and his eyes wild as he shaped up and bobbed before the momentarily stunned man. 'Come on then. Let's have yer.'

'Albie,' Chas called to him, chastened after his 'chat' with Bernie. 'Listen to yer dad. Yer don't wanna do that.'

'Why not?' one of the South Londoners jeered. 'We might as well bet on that great Jessy instead of them mangy-looking dogs.' He turned to his friends. 'Even if the bloody dogs are prettier!'

At the sound of the men's laughter, Albie's temper snapped and he lunged at his opponent.

Chas tried to stop him, but Bernie wouldn't let him.

'You're all right, Chas, leave him.' Bernie, with his infallible instinct for a willing punter, noted the eager faces of the men; they'd be just as happy to lose their wages on the outcome of a fist fight as they would on the speed of a dog.

Albie's opponent shook his head as though to clear his thoughts and then wiped the blood from his face with a sinewy forearm. 'Yer don't wanna get that pretty face of your'n messed up, do yer?' he said, bending slightly at the knees as he weighed up his chances of landing one on Albie's nose.

With a sudden lunge, the two men laid into one another. The others formed a ragged circle round them, hollering for blood, while the dogs yelped hysterically and Bernie calmly offered odds on the outcome.

The South Londoner was big but he was no match for Albie and he was soon curled up on the grass trying to protect himself from Albie's vicious blows.

'That's enough,' said Bernie shoving Chas forward, the only one brave, or stupid, enough to get close to Albie to stop him. The punters had had a good show for their money but Bernie didn't want to antagonise the loser's mates by having him get too bad a beating.

'Time to stop, Al,' Chas said, standing behind Albie and wrapping his arms round him. 'Come on, mate.'

But Chas's pleas didn't get through to Albie; before he knew what was happening, he felt as though he had been shot out of a cannon. He exploded backwards into the crowd as Albie threw his arms wide and got back to his task of finishing off his opponent. It eventually took three men to pull him off his now unconscious victim.

Albie stood, his chest rising and falling, his face covered with sweat and splashes of blood, none of them his.

'That temper of your boy's, Bernie,' said Jack, an elderly man who was squatting down next to his greyhound, trying to soothe the quivering creature by fondling its silky, brindle ears. 'It's gonna get him in trouble one of these days if he ain't careful.'

Bernie laughed. 'Yeah, takes after his old man, Jack. In lots of ways.'

Albie took the cloth from Chas that had earlier caused all the trouble and wiped his face. Then he straightened his tie and threw his jacket over his shoulder ready to head back to the Riley.

Chas nudged him and nodded over at a young couple who were walking towards them in the now bright morning sunshine. 'Better warn yer dad. Hold up, lads,' he called out to the little crowd huddled round Bernie who was sorting out the winnings. 'Strangers about.'

'Here they all come.' Jack took his watch out of his pocket. 'All out for their Sunday morning stroll.' He wound the watch and put it back in his pocket. 'Time we was off, anyway. It's getting on for half past eight already.'

'What, no racing?' complained a disappointed punter.

38

'None today. No time. Anyway, I dunno what yer complaining about. Yer all did all right out o' my boy winning that fight.'

'Yeah, but we know you, Bern,' someone else chipped in. 'Yer let us win a few bob one week then rob us blind the next.'

All the men except the two who were seeing to their badly beaten mate joined in the good-natured ribbing. 'Yeah, you and that old woman of your'n must be loaded. 'Bout time yer let us poor mugs have a few weeks' luck in a row, ain't it? How 'bout a few wins next week and all?'

'Yer'll just have to wait till then and see what happens, won't yer?'

'If the Germans don't get us first,' one of the men laughed. They began to move away from the secluded corner of the Hackney Marshes, back towards their cars and vans and to whatever they were intending to do with the rest of the bright Sunday morning. Two of the dog owners called their goodbyes and then disappeared behind a thick clump of gorse with their hounds. The hissed shout of 'Go fetch 'em', followed by a sudden squeal, told the others that the men were rabbiting.

Albie curled his lip contemptuously. 'Who'd be bothered with rabbiting?'

'If it's gonna be anything like the last war,' said old Jack, pulling his cap firmly down on his head despite the growing heat, 'we might all be glad of a few rabbits.'

'Yeah, right, about as glad as that idiot I give a walloping to,' smirked Albie.

Jack shrugged and strode away at surprising speed for an old man, easily keeping up with the loping gait of his dog. 'See yer next week then,' he called back to them. 'Gawd and the Jerries willing.'

Albie laughed. 'Yeah, see yer, Jack. If war ain't broke out.' He turned to Chas and shaped up like a boxer. 'I'd

39

have finished him off proper if them mates of his hadn't been there to pull me off.'

'That why I stopped yer, son,' Bernie said. 'Old Jack's right, that temper of yours is gonna get yer into right trouble one of these days.' He pulled the now rather thinner wad of money from his pocket and handed a couple of notes to Albie. 'You earned that – they'll all be back for more and bring plenty of mates with 'em. You and Chas go and get yerself a bit o' breakfast.'

'Ta, Bern,' Chas said politely. 'Appreciate that.'

Bernie ignored him. 'And there's yer mother's takings.'

Albie took the money and put it in his inside pocket. 'Yer driving, Dad?'

'No, Barmy Bill brought me in his shooting break with his greyhound.'

'Cor,' grinned Chas. 'Way he drives, yer'll wanna lift with us if yer wanna get home in one piece.'

'No, yer all right,' said Bernie. He nodded towards the hare-dragging gadget. 'You boys just make sure yer get that gear back for me. I'll be home later, I've gotta bit o' business to attend to first. So I'll love yer and leave yer, boys.' He winked and tipped his hat to them, then walked off in the direction of Clapton.

Albie shook his head. 'And he's got the cheek to moan at me about going out birding.'

'Yer've gotta hand it to him though, Alb. Even at his age he's still getting all the birds he wants. Wish I knew how he did it.'

'It's obvious,' grinned Albie, studying the grazing on his knuckles. 'It's the old Denham charm, innit? Kills 'em every time.'

Chas nodded thoughtfully, or what for him passed for thoughtfully. 'I think I did all right with that twin last night, Al, what d'yer reckon?' he asked as they loaded the racing equipment. Before Albie could give his opinion, Chas continued, 'I could murder me breakfast, couldn't you? I'm starving.'

'Yer gonna have to wait a bit longer, Chas. We've got an errand to do first.'

Chas got into the Riley without complaint and waited patiently to see where Albie was taking him. Huge as he was, he was used to following where Albie led without question, but he couldn't hide his surprise when Albie drew up in Grove Road at the top of Darnfield Street. 'Here, ain't this where the twins come from?' he blurted out as their destination dawned on him.

'Well done, Chas,' said Albie, slapping him hard on the shoulder. 'Now. See this?' He held up an envelope.

Chas replied with a silent nod.

'Good. You put it through the letter box of number six. Got it?'

Chas nodded again, took the envelope and got out of the car, soundlessly repeating to himself, 'Number six, number six.' He had taken only two steps away from the car when he turned round, ducked his head and looked at Albie through the window. 'Number six *Darnfield Street*, would that be, Al? Where the girls live?'

Albie wearily exhaled a stream of blue-grey cigarette smoke. 'Yes, Chas,' he sighed. 'Number six Darnfield Street. Where the girls live.'

'Right.'

Chas might have been slow in some ways but he was quick enough on his feet. He was soon back in the car, his errand run, waiting to see where Albie was taking him next.

'Breakfast?' Chas wondered hopefully.

'Breakfast,' confirmed Albie.

Within two minutes they were walking into a cafe on the Mile End Road; even at ten to nine on a Sunday morning, it was crowded with customers.

41

'Hello, Paulo, mate,' said Albie. 'Why ain't yer in the kitchen?'

'I am, and I'm out here and all. I'm doing everything this morning. Bloody madhouse, it is.'

'So where's your Gino then? Not at church surely? I know he's a bit of a holy Joe even for one o' you mob, but even Gino puts his business first.'

Paulo wiped his hands down the front of his white, starched apron. 'He's gone back home for a few weeks,' he whispered nervously.

Albie frowned. 'He never mentioned nothing to me.' Suddenly he didn't sound so friendly. 'Here, yer don't mean home as in Italy, do yer?'

'Yeah.'

'But he ain't been there for years.'

'It's Mama.'

'Old lady sick, is she?' asked Chas with a concerned frown.

'No. She's fretting about war breaking out 'cos she's heard how there's been trouble over here for some of the Italian families with cafes and that.'

'But yer know nothing like that'll happen around here, Paulo, me old son,' said Albie, brightening up again. 'Not while yours truly's here to look after yer.'

Paulo nodded gloomily. 'Right. That's what Gino said.'

Albie winked and pinched Paulo's cheek. 'So long as you remember that, then everything'll be all right, won't it?'

Paulo nodded again, this time with resignation, then he swallowed hard. He looked over his shoulder to make sure that no one was listening. 'Gino told me about the payments.'

'Good, so there won't be no misunderstandings then. Right. That's settled. Now give us two breakfasts. Matter o' fact, I think I could manage the full works this morning, so make sure yer give us all the trimmings.'

42

'Right, Albie, sure. Straight away,' Paulo said and headed quickly towards the kitchen, ignoring a customer in the corner who was asking for another cup of tea.

Albie and Chas settled down at a table near the window. Albie lit a cigarette and made himself comfortable, enjoying the sun warming him through the glass. It looked like being another nice day, maybe even the start of an Indian summer after the wet and windy weather of the last few miserable weeks. But the moment was spoilt for Albie. 'Aw, no,' he said turning away from the window. 'He ain't seen me, 'as he, Chas?'

'Who?'

'Him. Out there. Doctor sodding Reider.'

'He's seen yer all right,' sniggered Chas. 'And just look at the state of him trying to cross that road. Pissed as a fart and it ain't even nine o'clock yet.'

Albie shook his head as the man came stumbling into the cafe. 'You watch.' Albie winked at Chas. 'He's on the tap again. Guaranteed.'

'Albert,' slurred Dr Reider, his eyes swivelling in and out of focus as he tried to find his way towards Albie's table. 'Just the chap.' He slumped down on the chair next to Chas and leaned across the oilcloth-covered table towards Albie. 'Was out to a bit of a party last night and I seem to have found myself a bit short of the readies. Wonder if you might . . .'

'I've told yer, Dr Reider,' said Albie standing up and reaching into his trouser pocket. 'Yer wanna keep away from them spielers or yer'll never have no dough.'

'What makes you think I've been gambling?' the doctor asked in an offended voice.

'Just a guess,' said Albie and slowly folded up a large white five pound note before handing it to the doctor. 'It'll have to go in the book, yer know.'

'Of course, of course,' Reider agreed willingly. Then he rose shakily to his feet, pocketed his loot and wove his way unsteadily out of the cafe.

Albie watched him pass the window, heading straight back in the direction of Whitechapel and its illegal gambling clubs, exactly as Albie knew he would. 'Mug,' he sneered.

'Watch yer backs.' Behind them Paulo appeared with two plates piled high with fried bacon, sausages, eggs, tomatoes and black pudding. 'On the house, Albie,' he said uneasily.

'Nice. Very nice. I like a bit of respect.' Albie nodded for Paulo to leave as he pulled his plate towards him and stuck a fork into the crisp, dark brown skin of a sausage, making it spurt a jet of hot fat across the table. He raised the sausage to his lips and blew on the hot meat. 'He must owe me mum nearly a hundred quid, that Reider. Drinking and gambling can be very dear hobbies.'

'What, even on a doctor's wages?' Chas asked, his mouth full of black pudding.

'Specially on a good wage – more to lose, yer see. And if he knows what's good for him he wants to start thinking about getting some of that money back that he owes me mum. Yer know how she gets.' Albie chewed reflectively on the piece of sausage. 'Not bad,' he said, cutting through one of his eggs, releasing a thick pool of dark yellow yolk. 'It's different me and the old man having our little dip,' he continued. 'But she don't appreciate no strangers taking liberties.'

Chas laughed, a cold, dry sound that rumbled in his throat.

Albie didn't join in, he had a hurt look on his face as he put down his knife and fork. He raised his hand and snapped his fingers to attract Paulo who was hovering anxiously by the counter. 'No fried bread.' Albie's expression might have been one of disappointment but his simple statement sounded menacing enough to send Paulo rushing back to the kitchen.

'Mum, I've got the takings,' Albie shouted along the passage as he stepped inside the street door of the Denhams' house in Bow Common Lane.

Even though everyone in the area knew that Queenie kept all her money indoors – like most moneylenders she had no time for banks and had no intention of bothering herself with things like tax – nobody would dare go through the ever open front door without being invited in, not when she had an old man like Bernie and definitely not with a son like Albie around the place.

'Yer'll have to wait a minute if yer want yer breakfast,' she yelled back at him from the front parlour. 'I'm in here just seeing to this. Trying to make sense of all these bleed'n bits of paper.'

'It's all right, Mum. I've had some already.' Albie went into the dingy parlour. The small room was made to seem even tinier by its clutter. There was not a space that didn't have a dust-covered ornament, a vase of drooping, dead flowers or a pile of unidentifiable clothes which could have been dirty or were maybe waiting in their crumpled heaps to be ironed into more recognisable shapes. Albie lifted a toppling pile of papers from the greasy seat of an overstuffed armchair that stood by the table at which his mother was working, and sat down. He puffed out his handsome cheeks and patted his middle contentedly. 'Right full up, I am.'

'Aw yeah. And where'd you have that then? Round some silly tart's house while her old man's away at sea, I suppose.' Queenie looked up and smiled proudly at her son, her face folding into deep, thickly powdered creases. She had bright crimson circles of rouge on her cheeks that matched her painted lips, and black, pencilled eyebrows which rose into extravagant arches high above her actual brow line. With her startlingly unnatural orange curly hair and the material of her vivid floral frock stretched tight across her bosom, Queenie bore more than a passing resemblance to a pantomime dame. 'Yer a lad with the girls,' she beamed at her son. 'New one every week. Just like yer old man,' she added fondly and then went back to trying to make sense of the accounts over which, she knew, her husband and son bamboozled her.

'If yer must know, I had me breakfast in a cafe. But I have got meself a new girl.'

'Oh yeah? So who's this one?' Queenie frowned at yet another indecipherable pencilled note from the pile in front of her, then shrugged and stabbed it down hard onto an already overspilling spike.

'Right looker she is. Blonde. Very tasty.'

'After me dough, I suppose, like all the rest of 'em.'

'Leave off, Mum. Even if I was boracic lint, yer know I could get any girl I wanted. Can't resist me, can they?'

'Hark at you,' Queenie said rolling her eyes. 'Yer sound just like that bloody father of your'n. I dunno. Men!'

The cackling of sudden laughter coming from behind him made Albie start. He twisted round in his armchair to see one of Queenie's many customers, an elderly woman in a baggy, navy blue serge coat and a headscarf, grinning at him from the corner of the room.

'Yer right there, Queenie,' the old woman cackled, exposing her stained and broken teeth. 'They're all the same, men, the bloody lot of 'em. Least they are in the dark with their trousers down!'

3

'D'yer think Dad heard us coming in last night, Eve?'

'Bloody hell, I hope not.' Evie glanced sideways at Babs and pulled a face. 'Anyway, it was hardly last night, was it? This morning, more like.' She carelessly dropped the dirty plates from their Sunday dinner onto the draining board and stretched luxuriously, lifting her arms high above her head. 'Can't be helped, Babs, but yer gonna have to do the washing up all by yerself 'cos I've gotta get ready. I'm seeing Albie tonight, so I wanna look me best, don't I?'

Babs silently carried on with what she was doing. First, she covered her dress with the cross-over apron that she took from the nail behind the kitchen door, then she lifted the kettle from the stove and poured boiling water into the enamel basin which stood in the big butler sink, threw in a handful of soda, and topped up the basin from the single brass cold-water tap. She slipped the plates and cutlery into the bowl and began scrubbing them clean. Evie made no effort to help her.

'So when was all this decided then?' Babs asked over her shoulder. 'I didn't hear no one say nothing about going out with him while we was in the car last night, apart from the stuff you told me about him asking yer to go flapping.'

'You was too busy with that Chas,' Eve said, shoving Babs in the back so that she slopped water onto the kitchen floor. 'Saucy cow. Yer was making a right meal of it, weren't yet? All over him.'

'Don't tell lies, Evie. Yer know it wasn't like that. And yer can stop yer joking around and all. I'm just about fed up with you always getting out of doing everything.'

'You ain't gonna start, are yer?' Evie levered herself onto the scrubbed kitchen table and swung her legs restlessly backwards and forwards. She hesitated for a moment then said, 'Tell yer what, I'll put the kettle on and we can have a cup o' tea before I take meself upstairs to get ready. How about that?'

'All right,' sighed Babs. 'At least yer'll be doing *something*.' She wiped her cheek with the back of her wet and greasy hand. 'And yer can take one through to Dad while yer at it. Before he closes his eyes for his afternoon kip.'

Eve reached across Babs to fill the kettle from the tap and then set it back on the gas stove.

'Yer still never said when he asked yer.' Babs leaned sideways out of Evie's way so she could reach the cups and saucers stacked on the single shelf that ran along the wall above the sink.

Evie took an envelope from her dress pocket. 'It's a letter,' she explained, holding it out to her sister.

Babs didn't take it from her. 'Me sister's a genius and she's got a boy friend what can write,' she sniped sarcastically.

'All right, clever clogs,' Eve sneered back at her. 'So that means yer won't be wanting to share the fiver that he put in the letter, does it? Shame, 'cos he said we should both get ourselves a little treat, and all.'

'A fiver?' Babs almost dropped the plate she was washing. 'Evie, has that peroxide sent you completely out of that head o' your'n? What on earth's possessed yer to take money off the likes of Albie Denham?'

48

'Aw, leave off, Miss High and Mighty. Why shouldn't I take it?'

Babs's voice rose with her anger. ''Cos he's a crook and he pulls all kinds o' dodgy strokes that you don't wanna get mixed up with. That's why.'

'Aw yeah, and what kind o' dodgy strokes are they then? Seeing as you know so much about it all.'

'You know as well as I do, Eve.' Babs turned to her sister and began counting on her wet fingers. 'There's the flapping, for a start. Then there's his dad, he's a bookie, and his old girl's a moneylender. And then there's the talk that he's involved in the protection racket.'

'Well,' answered Eve pertly. 'I should do all right for meself then, shouldn't I? What with all that dough coming in.'

'Evie! I don't believe this. What the bloody hell's got into you?'

'Don't be such a hypocrite, Babs. I never saw you complaining when we was in that club last night.' Evie narrowed her eyes. 'I know. How about you coming along with us tonight? Shall I tell him to bring Chas along for yer?'

'You are kidding, ain't yer? It was all right for one night, just for a laugh, but what would I wanna get mixed up with the likes of them two lairy bleeders for? Chas is a bleed'n ape and that Albie . . . Reckons he's George Raft, how he struts about.' Babs turned back to the washing up. 'It's just asking for trouble going around with that pair.'

'Suit yerself.' Evie shrugged dismissively and slipped down from the table onto the lino-covered floor. Very deliberately she went over and turned off the gas. 'I'm going up to get ready.'

This was too much for Babs. 'How 'bout the tea, yer lazy cow?' she screamed. 'Can't yer even do *that*?'

'How *'bout* the tea?' Evie screamed back at her. 'Make

it yerself. I ain't got the time.'

Babs slapped the flat of her hand down into the washing-up bowl, sending a greasy spray of lukewarm water jetting across the floor. 'Well, if yer want yer dinner things washed up, yer gonna have to tell that no good Albie Denham to get yer a bleed'n maid, ain't yer?'

'Oi, what's all this row about?'

The sound of their father's voice silenced both girls immediately; they knew better than to upset him after he'd been drinking. He stood in the kitchen doorway, his shirt hanging out of his trousers, his braces dangling round his knees.

'Can't a bloke even have a kip in his own front room of a Sunday afternoon without you pair shouting and hollering like a pair o' bloody fishwives?'

'It's her,' snapped Babs. 'She's a rotten, lazy cow.'

'Me? You was the one what started it,' Eve shrieked back at her.

'Shut up!' Georgie hollered above both their voices. 'Now, what's all this yer was shouting about Albie Denham?'

'Nothing,' said Babs, staring down at her feet.

Evie lifted her chin haughtily in the air. 'If yer must know,' she said, 'I'm going out with him tonight.'

'Aw no you ain't, my girl.'

'And why's that then, Dad? You gonna stop me?'

'If I have to.'

'Don't make me laugh.' Evie folded her arms and tapped her toe impatiently on the thin, dull red lino that covered the kitchen floor. 'Anyway,' she demanded, flapping her hand in the air, 'what you got against Albie Denham?'

'As if you don't know.' Georgie hooked his braces up over his shoulders. 'As if the whole of the bleed'n East End don't know. They're no-goods, the lot of 'em. Him with his flash clothes and his shiny motors, and his old girl with all her diamond rings. Never done a stroke o' work in their life. None of 'em. Crooked bastards. And his old man's just as monkey as his mother. If they X-rayed the whole lot o' that family they wouldn't find a stroke of work in any one of 'em.'

Evie strode furiously across the little kitchen and stood right in front of her father, her face like thunder as she glowered up at him. 'Just hark who's talking.' She paused, hardly able to form the words. 'I know what it is, yer jealous of him, ain't yer? Just 'cos he's made something of himself and not wound up a useless drunk like you.'

Babs grabbed hold of Evie's arm and swung her round. 'Shut up, Eve. That's enough.'

'I ain't even *started* yet,' hissed Evie, turning back to face her father.

Georgie hung his head. 'Yer wouldn't talk to me like that if yer mother was still around,' he mumbled pathetically.

'You, you're a hypocrite just like her!' Evie screeched at him, jerking her thumb in Babs's direction. 'No wonder yer can't look me in the eye.'

'Evie, shut up, please! Don't talk to Dad like that.'

'No. *You* shut up, Babs. What does he know about what Mum'd have let us do? If it wasn't for him, Mum'd never have left us in the first place.'

Babs sat down on one of the hard kitchen chairs and stared at the floor, wishing that her sister would just be quiet and leave it alone before she said something they might all regret.

But Evie couldn't stop herself, not now; she had to carry on shouting. She didn't care who could hear her or what they thought, or what pain she caused. She considered herself too badly hurt for any of that to matter. And so it all come blurting out. 'We might have been little but we heard yer rowing the night before she left us. Did yer

51

know that?' She spat the words at him. 'And who could blame her for going? Just look at yer. You ain't had a shave for days and yer stink o' beer. I bet she couldn't stand the sight of yer, just like I can't. Yer make me sick just looking at yer.'

'I never used to be like this.' Georgie said the words so softly the girls could barely hear them. 'Not till she run off and left us for that bloke down the market.'

'Don't give me that.' Evie's voice quavered as she fought back the tears. 'If it wasn't for you, me and Babs'd still have Mum here with us now. And everything'd be . . . Everything'd . . .' The tears won and began flowing down her cheeks. 'Aw, just get out of me way, can't yer.'

Georgie moved placidly to one side as Evie stormed out of the kitchen. They heard her crash her way up the uncarpeted stairs and almost smash the bedroom door as she swung it back on its hinges.

'She'll calm down in a minute, Dad,' said Babs softly. 'Fancy a cup o' tea?'

Georgie sank down in the carver chair that stood by the stove and nodded.

'I'll see if Evie wants one.' Babs went to the bottom of the stairs to call up to her sister. 'Wanna cuppa, Eve?'

Evie appeared on the tiny, unlit landing; she was wearing her hat and jacket. 'No thanks,' she answered tersely, wiping her nose on the back of her hand. 'I've decided to go out early.'

Babs stood to one side to let her past. 'Don't be too late, Evie,' she said quietly. 'Remember it's work in the morning.'

Evie waited till she had opened the street door before shouting down the passage loud enough to ensure that Georgie would hear, 'I hardly think I'll be working in that rotten workshop much longer, do you, Babs?'

'Evie,' Babs pleaded. 'Keep yer noise down. Please.'

'What's the matter, Babs, worried that gossiping old cow over the road'll hear?'

'I couldn't care less about her, I just don't want yer getting Dad going, that's all.'

'Well, perhaps he won't have to put up with me for much longer. 'Cos now I'm seeing Albie Denham, I don't reckon I'll stay a machinist in no poxy dress factory. Albie's got class, yer see. So I'll be leaving here soon, and I won't be around to upset none of yer no more.'

'Do us a favour and leave off, Eve,' Babs said wearily. 'Yer really getting on me nerves.' She rubbed her hands over her face; she didn't know what to do, but she knew it was pointless to try and argue with her sister. She shook her head and sighed. 'Just leave off.'

'No, *you* leave off, Babs.' Evie was shouting even louder now, her fists tucked tight into her waist. 'D'you know what's really sad? You've got the chance to get on, just like me, 'cos his mate Chas really fancies yer. But yer too scared to take a chance. Just like you always are.'

Evie stepped out into the street and slammed the door behind her with an almighty bang, making the photograph of her and Babs as identical cuddling five-year-olds jump off its nail in the hall and go crashing to the ground.

Babs closed her eyes for a moment and took a deep breath before bending down to clear up the broken glass. She held out the bottom of her apron and dropped the shards into it, then picked up the photograph. It hadn't been damaged but it looked forlorn and faded without the shiny covering of glass. The clips and wooden backing were still intact so she hung the now dull picture back on the wall and then walked slowly, head down, back to the kitchen. She stood in the open doorway and looked at Georgie slumped in the chair by the hearth, his legs stuck out in front of him, flicking half-heartedly though the Sunday paper.

'All right, Dad?' she asked softly.

Georgie folded the newspaper back on itself. 'Full of bloody war again,' he muttered furiously, his lips tight. 'What's wrong with people? Yer'd think they was looking forward to it.'

'D'yer wanna go in the front room and have the wireless on?' Babs asked over her shoulder as she wrapped the pieces of glass in an old blue sugar bag and put it in the rubbish bucket outside the back door. 'I can do the washing up later on,' she said.

'No,' he sighed, tossing the newspaper onto the floor. 'You go in and listen if yer like.'

'Tell yer what, I'll turn it up so we can hear it in here, shall I?'

'I said *no*.'

The anger in his voice made Babs flinch. 'Sorry, Dad, I only thought—'

'It don't matter. It's that Evie – she's got me right hot and bothered. Just like her bloody mother, she is.'

Silently, Babs reached over and took her darning mushroom and a grey woollen sock down from the crowded mantelpiece. She sat down at the table and started mending the hole in its heel. She was going to suggest that they might take their chairs and go and sit out in the street instead, but she thought better of it considering his frame of mind and knowing that he was still recovering from one of his boozy lunchtime sessions in the pub.

Georgie carried on speaking, although he seemed hardly aware of Babs sitting there sewing. He wasn't really addressing his daughter at all. 'I've always said it,' his words dripped venom, 'there's needy and there's greedy, and then there's the no-good sods like your no-good mother and that fancy no-good feller of hers. Just like that no-good bastard Albie Denham and the rest of his stinking family.'

Babs sat quietly darning, trying to lose herself in the

54

rhythm of working the grey thread back and forth while Georgie ranted and raved about life's injustices. Gradually his bellowing subsided and was replaced by loud alcohol-induced snores as he lay back in the chair, his mouth open, a line of drool dribbling onto his unshaven chin.

When she was sure he was sound asleep, Babs put the mended sock in her apron pocket ready to match up later with its partner in her Dad's tallboy and stood up. She put the darning mushroom back on the mantelpiece then picked up the newspaper, folded it neatly and put it on the table close to Georgie's chair.

'Right,' she said to herself. 'No point sitting about. Someone's gotta do it.'

She boiled some fresh water and finished the washing up. Then, when she had put all the dishes away, had wiped round the sink and draining board and was satisfied that the kitchen was tidy, she sat down at the table to have a look at the paper. Neither she nor her twin usually bothered much with the papers, and the news on the wireless always made them groan; as far as they were concerned the only thing worth listening to was the dance band programmes. But what with all the talk about Germany, she decided maybe she would have a little look this evening, just to see what all the fuss was about.

She spread the paper out on the table and slowly turned the pages. Dad was right, she thought, it was full of talk of war; she really hadn't realised how serious it all was. Why hadn't she? she wondered. There'd been plenty of talk, of course, but she'd dismissed most of it as scaremongering only worthy of the likes of the more gossipy of the elderly neighbours. But perhaps it was time she did start taking it seriously. Almost everything in the paper seemed to be about gas attacks and air raids. And the pictures, nearly every one was of men in uniform.

Babs swallowed hard as she looked closely at the grainy black and white photographs; some of the men were so young, not much older than Micky Clarke by the look of them, just like the boys from the streets around Grove Road who'd all rushed to join up, most of them boys that she and Evie had been out with at one time or another. Maybe Evie was right as well, she thought. Maybe it did make sense just to go out and enjoy yourself, no matter what. Say there was no tomorrow, what would it matter then if she went out with Chas, or even Albie Denham himself? What was the point in behaving yourself if the whole bloody country was going to be blown to bits or gassed to death?

Now even more depressed than she'd been after rowing with Evie, Babs closed the paper and went over to refill the kettle. That was always the answer, she laughed humourlessly to herself. 'Have a cup o' tea – that'll save you from Hitler's bombs.'

Babs made a full pot and poured two cups.

'There's a cup o' tea for yer there, Dad,' she said touching him on the arm. She soon wished she'd let him go without; almost the moment he opened his eyes he was back to moaning about the Denhams.

'I don't know what's got into her,' he complained. 'What's she wanna get herself hiked up with that moody bastard for?'

'He might not be moody, Dad. Yer don't know for sure.'

'What, coming from that family? I know I ain't been much of a dad, but I have got some feelings, and I'm worried about Evie, Babs. Right worried.'

She crouched down by his chair. 'Listen to me, Dad. Evie's always been a bit wild, we both have at times. But she ain't daft. She knows how to look after herself. Anyway, she's only having a good time. What's the matter with that?'

'I suppose yer think yer mother was only having a good time and all.'

Babs stood up. She went over to the sink and grabbed its cold, hard stone edge. Keeping her head bowed and her back to Georgie she said quietly, 'That was spiteful, Dad. There was no need to say that.'

'Yer right, I'm sorry.' Georgie ran his hand through his thick, greying, though still glossy dark brown hair and down over his unshaven chin. 'I'm a bit out o' sorts, that's all, girl.'

'Yeah. Course.' Babs went to say something, then hesitated. She stood silently for a minute. 'Well,' she said briskly, the moment past, 'I'll be going up now. I've gotta put me hair in pins for work in the morning.' She turned to face him. 'Don't fall asleep in the chair again, will yer? Yer'll give yerself a bad back.'

'No, I won't,' he said smiling weakly. 'Yer a good kid for worrying about yer old dad.'

Babs smiled back at him, her own effort even fainter than his.

Georgie grasped the arms of the chair and stood up. 'I thought I might have a walk down the Drum for a quick half before I get meself up to bed.'

'I ain't got no money for yer, Dad,' Babs said quickly, knowing that she had her bus fare for the week, the shopping money for food and very little else.

'Don't need none,' said Georgie, inspecting his unshaven chin in the overmantel. 'Jim and Nellie said to pop down and clear the tables for 'em. They'll see me all right for a drink or two.'

With her hair set in pins ready for the morning, and with her dad and sister both out, Babs couldn't think what to do next. She didn't feel like reading any more of the paper and there was nothing on the wireless worth listening to. The house was still and silent.

She flopped down on the bed and lay listening to the sounds coming from the street below. Even though it would soon be dark there was still the happy laughter and shouting of children playing outside, making the most of the warm, late summer evening, while their mothers sat on their stone window ledges or on chairs they had fetched from their kitchens, exchanging the news and gossip of the day. The lively noises coming from outside made the silence inside the house seem even more depressing. Half-heartedly she levered herself up onto her elbows, deciding whether she could summon up the energy to get dressed again and go down to join her neighbours; but she couldn't be bothered. She couldn't even be bothered to turn on the lamp. She just flopped back down onto the pillows, pulled the eiderdown over her legs and lay there in the gradually darkening room trying to remember when she had last been entirely alone.

Her thoughts wandered and soon nagging worries about what Evie was getting herself into with Albie Denham crept back into her mind. But, Babs kept reminding herself, why should *she* be bothered what Evie was up to? She'd gone through all that earlier and look at the trouble it had caused. And Evie was seventeen after all, Babs tried to reason to herself, definitely not a kid. She could look after herself.

Still Babs couldn't sleep. No matter how she tried to convince herself otherwise, she finally had to admit that it wasn't only the idea of Evie getting involved with a crook that bothered her – after all, there were plenty in the East End who got by in all sorts of ways. No, what she really didn't like, what she really hated, was the idea of being without her twin. The gnawing pain deep inside her felt as though half of her very being had been ripped away. It had always been her and Evie together, the Bell twins, that was how it was.

Her thoughts drifted and she remembered how she and Evie had shared the back bedroom and then, on the very night their mother had left them, how they had moved into the front. A terrible sadness came over her as she heard the sound of their parents' rowing filling her head and her dad begging her mum to stay.

She stared up at the ceiling, not moving as tears trickled down her cheeks and ran down into her ears. Would she be like Georgie? Would she fall apart if Evie left her?

She must have eventually dropped off to sleep, because the next thing she knew was being woken by the sound of sparrows squabbling in the gutter outside the bedroom window and the sky bright with sunshine. She blinked the sleep away from her eyes and reached for the alarm clock on the side. Nearly half past seven – she'd forgotten to wind it.

She threw back the eiderdown and swung her legs onto the chilly, lino-covered floor.

'Get a move on, Eve,' she said automatically. Turning to look over her shoulder to her sister's side of the bed, she added her usual brisk words of encouragement, 'Come on, we're gonna be late if yer—'

The words froze on her lips. Evie wasn't there.

4

Lou, a freckle-faced, pink-cheeked young woman of about eighteen, looked up at the calendar on the factory wall. 'First of September.' She sounded relieved as she shouted the date to Babs over the sounds of the workshop. 'Thank gawd it's Friday at last,' she added as she whizzed a strip of folded floral material under the foot of her sewing machine and then tossed the resulting sleeve onto a growing pile by the side of her chair, ready for another machinist to fix to the blouses. 'I wish we could get a bit more of this piecework, Babs.' She snapped the foot closed over another folded length of cloth. 'Yer know, I just can't seem to get by from one pay day to the next lately without having to have a sub off me mum. And she's getting right cheesed off with it, I can tell yer. Still, I promised her I'd help when I get in tonight – to sort out the blackout curtains and taping over the windows and that. Bloody waste o' time, if you ask me. You done your'n yet?' Lou bent forward to bite through the thread of yet another completed sleeve, turning her ginger curl-framed face towards Babs as she did so. 'Oi! You listening to me, Babs?'

Babs nodded.

'Well, I only hope you are. The wardens are gonna make sure we're all keeping the blackout from tonight, remember. Pathetic.' Lou smiled happily to herself. 'Still, at least it means I'm in Mum's good books for saying I'd help her; not that I intend doing very much, mind. Not after working here all day, I don't.'

Lou continued to chatter away ten to the dozen while Babs sat silently working at the machine next to hers. Lou did not appear to be overly concerned that her friend was so much quieter than usual. But the machinist who sat on Lou's other side – Ginny, a tall, thin-lipped gossip in her mid-twenties – seemed only too interested in Babs's unusually subdued manner.

'I see that Evie Bell ain't in again yet,' Ginny hissed slyly to Joan, the slow, fat, easily led girl of fifteen who sat next to her. 'Since she bleached that hair of hers last weekend she's been late every single morning. Now, let me guess why.'

Joan giggled lewdly. 'I dunno, Ginny. Why do you reckon?'

''Cos she's no better than she ought to be, that's why,' Ginny muttered back. 'Exactly like her mother, see.'

Not being a practised gossip like Ginny, Joan made the mistake of talking about other people's business in far too loud a voice for her own good. 'What's the matter with Evie and her mother then, Gin?' she asked, agog at the possibilities. She gasped: 'Here, they ain't a pair of old brasses or nothing, are they?'

Lou's eyes widened as Babs stopped her machine dead, threw back her chair and strode along the bench to where the unfortunate Joan now sat shaking in her seat.

'*What* did you say about me sister and me mum?' demanded Babs. 'I don't think I could have heard yer right.'

Ginny, whose machine was now the only one in the workshop still going, kept her head down, apparently engrossed in the Peter Pan collar she was making. Even Maria, a quiet, second-generation Italian girl who always kept herself to herself and concentrated on her job of hand-finishing the garments, had stopped working and

62

was now staring at the sight of Babs advancing on Joan with a pair of pinking shears in one hand and a heavy wooden yard stick in the other.

'I never meant nothing, Babs.' Joan tried backing away, desperately looking to Ginny for support.

'Well, if yer never meant nothing why d'yer say it?'

'What yer gonna do with that yard stick and them pinking shears, Babs? Measure her up for a wavy haircut? She needs something to liven her up, big-mouthed little mare. Just look at her. She's as plain as a plum pudding with no currants.'

Babs knew the voice immediately; it was as familiar to her as her own. She looked round to see Evie standing in the doorway of the workshop, hands on hips, grinning from ear to ear.

'Morning, everyone,' she chirped, hanging her jacket and hat on the stand by the time clock. 'Don't s'pose it was you clocked me in, was it, Ginny?' she asked sarcastically as she settled herself in the vacant seat at the end of the workbench. Up until Tuesday, the seat had been Lou's, but when Evie had been so late in on Monday after staying out all night with Albie and had had her pay docked for her trouble, she had persuaded Lou to swap places and let her sit closest to the door. Now she could sneak in if she was late again, as she had been on every morning since and as she fully intended being on many other mornings.

'Course she didn't clock you in. *I* did,' Babs glared at Evie as she settled herself back down next to her at the workbench. 'So what was the matter with you this time? I couldn't wake yer this morning, no matter what. Even with the cup o' tea I went to all the trouble of bringing up to yer. And I suppose that's still on the floor by the bed and all.'

'You don't half go on, Babs.' Evie sighed and rubbed the backs of her shapely calves. 'The roads was so busy

63

out there, what with all them blokes painting white lines on all the kerbs and everything, I had to get off the bus at Vallance Road and walk all the way up here to bloody Aldgate.'

'Cor, you had to walk a couple of hundred yards! Mind yer don't wear yerself out.'

Evie scowled at Babs and unenthusiastically picked up the front panel and the facing of a blouse. She stuck one on top of the other then wearily plonked them under the foot of her machine. 'I dunno what's the matter with you, Babs. I got in late and overslept, that's all.'

'That's all?' Babs whispered fiercely. She felt like hollering, but wouldn't give Ginny the satisfaction of hearing that she and Evie were rowing. 'That's *every* single night yer've been in late – if yer've bothered to come home at all. Every single night since Sunday.'

'Since Saturday, don't yer mean?' Evie corrected her with a saucy grin.

'Watch it, you two.' Lou tapped Babs urgently on the arm. 'Get yer machines going. It's Silver.'

Babs and Evie immediately stopped their row and became pictures of industry, furiously working away at their machines. But young Joan wasn't quite so quick on the uptake. 'Silver? So what's he want then?' she called along to Lou. 'Here, you sure? He hardly ever comes up here to the workshop.'

'Yes, I'm sure,' hissed Lou through clenched teeth. 'Now pipe down.'

'Well, what's his game then? Why's the four eyed old . . .' Joan's words faded away and she sat there, open-mouthed as though she was at the dentist's. The bespectacled object of her abuse was standing listening to her from the doorway.

Mr Silver removed his glasses and slowly polished them on his pocket handkerchief. 'My "game", Joan, for your information,' he said as he walked into the workshop and

64

replaced his spectacles on the end of his nose, 'is to keep you lot in employment, so perhaps you could manage a bit of courtesy'. He was addressing Joan but his eyes were fixed on the astonishing sight of the Bell twins with their contrasting hair colours. With an approving nod in their direction, he strolled up and down the line of workers, peering over their shoulders at the piles of work by their chairs.

'Sorry, Mr Silver,' mumbled the red-faced Joan. 'I didn't mean nothing.'

Ginny gave Joan a crafty nudge and whispered hurriedly in her ear. Innocent as ever, Joan did as she was told. 'So what *are* yer doing up here in the workshop then?' she asked, looking puzzled when the girls – all except Ginny – started laughing.

Ginny merely looked out of the corner of her eye, along the row to where Maria sat at the far end of the bench surrounded by a heap of blouses ready for finishing.

'If you could possibly do me the honour of waiting a moment, Joan,' Mr Silver said with an exaggerated politeness that had all the girls laughing again, 'until the chaps from the warehouse join us, then your curiosity will be satisfied.'

The thought of the warehouse workers coming upstairs had the girls giggling and whispering to one another; even Ginny patted her hair to make sure it was tidy.

'That's enough,' said Silver wearily. 'They're coming up to listen to what I've got to say, not to ask you lot to a dance.'

'Here they are, Mr Silver.' Joan pointed excitedly at the door. 'Look, they're here.'

Silver turned to acknowledge the warehouse staff who had just arrived. 'Right, in you come, chaps,' he said, beckoning them in with a tilt of his head.

There were five of them who variously sloped, strutted

or walked slightly warily into the workshop and stood along the far wall from the workbench: one gangling, fair-haired youth who looked as if he'd just left school that morning and, from his bright red cheeks, wished he was still there; two good-looking young men – the very obvious objects of the workshop's adulation; one much older man, Dick, who looked fit enough for work but also old enough to have retired to an armchair by the fire many years ago; and finally Tiddler, a handsome-faced man in his late thirties, who because of a diseased and sickly childhood reached barely four feet ten in height.

Turning back to face the whispering young women at the workbench, Silver raised his hand for silence. 'Do us all a favour and shut up, ladies. I've got an important announcement to make. One you *all* should hear.'

Ginny muttered something to Joan who, without a second's thought, piped up, 'Here, no one's getting the push, are they, Mr Silver? You ain't sacking no one?'

Silver looked exasperated. 'Let me get a word in edgeways, eh?'

Joan tutted and put her hands primly in her lap. 'I only wondered,' she said to herself.

'Right, now if I've got your attention. I don't think any of you would disagree that I've been easy on you lot for too long. I know you all reckon I'm a soft touch as a governor. But all that's going to finish.'

Hurried, concerned glances passed between the workers.

'Men out there are joining the army, they're ready to fight for what's right. And what do you lot do? You slope off early, you get in late.' He stared at Evie, who didn't even have the grace to blush. 'And you nick gear out of the warehouse.' He turned to the two good-looking men and nodded at them. 'I'm not stupid, I know about the odd rolls that get "damaged".'

The two men shuffled uncomfortably.

Mr Silver turned back to the machinists. 'And yes, I know all about the cabbage. Sometimes I think there's more of my garments on sale off bent stalls down the Lane than I've got in the whole of my showroom.' He paused, letting them all squirm. 'Well, that's always been part of the rag trade, I suppose, but, like I said, things round here are going to change.' He held up his hand. 'Please, just listen, Joan.' Silver clasped his hands behind his back and rocked backwards and forwards on his heels. 'Now it's going to be *your* turn. I'm giving you lot the chance to do your bit in fighting that, that . . .' Silver ran his hand through his sparse grey hair. 'That bastard Hitler,' he finally managed to say.

Looks of surprise flashed round the workroom at the shock of the usually gentlemanly Mr Silver using bad language.

'Because,' he continued, 'from now on we're making uniforms.' He paused again, listening to the workers' discontented mutterings about the war not even having started yet, and what was he on about, and how were they meant to be able to handle all that heavy cloth. 'Oh, and I should mention that it's all piecework, and I'm personally going to see that there are some very attractive bonuses.'

All Mr Silver's workers cheered, whether from patriotism, relief that nobody was getting sacked, or delight at the prospect of all that piecework wasn't clear, but cheer they did. That is, all except Ginny. She raised her hand. 'Mr Silver,' she said in a low, wheedling voice.

'Yes?'

'What's Italy gonna do in this war, Mr Silver?' Ginny flicked her eyes along the row towards the olive-skinned Maria. 'Not on our side, are they? More like friends of the Jerries, me dad says. Something about what they did in Spain, or something. Is he right?'

Silver shook his head sorrowfully. 'Isn't there enough hatred in this world?'

Ginny sucked in her cheeks and looked pained. 'I only said what me dad reckons.'

'Just get on with your work.' Silver walked towards the doorway then stopped. 'We'll have to get this blouse order finished quick as we can,' he said to them. 'Then we can sort out converting to the heavy-duty machines.'

With the knowledge that their jobs were safe, the warehouse workers readily followed their boss back down the iron stairs to get on with their duties and the machinists set about polishing off the blouse order with renewed enthusiasm. But even with all the machines going full pelt, they could all still hear Ginny's moaning voice above the noise.

'I don't understand that Silver,' she said sharply. 'He's such a mean old bastard. He's never give us nothing, yet he give all that gear away to the refugees last month and now he's doing uniforms and giving out bonuses when he don't even have to.'

'Well, I don't think he's mean. He's always seemed very fair to me,' Evie said, raising her eyebrows at Babs.

'More than fair,' Babs agreed.

'Aw, yeah,' sneered Ginny. 'I'm sure you two do think he's fair. And I'm sure fellers always are fair to the likes of you and yer sister, Blondie.'

Evie laughed disdainfully. 'I'll ignore that, Trappy.'

Ginny's machine stopped. 'Who you calling "Trappy"?'

'Dunno,' Evie answered airily, and tossed another almost completed blouse onto her pile. 'They don't label rubbish.' She leant forward and called along to the far end of the row. 'Here y'are, Maria. Another bundle for yer.'

Maria pushed back her chair and stood up.

Babs looked at Ginny then at Evie – they were both glaring as though daring each other to say something else.

'Why shouldn't Mr Silver give stuff to the refugees if he

feels like it?' Babs said as she watched Maria move along the row towards them. 'They're his own people, ain't they? It's only right to help yer own.'

'Tell that to the Italians,' jeered Ginny.

Evie slammed her hand down on the bench. 'Can't you just *shut up* for five minutes?'

'Yeah, shut yer row and get on with yer work, Ginny.' Babs winked at Maria who had stopped between her and Evie to collect the pile of blouses. 'Yer giving me a headache.'

'Take no notice of her.' Evie touched Maria gently on the arm. 'She's jealous 'cos yer so pretty and 'cos of that lovely figure of your'n.'

'Yeah,' agreed Babs. 'She's just a jealous, hatchet-faced old bag.'

Maria picked up the blouses and smiled wanly at the sisters and walked slowly, head down, back to her place.

Ginny snorted with disgust and got back to her machining.

Evie nudged Babs to get her attention and then she rocked her chair onto its back legs, poked her tongue out and stuck her fingers up behind Ginny's back. Not caring if Ginny had seen what she had done, Evie turned back to Babs. 'Here, look what I've brought in.' She held up a tightly rolled parcel of black material that she produced from her bag.

'What yer doing with them?' Babs sounded flabbergasted. 'They're the bloody blackout curtains.'

Evie rolled her eyes. 'Aw, ain't they pork chops? And I was gonna do 'em for dinner and all. What we gonna have now?'

'So what yer brought 'em in here for?' Babs frowned. 'Oi, Eve, you ain't gonna make a dress or nothing out of 'em, are yer?'

'No.' Evie sounded indignant. 'The way you talk to me sometimes. If yer must know, I'm gonna line 'em with a

69

bit of that flowery stuff we've been using for the blouses. Might as well have the house looking pretty inside, eh?'

'Don't you let Silver catch yer.' Babs looked warily over Evie's shoulder. 'Not after what he said.'

'Shame, I was gonna ask him to help me do the hems and all,' Evie said as she expertly pinned pieces of the floral material to the inside of the curtains. 'I told yer, Babs. I ain't stupid.'

'I dunno sometimes.'

Evie ignored her sister's concern and got on with machining the brightly coloured backing to the dull blackout cloth, accompanying herself as she did so with a tunefully boisterous rendition of 'Roll Out The Barrel'.

Lou nodded towards Evie, her ginger curls bobbing. 'She's happy.'

'Still with her new bloke, ain't she.'

'Yer don't sound very happy about it.' Lou frowned in surprise at Babs. It wasn't like the Bell sisters not to support one another, no matter what either of them had got up to. They could have a tiff over something, and they often did, but it never lasted and was never, ever serious. And there had, up until now, been an unspoken rule that the twins would never speak ill of one another, even in a joke, to any outsider, no matter how well they knew them.

'Can't say I am very happy about it.' Babs spoke so that Evie could hear what she was saying. 'But I don't suppose it's nothing to do with me.'

'Yer right, Babs.' Evie smiled sweetly as she guided the curtain material forward. 'It ain't. And nor has the fact that I'm going out with him again tonight either. And tomorrow night. *And* probably the night after that and all. Yer wanna get yerself out more, Babs, yer must be bored silly sitting in every night by yerself. Yer getting a right little stay-at-home.'

Babs's cheeks reddened; she had missed going out with

70

Evie and they both knew it, but it hurt her to hear Evie say it so bluntly, and in front of Lou.

Lou bent her head towards Babs so that Ginny couldn't hear. 'I know, Babs,' she said quietly. 'Let's me and you find ourselves a couple of chaps to take us to the pictures tomorrow night. What d'yer think? I ain't got nothing to do and I don't fancy sitting in on a Saturday night. Specially not with me dad going on about war all the time and me mum moaning about all the money I owe her. What d'yer say?'

'I'm not sure if I feel like it,' Babs said noncommittally. She didn't want to prove Evie right quite so easily.

'Go on, that good-looking Freddy from down in the warehouse right fancies you, Babs, yer can see it all over his face. Tell yer what, we'll go down and see him after work and tell him to bring that mate of his for me.' Lou, increasingly warming to the idea, beamed at Babs then closed her eyes and, with a sigh, slowly shook her head. 'Cor! What a pair of lookers them two geezers are.'

Babs looked at Evie who was feigning ignorance of the conversation between Lou and her sister. 'Go on then. Yer on.' Babs said it reluctantly but she, too, was smiling now. 'I'd like that, and yer right, that Freddy is a bit tasty. But you're gonna have to go down there and sort it all out, Lou. I've gotta get off home sharpish tonight to sort out this stupid blackout stuff.'

'Can't you help her get it done, Evie?'

Babs looked at Lou as if she was mad and Evie just carried on singing as though she had heard nothing.

Lou got the sisters' message loud and clear. 'Sorry. Daft question.'

Evie folded up the finished blackout curtains and slipped them back in her bag. She ended her song as she started working on making up a sleeve. 'Lou,' she said casually.

'Yes, Eve?'

71

'When yer go down the warehouse to see Freddy later on, don't let Tiddler hear yer making no plans to go out, will yer?'

'Eh?' she said, winking at Babs. 'I didn't think you'd heard me and Babs having our little chat.'

'Leave off, Lou. I mean it. Yer know how the poor sod gets himself all upset 'cos he ain't got no one. And he's a decent bloke.'

'All right, Eve.' Lou chuckled and said to Babs, 'That twin o' yours is a right softy underneath, ain't she, Babs?'

'She ain't a bad old cow really,' Babs said affectionately.

'What, me?' Evie put her hands to her chest and pulled a face of mock horror. 'Yer both wrong there, girls. Right hard case, I am.'

'Yeah,' smiled Babs. 'Course you are.' She nudged her sister playfully. 'Come on, Evie, how about another song? Tell yer what, I'll do all the girls a favour and join in with yer. My voice'll cover up your rotten squawking and give their ear'oles a rest.'

Babs stood on the pavement outside number six, her hands on her hips and her head tilted to one side, staring at the front window. 'I dunno,' she said to herself. 'It still don't look right.' She went back inside and called up the stairs: 'Can't yer come down and help us just a minute, Eve?'

'I told yer once,' Evie called back and stepped out from the bedroom onto the upstairs landing. She was wearing only her underslip, and had a hairbrush in one hand and a mirror in the other. 'I did my bit when I lined the curtains this morning.'

'And yer didn't even do that right 'cos yer rushed 'em. Typical o' you. Yer start something all nice then get bored with it and wind up mucking it all up. The upstairs ones are fine, they're hanging just right, but

72

them downstairs ones, the ones that really matter, they're all rucked up in one corner. The light's gonna come right through and Frankie Morgan'll just love that.'

'Does it really matter? You said yerself it was all a waste o' time.'

'I know that, and you know that. But Frankie Morgan knows he can fine us if we don't do it right.'

'Yer finished?' Evie shook her head. 'Gawd, Babs, ain't yer got nothing better to worry about?' She tutted loudly and went back into the bedroom. 'Now just leave me alone,' she shouted. 'Albie'll be here soon and I ain't even got me frock on yet.'

Babs fumed silently as she stomped into the front room and climbed onto the kitchen chair she'd been using as a stepladder. 'Bloody things,' she complained to herself and began unpicking the offending seam. She worked quickly and skilfully and, when she had finished resewing the cloth, she stuck the needle through the front of her apron for safekeeping and went back outside into the street to see if the curtains were now hanging properly.

'Taped yer windows, I see.' It was old Alice Clarke from over the road. She was sitting on a kitchen chair by her street door, her short skinny legs dangling, her narrow little shoulders hunched and her scrawny arms folded tight across her chest. She was in her customary 'on duty' position from where she could take note of all the comings and goings in Darnfield Street.

'Yes, Alice, I've taped the windows,' Babs answered her, but she didn't turn round to face her. The last thing she wanted was to give Alice the opportunity to get started on the neighbours and their misdoings.

'Looks like rain.' Alice tried again to engage Babs in conversation. 'Reckon this fine weather's over.'

'Yeah,' Babs said, and went to go back indoors.

'Yer'd do that a lot quicker if yer dad and sister helped

yer.' Alice shouted the words just as Babs put her foot on the street doorstep.

Not wanting to get involved in a row that could, if Alice's past form was anything to go by, go on for weeks, Babs decided it was best not to be outright rude to Alice, but to hover in the doorway just long enough for Alice to have the chance to say at least part of her piece before she went inside.

'Our young Micky come round to help Nobby put up our blackout, yer know. Good boy, he is. Always helps his nan. Always—'

'Very nice, Alice,' Babs interrupted her. Having agreed that Micky was indeed a wonderful grandson, she'd intended to dash inside before Alice had the chance to start pumping her, but she should have known better. Long years of gossiping on street corners had made Alice a formidable interrogator, and before Babs even moved a step Alice had launched into her questions.

'Ringer and yer sister too busy to help you, I suppose. Better things to do than help you, have they? Out somewhere or other, are they? All right for some, eh? Don't it give yer the hump, you staying indoors grafting while them two are out and about?'

Babs knew that if she was ever to get away from Alice, she had to offer her at least some nugget of information that she could pass on. If she didn't, Alice would only make up her own stories about them. Babs sighed loudly, wild with herself for ever getting into this. 'If yer must know, Alice, Evie's indoors. She's upstairs getting changed and Dad's popped out for a bit.' Babs folded her arms and stared at the nosy woman. 'As if you didn't know most of that already.'

Satisfied that she now had Babs's full attention, Alice got into her stride. 'I *thought* I saw yer dad go in the Drum, must have been, what, nearly two hours ago – about five o'clock? But yer've still gotta do this blackout stuff proper, yer know, whether yer've got help or not, 'cos when that bloody Frankie Morgan starts on the prowl tonight,' she jerked her head towards number eight, Frankie and Ethel Morgan's house, 'yer'll never hear the end of it from that one if it ain't done right. I mean, he's enough of a know-all as it is, but now they've give him that tin hat and blinking armband of his, he'll drive us all mental. That's the trouble when yer give a know-all like him a uniform, goes to their heads, yer see. Here, that's a good'un, goes to their heads, and he's got a helmet!' As Alice laughed, her thin lips practically disappeared altogether, exposing her dark pink gums and the few teeth she still had left.

Babs didn't join in with her laughter, she just stood there, a glazed expression on her face while Alice got on with talking at her from her perch across the street.

'What with that tin hat and his stories about what a blinking hero he was in the trenches. Load of old toffee, if yer ask me. I'm telling yer, girl . . .' Alice was suddenly distracted by something far more interesting than the veracity of Frankie Morgan's famous wartime stories – the arrival in Darnfield Street of a shiny black motor car.

'Here, twin, ain't that Albie Denham?' Alice got up from her chair and craned her neck to get a better look at the driver. 'Yeah, I'm sure that's Queenie's boy. I've seen that car round here a few times lately, ain't I?' She dragged her gaze away from the car and flashed a quick look at Babs. 'Well? Is it him?'

Babs didn't bother to answer Alice's question. The moment Albie tooted the car horn to announce his arrival, she turned on her heel and disappeared into the passageway of number six. She might not be able to stop Evie seeing Albie Denham, and she'd come to the conclusion that she probably had no right even to try, but that didn't mean she had to speak to him or even acknowledge his existence, for that matter.

'Oi, mind yerself, Babs, yer in a bloody dream.' Evie ducked neatly past Babs as they nearly collided in the narrow passage. 'Don't wait up,' she added as she skipped nimbly over the step and out into the street.

'Don't worry, I won't,' snapped Babs. 'Why should I?' As soon as she'd said the words, she wished she hadn't. Why had she said that? The last thing in the world she wanted was to fall out with her sister again; when all was said and done, Evie and her dad were the most important part of her life.

She went to the street door and watched Evie greeting Albie, smiling wryly to herself as she saw Evie look round to make sure that all the neighbours could see that she was being collected in the gleaming black motor. But Babs's smile didn't last; she bit her lip as she felt a red flush of shame creep over her throat. The guilty thought had crossed her mind again that she was more jealous of Evie going out every night and leaving her than she liked to admit. She took a deep breath and, hoping to make amends, called out, 'Have a nice time, Eve. See yer later.'

But Evie was too busy to notice her sister. She was looking up at Albie from the front seat of the Riley as she flirtatiously arranged her skirt round her long, shapely legs, while Albie watched her appreciatively.

'Bloody hell, Evie, at least I tried!' In childish fury at what she took to be her sister's indifference, Babs slammed the street door, sending the still unglazed photograph of her and Evie crashing to the floor. She didn't stoop to pick it up this time; instead she kicked the wooden-backed portrait all along the passage as she strode towards the kitchen. 'Awwww!' she fumed, balling her fists tight to her cheeks, so frustrated that she didn't know where to direct her fury.

'Pull yerself together, for gawd's sake,' she said, her jaw aching with tension. With a final kick at the photograph, she marched over to the hearth and rested her arms on the mantelpiece. She stared hard at herself in the speckled glass of the overmantel, turning her head this way and that.

'What's got into you, Babs Bell?' she demanded of her reflection. 'Yer acting like a stupid, spoilt rotten little two-year-old brat. Yer gonna have to pull yerself together if yer don't wanna scare Freddy off before yer even started.'

Babs pinched her cheeks, bringing a flattering pink glow to her creamy complexion. 'See,' she told herself, 'yer look good when yer ain't going mad. And it's your turn to be out with the fellers tomorrow night, so yer wanna look yer best, not like some sour-faced old moaner.' She laughed sceptically as she wagged her finger at her reflection in the glass. 'And remember, it'll be Evie's turn then to be worried about you being out till all hours.'

She bent down and picked up the photograph. There they were, the two little girls, like two peas in a pod, arms round each other, and both with that special look that said that nothing would ever come between them. That was how they'd been and that was how Babs wanted it to be again. She knew that she would have to make some sort of an effort at least to try and understand what Evie was doing with Albie Denham or else she was sure she'd regret it in the long run. She smoothed the faded photograph with her hand and went out to the passage to hang it back in its place on the wall.

'Come on, Evie.' She dragged the covers off her sister. 'Up yer get.' Babs stood by the bedside already dressed and ready to go.

Evie pulled the bedclothes back over her head. 'Tell Silver I'm ill, Babs. Please.' She groaned pathetically. 'I can't face work this morning. I'm ill. I really am.'

'Number one,' Babs puffed from the exertion of trying to wrestle the covers away from her twin, 'it's Saturday, so there ain't no work. And number two, it ain't this morning, it's nearly one o'clock, and if yer don't shift yerself, Evie Bell, the stalls'll all be packed in and we won't get no pie 'n' mash neither.'

'Well, why didn't yer say so before?' Evie was suddenly sitting up, now apparently wide awake. She sprang out of bed and dashed downstairs to have a wash at the kitchen sink, leaving the bedclothes behind her all balled up in a tangle of sheets, pillows and pink satin eiderdown.

Within minutes the sisters were strolling arm in arm along Grove Road, making their way towards the Roman Road street market.

Babs lifted her chin and sighed happily. 'Feel that sun on yer face, Evie. Don't it make yer feel glad to be alive? And look how it makes them barrage balloons shine, like great big silver fish in the sky, ain't they?'

'Blimey, what's got into you?' Evie looked at her sister as though she'd grown another head. 'You've perked up a bit, ain't yer?'

'How d'yer mean?' Babs felt oddly shy with her twin.

'Well, yer ain't exactly been the life and soul o' the party over the last few days, have yer? Yer've been a right moaner over every little thing.'

Babs didn't answer. Just thinking about her childish behaviour the night before made her bite her tongue. She didn't like to think what Evie would say if she knew how she had kicked the photograph along the passage. Babs forced herself to smile. 'How can I have the hump on a day like this?' she asked breezily. Even though Evie hadn't actually witnessed the tantrum, Babs was determined to make amends for her sulky attitude towards Albie. 'So what did yer do last night? Have a good time, did yer?'

Evie stared at Babs as they turned into the market.

78

'Yeah,' she said with a frown. 'I had a great time.'

'Good.' Babs patted Evie's arm and smiled – a bit easier this time. 'So, tell me all about it.'

As the girls moved between the crowded stalls, Evie made Babs laugh out loud as she told her about being out with Albie on the first night of the blackout.

'What a performance. I heard some bloke really swearing, not just bloody this or sodding that I don't mean, but really having a go, 'cos he'd walked smack into a pillar box. No one had put a band round it or nothing and he'd gone crashing right into it. Bashed all his chest and shins, he did. And the roads! Yer wouldn't believe it. All yer could hear up West was bloody car horns going. "Get out me so-and-soing way" they was all hollering. Yer should have heard 'em. They'd have made even Jim from up the Drum blush, I'm telling yer.'

Babs chuckled. 'Not if he'd have heard our dad first. Yer should have heard him trying to get his key in the lock with no lampposts alight last night. Yer'd have known about language then. He said words I bet sailors ain't never heard of.'

'Oi, oi, girls! What a pair o' little darlings.'

As one, the twins turned to see who had called out to them.

The stallholder's mouth dropped open when he saw that it was the Bell twins. 'What yer done to yer barnet, twin? The pair of yer look even more gorgeous than ever.'

'Like it?' Evie did a twirl.

'Not half. Here, look, Arch, cop a load of this.'

'What's that then, Bob?' Archie Simpkins, his mate on the opposite stall, who was also the twins' next door neighbour, turned round to look. 'Bloody hell.' He sounded impressed. 'What a sight for sore eyes you two are. Yer wanna show my Blanche, see if she'll do hers.'

'Yer don't mean that,' grinned Babs. 'You love Blanche just the way she is.'

'Yer right there, twin,' said Archie proudly. 'I wouldn't change my old woman for the world.'

'But these two they're a geezer's dreams come true.' Bob took off his cap and scratched his head. 'Here, girls, have these on me.' He handed Evie an armful of cabbage and filled Babs's basket with big soil-covered King Edwards. 'Take them home and make the cat laugh,' he said. 'Now I can die a happy man. The Bell twins turned into a blonde *and* a brunette, now I ain't gotta choose between yer. I can fancy yer both!'

The girls smiled their thanks and strolled away, the vegetable man's compliments ringing in their ears. At ease with one another once again, they took their time looking at the stalls that caught their fancy, picking up and discarding a pair of tortoiseshell combs, refusing the offer of a tray of cracked eggs, hesitating over a pair of satin cami-knickers. Finally they decided that they'd have to sustain themselves with pie 'n' mash before they could go another step.

Carefully balancing the deep plates piled high with pie, mash and liquor, Evie and Babs edged sideways between the wooden bench and the marble-topped table.

They both shook generous amounts of chilli vinegar and salt over their food and got stuck in with their spoons and forks.

'Bloody handsome,' said Babs after the first, delicious mouthful. 'Can't beat it, can yer?'

'Yer right there, Babs.' Evie used her fork to pile her spoon with another helping of pie. 'Me and Albie was saying that when we was in some posh place he took me to the other night.'

Babs had swallowed the mouthful of food she had just taken, but she didn't say anything.

Whether Evie noticed her sister's silence or not, she

didn't react as though she had. 'So, are you doing anything tonight then, Babs?' she asked with a smile.

'Yeah. If yer wasn't so wound up with what you was doing all the time yer'd have remembered that I'm going with Lou to meet Freddy and his mate.'

'Aw, yeah.'

The awkward silence that rose like a brick wall between the sisters was broken by a woman carrying two plates of pie and mash and a bowl of mash and liquor, who came to a halt by their table. With her was a boy of about nine and a toddler.

'Hello, twins,' she said. She sounded exhausted. 'Let's sit down.'

Evie and Babs slid further along the bench towards the tiled wall.

'Watcha, Blanche,' Babs said to the woman and reached out to the toddler. 'Here, come on, Janey. You sit with yer Auntie Babs and let yer mum have her dinner.'

Evie ruffled the boy's hair. 'And you sit next to me, darling, and yer mum can sit there.'

Blanche Simpkins was the wife of Archie, the stall-holder the girls had been talking to; she lived in number four Darnfield Street, between the Bells on one side and the baker's shop on the corner. She dropped down gratefully onto the seat on the opposite side of the table and rubbed the back of her neck, appreciating the luxury of having a bit of space around her as only the mother of young children could. 'Thank gawd for that. I'm bloody whacked out, it's so warm out there. Right muggy and stormy it is.' She nodded towards the front of the shop where a heap of shopping in a pushchair was tucked behind the open door. 'And I've lugged all that lot from the other end of the market. My Archie did some sort of a deal with one of the other stallholders and got all that veg off him. We'll be eating bloody carrots and cabbage for weeks.'

Babs nodded towards her basket and grinned. 'We just saw him and all.'

'He liked me hair,' said Eve, flicking her waves away from her face.

'I feel too tired to even brush me hair some mornings,' Blanche sighed. 'I've been that busy. I've missed our chats, Babs.'

'Good job I'm here to help yer carry all the shopping then, ain't it, Mum?' piped Len.

'Yeah, yer me little helper, ain't yer Len.'

Len smiled angelically. 'Not like Mary and Terry, eh, Mum?'

'No.' Blanche tutted. 'I ain't seen hide nor hair of them pair since first thing this morning. Now come on, Len. Get on with yer dinner.'

'They'll be out somewhere with Alice's grandson,' Babs said reassuringly. She shifted Janey, Blanche's toddler, to a more comfortable position on her lap and fed her another spoon of mash and liquor. She waved the emptied spoon at Blanche. 'I reckon Micky Clarke fancies your Mary.'

Blanche laughed. 'Kids. They grow up so fast nowadays. Nearly fourteen, she is. Dunno where the time goes lately.'

'Pretty girl and all,' said Evie. 'Lovely hair.'

'She got a job lined up yet?' Babs asked. 'There might be something going at Styleways. I could ask Mr Silver for yer if yer like.'

Blanche flashed a look at her son who was contentedly tucking into his dinner. 'Thanks, but not yet,' she said quietly, with a nod towards Len. 'Archie's worried about there being a W-A-R.' She spelt the word out almost soundlessly. 'And he'd want me to take the kids, yer know, somewhere safe.'

'W-A-R,' Len repeated. 'Dad said there's gonna be a

82

war when he was talking to Mr Morgan about the blackout.'

Blanche rolled her eyes. 'Bloody kids, can't keep nothing from 'em. Don't you two have none, they drive yer bloody barmy.'

Babs looked at Blanche's tired face. 'Yer wanna make a bit of time for yerself, Blanche. Pop in for a cuppa when you get a minute, we ain't had a good old chin-wag for ages.'

'I'd like that Babs. Ta.'

'Sure me and Albie can't give yer a lift, Babs?'

'No, it's all right, I'm only meeting Lou at the corner of Burdett Road.'

At the sound of a car pulling up outside, Evie reached above the dressing table and lifted the net curtain. 'It's up to you, but it looks like it's gonna tip down out there.'

'I'll be all right. See yer later.' Babs lifted her chin so that Evie could kiss her on the cheek. 'And don't forget yer torch.'

When she was satisfied that Albie and Evie had gone, Babs grabbed her jacket, hat and bag from the bed, checked that all the blackout curtains had been drawn – her father would never remember when he got back from the pub – and rushed off to meet Lou.

By the time she was less than halfway along Grove Road, there was an almighty crash of thunder followed almost immediately by a brilliant streak of lightning that slashed across the darkening evening sky. And then the heavens opened. Raindrops the size of coins plopped onto the pavement. 'Aw, blimey!' wailed Babs and, holding her handbag over her head, she began running towards Mile End.

She was quick on her feet and within moments was dodging across the busy Mile End Road to where Lou was sheltering in a shop doorway on the corner of Burdett Road.

'Watch out!' yelled Babs as a cyclist skidded round her. 'Yer'll splash me stockings.' She shook the rain from her sleeves and joined Lou in the doorway. 'The roads are a bloody nightmare,' she said dabbing the mud from her legs with her hankie. 'Gawd knows what it'll be like when it gets properly dark.' She straightened up and winked at Lou. 'Still, Freddy'll make it all worth it, eh? And there's always good films on at the Troxy.'

'Er . . .' Lou nibbled her bottom lip nervously. 'Freddy's gone and joined up, Babs.'

'Do what? Not another one?'

'Yeah. And his mate. Apparently they both went off yesterday afternoon.' Lou stared down at the rain spots on the toes of her suede shoes. 'Tiddler told me when I went down the warehouse after work. They hadn't told no one about it before 'cos they didn't want the governor to find out in case they didn't get their wages, see.' She looked cautiously at Babs before she went on, trying to gauge her response to the news that she had let her down. 'But after Silver went on about us doing our bit and all that, they thought they'd be safe telling him.'

'And were they?'

'You ain't kidding. He made a right fuss of 'em, even give 'em a few bob extra to get 'emselves a couple o' drinks on him.'

'Why was they in such a hurry?'

'They didn't wanna wait till they was called up and then have to wind up going in with people they didn't know. Least this way they'll be together, Tiddler said.'

Babs puffed out her cheeks and sighed. 'Well, this is gonna be a fair old Saturday night out, innit? Tiddler and old Dick'll be the only fellers left in the whole of London soon. Aw, mustn't forget that spotty little Herbert they've got down in despatch now, must we. He might start seeming a bit better looking if we get really desperate.'

Another clap of thunder boomed above them. Babs shook her head and gazed out from the shop doorway at the crowd of people who had just spilled out of Mile End Station and were now staring disbelievingly at the pouring rain. She turned to Lou and laughed weakly. 'So, yer telling me I've got all cased up in me best gear, got soaking wet, and all to come and see you? I could have waited till Monday morning and seen yer at work.'

'It ain't all bad news, Babs.'

Babs didn't look convinced.

'Me brother Bob's mate Ernie, and some bloke called Sid, another pal of his, they're gonna meet us instead. Down the Aunt Sally for a drink.'

'Yeah?' Babs sounded sceptical.

'I know Bob can be a bit unreliable sometimes, but I threatened him, and from what he said, they sound all right. They're sailors, he reckons.'

Babs linked her arm through Lou's and grinned. 'Well, I ain't never kissed a sailor before. Meant to be good luck, innit?'

Lou grinned back. 'Well let's get going or we'll never find out, will we?'

They hurried along Burdett Road, jostling each other for space under Lou's umbrella. They had almost got to where they had to cross the road to get to the pub when Babs pulled Lou to a sudden halt. She had stopped by a crowd of people grouped round a newspaper stand selling the late evening editions.

'Any news yet?' Babs asked, standing on tiptoe and peering over a man's shoulder trying to get a look at the headlines on the billboard.

'Blimey, Babs, yer as bad as me bleed'n dad,' complained Lou.

Babs ignored her but Lou was determined, dragging

Babs reluctantly away. 'Look, there's still a chance that this war might not even happen,' she said with a shrug. 'Let's forget all about it, eh? Just for tonight anyway.'

Babs pointed across the street to where two blue-uniformed sailors stood in the pub doorway. 'Don't think there's much chance of that,' she laughed. 'Not with the navy buying our port and lemons.'

'Ship ahoy!' giggled Lou in reply and they both dashed across Burdett Road to the shelter of the Aunt Sally.

'So which one o' you fellers is which?' Lou asked as she shook the rain from her umbrella. 'I'm Lou, Bob's sister.'

'I'm Ernie,' said one of them.

'Right,' said Lou, taking his arm. 'You're mine.'

'And I'm Sid,' said the other man. He seemed delighted at the way things had turned out.

'And let me guess what you do for a living.' Babs grinned at Sid and touched his collar for luck.

'Ne'mind what I do, you just tell me all about yerself, darling.' Sid pushed open the pub door to let her inside. He followed her in, not thinking about Lou and Ernie behind them.

'Oi!' A voice shouted from behind the bar. 'Ain't you heard of the blackout, moosh? Get that door closed.'

Sid didn't flinch at the reprimand, he hardly even heard it; he was too busy trying to believe his luck. His own eyes were out on stalks as he watched all the heads turn to gaze at Babs as she walked over to a table in the corner of the crowded bar. The best part was that he'd turned up at the last minute only as a favour to a mate, with no idea what sort of a girl he'd be meeting, and he'd wound up landing himself a real, genuine beauty. He pulled out a chair for Babs and said, 'They say yer get paid back if yer do someone a favour.'

'Do what?'

Sid didn't have the opportunity to explain. Lou and Ernie had joined them at the table and Ernie seemed as impressed as Sid by Babs's looks.

'Can I get you a drink?' he asked, staring at Babs.

'Port and lemon, eh, Lou?'

'Lovely.' Lou sounded fed up as she plonked down in the seat next to Babs, while Ernie went up to the bar.

Sid pulled a chair from another table and squeezed it in between the two girls.

'I dunno, Babs,' Lou said, glaring at Sid. 'I might as well not be around whenever you or Evie are about.'

'Who's Evie?' he asked.

'Her twin,' said Lou with a resigned sigh.

'Not identical?'

'Yeah.' Lou folded her arms.

'Blimey!' Sid stood up to take the tray of drinks from Ernie. He jerked his head towards Babs. 'She's only got a twin, Ern.'

Babs squirmed and flashed a warning look at Lou not to start. In defiance, Lou picked up her glass and tried to down her drink in one long swallow, almost choking herself in the attempt.

'I think we might wanna go to the you-know-where, don't you, Lou?' Babs hissed at her friend and, reaching across the bedazzled Sid, she dragged Lou up from her seat.

In the privacy of the Ladies, the girls had a little chat: Babs told Lou to grow up and Lou told Babs to stop showing off. Then they both sulked and then they both laughed, at themselves and at each other, and finally went back to the table whispering happily. And once they had all had a few more drinks, the girls and their sailors settled down and seemed to be getting on fine with one another.

Sid chatted away to Babs about all his hopes and fears and ambitions and sounded genuinely interested when he asked her what she wanted to do with her life.

As for Ernie, he was more than a little impressed, not

to say surprised, when he found out that Lou wasn't only a keen but a formidably knowledgeable Arsenal fan. 'A pretty red-headed girl with gorgeous freckles and a brain and all,' he said in awe as she discussed in detail the triumphs and tragedies of the Gunners' previous season. 'And not one single word about no rotten war.'

All too soon for the four of them, last orders were called and they had to leave the comforting fug of the bar. As they stepped outside, the effects of the blackout hit them like a solid barrier of darkness.

'Bloody hell.' After two attempts, Sid slipped his arm round Babs's shoulder. 'I ain't never seen nothing as dark as this.'

'Least that rain's stopped,' Ernie said happily and wrapped his arm protectively round Lou.

'I was gonna say yer could leave us up the corner, but I think I've changed me mind,' whispered Lou, cuddling up to Ernie.

'I wouldn't leave you in the dark, darling.' Ernie bent his head and pecked Lou gently on the cheek.

'I'm going to Eric Street, and Babs wants Darnfield Street, if that's all right with you boys.' Lou breathed the words, hardly making a sound. 'But I don't know why I'm whispering.' She burst into a fit of loud joyful laughter, brought on by a combination of one too many port and lemons, the feeling of Ernie's muscular arm wrapped round her and the added spice of fear of the unfamiliarly intense darkness.

'Eric Street'll do me and all, ta, Sid.' Babs said it a bit more briskly than she'd intended.

'But I don't mind.'

'No.' She said it firmly, shaking her head in the dark. 'I'm staying there the night.' The thought of the possibil-ity of turning up at number six and her dad being the worse for wear after a night in the Drum made her determined, no matter how dark it was, that Sid wouldn't take her anywhere near her street door.

'News to me,' Lou said. 'But yer welcome.'

'Here,' Sid sounded suspicious. 'You ain't married, are yer, Babs?'

'No I bloody ain't!'

Lou sniggered in the darkness.

'Yer might have been.' Sid now sounded sulky.

'Well, I ain't.' Babs fiddled around in her handbag. 'I've got a torch in here somewhere.' She jabbed it towards Sid. 'And no, me husband didn't buy it for me. I got it meself, down the Lane.'

Sid took the torch and shone the pale beam at their feet as the four of them walked along Burdett Road in the direction of Mile End Station. Their footsteps striking the flagstoned pavement sounded strange, too loud, in the blackness; in fact all the sounds around them were more intense, stronger, sharper than they ever remembered them being. Every few yards they would hear a yell from somewhere close by, either a curse or a warning as someone misjudged their step or bumped into what, in normal times, would have been a perfectly familiar lamp post but in the blackout had became a phantom street robber or even a murderer lurking in wait.

Lou screamed as the torch suddenly went out. The four of them stopped dead. Ernie bashed into Sid, nearly knocking him over.

'I was sure them batteries was all right,' Babs said apologetically.

'They are,' said Sid, and before she or Lou knew what was happening, the girls were standing in adjoining shop doorways having their chance to find out if kissing a sailor really did bring good luck.

'Sid. Sid.' Ernie tapped his friend on the arm. 'We'll have to be getting back or we'll be in right bother.'

Sid gave Babs a last, lingering kiss. 'Come on then,' he

said reluctantly. 'I suppose we don't wanna get chucked out before we've even been to sea.'

They walked the last fifty yards to Eric Street in silence, each with their own thoughts about what had happened that evening and each with their own ideas about what was likely to happen to them in the future. Not one of them was yet out of their teens but they all felt they were growing up fast.

'This is me,' sighed Lou and they stopped outside a narrow, terraced house.

'And me.' Babs didn't have the chance to say any more. Sid had already pressed his lips against hers. 'All right, Jack Tar,' she said, shoving him away good-naturedly. 'Mind how yer go.'

After several more urgent minutes of kissing and cuddling and passionate whispers and promises, Sid and Ernie reluctantly dragged themselves away and disappeared down the road into the blackness. The girls could no longer see them but they heard Sid call out, 'Remember to make sure yer listen to yer wireless tomorrow, girls. Yer never know, old Chamberlain just might mention us two brave sailor boys by name.'

'Some hope,' Lou shouted back fondly.

'Shut up down there, can't yer?' came a gruff disembodied voice from an upstairs window.

Lou pulled Babs by the arm and they settled back against the window ledge. 'What was all that about you staying here the night?' she said quietly, so as not to disturb the complaining neighbour. 'You had a row with yer dad or something?'

'No, I just didn't wanna get too involved with Sid, that's all. They'll be going away soon, so there didn't seem no point in getting serious for just one night.'

'Aw, I see.' Lou didn't sound in the least convinced.

'Nice bloke though. How d'yer reckon your Bob managed to get something right for once?'

Babs couldn't hear Lou's answer; every sound disappeared inside the tremendous crash of thunder that ripped though the air around them. The sky then flared with a flash of blue and yellow lightning that, for a split second, illuminated everything, including Lou's terrified expression, with a sickly, ominous light.

'Sod me! It's like the world's coming to an end.' She shoved her rolled-up umbrella at Babs. 'I'm going indoors. D'yer want this or are yer coming in with me?'

'I'll take the umbrella. Ta, Lou.'

'Right,' said Lou, disappearing into the blacked-out passage of her house. 'Suit yerself. But mind how yer go.'

'I'll be all right. See yer Monday,' Babs called over the sound of the rain that was now sheeting down.

As she dashed off into the pitch-black of the stormy night, Babs heard Lou's faint reply floating behind her: 'If we're still here, girl . . .'

5

'So, what did yer think of the film last night, then?' Evie
was sitting at the kitchen table preparing potatoes for
their Sunday lunch. She held her head to one side as she
carefully cut round the vegetables and let each long strip
of peel fall onto a sheet of old newspaper. 'Good, was it?'

Babs, who was standing at the sink, kept her back to
her sister and carried on cleaning and chopping the
cabbage they had been given in the market the day
before.

'Well?'

'Dunno. Didn't really see no film.'

Evie laughed. 'I thought yer was looking pleased with
yerself. Freddy that good a kisser, is he?'

'I dunno, I didn't see Freddy.' Babs looked over her
shoulder and rubbed her nose with the back of her wet
hand. 'Only gone and joined up, ain't he?'

'Blimey.' Evie dropped the potato she had just peeled
into a saucepan of clean water which stood on the table.
'Another one.'

'That's exactly what I said.'

'Don't let's get all humpy,' Evie said with an encouraging grin. 'Come on, tell us. What did yer get up to after
all? And don't say yer went out with Lou, 'cos yer know
what I mean. I can see from yer face yer saw someone.'

She leaned back in the hard kitchen chair and folded
her arms. 'And from how yer've been twittering away like

93

a bleed'n canary since yer woke up, yer must have had a good time.'

Babs turned round to face Evie. She leant back against the sink and she, too, folded her arms. 'Lou's brother Bob fixed us up with a couple of sailors he knows from somewhere or other. Yer know Bob and all his mates.'

'Blimey, if Bob sorted it out, yer was more than lucky it turned out all right.'

Babs laughed. 'I said that and all.'

'But sailors, eh?' Evie nodded her approval. 'What was your one like – nice?'

'Yeah. He was all right. Not bad looking and he really talked to me. I've always liked that in a bloke.'

'Seeing him again, are yer?'

Babs moved over to the table and sat down opposite her sister. 'No.' She picked up two potatoes, handed one to Evie and started half-heartedly peeling the other one herself. 'Shame really. I felt a bit sorry for him. Him and his mate's going off on their first trip in a couple o' days and he's never even had a proper girl friend.'

Evie looked dubious. 'How old is he?'

'About nineteen, twenty maybe.'

'What yer mean, he's going away to sea and he's never—'

'Evie!' Babs opened her eyes wide. 'Shut up or Dad'll hear yer.'

'No he won't.' Evie jerked her head towards the door. 'He's through in the front room. Got his nose stuck in the paper before he goes down for his pint. And he's got the wireless on. He won't be able to hear a thing. So, come on, tell us about this sailor.'

'Well, keep yer noise down and I will.'

Evie rolled her eyes impatiently. 'Gawd, it's like pulling teeth.'

'We went for a drink in the Aunt Sally.' Babs glared at her sister's sudden change of expression. 'And there's no

94

need to turn yer nose up like that, neither. We can't all have fellers with motor cars.'

'All right, get on with it.'

'And then they walked us back to Lou's in Eric Street.'

'In the blackout, eh?'

'And yer can take that expression right off yer face and all.' Babs's tone was prim, but she was smiling as she spoke. 'All right,' she relented. 'They did the obvious. They pulled us into a shop doorway.' She leant across the table towards Evie and whispered, 'And yer know how dark it is out there now.'

'Babs Bell, you didn't? Not in a shop doorway in Burdett Road!'

'No, I did not.' Babs laughed out loud. 'Still, a bit of a kiss and cuddle can't hurt no one, can it? Cheered him up, anyway.' She studied the potato that she had almost whittled away to nothing. 'He's gonna love me for ever, he reckons. Been looking for a girl like me all his life.'

Evie reached across the table and shoved Babs on the shoulder. 'So what's his name then, this sailor boy who's gonna love yer for ever and take yer away from me?'

Babs put her hand to her face and stared up at the ceiling. 'Er . . . Sid, I think. Or was it Joe? No, hang on, it might have been Cyril . . .'

Evie nudged her again and they both burst into a fit of giggles.

When they'd got themselves under control, Babs said quietly, 'No, be serious a minute. I don't mean Sid necessarily – that *was* his name by the way – but yer know, I really would like to have someone like him. Someone who's really interested in me. Who cares.' Babs dropped the now tiny piece of potato into the saucepan. 'Who knows what might have happened if these had been different times.'

'Hark at you, yer daft mare. We've got the pick o' the fellers round here. Just like we always have. Yer could be

95

out with a different one every night if yer felt like it.'

'I weren't talking about that.' Babs stood up and went back to the sink. She fiddled about with the colander, draining the water from the chopped cabbage leaves. 'Evie, I know I've been a bit horrible lately – about you and Albie, I mean.'

Evie was immediately on the defensive. 'You ain't gonna start on that again, are yer?'

'No. I just wanna say something that's been bothering me.' She sighed and turned round from the sink to face her sister, but she changed her mind and looked down at the lino instead. 'Yer know when yer was joking about Sid taking me away from yer, well, that's how I've felt about Albie and you.'

'Babs, it was a joke. I never—'

'No. Please, let me say it. I said I was worried about yer seeing him, and I am, but it's more than that. I think I'm jealous of him.' Babs swallowed hard, trying to stop her voice from cracking. 'Jealous that he was gonna take yer away from me and I was gonna be left all alone. We ain't never been apart like this before, have we?' She took a long deep breath and looked up at her sister. 'I'm scared that everything's gonna change, Evie.'

'Yer silly cow.' Evie pushed back her chair and threw her arms round her sister. 'No one could ever take us away from each other, Babs. No one.'

Babs looked up through her tears. 'I hope not.'

The sound of their dad's loud complaints from the front room made them both look towards the open kitchen door.

'Bloody load of old nonsense,' they heard him holler. 'What's flaming Poland gotta do with us over here? That's what I wanna know.'

The twins frowned questioningly at each other. 'Poland?' they both said.

'Sod me!' Ringer shouted even louder this time.

On her way into the front room to see what was wrong, Babs rolled down one of the sleeves of her blouse and wiped her eyes on the flowery material.

'What's the matter, Dad?' Evie sat herself down on the arm of his over-stuffed chair.

'It's the Prime Minister speaking from Downing Street.'

Babs smiled at Evie. 'Sid told me that Chamberlain'd be on the wireless this morning.'

'Sssh!' Georgie shook his head urgently then looked at each of his daughters in turn. 'It's the Germans. They say they ain't gonna pull their troops out o' Poland.'

Babs was about to say something else, but Evie got in first. 'What's Poland got to . . .' she began, but the Prime Minister's ominous words echoing from the wireless in the corner of the room silenced even her.

'. . . consequently,' he went on, 'this country is at war with Germany.'

The words stunned the three of them, just as they were stunning people all over Britain.

'But . . .' Babs dropped down into the armchair across the hearth from the one in which her dad and sister were sitting. 'But how can we be at war? He did say war, didn't he, Dad?'

Georgie nodded silently.

'But war can't happen, not on a day like this.' Babs stared up at the window where only two nights ago she had thought that hanging the blackout curtains had been such a waste of time. 'Look at that lovely blue sky now that that storm's blown over. How can war happen when the sun's shining?'

Evie stood up and went over to the window, moving slowly as if she were in a dream. 'What've we gotta do, d'yer suppose?'

'Remember,' Georgie said solemnly, 'that's what we've gotta do.'

'Remember what?' Evie turned round; she looked confused.

'How things are this morning, 'cos nothing's ever gonna be the same again.'

'Dad!' Babs looked at Evie who had now gone as white as the lace edging on the chairbacks had once been. 'Don't talk like that, yer frightening her.'

Georgie stared into the empty grate. 'If half the stories the old boys used to tell us about the Great War were true, she should be bleed'n frightened.'

'Don't, Dad, now yer scaring me and all.' Babs went over to Evie and put her arm round her sister's shoulders.

Less than a quarter of a mile from Darnfield Street, Maudie Peters was in St Dorothea's Church playing the piano for the morning service. She had just struck up the opening chords of 'Now Thank We All Our God' when the local beat constable poked his head warily round the metal-studded, heavy wooden door. Not being a religions man himself he always felt awkward in churches, not sure quite what to do or how to behave. He hovered around the doorway for a moment but, knowing that action was called for, he took a deep breath, removed his bicycle clips and strode self-consciously up the aisle with his tin hat tucked under his arm. First he went over to the piano and whispered something to Maudie who immediately stopped playing. Then he shuffled sheepishly over to where the vicar was standing by the pulpit. ''Scuse me, Mr Forsythe, sir,' he said to the vicar. 'Sorry to interrupt the service and everything. But I thought you ought to know that just a minute or two ago it was announced that we're at war with Germany, sir.'

Gasps of horror echoed around the high, vaulted stone ceiling of St Dorothea's as the appalled parishioners took in the constable's mumbled words. Like the Reverend Clifford Forsythe, many of the mainly elderly congregation were old enough to have nightmare-inducing memories of the Great War. In fact it had been the part the vicar had played as a young officer in that conflict that had resulted in his determination to enter the Church in the first place. He had made up his mind to dedicate his life to serving a parish where the congregation was made up of working people just like those whose sons, husbands and brothers he felt he had sent to such terrible, wasteful, pointless deaths in the mud and gore of no-man's land.

He closed his eyes and the all too familiar images of death came flooding back to him. When, only a few seconds later, he opened his eyes, he was momentarily surprised to find himself not in the death-stained fields of Flanders but in the cool, stone interior of the church where he had served for almost twenty years. With an almost imperceptible shake of his head in an attempt to clear his mind, he stepped forward and grasped the edge of the front pew, trying to disguise the trembling in his hands. 'Those of us here today with memories of war will understand that there will be no sermon today.' He spoke in what he hoped was a reassuring tone but he could barely hide the quaver that threatened to crack his voice. 'Prayers are all that are needed today.'

Many of his flock who were already standing, unsure whether they should leave, hastily sank to their knees.

'But prayers can be said anywhere. This is a time to be with those you love, so go home to your families and may the Lord go with you all.' With a gesture of blessing, Clifford Forsythe turned on his heel and disappeared into the vestry.

With those words of permission and following their vicar's example, everyone rushed out as quickly as they dared without looking impious, everyone, that is, except Maudie Peters. She stood up and carefully folded her music, put the tidy sheaf of loose sheets away in the piano seat and then walked slowly outside into the cramped churchyard of St Dorothea's. She walked, almost reluctantly, over to the black-painted iron railings where her bicycle rested, its empty basket turned towards her. She didn't even have anything to put in it, she thought, not a bag, not a bunch of flowers, nothing. It was empty, just like her house in Darnfield Street. She wished, as she wheeled the high-framed bicycle to the gate, that she had left it at home; people must have thought it a ridiculous thing to do, riding the thing such a short distance. But worse than what people thought was the choking feeling of depression which filled her chest when she admitted to herself the real reason she had brought her bike – to support her pathetic pretence of having somewhere to go after the service, so that no one would feel sorry for her. All she was actually going to do was ride round and round Victoria Park for an hour or so in order to put off the dreaded time when she would eventually have to go home to her lonely Sunday lunch of bread and cheese and maybe an apple – if she could be bothered to eat anything at all. But after what the constable had told them, she supposed that she should go straight home.

As Maudie freewheeled along Grove Road, slowing down for the turn into Darnfield Street, she, and all the other people who heard them, could hardly believe it – the air raid sirens started their wailing, flesh-creeping warnings. It was impossible to accept that only seven short minutes after war had been declared, the country was already under threat from what everyone would now have to think of as the Enemy. Maudie wasn't sure why she did it, but she got off her bike outside the Chambers' baker's shop on the corner of Darnfield Street and stood watching her neighbours, most of whom she hardly knew, as they reacted in their own ways to the threat of attack. Frankie Morgan appeared in his doorway at number eight, the last house but one from the canal end of the street. He was not a young man, but he went hurtling into the middle of the road barking out his official orders as he fastened the buttons of his jacket.

'For Christ's sake, take cover!' he yelled, frantically signalling with his arms. He started to make his way up the street towards the open Grove Road end, but he only got as far the Bells's when he skidded to a halt and turned back the way he had come. He sprinted over the road to the Jenners's at number nine and bashed on the already open street door with his knuckles. 'Turn yer gas off in there, Liz,' he shouted at the top of his voice, trying to make himself heard over the eerie scream of the sirens. 'Yer can forget cooking yer dinner, there's a raid on out here!'

Liz's husband Ted came to the door in his vest with his braces dangling round his knees. 'We ain't deaf, Frankie. Now keep it down, for gawd's sake. I'm having enough trouble trying to keep the kids calm.'

'Don't give me calm,' hollered Frankie, pointing at his warden's armband. 'I'm an official, I am.'

Ted's wife Liz came to the door, jiggling a crying baby up and down in her arms. 'Ted, yer'll have to do something. They're all in a right state in there. Yer gran's going on about Zeppelins and all that stuff in the papers about gas and bombing raids and everything. Aw, Ted, what we gonna do?'

'Get 'em all in the bleed'n surface shelter, that's what,' shouted Frankie. He jerked his thumb angrily towards a makeshift-looking brick building that the council had erected in the middle of the road between the Jenners' place and number ten, the house opposite that had been empty for years because of the water that had leaked in from the canal practically since the day it had been built.

Liz looked pleadingly at her husband. 'Should we, Ted? What d'yer think? It don't look very safe to me.'

'Don't bloody ask him.' Frankie was fuming. 'I'm the

101

sodding warden round here, not yer old man. Now, Lizzie Jenner, are yer gonna get them kids and Ted's old granny in that shelter, or d'yer wanna get their heads all blown off?'

Liz burst into panic-stricken tears. 'Are yer sure it's safe in there for me kids, Mr Morgan?' she sobbed.

Frankie didn't answer, he had other things to worry about; with a flourish of his armband, he straightened his tin hat and made off up the street to check on the rest of his charges.

'I bet yer ain't made your Ethel go in there, yer wouldn't dare!' Ted shouted after him and led his now trembling wife back into the house to try and persuade them all to go into the shelter, or at least to stop crying.

Frankie didn't hear, he was too busy banging loudly on Maudie Peters's street door. If he hadn't got himself so worked up with the Jenners he would have noticed that Maudie had been standing outside the baker's and was now wheeling her bike along the road towards him.

'It's all right, Mr Morgan,' she called to him. 'I'm here. I'm going straight into the shelter.'

'Well, you make sure yer do,' blustered Frankie and started bashing on the door of number five instead. When he got no reply there either, he ducked furtively inside the last door on that side of the road, which just happened to be the Drum and Monkey.

Frankie knew that Nellie and Jim planned to use the pub's cellar as a shelter for themselves and any customers who were in the pub during a raid, but, he reasoned to himself, he'd better check anyway. Inside the empty bar – purely in the interest of steadying his nerves – he helped himself to a tot of whisky which stood untouched on one of the tables. But, with his responsibilities as a warden in mind, he refused Nellie's shouted offer that whoever it was up there in the bar was welcome to join them in the cellar.

As Frankie took a few more moments to check that there was nobody left in the pub who had missed the warnings – or who might just have left another Scotch going begging – the neighbours on the other side of the street were having to sort themselves out without the benefit of their warden's advice.

Across the road, on the opposite corner to the pub, where just a moment ago Maudie had been standing with her bicycle, Rita and Bert Chambers had taken refuge in the big basement cook-house below their bakery. They had their arms round each other, fretting about their only son, Bill, who had only recently joined the air force. Next door at number four, no one was in, as Blanche and Archie Simpkins had already made their way with their four children to what Blanche could only pray was the safety of the surface shelter. In number six, next door to the Simpkins, while the siren screamed the teeth-jarring notes of its two-minute-long warning, Babs was agitatedly struggling with her gas mask.

Evie peered nervously out of the kitchen window up at the sky. 'Hurry up, Babs, that warning ain't no joke, yer know.'

'I told yer. I ain't going out without me gas mask on.' Babs was now getting furious, not only with the strap adjuster that would not budge, but with herself for not having practised putting on the stupid thing when she had the chance.

'I hope Albie's all right,' Evie said and turned round from the window to tell Babs that she *had* to get a move on, but instead she burst into wild laughter, her fear making her shrill. 'Yer look just like a pig with glasses on in that thing. Blanche was saying she couldn't get her youngest to even try hers on. Don't blame her though. If you could see yerself. Right idiot yer look. Really stupid.'

Babs muttered something unintelligible.

'Eh?'

Babs ripped the mask from her face. 'I said, sod Blanche and her kids. Where's Dad?'

Gas mask in hand, she rushed into the front room calling out urgently for him, while Evie hollered up the stairs. But there was no reply to either of them. The girls looked at each other. Without another word Evie ran after Babs out into the street.

'I don't believe this.' Evie went over to where Georgie was standing in the middle of the road staring up at the sky, his hand shading his eyes from the bright morning sunshine. She grabbed his arm. 'Are you barmy, Dad? Come on, yer coming with us.'

He didn't protest, he just looked bewildered as, with one of his daughters on either side of him, he let himself be frogmarched along the road to the shelter. 'It's like Babs said, it don't seem right, do it? Not on a day like this. Yer know, the morning yer mum left us was a nice day like this.'

The twins said nothing.

When they reached the shelter, Babs grasped the handle and pulled the door open wide for Georgie.

'Shut that flaming door, can't yer?' someone shouted from the dimly lit interior which was thick with the smells of paraffin, cigarette smoke and fear.

Babs shoved Georgie inside and slammed the door shut behind her and Evie.

Their eyes quickly became accustomed to the pale light coming from the single oil lamp which swung from a hook in the ceiling. There was barely room for them on the narrow wooden benches which ran down either side of the rough brick walls, and almost every part of the floor was covered in possessions or children.

Blanche Simpkins shifted closer to her husband Archie and patted the bench. 'Here y'are, Ringer,' she said. 'You sit here between me and Miss Peters.'

Georgie nodded silently and slumped down onto the

hard unpainted seat between the two women.

'Not exactly luxury, is it?' Evie said solemnly as she picked her way over the various little Jenners and sat down on the floor in the corner by Blanche's two oldest children, Mary and Terry.

Babs stayed where she was, standing uneasily by the door, listening for any unfamiliar sounds coming from outside.

'As I was saying before we was interrupted,' said Alice Clarke. The street moaner and gossip fixed her accusing gaze on Georgie. 'I didn't know whether to stay indoors and die in me own front room or come into this death trap. I listened to the wireless for instructions but that was useless, so I went outside, and then I see that bleed'n idiot of a copper on his bike going past the top of the turning. Placards he had on him, if yer don't mind. On his chest and back. Lot of bloody good that is after the sirens had already gone. And as for that Frankie Morgan, we might all have been bombed to death by the time that old goat got himself moving.'

'Well, we're all in here now, Alice. So why don't you shut your cake hole and give us all a rest?' Blanche rolled her eyes at Ethel Morgan, trying to convey to her that, no matter what Alice said, the rest of them all knew that Ethel, determined as she was, couldn't be held responsible for her Frankie's aggravating habits. 'All safe and sound, ain't we?'

'Safe?' Alice snorted. 'I don't think so. Not in here.'

Blanche lifted her chin in the direction of Liz Jenner who was rocking her baby to and fro, looking ready to start crying again at any moment. 'Can't yer see yer upsetting everyone?'

'I ain't upset,' said Blanche's son Terry, doing his best to impress Evie, who rewarded his bravado by ruffling his hair and smiling at him.

'Hope we ain't in here long,' Alice Clarke's husband

105

Nobby said in his doom-laden voice. 'Our young Micky's meant to be coming over to help me whitewash the lav *and* I never brought me embrocation with me. I'm a martyr to me chest if I don't rub it in regular. But Alice said we had to come straight here once she'd made up her mind what we had to do. So I had to leave it on the mantelpiece. Hope no bombs don't fall on the house or nothing, 'cos the chemist won't be open till the morning and I won't be able to sleep tonight without me embrocation.'

Blanche shook her head disbelievingly at Babs, who was now, despite her fears, hardly able to suppress her laughter.

'Did you manage to bring anything with yer, Blanche?' Babs asked, spluttering the words as she tried to keep a straight face.

Blanche squeezed Archie's arm. 'Only me old man and me kids. That's all I need.'

'I brought me knitting.' The tiny voice that came piping from near where Evie was squashed on the floor with the kids came from Ted Jenner's old granny who'd lived with her grandson since he'd got married.

'Gran loves her bit of knitting, don't yer?' Ted said gently.

'I grabbed this off the table,' laughed Archie and pulled a quart bottle of pale ale from under his jacket. 'Wanna swig, chaps?'

Ted Jenner gladly accepted the offer but Nobby, after a sharp, tight-lipped glare from Alice, reluctantly refused.

'I didn't think to bring nothing with me,' said Babs with a shrug.

'I brought this.' Evie held up the photograph of herself and Babs. 'I just grabbed it off the wall as we run out.'

Babs picked her way between the children and, squatting down next to Evie, kissed her on the cheek. 'Yer a soft hap'orth,' she said affectionately.

Evie frowned as she wiped the dull surface of the picture. 'Dunno what's happened to it, though. Could do with some new glass.'

'I never thought to bring nothing neither,' said Ethel thoughtfully. 'When I heard my Frankie shouting the odds and ordering everyone to either get in here or back indoors, I went to the street door to see what all you lot was doing.'

Alice sniggered. 'What, didn't your Frankie make sure you was all right first then, Ethel?'

Ethel was indignant. 'He told me exactly what to do, just like in the instructions he's been given. I told yer, I was just seeing what everyone else was up to.'

'Yeah, right. Course he did.' Alice looked knowingly at her neighbours. 'I can just imagine Frankie being bothered or brave enough to hang around to tell you what to do.'

Evie winked conspiratorially at Terry and Mary Simpkins. 'Here, Ethel, I wonder where he is now. Wonder what he's up to while you're stuck in here with us.'

'Ssshhh, shut up, can't yer, Eve,' said Babs and found just enough room to elbow her hard in the ribs. 'Aw, sorry,' she hissed sarcastically at her sister. 'Cramped in here, ain't it?'

'Bloody cramped,' complained Alice. 'If we had decent gardens instead of them piddling bits of back yards we could all have our own Anderson shelters. It's all right for some.' She sighed loudly. 'Still, me and Nobby'd even have to share that with them upstairs.'

'Where are Minnie and Clara?' It was the first time that Maudie had spoken.

'They wanted to stay indoors,' said Alice with a sneer. 'Said they was gonna shelter under their bed. Gawd knows how they think they'll get under it though. Pair of bloody great porpoises.' She leaned towards Maudie, her skinny claw of a finger jabbing the air to emphasise her

107

point. 'They might have been married once upon a time, the pair of 'em. But they've lived together for years, they have, if yer know what I mean. And we have to have 'em living upstairs, decent people like me and Nobby.'

'You big-mouthed old bu –' The rest of Evie's words were drowned in a sudden, loud, high-pitched monotone which came droning from the street outside.

'Here, ain't that the all clear?' Ted Jenner stood up, bashing his head on the Tilly lamp. 'Yeah, it is. Listen. Listen, it is!'

Within a few seconds the shelter was empty and the neighbours were standing around aimlessly in the road as though unsure what they should do next.

'That it then?' asked Alice. She sounded disappointed that events hadn't been more dramatic.

'Well, I dunno about the rest of yers,' Georgie said. 'But I need a drop of something.'

'Yer on, Dad.' Evie turned her nose up at Alice and took Georgie's arm. 'Come on, Babs, I'll treat us all to a drink.'

'I'll just go and knock for Minnie and Clara,' said Babs, with a defiant look at Alice. 'I'll be with yer in a minute.'

Five minutes later Babs walked into the Drum with Minnie and Clara clinging weakly to either side of her.

'I thought we'd find him in here,' Babs laughed and nodded towards Frankie Morgan who was holding court at the bar. 'Left Ethel all on her tod, the old devil.'

Minnie smiled feebly. 'Not surprised, the ruckings he gets off her. Still, who can blame her, he's such a flipping nuisance. And, speak as I find, I've never heard her moan at no one else.' Minnie suddenly went very pale and held her hand to her forehead. 'I think I'd better sit down, Babs.'

Babs settled the two large women at a table and went to fetch them a drink.

Georgie had already downed a couple of Scotches and

was halfway down a pint of half and half while at the same time busying himself acting as potman, a job that Jim and Nellie Walker let him do for a few shillings a week and to pay off his slate. They were nobody's fools but they tolerated Georgie's drunken unreliability, letting him get away with more than enough, because of their fondness for the twins. They'd never had children themselves and since the girls were small they'd had more than a soft spot for them.

'I think it's nerves, but Clara seems more worried about their dinner getting ruined than any bombs falling on her,' Babs said as she slipped into the space at the bar between Rita and Bert from the baker's. 'Yer made 'em turn the gas off, didn't yer, Frankie?'

'Bloody right I did. It's me duty.'

Bert, his hair white with the flour that he never quite managed to brush from it entirely, called over to Minnie and Clara, 'Yer know yer always welcome to put yer Sunday dinners in me ovens, girls, don't yer? Life's gotta go on, eh? Can't have me two favourites going without their grub, now can I?' He laughed good-naturedly, his round cheeks glowing like apples, and took a swig from his pint. 'Just so long as Jim's beer don't run out, eh? Then we'll all be happy.'

'Don't you worry yerself, Bert,' Jim answered him back as he handed Babs the drinks for Minnie and Clara. 'I'll just put a bit more water in than usual.'

Nellie the landlady shoved her husband Jim unceremoniously out of the way and leant across the bar to where Evie was standing. 'Got yerself a new chap, I see.' She touched Evie gently on the side of her face. 'Nice motor and all. Good luck to yer, darling. Pretty little thing like you deserves the best. And look at yer lovely blonde hair and all.'

'Yer'll have to get yerself a nice geezer sorted out, twin,' Jim called over to Babs as she sat down with

Minnie and Clara. 'Can't have yer letting the brunettes down, now can we?'

'I dunno why everyone sounds so bleed'n cheerful,' Frankie complained. 'But then I don't suppose none o' you lot remember the Zeppelin raids.'

'Blimey, yer sound just like me old granny.' Archie winked at Nellie. 'Watch it, or he'll frighten all yer customers away, Nell.'

Frankie wasn't put off by either Archie's sarcasm or everyone else's laughter. 'Terrible, it was, the Great War. Dropped bombs right out o' the sky on ordinary people, just like us.'

'Don't be soft,' Jim said as he pulled Georgie another pint. 'All this won't come to nothing, you just wait and see. Bit of a ruck between the politicians and that'll be that. Anyway, why'd the Germans wanna bomb ordinary people like us?'

'Yer could ask why they wanted to bomb them poor sods in Spain a few years back,' said Frankie, nodding wisely to himself. 'Front line we'll be here, you just wait. Too near the docks and the City for our own good, you mark my words. I shouldn't mention it, but it's what they've been saying down at the ARP centre for months.'

Doubting hisses and boos were the general response from all round the bar to Frankie's pessimistic warning.

But not from Clara. She rose unsteadily to her feet, her eyes full of tears and said loudly to everyone, 'But yer should listen to him. He's right. There was bombs over London. People got killed and all, so what does me Sunday dinner matter?'

Minnie put her glass down on the table and stood up also. She put her arm round her usually quiet friend. 'Don't get yerself upset, Clara. Yer don't really think they'd attack *us*, do yer, love? Not us here in Darnfield Street?'

The bar suddenly went very quiet and everybody seemed to be staring into their drinks.

6

What with the glorious September weather and the absence of any bombs, it was as though the panic caused that morning by the first air raid warning of the war had never happened. As on any other ordinary warm September evening in Darnfield Street, and most similar turnings all over the East End, street doors stood wide open, men strolled down to their local, women sat by their steps on kitchen chairs chatting, knitting and mending, and children dashed about, playing riotous games of Outs and High Jimmy Knacker or got up to no good down by the canal.

'Yer there, Babs? Eve?' Babs heard someone call along the passage.

'Hold on, coming.' Babs went to the door to find Blanche Simpkins standing there. A good-looking woman in her early thirties who always had a smile for everyone, despite the effort needed to keep her brood in order, today she looked unusually serious and, even more strange for her, she didn't have Janey, her two-year-old, hanging on to her skirts.

'Fancy a cuppa?' asked Babs, jerking her thumb back towards the kitchen. 'I was just making one.'

'No ta, Babs, I ain't stopping. I've got a lot o' things to sort out indoors. I just come to ask a favour.'

'Course.'

Blanche looked up and down the turning, making sure

that no one could overhear. Her eyes fixed on the house opposite where Alice Clarke was perched on a squat stool shelling peas for the next day's dinner. 'I've been talking to Archie,' she said quietly, then took a deep breath and opened her mouth as though she was about to say something else, but she apparently changed her mind and instead sat down on the stone step.

Babs sat down next to her. 'Yeah, what is it, Blanche?'

'Me and Archie've been talking about this evacuation lark.'

Babs nodded. 'Yer said they'd written to yer.'

'Yeah, we've even got a place all sorted out for us and everything. Through someone me little sister Ruby knows from work.'

'But yer not going? Yer said yer wouldn't.'

'I know I did. There was no way I was gonna leave my Archie by himself, but I mean, Babs, since that fright this morning, I dunno what to think no more. It'd be all right if it was just us two but we've got the kids to think about.'

Babs shook her head. 'I thought you was determined not to go.'

'I was, but Archie thinks different.'

'What's Archie got to say about it?'

'Yer know him, never refuses me nothing if I've set me mind on it, and I'm that stubborn he wouldn't have much chance to anyway. But there's no telling him this time about what I do or don't wanna do. In fact I can hardly believe it's him, Babs. Once that warning went this morning, that was it. He's been right firm. Told me I've gotta go, and I've gotta take all the kids with me and all.'

'Even the big'uns?'

Blanche nodded. 'Day after tomorrow.'

'Bloody hell, Blanche. That soon? What do Mary and Terry reckon about it?'

'Well, to be honest, our Terry hates the idea, thinks he's too grown up.'

'He's thirteen now, ain't he?' Babs frowned. 'Here, do they let 'em go that old?'

'If they're with their mums and the billeting people say there's room they do. And there's plenty o' room in this place Ruby's organised. I wish she'd have kept her flaming bright ideas to herself instead of telling Archie. Cornwall or somewhere, it is. Back of bleed'n beyond. Never heard of the bloody place.'

'So, will Terry go?'

'Don't think he's got no choice the way Archie's dug his heels in. But I've promised Terry that if he'll come with me and stay just for a while, then soon as he's a bit older he can come back and work in the market with his dad.' Blanche picked at the stitching on the bottom of her cross-over apron and laughed feebly. 'That's all he's ever wanted to do, that one, have a stall of his own down the Roman, just like his dad.' She rubbed her red, work-worn hands over her face. 'But I can't kid our Mary like that, she's nearly fourteen already, and stubborn just like me. Or like I usually am.'

'And she's a pretty girl, just like her mum, and all,' said Babs, trying to cheer her up.

'I dunno about me being pretty,' said Blanche tucking a stray hair under her turban, 'but being pretty's half our Mary's trouble. Her and that Alice's grandson, Micky, right fancy each other, they do. That's all I hear about, Micky this, Micky that, Micky the bloody other.' She shook her head. 'I can just imagine what Alice would say if she found out.'

'Don't she know?' asked Babs.

'Yer kidding, ain't yer?' said Blanche. 'And there's our Terry. He worships Micky and all. Yer know what they're like at that age. Just 'cos Micky's fifteen, Terry thinks the sun shines out of him. Micky ain't a bad kid, I like the way he's always round here helping his nan and grandad, but I wish my Archie had never let him work on the stall.

Mary's seeing too much of him for my liking.'

'Look, Blanche, yer don't wanna fret about that, yer know what young girls of her age are like. Soon as yer go down wherever it is yer going she'll have met someone else in a couple o' days, you just wait and see.'

'I wouldn't bank on it. I was her age when I met Archie and no matter what no one said I wouldn't change me mind, I knew he was the one.'

'Well, she can't stay here without yer, can she?'

'Can't she?' Blanche sighed. 'Remember when we saw you and Evie in the pie shop?'

'Yesterday, yer mean?'

Blanche shook her head. 'No . . . Yeah. Hang on, wait a minute.' She thought for a moment. 'I suppose it was yesterday. Seems longer ago, don't it, with everything what's happened?'

'Yer right there,' said Babs, running her hands through her thick, dark brown hair. 'A lot of things have happened since then all right.'

'Anyway, that Len o' mine, he might only be nine years old but he's got a right old man's head on his shoulders, figures out all what's going on, he does. Now yer mustn't blame yerself, Babs.' Blanche hesitated, nibbling her lip while she thought how to put what she had to say. 'Yer see, Len told Mary all about you offering to ask about a job for her at Styleways.'

Babs screwed up her face. 'Aw, Blanche.'

'Yeah, and now that's all I've had out of her since this morning. "I'm getting a job with the twins." It was only me warning her to shut up in front of her dad that she never started on about it when she saw yer both in the shelter this morning.'

'Aw, I'm really sorry.' Babs clasped Blanche's hand in hers. 'I wouldn't interfere or nothing for the world, yer know that.'

'I know and I told yer, it ain't your fault, it's Len's. But it don't matter anyway. She ain't got no choice, at least not for another few weeks till she's fourteen. After that we'll just have to see.'

'How about Len, does he wanna go?'

'I told him it was in the country and he said he'll go anywhere if there's gonna be animals. Yer know him. He'd have a barn yard out the back if I'd let him. And Janey's too little to argue. She don't know no better, so she's all right. But, to tell the truth, Babs, it's Archie I'm really worried about.'

Babs smiled encouragingly. 'It'll be a lot quieter without you lot. He'll think he's on his holidays.'

Blanche didn't smile back. She turned to Babs but then dropped her gaze and started picking at the hem of her apron again. 'Babs, would you keep an eye on him for me?'

'How d'yer mean?' Babs sounded really shocked. 'Here, yer don't think he'd muck around while yer away, do yer, Blanche? Not your Archie.'

For the first time since she'd sat down on the doorstep, Blanche smiled as if she meant it. 'No, yer daft cow, course I don't.' She put her hand over her mouth to stop herself laughing out loud at the very thought of it. 'Can yer imagine?' she spluttered. 'My Archie with a girl friend.'

'Not really.'

'What I meant was could yer make sure he don't starve or nothing? Yer know what blokes are like.'

'If yer want an expert on blokes . . .' came a voice from behind them.

They looked round to see Evie standing in the passage, dressed up to the nines and striking one of her favourite glamour girl poses that she got from the films.

Blanche laughed. 'It wasn't that sort of expert I was after.'

'Move over.' Evie squeezed between her sister and

Blanche and, despite her new outfit, sat down on the narrow stone step.

Blanche touched the bouncing waves of Evie's hair. 'Yer know, I still can't get used to you being blonde, Eve.'

'No, but yer know the difference between us now, don't yer?'

'I always knew the difference between you two,' she laughed.

'What, I'm the madly glamorous one, yer mean?' asked Babs, affecting a deep sultry voice.

'No, stupid, you're the ugly one,' said Evie nearly falling backwards into the passage as Babs shoved her in the ribs.

Babs narrowed her eyes at Blanche. 'If you say I'm the one who usually wears the pinny . . .'

'Or, I'm the one who's got the fancy man . . .'

'Yer both wrong,' said Blanche triumphantly. 'It's yer dimples, they're on different sides, ain't they?'

'Yer know what, Blanche, yer a bloody marvel. I thought it was only me and Babs what knew about that.'

'And a couple of blokes we tried to con once,' Babs reminded her sister.

'It comes from being a mum, yer see,' Blanche said with a shrug. 'It was easy, yer notice all sorts of things about kids.'

'Kids? Bloody liberty!' Babs nearly exploded. 'We're gonna be eighteen in May.'

Blanche pinched Babs's cheek. 'Yeah, but yer still young'uns to an old married lady of thirty-two like me.' Blanche's gaze was drawn to the end of the turning. She put her hand up to shade her eyes from the still bright evening sun. 'Talking about marriage, here comes your feller in his motor car, Eve.'

'Marriage?' Evie got up from the step and brushed the dust off the back of her pale blue crepe dress. 'Yer've

116

gotta be kidding, ain't yer? I'm only out for a good time.'

Blanche grinned. 'It gets us all in the end, girl.'

Babs said nothing, she just sat there as the gleaming black Riley drew to a smooth halt at the kerb beside them, knowing that all eyes in the street were directed at number six.

'Well, I'll love yer and leave yer,' said Evie, bending down to plant a kiss on her sister's forehead. 'And—'

'Yeah, I know,' Babs interrupted her. 'Don't wait up.'

Evie winked and clicked her tongue. 'Got it!'

Babs looked up into her sister's face, seeing herself in the familiar mirror image of her twin but also seeing something new in Evie's expression, something she hadn't seen before. It was a sort of toughness, and it excluded her because she didn't understand it. 'Yer will be careful, Eve, won't yer?'

'It's all right, Babs,' said Evie, rolling her eyes at Blanche. 'I've got me gas mask with me.' She held out the stiff card box that was slung on a cord across her shoulder. 'It's a new one, right pukkah and all. Albie got it for me.'

'It wasn't gas attacks I was worried about.' Babs's face was grim.

'I thought we'd sorted all this out,' said Evie wearily.

'I know, and I don't mean to go on again, but be careful. For me. I'm serious.'

'Well, I'm not.' Evie poked out her tongue and sashayed over to the Riley where Albie was sitting waiting, her high heels clicking on the paving stones. 'Fusspot,' she called over her shoulder.

Blanche leant back with her arms folded and watched Evie climb into the luxurious interior of the car. 'What would yer give to go for a ride in something like that?' she said wistfully.

'She's giving more than enough, I reckon,' Babs muttered under her breath. 'And it's changing her.'

'What did yer say?' asked Blanche, enthusiastically returning Evie's wave of farewell.

'Nothing.'

Blanche laughed as the younger children gathered in a huddle on the pavement to watch Albie turn the car round.

'Look at them,' she said fondly. 'They all love motors, don't they?'

Babs didn't answer.

'What's the matter with you?'

Babs shrugged.

Blanche patted her knee. 'Yer wanna get yerself a new bloke, Babs. That's your trouble. I ain't seen yer out with no one regular for quite a while now, have I?'

Babs shook her head as she watched Albie steer the car out of the turning and off into Grove Road. 'No, no one regular.'

'I thought yer was keen on that Percy Bennett from round Haverfield Road, wasn't yer?'

'He's all right. I go out with him now and again.'

'Nothing more? Nothing gonna come of it?'

Babs sat up very straight, staring after the Riley as it pulled out of the turning. 'He always wants to see me again,' she said flatly, 'but I think of him as more of a mate. It was going to school with him, I suppose.'

'He's nice though, ain't he?'

'Yeah.' Babs's voice was clipped. 'Really nice feller, but . . .' she paused, trying to find the words to express what she felt. 'There ain't nothing special, nothing that makes me . . . I dunno. Just ain't my type maybe.'

Blanche glanced sideways at Babs, noting the tension that was making her lovely face as rigid as a mask. 'Evie went out with his mate Joe for a while, didn't she?' she asked casually. 'Like, yer know, the four of yer together?'

'Yeah. That's right.' Babs stood up and made much of

118

stretching and yawning. 'We always used to go out in foursomes.'

'Before Albie Denham come along.'

Babs looked down at Blanche. 'I'd better be getting on,' she said with a tight-lipped smile. 'I bet Evie's left a right mess in there.'

Blanche stood up and sank her hands into the deep pockets of her apron. 'I'll be over to see yer before we leave, to say goodbye properly.'

'Yer definitely going then?'

Blanche took a deep breath and then exhaled slowly. 'Yeah. Archie's right, it's for the best. And he'll be all right with you keeping an eye on him.' She gently brushed Babs's hair away from her face with her hand. 'Yer'll find out one day. It's like a lot o' things when yer a mum, yer don't have much choice. Yer do what's best for yer kids and sod what you want.'

Babs felt the tears prick at her eyes. Without another word she was over the step and striding angrily along the passage. But before she went into the kitchen she stopped and, without looking round, demanded in a loud, trembling voice, 'What, like our mum always thought of us, yer mean?'

At a few minutes before six on Tuesday morning, most of Darnfield Street was standing outside on the pavement, waiting to wave goodbye to Blanche and the kids as they left for Paddington all packed into Archie's little market truck. Just like their neighbours, Babs and Evie were by their street door, yawning and shivering in the early morning chill even though they had their coats on over their night things.

'Mind how yer go,' called Clara tearfully.

'Yeah, watch out for them country people, Mary,' shouted Minnie. 'I bet they can't skip like we can.'

'I'm too old for skipping,' snapped Mary Simpkins and

climbed sulkily onto the back of the truck.

'Yer never too old,' laughed Minnie. 'Right, twins?'

'Right,' Babs said, trying to force herself to smile. But like Clara, she was close to tears. She had been over to see Blanche after what had happened on Sunday but things hadn't been right between them since she'd shouted at Blanche like that about her mother. She wished she'd said sorry. Blanche had been good to her and Evie; she would really miss her. And the kids. She bit her lip trying to stem the tears. She hated the way everything was changing. Why couldn't things just stay the same?

'I wish I was more like you, Eve,' Babs said suddenly, as the tears began flowing down her cheeks.

'What?' Evie shivered. 'Blonde, yer mean?'

'No, yer dopey sod,' Babs sniffled. 'Not taking things to heart so much and going out and having a good time with whoever comes along.'

Evie scowled at her. 'Thanks very much. Yer make me sound lovely, like a right old whatsit.'

'Aw, you know what I meant. It just come out wrong.'

'It's too early for all this, Babs.' Evie opened her mouth wide and yawned loudly. 'Look, they're pulling away, we nearly missed 'em with you and yer moaning.' She grabbed her sister's hand and waved it. 'Come on, Babs, let's say bye bye and then we can get back in and get our heads down for another hour. I dunno if I can face work. I'm bloody knackered. Wish I'd stayed in bed like Dad. He ain't daft.'

Before the truck was even out of Darnfield Street, Evie was halfway up the stairs, leaving Babs to close the street door.

Babs threw her coat over the end of the banister. 'I'm gonna make meself a cup o' tea,' she called. 'Want one, Evie?'

'No thanks, all I want's me bed.'

Babs sat at the kitchen table and stared into her cup. She had to pull herself together, she couldn't keep blaming other people for making her miserable. She gulped down the hot tea and went into the front room. From the sideboard drawer she took a small cardboard case which held writing paper, envelopes and a fountain pen. It had been the first prize in a story writing competition at school that she and Evie had won. She smiled wistfully to herself as she remembered how she and Evie had just accepted that because they were joint winners they should share the prize. That was all part of being a twin, she thought to herself, and something that she had once thought would never change.

She settled herself down at the kitchen table with a fresh cup of tea and began writing a long rambling letter to Blanche, the gist of which was that she wished she hadn't been so rude to her and that she hoped they could still be friends.

The following Tuesday she was sitting at the table before she went to work having tea and toast for breakfast and reading Blanche's reply:

Dear Babs,

It's bloody lively down here. Terry's moping, Mary's sulking and young Janey's got the hives from all the butter and cream she's been eating. I ain't had a wink of sleep with her scratching and fretting all night. The only one who's happy is our Len and I don't see him from the time he gets up to when it's time for bed. He even likes the school here. Less than forty kids in the whole school there are, funny old turn out. Mind you, the whole bloody place is funny, to tell you the truth, Babs.

And me, I'd kill for pie and mash or a proper wing of skate and chips. All they have down here is pollock. Don't laugh, honest, that's what it's called.

Pollock. And the batter! Vile it is, don't know what they cook it in but it tastes horrible. And they don't even have a drop of onion vinegar to pour over it. There's no Woolworth's and it's bloody miles to the nearest pictures. And the way they look at you when you open your mouth and they realise you're a Londoner. They think that we've all got nits, that the kids are gonna piddle the bed every night and that we're going to thieve everything out of their rotten little shop. Shop! I don't know how they've got the cheek to call it that. It ain't no bigger than someone's front room. What a dump. And I know we've got an outside lav back home but down here you have to walk right down this really dark path, past all these horrible bushes. It's right creepy here at night, I can tell you. Horrible. And Mary was going on about grey ladies hiding in the trees. I'd rather use a poe, honest I would.

But to be fair, the people are doing their best, I suppose, and if Terry and Mary weren't me own I wouldn't put up with the pair of them. They ain't stopped going on since the minute we got here. When we going home, Mum? When? Eh, Mum? I'm sick and tired of it, Babs, I really am. Still, don't do moaning, does it, that don't help no one. Only makes people fed up with you. By the way, how are you and your Evie getting on now? It must be hard for you, her getting close to someone else and you being twins and everything. And what with all the changes 'cos of the war.

I'm surprised, you know, Babs, that the Jenners have stayed in the street with all their little brood. Thought they'd have got right away from London. Mind you, I never really got to know Liz and Ted, they've always kept themselves to themselves, maybe they've got plans to go away soon and haven't said nothing to no one. The way things are going according to my Archie, there won't be no one left in the East End except a few old fellers and their old girls. Have any more of the young blokes from round our way joined up yet? You want to get a move on, girl, and find yourself a chap before they all bugger off! Are Rita and Bert still telling everyone about their Bill joining the Air Force every time they sell you a loaf of bread? They must be right proud of him, he's done so well for himself. A kid from Darnfield Street. Rita always said he was too clever a boy to have been happy working in the baker's with them.

I've been putting this bit off so I don't get myself all worked up. How's my Archie doing? I don't half miss him, Babs, specially at night when we used to lay in bed and chat about what had happened during the day and with the kids and everything. Even though he wrote and said he was all right, I bet he ain't. He told me how you pop over there and check on him. I really appreciate how you're making sure he's had a bit of dinner and see his washing's done and that. And your Evie and all. That surprised me. Wonder she's had the time from what you said about her going out every night with Albie Denham. Still, she's like you, Babs, good-hearted. I know how you both always like to see that other people are all right, and that they're happy and that. You're a good pair of girls and lucky to have one another. There's a lot of people who haven't got no one. Like that Miss Peters living all by herself in number seven. We should count our blessings, I say, make the best of life and be glad that other people are able to enjoy themselves.

Give my best to Ringer and thanks, Babs, to you and your Evie for all what you're doing. Keep well, darling. I remember you all every night when I pray that this is all over soon and I can get back to my Archie.

With love from your friend, Blanche.

Babs finished her tea and smiled to herself. Folding the letter and slipping it back into the envelope she said to herself, 'Yer a clever one, Blanche Simpkins. It ain't only dimples yer notice.'

7

Georgie sat up at the bar of the Drum, his expression morose, his pint glass nearly empty. 'How long we been in this war now?' He paused, not to wait for a reply but to drain the last of his beer. 'And what's happened, eh? That's what I wanna know.' He jabbed his nicotine-stained finger at the newspaper that Jim, the landlord, was reading on the other side of the bar. 'Nothing, that's what. All a bloody load of old rubbish. What we gonna do, tell me that if yer can? Nothing, that's what. And do you know what we *should* be doing?'

Jim looked over the paper at Georgie but Nellie shook her head at her husband to silence him. She put the glass she had been polishing onto the mirror-backed shelf. 'I dunno, Ringer,' she said in her practised landlady's voice that persuaded the listener that she was actually interested. 'You tell me.'

'I will,' said Georgie. 'I will tell yer. I'll tell you that we've been in this bloody war since . . .' He paused, the alcohol befuddling his memory. 'Since . . . well, what's today?'

Nellie checked the date on Jim's newspaper. 'November the twenty-seventh,' she said with a weary sigh. 'So it's over two months now.'

'Right, November the . . . whatever. And I'm telling yer, what's happened? Nothing, that's what. Bloody Warsaw fell – wherever that is. And that other place is in

125

trouble and . . . and what're we doing? Nothing.' He waved towards Jim's newspaper. 'No attacks from our lot, no support from the army. What was the point of all them geezers rushing to join up, eh? Bloody waste o' time and money.' Georgie slapped the flat of his hand down hard onto the polished wood of the bar. 'Ouch.' He blew on his smarting palm. 'That bloody hurt.'

'Yer gonna chuck a bit more coal on the fire, Ringer? It's got really parky in here. And yer can collect a few more glasses when yer've done that. We'll be opening up again soon and this place is still in a right old mess.'

Nellie was trying to sound reasonable; she didn't want to sack him for the girls' sake, but he could try the patience of a better woman than she'd ever be and Jim was more than fed up with him. Nellie's husband wasn't such a soft touch as she was and Jim had been ready to give him the push months ago.

'I'm warning you, Ringer,' Jim said. He was speaking quietly but Nellie could see that he was working himself up into a temper. 'You either buck your ideas up and do what Nellie tells yer or—'

'No bombs, no fighting here, no nothing.' Apparently oblivious of the fact that Jim was giving him a warning, or even talking at all for that matter, Georgie carried on along his line of alcohol befuddled thought. 'What are we meant to be in this lot for, eh?' He stared into his empty glass. 'Why don't we either get stuck in or pull our troops out and just let 'em all get on with it, eh? Let 'em all blow 'emselves to bloody bits.'

'That's it!' yelled Jim.

'Yeah, bombs, good idea,' said Nellie wearily as Jim went storming round the other side of the bar, intending to tell Georgie his fortune good and proper this time. 'Get rid of the lot of 'em. And all my bleed'n customers and all their dirty glasses with 'em, with a bit o' luck.'

★ ★ ★

126

Although it was bitterly cold out, the coldest winter that anyone could remember and with still more snow about to fall from the unnaturally yellow look of the sky, Albie parked the Riley on the corner of Stepney Way and, leaving Chas to keep an eye on the car, walked the final, freezing hundred yards to Dr Reider's surgery. Albie wasn't keen on anyone knowing he was there and the sound of the Riley's powerful engine roaring along the slum streets of the East End made his now trademark gleaming car stand out like a cabaret singer in a church choir. Even in the gloom of the winter blackout he was cautious and checked over his shoulder that there was no one he knew in the street before ducking through the shabbily painted doorway that led into the even tattier waiting room of Reider's rundown surgery. It had just gone four o'clock in the afternoon, at least an hour before the evening patients would be arriving and also early enough for Reider to still be hungover from his lunchtime session in the George. The whole situation suited Albie's purpose very nicely.

Albie shoved the consulting room door back on its hinges and strode into the cramped interior. Through the chaotic dinginess, Albie could make out the outline of Reider slumped forward in his battered leather chair, his head jammed up against a pile of books on his desk. 'Hello, Doc. I've come to see yer on a bit of business.'

Reider lifted his head, sending the books crashing to the floor. In the dull bluish light of his desk lamp he looked terrible. His red-rimmed eyes were out of focus and from the stubble on his chin it looked as though he hadn't bothered to shave for at least a couple of days.

Albie made no attempt to remove his hat, scarf or gloves. He picked up a rickety bentwood chair and stuck it down, facing the wrong way, by Reider's desk. He lifted his leg across the seat and mounted it as though he were straddling a horse. 'Yer don't look like Lady Luck's been treating yer very well, Doc.' Albie gave a sad, slow shake of his head. 'She can be a right bastard, can't she?'

'Listen, Albert . . .' Reider was doing his best to concentrate on what he was trying to say but his words were thick with sleep and booze.

Albie reached across the desk and took Reider's lapels in his huge fists. 'No, Doc, it's *you* what's gonna listen. Yer gonna do me a little favour.'

Reider attempted to nod but couldn't because Albie had him trapped by the collar of his jacket. 'Whatever you say, Albert,' he gasped.

Albie smiled. 'Good.' He let Reider go and brushed his leather-gloved hands against one another. 'Don't want no nastiness, do we now?'

Reider rubbed his throat and tried to straighten himself into some semblance of dignity.

'You owe me mum a lot of money, Reider.'

'Yes, and I have every intention—'

'What, just as soon as yer luck changes?'

Reider said nothing, he just bowed his head in self-pity.

Albie smirked at him. 'Least yer've got the decency to blush. But don't worry, I ain't after no dough – not today anyhow. Like I said, it's a bit of business I've come here to see yer about.'

Reider looked scared.

'Yer see, it's about this war. I don't fancy going in no army or nothing, not when it means leaving me poor old helpless mum and dad to fend for 'emselves. And I got to thinking. I reckon you might be just the feller to help me.'

With an expression of sheer relief, Reider hurriedly took a sheet of writing paper from his drawer and began writing in a shaky scrawl.

Albie examined the completed letter under the lamp. 'Rheumatic fever as a kid, eh? Give me a weak ticker, did it? Nice touch that, Doc. Make 'em feel sorry for me.' Albie stood up and leant forward on the desk, looming over Reider. He tossed the letter at him. 'Get that sent off, Doc, or whatever it is yer have to do with it, and remember, this is our little secret, all right? And make sure all yer records show what a poor little bleeder I was and how I suffered.' Albie straightened up and turned to go. 'Yer know,' he said, as he stood in the doorway, his big, menacingly muscled body almost filling the door frame, 'I reckon there's a few other blokes might appreciate a letter like that. Matter o' fact it could be a nice little sideline for us, Doc. Help yer pay me mum some of that money what you owe her.' Albie winked at Reider. 'Keep well, Doc.'

Under the pale light of the big wintry moon, Evie tottered gingerly across the snow-covered pavement and shivered as she climbed into the car next to Albie. She leaned across and kissed him hurriedly on the cheek. 'Christ, it's freezing out there,' she said, shrugging down into her coat. 'I hope we're going somewhere warm tonight.'

Albie took a tartan travelling rug from the back seat and draped it over her legs. With a broad wink he said, 'Yer'll have to make do with that while I'm driving, darling, but I promise I'll warm yer up later.'

Evie pulled the rug up to her chin and snuggled down into the seat. 'I'll look forward to that,' she said, peering coquettishly over the soft woollen tartan. 'But where we going first?'

'We, my lovely, are gonna go out to celebrate.'

Evie opened her eyes wide and cooed at him, 'What, on a Monday? And it ain't even me birthday, is it?' She lowered her chin and peered up at him through her lashes. ''Cos yer said it was me birthday last night when we, you know, in the back seat . . .' She giggled. 'Me feet still ain't warmed up yet. So what else could there be to celebrate?'

'Me and this joining up business.'

'What?' Evie sat bolt upright, letting the rug fall to the floor.

He laughed. 'Or should I say, *not* joining up.'

Evie's hands flew to her face. 'Yer fixed it then?'

'Told yer I would.'

Evie threw her arms round him and kissed him noisily on the lips. 'Mmmmm! I'm so pleased yer won't be going away and leaving me.'

'Watch it,' Albie said, playfully pushing her away. 'Yer'll have the hand brake off.'

Evie clapped her hands excitedly. 'Blimey, Al, this really is something to celebrate. Come on, let's get going. Let's go and dance.'

Albie engaged the gears and moved the car forward, sending a spray of slush spurting over the pavement.

'How about going out for something to eat?'

'Lovely. Shall we go to the Corner House?'

Albie turned to her in the dark and grimaced. 'Corner House? Do me a favour. Yer out with Albie Denham now, girl. Only the best for us.'

Evie was impressed. 'Smashing.'

Albie stopped at the end of Darnfield Street waiting for a gap in the traffic on Grove Road.

'Come on, get a move on,' he said, drumming the steering wheel impatiently as a bus crawled past in the snow.

In the few months she had been seeing him, Evie had grown to recognise the tone that had crept into Albie's voice and knew the tempestuous fireworks it could lead to. 'One thing yer can say about this weather,' she said brightly in an effort to lighten his mood, 'least yer can see something in the blackout, even if it ain't very much.'

She was relieved when Albie turned to her and smiled

130

and playfully brushed her chin with his fist. 'Yer good for me. D'yer know that, Evie? Yer calm me down. Help me keep me feet on the ground.'

'Glad to oblige, I'm only here to . . .' She stopped speaking when she saw that Albie had lost interest in what she was saying and was looking over her shoulder instead, concentrating on something behind her. 'What?' she asked, turning round. 'What yer looking at?'

'I just saw your twin, I think,' he said. 'Going in the Drum with a couple of blokes and another girl.'

Evie was silently fuming; she didn't like the interest he was showing in Babs. 'It might have been her,' she said carelessly.

'Yeah, I'm sure it was. I ain't seen her for a while. She's looking good. Real smart.'

Evie paused, considering what to say next. 'Yeah, yer right. It probably was her, thinking about it. She said she might be going in there tonight.' She looked at Albie. His expression was intense, his dark eyes focused on the unlit exterior of the pub.

'Even with the moonlight and the snow and everything, you must have bloody good eyesight being able to make out who it was out there.' Her tone was cool.

'I've always had an eye for a pretty girl.'

Evie frowned. He hadn't been looking at her when he spoke.

'Well, make sure it's only yer eye, yer cheeky bugger.' She said it lightly, knowing that she was chancing her arm by talking to him like that, but also knowing she couldn't say what was really on her mind, that she hated the way he always looked at other girls all the time, and now her own twin. 'So are we gonna get going or are we gonna sit watching buses go by all night?'

'How about going in the Drum for a quick one before we go?'

'All right,' she said, doing her best to sound enthusiastic. 'If yer like. But keep them big brown eyes of your'n to yerself, eh?'

Albie turned off the engine and got out of the car. He went round and opened Evie's door for her. 'She seeing anyone regular?' he asked as he offered her his hand.

Evie barely touched his fingers with hers as she stepped out of the car and onto the pavement. Her heart was racing. 'She is actually.' She blurted the words out. 'Well, not regular exactly. Loads of fellers, more like. Took it in her head lately to start enjoying herself again. Her and this girl, Lou, from where we work, they go about together. Probably who she's with tonight. They see different blokes all the time. Out nearly as much as I am, she is. That what yer wanted to know? That a good enough answer for yer, is it?'

'Blimey, I only asked,' said Albie. He slipped his trilby onto his head and then lit a cigarette, while Evie straightened herself up, brushing quite unnecessarily at nonexistent fluff on the collar and sleeves of her coat.

'Put that match out!' a gruff elderly man shouted at him from somewhere in the darkness back along the road.

Albie chuckled at the old man's quavering voice. 'Aw, please, don't frighten me, I'm shaking in me boots,' he sniggered and flicked the still burning match into the snow at his feet.

'I told you . . .' the voice came again.

Albie ignored him and concentrated instead on watching the match flame fizzle and die away in the snow, but he looked up sharply when Evie yelled at the top of her voice, 'Piss off, Frankie, can't yer? I'm sick of people bloody interfering.'

'Charming,' they both heard Frankie Morgan reply.

'What's got into you?' Albie asked and went to take her arm but she pushed him roughly away. Wearing such high heels, that was a mistake, and she went skidding across the pavement, nearly crashing into the wall of the pub. It was only the row of soaking wet sandbags that saved her.

'Now look what yer've bloody done. Look at the state of me legs.' She was so angry she would have taken her life in her hands and thrown something at him if it hadn't been too dark for her to find something to throw.

'Me? What have I done?' Albie wouldn't be pushed away again. He took her firmly by the elbow and guided her towards the door of the Drum. 'Come on, I thought it was you what was meant to calm me down. Let's go in and have a drink.'

'I can manage,' she hissed through her teeth.

As soon as they were inside the door Albie said, 'Get some seats by yer sister,' and left Evie standing there while he went over to the bar.

She strode angrily over to the table in the corner where Babs was sitting with Lou, Percy Bennett and his mate Chalkie. She shoved past Chalkie – who looked her appreciatively up and down rather than complaining about her rudeness – and angrily plonked herself down between him and Babs on the red leather bench seat that ran along the wall.

Babs looked at her twin with a surprised smile. 'Hello, Eve. Didn't expect to see you in here tonight.'

'I'm out slumming,' she snapped as she rummaged in her bag for her handkerchief. 'What's your excuse for being in this dump?'

'We're having a drink to see the fellers off. They're leaving for their camp the day after tomorrow.'

'You know how to have a good time, don't yer?' Evie sneered sarcastically.

Lou, who was sitting on the opposite side of the table across from Chalkie, glared at her then rolled her eyes at Chalkie to show her disapproval of Evie's rudeness. He didn't even notice her do it. Lou was seething. It was she who was meant to be with Chalkie, after all. It had been *him* who had asked her out for the evening, and she'd been enjoying herself up until now. Up until Evie had come in and started flaunting herself and her blonde hair.

'What's the matter with you, Eve?' Babs asked. 'Can't yer behave yerself?'

Evie spat on her hankie and started wiping her shins. 'I nearly slipped over out there, that's what's the matter with me. I could have broke me neck for all anyone cares.'

Babs looked over to where Albie was standing at the bar waiting for Jim to serve him. Albie pointed discreetly at Evie and mouthed to Babs, 'What's up with her?'

Babs blushed and looked away.

Albie smiled.

Evie didn't notice the exchange between Babs and Albie, she was too busy checking her stockings for splashes.

From where Lou was sitting, however, it was all too obvious that Chalkie had definitely noticed Evie. His eyes were practically bulging out of his head as he watched her rubbing her legs. 'If I'd have been out there when yer stumbled,' he said, with a stupid grin, 'yer'd have been all right. I'd have caught yer in me arms like yer was a little feather.'

Lou grimaced as she muttered to herself, 'Here we go, Lou. Evie's about, yer've turned invisible again.'

Evie glanced up at the young, fair-haired boy in his ill-fitting khaki uniform, then turned to her sister. 'Who's this then?' she asked, jerking her head at Chalkie.

'You know Chalkie, Eve,' Percy said amiably. 'From along by me in Haverfield Road.'

Evie looked blank. She tossed her hair over her shoulder and sighed wearily. 'No.'

Percy nodded at her. 'He went to school with us. He's Johnno White's brother.'

'Aw him,' said Eve flatly. 'Didn't recognise him in his little soldier suit.'

'Like soldiers, do yer?' Chalkie asked, puffing out his narrow chest and sliding his arm along the back of the bench chair so that it was behind her head.

'Not much,' said Evie, putting her hankie back in her bag. She looked towards the bar. 'Where's that Albie got to with my drink?'

'Albie?'

'Yes,' said Lou with a derisive smirk. 'Albie. Up at the bar. The great big bloke. The handsome one in the posh-looking camel overcoat.'

Chalkie followed Evie's gaze. 'You with Albie Denham?' he asked. He was no longer quite so full of himself.

Lou brightened up. 'Been seeing Albie quite a while now, ain't yer, Eve?' she said, sounding very pleased with herself. Her red curls bounced round her face as she nodded towards the approaching bulk of Albie Denham. 'And here he is, the man himself.'

Chalkie whipped his arm from behind Evie and placed his hands firmly on the table in front of him, making sure they were in full view of everyone. 'Wanna sit here?' he asked Albie, scrambling to his feet and going off to find a chair.

Albie took Chalkie's seat next to Evie without a word of thanks or acknowledgement. He slid a gin and orange in front of Evie and took a long swallow from his own glass which was three-quarters full of Scotch.

Chalkie returned to the table with a chair which he put down between Percy and Lou, opposite Babs.

For a long moment nobody said anything. Then Albie leaned forward on the bench and spoke right across Evie to Babs. 'How yer doing, girl? All right? I ain't seen much of yer lately.'

'I'm all right,' Babs said. 'Thanks for asking.'

'Don't mind me, will yer?' Evie gulped down her gin

135

and orange and pushed her empty glass in front of Albie. 'Can I have another one?' she snapped.

'Course.' Albie reached under his overcoat and into his jacket pocket. He took out a thick wad of notes and raised his eyebrow at Babs. 'How about you, darling? Drink?'

Babs held up her glass to him. 'Got one, thanks.'

'Yer've nearly finished it.' To Evie's increasing annoyance, Albie was looking directly into her eyes.

'I ain't greedy,' she said and turned away from him. She looked across the table and smiled deliberately brightly at Percy. 'This'll do me.'

'Suit yerself.' Albie stood up and held out his hands. 'Now, how about the rest of yers?'

He took their orders and went to the bar to buy the drinks. While he was gone, Evie studied her face in her powder compact, Percy chattered away to Babs about his mum and dad's reaction to him joining up, and Lou stared at Chalkie. Chalkie didn't respond, he just concentrated on the table top, running his finger round and round in a sticky pool of beer that had been spilt on its chipped surface.

When Albie returned from the bar with double what everyone had ordered but with nothing for Babs, Evie cheered up a bit.

'Yer a spoilsport, you, Babs,' she said, sipping at her drink. 'You always was.'

Babs ignored her teasing and carried on talking to Percy.

'She wasn't a spoilsport when she got up and sung with yer that time,' Albie said, looking at Babs over the edge of his glass. 'Tell yer what, why don't yer both get up and sing us a song now? Come on, Babs, how about it?'

Babs said, 'Excuse me a minute, Perce,' and looked round at Albie. 'Albie,' she said slowly, 'yer can see I'm talking to Percy so why don't yer get on with talking to

Evie or whatever yer doing and leave me alone?'

Chalkie's mouth dropped open at her courage, Lou stifled a frightened gasp and Percy shook his head. 'You always was a bold pair, you Bell sisters,' he said admiringly.

'Yeah. I've always liked that in a girl,' said Albie surprisingly affably, winking at Babs.

Evie looked fit to burst. She stood up and pulled her coat tightly round her. 'Are we going or what, Albie Denham?' she demanded. 'I ain't sitting in this dump all night. I'm used to better.'

Chalkie, emboldened by Babs's display of daring and the double Scotch he had just swallowed, folded his arms and rocked his chair onto its back legs. 'Where yer off to then, Albie? Somewhere nice that us soldiers what are gonna fight for our king and country couldn't afford?'

Albie stood up and began carefully fastening the buttons on his overcoat. He looked at Babs and winked at her again. 'Sorry, mate, can't tell yer.' He tapped the side of his nose with his finger and leaned down towards the now scarlet-faced Chalkie. 'Secret war work, yer see. Can't go talking to no private about it, now can I?'

With a tense smile, Evie linked her arm though Albie's and said through barely parted, red-painted lips, 'We'll be off then. Night, night, all.' She looked down at Babs. 'I'll see *you* later.' She practically spat the words at her sister.

'Yeah. See yer,' Babs answered with a frown.

Evie slammed the pub door shut behind her.

'Take care yer don't slip over in the snow and ruin yer stockings, Eve,' Lou called after the departing pair.

Babs tutted. 'Why's everyone being so bloody childish tonight?'

Almost immediately the door opened again.

'Now yer for it, Lou,' said Percy, laughing at Lou's horrified expression. 'Evie must have heard yer.'

But whoever it was outside, they couldn't get in. They were obviously having trouble getting past the triple layer of blackout curtain that hung in the doorway.

'Shut that bleed'n door, can't yer?' Everyone in the pub could hear Frankie Morgan's gruff hollering from out in the street and then the slurred voice of Georgie Bell answering him. 'I'm having a bit o' trouble with this curtain thing, Frankie boy. Ain't no one gonna help me?'

Babs covered her face with her hands. 'Aw, no,' she groaned. 'It can't be.'

Lou leant across and whispered to Babs, 'It's yer dad, ain't it? I thought yer said he'd gone down the Aberdeen 'cos Jim had shouted at him.'

'They must have chucked him out and all.' Babs bowed her head. 'This is turning out to be a right night, innit?'

Percy took Babs's hand in his. 'Don't worry. Yer dad'll be all right.'

'It ain't just him.' Babs looked nervously towards the door where Georgie was still wrestling with the blackout material. 'It's Evie and all. I dunno what's got into her, the way she was acting.'

Chalkie butted in. 'Ain't it obvious? It's that ugly brute Albie Denham. Right fancies yer, he does.'

Babs looked appalled.

Lou shoved Chalkie in the chest. 'Why don't you shut up? Yer getting right on my nerves, you.'

'I'm gonna get some more drinks,' snapped Chalkie. He stood up and went storming over to the bar. He was closely followed by Georgie who, having finally fought his way inside, had come stumbling in, almost dragging the curtain down from its pole.

'Hello, Ringer,' said Nellie. When she saw that her husband was about to say something to him, she nodded over towards Babs and shook her head. 'It's all right, Jim, I'll deal with this.' She handed Georgie his usual pint of half and half. 'Thought yer'd deserted us. Where yer been?'

Georgie took a deep swig of the foaming beer and wiped his mouth on the back of his hand. 'Down that Aberdeen, but couldn't stand it in there. Yer should have heard 'em all going on about all the bloody heroes going off to war. Dunno what all the fuss is about. London's as safe as houses and they're all acting like a right load o' nancies fretting and fussing about invasions and gas and gawd knows what else. But just look at all them barrage balloons.' Georgie waved his arm vaguely in the direction of the Gents. 'And the ack-ack guns and everything. All over the place, they are. Even if he was interested in us, Hitler wouldn't stand a chance with that lot. I mean—'

'Two pints of best,' Chalkie said loudly, leaning across the bar, 'and two port and lemons.'

'Oi!' Georgie tried to focus on Chalkie as he spun round to confront him. 'I was talking, if yer don't mind.'

'And I was ordering a round.'

'Just 'cos yer in uniform, it don't impress me, son.'

'I'll have to get Dad home,' said Babs and went to stand up.

Percy stopped her. 'I'll go,' he said with a sigh.

Lou patted Babs's arm. 'You stay here with me.'

'All right, Mr Bell?' Percy smiled at Nellie who smiled gratefully in reply.

'Who wants to know?'

'It's me, Percy Bennett. Didn't yer recognise me, all grown up in me uniform?'

The smile disappeared from Nellie's face. 'Yer said the wrong thing there, Perce,' she said and went to the other end of the bar to serve a customer. 'You keep an eye on them lot,' she said to her husband, jerking her head towards Georgie and the two young soldiers.

'Thanks,' said Jim.

'Uniform? I'll tell yer about uniforms.' George's words

139

might have been slurred but the menace in his voice was all too clear.

'What do you know?' Chalkie jeered. 'Yer ain't even in the bloody Civil Defence. Even old Frankie Morgan's doing something.'

'You saying I'm too scared to do me bit?'

Chalkie took another gulp of his beer. 'You work it out for yerself.'

'Listen here, son.' Georgie poked Chalkie on the shoulder. 'I was in the Great War.'

'Aw yeah?'

'Yeah, only a kid I was but I did my bit driving down the docks.'

'Aw, pardon me, right bloody hero,' Chalkie sneered.

Percy went to take Georgie's arm but he was having none of it. 'Leave me be,' he roared, 'while I tell this snotty-nosed kid about heroes.' Georgie was swaying alarmingly. 'My mate Ron, who I used to work with, he was a hero. Went off to Spain, he did, to fight with that International Brigade lot. What a brave feller, everyone said. Fat lot of good it did him. Lost a leg out there and when he come home he'd lost his wife and his job and all.'

'Least he could say he'd done something.' Chalkie finished off his drink and slammed his glass down on the counter. 'Yer lost yer wife and yer job and all. So what was your excuse?'

'You little . . .' Georgie pulled his fist back as though about to land a right cross to Chalkie's jaw, but Percy grabbed him and pushed him forward, sending glasses flying across the floor.

'That's it.' Jim lifted the flap in the counter and stepped round the other side of the bar. 'That's enough.' He grabbed Georgie by the collar of his jacket. 'I've had enough of yer, Ringer, yer making a right fool of yerself.'

Nellie joined her husband. 'Don't start, Jim, yer know young Babs is over there.'

140

Jim looked at Georgie disgustedly. 'I dunno how them girls put up with yer. If I was lucky enough to have kids . . .'

A fat, self-pitying tear dropped onto Georgie's cheek.

'For gawd's sake.' Jim pulled a red-spotted handkerchief from his trouser pocket. 'Pull yerself together, man.'

Babs bowed her head in humiliation.

Lou beckoned to Percy and then touched Babs gently on the shoulder. 'Come on, let's get out of here.'

'Sorry about the glasses, Jim,' said Percy, taking a half-crown out of his trouser pocket. 'Will this be enough?'

'Don't worry, son,' said Nellie. 'You just look after Babs.'

Percy nodded his thanks and goodbyes to Jim and Nellie and, taking Chalkie by the arm, guided him towards the door. 'We'll have one over the Railway,' he said and ruffled his mate's hair affectionately.

Georgie was unable to resist getting in the final word. 'I wouldn't waste me time going over there,' he slurred. 'Beer's like piss over there.'

'Yer mean you was barred from there, don't yer?' Jim said with a weary shake of his head.

Nellie went over and said goodnight to Babs, Lou and the boys, assuring them that it was all nothing, and closed the door behind them.

Then she went back behind the bar and poured herself a straight gin which she drank down in one, throat-burning hit. 'Yer know, Ringer,' she said, 'it really beats me. Yer've got two smashing girls there, and like my Jim said, we should all be that lucky. And what do you do? Act like a bloody fool, that's what. And what d'you have to start on them boys for, eh? Tell me that? Off to bloody training camp in a couple o' days and then off to gawd

141

alone knows where. Why d'you have to go on at 'em like that?'

Georgie looked round at all the stern faces in the bar. 'It ain't my fault.' He looked and sounded pathetic. 'If Violet hadn't have gone and done a runner like that and left me with the kids, I'd never be in this state.'

'Aw, stop moaning, Ringer.' Jim shoved a wet rag in his hand. 'Yer'll drive all the bleed'n customers away. Now come on, buck up yer ideas and clear them empty glasses off the tables or this is another job yer'll be losing.'

'That you, Eve?' Babs fumbled around in the dark trying to find the switch to turn on the bedside lamp.

'Who d'yer think it was, bleed'n Father Christmas?'

'There's no need to talk to me like that. You're back early, that's all.' Babs sat up in bed blinking in the light. 'Here, is everything all right? You look terrible.'

'Thanks.' Evie kicked off her shoe, sending it crashing across the room. 'I'm fine.'

'Sounds like it.'

'We had words. Satisfied?'

'Wanna talk about it?'

'No.'

'Suit yerself. Come on, yer must be perishing. Hurry up and get in.' Babs lifted the bedclothes. 'The bottle's still nice and warm.'

Eve got into the bed she shared with her sister and dragged the covers roughly out of Babs's hands. 'Do you have to be so sodding nice all the time?'

'Eve?'

Evie didn't answer her; she turned her back on her twin and pulled the eiderdown up over her head.

Babs switched off the lamp and said softly, 'Good night, Evie, see yer in the morning.'

She was just about to lie down when Evie sat up and

shouted, 'The whole bloody night, that's all I heard from him – that sister o' your'n, what a good girl she is.'

'Eh?'

'All he wanted to know about was you. That's why I come home. I'd had enough. Happy now?'

'Don't be daft, he was just getting you at it, that's all.'

'And what're you defending him for? I thought you couldn't stand him.'

Babs turned the lamp back on. 'Eve. Don't be so—'

'You've been crying,' Evie interrupted her.

Babs smiled. 'I'm all right. Dad come in the pub and caused a bit of a scene, that's all.'

Eve's angry expression softened to one of concern. 'Aw, Babs. Was he horrible?'

'Yer could say that. Yer was well out of it.'

Evie flopped back onto the pillows. 'Turn the light out, eh? Let's get some sleep.'

'Yeah, night night.'

They lay there in the dark, the only sound coming from their breathing, but then Evie suddenly said, 'I ain't like Dad, yer know, Babs.'

'What?' Babs sounded half asleep.

'If I ever found out Albie was seeing someone else, I wouldn't be like Dad and just sit back and take it.'

Babs yawned. 'Wouldn't yer?' she asked sleepily.

'No. And it wouldn't matter who it was neither. Cos I'd kill her, whoever she was.'

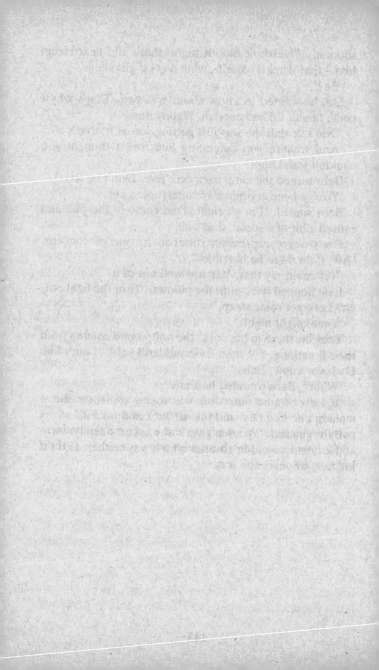

Life in London was really getting people down. The winter of 1939 had been the coldest for more than fifty years and, even with the coming of the New Year, there looked to be no improvement; if anything, the weather in early 1940 was even colder and the snow continued to fall. To make matters worse, rationing had begun. At first it was butter, sugar, bacon and ham, but there was the constant threat of further shortages to come. Worse than having to make do all the time was the frustration of having to put up with hardships that seemed so out of proportion to anything that was happening. Not only the dearer food and the shortages but the queuing up while short-tempered shopkeepers cut out coupons, the messing around with the palaver of the blackout and all its petty regulations every night, and of course the sadness and loneliness felt by those who were parted from their loved ones. And all for no apparent reason.

More and more were asking exactly why they had to put with all these things when there was still no actual sign of war, or at least not the sort of war that everyone had expected. The Phoney War they were calling it, whatever that meant. And people were just about sick and tired of it. The only casualty that Darnfield Street had seen was Georgie Bell blacking his eye when he'd walked into a wall of sandbags in the blackout on his way home from an unfamiliar pub. It didn't exactly make the street feel that they had a war hero in their midst. Bill Chambers, Rita and Bert's boy who had joined the RAF, hadn't sent home any stories that could make even a mother feel proud. So it was with rude replies rather than a feeling of inspiration or patriotism that most Londoners responded when, from February, posters of Britannia began to appear all over the place exhorting her subjects with the cry: It's up to you!

If only they could have seen some results, of whatever kind, coming from all the deprivations and inconvenience they were suffering, then it might have made a bit of sense to carry on making do, but most people were just feeling angry.

Most people, that is, except for the likes of Albie Denham. The weather and the war might have been bleak for others, but the outlook for Albie had never been brighter. He was in his element, raking in more money than ever before and he was enjoying flaunting it – taking gifts round to the Bells was one of his favourite ways of doing so.

Albie had been sitting in his car in Darnfield Street, waiting for opening time, when he knew Georgie would be leaving the house. He checked his watch. Any minute now.

Inside number six, Georgie had also just checked the time. The Drum would be open in a couple of minutes. He made sure his overcoat was tightly buttoned up to his neck and then slipped behind the blackout curtain that shielded the street door. Practice and Frankie Morgan had made all of Darnfield Street experts at ducking out of their houses without breaking the blackout, but even he hadn't managed to solve the problem of bashing into people and things in the time it took for his eyes to become accustomed to the darkness.

'Bloody hell! Yer nearly give me a heart attack.' Georgie stumbled back into the passage. 'Who is it?'

'It's me.' Albie stepped into the passageway and shut the door behind him.

'Stupid sod,' muttered Georgie. 'Yer should look where yer going.'

'How did I know yer'd be coming through the street door just as I was knocking?' Albie winked. 'Here y'are, Georgie boy, perhaps these'll make up for yer shock.' He dangled two plucked chickens by their legs, holding them up to Georgie's eye level. 'I know a feller down Laindon way with a smallholding, what owes me a few favours.'

The sound of Evie giggling made both men look up the stairs. 'I bet you do,' she said. 'Yer know everyone, don't you, Al?'

'Sure do, babe, and with me around you won't have to worry about no rationing.'

'You make me sick, Denham,' sneered Georgie, shoving his way past Albie. He opened the door and was just about to go into the street when he turned round and said, 'Yer know what yer have to do with chickens, don't yer? Stuff 'em. And that's exactly what you can do with 'em. Stuff 'em right up your arse.' With that he slammed the door behind him.

Evie ran down the stairs and threw her arms round Albie's neck. 'Hello, Al,' she said, her eyes shining.

'I don't think your dad likes me,' grinned Albie.

Evie snuggled into his chest. 'He's jealous,' she whispered. 'Just like everyone else is, 'cos yer so big and handsome and rich.'

Albie lifted Evie's chin with his finger and looked into her face. 'We ain't gonna have no more o' that old jealousy nonsense again from *you* though, are we?' His voice was cool, menacing.

Evie shook her head. She knew better than to speak when he was like that.

''Cos I told yer, didn't I? I don't like no one telling me who I can talk to or who I can look at. Right?'

147

Evie nodded again.

'Good. Now stick these somewhere and we'll be off.'

Evie took the chickens into the kitchen where Babs was leaning over the sink pouring a jug of rinsing water over her hair.

'Do something with these, Babs,' Evie commanded her.

'What? I can't hear yer.' Babs peered round, her soaking wet hair over her eyes.

'Nothing,' Evie called. 'See yer later.'

Babs groped on the draining board for the towel and wrapped it round her head. She rubbed her eyes dry with the flannel. 'Now, what were you saying?' She looked round but there was no one else in the kitchen. She heard the street door slam shut. 'See yer,' she said to herself and dropped down onto one of the wooden kitchen chairs. 'And what the hell're these?' She stood up and carried the two chickens to the back door, intending to put them in the meat safe in the yard. She only opened the door a crack and a swirl of snow flew in. 'Blimey,' she said to the two plucked birds as she put them back on the table. 'Yer'll have to wait till I'm dressed before I put yer out there.' She looked up at the clock on the mantelpiece – seven o'clock, and Lou wasn't coming round until eight. She lit the two front gas rings, one to boil the kettle on and one to warm herself by, and pulled a chair over to the stove. Then she sat down again and began lethargically towelling dry her hair.

She again looked up at the clock on the mantelpiece – nearly a quarter past seven. Listlessly she poured herself another cup of tea. She could just about be bothered to drink it. She stared at the chickens. She'd have to shift herself and get dressed soon or they'd start cooking right there on the table, the stove was making the kitchen so warm. Babs sighed to herself; it wasn't just the heat that was making her feel listless, it was everything. Everything seemed so pointless. She and Lou had been out with so many fellers lately, some really nice ones, but they'd all been on their way somewhere, not staying or coming, but going, every single one of them. She sipped the tea. It was nearly cold. She got up to refill the kettle. Just as she turned on the tap, there was a knock on the door. She looked at the clock – twenty past. Surely it couldn't be Lou already.

'Hang on,' she called as she took her coat off the banister and slipped it on over her underclothes.

She opened the door and peered round the blackout curtain. 'Bloody hell, what are you doing here?'

'Charming. Ain't yer gonna let us in then?' It was Blanche standing there on the doorstep, her head and shoulders gradually being coated with a layer of snow.

'Course, come in.' Babs practically dragged her in by the arm. 'You're a real sight for sore eyes, Blanche Simpkins. I've been that fed up about everything.'

Blanche kissed her on the cheek and laughed. 'So you ain't pleased to see me but just glad I'm here to sort yer out and tell yer yer fretting about nothing as usual. Right?'

'Right,' said Babs with a grin and took Blanche's and her own coat and threw them over the banister rail. 'Come in the kitchen and have a cuppa and tell me all about it.'

When they'd settled down at the table, Babs pushed a cup of steaming, freshly brewed tea towards Blanche. 'So? Get talking.'

Blanche blew across the top of her cup then sipped gingerly at the scalding brew. 'Handsome.' She set the cup back in its saucer and stared down at her feet. 'Where shall I start? The people down there was such snobs. They didn't like us Londoners at all. No, that's not fair, it wasn't all of 'em. The people we was staying with, they was all right – well, in their way. But some of the others . . .' She pulled a disgusted face. 'Right lot they were. And, I've gotta be truthful, there was fault on my side as well. I hated the countryside. The animals stink and make funny noises.' She took another sip of tea. 'It ain't like hopping when you've got all your mates with yer and yer sharing and that. It's like yer the odd ones out, a freak or something. When we got there, to the station, we was all right 'cos, as yer know, our Ruby'd already sorted out somewhere for us to stay. And I've got a few things to say to her and all when I catch up with her.'

Babs nodded. 'I'll bet.'

'But I wouldn't leave the station till all these little ones had got sorted out. There was a bunch of 'em, tiny little nippers some of 'em were, standing around waiting to be chosen. Like dockers waiting on the stones to be called for work, they was, poor little devils. Terrible it was. I could have cried for 'em. They stood there, all scared without their mums, with little labels on their coats, and little brown paper parcels with their bits and pieces. And these old girls come and looked 'em over like they was cattle or something. Should have seen 'em, the old bags. Like bloody schoolteachers they looked. One or two of the kids was really sad to see. Yer can imagine, them – what had the scabby knees and runny noses, yer know what I mean?'

Babs nodded over the rim of her cup.

'They got left till last, of course. None of the old cows wanted to take *them* home. Poor little sods.' She shook her head at the thought of it. 'But it was funny, yer know. Our Len, he loved it down there. I don't think he was all that keen to come home.'

'He's always been a bit different to the others, ain't he though, Blanche? How he likes animals and reading books and that.'

'Yer right there. He really got on at the little school down there. Loved it, he did. Mind you, he ain't best pleased that the schools are open up here, he was positive they'd still be shut. He hates going to Olga Street.'

'Can't blame him for that.' Babs ran her fingers through her hair and was surprised to find that it was bone dry. 'But I bet your Mary's delighted, ain't she, being back near her Micky?'

'You ain't kidding. Straight round his she went, didn't even take her coat off, just kissed her dad and legged it.'

'She wants to be careful in the blackout, there's been so many accidents on the roads.'

'Call this a blackout? Yer wanna see it down there. Can't see yer hand in front of yer face, yer can't. She'll be all right.' Blanche smiled wistfully. 'Yer forgetting how grown up she is, Babs. She's left school now, yer know.' Blanche drained her cup. 'Now, there is something yer don't know. She's only gonna start in the bloody munitions with that stupid sister o' mine Ruby. As if she ain't caused us enough aggravation already, sending us down to that hole. She has to bloody interfere. I could have killed her when she kept going on in all her letters about how much Mary could earn at the factory with her.'

Babs poured more tea into Blanche's cup. 'Mary could have earned herself a fair bit at Styleways and all. What with the piecework we're doing, we're earning a fortune compared to our usual money.'

'So something good's coming out of all this war lark then?'

'I suppose there's always a good side to everything.'

Blanche's eyes opened wide and she snorted. 'I can't see nothing good about being bloody evacuated.'

By the time Blanche had launched into another round of stories about the horrors of rural living, Babs had topped their cups up for the third time. 'It really was that bad then?'

'Well, I suppose I'm exaggerating a bit but, be truthful, Babs, what was the point of being stuck down there when it's as safe as houses up here? All them rumours about gas attacks and fire bombs – what a load of old rubbish that all turned out to be. Yer dad was right, after all.'

'And I don't suppose your Archie being stuck up here in London had nothing to do with yer wanting to come home?'

Blanche laughed. 'I'm the one who's meant to be able to read you like a book, not the other way round.'

'I have me moments.'

Blanche leaned back in her chair and folded her arms. 'I think it was being away from Archie over Christmas that was the last straw. Even though he got down for a couple of days afterwards, it still didn't feel right.' Blanche reached across and chucked Babs under the chin. 'I hope yer lucky enough to find someone as decent as my Archie to settle down with, Babs. Yer won't go far wrong if yer do.'

Babs said nothing.

'I imagined you lot, all in the Drum having a right old knees-up over Christmas, while we was singing bleed'n carols with the old couple what owned the house. Parsnip wine they give us.' Blanche pulled a face and shuddered. 'Bloody horrible, it was. They did their best for us, but they were a funny couple.' She bit her lip, trying to stop herself laughing. 'Honest, Babs, I couldn't even understand half of what they said.'

Babs joined in her laughter. 'You'd have all been talking like swede bashers if yer'd been there much longer.'

Blanche grimaced. 'Some hopes. Come on, Babs, make me wild, tell me what a good time you all had at Christmas.'

'Seems a long time ago now.' She paused then raised her eyebrows. 'Evie enjoyed herself all right. Got herself a fox fur. And not just a jacket neither. A proper full-length job.'

Blanche's mouth dropped open. 'What bank did she turn over?' She paused. 'Here, she ain't still with that Albie Denham, is she? When yer never mentioned him in yer letters I thought he'd moved on to drive the next poor cow barmy.'

'She's still with him.' Babs nodded towards the chickens. 'I presume that's where they come from.'

'I meant to ask yer about them.' Blanche's attempt at a smile couldn't disguise her concern. She took Babs's hand. 'Why didn't yer write and tell me? I bet yer've been bottling it all up. I know you.'

Babs looked down at Blanche's big, work-worn hand covering her own much smaller and softer one. 'I was trying to take yer advice, Blanche, leave her to it and get on with me own life.' She shrugged. 'And Evie ain't daft.'

'No, course she ain't, and neither are you, but . . .' Blanche shook her head. 'Albie Denham.'

'Yeah, Albie Denham. I've tried, Blanche, I really have, but I can't help fretting about her being with him. I don't like him, I really don't. And it's getting worse. I know I was jealous at first, about him taking her away from me and that, but I got over that part of it.' Babs lifted her chin and tried to smile but she was too close to tears. 'You always was good at giving advice, Blanche, but it ain't always easy for me to take it. I did me best.'

'I don't blame yer being worried, darling, but yer mustn't get yerself all worked up. And like yer said, Evie ain't daft.' Blanche stood up and busied herself at the sink, refilling the kettle. Before she turned round to Babs, she fixed a tight smile on her face. 'Don't let's get all humpy,' she said over her shoulder as she set the kettle down on the stove. 'I could've stayed down in the bleed'n sticks if that was what I wanted. Come on, give us all the gossip about who's doing what to who. I've missed that nearly as much as I've missed me pie 'n' mash.'

Babs managed a smile this time. 'Well, there's plenty

what ain't changed, yer'll be glad to hear. Alice is exactly the same.' Babs stood up, stuck her fists into her waist and screwed up her face. "'My girl wouldn't have let *her* Micky be evacuated to no strangers if he'd still been at school,'" she whined in a creditable impersonation of Alice Clarke. "'And so long as people like Frankie Morgan do their duty proper, that Hitler'll never get through.'" Babs took the cups and rinsed them under the single cold tap. 'Can you imagine, Frankie Morgan fighting the Germans? He must be ninety if he's a day.'

Blanche laughed. 'Well, us lot are back now, that'll give her something else to go on about.'

Babs wiped the cups dry and put them back on the table. 'Yer don't know how good it is to see yer back, Blanche. And I know Minnie and Clara'll both be right pleased to see the kids around again. They asked after yer all the time.'

Blanche was about to answer but she was cut short by someone knocking at the door.

Babs looked up at the clock. 'Bloody hell.' She ran out into the passage and let Lou in.

'New fashion?' she said, looking Babs up and down. 'It would never have occurred to me to go out in me slip and drawers.'

'I'm sorry, Lou, I didn't realise the time had gone so fast.'

'That's all right. They can wait.'

Babs guided Lou into the kitchen. 'Look who's here,' she said, going over to Blanche and kissing her on the cheek.

A broad smile spread over Lou's chubby face. 'Hello, Blanche, good to see yer. How yer doing?'

'All right, now I'm home.'

'Ain't just a holiday then?'

Blanche shook her head emphatically. 'Definitely not. I'm home for good. Wouldn't worry if I never saw another bloody sheep in me whole life.'

'Yer don't mind if I just do me face, do yer?' asked Babs, setting up a little hand mirror against the teapot and taking out lipstick, rouge and mascara from her handbag.

'No, you carry on,' Blanche said. 'Wouldn't want yer going out without a bit of colour in yer cheeks.'

Lou perched on the edge of the table next to Babs. 'I'm glad yer back, Blanche.' She hesitated, watching Babs stroke her lashes with the sticky mascara. 'I'm glad for Babs's sake.'

Babs didn't shift her gaze from the mirror. 'Don't go getting all dramatic on me, Lou. Cheer up, everything's fine.'

Lou swallowed. She glanced sideways at Blanche. 'I ain't so sure about that, Babs.'

Babs put down her mascara brush and looked at Lou. 'What yer talking about?'

Lou looked away as though she couldn't face her friend. 'I don't wanna worry yer,' she said quietly, 'But I don't think that everything is fine.' She glanced at Blanche. 'I didn't say nothing before but I reckon I can tell yer now Blanche's back with yer.'

Lou took a deep breath before the words came tumbling out. 'If half the stories are true that our Bob's been telling me about Albie, Babs, then things *definitely* ain't fine. Evie wants to watch her step. I think she's getting in well over her head.'

9

With the coming of spring, the weather in 1940 took a definite turn for the better, but even that did nothing to lift Babs's spirits. Her doubts and worries about Evie seeing Albie Denham, confirmed so worryingly by Lou, had now deepened into a real fear for her twin. No matter how she tried to get through to her, she couldn't. Evie was totally obsessed with Albie, refusing to listen to a single question about what he was up to and how he seemed to be growing richer by the day. And Georgie didn't help matters; if anything, he was drinking even more than usual. So what with Evie being out every night with Albie and Georgie being either in the pub or sleeping off his latest binge, Babs was just about fed up with the situation. It helped having Blanche back home, but Babs couldn't keep running to her; she had worries of her own, and not only about her children.

Blanche was having to face the increasing possibility that Archie, even though he was over thirty, might be called up. People had been keen for something to actually happen in the war, and now it had, with a vengeance. The so-called Phoney War was over. On 9 April, Hitler's forces had invaded Norway, and British military help had failed miserably. It definitely wasn't what the British public had wanted or expected to hear when they called for action; they were stunned by the defeat of Norway.

And then on Friday, 10 May – ironically another

beautiful spring day – a further crisis loomed to reduce the spirits. Germany invaded Belgium and Holland; the Germans were moving inexorably through the battered towns and villages towards the Channel and Britain itself. There was a feeling of disbelief, even panic in the air that perhaps the stories and rumours from the early days of the war about a German invasion weren't just cowardly, defeatist talk after all. Chamberlain was blamed from all quarters for his weak leadership, and at six o'clock that evening, Winston Churchill replaced him as Prime Minister and became leader of the new coalition government.

For a while at least, people once again had a focus for their feelings of patriotism, even if it was only Churchill's big, triumphant cigar and his rakish siren suit.

Two weeks after Churchill became Prime Minister, on the evening of Saturday, 25 May, Darnfield Street was witness to the increasingly unusual spectacle of Evie and Babs Bell walking along arm in arm towards the Drum.

They might have looked a blooming picture of family happiness, the two lovely girls strolling along in the late spring sunshine, but Evie for one wasn't in a very good mood. 'I'm warning yer, Babs,' she sniped, 'if Dad turns up drunk and starts, or if he comes over all sentimental, I'm straight out of that pub, right? I really mean it. I ain't having him show me up in front of Albie.'

Babs had to bite her tongue. Instead of saying what she really felt, she smiled and said, 'Don't worry, Eve, Dad won't start. Not tonight, he won't. Not with Nellie specially inviting us in for a drink like this.' She cuddled closer to her twin. 'Don't let's be miserable, eh? Not today. Try and enjoy yerself. For me.'

'I mean it,' Eve repeated.

Babs flinched, her sister sounded so hard. 'He's probably forgotten it's our birthday anyway,' she said quietly.

When the girls stepped inside the Drum, they couldn't

believe it; it was as though all the street was in the pub waiting for them. Jim and Nellie had obviously turned a blind eye to young Mary and Terry Simpkins slipping in with Blanche and Archie because there they were sitting at a corner table with Alice and Nobby's grandson Micky. Alice and Nobby themselves had a central table with a good all-round view, which they shared with Ethel and Frankie Morgan – who was sitting there complete with his tin helmet and armband. Rita and Bert had popped across from the baker's and were standing at the bar, and even Miss Peters was sitting there sipping a sherry with her next door neighbours, Minnie and Clara. The only people from the street who were not there were the Jenners, although nobody really expected them to be in the pub, and Georgie was still on the missing list, not having been seen or heard of by anyone since lunchtime.

.'Here y'are, girls, over here.' Lou was calling to them from the far end of the bar. 'I've had these lined up waiting for you two for nearly half an hour.'

The twins went and stood either side of her as she slid a port and lemon in front of each of them.

'Thank gawd yer here at last,' Lou said, raising her glass before she sipped gratefully at it. 'Nellie and Jim asked all the street in for a birthday drink for yer and they thought the guests of honour wasn't gonna show.'

Evie and Babs frowned at each other. 'Did you know?' they asked each other. They both shook their heads.

'And all these old moaners in here,' Lou carried on, with a general wave round the bar, 'they've been driving me flaming barmy. It's as bad as being at home with me dad. Honest, if I'd have heard another word about fifth columnists, Holland capitulating or that bleed'n Mosley geezer, I swear I'd . . . I dunno, but I would have.'

'Ain't stopped yer talking though, Lou,' grinned Evie.

'Shut up, Eve,' Babs giggled then turned her back to the bar and raised her glass to the neighbours. 'Sorry

159

we're late, everyone. We didn't know yer was all expecting us.'

'We'd have been in before,' Evie added, 'but we've been waiting for Dad. It's really nice to see yer all here. Cheers.'

Calls of 'Happy birthday, girls' echoed round the pub and glasses were raised.

The twins turned back to the bar. 'Ta, Nell,' they both said. 'It's right good of yer, thinking of doing this for us.'

'There's a bite to eat later and all,' said Nellie with an affectionate smile. 'I thought everyone could do with a bit of a celebration, what with all the bad news lately, and today seemed just the day to do it.'

Lou whispered to Babs out of the side of her mouth, 'If she starts on about the war . . .' But she needn't have worried. Nellie wasn't about to give a speech about the enemy or troop movements, she was much more interested in the twins enjoying themselves.

'I've done a few sandwiches and I got in a couple o' bowls of eels and Rita's made yer a smashing cake. Nice little spread, it is.'

'Aw Nellie, what can we say?' Evie turned to her sister. 'You say something, Babs.'

'Yer always so good to us, Nell. What *can* we say?'

'That's all the reward I could ask for,' said Nellie. She sounded choked. 'Your two beautiful, dimpled faces smiling at me.' Nellie never tried to hide her fondness for the twins; she had spent many wakeful nights thinking what it would have been like if she and Jim had been fortunate enough to have had children like them; or even one child would have been a dream come true. But it was never to be. She looked along the bar to where her husband was sharing a joke with Bert. If things had turned out how she had always hoped they would, he'd have been a good dad, she thought to herself. He was a kind, decent man, better than that Ringer had turned out to be. He was such a lucky bugger having the girls but he was too stupid lately to realise it. Life wasn't fair, she'd learnt that years ago.

She took a gulp of her lemonade. 'Dad not around then, girls?' she asked.

Evie shook her head. 'No. He cleared off somewhere hours ago.'

'He'll be along soon,' Nellie said with more sincerity than she felt. 'He wouldn't miss his girls' birthday now, would he?'

Frankie Morgan came up to the bar and pushed in between Lou and Eve. 'Pint and half of bitter shandy, please, Nell.' He leaned his scrawny arms on the polished counter. 'Hear the wireless?' he asked no one in particular.

'Aw no, not again,' wailed Lou. 'Here we go, more bloody war talk.'

Frankie wasn't deterred. 'Germans have got as far as Boulogne. We've gotta be on the ready.' He pointed at the stony-faced girls. 'Specially pretty little things like you three. Yer never know what might happen if they ever do get over here.' He shook his head ominously and leaned closer to Lou. 'Yer hear all sorts of terrible stories about what them foreign soldiers get up to.'

'That's nice talk in front of young girls, I don't think,' said Nellie angrily and shoved the two glasses in Frankie's direction.

Frankie made a show of digging deeply into his pocket.

'Have this one on us,' Babs said winking at Lou. 'For our birthday.'

'Good luck to yer, darling,' said Frankie, raising his pint glass to his lips. 'And yer don't need to have no worries about invaders,' he said, lifting his elbow so that they could all see his Civil Defence armband. 'Not with Frankie Morgan around.'

'Frankie!' Ethel shouted from the other side of the

crowded pub to her husband. 'Stop bothering them young girls and fetch them drinks over here.'

'Yes, my sweet,' he called to her. Then, with a smile on his face, he muttered to the girls under his breath, 'They could use her as a secret weapon. Hitler'd shoot back to Germany so fast yer wouldn't see him for dust.'

Evie, Babs and Lou turned back to the bar to stop Ethel from seeing them laughing, but it also meant that they didn't see Georgie come into the pub.

Babs jumped as he tapped her on the shoulder.

'Happy birthday, girls,' he said with a soppy look on his face.

Evie smiled with relief when she registered that there was hardly a whiff of booze on his breath.

'I bought yer both a little present,' he said holding up two identical, flat cardboard boxes. 'They ain't much. But they're all I could afford.'

'That's where yer've been, ain't it?' Babs said, taking the box from him. 'Yer a daft old thing.' She kissed him tenderly on the cheek. 'Aw look, Lou, ain't it pretty?'

She held the open box out to show Lou the necklace of sparkling glass beads fixed in a dull, gold-coloured setting.

'Help us on with it, Dad,' Evie said. She handed him the necklace and turned her back to him.

When both girls had their presents secured round their necks, they went round with Lou, showing them to everyone in the pub.

'Yer not a bad bloke at times,' sniffed Nellie, wiping her eyes with an extravagantly frilled hankie. 'Here, you old sod, have a Scotch.'

Georgie took his drink and went to the end of the bar to stand with Bert and Rita.

The twins were just showing their glittering gifts to Miss Peters, Minnie and Clara when Albie made his entrance. As usual when he came into a room full of people, he made it into a production. He swaggered, back as straight as a rod, his camelhair overcoat slung across his broad shoulders, carrying a black velvet box in one hand and his trilby in the other. The only difference in his typically boastful demeanour was that on this particular evening, rather than looking smug, he was looking decidedly fed up.

As was his habit, he stared around the room, gauging the impact of his arrival, then he leant forward and kissed Evie briefly on the lips. He turned to Babs. 'Hello, doll face,' he said to her without the trace of a smile. 'Aw, and a happy birthday to both of yer,' he added flatly.

Evie immediately lost all interest in showing her necklace to the neighbours and when Albie went up to the bar, she followed, trotting along behind him like an eager puppy.

While Babs waited for Minnie to have a good look at her birthday necklace, she kept her eye firmly on Evie. When Minnie had finished admiring it, Babs smiled and said, 'I'll send a drink over to you three ladies in a minute. I'm just going over to see Eve.' With Lou in tow, Babs joined her sister.

Albie's mood had grown even darker. He was sipping a large Scotch and complaining to Evie. 'Bloody hundreds of stakes they've hammered in,' he fumed, 'right across Hackney Marshes.' His handsome face was rigid with anger. 'Put 'em in to stop enemy landings, they reckon, if ever yer've heard such total shit. As if the bleed'n Germans wanna go to a piss hole like Hackney.'

'Don't matter, does it?' Evie asked sweetly, looking up at him through her thickly mascaraed lashes. 'Don't affect us over here.'

'Don't affect us? Don't matter?' Albie looked at her as though she was stupid. He turned to Babs and Lou. 'Don't she know nothing, this sister o' your'n?'

Evie flushed scarlet with shame.

Albie shook his head. 'Only stopped all the flapping, ain't it, yer silly mare. Good little earner that was and all.' He swallowed the last of his Scotch and pushed it across the counter to a tight-lipped Nellie. 'Kept the punters happy. Now what am I gonna do for 'em?'

Lou pulled a face at Babs, signalling frantically that they should leave Albie and Evie to it. But Babs wasn't moving. She didn't like to see her sister upset, and especially not by the likes of Albie Denham.

Albie snatched up his refilled glass and took a long swallow of the whisky. 'First thing in the morning I'm gonna get rid o' that poxy greyhound the old man brought home. No point feeding the bastard if it can't earn its keep.' He rested his brawny forearms on the bar. 'That can go straight in the canal.'

Evie looked shaken; she touched his sleeve but he shook her off. 'Yer don't mean that, Albie, do yer?'

'Don't I?'

'But I was getting to really love that dog.'

Albie sneered and took another swig from his glass. 'How can yer love a bloody dog?'

Babs took a deep breath and said, 'I'll have it.'

Albie straightened up to his imposing full height and turned towards her. He stared down into her eyes for what seemed like ages before he spoke. 'All right then,' he said, with a surprisingly charming smile. 'The bloody thing's yours. Happy birthday.'

Evie shook her head agitatedly. 'No, you can't have her. You can't,' she said loudly. 'I'm Albie's girl friend, and if anyone's gonna have Flash it's me. It's only right.'

'All right, Eve,' Babs said, trying to calm her down. 'I was only trying to save the bloody animal 'cos I thought yer was upset. You have it if you're so keen.'

Evie opened and closed her mouth like a fish washed up on the shore trying to breathe.

Nellie came to her rescue. 'Come on, girls. Ain't yer

gonna take these drinks over to the ladies?' She shoved a tray towards Babs and nodded towards Minnie, Clara and Miss Peters. 'Yer've kept 'em waiting long enough, haven't yer?'

Babs picked up the tray and nodded to Lou. 'Come and help me.'

Gratefully, Lou followed her over to the table.

Next, Nellie filled a squat glass full of whisky, held it up and called along to where Georgie was standing talking to Rita and Bert from the baker's. 'For you, Ringer, Evie'll fetch it.' Then she shoved the glass into Evie's hand. 'Take that for yer dad. Go on.'

With her cheeks flaming, Evie meekly took the glass but she didn't have the chance to take it to her father. Albie had grabbed her arm.

'What yer doing with that bit of brass junk round yer neck?' he demanded loudly.

Evie bowed her head and touched the necklace that she had only moments ago been so pleased with. Now she felt as though it were burning its way through her flesh.

Babs was just about to give Miss Peters her sherry, but at the sound of Albie's dismissive sneers, she stopped in her tracks. She handed the tray to Lou. 'You sort this out, Lou. I won't be a minute.' And with that she marched back to the bar.

'Dad bought these for our birthday,' she said, her chin high.

'Bloody hell, yer both wearing 'em.' He burst into derisive laughter. 'Green necks the fashion round here, are they?'

Babs looked along the bar to where Georgie was standing with Bert and Rita. His face had drained of colour.

'Get that off,' Albie instructed Eve.

'Don't, Eve. Don't,' Babs pleaded. She could hardly believe it as Evie ducked her head and reached back to unfasten the necklace. Babs looked along at Georgie. His eyes were fixed on Evie.

Albie grinned triumphantly as Evie carelessly let the now rejected gift drop from her hand onto the bar. 'These are more like it,' he said, brushing Georgie's present onto the floor and putting down the velvet box he had brought with him in its place. From out of the box he took a string of plump, creamy pearls and held them high for everyone in the pub to see. 'These are more like what Albie Denham's girl should be wearing, not a piece of crap like that.'

As Albie fastened the pearls round the now beaming Evie's throat, Georgie slammed his glass down on the counter and stormed out.

'Dad!' Babs called after him, but he was already out of the door. She stood there, defeated.

Alice Clarke turned to Ethel Morgan. 'You wait and see,' she said, nodding wisely, 'just you mark my words, there's truth in it as sure as I'm sitting here.' She gulped down the last of her milk stout and peered at Ethel across the rim of her empty glass. 'Sure as I'm sitting here,' she repeated, her eyes narrowed with meaning. 'Pearls bring tears.'

10

When Evie eventually got up the next day, it was getting on for half past three in the afternoon. Sunday dinner had been eaten long ago, Georgie was asleep in the chair in the front room and Babs was sitting at the kitchen table reading the papers and drinking tea.

Evie shuffled into the kitchen, wrapped in a candlewick dressing gown. Her blonde hair was all over the place and the remains of the previous day's make-up were smudged around her eyes and lips.

'It's in the oven if yer want it,' Babs said without looking up from the paper. 'It'll be all baked up by now and serve yer right.'

'What's the matter with you?' Evie slumped into one of the hard kitchen chairs opposite her sister.

Babs put the paper down on the table. 'Don't nothing get through that thick skin of your'n no more?'

Evie rolled her eyes and scratched her head. She yawned loudly. 'Any tea left in that pot? The inside of my mouth's like the bottom of a shoe.'

'That's it,' snapped Babs. 'It's always the same, always what's wrong with *you*. How you feel, what you want. How about other people, eh, tell me that?'

'You finished?'

Babs leant across the table and pointed her finger close to Evie's face. 'There's more things to worry about than the taste in your bloody mouth.' She flicked the paper open. 'Look at all this about the poor bloody soldiers in Dunkirk. Look at all this about the French people. Look, go on, look.' Babs threw the paper across the table at Evie. 'And now let's get a bit closer to home.'

Evie crossed her legs and concentrated on her foot as she jiggled it up and down.

'Can't look at me, can yer?' Babs stood up and grabbed her sister's arm. 'Have you got any idea how you must have made Dad feel last night?'

Now Evie stood up too. She pushed Babs away from her. 'Has he got any idea how he's made *me* feel for the last twelve years since Mum left us?'

'Here we go, me, me, me. I'm sick of yer, Evie. Yer've changed and I don't like it.'

'Aw, come on, we gonna start on about Albie again, are we?' Evie moved closer to Babs. She stared into her face. 'If you wanna wear a bit o' glass round yer neck, that's fine by me. But I'm gonna have nice things. Real things.' Evie held out the pearls that she was still wearing from the night before. 'Things like this. Things that're worth a few bob.'

Babs sneered and turned away.

'Jealous again, eh?'

'Shut up, Evie, and grow up, can't yer? Can't yer see the way he's treating yer? It's like he owns yer. Like yer another one of his things to do what he likes with. He's no good, Eve, can't yer see that neither? Can't yer see how he's making yer look?'

'I don't wanna choose between you and Albie, Babs, but if you make me, I don't think there'd be much competition.'

Babs snorted scornfully. 'How long do you really think it's gonna last with him, Eve? Be truthful. You know how he goes through girls. Uses 'em up and chucks 'em away. Why d'yer think Dad's been so worried about yer? A couple of months ago yer was gonna leave work and

168

move into a posh flat. What's become of all that, eh?'

'Leave off, can't yer. Yer jealous, the pair of yer. You and Dad.' Evie sat back down at the table. Her chest rose and fell as she breathed deeply, trying to control her anger. 'You ain't got no right to talk to me like that, Babs. Not you, not no one. And anyway, I wanna go to work, it gives me something to do.'

'Huh!'

'You shut up, Babs, do you hear me? I'm Albie Denham's girl, and I expect to be treated with a bit of respect. I won't be spoken to like that.'

'Don't be so pathetic.' Babs shook her head. She felt as if she was speaking to a stranger. '"I won't be spoken to like that",' she mimicked. 'Just who do you think you are?' Babs was shaking with anger. 'Perhaps this little problem'll bring yer back to reality.' She went over and flung open the door that led into the back yard. 'What yer got to say to that?'

A large, brindle-coloured greyhound bounded into the kitchen and went skating across the slippery lino, coming to a lolloping, ungainly halt by the stove. It turned round and sat up on its haunches, its tongue hanging down from its excited, grinning chops as it pricked up its ears and looked eagerly from Babs to Evie and back again.

'What the hell . . .' Evie drew her legs up on the chair, away from the slobbering animal.

'Come on, Flash,' Babs said through lips stretched tight across her teeth as she dragged the hound by its collar over to Evie. 'Come and see yer new mummy.'

The dog rested its silky muzzle on Evie's thigh.

Evie's mouth dropped open.

Babs smiled and started walking towards the kitchen door.

'Babs!'

She raised her eyebrows and shrugged. 'You wanted it,

169

and whatever your little heart desires . . .'

'He didn't. He wouldn't.'

Babs nodded. 'He would and he did. Fetched it round at dinner time while you was still snoring.'

Evie had never been one to let people see that she was beaten; with her combination of stubborn pride and sheer bloody-mindedness, she was determined that everyone would think that having Flash to look after wasn't just a childish whim but was exactly what she wanted. And so she began a whole daily routine that now revolved not only round seeing Albie and, usually, going to work, but also round caring for the dog.

Blanche was out on the pavement sweeping when Evie dashed past her house at the end of Flash's lead, the long-legged hound dragging her along almost faster than she could run to keep up.

'Can't stop, Blanche,' she panted with a hurried wave. 'Gotta get Flash home and get meself off to work.'

Just as Evie came to a skidding halt at the front step of number six, Babs came out of their door.

'I'm leaving right now, Eve,' she said briskly. 'So it's up to you whether yer come with me or not, 'cos I ain't missing that bus.'

'Be right with yer,' Evie said with a brave smile as she and Flash shot past her and along the passage.

Babs stepped out onto the pavement and stretched her arms high above her head. 'Morning, Blanche,' she said with a leisurely yawn.

Blanche stopped sweeping and leant on her broom. 'Morning, darling.' She took a deep lungful of air. 'And what a lovely morning it is, eh.' She sat herself down on the step and laughed. 'That Evie's come up smelling of roses again, ain't she? The sun ain't stopped shining since she got that dog. Not rained once since she's had to walk it.'

A bit reluctantly, Babs laughed with her. 'Typical, ain't it?'

'Keeps on like this,' Blanche said, 'and it's gonna be a summer just like we used to have when I was little. I was saying to my Archie, it's a shame they had to go and close the lido over Vicky Park, it'd have been smashing over there for the kids in this hot weather.'

'Not only for the kids. I'd have loved to have gone over for a bit of a muck-about in the water. I was thinking how it would've been nice to have gone down to Southend for the day like me and Evie used to.' Babs grinned. 'We've had some right laughs down there.' She plonked herself down on the step next to Blanche. 'Yer know,' she said, cupping her chin in her hands, 'I'll be glad when everything gets back to normal.'

Blanche brushed her hair back off her forehead and sighed. 'Me and all, darling. I dunno why everything has to be like this.'

Babs puffed out her cheeks and thought for a moment. 'Why does everything have to be so complicated? Why can't it be like it was when we was little? Simple. Not horrible like it is now. I liked it how it used to be.' Babs's lip began to tremble and she struggled to keep her voice from quavering. 'It used to be so good.'

'Seems daft, don't it?' Blanche said. She picked absent-mindedly at the peeling paint on the broom handle, her expression now as serious as Babs's had become. 'All this beautiful weather and us sitting around going on about how we wished things was all like they used to be before the war started.' Blanche flicked the broom at a cigarette end that had escaped her earlier sweeping. 'Mind you, all that about them poor sods in Dunkirk, I suppose it really is something to get worked up about.'

'I think yer've got me wrong, Blanche.' Babs sounded guilty. 'I know it makes me sound selfish and rotten, but I've gotta admit, I didn't really mean things like that.

What I meant was that I wished things was like they was before that rotten Albie Denham was around.' Babs brushed her thick dark hair off her face. 'But yer right as usual, Blanche. What really matters is all the terrible things that're going on, the real things that we should be worried about.'

Blanche put her arm protectively round Babs's shoulders. 'Don't go blaming yerself, yer wouldn't be human if yer didn't let yer own worries get yer down. Take my Archie, he's been right fretting himself.' She made a rueful little attempt at a smile. 'He's daft, but he reckons that working down the market means that he ain't doing his bit, with the war and everything. But I said to him, I said, people have still gotta carry on living, Arch, even if there is a war going on. I'd rather he was down there than away at some army camp, and the way things are going that might happen before long.'

Babs opened her mouth to say something comforting to Blanche but instead she jumped as someone tapped her on the shoulder. It was Evie.

'Yer frightened the life out o' me,' Babs gasped.

'Yer know what they say,' Evie said, winking at Blanche. 'It's a guilty conscience what makes yer act like that. What was the pair of yer talking about? Me?'

'Course,' said Babs, standing up and dusting down her skirt. 'What else is there to talk about but the Blonde Bombshell?'

Evie flicked her hair over her shoulder. 'I can't help being gorgeous.' Then she stuck her hands on her hips. 'So are yer gonna hang around here gassing all day, Babs, or are yer coming to work with me?'

Babs looked at her watch, then pulled a shocked face at Blanche. 'Blimey,' she said, 'we're gonna be on time, two days in a row. Mr Silver'll think his luck's changed.'

Evie and Babs settled down at the work bench and picked

172

up the first of the heavy front panels of the army greatcoats they were now working on at Styleways.

Lou looked blissful as she eased the thick khaki cloth of a collar under the foot of her machine. 'I love doing these,' she said happily. 'I ain't never been so well off.' She laughed as she threw the finished collar onto an already toppling pile. 'And me mum likes it and all. I ain't hardly mumping off her at all now.'

'Well, I think the bloody things are a right sodding nuisance,' Ginny moaned as she heaved another completed sleeve onto the pile that was next to her seat. 'As if soldiers need these bloody heavy old things in this weather.'

Evie carried on with her machining as though Ginny hadn't spoken, but Lou and Babs rolled their eyes at each other. 'Flipping missog,' Lou mouthed at Babs so that Joan, who was sitting next to her, couldn't hear what she said. At the far end of the bench, Maria, who was sitting next to Ginny, said in her quiet, unassuming way, 'Some of the places where the soldiers have to fight might be very cold. I bet they're glad of coats like these.'

'What did you say?' Ginny asked incredulously.

Maria repeated what she had said, then added, 'I like to think that the coats are keeping some brave soldiers warm.' She held up a piece of paper and looked at it shyly. 'I put these little notes in the pockets, saying I wish 'em all well and that.'

Ginny shook her head in disbelief and turned to Joan who was sitting on the other side of her. 'I did, I heard her right the first time.'

Joan giggled.

Ginny turned back to face Maria. 'I really thought that I must have heard yer wrong 'cos, honestly, I just couldn't fathom out how yer could actually say them things.' Her voice and her expression were savage as she leaned close to Maria. 'You just don't understand, do

173

yer, yer stupid bloody Eytie. As if they'd wanna have notes in their pockets from the likes of you, the bloody enemy. No better than the Jerries, you mob.'

Evie was on her feet before Ginny had finished speaking.

'You wanna pick on someone, Ginny, you try me for size.'

'*You* ain't a dirty foreigner, are yer?' Ginny still sounded cocky but she didn't look so confident.

'Nor's she, not that it's got anything to do with it,' said Babs, joining Evie behind Ginny's chair.

Ginny kept her head down as she spoke. 'Her old man's dad was an Eytie, weren't he? That's the same as being a foreigner.'

Now Maria was standing up as well. 'My grandad was Italian, yeah, but he lived over here since he was two years old.'

Evie put her arm round Maria's shoulder. 'Yer don't have to explain yerself to that mean-minded, hatchet-faced old tart,' she said. 'And *you* don't have to side with her neither,' she said, looking at Joan.

Joan gulped and started working on making up a stack of pocket linings.

Ginny poked Joan on her flabby arm. 'Yer know there was all fighting up Clerkenwell way again last night, don't yer? And in Soho, my dad reckons.' She turned back to Maria. 'They've been smashing up all the Eytie shops and cafes 'cos of them joining up with Hitler in that Axis lot.'

Joan looked round. Evie and Babs were still standing behind Ginny's chair. Joan might have let herself be easily led by Ginny but she wasn't stupid; she knew when the odds were against her. 'I don't think people should be horrible like that,' she ventured. 'Not to people they know. They ain't all bad.'

Ginny glared at Joan, furious at her disloyalty, then turned her stare back on Maria. 'What do you think,

Axis?' she demanded, but she didn't give her the chance to reply. 'Course, they don't smash up the places what've got protection from crooks and gangsters,' she went on, glancing slyly under her lashes at Evie. 'There's a lot of blokes making plenty o' money out of protection, so I've heard.'

'That's it,' fumed Evie. 'I've had enough.' She drew back her fist and was just about to let Ginny have it on the nose when Mr Silver walked in.

'Not working, ladies?' he asked, perfectly calmly.

'You don't know how lucky you were,' Evie hissed at Ginny as she and the others returned to their seats.

'I just wanted to let you know the news I've just heard.' He paused, took off his glasses and pinched the bridge of his nose between his thumb and forefinger. 'Paris has fallen. We're all going to have to do our very best in whatever way we can. It seems like the war's getting nearer every day.'

Everyone was silent, shocked; with news like that, even Ginny didn't have the heart to make a sarcastic or clever-dick remark.

Two days later, when Georgie was crossing the street on his way to his regular Sunday morning session in the Drum, he almost ran into Maudie Peters as she made her way to church.

'Good morning, Mr Bell,' Maudie said with a shy dip of her head.

Georgie nodded. 'Morning, Miss Peters.' He felt the colour rise in his cheeks as he remembered that the last time he'd seen her was three weeks ago when she'd been in the pub on the twins' birthday. He smiled sheepishly. 'Ain't seen yer around for a while,' he said, taking off his cap.

Maudie smiled. Georgie was surprised at how nice it made her look.

'Well, I suppose I'm like everybody else at a time like this, Mr Bell, I'm doing what I can to help. Nothing much, just things through the church. Sending parcels and going to comfort families whose sons or husbands are away.' She flashed her surprisingly girlish smile at him again. 'In fact, I'm on my way to church now. It's the National Day of Prayer for those poor, suffering people in France. You'd be very welcome to join me.' She looked away and added softly, 'If you'd like to, I mean.'

Georgie wrung his cap round and round in his hands. He didn't know what had got into him, he was blushing like a schoolboy. 'I'd love to come,' he stuttered, 'but I've got a lot on at the minute.'

'Of course,' Maudie said hurriedly. 'I wasn't thinking. It must be so demanding bringing up two girls all alone. I've often thought what a good job you've made of such a difficult task, Mr Bell. You must be very proud of them.'

Georgie nodded dumbly.

'I must be going now, I hate being late.' Maudie straightened her already perfectly placed hat. 'Perhaps you could join me at church some other time.'

Georgie nodded again. 'I'd like to, thanks,' he mumbled, barely audibly.

As he stood and watched Maudie walk away from him along Darnfield Street and then turn into Grove Road, he shook his head, totally bemused with himself. Why had he said that?

11

The next evening, Monday, at nine o'clock, the news that everyone had been dreading was finally broadcast on the wireless: France had surrendered to Germany. In the baker's the following morning, it was all that Minnie and Clara could talk about when they went to buy their bread from Rita Chalmers.

'Hitler?' said Minnie in a cross between a sneer and a gulping sob. 'Don't talk to me about that crafty-looking, swivel-eyed rotter.' She folded her arms across her broad, aproned front and tapped her toe as though impatient to be let loose on the object of her hatred. 'I know what I'd do with the greasy-haired rat if I got hold of him.' She jerked her head in what she thought might be the general direction of the Continent – which was actually more towards Bethnal Green way – then sighed sadly and said, 'All them poor sods over there in France. Terrible, it is. Terrible. Fancy having to surrender to that no good, ugly-headed worm.'

Rita nodded her agreement as she sliced up a large slab of bread pudding that Bert had just carried up from the basement in a big, blackened tray. 'I have to say that I . . .' she began, but a sudden rush of assorted little Jenners bursting through the shop doorway stopped her.

'Got any broken biscuits, missus?' piped up the tallest of the tiny troupe.

'Yeah, I have,' Rita sighed, waiting for the inevitable retort.

'Well mend 'em then!' they screeched in gleeful unison and darted out of the shop, shrieking and squealing like little piglets.

'Them kids,' said Clara kindly.

'Yeah, they're all right, bless 'em,' said Minnie with an indulgent smile.

'Yeah, nice to see 'em enjoying 'emselves,' said Rita, who was actually more preoccupied with sniffing appreciatively at the bread pudding than worrying about the youngsters and their games. 'Yer know,' she said wistfully, 'if he wasn't me husband already, I'd propose to that Bert o' mine tomorrow, this smells that good.' She smiled happily to herself as she wrapped two hefty chunks of the dark, greasy confection in a piece of stiff, waxed paper. 'Plenty o' currants and spice in that,' she said with a wink, handing the parcel over to Minnie to put in her string bag. 'Nice and tasty with a cup o' tea for yer.'

'We'll have that this afternoon,' said Minnie, hooking the bag over her plump forearm. 'After we've finished all our cleaning jobs, me and Clara get indoors, put the kettle on and like to have a little sit-down before we get on with our bit of knitting.' Minnie looked at her friend. 'We're both doing loads of knitting, ain't we, Clara?'

Clara nodded with a self-effacing smile. 'Yeah, we are. Loads.'

'It's our way of doing our bit, yer see.' Minnie's voice had a catch in it as she continued, 'Makes us think about the last war and how we tried to help by doing our bit then, don't it?' Minnie patted Clara's arm affectionately and said to Rita, 'Not a day goes by when we both don't say and think something or other about our husbands, does it?'

Clara shook her head.

'They say time heals, but I ain't so sure. It still hurts me

178

to think about my Fredrick, and I know Clara feels the same about her Alf, God rest their souls.'

'That's right,' sniffed Clara.

'Yer know, Rita,' Minnie said, trying to be brave, 'I'll bet there's plenty of other widows what was left from that terrible time who feel exactly the same as me and Clara, but it don't make it no easier to know that you're not the only ones.' She stood there silently for a moment, lost in her heartbreaking thoughts. Then, briskly pulling herself together, she patted her tight, steel-grey perm, leant across the counter to Rita and said in a loud, exaggerated whisper as though what she had to say was a state secret: 'We're giving all the socks what we knit to Miss Peters so's she can take 'em round the church and then they send 'em abroad to all our boys over there.' She acknowledged the existence of the Continent – and abroad generally – with another vague nod, this time in the direction of Victoria Park. 'Or wherever they are. You know.'

Rita smiled, showing that she did indeed know.

Minnie pointed up to the photograph of Rita and Bert's son in his RAF uniform, which was pinned in pride of place on the back wall of the little shop. 'You just let us know where your young Billy's stationed and we'll send him a few pairs, special like, made out o' nice soft wool so's his feet won't rub in them big boots they have to wear.'

Rita struggled to keep smiling as she thought of her only child all those miles away from her, going through who knew what deprivations and dangers. 'That's very nice of yer,' she said gratefully. 'I'm sure he'd appreciate it. And I know I would.'

'Who'd appreciate what?' The familiarly suspicious voice of doom came from Alice Clarke as she entered the baker's shop, her sharp, red-tipped nose ready to sniff out any hint of a story that might try and escape her inbuilt radar for a bit of juicy gossip.

Rita rolled her eyes at Clara while Minnie rounded on Alice. 'What we'd *all* appreciate,' Minnie snapped, with only a hint of the sarcasm she felt actually showing, 'is people being pleasant to one another and not running no one down.'

'How can you expect people to be pleasant in these times?' Alice threw up her arms in despair as she positioned her scrawny backside on the wooden chair left beside the counter for customers to rest on. 'I've got more than enough to put up with without having to worry about other people and their bloody problems.'

As Alice set about listing her personal hardships, Rita, Minnie and Clara flashed disbelieving looks at one another. 'What with marge and cooking fat on ration now as well, not to mention tea.' She waved her ration book threateningly at Clara. 'I mean, a quarter a week between me and Nobby. How we meant to get by on that, eh? You just tell me that. Go on, tell me.'

Clara blinked, not knowing what to say.

But Minnie knew all right, Alice couldn't intimidate her. 'So how d'yer think Rita and Bert manage?' she demanded with a querulous raising of her eyebrows. 'Or me and Clara?'

'You two are a different case, two women living together.' Alice looked Minnie and Clara up and down with a distasteful shudder. 'And I've got me grandson to think about. Not that you pair'd know anything about normal families with grandchildren, but whenever our young Micky comes round he always wants a bit o' grub. That's what youngsters are like, yer see. Can't fill 'em up. Terrible, it is, how I'm having to manage like I am.'

Minnie and Clara shook their heads in wonder at Alice's gall, but it was left to Rita to voice the feeling of disgust that all three women felt for Alice's sneering prejudice. 'Yeah, course, we forget you're the only one with a normal family, Alice, and how you're suffering's far more serious than them poor buggers in France having to surrender to the Germans.'

Apparently oblivious of their scorn, Alice pursed her lips and continued with her grouching. 'I dunno about no Frenchies,' she snorted, tightening her already closely-knotted turban, 'but if this hot summer goes on like I bet it will, I dunno how I'm gonna cope. Yer know, I reckon it's hotter indoors over there in number five than it is in your ovens. The heat's terrible. I dunno how I'm managing at my age.'

Minnie was tempted to point out that she and Clara were only a couple of years younger than she was and that they actually lived upstairs in number five where it was much hotter anyway, so they did indeed know about the discomfort, but she thought better of it. She had more important things to do than get into arguments with Alice.

'And sitting outside on your doorstep's a waste of time,' Alice went on, "cos soon as yer settled, that bleed'n siren goes off again. I wouldn't mind if it served a purpose, but it's as pointless as that Frankie Morgan and all his hollering and hooting to make us get in that bloody shelter. And that's another thing, that shelter. What a rotten hole that is, stifling it is in there. Stifling. I dunno why I bother.'

Usually a quiet soul who tended to let Minnie speak up for her, Clara could take Alice's self-centred whining no longer. 'Well, why don't yer stay outside on yer street doorstep nosing when the warning goes again? See what happens to yer then.'

'And what d'yer really think would happen, eh? Tell me that.' Alice's already hatchet-sharp features hardened alarmingly as she leant forward in the chair and began prodding her skinny finger at Clara. 'Nothing, that's what.' She leant back again and mumbled to herself, 'Silly bloody cow, nothing, that's what.'

181

Clara looked to Minnie for support.

Minnie didn't let her down. "'Nothing", yer say. Well, tell that to the poor sods what lost their homes in them raids the other night. And to the boys like Rita's Bill what're protecting us all.'

'Protecting us?' sneered Alice. 'Protecting us from what? That's what I'd like to know. I dunno what everyone's getting 'emselves so excited about.' She flapped her bony hand in a dismissive wave. 'The way everyone's been going on, yer'd think we was gonna have the bloody war right here in the East End on our flipping doorsteps. It's all scare-mongering, you mark my words. We won't have any trouble round here. No chance. This whole war lark'll all come to nothing. It'll all be over before yer know it, and all them panic merchants are gonna feel right idiots.' She grimaced at the photograph of Rita's son Bill. 'And all this performance with shelters and wardens and bloody aeroplanes. You see, it'll all have been a complete waste o' time. And money.'

It had just gone eleven o'clock on a warm, late August evening and the residents of Darnfield Street were, like many other Londoners, either settling down to sleep or making their way home in the blackout from a sociable Saturday night out. The daylight raids that had, at first, so scared and alarmed everyone had become such a familiar sight that people were no longer worried about sheltering. And when the sirens went for the sixth time since the first, aggravating blast had gone at six o'clock that morning, many simply ignored them.

Babs was just about to put her key in the lock to let herself indoors after spending the evening with Lou when she heard the warning. She stood there for a moment, wondering what to do. Should she go indoors to the loneliness of an empty house, or into the stifling heat and discomfort of the shelter where Blanche would probably be with the kids, so at least she'd have a bit of company.

The decision was made for her; within moments of the warnings beginning there was a sound she didn't at first recognise but the meaning of which she soon guessed. A blitz of bombs was whistling down over London from out of the black night sky with unprecedented ferocity. Babs made a dash for the shelter, pleading heavenwards to whoever might be listening that Evie and her dad were somewhere safe and that none of the missiles would fall on Darnfield Street. Just as she got to the shelter door, she turned on her heel and sprinted back to number six. Frantically fumbling in the dark for her key, she called loudly, 'OK, Flash, don't worry, I'm here.' Inside, the terrified greyhound howled pitifully.

With the door finally open, Babs flew along the passage and into the kitchen. 'I dunno what Alice is gonna say about you going in the shelter,' she said, as she snapped Flash's lead onto her collar and dragged the quivering animal towards the front door.

The next day there were enough rumours flying around about fire bombs, high explosives and the terrible death toll to ensure that on Sunday evening nearly everyone in the East End was glued to their wireless sets, waiting for any scrap of comfort, information or instruction – anything, in fact, to tell them what was happening.

In Darnfield Street, Frankie Morgan's previously dismissed warnings and directions were being taken seriously or at least considered carefully. Even those like the Jenners with their brood of little ones and their elderly grandmother, who still didn't fancy the idea of going in the shelter, followed Frankie's instructions and were sleeping downstairs, away from the threat of unsuspected fires starting over their sleeping heads.

At a quarter past eleven on that Sunday night the sirens went again. This time people didn't hesitate; they threw their coats on over their nightclothes and headed for the public shelter.

By the time Babs got to the shelter, it was almost full. Blanche sat Janey on her lap, making room on the bench. 'She's half asleep anyway.'

Babs took off her soft felt hat and shoved it in her pocket. She shook her hair over her shoulder and stared at Alice. 'Not got nothing nasty to say about Flash tonight?' she asked before Alice had a chance to say anything.

Alice surprised them all by shaking her head and not saying a word.

Blanche raised her eyebrows at Babs. 'Blimey, what's up with her?' she whispered under her breath.

Babs shrugged. 'Dunno, but she's got the needle over something.'

'Are your dad and sister all right?' Maudie Peters asked suddenly. 'If I'm not being nosy.'

'Course you ain't. Nice of yer to ask.' Babs glared at Alice, daring her to make a comment as she added, 'Dad'll still be in the Drum, he's working tonight, so Nellie and Jim'll take him down the cellar with them, and Evie's out with her feller up West.'

'So he'll look after her,' said Maudie reassuringly.

'Yes,' said Babs with a sideways glance at Blanche. 'He will.'

'Here they come,' sighed Minnie as the droning sound of approaching aircraft made everyone look anxiously up at the ceiling of the shelter as though they could see through it into the blackness of the night sky. 'Let's hope there's no surprises for us tonight, eh?' She patted Clara's shaking hand. 'Don't worry, we'll be all right in here,' she reassured her terrified friend, then she turned to Babs and gestured silently to Clara. 'Why don't yer give us a song, Babs? Cheer us all up.'

'Yer on,' said Babs. She stood up and handed Flash's

lead to Blanche's Len who was squatting on the floor by his mum's feet. 'I think yer all know this one,' she said and started singing the opening notes of 'Bye Bye Blackbird'. Babs was slightly shocked when Maudie Peters began clapping along, but was delighted when she got everyone – everyone except Alice and Nobby – joining in.

'This has turned into a right old sing-song,' beamed Minnie as she and Clara swayed in time to the tune. 'More like a Saturday night in the Drum than a Sunday night in the shelter.'

By the time the all clear sounded at dawn the next morning, Babs had gone through just about every song that they all knew and Miss Peters had sung one or two that they didn't.

Archie stuck his head out of the shelter first. Satisfied that it was safe, he let Mary and Terry slip out past him. 'I'm just gonna have a word with Frankie then I'll go and put the kettle on,' he said to Blanche, pecking her on the cheek and ruffling Janey's fluffy baby curls.

'Ta, darling,' Blanche said sleepily. 'I could murder a cuppa tea that ain't been in a flask.'

Blanche let most of the others file out of the shelter before she herself got to her feet and stepped out into the bright, early morning sun. She handed Janey gratefully to Babs while she stretched her aching limbs. 'Monday morning and the world's still here,' she yawned. 'Look at it, it's like nothing's happened.' Smiling down at Len she said, 'What a weekend, eh, son? But it weren't too bad, was it? I mean, if that's all that's gonna happen, we ain't got nothing to worry about, have we?' Blanche flinched as she felt someone poke her hard in the side. 'Oi! What the hell was that?' She spun round to see Alice standing there, fists on her tiny hips, scowling with fury. 'I might have known it was you, Alice,' Blanche said, rubbing her side. 'I thought yer'd been too quiet all night. Now what d'yer want?'

'I wanna know how you can have the gall to stand there and say we ain't got nothing to worry about.' Alice was speaking nine to the dozen. It was the first time she had said anything since the warning had gone the previous night and she had a lot of catching up to do. 'There was bombs and gawd knows what falling out here and you have the cheek to say that. And her,' she jabbed her finger towards Babs, 'she had the bloody sauce to sing. And that Miss Peters. I thought she'd have more sense, her a church-goer and all.' Alice's eyes blazed. 'We could all have died in there last night.'

Blanche took a deep breath, then said as calmly as she could, 'Babs, all right if Len takes Flash for a little run?'

Babs nodded. 'Course. Go on, Len, and watch she don't pull yer over.'

Blanche watched her son as he raced off happily at the end of Flash's lead. Satisfied that he was out of earshot, Blanche folded her arms and rocked back on her heels. 'Ain't you got no brain at all, Alice? We was all doing our best to keep cheerful, and me, I was trying to kid Len along that it was all safe and sound out here. And you have to go and put the bloody willies up him. What's the matter with you?'

'What's the matter with *me*?' Alice was now yelling as loud as her reedy little voice let her. 'What's the matter with *you*, yer mean. Yer should still be evacuated with young kids like your'n.'

Blanche looked at Babs. 'Have I heard right?' She didn't wait for Babs to answer. 'You hypocritical old bag, Alice. If you wasn't such a little runt, I swear I'd . . .' She could barely get the words out she was so angry. 'It wasn't no time ago that you was running me down for going away and mouthing off about how your precious girl wouldn't have let her kid be evacuated. And *now*.'

Alice stuck her chin out. 'That's before my Micky told me about Southern Grove.'

'And what exactly did your Micky tell yer about Southern Grove?'

'They had bombs there. Loads of 'em. Fire bombs and big exploding ones that wrecked all the houses and blew great holes in the road. He said he'd never seen nothing like it.'

Blanche shook her head in wonder. 'I don't believe you, Alice. Yer always such a sodding know-all. But this time we all know yer wrong 'cos yer can ask anyone, it was only the docks what got it.'

Alice was silent for a moment, then she said quietly, 'Say what you like. I know different.' Then she marched off towards her house.

Blanche stared after her. 'Gawd only knows what she'd say if she found out how serious her Micky's got with my Mary.'

'I'd better go and see if Dad and Evie have got back,' said Babs, holding Janey out to Blanche.

'Right.' Blanche sounded distracted as she took the toddler from her. 'I'll send Len over with the dog soon as he gets back.'

'When he's ready. I won't be going into work till later.' Babs began walking away.

'Babs,' Blanche called after her.

Babs stopped and turned back. 'Yeah?'

'They ain't interested in hitting houses and people like us, are they?'

Babs shrugged. 'No. I don't suppose so.'

'I'm not so sure.' It was Clara. She and Minnie had left the shelter straight after Archie but they hadn't gone indoors yet. It had been only the second time that they'd spent the night in there and they both needed some fresh air. 'I heard the kids talking in the shelter about how Southern Grove got it. It's true what she said.'

Blanche held Janey tight to her chest. 'No it's not, it's just more stories. And yer don't wanna listen to kids no more than yer wanna listen to Alice.'

Clara sniffed. 'I wish I'd stayed under the bed like I wanted,' she said tearfully. 'Then I wouldn't have heard all this horrible stuff in the first place and I wouldn't have to tell all you.'

'Don't upset yerself.' Minnie handed Clara a hankie and wrapped her arm round her friend's broad shoulders.

'But I heard it from someone else and all,' wailed Clara.

'Who from?' Minnie frowned. 'Yer've been with us all night in the shelter.'

Clara blew her nose noisily. Staring down at the pavement, she said softly, 'Frankie Morgan was saying about it to your Archie when we left after the all clear just now.'

Blanche swallowed hard. 'You know how people exaggerate, Clara,' she said, trying her best to smile. 'Always gotta have a story to tell. I'll talk to Archie. You'll see, it'll all be a load of old toffee.'

'Well, let's hope that's all it is, 'cos I'm scared, scared stiff. I knew it was gonna be like this from the minute that war broke out, when them rotten sirens went off for the first time.' She looked up, her eyes full of tears. 'Say something happened to one of us, Min, to you or me, think what it'd be like to be left all alone.'

'Shut up, Clara, or yer'll have me grizzling and all.' Minnie took the hankie from Clara and blew her own nose. 'What's got into you? Yer giving me the creeps.' She looked to Blanche and Babs for support. 'Please, tell her there's nothing to worry about.'

But it wasn't Babs or Blanche who spoke next, it was Evie. While Clara had been speaking, Albie had dropped her outside number six and as soon as she'd seen Babs she'd come running over to her. 'Thank gawd yer all right,' she said, throwing her arms round Babs. 'When I saw all the bomb damage to them little houses as we was driving along, I made Albie drive like a nutcase to get me back to yer. I nearly had kittens worrying.'

Clara burst into loud noisy tears.

'Evie!' snapped Blanche.

Evie looked bewildered. 'What? What have I said?'

12

After a few edgy days, things rapidly got back to normal
for the residents of Darnfield Street, or what passed for
normal at the beginning of September 1940. The weather
was fine, more like high summer than autumn, and the
fact that there had been no warnings so far that day, not
even the by now expected false alarms, had helped lift
everyone's mood. But as Babs hurried along Grove Road
on that sunny Saturday morning, loaded down with
shopping, her mood was not very sweet at all. In fact, she
was getting herself worked up into a real temper.

'You promised me, Evie,' she muttered to herself.
'You said you wouldn't let me down again.'

But Evie had let her down. For the last goodness only
knew how many weeks, her sister had failed to come in
after going out on a Friday night with Albie Denham,
leaving Babs by herself to sort out the shopping and
cleaning that had to be done over the weekend.

Babs was so busy complaining to herself that at first she
didn't hear her name being called, but when she eventually stopped and looked over her shoulder to find out who
wanted her, she saw it was Blanche and Len staggering
towards her. They were even more laden with bags than
she was.

'At last,' Blanche shouted to her. 'I've been trying to
get yer to slow down since yer left the market.' She
puffed loudly as she dumped her bags on the pavement. 'I

always say it, but this time I really mean it, it's a good job I've got my Lenny here to help me, ain't it?' Blanche winked affectionately at her son and rubbed at her aching back.

'Yer right there, Blanche,' said Babs, doing her best to smile at Len as she too let her bags drop to the pavement. 'I could do with a bit of help meself.'

'It ain't like you to go down the Roman on yer own.'

'No,' Babs said flatly, 'it ain't usually, but it's becoming something of a habit lately and one that I ain't very keen on, to tell yer the truth.'

'Evie not come home again?' Blanche asked quietly, almost mouthing the words, so that Len couldn't hear.

Babs shook her head. 'No.' After a moment of uneasy silence, Babs spoke to Len. 'So what you been up to then, apart from helping yer mum?'

'I've started a collection,' said Len, his eyes shining at the thought of it. 'Look.' He dug into the pocket of his shorts and pulled out a chunk of metal. 'Shrapnel, that is. I think. Or part of an aeroplane anyway.'

'Fancy that,' said Babs, looking at it closely.

'I found it out walking along the canal—'

'You what?' demanded Blanche. 'Yer know you ain't allowed down there.'

'Not *by* the canal *exactly*, Mum,' Len quickly corrected himself. 'But down that sort of end of the street.' He turned back to Babs. 'There was this dogfight, see.' Len waved his arms excitedly in the air. 'Vapour trails right across the sky and Spitfires and Hurricanes and everything all fighting the Jerries in their Messerschmitts. Then they got him! Bull's eye! And I'll bet my mum's kettle was used to make the Spitfire what got him.'

Blanche was frowning. 'Are you telling the truth, Len?'

'Yeah.' He sounded hurt that his mum would doubt him. 'You give yer kettle in when the lady come round collecting 'em.'

'Yer know I don't mean about no kettle.'

Len swallowed hard and looked down at his boots.

'There ain't been no planes come down anywhere near here, Len. So where yer been? You been off on that old bike of your dad's again?'

'When we was in Cornwall yer let me go for miles without having a go at me.'

'Well, we ain't in Cornwall now, thank gawd.'

'I wish I was still there. It was smashing.'

'Don't start crying, Len.' As always, the sight of any of her children even close to tears immediately mollified Blanche's temper. 'Tell yer what,' she said gently. 'I'll talk to Dad about you getting that rabbit yer wanted, how about that?'

'Would yer, Mum?' His tears forgotten, Len was now beaming.

'Course, and why don't yer ask Babs if she'll let yer take Flash out for a walk later?'

'I'd be grateful if yer would, Len,' said Babs, smiling down at him. 'It'd save me a job.'

'If I take these bags home now, Mum, and put the stuff in the cupboard, can I take her out straightaway?'

'Go on then. And tell Mary to get the kettle on.'

Len picked up the two bags he had been struggling with earlier, their weight no longer a problem, and raced off as fast as he could towards Darnfield Street.

'She's out the back in the scullery,' Babs called after him. 'The key's on the string.'

'Righto!' Len shouted back.

'He's such a good kid, Blanche.'

'Yeah. I wish he was a bit happier, that's all. Then perhaps he wouldn't go wandering. He was like a different boy when we was down there.' Blanche looked down at the shopping round Babs's feet. 'You looking after the dog and all now, Babs?'

'What do you think?'

'I think you're letting Evie get away with murder.'

Babs shrugged. 'Ain't got much choice, really. Someone's gotta do it.'

Blanche studied Babs's face for a moment; she looked tired. Doing her best to sound cheerful, she said, 'Here, I saw Ringer talking to Miss Peters again the other day. Looked like they was getting on right well and all.'

Babs looked surprised. 'Me dad and Maudie Peters? You sure, Blanche?'

'Yeah, didn't yer know? That's a few times I've seen 'em chatting lately.'

'What am I meant to be, on the Brains Trust?' snapped Babs. 'Course I didn't know. How am I meant to know anything?' She kicked at one of the shopping bags, sending a stream of potatoes rolling towards the road. 'I'm too flaming busy working and cooking and cleaning to have a chance to know anything.' She bent down and started picking up the vegetables. 'Bloody things.'

Blanche bent down to help her. 'Sorry, Babs, I didn't mean to upset yer,' she said, stuffing them back in the bag.

'No, Blanche, I'm the one who should be sorry. I'm tired, that's all.'

'Yer doing too much.'

'Got yer eye on me, have yer?'

'I ain't poking me nose in, Babs.' Straightening herself up, Blanche handed her the last of the potatoes. 'I'm just a bit worried about yer.'

'I know you are, Blanche, and I'm grateful to yer.'

Blanche smiled and picked up her bags. 'Come on, let's get this lot home. I tell yer what, why don't you do a list of what yer want every morning, drop it in through me door, and I can get yer bits for yer while yer at work. I bet yer spend all yer dinner time in them bloody queues.'

'That's right kind of yer, Blanche,' said Babs, heaving her bag onto her arm, 'but I'll be all right. I don't suppose 'it'll last much longer with Albie Denham,' she added with a loud sigh as they started walking slowly along Grove Road.

'I ain't so sure about that, it's been about a year now, ain't it?' Blanche glanced sideways at Babs, waiting for her response, but she said nothing. 'I've gotta admit, it ain't turned out like I thought it would.'

'Yer right there. I thought he'd have had it away a long time ago.'

'Maybe he's changed and they'll settle down together.'

'D'yer reckon?' Babs asked sceptically.

'No. Not to be honest with yer, Babs. I don't.'

They walked along quietly for a moment, Blanche doing her best to think of something to say, anything to change the subject away from Albie Denham. 'Have you heard?' she said suddenly. 'They're saying how the King and Queen and all the government are doing a runner to Canada.'

'Wish I could go to bloody Canada.'

'I like them slacks yer wearing,' said Blanche, trying again. 'Always fancied meself in a pair of trousers. And Archie reckons I've still got the figure for 'em.'

Babs looked down at her legs as though the trousers were a surprise to her. 'These? I made them out of a remnant at work.'

'Big remnant,' laughed Blanche, relieved that she'd distracted Babs.

Babs laughed with her.

'I'd love some new things,' said Blanche wistfully. 'But there just don't seem to be the gear around to buy like there used to be.'

Babs stopped dead and turned to Blanche. 'If yer worked at Styleways yer could make yerself anything yer want.' She paused. 'Well, within reason.'

'Me? Work?'

'Why not? The governor's looking for people, to work

on uniforms. Good money it is and all. And there's some really nice girls, yer'd like 'em. One horrible one, but you get that anywhere.'

'How about the kids?'

Babs put down her bags again and thought for a moment. 'Janey can go to the nursery they've opened up at the school, and the rest of them are old enough to sort themselves out.'

'I'm not too sure about Len.'

'He'll be all right. Archie'll be there for him. He's always finished early down the market before school packs up.'

'Shame Mary never took that job at Styleways. I could have killed her starting on them munitions. That's our Ruby's fault, interfering as usual.'

'I ain't talking about Mary, I'm talking about you. Perhaps when she knows you'll be working there she'll wanna job and all.'

Blanche laughed. 'I don't even know if I'm gonna say yes yet, nor's yer governor. But I know if I do go there, it'll make Mary even keener to stay on munitions.' She frowned. 'And what'll my Archie say? I've not worked since we got married.'

'Has he ever refused you anything?'

Now Blanche was laughing again. 'Can't think of nothing, except about that bloody evacuation lark, of course, and Archie says now how he should have listened to me about that anyway.'

'Good, that's settled then. I'll go in to Mr Silver first thing Monday morning and see about it.'

Blanche looked a bit wary. 'Suppose I could give it a go.'

'Course yer could.' Babs picked up her bags and they began walking again. 'And yer don't have to stay if yer don't like it. But I know yer will, 'cos Mr Silver's right nice, ever so easy to work for.'

196

'He must be,' Blanche said with a chuckle. 'What he lets your Evie get away with.'

'He is good to her, but she works hard when she is there.'

'Even so, he must be a bit of a soft touch.'

'He ain't silly, Blanche, but he's good to all of us girls in the workshop. Dunno what he's like to the homeworkers, but I bet he's the same with them.'

'I could do that. Homework. That might suit me better.'

'Don't be daft, going out to work's the whole point of it. It'll do you good to get out.'

'Hark at us. I never even thought about working five minutes ago, now I'm deciding whether I wanna work in the factory or indoors.' She shook her head. 'Going out tonight, Babs?'

'I know you, Blanche, I know yer just trying to change the subject, but I ain't gonna let yer. Yes, I am going out tonight, and I'm going out with Lou *from work*. You like her. You'll like working with her and all.'

'*If* I ever work with her,' grinned Blanche, now almost resigned to the fact that she'd at least have a talk to Archie about going to Styleways.

'You will,' Babs grinned back. 'I've left it to Lou to sort something out for me and her to do tonight. Should be good. Her brother Bob's been coming up trumps with all sorts of fellers for us. You name 'em, soldiers, sailors, airmen, we've been out with the flipping lot!'

'It's good to see you laugh. You go out and enjoy yerself, make the most of it.'

'I think I'll have to. Bob's off to training camp himself soon, so there won't be no one around to find fellers for us.' Babs's laughter was no longer quite so convincing.

'As if you'd ever have any trouble finding yerself a bloke,' scoffed Blanche.

'I dunno so much. I always used to think that Evie was

barmy when she used to worry about being left an old maid. Now it's me what's worrying.'

'Now you really are being daft.'

'Am I?' Babs said softly. 'Am I really?'

13

Later on that hot, sunny Saturday afternoon, Babs and Blanche were both out in their back yards taking in the washing.

Babs shifted the clothes prop, letting the line slacken so she could reach the sheets that she'd pegged out before she went to the market. 'How d'yer feel about starting work now yer've had a couple of hours to think about it?' she asked, looking over the wall at Blanche.

'What time have I had to think about anything with all this to do?' Blanche mumbled, the wooden pegs she held in her mouth wobbling as she spoke. 'I ain't even spoken to my Archie about it yet.'

'You know what he'll say anyway.' Babs doubled the clean white sheet over her arm and laid it carefully in the washing basket; if she didn't crease it too much she'd be able to get away with only having to rub the iron over it.

Blanche took the pegs from her mouth and dropped them into the little checked bag that hung on the line. 'So, have you heard from Lou yet about what you pair are getting up to tonight?'

'Yeah, it's all sorted out. She popped round a little while ago to tell me.'

'Good. I told yer, yer should go out and enjoy yerself, single girl on a Saturday night. And you wait and see, I bet yer find yerself a right nice chap and all.'

'All right, Grandma,' Babs laughed as she took down

the next sheet from the line. 'I shouldn't have said them things this morning, should I? 'Cos I know you, yer'll be after me, seeing if I've got a feller and about settling down every five minutes now.'

'We'll see,' Blanche said, unpegging Janey's little vests. 'So, what are yer doing?'

'Going to see that new Cary Grant and Irene Dunne film.' Babs paused. She let the pillow case she was just about to fold drop into the linen basket and put her hand to her chin. 'Now, what's it called? I bet you know.'

'*My Favourite Wife*?' asked Blanche with a grin.

'That's the one,' chuckled Babs.

Blanche narrowed her eyes. 'Cor, Cary Grant. I wouldn't mind being his favourite wife.'

Babs got on with her folding. 'Don't let your Archie hear yer.'

'It's all right, Cary can nip round for a few hours and Archie won't know a thing about it. He won't be in for ages yet. Gone to see the Arsenal, ain't he. Him and Micky packed the stall away a bit early so's he could go and—'

The unmistakable sound of the air raid warning interrupted her.

'Aw no,' she hollered to Babs, tossing the clean vests carelessly into the washing basket and scooping up Janey from where she was playing by her feet. 'Here we go again, bloody thing. Grab yer ration books, Babs.'

'I'll go out the front and get Len,' Babs called over her shoulder as she dashed for the back door.

'I wish they'd drop a bomb on that scullery and get rid of the copper, the washing board and the tin bath with it, so I never had to do another bit of washing again,' laughed Blanche as she too disappeared indoors.

As she and Babs hurried along to the surface shelter at the end of the road, Blanche said, 'I wouldn't bother if it wasn't for these two little'uns.'

'I ain't a little'un,' said Len indignantly.

'But you've gotta come with us, Len, 'cos you have to look after Flash for me,' said Babs, ushering him inside.

'Ta, Babs,' whispered Blanche. 'I just hope Archie and them other two are all right.'

'Course they will be,' said Babs, settling herself down as best she could on the uncomfortable wooden bench. 'It'll all be another waste of time, you see. Still, better than getting in the washing, eh? And it's definitely better than having to do the rotten ironing. All them sheets and pillow cases.'

'I hope yer right,' said Clara.

Minnie patted her hand. 'I wanted to stay indoors, but Clara thought it best to be on the safe side.'

Blanche smiled reassuringly. 'Not worth the risk, eh, Clara?'

The siren faded, but it was immediately replaced by another sound that had everyone who wasn't in the shelter rushing to their doors to see what was going on. It wasn't the familiar droning of the aircraft that made them curious, they'd heard that nearly every day, it was the number of planes that had everyone looking up into the clear afternoon sky.

Blanche's fourteen-year-old son Terry, his sister Mary and Micky Clarke were hanging around chatting and smoking on the corner by the baker's shop.

Terry put up his hand to shade his eyes. 'Here, will yer just look at them.'

Mary copied her brother. 'I ain't never seen so many planes in one go before. And all in lines. Wonder what that's in aid of.'

'Sodding hell,' gasped Micky. 'There's flipping hundreds of 'em. Here, hang on.' He squinted up at the aircraft and gulped. 'Shit, they're only Jerries, ain't they. And look at that,' he pointed to a group of planes flying in the opposite direction. 'There's our planes heading right for 'em.'

Micky's words were immediately followed by the sound of a hail of empty bullet cases bouncing around on the cobbled street right where they were standing.

Terry stared down at them with his mouth open. 'Blimey.' Then he bent down and picked one up. 'Len'll like this,' he said, holding it out for Micky to look at.

'For gawd's sake, Terry, just take Mary and run for it! I'm gonna get me nan and grandad.'

As Micky raced across the street, he shouted at the top of voice for everyone to take cover, then threw himself into the passage of number five where Alice and Nobby were standing, trying to decide what to do. He grabbed his nan by the arm. 'Come on, quick!' he yelled. 'And you, Grandad. Yer've gotta get in the shelter.'

As they got to the street door there was a massive explosion that shook the house. It sounded and felt as though it was right on top of them.

Alice's hand flew to her mouth. 'We've been hit,' she shrieked.

'No, Nan, it's just the blast. Come on.'

Micky was right, the bomb had fallen several streets away, on the other side of Grove Road. But even so, there was still some damage – the big front window of the baker's, where only seconds before he, Mary and Terry had been standing chatting had been completely shattered. Alice went to rush over there.

'Ne'mind that,' said Micky, pulling her along. 'You're going in the shelter.'

'But Rita and Bert—'

'Don't worry, Nan, they'll be down in the bakehouse.'

Ethel Morgan, Maudie Peters, Terry and Mary Simpkins and the whole Jenner brood all got to the shelter together, just as the baker's window shattered.

'Gawd above!' gasped Ethel as they all hurled themselves inside.

Everyone sat where they could, while Terry and Mary huddled round Blanche, fussing over Janey and annoying Len with their concern.

Blanche shook her head with relief. 'Am I glad to see you two.'

'Micky'll be here in a minute,' Mary said to her mum. 'He's gone to fetch his nan and grandad.'

'Let's hope they hurry up,' said Minnie. 'It sounds nasty out there.'

Maudie looked across to Babs. 'How about Evie and your dad?'

Babs nibbled her bottom lip. 'Both out, Miss Peters,' she said.

Maudie nodded. She looked concerned; they all did. The continual drone of the waves of planes going over and the sound of guns firing could be heard all too clearly inside what now seemed a ridiculously fragile building.

The planes might have been loud but they all heard Micky and Frankie Morgan rowing outside the shelter.

'I'm enforcing the regulations,' Frankie shouted, barring the way to the door and pointing to a small blackboard that he'd fixed to it. 'Can't you read? That says that this shelter is full. And that's what it means. There's too many liberties been taken round here. And now people from other streets thinking they can—'

'Are you gonna move?' Micky said calmly.

'Yer supposed to go to the shelter shown on the sign when this one's full.'

Micky ripped the board from the door, and rubbed out the chalk writing. 'Now, get out of me way.' He took his nan's arm, forced Frankie to one side and led Alice and Nobby inside, letting the door swing shut behind him in Frankie's face.

But Frankie was having none of it. He immediately

slammed it open, straight back on its hinges, and stood there in the doorway, hands on hips.

'Yer meant to be the bloody warden, yer silly sod. Shut that flaming door,' snarled Ethel at her husband. 'Ain't you got no brains?'

Still fuming, Frankie did as he was told but when he turned back round to confront Micky, he was furious to see that Nobby and Alice had already sat themselves down next to his wife and that Micky had squeezed in on the bench next to Mary Simpkins.

Micky looked up at Frankie and sneered, 'I thought yer said the shelter was full.' Then he said to Alice, 'You all right, Nan?'

'Yes, thank you, darling,' answered Alice, glaring at Frankie as though she'd like to wring his neck for him.

Ethel was still furious with her husband. 'How could yer think about turning 'em away?' she demanded, glowering at him. 'You just wait till I get you home.'

'I thought it was full,' Frankie said pathetically. 'I thought all the street was in here. And if the other twin and Ringer had been in, it would have been.'

'And how about Nellie and Jim, and Rita and Bert?' demanded Minnie.

'I was only doing me duty.' Frankie looked about him, miserably seeking some sort of support for what he had done.

Alice wasn't going to give it him. 'My grandson's entitled to come in here if he wants,' she insisted, her eyes hard with anger. 'And I'll make sure he does and all, whenever he feels like it.'

Ethel nodded in agreement. 'I'll make sure and all, Alice. You just see if I don't.'

Frankie knew when he was on to a loser. Crestfallen he turned round in the cramped shelter, nearly falling over Janey who was playing on the floor with her dolly. 'I better get back to me duty out in—' A gigantic crash drowned out the rest of his words.

Alice screamed and Blanche grabbed Janey. The vibration loosened the hook in the wall where the Tilly lamp had hung. It went clanging to the ground and the shelter was suddenly plunged into pitch darkness.

'Grab that lamp!' yelled Micky.

'I'm in charge here,' Frankie bellowed at the top of his voice. 'Now everyone calm down. We don't need a light.'

'Yer silly old bastard,' shouted Micky, feeling round on the floor for the lamp. 'We don't wanna have a bloody fire in here, do we?'

'Don't you talk to me like that, young man,' said Frankie indignantly, but his anger was quickly replaced by fear as another loud crash sounded and the floor began to quake beneath them.

'Aw my good gawd,' groaned Alice.

Clara grabbed Minnie's hand, and the Jenner baby started to scream.

Liz Jenner stared into the darkness. 'I dunno why I let you persuade me to come in here, Ted,' she whimpered. 'I knew we should have stayed indoors.'

'There.' Micky hung the relit lamp on the hook he had screwed tightly back into the wall, then he sat back down and slipped his arm round Mary who, with a defiant stare at Alice, cuddled into his shoulder and looked adoringly up into his eyes.

Everyone except Frankie sighed with relief, but the shelter was soon rocking again. Flash howled, cement dust rose from the floor making everyone cough and their eyes sting, and one of the younger Jenners wet herself.

Babs closed her eyes and took a deep, choking breath of dust-filled air, then, with a quiet, quavering warble, she started singing, 'Pack up all my cares and woe, here I go, singing low, bye, bye, blackbird . . .' She felt someone grab her hand; it was Len.

'I'll sing with yer, twin,' he said.

'Good boy,' croaked Babs, squeezing his hand. 'Come on, you lot, join in with us. Like yer did the other night.'

'This ain't like the other night.' Nobby could barely speak for coughing.

Another crash came, louder this time. Liz Jenner cringed in the corner, her fingers digging hard into Ted's arm as she clung on to him desperately.

'All right, Liz,' he whispered to her. 'Come on, don't let the kids or Gran see yer scared.'

'Christ, that was near.' Frankie sounded close to panic. 'Wonder what poor bugger got that one.'

'Shut up, can't yer?' Ted said as evenly as he could, forcing himself not to get up and punch Frankie on the nose. 'Yer scaring the kids.' Another one of his youngsters started crying. 'It's only God having his coal delivered,' Ted Jenner said gently.

'No it's not,' Len piped up. 'That's when it's thunder and lightning.'

'No. It thunders when God moves his furniture,' said Minnie. Her voice, like her legs, was shaking but she was doing her best to cheer up the kids.

There was a sudden, enormous cracking sound; it felt as if the whole world was being ripped apart from under them as the brick building shuddered on its foundations.

Blanche held Janey close to her. 'What have I done, Babs,' she said flatly, 'bringing the kids back to this? I just hope my Archie's all right.'

When the all clear sounded at six o'clock that evening, they felt as though they had been in the shelter for days.

When they stepped outside, the sky was dotted with thick dark plumes of smoke from the fires that had started all over the East End.

Blanche looked dazed and exhausted but she soon came to when Janey shouted, 'Daddy!'

'Thank gawd, Babs,' she said, holding Janey tightly to

her. 'It's Archie.' She paused then said, 'I'm going to wait and think about it a bit before I talk to him about going to work. You understand, don't yer?'

Babs nodded. 'Course, that's the last thing yer wanna worry about. Listen, Blanche, I'll talk to yer about it later. I've gotta go, I'm gonna check that Dad's in the Drum.'

'He will be, love.'

'I know, but I just wanna make sure. Then I'll see to Flash and get straight over to Lou's. I'll get ready over there.' Babs shook her head wearily. 'I could do with getting out.'

'You get off soon as yer like, Babs. Len'll look after Flash for yer.'

Babs hurried away just as Archie came puffing up to Blanche. He folded his arms round her and Janey. 'I can't tell yer what a relief this is, darling.' He and Blanche stood there not needing to say anything more, just glad to be holding each other.

Mary came up behind them and tapped Archie on the shoulder. 'If yer in such a good mood, Dad,' she said with a cheeky smile, 'yer won't say no to me going to the pictures with Micky tonight, will yer?'

'You go and enjoy yerselves,' said Archie before Blanche had the chance to object.

'Say there's another raid?' Blanche sounded alarmed.

'Don't worry yerself, they can't have any more bloody bombs left after that little lot,' he reassured her.

But Blanche didn't look convinced as she watched Mary and Micky walk off down the street hand in hand.

'Archie?' Blanche looked fraught.

He had to do something to comfort her. 'Hang on!' he called after them. 'Micky, make sure you get Mary safe into a shelter somewhere if that warning goes. D'you hear me?'

Micky responded with a quick thumbs up and a grin

and they were on their way again.

At half past eight that evening, just as Archie and Bert had finished patching up the window of the baker's with plywood sheets, proof came that there were plenty of bombs left to drop over the East End. There was no hesitation this time; the siren had hardly got going before the shelter in Darnfield Street was packed.

'Tell yer what, Blanche,' whispered Archie. 'If this carries on we'll have to find somewhere better than this surface shelter. It can't be much use, the way it's shaking. Perhaps we should have taken up Bert's offer of going down into his bakehouse.'

'It's cramped and hot enough in here as it is,' said Blanche, frowning. 'I dunno how the kids'd rest in all that heat down there from the ovens.'

'Perhaps when the weather gets a bit colder.'

'Don't even think that this is gonna last, Archie. Please,' Blanche pleaded.

'Only kidding,' he said, as another loud crash shook the walls. 'Come on, rest yer head on me, yer gonna have to try and get some kip.'

'I just hope that Micky did as he was told and looked after Mary,' fretted Blanche. 'They could be anywhere, the pair of them.'

Alice sat opposite Blanche, her chest rising and falling as she breathed rapidly in and out. 'If anything happens to my Micky,' she muttered menacingly, 'then we'll all know who's to blame, won't we?'

'I'll ignore that, Alice,' Blanche said through tightly-pursed lips. 'But if I didn't have my kids here . . .'

'All right, Blanche,' Archie pacified his wife. 'Just try and relax, you're worn out.'

It was the early hours before everyone managed to doze off, albeit fitfully. Young Terry Simpkins woke with a start, not sure where he was. 'Dad?'

'It's all right, son, you go back to sleep.' Archie pulled

his pullover off, rolled it up and tucked it under his son's head. 'Come on now, yer all right, yer dad's here.' Satisfied that Terry had dropped off again, Archie leant back against the rough brick wall of the shelter and closed his own eyes. 'At least we won five nil this afternoon,' he said to himself with a grin. 'I'd hate to die knowing we'd lost to Fulham.'

When the final all clear came at five o'clock the next morning, the scene outside was even worse than that on the previous afternoon. There was no damage in Darn-field Street itself, apart from Rita and Bert's broken window, but the sky was full of smoke that came belching up from the direction of the docks.

As the neighbours staggered out of the shelter, Frankie Morgan held court in the street. It was about time, he thought, that they showed a bit of regard for his official status, and he was revelling in having information – strictly secret, of course – from his ARP controller about what had happened the night before. He was only too willing to pass it on in exchange for a bit of respect.

'Almost three hundred planes there was,' he said, grasping his lapels and rocking back on his heels. 'Bomb-ing from early evening till near dawn.' He accepted a cigarette from Ted Jenner. 'The fires down in the docks, massive they reckon they are, and uncontrollable, started before it was even dark.'

'Any casualties?' Blanche asked, her face pale with tiredness and strain.

'Already been estimated that fifteen hundred people at least have been hurt.'

'Mary . . .' Blanche gasped. She felt her legs go weak as Archie led her back to number four.

When Mary eventually put her head round the kitchen door at nearly half past seven that morning, Blanche didn't know whether to kiss her or clip her round the ear.

Instead, she slammed her cup of tea down on the table. 'Where the hell were you? I thought you'd got bloody blown up.'

Mary sat down next to her dad, well away from her mum on the opposite side of the table. 'We was in the Troxy when that second warning went, so we stayed there. Yer told us to shelter somewhere safe.'

Blanche sighed loudly and rolled her eyes heavenwards. 'Me and yer dad was that worried.' She reached out to take Mary's hand, then suddenly changed her mind. 'You go through now, Arch, try and get a few hours' kip. I wanna have a word with Mary.'

'All right. I could do with getting me head down for a bit.' Archie bent forward and kissed Mary on the forehead. 'Good to see you home safe and sound, sweetheart.'

'Ta, Dad,' Mary smiled up at him. 'I'm glad to be home and all.'

As soon as Blanche heard him close the door to the downstairs front room which she and Archie used as a bedroom, Blanche hissed across the table at Mary, 'You *sure* you was in the Troxy all night, Mary Simpkins?'

'Yeah.' Mary was taken aback by her mother's anger. 'Course. Where d'yer think we was?'

'Never you mind,' Blanche said warily. 'You just tell me about it.'

'Well, when the warning went outside, we couldn't hear it but they put a sign up on the screen what said there was a raid. After what had happened in the afternoon, some people started getting a bit scared.'

'I *knew* I shouldn't have let yer go.'

'Calm down, Mum, nothing happened. They just panicked a bit. So the manager got up on stage and said that it was safe there in the picture house, but people was still scared, so he shouted out, "Come on, let's all sing".'

Blanche still looked dubious. 'Sing?'

'They was a bit slow getting going but when he started on "There'll Always Be An England", yer should have heard them then. Singing their hearts out, they were. Me and Micky and all.' Mary grinned. 'Right laugh it was. We all sung all night. Some of 'em even got up and did a turn. The twins should have been there, they'd have gone down right well.'

Blanche looked at Mary through narrowed eyes. 'So long as yer sure that's all yer got up to.'

'When we was walking home just now, me and Micky . . .' Mary had sounded completely composed up until then, but now tears filled her eyes. She sniffed, stared down at her hands and then went on, 'There was all these people sitting along the kerb outside where their houses had been; they looked really sad, all their homes ruined. Yer should have seen 'em. I kept thinking, say that's happened to our house, what'll I do then if Mum and Dad and the kids are hurt.' Mary's tears started flowing. 'Blimey, Mum, I didn't think yer'd have a go. I thought yer'd be glad I was home here safe.'

'Course I'm glad yer all right, yer great daft hap'orth.' Blanche was crying too. 'Come and give yer mum a cuddle.'

14

By the Thursday, after four days of what seemed like total madness, so much of what had been familiar lay abandoned and in smoking ruins. People tried to do the best they could, to make sense of what was going on: making their way to work through bomb-shattered streets and roads pocked with craters, shopping in places with no windows and very little stock, cleaning and sweeping, caring for children, just getting on and doing all the different things that made up the everyday existences of ordinary people. But something that had changed was that all the talk now was of one thing only: the terrible raids and their effect on friends and relatives.

The exact figures weren't being released to the newspapers or on the wireless, but with people like Frankie Morgan living in the midst of close-knit East London communities and the strong family ties which linked so many streets, it soon became widespread if unofficial knowledge that in the first three days of the Blitz nearly a thousand people had been killed. The estimates for injuries hadn't even been guessed at yet.

Many people took the decision to stop going to the street shelters; after the terrifying couple of nights they had had to spend in them, they believed them to be useless. Instead, they took their chances under dripping railway arches, in dusty, rat-infested warehouse basements, bleak, uncomfortable Tube station platforms, and even the pews of neighbourhood churches.

Maudie was on her way to her local church on that Thursday morning when Georgie bumped into her on the corner of Darnfield Street as he was going into the pub.

'How are you, Mr Bell?' Maudie asked. 'I haven't seen you for a few days and I was wondering.'

'I'm all right, thank you, Miss Peters,' Georgie answered shyly. 'And yerself?'

'I'm fine. I've been sheltering at the church. You know, St Dorothea's.'

Georgie nodded.

'Ever since the surface shelter . . .' She paused and pointed back down the road to the deserted brick building. Then she flashed the smile that lit up her face. 'Ever since it proved so useless.'

Georgie looked concerned. 'Is there a crypt or something there in the church?'

Maudie shook her head. 'Nothing so grand. We spend the night in the pews.' She smiled again. 'Praying and hoping.'

'But is that safe?'

Maudie shrugged. 'Is anywhere?'

Georgie jerked his thumb over his shoulder to the door of the Drum. 'Everyone else from the street, except you and the Jenners that is, are going in here. There's a big cellar and it keeps nice and cool. Not like that bloody . . .' he hesitated. 'Excuse me, not like that rotten shelter. And Rita and Bert have said we can go down into the basement of the baker's if there's still raids on when the weather gets colder.'

'That's very kind of them all.'

'That's why I'm going in there now, in the pub I mean.' Georgie blushed, he was getting himself all tongue-tied. 'Me, old Nobby and Jim have been knocking some bunks together to make it a bit more comfortable.' He held up the claw hammer and screwdriver he was carrying as proof.

She flashed her smile at him again.

'The Drum's a lot closer than the church or the Tube station, Miss Peters.'

'Yes, it is.'

'I can understand if yer ain't very keen. At first, my girls said they wouldn't come in the Drum. They said they liked their bit of privacy, so they made a bed under the table instead. Right uncomfortable that must have been.' Georgie had started to babble, he could feel himself talking quicker and quicker but for some reason he just couldn't stop himself. 'I think they was really worried, yer see, worried that . . .' Georgie stared down at his boots '. . . worried that their old dad was gonna have a few too many and show 'em up. But after all these things have been happening I've been trying to pull meself together. We've all gotta try and do something.' He raised his eyes, a horrified expression on his face. 'I dunno why I said all that, Miss Peters. You have that effect on me somehow. Yer make me come out with things.'

Maudie smiled. 'I don't mean to.'

'They prefer the Drum now anyway,' he said hurriedly.

Maudie put her head on one side and Georgie felt his cheeks burning.

'They're a nice couple, Jim and Nellie,' she said. 'Seem to be very interested in the girls.'

'Yeah, when Violet run off they come along and told me that if ever the girls needed anything, just to let them know.'

'That was really kind of them.'

'They never had kiddies of their own. Shame.'

'Yes, it is. It's a blessing to have children.'

There was a brief pause; Georgie racked his brains for something, anything not too stupid, to say. 'I reckon they should have cleared off down hopping with that lot from Grove Road, yer know,' he finally blurted out.

'Who?' Maudie looked confused.

'The girls, but yer know how wilful girls can be. Specially my Evie. Not that I see much of her now, although she does try to be home at a reasonable hour what with the warnings and knowing how me and Babs worry about her. Then there's that dog of hers . . .'

Another pause fell between them.

'I've never been hop picking.' This time it was Maudie who filled the silence. 'Is it good?'

'More of a women's thing really,' George said. Suddenly he grinned. 'Yer a funny one, you, Miss Peters.' His eyes opened wide. 'I didn't mean to be rude or nothing.'

'I know.'

'Do you, er, do yer listen to the wireless much, Miss Peters?' She'd think he was a right idiot, why had he asked her that? Of course she did. Everyone did.

'No,' she answered with a small shake of her head. 'My wireless doesn't seem to be working. I miss hearing the news.'

Georgie cheered up immediately. 'Is it the accumulator wants changing? I could do it for yer.'

'No. I don't think it's that.'

'You'll have to come indoors and have a listen to ours.'

Now it was Maudie who looked shy. 'I'd like that. Thank you, Mr Bell.'

'Or I could have a look at your set for you.'

'Oh, if you'd rather I didn't come in . . .'

'No. No. No, I didn't mean that.' Georgie could have bitten off his tongue. Why didn't he think before he opened his mouth? 'Tell you what, I could look at it now. Jim and Nobby can manage for a bit without me. It'll only take me a minute.' He waved the hammer and screwdriver. 'I'm quite good with me hands.' He hesitated.

'Aw, I didn't think, yer was on yer way out.'

'I was just going to see if there was anything I could volunteer to do round at the church. You know, anything to help. It makes me feel a bit less like an unwanted spare part.' Maudie let out a little sigh. 'But I suspect that the vicar only finds me jobs to keep me occupied. And I'm sure that can wait.'

'I'll come now then, shall I?'

As Georgie stepped timidly into the kitchen of number seven, he took off his cap and looked round at the bright little room dotted with colourful pictures and jugs full of branches and twigs and, yes, he was right, dandelions. 'Nice place yer've got here, Miss Peters,' he said, staring at one of the packed vases.

'I see you've noticed my "wartime roses",' she said with a surprisingly girlish laugh. 'Don't worry, I'm not mad, I know they're twigs and weeds, it's just that I like to have flowers around me to liven the place up. Make it a little less . . .' She didn't finish the sentence. 'I used to grow my own flowers, you know, out the back, but now I grow vegetables. And even I wouldn't put a potato in a vase.' She turned and looked out of the kitchen window. 'There's not much space out there, but it's just trying to do my bit again.'

'Time I did my bit, I think,' Georgie said, pointing to the set in the corner. 'This the wireless?'

Maudie turned back to face him and nodded. 'Yes. I'll put the kettle on.'

She took off her coat and busied herself with making the tea while Georgie poked around in the back of the wireless. After only a few minutes he had the dial lit up and the set tuned in to the painful strains of a strangulated tenor warbling about his mother.

'That's wonderful.' Maudie's smile radiated warmth. 'And just in time.' She held out a cup of steaming tea to Georgie and then pointed to the wireless. 'I meant it

217

was wonderful that you'd mended it, not that I liked that terrible noise.'

Georgie grinned back and turned the knob to off. 'He was a bit strong.'

'Sit down, please.'

Georgie settled himself awkwardly at the lace-cloth covered table.

'I'm very grateful to you, Mr Bell. I do like to hear the news.'

Georgie was about to sip his tea, but he halted the cup inches from his lips so that he could answer her. 'Me too.'

'Not that there's much good news lately.'

This time Georgie already had the tea in his mouth, so he shook his head in reply.

Maudie also shook her head, but more in despair than anything else. 'I heard some terrible news round at the church yesterday. About the families who were bombed out in that first big raid last Saturday.'

'What was that then?' asked Georgie.

'They were using a school in Canning Town as a temporary rest centre. They were all staying there the night and were told that evacuation transport was coming to pick them up on the Sunday afternoon. But by Monday night, still no one had come for them.' Maudie stopped speaking for a moment. She fiddled with her cup, turning it round and round in its saucer. Then she took a sharp intake of breath and continued. 'And on early Tuesday morning the school was bombed. They were all killed. Every one of them. The officials said that seventy-three had died in there.' She looked across the table at Georgie. 'I don't believe them. I think it was many more. One of the women from the church told me that her niece's little family were in there and they certainly weren't on any official list, they'd just gone there on Monday night when their house lost its roof after an incendiary attack. She says she'll never forgive herself, that *she* should have

218

taken them in. But it wasn't her fault. She'd already taken a young woman and her baby in and she didn't have any more room.' Maudie drained her cup. 'But it's no good arguing with her. And I do know how she feels. When people are suffering and you're not, it's all too easy to feel guilty.'

'Yer right there,' Georgie said abruptly, surprising himself. 'I've been thinking that I should be doing more.'

'Have you, Mr Bell?' Maudie asked as she refilled their cups. 'What sort of thing were you thinking of?'

Georgie hardly faltered. 'I thought I'd become a volunteer fireman,' he said, not having a clue how that particular idea had popped into his mind. In fact, he couldn't think why he'd said it at all.

'What a wonderful idea,' said Maudie, her smile of approval making Georgie feel for once he'd said the right thing.

Georgie decided to waste no time putting his thoughts into action. Within forty-five minutes of leaving Maudie's house, he was standing in front of Sub-officer Smith's desk in the temporary fire sub-station that had been set up in a requisitioned school off Old Ford Road.

Sub-officer Smith looked at the form that Georgie had filled in. 'Says here you were a lorry driver, Bell. That you'd like to volunteer as a driver of a heavy-unit fire appliance.'

'I talked to a few of the fellers out there in the yard and that seemed a sensible sort of thing for me to do.'

Smith nodded noncommittally. He looked at Georgie's details again. 'Married man, are you, Bell?

Georgie frowned. 'Married?' He wondered what this was leading up to.

'Yes, you'll be expected to stay here you see, to sleep, when you're on shift. We need as many men as we can get, but some men might be more suited to a different kind of volunteering. I can't be doing with any shirkers or problems. Too busy for that.'

Georgie sucked in his lower lip and twisted his cap into a tight roll behind his back. 'I am married, in a way, but the wife, she's not exactly around. Not seen her for more than ten years now.'

Smith didn't say anything, knowing that by letting Georgie take his time he'd tell him more than any questioning would glean.

Georgie didn't disappoint him. 'Might as well be honest. Everyone knew me, Georgie "Ringer" Bell. I was a happy man with a lovely wife and beautiful little twin daughters. Good job, nice little house. I had it all. Or so I thought. Then me and Violet – the wife – started rowing. I didn't know what had got into her. Kept saying how she wanted something more in life. I didn't understand what she meant. If I had, I swear I'd have done something about it. But there was no talking to her. Then one day Violet never come home from the market. I left the twins with Nellie, a neighbour. They was only little'uns, eight, nine years old, and I wandered the streets looking for her. It was a stranger told me the strength of it. She'd upped and done a runner with a stallholder, bloke from down the next turning, if yer don't mind. I stopped bothering with things from then on. I took to drinking too much and I got in trouble with me job. It was a good job and all – driver with the Union Cartage – and it weren't long before I got the sack. They kept me on as long as they could because they knew I had the girls.' Georgie bowed his head.

'How did you manage?' Smith asked.

'I got by. Scraped a living working as a potman at the Drum and Monkey, that's the pub on the corner of our road. They've been good to me in there. And I did bits and pieces for the stallholders in the Roman Road. People felt sorry for me, I suppose. For the girls, really. Well, it's dawned on me recently, over the last few months or so, that I should stop feeling so sorry for meself. I realised I'd never amount to nothing, the way I was carrying on, never be no use to no one if I didn't do something. And quick and all. So, here I am. I've thought about it and I've decided it's time I pulled meself together and started thinking about something other than moaning about how hard done by I've been.' Georgie smiled mirthlessly. 'It'll make a change.'

'You really have been honest with me, Bell,' said Sub-officer Smith, flipping over the top sheet of a pile of pages on his desk. 'So I'll be honest with you too.' He lifted his chin and gazed steadily at Georgie. 'I'm a bit wary of you, Bell, about you not having much of a work record lately and about your self-confessed drinking. But being short of manpower means that beggars can't be choosers.'

Georgie grinned. 'Thanks very—'

'Not so fast, Bell.' Smith held up his hand. 'I'm going to take this a bit careful. So there are conditions. First of all, I've got no intention of starting you off on the heavy unit. We've got just the one here and it's too precious to take any risks with. We'll just have to carry on making do with the bloke who's doing his best on that for now. No, we'll try you out on one of the taxi cabs we've requisitioned to tow the trailer pumps. You'll be driving that. They've got small crews, so they'll be able to keep an eye on you.'

'Ain't I seen them cabs being driven by women?'

'By women *what*, Bell?'

Georgie looked puzzled, not understanding at first. Then he realised. 'By women. Sir.'

Smith gave the briefest of nods. 'That's right. Any problems with that?'

'No, sir.'

'Good. So let's see how you do. Now, the second condition. The training's not what it was before this little

221

lot started, so I'm going to be watching you closely, Bell, to see how fast you learn. It'll mean having to sort yourself out quite a bit. Picking things up as you go along. And finally, I expect to see you quite a bit smarter and fitter than you are now. Work on it. Maybe a drop less ale would be a start. And a shave.'

'Yes, sir.'

Smith stood up and came round his desk to Georgie. 'I'll put you in with Volunteer Fireman Johnson, he'll show you the ropes. Now, I don't want to be made a fool of, Bell, giving you this chance. Let's see you prove yourself.'

When Georgie got back to Darnfield Street, Babs was standing at the kitchen sink getting the tea ready.

'Hello, Dad,' she said, looking up at the clock on the mantelpiece. 'It's only sausage and chips so it'll be ready about quarter past six, all right?'

'Lovely, girl,' he said.

Babs turned back to the sink and got on with chipping the potatoes. She could tell by his voice that he hadn't been drinking. 'What you been up to then?'

'I've joined the fire brigade.'

'Blimey!' Babs dropped the half-peeled potato into the sink, wiped her hands on her apron and sat down at the table.

'I'll make us a cuppa, shall I?' Georgie said.

'Yeah, that'd be nice.' Babs could hardly believe it as Georgie took his jacket off, went out in the hall to hang it over the banister, then came back into the kitchen, filled the kettle and set about making a pot of tea.

'Evie in?'

Babs nodded. 'Yeah.'

'I'll make a cup for her and all then.'

'Am I dreaming? There's Evie – she actually come home from work with me and said she'd stay in for a bit of tea before she goes out tonight. Now here's you saying yer've joined the fire brigade.'

'It's true.' Georgie took cups and saucers down from the shelf and put them on the table.

'And yer using saucers and all. Yer never bother with saucers.' Babs sounded flabbergasted. 'Here, Dad, what's going on?'

'I'm gonna be training with this feller. Vic Johnson, he's called. Nice bloke. You'd like him. Family man.'

'No, Dad, you know what I mean. What's going on with you? Why d'yer do it? What's got into you?'

Georgie filled the pot with boiling water and covered it with the tatty old cosy that they'd had ever since Babs could remember. 'We need a new one of these,' he said, looking at it distastefully.

'Never mind the tea cosy, Dad, just sit down and tell me what's going on. Please.'

Georgie sat down and rubbed his hand over his stubbled chin. 'I was talking to Miss Peters and I realised that I wanted to do me bit. I've been a right slob lately. A self-centred old drunk, if I was truthful.'

Babs said nothing, she just raised her eyebrows and poured the tea.

'I was wondering if yer had any idea where me suit is? Is it still in the wardrobe in your'n and Evie's room?'

Babs thought for a moment. 'Don't think so. No, it must still be in the pawn shop.'

'Aw yeah, suppose it is.' Georgie sipped at the scalding tea. 'Wonder if they've still got it.'

'Shouldn't think so. It must have been years ago the last time me and Evie took it round Uncle's for you.'

'Perhaps I'll have to see about getting meself a new one.'

'New what?' It was Evie standing in the kitchen doorway. Her bright blonde hair was pinned tight to her head in sausage-shaped curls, and she was dressed only in her underslip and the string of pearls that Albie had given her.

Babs nibbled at her lip. 'Dad's gonna get himself a new suit,' she said, trying not to giggle in amazement at the idea of Georgie caring about what he looked like.

Evie frowned. 'A suit?'

'Yeah.' Babs was now having trouble not bursting out laughing. 'And he ain't been to the pub.'

'No?'

'No. He went and joined the fire brigade instead.'

Evie's mouth fell open. She looked at Babs, but immediately glanced away again, knowing that her twin would only set her off. She did her best to compose herself and said, 'Fire brigade, eh, Dad? That'll be nice for yer.'

That was too much for Babs, she hugged her sides and tears of laughter streamed down her cheeks. 'Aw, Dad,' she gasped. 'It's gonna be so good to have yer back.'

Now it was Georgie's turn to look confused. 'But I ain't been nowhere.'

'Aw yes you have,' said Evie with a tearful smile. She threw her arms round his neck and planted a kiss on his unshaven cheek. 'Welcome home, Dad.'

15

After the glorious summer, the winter of 1940 came as a sudden, sharp shock; not only was the cold weather itself a chilling contrast to the long, warm days that had gone before, but it had started so early. It was only the second week in October and was already bitterly cold. But the weather was only a minor inconvenience; it was the Blitz that was the main and very real concern in most Cockneys' lives. Getting ready every night became second nature, a routine got down to a fine art of collecting blankets, folding chairs, slippers, knitting, books, sandwiches, cigarettes, hot water bottles and flasks of tea – everything, in fact, that might be needed to pass a long night listening to the aircraft overhead and explosions nearby, while everyone did their best to rub along together, help each other out and muck in, in the odd assortment of crowded places that had been taken over as shelters.

But even the most fervent of community spirits could be sorely tested when, exhausted from having to carry on despite lack of sleep, people emerged from their makeshift shelters to be faced with the cancellation of yet another delivery to the already half empty local food shop, or having to put up, again, with the disruption of their usual transport to work, or finding out that the mains had been struck and that there wasn't even any water with which to make a cup of tea.

Blanche would gladly have put up with all those things, and more, if only she could have swapped them for the letter that had come for her Archie. It was the letter she had been dreading, telling them that Archie was to go away to army training camp.

Archie and she had argued about it, argued more than at any other time in their married life, but he had been insistent. He said that with all that was going on around them, on their very doorsteps in the East End, he had to do something more than work down the market, something that would contribute somehow to the fight that was now as much about protecting his own family as trying to help unknown foreigners across the Channel. Blanche had begged Ted Jenner to try and get him work in the docks, loading supplies or anything that Archie would consider proper, worthwhile war work, but it was no use, there was nothing for him there. So Archie had made his decision. He had joined up. He had even knocked a couple of years off his age to make sure they would accept him. The recruiting sergeant, a tough, no-nonsense York-shireman with a neck like a bull, had approved of Archie's attitude and had turned a blind eye to his claim that he was in his twenties. And now, on a cold, grey October morning, Archie was leaving for camp.

'Blanche?' Babs called through the letter box of number four. 'I'm here.'

Blanche opened the door and pulled back the blackout curtain to let Babs in. She smiled bravely. 'Thanks for doing this for me, Babs.'

'Daft,' said Babs, pulling Flash in after her. 'As if yer ain't never done nothing for me and Evie.'

'Even so, I appreciate yer taking the time off work. Archie couldn't have stood having to say goodbye to the little'uns at the station. It's gonna be hard enough saying goodbye to me and the other two.'

Babs followed her along the passage into the kitchen. It

was exactly the same as the Bells' kitchen in number six, but seemed much smaller with the extra chairs round the table and all the things belonging to the children.

Blanche fussed around, wiping every available surface with a damp rag that she had in her hand. 'I've left a sheep's head stew on the stove for their tea and there's plenty in there for you and all. Help yerself, won't yer?'

Babs nodded. 'Right.'

'And Len wants to feed the scraps to Flash, if that's all right with you.' Blanche's face crumpled and she let the cloth fall to the floor. 'What am I gonna do, Babs?'

'You just go. Go on.' Babs went over to the high chair in the corner where Janey was gnawing happily on a crust of bread and chucked the toddler under the chin. 'We'll be all right, won't we, darling?'

'Hello, Babs.' Archie was standing in the back door-way with his arm round Len's shoulder. 'It's cold out there.'

'Freezing,' said Babs.

'We've just been checking that Len's rabbit hutch ain't got no leaks or nothing. It looks like it's gonna be a bad old winter.'

'We'd better be going if yer gonna get that train,' Blanche said briskly, and ran out of the kitchen.

The taxi journey to Waterloo was difficult to say the least. Archie tried a few times to make conversation, but he got no response from Blanche, Mary or Terry. The three of them just stared wordlessly out of the windows at the grey London streets; even the shocking scale of the bomb damage couldn't provoke a single remark.

At the station, the platforms were crowded with men in uniform and women and children jostling for places to say goodbye as soldiers, sailors and airmen hung at precarious angles from open carriage windows. The goodbyes weren't whispered, everyone was shouting, trying to be heard over the noise of trains pulling out from other platforms and steam hissing from the engines as they prepared to leave. The smell of coal and cigarette smoke, mixed with the unmistakable scent of Evening in Paris, was everywhere.

As they pushed their way along the platform, looking for a carriage with an empty seat, Archie tried to say what he was feeling but it came out more like a list of instructions. 'Terry, you do what you can to keep that stall going with Micky. It's been a little goldmine for us and I don't want it ruined.'

'Yes, Dad.'

'Micky knows all about the wholesalers and everything, so you just listen to him, he'll make sure that side of it's all straight.'

'Yes, Dad.'

'And most important of all, you look after yer mum. You're gonna have to be the man of the house while I'm away. And you, Mary, I know yer working hard in that factory but that's no excuse not to do what yer can for yer mum. All right?'

'Yes, Dad.'

'Promise?'

'Promise. I'll do me best, Dad.'

'Good.' Archie stopped fighting his way through the crowd and stood by an open carriage door. 'Now you two go and amuse yerselves for a couple of minutes. I wanna have a word with yer mum.'

Mary pecked Archie on the cheek. 'See yer, Dad,' she whispered and started sniffling into her hankie.

Terry threw his arms round Archie and slapped him on the back. 'Yeah, see yer, Dad. Bring us back a Jerry's helmet.'

'Go on, you two. Wait by the gate back there where yer mum can find yer.'

Archie held Blanche's hand tightly in his as they

watched Mary and Terry disappear into the sea of khaki bodies. 'They're good kids,' he said, then he lifted Blanche's chin with his finger and looked into her eyes. 'Yer should be proud how they've turned out. It's all down to you, yer know.'

Blanche couldn't say anything, the lump in her throat felt as if it was choking her.

'I often wonder what would have happened to me if I hadn't met you over Vicky Park that Sunday afternoon. D'you remember, Blanche? There I was, Jack the lad, breaking that fence down with that mob o' boys from down St Stephen's Road and you come storming over, hollering and hooting about how we should leave it alone.' Archie laughed. 'Always been a fighter, ain't yer?' He pulled her to him and wrapped his arms tightly round her. 'And yer've gotta keep fighting. It ain't gonna be easy for neither of us.' He reached inside his overcoat and took a little box from his jacket pocket. 'Here, I want yer to wear this.'

Blanche opened it. Inside was a little marcasite brooch.

'It's an A,' he said, pinning it onto her lapel. 'For Archie, so yer won't forget yer Archie Simpkins's girl, and that yer always will be.'

Blanche couldn't hold back her tears any longer, but she had to say something. She struggled to speak. 'I just dunno what to say now the time's come, Arch.'

'Be brave, darling, and with a bit o' luck it'll all be over soon. And I want yer to remember, Blanche, this is not something I wanted to do, it's something I *had* to do.'

When they got back from the station, it was nearly dark, but Mary and Terry couldn't settle, so they took Len and Janey out for a walk with Flash while Babs sat Blanche down with a cup of tea and let her cry.

Blanche didn't say much but she made it clear that if there was still a job going at Styleways, she would take it.

Anything to fill in the long hours when she would be driving herself mad, missing Archie.

While Babs sat in Blanche's kitchen, comforting her and making yet another pot of tea, Georgie was chatting away to Vic Johnson at the fire station as they checked and rechecked the equipment ready for the evening shift. Georgie had been in the service only a month but he was enjoying having a sense of purpose again and the feeling of tiredness that came from working hard rather than from self-pity and too much ale.

Satisfied that the hoses had all been dried and re-coiled and the pumps had been inspected, Vic straightened up and stretched. He studied the night sky, watching the searchlights playing backwards and forwards across the solid blackness. 'With a bit of luck we'll have time for a brew before we get called out tonight, Ringer.'

But he and Georgie didn't even reach the classroom that the firemen used as a canteen before the bells went down, as they had both learnt to call the signal for action. Sub-officer Smith appeared out of the operations room with their orders.

'You're driving the heavy unit tonight, Bell,' he said gruffly. 'Don't let me down. And you're on it with him, Johnson.'

Georgie and Vic puffed up with pride as they scrambled into the cab of the big grey-painted fire engine with the rest of the crew.

'This old bus must have been a sight before the war, eh, Vic?' said Georgie as the engine shuddered into life. 'All shiny red against the gleaming brass.'

'Blimey,' Vic laughed. 'You ain't turning into a poet, are yer, Ringer?'

Georgie drove them as fast as he dared through the blacked-out streets where the only illumination came from the brief eerie light of explosions and the scattered fires that were breaking out after yet another series of incendiary showers. As they got closer to their destination, he was forced to swing the engine from side to side to try and avoid the craters made by the latest enemy surprise – land mines. The crew were more than grateful that Georgie was determined not to disappoint the sub-officer's trust in him. In fact, Smith would have had every reason to be impressed by Georgie's composure and skill as he negotiated the roads where, in places, even the tarry blocks of the road surface itself were now on fire.

Georgie leant forward, grasping the steering wheel as though it were the reins of a bucking pony, refusing to be distracted by the sounds of aircraft overhead, the bombs falling around them, the staccato anti-aircraft fire that abruptly punctured the rare moments of silence, or even the weird sight of barrage balloons shining in the night sky like enormous scarlet fishes as their silver skins reflected the fires below.

'That must be it,' Vic shouted, pointing to a great cloud of thick black smoke that belched from the now glowing skyline ahead of them.

Georgie pulled the engine as close to the fire as he dared. The crew leapt out and started unrolling the hoses, connecting them up to hydrants.

'We're gonna need all the water we can get tonight,' one of the crew called to Georgie. 'Let's just hope Jerry ain't split the water main.'

They breathed a sigh of relief when they found that the water main was intact, and more than one of the crew silently thanked God that the nearby emergency surface tank was also still in one piece, because they really did need a lot of water. The ARP report that the sub-officer had given them had been all too accurate: nearly the whole terrace of little two-up, two-down houses had received direct hits, and the tiny corner shop no longer had much of a roof or any windows.

The firemen wrestled with the huge hoses that buckled

and all but melted in the intense heat as they struggled to keep the powerful jets of water directed into the flames licking arrogantly round the shattered husks that had, only hours before, been people's homes. They ignored the burning brands that flew into their faces and the red-hot shrapnel that ricocheted off the roofs, glanced off the cobbles and seared into their clothes. For the crew, the night was one of smoke, sweat, excruciating heat and muscle-straining work; being almost knocked off your feet by the effect of high-explosive bombs going off nearby was just another part of the job.

But for the now homeless families who looked on, watching the paint blistering and peel, listening to the glass shatter and the huge roof timbers creak and rip apart, sending great bursts of sparks into the air, it was far from routine.

They looked on dumbly as one of the firemen clambered up the turntable ladder and fought his way through the smoke and fumes to get water into the roof spaces to stop the flames spreading further. Even the sight of the rats streaming out of the devastated buildings, desperate to escape the heat, wasn't enough to move the dazed and bewildered onlookers to speech; it took the bravery of two young female stretcher-bearers going into one of the blazing houses to rescue an elderly man to do that.

The neighbours who had once lived in the now ruined street gathered round as the young women laid the stretcher down and checked the old man for injuries.

'Well done, girls,' someone said, then he turned to the old man. 'Sam? How yer doing, mate?'

The old man's eyes flicked open. 'Me teeth,' he lisped. 'These bloody ambulance girls have left 'em on me bedside table.' He flopped his hand back towards the now caved-in shell that had been his home. 'Call one of the firemen, they might have a bit more go in 'em.'

'But Sam—'

'It's their job, ain't it? Go on, tell 'em to fetch me teeth. They're me best set and all.' With that, the old man passed out and the young women, arms straining, lifted the stretcher and set about carrying him to the shelter of their ambulance.

As they passed by, Georgie shook his head and gave them a wry smile. 'Ne'mind, girls,' he shouted over the combined din of water, fire and destruction. But the smile was soon wiped off his face.

'Looter! Get him!' hollered the duty constable who was helping the ambulance crew administer first aid, and pointed urgently towards the corner shop.

No one liked looters, including Ringer Bell. Being the nearest, he stuck his thumb up at the constable to show he had heard and then nodded to his colleague to continue handling the hose alone.

Georgie crept swiftly towards the shop, sticking as closely to the damaged wall as he dared. Sweat poured down his face; he tried to wipe it away with the back of his hand but all he succeeded in doing was rubbing grit into his already sore and scorched cheeks. He got to the splintered remains of the shop door. It hung drunkenly on its shattered hinges, the now pathetic sign boasting, 'Hitler won't stop us opening!' still nailed to its warped and twisted panels

Georgie peered cautiously inside, not fancying confronting a frightened looter armed with who knew what sort of weapon. It took a moment for his eyes to become accustomed to the dark, but then he saw him, crouched in the corner on a pile of rubble by what had once been the counter, his face lit up by the flickering of the flames – not a burly, desperate criminal, but a terrified, wide-eyed, skinny looking kid with a half-eaten apple in his hand. He was filthy.

'Got the bastard?' shouted the constable from over by the ambulance.

Georgie, still looking directly at the boy, called out, 'Must have been a trick of the light. Probably a cat yer saw. After all these rats that've been disturbed.' Then he leant forward and whispered to the boy, 'Go on, son, clear off before the copper sees yer.'

The boy crawled forward over the debris. He looked like a little frightened animal. He didn't take his eyes off Georgie once.

'Wait. Here y'are.' Georgie reached in his pocket and slipped the boy a shilling piece. 'If yer hungry, you buy yerself a bit of grub. Nicking's no way o' life for a kid.'

As the boy made to flee from the shop and into the shadows, he wavered for just a moment, long enough to hiss at Georgie, 'I think someone's in there, mister.' Then he was gone.

Georgie didn't hesitate. Wrenching the limp door from its frame, he threw it onto the pavement behind him, got down on his belly and listened. Was that a sound? A whimpering or moaning? *Listen*, he instructed himself. *Concentrate*. Then, going against all that he had learnt during training with the more experienced fire crews, he crawled further into the devastated shop, fumbling around inside his uniform to find his matches. He had no thought for possible gas leaks as he struck the third match. He saw the sparkle of a tiny stone; it looked as if it might belong to an engagement ring. And yes, the finger it was on looked like a young woman's finger, and it was twitching as it poked out from a pile of rubble beside what had once been the proudly dusted wooden shelves. She was alive.

Georgie crawled carefully back out onto the pavement, determined not to disturb the rubble, and then raced over to the constable to get help. To his dismay he was told the heavy rescue squads had already been called down to the docks.

'But we can't just leave her till they get here!' Georgie

shouted. 'That could be tomorrow.'

'No one's saying we should,' said the constable and ran back to the shop with Georgie, the pair of them ready to dig through the wreckage with their bare hands if necessary. But it soon became obvious that there wasn't enough room for the two of them to work together safely and Georgie insisted that it should be him who should carry on alone.

As Georgie dug, oblivious of anything but his task of rescuing the trapped young woman, he became the focus of attention for the homeless families who had little else to give them hope. They stood, alternately holding their breath and urging him on with silent prayers, as he dug through the debris. It took almost half an hour of back-breaking, painstaking effort before Georgie lifted the beam that had protected the young woman from instant, crushing death. As he heaved the heavy timber to one side to release her, a little terrier flung itself out from under the wreckage, snarling and growling at Georgie, determined to protect its mistress from further harm.

'No, Lady,' the girl whimpered. 'Down. He's here to help us.'

The little dog returned to her mistress's side and sat there vigilantly baring its teeth.

'What's yer name, love?' Georgie asked gently, his every muscle straining as he pulled a splintered plank from her legs and threw it to one side.

'Sal,' the young woman whispered. 'Sal Turner. Am I gonna be all right?'

'Yeah, course yer gonna be all right, Sal,' Georgie reassured her. 'And soon as I've got these last few bricks moved, yer gonna be out of here.' As he cautiously lifted a chunk of plaster, careful not to shift anything too quickly, Georgie tried to keep Sal calm. 'My daughter's got a dog,' he panted, wiping the grime from his eyes with his forearm. 'Out walking her, were yer?'

235

'Yeah,' Sal gasped. 'Lady is all right, ain't she?'

'From the look of her teeth, Sal, she's just fine.' Georgie felt his stomach turn as the unmistakable sound of timbers groaning came from overhead.

'When the raid started . . .' Sal was speaking in gasps as pain racked her chest. 'I come in here. The roof had already been hit, see. And they say lightning don't strike twice in the same place. So I thought it'd be safe. Well, they're wrong, ain't they?' Sal groaned again. She was in agony. 'It got another hit, and this lot fell in on us.' She started to cry, the pain more than she could cope with.

'Come on, Sal,' Georgie urged her as he looked over his shoulder, signalling for the constable to do something, anything to help him, before the roof caved in completely. 'Give us a smile. Come on, just to please me. Yer a right beauty as it is, but I bet you're even prettier when you smile.'

The constable shrugged hopelessly, his face full of fear. 'What can I do?'

Georgie closed his eyes, hooked his torn and bleeding hands under Sal's arms and said, 'Take a deep breath, darling. I'm gonna get you out. Now. One, two, three.'

Georgie took a deep breath himself, braced his leg against what remained of the wall and, with a superhuman effort, dragged Sal clear and out onto the pavement. As the debris shifted, the shop folded in on itself as if it were made of paper. Bricks, glass and timbers shattered around them, and Georgie threw himself over Sal to protect her.

The last thing he felt before he passed out was Lady sinking her teeth into his arm.

'Yer did what yer could, Ringer.' Vic was holding out a thick china cup full of tea that he'd fetched Georgie from the mobile canteen that had turned up.

'She's dead, ain't she.' It was a statement rather than a question. Georgie struggled to sit up.

Vic nodded. 'Sorry, mate.'

'What a sodding, bloody waste.' As Georgie took the lighted cigarette from the constable, he winced with pain. He looked down at the ripped sleeve of his uniform where Lady had attacked him in her loyal efforts to protect her mistress. 'Where's the little dog?'

'The girl driving the ambulance couldn't separate 'em. The little thing wouldn't leave the girl's side. So when they . . .' Vic looked into his cup, as though he would find the right words sitting there in the tea. 'When they took Sal away, they took the dog and all. The driver said she'd keep it till they found it a home.'

Georgie nodded, his jaw rigid to stop himself crying. 'I bet she winds up keeping it herself. 'Cos they're all the same, ain't they, young girls with dogs?'

Then, with his muscles stretched beyond what he thought they were capable of, Georgie held out his hand for Vic to help him stand up. Although he was almost dead on his feet, Georgie insisted on getting stuck in with the others as they finished their job, damping down and then rolling up the unwieldy lengths of hose. After the long hours withstanding such extreme water pressure, the seventy-five feet long hoses had become semi-rigid, the opposite but no less awkward problem to when they had almost melted in the intense heat when the fire had been at its peak.

It was the early hours before Georgie and the rest of the crew, faces black as coal, uniforms soaked through and weighing what felt like a ton apiece, were cheered for their bravery as they finally made their way home. But Georgie didn't hear the people's thanks as he concentrated on the road in the dawn light. All he could hear was the sound of Sal's voice echoing round his aching head.

16

Two days later, Georgie stepped out of his street door and began walking along Darnfield Street, his hands stuffed deep into his pockets and his collar turned up round his ears. It was seven o'clock in the morning, still not fully light, and it was freezing. He had been home for only half an hour after three long days on shift and had thought that all he wanted to do was to get into bed, but with the image of Sal Turner's pretty young face still going round in his head, he hadn't been able to rest. Instead, he had sat in the kitchen drinking tea and smoking, waiting for the girls to come back from the shelter to get themselves ready for work. He intended to see them first then go back to the sub-station to check if there was anything he could do to help out for a few hours. But the girls were taking longer to come home than he had expected, so he decided to go over to the pub to find them.

'Yer frightened the life out of me, Ringer,' Minnie said as she and Clara practically fell into his arms as they stepped out of the front door of the Drum. Minnie squinted at him more closely. 'Blimey, yer look like yer could do with a good night's sleep.'

Georgie smiled, pleased to see their familiar faces. 'Hello, ladies. And what's this?' He peered into the cage that Minnie was carrying. 'Yer know, I never knew you had a parrot.'

'We've only just got it, ain't we, Clara?'

Clara nodded her head. 'Polly, it's called.'

'This old girl in the ward, where we clean at the hospital,' Minnie explained, 'she died, poor old thing. Wasn't no one else who'd take it. So me and Clara wound up with it.'

'That's good of yer,' said Georgie. He touched the bite marks on his arm, thinking about Sal and Lady, the little dog who'd been left without a mistress. 'Kind.'

'Not really,' said Minnie, obviously pleased. 'You know how it is, Ringer. Wouldn't like to think of even a dumb animal suffering 'cos of the war. They didn't bloody start it, did they?'

Clara poked Minnie in the side. 'Language, Min.'

Minnie laughed. 'Aw yeah, I was forgetting. We've gotta watch every word we say now. The woman what owned this bird might have looked a nice old girl, but she must've had a tongue like a docker's tart. Yer wanna hear this bleed'n thing swear!'

Clara giggled. 'Come on, Min, we'll be late.'

Minnie rolled her eyes at Georgie. 'I dunno. She still worries about being on time, even in the bloody bombing.' She linked her big, plump arm though Clara's. 'Still, we'd better get this little devil indoors then get ourselves off to clean them bloody offices.' She looked back over her shoulder at Georgie and shook her head. 'Then we're off down to Bancroft Road to do the hospital. No peace for the wicked, eh, Ringer?'

'No peace for no one lately, Min.'

Georgie still didn't get inside the pub. Someone tapped him lightly on the back. He turned round. It was Maudie Peters.

'I'm glad I caught you, Mr Bell.' She was puffing as though she had been running. 'I saw you talking to Minnie and Clara and wanted to find out how you all were. What with one thing and another, I've not seen either of the girls for days.'

'Me neither. I've been on duty solid for the last three days.' Georgie suddenly looked concerned. He jerked his thumb at the pub door. 'Haven't you seen 'em in here? They promised me faithfully they'd go in here to shelter every night.'

'Don't worry, I'm sure they have been. It's me, I've not been in there. I've been round at the church, handing out blankets and tea.'

Georgie looked relieved. 'Aw, I see.'

'There's been plenty of little things to do round there lately. Mind you,' she said, looking up at him, 'I still feel bad when I see how much other people are doing.'

'We all do what we can.'

'Well, to be honest, it's a bit of a waste of time. There are more than enough volunteers at the church. Too many really, all getting on top of one another.' Maudie laughed ironically. 'With all the old maids like me around, the vicar's attracted himself quite a following, elderly though he is.'

'Yer shouldn't knock yerself so much, Miss Peters.'

'You're being kind.'

'No. No, I'm not. I mean it. And like I said, we all only do what we can.'

'I think that some of us are doing a lot more than others.'

Georgie looked down at his boots. 'I was thinking the other day,' he said quietly. 'There's something I'd like to do for you. If yer like.'

'Oh?' Maudie sounded intrigued.

'There's always loads of timber on the bombsites. And I was thinking that I could fetch some home and chop it up for yer, for firewood. 'Cos this cold weather looks like it's set in for the winter now.'

Maudie wrinkled her nose and blushed. 'Oh dear.'

241

'Is something wrong?'

'I've got a gas fire.'

Now it was Georgie's turn to blush. 'I don't suppose it'll be much use to yer then, firewood?'

Maudie burst out laughing. 'No.'

George grinned. 'Yer know, that is exactly what I could do with, seeing someone laughing, Miss Peters. And you have got a very nice laugh.'

'Thank you, Mr Bell.' She smiled up at him, meeting his gaze for just a little longer than Georgie expected. 'And I've also got very cold feet,' she added. 'In fact, I'm freezing. I'll see you later.'

Georgie watched her as she hurried off along the road towards her house, his breath making little clouds as he whistled thoughtfully to himself.

As Maudie disappeared inside number seven with a wave, the door of the Drum opened and Babs and Evie were standing beside him.

'You sound like yer in a good mood, Dad,' said Babs after she had kissed him on the cheek.

'Why shouldn't I be, with two lovely daughters?' He put his arms round their shoulders.

'Careful, Dad,' Evie groaned, pulling away from him. 'I ain't feeling too good.'

'No?'

'No. Must be having to sleep on them rotten, hard bunks.'

'Yeah,' he said cautiously, looking at the dark circles under her eyes. 'Must be. Well, I just wanted to see that yer was both safe and sound before I nipped back to the station for a couple of hours. You eating properly, Eve? Yer wanna get home and get yerself some grub.'

Evie's face turned even paler.

Later that day, Blanche Simpkins was coming to the end of her first day's work at Styleways.

'I know I've never met that young lad from the warehouse, but I hope he's all right. Fancy him getting trapped in that building like that. Must have been terrifying for him, poor little sod. And I can imagine how his mother's suffering.'

Ginny turned to Joan and said quietly, 'She ain't been here five minutes and hark at her. Yer'd think he was her kid the way she's going on.'

Blanche might not have been there for very long, but it was still more than long enough for her to have got the measure of Ginny. 'What was that yer said, Ginny? Something poisonous, I suppose. But yer wanna be careful what yer say in front of me, 'cos I don't take no lip from no one. Wouldn't do no harm for you to remember that.'

Babs cheered. 'Go on, Blanche, you tell her, girl.'

'Yer gonna have to watch that trap of your'n, Gin,' said Lou, happily. 'I've seen Blanche chasing her Terry down the street with a copper stick just for cheeking her before now. Gawd knows what she'd do with them tailoring shears.'

Ginny was fuming. 'I thought working with a bloody Eytie was bad enough, but now we've got sodding Mother Hen to put up with and all.'

'That's me finished,' said Blanche, pointedly ignoring Ginny's taunts as she snapped open the foot of her machine. Then she stood up and went to the end of the work bench where she picked up a stack of completed army trousers from by the side of Evie's chair and carried them along to the other end of the row to Maria. 'There y'are, sweetheart,' she said, smiling at her, and turned and walked slowly back to her place. 'Yer know what,' she said as she sauntered past Ginny's seat, 'I can hardly believe it's this time already. I never would have thought the day could pass so quick. Must be all the nice, friendly company.'

Everyone in the workshop, except Ginny, started snorting with laughter, but their amusement didn't last long – the all too familiar sound of the air raid warning had started its wailing.

'Aw, bloody hell,' said Lou, throwing up her arms. 'Can't they even wait for us to get home? I don't wanna be stuck here in the sodding basement for another night.'

'Perhaps it's not too bad,' said Maria, pulling back the corner of the blackout curtains and peering down into the street below. 'Blimey, it is. Will yer look at them fires? They ain't wasted no time tonight.'

Babs leant over Maria's shoulder to look for herself. 'Christ, Eve, we've gotta get home. Them fires. They're over Bow way. Look.'

Mr Silver came puffing into the workshop; he had run up the stairs to make sure that everyone was following the procedure. He knew what a fuss the girls made about having to go downstairs to shelter; in fact, he thought they had all started getting a bit too relaxed about the warnings altogether lately and he didn't want their injuries on his conscience.

'Come on, girls,' he urged them. 'Switch those machines off and get yerselves down to the basement.' He shook his head at Babs. 'Don't worry about yer bags and coats. Just leave them where they are. Please, just get yerself downstairs.'

'Sorry, Mr Silver, I can't. I've gotta get home to see if me dad's all right.'

Mr Silver couldn't stop her. Babs, quickly followed by Blanche and Evie, dashed past him and disappeared through the fire doors before he had the chance to open his mouth to protest.

'I knew I shouldn't have left the kids,' Blanche panted as they flew down the stairs.

'They'll be all right,' Babs said, jumping down the bottom three steps. 'Mary'll be sheltering at the factory with your Ruby. Terry'll have made Len go in the Drum with him. And Janey'll be fine at the nursery.'

'Will she?' Blanche didn't sound convinced.

'Course,' Babs reassured her, pulling open the door to the street. 'Now, come on, Eve, get yer coat done up, it's perishing out here.'

It wasn't only cold outside, it was dark, noisy and frightening. The three of them ran, the sound of their shoes hitting the pavement ringing in their ears. But Evie suddenly stopped.

'You two go on,' she gasped. 'I'll have to slow down.'

'If yer think I'm leaving you here, yer silly cow, yer even dafter than I thought yer was,' Babs said, trying to drag her along. 'What's the matter with you, Eve? Too much riding around in motor cars made yer soft?'

'I feel sick, Babs.'

'Yer wanna try staying in a couple o' nights and getting some rest. Now come on.'

'I mean it, Babs. And I ain't arguing with yer.' Evie leant back against the wall. She could feel the cold sweat trickling down her back. 'I told yer, I feel ill.'

Babs sighed in despair. 'You'll have to go on, Blanche. See to yer kids. I'll sort Evie out.'

'I will if yer don't mind,' Blanche agreed hurriedly and ran off into the dark. 'Look after yerselves,' they heard her call back to them.

'We can't stand here like flipping targets, Eve. We might as well have stayed at work.'

'I can't help it.' Evie's bottom lip was trembling.

Babs bowed her head and took a deep breath before speaking. 'Look, Eve,' she said slowly and deliberately. 'Yer gonna *have* to move. It ain't much further and we'll be at the station. If the trains're running we can at least get to Mile End.'

Evie nearly vomited at the thought of going on the packed, smoke-filled Tube. 'I can't, Babs. I'm sorry. I'll stay down on the platform till the all clear if that'll make yer any happier, but I can't go on no train. I really ain't well.'

Torn as she was between leaving her twin and finding out if their dad was safe, Babs knew that she had to get back to Darnfield Street. She had only been saying to Blanche that very morning how well things had been going for Georgie lately. Now, as she ran though the streets back to Bow, she felt she had been tempting fate.

Although he was now even more tired than he would have thought possible without falling asleep on his feet, Georgie was glad that he had gone back to the station. They needed all the help they could get during the night of almost nonstop raids. The word was that there were over twice as many planes as usual dropping their deadly cargoes over London; nobody knew if that was true, but it certainly seemed like it.

When he finally drove the heavy unit back into the yard at gone nine o'clock the next morning, all he was fit for was the short crawl from the engine's cab to the mess room.

'I'm gonna murder this cup of tea,' he yawned, as he slumped down at one of the trestle tables. 'Don't matter how much yer drink when yer out there, yer can never quench yer thirst while yer've got that stink of fire in yer nostrils.'

One of the women from the watch room came in and sat down next to him. 'I know yer knackered, Ringer,' she said to him gently. 'But I think yer wanna get home. We heard a couple of hours ago that Darnfield Street got hit.'

Without saying a word, Georgie sprang to his feet and, not even noticing the weight of his soaking wet uniform, sprinted off as though he was a man half his age who had had a full eight hours' sleep.

'They've gotta be all right,' he kept repeating to himself. 'They've gotta be.'

Georgie was frantic by the time he reached the corner of Darnfield Street. A group of his neighbours was sitting huddled over cups of tea on the pavement outside the Drum. He could barely force himself to look to see who was there.

He nearly collapsed with relief when he saw that two of them were his daughters.

He dropped down on the kerb between Babs and Evie and buried his head in his hands. 'When they told me back at the station that the street had got hit, all I could think of was . . .' He slowly let his hands fall from his face and looked along to the canal end of the road. 'I never realised that the demolition squad was here. They look hard at it.' He half rose to his feet. 'It wasn't number seven what got hit, was it?'

Babs put her hand on his shoulder. 'No. Sit yerself down, Dad. Don't worry. Miss Peters ain't hurt.'

'So where is she?'

'The pub's the only place with water, so she's inside helping Nellie make the tea for everyone. All them blokes working down there must be gasping.'

Evie stared into her cup. 'It was the house next door to Miss Peters what got it.' Her voice sounded flat, as if she was in a trance. 'The Jenners.' She gulped down a mouthful of her tea. 'Their baby. It's dead.'

'Aw, Christ. Not the baby.' Georgie shook his head, but all he could see was a picture of Sal lying in the rubble with a baby by her side instead of her little dog.

'And Ted's old nan. She's copped it and all,' Babs said, rubbing Georgie's back. 'Blimey, Dad. Yer uniform's soaked through and yer look that tired. Let me get yer a cup o' tea and then yer can go home and get some kip, eh?'

It was as though Georgie hadn't heard her. 'Them poor buggers.'

'I know, Dad. But how about that cuppa?'

'I'll have some tea in a minute,' Georgie said, struggling to his feet. 'I've gotta see if there's anything I can do to help.'

Just as he got to the wreck that had once been the Jenners's home, Maudie caught up with him.

'I saw the girls back there. They told me you were here.'

Georgie ran his hands through his gritty, smoke-clogged hair. He could imagine what a state he looked. 'How are you?'

Maudie shrugged. 'The back of my roof got hit, that's all. But, compared with this, that hardly seems to matter.'

Alice Clarke came striding over from where she had been standing right up the front by the rescue workers. 'Well, *you* might think it don't matter,' she snapped at Maudie, 'but yer wanna see the mess in my back yard. Half your roof tiles I've got in there. What yer gonna do about it?'

Maudie rolled her eyes disbelievingly at George. 'I'll make sure it's sorted out, Alice.'

'Well yer wanna make sure yer do.' Alice folded her scraggy little arms and nodded to where Ted and Liz stood in a daze, watching as the men brought a ragbag of smashed and broken things out of the ruins of the house. 'Should have gone in the Drum's cellar like the rest of us.'

Georgie ignored her. 'Don't make sense, does it, when that bloody empty house opposite's still standing.' He stepped a bit closer to Ted and Liz, not close enough to impose, but close enough not to have to shout. 'Anything I can do, mate?'

Ted hugged Liz to him and shook his head. 'Nothing no one can do, ta, Ringer.'

'Yer've only gotta ask.'

'Yeah. I know.'

Georgie stood there as the rescue squad workers clambered through the inside of what had been the privacy of the Jenners's home but was now exposed for everyone to see like the guts of a slaughtered animal. One of the men reached up and unhooked a looking glass that was hanging crookedly from a nail but had somehow not been smashed by the blast. He loaded it onto the pushchair he had just dragged from under a pile of bricks and pushed it, bumping crazily over the rubble, out onto the pavement.

When she saw her baby's pushchair, Liz pulled away from her husband and started laughing wildly. 'Look, the mirror's all right,' she shrieked. 'So at least we won't have seven years' bad luck, eh, Ted? Eh? Eh? Eh?' Then she let out a terrifying animal wail, folded in on herself like a rag doll and collapsed in a heap onto the cold, hard road.

One of the Jenner children, a boy of about six who was standing with his equally bewildered brothers and sisters, started to cry. His little arms hanging loose by his side, he made no attempt to wipe away the tears. 'Daddy?' he pleaded. 'What's wrong with Mummy?'

Maudie took off her coat and wrapped it and her arms round the crying child. 'Mummy doesn't feel well,' she said softly, soothing the petrified little boy.

'Needs to pull herself together, that one,' sniped Alice.

Ted bent down beside Liz and cradled her in his lap, rocking her back and forth as though she, too, were a frightened child. 'Everything'll be fine, darling, you see,' he said, his jaw rigid. 'I'll find somewhere for us. Don't you worry. I'll get us another home.'

Maudie glared at Alice, daring her to say another word, and then said quietly to Ted, 'I hope I'm not interfering, but the kids are all badly shaken. Let me take

249

them indoors. I can put you all up, for as long as you like.'

Ted looked up at her. 'That's kind of yer,' he said flatly.

'Yer wanna remember that yer've gotta clear up them tiles,' Alice butted in.

Maudie didn't even look at Alice. 'Not kind at all, Ted,' Maudie insisted. 'There's more than enough room.'

Liz lifted her head, her red tear-filled eyes darting around as if she was being hounded by some unseen predator. 'No. No, Ted. I wanna go to the rest centre round the school. I don't wanna stay here. Not here. Please. Not where my baby . . .' She pushed Ted away from her and staggered to her feet. She just managed to get to the drain in the side of the road before she threw up.

Maudie moved forward to help her, the child still clinging tightly to her side, but she stopped when Ted held up his hand to prevent her from getting any closer to his wife. 'We don't need any help. Thanks. We'll be all right.' There wasn't a hint of either hope or belief in what he said.

Liz looked up. Even though it was so cold, her hair was damp with sweat, stuck to her forehead in black, snaking tendrils. 'You could help out with the arrangements,' she said to Maudie as she swayed unsteadily from side to side. Her voice sounded harsh and rasping. 'You could speak to the vicar for me. I want it all done proper.'

'Of course.' Maudie wanted so much to reach out to her, but she knew she couldn't. All she could do was cling tight to the little boy. 'On the day of the . . .' Maudie struggled to find the right words, '. . . the day of the service, you could arrange for the cars to leave from my house. If you want, that is.'

Liz pressed her lips together and closed her eyes. Then she took a deep breath and stared directly at Maudie.

'Thanks, Miss Peters, I'd appreciate that.' She turned to her husband. 'Ted, I wanna get away from here. Now.'

Ted nodded. He took one of the Woodbines from the packet that Georgie held out to him and stuck it, unlit, into the corner of his mouth. Then he gathered up the few things that remained of their home and handed them to the bigger children to carry. Without a glance behind him, he took Liz by the arm and led her away. The little boy who had been standing with Maudie looked up at her. A final, single tear ran down his cheek. He wiped his nose on the rough sleeve of his hand-me-down jacket and ran over to join his brothers and sisters who were following their parents silently, their heads bowed and their arms full of battered and broken bits and pieces, for all the world like a group of refugees who had been ejected from their homeland.

All that was left of the Jenners in Darnfield Street was the baby's pushchair.

Maudie sighed loudly and blew her nose. 'How much more can people take?' She was asking herself as much as Georgie. 'What'll be left at this rate?'

Georgie stared up at the broken husk that had once been number nine. 'You know what they say, "London can take it". Just let's hope they're right, Maud.' Without thinking, Georgie put his arm round her shoulders, but almost immediately he pulled it hurriedly away. 'I'm so sorry,' he stammered. 'I didn't mean to do that. I must be tired. I didn't mean to take no liberties.'

Maudie looked up at him through her tears. 'With all this,' she said waving her arms helplessly around her, 'I think we're past all that now, George, don't you?'

Georgie nodded. 'I reckon yer right, Maud.'

'Maud? George?' sneered Alice. 'Do me a favour.'

From the look on Georgie's face, Alice was lucky that Blanche came running across the street towards them just then. 'Ringer, can you help us? Please.' Tears were streaming down her cheeks. 'If only my Archie was here. But I don't know what to do. When we went over home from the Drum just now, we found it. Look. Aw, Ringer. Is it . . .?'

Young Len held out his pet rabbit for Georgie to look. 'There's no marks on it or nothing, Mr Bell,' he said anxiously. 'I think it's just asleep.'

Georgie took the limp creature from the boy's arms and examined it. 'I'm sorry, son,' he said gently. 'It must have been the shock of the bombs what done it.'

'I should never have started that bloody job. We should have stayed in Cornwall.'

Len took the rabbit tenderly back from Georgie and buried his face into its still warm fur. 'I wanna go back there, Mum. Please, let me.'

Blanche stood there, helpless, not knowing what to say or what to do.

Maudie reached her hand out to Len. 'Come on, love,' she said. 'Let's go and bury him. We can put him in my back yard if you want. There's a lot of nice plants there. I bet he'd like that.'

Alice couldn't believe her ears. 'Do what? Yer gonna bury a rabbit? Yer wanna stick it in the pot with a few veg and a bit o' gravy.'

Maudie turned to face her mean-minded neighbour. 'Why don't you just shut your interfering mouth, Alice, before someone does it for you?'

Without waiting for Alice's reply, Maudie went to help Len bury his rabbit, and with it a piece of his childhood that she knew would never return.

17

'It was nice of that chap down the Roman to let you have all this ham.' Maudie put down the plate of sandwiches she had made on the big trestle table that Nellie had set up at the far end of the bar.

'People chip in at a time like this for poor sods like the Jenners,' said Nellie with a rueful smile. 'Brings out the best in 'em.'

Maudie wiped her hands on the apron that Nellie had given her to wear over her black crepe dress. 'What can I do next?'

Nellie looked up at the big, brass clock that stood on the shelf among the bottles of spirits and luridly coloured liqueurs. 'Sure yer've got enough time?'

Maudie looked at her watch. 'Ted's due to bring Liz and the children over to mine at about half past twelve. So I've got about a quarter of an hour.'

'Well, so long as it don't make yer late. Tell yer what, d'yer fancy making us all a cuppa? The kettle's already simmering on the hob, it only wants the gas turning up.' Nellie slumped beside Babs on one of the bench seats that ran along the wall. 'I dunno about you, Maud, but I could do with a cup. I'm whacked out.'

'I bet you are. You've not stopped since I've been here, and that was first thing. I'll make the tea then I'll nip back home to make sure I'm in when Ted and Liz arrive.' Maudie ducked under the counter flap and

253

went through to the kitchen.

Babs eyebrows shot up. 'You called her Maud,' she whispered. 'What's all that in aid of?'

Nellie shrugged. 'Don't ask me, it's what she told me to start calling her.' As she spoke, Nellie stood up and started fiddling about with the plates of sandwiches, the bowls of winkles, cockles and eels and the dishes of pickled onions and red cabbage. She moved them around on the cloth-covered table, critically eyeing the various rearrangements, until she was satisfied with the result. 'Changed woman, she is. Looks ten years younger. But as to what's done it . . .'

'You know as well as I do,' Babs said, also getting up and putting the sandwiches that Nellie had just moved back to where she had set them down in the first place.

'Well, I suppose I do. I reckon making friends with your dad's brought her right out of her shell lately.'

'It's done Dad good and all. He's been like a different person.'

Nellie smiled noncommittally. She wanted to see how long Ringer's new way of carrying on lasted before she was prepared to pass any judgement on it. 'Now let's both stop messing around with the food and take the weight off our feet.' Nellie sat down on the bench again and patted the place next to her. 'Come on. Sit down.'

Babs sat down reluctantly. 'I've got the right fidgets,' she said with a shudder. 'It's all this business. If yer keep going, yer don't have to think about it.'

'It's hard,' Nellie agreed, 'but try and forget all that for the minute. Tell me about your Evie. She looks terrible.'

'Yeah. Yer right there, Nell. But I dunno what's up with her. She's not been herself for a week or so now. Must be coming down with something.'

'Well, I just hope it's not 'flu, that's all.' Nellie jerked her thumb at the bar. 'I've been told some horrible stories

254

across that counter about all the flipping illnesses and things that're going around again.'

Babs looked worried. 'I hadn't thought about 'flu.'

'Well, yer should. 'Cos she needs to keep her strength up in case she does get a touch of it. Knocks yer for six, it does. I mean, the other night, when you and her went round to do the collection for the wreaths, I couldn't believe it. Rings under her eyes like an old girl's, she had. She's overdoing it, I'm telling yer. Yer wanna have a talk to her, tell her to stay in a few nights a week.' Nellie curled her lip into a sneer. 'I reckon Albie Denham can find something or someone to keep himself occupied.'

Babs didn't need to say anything, it was enough for her just to look at Nellie.

'Yeah, I know,' Nellie answered for her with a flap of her hand. 'Yer might as well talk to yerself as to try and talk to Evie.'

'Tea?' Maudie appeared from behind the bar and put the tray down on the table in front of Babs and Nellie.

'Make the most of this, you two,' said Nellie, speaking with the weary voice of experience. 'I've done enough funeral teas in this pub to know we're in for a long hard slog.'

'That wind cuts through yer like ice.' Minnie shivered as she stepped inside the Drum behind Clara. 'It feels more like January than the middle of October out there.'

'It's not only the wind that's making yer shiver, Min,' whispered Clara, following her inside. 'It was them coffins.' Clara's lip trembled. 'I'll never forget 'em, as long as I live. Old Nanna Jenner's was hardly bigger than the one that the baby was in.'

'And fancy being buried with yer great-granddaughter.' Minnie let out a long slow breath. 'Makes yer think, don't it, Clara?'

Like the rest of the neighbours, Minnie and Clara

stood aimlessly around while they waited for Ted and Liz to come into the pub. When the cars had pulled into the street, Liz had taken it into her head to take the children to have one last look at the bombsite that had once been their home. She wanted them to be able to replace their memories of their mother screaming and fainting with one of her standing there, still desperately sad, but at least in control of herself. Ted had tried to persuade her that it didn't matter, that it wasn't necessary, but there had been no reasoning with her. It's what she wanted to do for her children and for the baby she had lost.

Everyone agreed that it didn't seem respectful to start eating or drinking till the Jenners appeared – everyone, that is, except Alice Clarke. She was content neither to stand around in silence nor to show a bit of consideration for people's feelings by whispering quietly to Nobby. As usual she was far more interested in holding forth on whatever happened to be going on, allowing everyone within earshot to have the benefit of her views on events.

'I wouldn't mind a cup o' tea,' she began, as she surveyed the food table. 'And a sandwich wouldn't come amiss after standing round that grave in the perishing cold.'

She waited. When no one replied with the offer of either, she started on a different tack.

'I don't think she believes that baby's dead, yer know. I've seen it all before. They go mad when something like that happens. She'll be up there searching for it.'

Evie shook her head with disgust. 'Don't talk so stupid, Alice.'

'Well, why else did she wanna go up there? It's morbid, if you ask me.'

Thinking about what Nellie had said about Evie needing to rest, Babs put herself between her twin and Alice. 'Don't waste yer breath on her, Eve,' she said and pulled out a chair for her sister. 'Sit down,' she ordered her,

256

nodding towards the seat. Evie looked a bit surprised but sat down gratefully. Then Babs turned her attention to Alice. She folded her arms and looked down her nose at the old woman. 'She's being morbid, yer say, Alice?'

'Yeah, morbid.'

Babs unfolded her arms and pointed her finger very close to Alice's nose. 'She's just buried her baby and Ted's nan, course she feels sodding morbid. How d'you expect her to feel, like going bloody dancing?'

'Very nice talk,' said Alice with a haughty toss of her head. 'And what's she sitting down for, that sister o' your'n? That's what I wanna know. If old'uns like me can stand up till them two get back here, why can't she?'

Babs glanced over to Evie and saw that she was fuming. Babs held up her hand to silence her and answered for her. ''Cos she ain't been feeling well, that's why. I suppose she needs a note from the doctor to say she's allowed to sit down. Shall I get yer one? Or would yer rather she passed out on the floor in front of yer?'

'Not well?' Alice narrowed her eyes and stared hard at Evie. 'Looks all right to me. Too much gallivanting, that's all that's the matter with her. Wants to spend less time bleaching that hair of her'n and get in at a decent hour like other people and then she'd . . .'

Evie stood up slowly. 'Have you finished, you nosy old bag?'

'Eve.' Georgie touched his daughter gently on the arm. 'Don't upset yerself over her, darling.'

'I ain't upset.' Evie said the words very deliberately as though she had to struggle to pronounce each one. 'I'm bloody furious.'

Alice looked round at her husband who had been standing sheepishly by her side. 'Nobby,' she barked. 'Will you listen to her? I know what she's got herself all wound up about.' She turned back to face Evie. 'Yer know all about getting notes from the doctor, don't yer?

Or should I say that that crooked fancy man of your'n does? I've heard all about it. Too ill to join up. Pwuuhh!'

'You rotten, hatchet-faced old . . .' Evie lunged forward, ready to wrap her hands round Alice's skinny throat.

'Come on, Evie.' Maudie spoke calmly but authoritatively as she stepped forward and took Evie's arm. 'Come out the back and help me and Babs start making the tea.'

'You'd better watch what you say about my sister,' Babs mouthed at Alice before she followed Maudie and Evie into the safety of the kitchen.

Bert Chalmers from the baker's put his hand on Georgie's shoulder and winked at him. 'All right, Ringer? That Alice, eh? Make a saint swear, she would. Tell yer what, Ted won't mind, let's go up the bar and get a drink. I hate these things, don't you?'

'And I hate *these* things,' said Ethel Morgan, ripping the black armband off the sleeve of her coat. 'It was bad enough when it used to always make me think about who I wore it for the last time, and who I'd be wearing it for the next. But now it makes me think about him and his bloody ARP armband.' She lifted her chin towards her husband Frankie who had followed Georgie and Bert to the bar. 'And that's all I need, having to think about him more than I have to.'

As everyone else began to drift towards the bar, the door opened and Ted ushered Liz and the children through into the pub.

Liz stepped inside and just stood there, staring blankly. Everything about her looked pathetic: her arms drooped by her sides, her shoulders were hunched like an old woman's, and the black coat that Blanche had loaned her hung on her narrow body like an oversized dust sheet thrown over a footstool.

Nellie took Liz by the hand and sat her down at a table in the corner. She signalled for Rita to come over. 'Try and get Liz to drink this,' Nellie said, handing Rita the cup of tea she had ready for her. 'There's plenty of sugar in it – most of Jim's ration if he only knew – and a little drop of brandy. Good for her nerves. I'll take the kids through the back for a bit. They don't wanna be in here with all this.'

'Best thing,' Rita agreed and sat down next to Liz.

Ted was standing in the middle of the room. He started to speak, but seemed immediately to lose his train of thought. 'I'd, er . . .' He ran his hands through his hair and shuffled about. He looked perplexed, as though he wasn't quite sure why he was there. 'I'd like to, er . . .'

Everyone turned to look at him except Liz who carried on staring into the teacup that Rita had placed in her hands.

'I'd like to say a few words,' Ted finally managed to say.

Jim came round the bar and handed him a glass of Scotch. 'You take yer time, mate,' he said, patting him on the back.

Ted was unaccustomed to drinking spirits but even throwing back the whole glassful in two quick gulps didn't appear to affect him. He seemed to have trouble noticing anything beyond what was going on in his head. 'Me, Liz and the kids wanna thank yer for what yer've done. That's what I wanted to say.'

Murmurings went round the bar, reassuring Ted that they hadn't done anything at all, well, no more than anyone would have done in the same position.

'No, I mean it. Thanks.'

'Have you got somewhere to stay yet?' Maudie asked as she came through from the kitchen carrying a tray of tea, followed by the twins. 'You know my offer's still there.'

'Yeah, I know, Miss Peters. And I'm grateful to yer. But I've decided that it's best for Liz and the kids to go away. It's all been sorted out, they're gonna be evacuated to some place in Shropshire somewhere.'

'You going with 'em, Ted?' Blanche with her memories of her own evacuation and of Archie joining up was more sensitive than most to talk of separation.

Ted shook his head. 'I'd like to, Blanche, but I can't.' Ted sounded resigned to disappointment and pain. 'Me job in the docks is a reserved occupation. I've gotta stay put.'

'That don't seem fair,' Minnie whispered to Clara. 'Splitting up the poor buggers at a time like this.'

Clara grasped Minnie's hand. 'Terrible. Just terrible.'

'Well, yer've got no worries about finding yerself a place to stay, Ted. We've got space upstairs.' Jim pointed to the ceiling of the bar. 'Plenty of little rooms up there. Take yer pick. Whichever one yer like.'

Ted stared down at the floor. 'Yer all really kind.' He was close to tears. 'But I don't think I could stay in the street. Not now. I'll get lodgings down Poplar way. Near work.' He took out his hankie and blew his nose loudly.

Maudie waited for Ted to continue, but he just stood there, staring at the floor. She took a deep breath, determined to keep her tears till later, and said, 'Nellie told me you're all to have something to eat. Now, who wants tea?' She turned to Evie. 'Can you take a few bits of food out the back? Make sure the kids get something to eat.'

At the mention of food, Evie grasped the back of a chair to stop herself swaying. 'I think I'll sit down, if yer don't mind, Maud. Babs'll do it, won't yer?'

When everyone had helped themselves to food and drink, they sat around, as was the way with funerals, and talked about old times, present troubles and what might happen tomorrow.

'It's true,' Alice said, after she'd passed on a shocking tale of looting and scavenging that she'd heard from someone down the market. 'Stealing out of old girls' houses while they're in the shelter. That's all some kids know nowadays, getting something for nothing and don't care who they hurt.'

'Yer can't tar 'em all with the same brush, Alice,' Georgie said from the next table where he was sitting with Maudie. He was remembering the scared young boy in the bombed corner shop with the half-eaten apple. 'Some kids don't come from streets like this one where they've got a chance to go to someone for help if they need it. Some poor little sods have to get by whatever way they can. They don't have a choice if they're hungry.'

Alice sneered at his stupidity. 'Don't give me that.'

'He's right,' said Maudie.

'Who asked you?' Alice demanded.

Maudie continued, determined to have her say. 'It is special round here, the way people stick together. And we should be proud of it. Proud of what we manage to do for each other. If you ever get the chance, you should speak to the vicar about why he lives here. He'll make you really think.'

'Vicar!' spluttered Alice. 'Yer wanna sort out getting your roof tiles out of my flaming garden instead of wasting yer time round the church Bible bashing.'

Maudie put her cup down gently on its saucer, waited a calming moment before she spoke and then said, 'I've been to see the person at the council office, and she's promised to send someone round to come and inspect the damage on the roof from the incendiaries. And I'm sure they'll do something about the tiles. But they say, rightly, that leaks and shattered tiles aren't exactly dangerous and that I'll have to wait, just as you will, along with thousands and thousands of other Londoners.'

Alice looked round the room, her eyebrows raised halfway up her forehead. 'I thought you was gonna sort them tiles out.'

'I'll have a word with someone I know down at the station whose sister works at the council, if yer like. See when they think they'll be able to come to fix it.'

Maudie smiled at George. 'Thanks.'

'Till then we'll have to muck in and see what we can do for ourselves. I'll help yer clear up and I'll nail a bit of lino or tarpaulin over the damage.' Georgie raised his pint to Maudie. 'We'll muddle through, girl, don't you worry yerself.'

Alice narrowed her eyes. 'You two have got very friendly,' she said accusingly.

Babs had just arrived at Alice's table with a tray to clear away the dirty crockery. She winked across at her dad. 'That all yer got to say, Alice?' she asked, picking up the empty cups and plates. 'I thought yer'd have managed something a bit more spiteful or gossipy than that. Must be losing yer touch.'

Maud pressed her lips together trying to stop herself from turning on Alice. When she had got herself under control, she said to Georgie, 'I've got a few veg that you and the girls might like, and one or two eggs. By way of saying thank you.'

Alice wasn't best pleased that she hadn't got the response she had hoped for – she had expected at least a denial about their friendship, which she could then make something of. She had to find something else to be nasty about. 'Sounds like yer've got yerself a right little barn-yard,' she snapped.

'There's not much room but I do what I can,' Maudie answered coolly. 'If I had a bit more space I could do a lot more.' She turned and smiled at Georgie. 'I'd even put a few rosebushes back in.'

'Rosebushes!' Now that *was* something that Alice could make something of. 'What's the good of rose-bushes? If we had bigger back yards we could have had proper Anderson shelters and we wouldn't be sitting here now at a funeral. Mind you,' she said, looking over to where Liz still sat with Rita in the corner, 'don't suppose that one'd have gone into no Anderson shelter. Funny cow.'

Babs had to stop herself hitting Alice over the head with her tray.

Nobby finished his drink and looked thoughtfully at Maud. 'Hens yer've got, eh?' He spoke as though his wife hadn't even mentioned Anderson shelters or funerals. 'I've thought about getting meself a few hens. I wonder if there's any decent timbers left up at the Jenners's place. What d'yer think, Ted? Any wood left on the debris up there?'

Babs slammed the tray down on the table. 'I don't know what to say. I really don't.'

Alice looked around for someone to explain Babs's behaviour to her. But when she saw that everyone was glaring at her and Nobby instead, she protested loudly, 'What? What's up? He only wants a bit of wood. Gawd help us, whatever me or Nobby says is wrong.' Then she turned and fixed her scowl on Maudie and said pointedly, 'I dunno what's the matter with people round here lately.'

Maudie got up and went and stood right beside Alice. She bent down and said quietly, 'There's nothing wrong with people round here, Alice, nothing at all. Well, not with most of them. In fact, you'd go a long way to meet anyone like your neighbours. Anyone half as decent. You'd do yerself a favour if you remembered that.' Then she calmly turned round and went back to sit with Georgie at the next table.

Alice puffed the air from her cheeks and shook her head. 'Well! Hark at the church-goer. You can see she's been mixing with the Bells.'

18

It had been two weeks since they'd buried the Jenners's grandmother and Liz's baby but the funeral was still very much on Blanche's mind as she sat working at her machine in Styleways talking to Babs about her son.

'When I saw, close to, like, what happened to the Jenners, it made me realise that I had no right to stop young Len from going back to Cornwall.'

'You still don't fancy going back though?' Babs said. She sounded vague, distant.

'No. Aw, don't get me wrong, I miss Len, same as I miss my Archie. But they're both doing what they really – want and yer shouldn't stop them yer love from doing that, should yer? 'Cos that ain't loving 'em, that's owning 'em.'

Babs didn't say anything.

'Yer know, I'll never get over Len's little face as he held that dead rabbit in his arms.' Blanche doubled over the waistband of the pair of trousers she was making and pushed them under the needle. 'Kids. I don't know, who'd have 'em, eh? Don't get me wrong, I love my kids, too much sometimes, but they're such a worry, Babs. And a bind. See, they always have to come first. But you younger girls, things are different for you. Way things are nowadays, girls can take all these chances that're coming up and who can blame 'em? Take my little sister Ruby. I always felt she was a bloody waste of space how she carried on, a right useless lump, but now she's gone and got herself a right good supervisor's job at her factory, if yer don't mind. Earning nearly as much as her Davey. But that's the war for yer though, innit. She couldn't have done that before, I don't reckon, do you?'

Again, Babs didn't reply.

Blanche stopped her machine, turned to Lou and mouthed, 'Bloody miles away. D'you know what's up with her?'

Lou turned down the corners of her mouth and shook her head.

Blanche turned back to Babs. 'I can't stand all this. I've gotta come right out and ask yer. What's the matter with you, Babs? You ain't hardly said a word all day, and that must be the twentieth time yer've looked at that clock in the last five minutes.'

Babs shrugged. 'I wanna get away dead on five, that's all. I wanna get home.'

'So that's it. Yer hoping Evie'll be there when yer get in.'

'Yeah.'

'It's only been a couple of days. She'll be fine. And it ain't as if she ain't pulled strokes like this before, is it? You'll see, she'll have been off somewhere being wined and dined by that toerag of an Albie Denham and she'll come home with her arms full of parcels and about ten new hats to show off.'

Babs kept her eyes fixed on her machine. She swore angrily at herself as she let the row of stitching go zigzagging off the seam.

Until then, Ginny had just been listening and watching what was going on, but now she bent her head low and whispered somethingto Joan. Joan shook her head, but Ginny wouldn't be refused. She poked Joan spitefully in the arm, urging her to do as she was told.

Joan didn't look very happy as she said to Babs, 'Not

266

seen your Evie about, Babs. Still sick, is she?'

Babs ignored her.

But Blanche didn't. 'I've told yer before, Joan,' Blanche said, switching her machine back on, 'yer've gotta start thinking before yer speak. And yer've gotta stop letting other people make yer do their dirty work for 'em.'

Joan blushed and got on with working her way through the pile of trouser pockets she was making up.

Ginny tapped Joan on the shoulder. 'I'll go to the Ladies with yer,' she said.

'But I don't wanna—'

'I said I'll go with yer,' Ginny said, jerking her head towards the door.

When they came back a couple of minutes later, Ginny returned to her seat but Joan stopped by Babs's chair and said, 'If yer sister's missing, Babs, I bet yer really worried, ain't yer? Fretting that she's been killed in a raid or trapped somewhere like the young warehouse lad was. Must be rotten for yer.'

The silence in the workroom was brief but very uneasy as everyone sat waiting for Babs to erupt. But she said nothing.

Joan sighed with relief, kept her gaze fixed straight ahead and went to get on with her work.

The moment the clock touched five, Babs grabbed her bag and coat and ran from the workshop without waiting for Blanche or even saying goodnight.

Getting home in the blackout was a nuisance at the best of times, but that evening Babs cursed and fumed as she struggled to get home in the pitch dark. All the usual hindrances, like crawling buses, dawdling pedestrians and unexpected piles of soaking wet sandbags just waiting to trip you up or bark your shins had apparently been multiplied by ten just to get in her way. And now her torch had packed up on her. By the time she turned into

Darnfield Street from Grove Road, she had worked herself up into a foul temper and a raging headache.

As she fiddled around trying to get her key in the lock of the street door, someone tapped her on the back. She turned furiously.

'Yes?' she yelled. 'What?'

'All right, Babs, it's only me, Terry.'

'Sorry, love, what d'yer want?'

'I saw your twin just now, and—'

'You saw Evie?'

'How many twins yer got?'

'Just the one, thank gawd.'

'She had the right hump on her. I only asked her if she wanted me and me mates to take Flash out for a run for her. She hardly even managed to say hello.'

Babs ruffled Terry's hair. 'She didn't mean nothing, Terry. Yer know what she's like, and she ain't been very well. But I'm sorry. I'll go in and tell her.' Babs pushed open the door.

'Well, she ain't in there, she was going down to the canal.'

Babs stood in the doorway and looked at Terry with incredulous surprise. 'What, Evie was taking Flash for a walk?'

'No, she never had the dog with her. That's why I'm here. She said I'd have to see you when yer got in. About, you know, taking Flash out for a run.'

Babs stumbled down the step in the darkness. 'Lend us yer torch, Terry,' she said, snatching it from him, and then started running down the street towards the canal.

'I'll go in and get Flash, shall I?' Terry called after her.

'In the kitchen. Lead's on the hook,' Babs's voice shouted back from the darkness. 'Slam the door shut behind yer.'

Babs shone the faint beam of Terry's torch cautiously in front of her as she edged her way along the narrow

268

alley that led to the canal towpath.

In the dark she could hear the rhythmic sound of someone throwing pebbles, one by one, into the black waters of the canal. She lifted the torch to shoulder height. It was Evie. She was standing there, tears running down her face, not bothering to wipe her eyes, just making a slow swipe of her tongue at a drop that slid from her nose towards her lips.

'Eve?'

'Remember how I used to make yer come down here when we was little, Babs?' Evie's voice was raw from crying. 'Even though we both knew we mustn't go near the water. We used to chuck in stones and watch the rings grow wider and wider until they disappeared.'

'I remember,' Babs said gently.

'And how we tried to catch a fish by putting salt on its tail, like old Frankie kidded us yer could?' A shuddering sigh passed through Evie's whole body. 'Things was so simple then. Dad catching us down here by the canal was as serious as things got.'

Babs put her hand softly on her twin's arm; she could feel the dampness on the fox fur from the drizzle that had started to fall. 'Evie, what's wrong? Tell me, please.'

Evie pulled away from her sister's touch. She sniffed loudly. 'I've just heard that they've stopped selling silk stockings for the duration. And I'm heartbroken.'

'Don't be nasty, Eve.'

'Well, don't you be so stupid.' Again there was the plopping sound from the water. 'What d'yer *think's* wrong with me?'

'If that Albie's hurt you, Eve . . .'

Evie laughed contemptuously. 'Aw, he's hurt me all right.' The effort of trying to control herself was too much for her; she broke down into chest-heaving sobs. 'I'm pregnant, Babs. I'm bloody pregnant.'

'Christ, Eve, what yer gonna do?'

'Gonna drown meself, that's what. What else can I do?'

Now Babs was crying too. 'Why d'you always have to be so flaming dramatic?'

'Dramatic? Well, if you're so clever, you tell me what *you'd* do.'

'I wouldn't be in this state in the first place.' Babs felt like biting her tongue off. 'I'm sorry, there was no need for that.'

Again, the sound of something hitting the water. Babs shone the torch downwards to watch. 'D'yer wanna tell me where yer've been?' she asked, shifting the torch to follow the path of the widening circles as they spread out and finally disappeared across the water.

. 'Why not?' Evie said wearily. 'Albie's old girl went barmy. Reckoned how I was trying to trap her precious son.'

Babs restrained herself from shouting out loud what she felt about Albie Denham and his rotten family.

'So she sorted out this clinic for me to go to. To get rid of it. "Private nursing home", Queenie called it. Yer ought to have seen it, Babs. It was a rat-infested, filthy hole. Honest, yer wouldn't have let Flash stay there the night. One look of the place should have been enough – I should have had it away there and then. But I did as I was told and went in like a good little girl.'

'I should have been with yer.' Babs tried to take her hand

'Don't.' Evie pulled away. 'They stuck me in this room and I saw one of the so-called doctors. I said then, I wasn't having none of it. The room, it was disgusting. And he had this filthy old suit on. I got me fur back on and said I was off, but he went outside and brought Albie in. They told me I was being emotional, and how it was only natural, and that if I spent the night there, got some rest, I'd see sense in the morning. They took me into this little ward with four beds. There was just one other

270

woman in there, she was asleep. They told me to get into bed and then Albie buggered off with Chas on the piss somewhere. Said he needed a drink. *He* needed a drink.'

'But you stayed?'

'I stayed all right.' She paused. 'I sat on the edge of this lousy, rotten bed they give me. Too frightened to lay on the pillow 'cos of what I might have caught. The next morning they brought another woman in. Right state she was, like a right old whatsit. She was laughing, going on about how she was back in there again for her little holiday . . . Then the other girl woke up.' Evie closed her eyes for a brief moment then carried on. 'I tell yer what, Babs, I couldn't get out o' there quick enough. It weren't the abortion or nothing what worried me, I'd do anything not to be having it, but yer know what a coward I am. I looked at the state of them two and the place and the beds and I knew I couldn't let them butchers get their hands on me. I couldn't.'

'Why didn't yer, you know, use yer loaf a bit? Be careful and use something so's yer didn't get in this mess?'

'Leave off, Babs. It's a bit late to start thinking of that now, ain't it?'

'Yeah, I'm sorry. I'm upset, that's all.'

'You're upset. That's a good'un.'

'Don't let's start rowing, Eve – aw shit, that's all we need, the bloody air raid warning. Come on, shift yerself, the planes'll be over soon.'

'I'm not coming.'

'Aw yes you are.'

Evie sighed. She sounded sad and exhausted. 'I just don't care any more, Babs.'

'Well, I bloody do. Christ, there's the bloody guns started up now. We've gotta get to the shelter.' She tried to grab Evie's hand to pull her along, but her fist was tightly clenched round something.

271

'Chuck them stones down and come on.'

'They ain't stones.' Evie sounded oddly calm. 'They're the pearls what Albie give me for me birthday.' She opened her hand and tossed the remaining milky pearls into the water. 'It's true, yer see, what they say. Pearls do bring tears.'

Overhead, the searchlights had started trawling the night sky for enemy aircraft and the staccato clatter from the ack-ack defences in Victoria Park echoed eerily across the water as though it was coming from the canal itself.

Babs took her twin's hand in hers. 'We've gotta go, Eve.'

'No.'

'D'yer wanna get me killed and all? 'Cos if you stay, then so am I.'

'Not in the Drum then, Babs. I ain't going in there. Not with everyone from the street.'

'Don't worry. We won't see no one. Now, just start walking and we'll go indoors.'

Evie let her sister take her hand and Babs led her as fast as she could back through the alley and along Darnfield Street. By the time they had got indoors and into the kitchen, the siren had long since stopped and that evening's episode of the Blitz was well under way.

Babs made sure the blackout curtains were pulled and then she turned on the kitchen light. She could hardly believe how awful her sister looked. She pulled the wet fur coat off Evie's shoulders and threw it down on the floor under the table.

'Get under there, Eve. Now.'

Evie crawled under the table without a word and sat there silently while Babs, with a constant ear to how close the planes sounded, rushed around the kitchen making tea.

Babs crouched down, careful not to spill the tea, and

squeezed under the table next to her sister. She put the cups down on the floor and wrapped a tea towel round the end of her finger. 'Well, at least I know what the matter is now,' she said as she gently tried to wipe the streaks of mascara away from Evie's eyes with the cloth. 'Now drink yer tea while it's hot.'

Evie looked up at her sister pathetically. 'What am I gonna do?'

Babs put her hand over her mouth to stifle her giggles. 'I'm sorry, Evie, I don't mean to laugh, but I thought . . . I thought you had the 'flu.'

Evie's face crumpled and she dissolved into loud, heart-rending sobs.

'Aw, Eve, don't cry. I wasn't laughing at you, I was only laughing 'cos I'm relieved yer home. And 'cos I'm nervous. And 'cos I'm worried. And . . . Aw, Evie, don't. Please.'

'I love him so much, Babs. I really love him.' Evie threw her arms round Babs's neck and cried as if she would never stop.

19

Even though it was only the beginning of November, it already felt as if the bad weather had been going on for ever. But it wasn't only the exceptional cold that was making life in London difficult and unpleasant. It was also the dark, the shortages and the continual danger from the Blitz. But people carried on, and most had resigned themselves to accepting the fact that it was going to be a long, hard winter.

In the kitchen of number six, Babs was dishing up two bowls of neck of lamb stew and dumplings, while Evie sat listlessly at the table with her chin resting on her hands. Babs put one of the plates down in front of her twin.

'Get stuck in, Eve. Dad won't mind if yer start. Go on, while it's hot. Yer've gotta keep yer strength up.'

Evie picked up her fork and stuck it in one of the dumplings. She examined it wearily, making no attempt to put it even near her mouth.

Babs put her own plate on the table and sat down. 'Fancy coming to the pictures with me and Lou tonight?'

'Not really.'

Babs picked up one of the lamb bones and began nibbling at the meat. 'Yer don't wanna stay in on a Friday. Dad's only gonna wanna go to bed after being on shift. So yer'll be sitting moping by yerself.'

Evie let the dumpling fall from her fork back into the stew. 'I said no.'

Babs carried on eating, sucking the meat clean from the bone then forking up the vegetables. 'Why not?' she asked between mouthfuls.

'I'm exhausted, that's why. You don't know what it's like. Being sick and wanting to wee all the time.' Evie pushed the plate of food away from her and Flash jumped up eagerly, hoping for leftovers. 'Bloody get down, yer rotten hound. Look at my stockings.'

'I'm just about fed up with all this, Evie.' Babs threw her fork into her bowl, splashing hot stew across the oilcloth-covered table. She got up to fetch a cloth from the sink. 'I'm doing me best, working me fingers to the bloody bone and are you even a bit grateful? No. Course yer not.' She rubbed vigorously at the spills. 'And d'you care how long I queued up to get that meat? No. Well, all bloody dinner time I stood there in the cold, never even had a cup of tea, while you stayed in the workshop all nice and warm.'

'What, d'yer want me to go out and stand in the queue? Look at me, I look like a sodding elephant.'

Babs tossed the cloth into the sink and sat back down at the table. 'Eve, you are four months' pregnant. You don't even show.'

'Liar.'

'Come on, cheer up. Come out with me and Lou. We'll have a laugh.'

'No, I can't.' Evie ran her finger through the gravy that was congealing round the rim of her bowl. She avoided looking at her sister. 'I'm probably seeing Albie tonight.'

Babs nearly choked. 'So that's it. He's back on the scene, is he? I thought he'd disappeared up his own—'

'Shut up, can't yer, Babs,' Eve snapped. 'I've got enough on me mind wondering what to do next.'

From the passage came the sound of the street door opening.

Babs stood up and filled a third bowl with stew. 'Well,

'yer gonna have to tell Dad soon for a start,' she said, putting the food on the table.

'Tell Dad what?' Georgie asked as he peeled off his uniform jacket and hung it on the back of his chair. 'This grub looks nice.'

'I'm having a baby.' Evie blurted the words out, more as a challenge than as a statement.

'I know that,' said Georgie, sprinkling salt over his stew. 'I ain't stupid. I've been wondering when yer'd get round to telling me.' He reached across and patted Evie's hand, while Babs gaped at him in astonishment. She'd never have believed he would take it so calmly. 'Now get that dinner down yer,' he went on. 'Yer've gotta look after yerself in your condition. And my grandchild.' He waved his fork at Evie to emphasise his point. 'And don't you let me catch you worrying yerself about that no-good rat Denham dumping yer like that. Yer old dad'll see yer all right, sweetheart. You don't need the likes of him.'

Evie flashed a warning look at Babs not to mention that she was seeing Albie again; she couldn't face another row.

She was more than thankful that Georgie had already gone up to get some sleep when Albie turned up to collect her.

The next morning, Evie astonished Babs and Georgie when she called upstairs for them to come down for breakfast. When they got to the kitchen, the table was set and the toast had been made.

'What's all this in aid of?' yawned Georgie, scratching at his unshaven chin. 'Ain't me birthday, is it?'

Babs dropped down onto one of the chairs. Sleepily she lifted the teapot lid. The pot was full. 'Someone ain't hit you over the head and sent yer crackers, have they, Eve?'

'Say what yer like to me, you two, nothing could upset me today.' Evie held her left hand out and wiggled her finger at Babs. 'I'm engaged.'

277

'You're what?' Georgie was now wide awake.

'Last night. I saw Albie and he asked me to marry him.'

'Him, doing the decent thing? Never.'

'That's it, try and spoil me day for me. Yer make it sound like he's doing me a favour.'

'Dad didn't mean it like that,' Babs said. Shivering, she wrapped her dressing gown tightly round her and went over to turn the gas higher. 'But yer've gotta admit it's a bit of a turn up. He ain't even been around for the last couple of weeks.'

Evie took a bite out of a piece of toast. 'If yer must know, he said us being apart give him the chance to think and he realised that he wants to marry me.' Evie paused. 'No matter what his old cow of a mother says.'

Georgie folded his arms and leant back in his chair. 'So that's what it's all about. He's had a ruck with the old lady about yer and now he's showing her who's boss.'

'Why d'yer have to be so horrible to me? If it was like that, why'd he get me this?' Evie gave them another flash of her ring.

Georgie looked at the sparkling stones.

'They're real diamonds. Not rubbish.' Evie admired the ring. 'Got it off some bloke he knows. A contact of his.'

'Wonder if the owner had any say in it?' Georgie's voice was hard, unrelenting. 'Or was she laying dead in some bombed-out house somewhere?'

'You ain't gonna ruin this for me, no matter how hard yer try.' Evie bowed her head sadly. 'I really thought yer'd got over all that jealousy. Can't yer just admit that Albie's done well for himself and be pleased for me, Dad?'

Georgie leant across the table to her. He lifted her chin in his hand. 'Look at me, Eve. All I could ever ask out of life is that you and Babs are happy. I'd give the world to make things right for you two after all the time I wasted and what I put yer through.' Georgie spread out his hands, trying to find words to express what he was feeling. 'Look, darling, I know yer think the sun shines out that no-good bastard, but why don't yer wait a while, see how yer feel? Yer don't have to rush into it or nothing. Be sure of what yer doing before yer marry him. There's plenty of room for a baby here. Me and Babs'd help yer. Please, Eve, don't get hiked up with him.'

'Yer just don't understand. Yer've got him entirely wrong.' Evie pulled out a necklace that had been hidden under the collar of her dressing gown. 'Look, he's bought me new pearls and everything.'

'Yer've changed yer tune,' Babs jeered. 'Don't I remember you going on about how pearls brought tears? But that was what – getting on for a fortnight ago now, wasn't it? I forget sometimes how you can change yer mind like a bloody seesaw.'

'I don't care what either of yer say. I love Albie and he loves me. And I'm getting married as soon as possible and it's up to you two whether you're there or not.'

Georgie stood up and pulled Evie to her feet. He put his arms round her and kissed the top of her head. 'Course we'll be there, sweetheart.' He looked over her shoulder at Babs and raised his eyebrows in a gesture of resignation. 'You just try and keep us away.'

The wedding preparations got under way that very morning with Maudie agreeing to have a word with the vicar to see if he was prepared to conduct the service even though Evie was pregnant. Evie had insisted on telling Maud that she was expecting, to show Georgie that she was going to keep everything above board and have no more deceit.

By the time Maudie got back from the church with the vicar's answer, Evie was prowling nervously around the house not knowing what to do with herself. When Maudie gave her the news that the vicar had agreed to marry them in the middle of November, Evie practically threw herself at Maudie with relief.

'I appreciate yer help, Maud,' Georgie said.

'I'm only too glad to help.'

'You'd have made a good mother, I reckon, Maud.' Evie was glowing with happiness. 'Yer kind and yer not like some people, yer don't judge no one.'

'Don't be silly.' Maudie blushed, she felt almost as happy as Evie. 'But before you get too carried away, you've got to think about sorting things out. There are barely two weeks until the big day. There's going to be a lot to organise.'

Evie pulled a face. 'Yeah.'

'I could help some more if you like.'

Evie kissed her noisily on the cheek. 'I would like that, Maud, I really would. I need someone to stick up for me.'

Maudie was now blushing even deeper. She was elated. It was a long time since she had felt really needed, or even useful. It was almost like being part of a family. 'We'd better get organised then,' she said, beaming at Georgie.

As they made their way through the bomb-damaged London streets to Styleways on Monday morning, Evie told Babs and Blanche that she was going to speak to Mr Silver about handing in her notice.

When they got to the workroom, Babs and Blanche hung up their coats and hats and settled down at their machines. But Evie kept her coat on and stood by the double swing doors that led through to the stairs and the offices.

'Wish me luck, Babs,' she said, holding out her crossed fingers as she backed through the doors. 'I'm gonna get it over with right away.'

'Just remember not to strong it too much,' Babs hissed at her. 'He ain't a fool.'

'She's right, Evie, you watch what yer say,' Blanche called after her – as much to intrigue and infuriate Ginny as anything else. 'Good luck, babe.'

Evie knocked on her boss's door and poked her head inside his office. 'Could I have a private word with you, d'yer think, Mr Silver?' she said, peering at him through her heavily mascaraed lashes. 'It's about handing in me notice. I'm getting married, yer see.'

Mr Silver didn't seem very surprised. 'Sit down, dear,' he said with a warm, avuncular smile. 'Good-looking girl like you, I can't believe you've not been snapped up before. It'll be that twin of yours next.'

Evie smiled sweetly back at him.

'So. When did you want to leave?'

'Soon as possible really, Mr Silver.' Evie gave him the full dimple treatment. 'See, me fiancé's only gonna be on leave for . . . for . . .' She rummaged around in her bag looking for her handkerchief. 'I'm sorry.' She sniffled pathetically as she peered over her hankie at him. 'You know what it's like with these brave soldiers going off to fight for their country . . .'

Evie was back home before midday with a ten pound note by way of a wedding present from Mr Silver tucked in her bag, and his best wishes for her brave husband-to-be.

'Dad. It's only me.' Evie found Georgie and Flash out in the back yard. They were both covered in white specks and splashes of varnish – Georgie had been whitewashing the back walls and painting the wooden lavatory seat.

'Want it to look respectable, don't we?' he said with a wink.

'Blimey, Dad, no one's done that since . . .' She stopped short of saying it.

'It's all right, Eve. I know what yer mean. Since yer mum buggered off.'

'Sorry, Dad.'

'Don't be daft, love. You go in and put the kettle on while I just finish this last bit here. And you wait and see what else I've got and all. A bit of carpet for the stairs. That feller Vic from the station, who I went to see last night, he used to be in the carpet game before the war. Let me have the whole roll for next to nothing.' He leant towards her and whispered. 'No coupons neither.'

'No coupons? You, Dad?'

He grinned. 'Special occasion, girl. Vic brought it round this morning. I was gonna lay it before yer got in as a surprise. Here, I ain't thinking, what yer doing home so early?' Georgie frowned. He dropped his brush in the bucket and rubbed his arm across his cheek, spreading the flecks of whitewash all over his face. 'Yer not sick or nothing, are yer?'

'No.' Evie shook her head gleefully. 'Much better than that, I'm a lady of leisure. I handed in me notice and Mr Silver said I could leave straightaway as me boy friend was gonna be leaving for the front soon.'

Georgie slapped his palms together. 'I've gotta hand it to yer. Yer never fail to amaze me, young lady. Still, now yer've got all this time on yer hands, yer can get stuck in with me. It's about time we jollied this place up a bit. How about having a few flowers about the place? I reckon we've got a few vases somewhere. Make it look nice for the wedding.'

'That's a lovely idea, Dad.' Evie leaned back against the back door and sighed wistfully. 'Wish I looked nice though. Just look at me, I'm like a barrage balloon.'

'Daft. You hardly show yet. Anyway, that might not be a problem. Might have another little surprise for yer later on. A present.'

Evie's eyes lit up as they always did at the thought of gifts. 'What? Tell me.'

'A frock that might do yer for the wedding.'

Evie giggled. 'Here, that Vic don't do dressmaking in his spare time, do he?'

'I don't think I could see Vic doing sewing, he's built like a bloody bus. No, it's Maudie. She says she's got a nice dress yer can have.'

Evie's smile disappeared. 'It's all right, me and Babs're gonna make me something. Babs'll get some material from work. Old Silver'll turn a blind eye if it's for me. Who knows, I might be the first bride in a khaki wedding dress.'

'But she wants yer to have it. As a present, like. Yer can't turn her down.'

'It's ever so kind of her, Dad, but I ain't even seen it yet. So I ain't gonna promise I'll wear it or nothing.'

'I bet it'll be just the job, you see,' Georgie said eagerly. 'Now, sit yerself down, take the weight off yer pins and I'll go straight over there now and tell her to bring it over for yer to have a look at.'

George was back with Maudie within five minutes.

Maudie nibbled her bottom lip nervously as she put a big, flat cardboard box down on the kitchen table and lifted off the lid. 'Alice was breaking her neck trying to see what I had in here,' she said, taking out layer after layer of tissue paper. A smell of sweet lavender filled the kitchen. 'There, what d'you think?' Maudie took out a shimmering white lace wedding dress and draped it over her arm.

Evie gasped. 'I think it's the most beautiful thing I've ever seen.' Her voice was hushed. 'Look at that stitching.' She turned to Georgie. 'Look, Dad, ain't it beautiful?'

Georgie looked at the dress then at Maudie. 'Beautiful,' he said flatly. 'I never realised it was a proper wedding dress.'

Evie pulled at the bodice, staring at it through narrowed eyes, guessing at the waist measurement. She lifted her gaze to Maudie. 'D'yer reckon I'll be able to get into it?'

'You're still very slim. But when you're ready, try it on, and if it needs adjusting, me and Babs can sort it out between us. We'll make it fit. We can let it out or put a panel in, if it needs it.'

'If yer sure that'll be all right?'

'Of course. It's yours. I want you to have it.' Maudie folded the dress carefully back into the box. 'I'm so pleased you like it.' She touched Evie gently on the cheek. 'I'll pop round later when Babs is home and we'll see what needs doing.'

When Georgie came back into the kitchen after seeing Maudie to the street door, he looked serious, almost stern.

Evie was stroking the dress lovingly as though it was a living creature. 'I dunno where she got it from, Dad, but ain't it the most beautiful thing yer've ever seen?'

Georgie didn't answer her; he felt too choked to speak.

It was the morning of the wedding. Evie was stretched out soaping herself in the tin bath in the kitchen, her blonde hair tightly wound in curlers and her face covered with vanishing cream. The cooker door was wide open and the gas blazed on full heat, keeping the little room as warm as if it were a summer's day. Blanche and her daughter Mary sat at the table cutting up one of Maudie's precious gardening magazines into tiny pieces to make confetti, while Blanche's toddler, Janey, lay snuggled up asleep on the rug next to Flash. Maudie was in the front room giving Evie's wedding dress a final pressing and humming to herself, over and over again, the order of hymns that she was going to play at the service.

'What with the salvage rules and us making this confetti,' Blanche said to Evie, 'and all that grub that Ringer got hold of from somewhere and,' she lowered her voice, 'the mystery wedding dress – gawd alone knows where that come from – let's just hope no coppers turn up at this do, Eve, or we'll all be spending the night in the nick.'

'Don't think there's much danger of that,' chuckled Evie. 'Can you imagine Albie inviting the law?' She ran her hands over her gently swelling middle. 'I don't look too fat, do I?'

Blanche tore another page from the magazine and started cutting it into squares. 'You look as gorgeous as ever, darling. Here, I didn't tell yer, my little sister's in the family way.'

Evie nearly dropped the soap. 'Not your Ruby?'

'Yeah, a little present her Davey left her last time he come home on leave.'

'But I thought she was planning to be running that munitions factory single-handed by the end of the year.'

'That's what she thought and all, but this being pregnant's put a stop to all that. She don't care though, she's so happy about the baby. Looking after herself all proper, she is. Even gone to stay with Mum's sister down East Ham way. It's safer down there, she reckons.'

Evie twisted round in the bath to face Mary. 'You gonna give up working there now Ruby's left?'

'You kidding?' Mary shook her head determinedly. 'I'm after her supervisor's job, ain't I?'

Blanche and Evie grinned at each other.

Babs came into the kitchen, rubbing her hands together. 'Flaming perishing outside, it is.' She went and stood by the cooker and warmed her hands. 'That's the cake sorted,' she said, blowing on her tingling fingers. 'Yer've had a right touch there, Eve.'

'How's that?'

'When I went in the baker's to collect it, Rita winked and told me to look under the cardboard. When I lifted it up there's only a whole bottom layer made out of proper cake.'

Evie sat upright in the bath. 'What, real cake?'

'Yeah, hidden under that cardboard one they rent out. I asked where the stuff had come from to make it, but Bert just tapped the side of his nose with his finger and said "Careless talk!" and then he winked at me and all.'

'Luck of the Irish, you've got, Eve,' laughed Blanche. 'He's a good'un, old Bert.'

'Real cake,' Evie repeated. 'Well, let's see it then.'

'I took it straight down the Drum, miss,' Babs said, dropping a mocking curtsey. 'If that's all right with you.'

Evie waved her hand regally at her twin and slipped her shoulders down under the water. 'Just so long as you ain't been shirking.'

Babs sat at the table between Mary and Blanche and started tearing pages from the magazine into strips. 'Guess who I saw in the Drum – the old trout herself.'

'Queenie Denham?' Blanche guessed.

'Got it in one. Should have seen her. She swanned in with these two women, laden down with boxes of food they was, looking down her nose at everyone. Even at Nellie.'

Evie held the flannel up to her face and peered round it as if she was in pain. 'Tell me the worst, Babs. Did she look like she had her wedding outfit on?'

'Fraid so.'

Evie groaned. 'Lairy?'

'Yer could say that. And her hair's very orange.'

'*Very* orange?'

'Very.'

'What a show up.'

Mary sniggered and Blanche tapped her across the back of her head. 'You ain't too big to feel the back of my hand, madam,' she warned her.

'Yer can't blame her, Blanche.' Babs nibbled her lip to stop herself laughing. 'You just wait till yer see her. She looks like she should be on top of a Christmas tree. And when she had the cheek to get all hoity toity with Nellie, after all she's done for us, I thought Nellie was gonna land one on her. I mean, there's Nellie, done all that food what Dad brought, and she's done it lovely and all. Then Queenie turns up with all this gear. And she kept saying, "I wanna do my boy proud, he's used to decent things, my Albie." And looking down her nose at what Nellie'd already laid out.'

Evie snorted. 'Used to decent things! What a load of old toffee. Yer should see their place, Blanche. It is soapy. She's a right filthy mare, that Queenie.'

Mary giggled.

'Truth. Yer should see their front room, they have a fire burning all weathers. It's all right now, when it's cold like this, but when it's warm it's horrible. Stinks like hell. They burn these great big lengths of quartering that they make Chas fetch from the bombsites. They stick one end in the fireplace and the other end goes right up the passage. As it burns away, the old girl kicks it further onto the fire till it's all used up. Then they put on another one.'

'Never.'

'Honest, Blanche. It's just like having a bonfire inside the house. You ask Babs. I've told her all about it.' She turned to Babs. 'And how about Bernie, the old man?'

Babs tutted and rolled her eyes. 'You listen to this, Blanche.'

'See, their lav's got no roof,' Evie continued. 'Not had one since I first went round there. And that's what, fourteen, fifteen months ago? And they ain't never bothered to do nothing about it. So when it's raining, Bernie goes out there with a bloody umbrella.'

'Liar,' Mary spluttered.

Evie's already big blue eyes widened. 'I swear on my life. And the lav door, that's as bad. It ain't got no hinges so you have to kind of lift it to one side to get in and out.

But Bernie can't be bothered to pull the door over to shut it or nothing when he's in there, so he just sits there reading the racing papers like a king on his bloody throne and anyone going past can see him. They're so used to it they even call out good morning to him.'

'It's smashing to hear you all laughing, girls,' said Maudie as she came into the kitchen. 'And I don't wanna be a spoilsport when you're having such a good time, but I think you should think about getting dressed soon, Eve. Your Dad'll be here with the taxi in less than an hour.'

Babs looked up at the clock. 'Blimey, Eve,' she said, undoing the buttons of her blouse. 'Come on, get out of that bath and let me get in. Hurry up, I ain't even ironed me bridesmaid's frock yet.'

'It's done,' smiled Maud. 'All you two've got to worry about is your hair and lipstick. I'll be back over when I've got changed.'

'We'll be off and all,' said Blanche, scooping the homemade confetti into old blue paper sugar bags. 'Mary, try and pick Janey up without waking her or she'll be grizzly all day.'

Forty-five minutes later, Babs and Evie sat side by side at the dressing table up in the front bedroom, looking at their twin reflections in the triple-framed mirror, Evie in her white gown and Babs in her pale blue bridesmaid's dress.

'Them flowers look right pretty in your hair, Babs.'

'They was Maudie's idea.'

'So long as everyone don't look at you instead of me,' grinned Evie, and shoved Babs in the ribs, nearly knocking her off the dressing table stool. 'Yer'll have to wait till you get married for that. This is my big day, not your'n.'

'I'm gonna miss yer so much, Eve.' Babs grabbed her twin's hand.

'Don't, Babs. Don't make me cry, yer'll spoil me make-up.'

Georgie knocked on the bedroom door. 'Can I come in?'

The girls both turned round to face him.

Georgie stood there a moment, looking at his daughters. 'I can't tell you two how beautiful you both are. Just look at the pair of yer. Like a painting.'

'You look smashing and all, Dad,' Babs said. Her lip quivered as she spoke.

Georgie sniffed. 'Bit o' luck I bought this new suit, eh?'

'Yeah.' Evie stood up and kissed him on the cheek. 'Yer look really smart, Dad. I'm gonna be proud to be on yer arm.'

'I'm the one who should be proud, Eve.' He blew his nose loudly. 'Yer do know it's not too late to change yer mind?'

'Don't, Dad, not today.'

'All right, darling. Not today. But yer know yer've always got a home here with us.'

'I know, Dad.'

Georgie took a deep breath. 'Right, you'd better go down, Babs, the cabs are waiting. Maudie's going with you, and me and Eve'll be in the one behind.'

As Babs stepped out into the street, Maudie was waiting for her.

'I'm sure you've already heard it from your dad, but you look a picture.' Maudie squeezed Babs's hand and led her to the waiting taxi.

They both smiled at the little crowd, including Alice and Ethel in the prime spot along the wall by the street doorstep, who had gathered to watch the bride leave the house before they ran round to the church for the service.

'Getting married.' Alice managed to make the words sound like an insult. 'All happened a bit quick, if you ask me.'

Now it was Evie's turn to leave the house. The

onlookers oohed and aahed at the beautiful bride on the arm of her proud father.

'Bit quick?' Ethel didn't bother to lower her voice. 'Will yer look at the size of her. That frock ain't fooling no one. I always knew that she'd bring trouble home. Just like her mother.'

Evie stopped right in front of her.

Ethel drew herself up to her full height and stared over Evie's shoulder. 'And I'd like to know where that frock come from and all.'

Evie lifted her veil and flashed her most dazzling smile at Ethel and Alice. 'March it's due,' she said sweetly, patting her stomach. 'And don't forget, me and Albie's really looking forward to seeing yer at the wedding party in the Drum.' She winked then dropped the veil. 'See yer, ladies.'

Georgie squeezed her arm and whispered, 'Good for you, darling. No one takes liberties with us Bells.'

'I'll be a Denham soon, Dad,' Evie reminded him.

Everyone, even Alice and Ethel, had to agree that the do afterwards at the pub was a success, a proper knees-up like they used to have before the war. Although the two old gossips wondered, loudly and rudely, about where all the grub came from, they were both more than happy to get stuck in to the shellfish, pies and pickles, the sandwiches, cold meats and trifle, and aggressively encouraged their husbands to do the same. Queenie showed a grudging approval of the cake, and took a large slab of it for herself, claiming that she had clients she wanted to treat to a little taster of her boy's wedding breakfast. No one was clear what Bernie thought of the proceedings as he was slumped, drunk, in the corner.

Even when the siren went the party continued; they all trooped down to the cellar and, because they couldn't carry the piano downstairs, Babs and Evie sang instead, bringing tears to their dad's eyes.

But as soon as the all clear sounded, they were back up in the bar and the dancing began, with Maudie surprising them by playing all the latest dance tunes as well as the old favourites.

Rather than cause a scene, Babs agreed to take to the floor with Albie when he made a show of asking her, as the bridesmaid, to dance with him.

She wasn't too happy when Maudie began playing the slow opening bars of 'Night and Day'. 'Remember that first night when we all went to the club?' Albie breathed into her ear. 'Yer sister sang it to me. D'you wanna sing it to me?'

Babs squirmed in his arms. She felt like kneeing him in the groin, but she knew she couldn't even walk away from him what with everyone watching. But she didn't have to put up with him holding her so close.

'What's up, darling? Gutted that it's not you what's gonna be in me bed tonight? If you play yer cards right . . .' His voice trailed off, his sickening meaning left dangling in the air between them.

'You pig,' she hissed under her breath. 'Just get away from me.'

Albie laughed at her. 'Keep smiling, girl, we've got quite an audience.'

'Chas!' Babs called as she looked round Albie's massive shoulders. She smiled seductively at Albie's handsome but dim mate who was standing propping up the bar. 'Ain't yer gonna cut in?'

'Stupid bitch,' sneered Albie as Chas, surprised but delighted, took Babs in his arms and waltzed her away, leaving Albie standing there.

By the time Evie and Albie were ready to leave for their honeymoon – in the rooms in the Mile End Road that Bernie had taken as part pay-off for a gambling debt and had then given them as a wedding present – Babs had danced with Chas a dozen times and she was uneasily aware he was getting quite the wrong impression.

As the guests threw handfuls of homemade confetti at the departing Riley which Frankie, in his role as ARP warden, had threatened to confiscate because of the noise made by the tin cans tied to the back bumper, Chas slipped his arm round Babs's shoulders.

'Yer must be freezing in that flimsy little frock,' he leered at her. 'I could keep yer warm if yer like, darling.' Before Babs realised what he was up to, he was trying to shove his hand down the front of her dress.

'Yer lucky, Chas, 'cos I'm putting that down to yer being pissed,' Babs snarled, pushing him away from her. 'And yer can bugger off now that bastard's gone.'

'I don't understand.'

'No, I don't suppose you do,' said Babs and went over to Georgie who was standing on the edge of the kerb still waving into the pitch dark of the blacked-out street.

'I think they've gone, Dad,' she said gently.

'Yeah.' Georgie sighed.

'Ready to go home?'

Georgie nodded in the dark. 'I said I'd walk Maudie home but that lot in there won't let her go.' He took off his jacket and draped it round Babs's shoulders.

'Just me and you now, eh, Dad?'

They walked slowly across the road back towards number six. The sounds of the party still going strong in the Drum echoed through the empty street.

'Never knew Minnie could dance like that,' Georgie said with a quiet, muted laugh.

'No. Nor did I.'

They stopped by the street door.

'I hope I'm wrong about Albie, Dad.'

'Yeah. Me too.'

'She looked lovely though, didn't she?'

'Beautiful.'

292

'You're ever so quiet, Dad. But it's no good upsetting yerself, she's gone and done it now.'

Georgie took the key out of his pocket. As he put it in the lock he said almost to himself, 'It's not that. I was just wondering where Maudie got that frock.'

20

It was now mid-December, just a month after her wedding day and Evie's life had changed completely. But not for the better. Instead of the glamorous life she had imagined, based on ideas she had got from seeing the Thin Man films with Myrna Loy and William Powell at the Troxy, her life was miserable, boring and lonely. In fact, the only similarity between the lives of the movie characters and her own was that she too had a dog. But even that wasn't a cute little terrier like the one who slept on the satin covers in Myrna Loy's swanky bedroom; it was a great lolloping greyhound that wanted walking every five minutes and howled every time the air raid warnings went off.

Being Albie Denham's missus was definitely not measuring up to the life of wedded bliss that she had expected. Not only was he out till all hours nearly every night of the week, either with Chas or on yet another 'bit of business' that he had to see to, he had taken it into his head that he didn't like being seen in public with a pregnant woman, which meant that Evie had no choice but to stay indoors night after night with only Flash for company. Most days Albie went out some time during the morning and didn't get back home until way past midnight. So it was with some surprise that she heard the knock on the door at half past five in the afternoon.

'Hello, Babs, what you doing here?' Evie smoothed

back her unbrushed hair and pulled her dressing gown round her – she hadn't bothered to get dressed yet, there seemed no point when there was no one there to see her.

'Yer don't mind me coming, do yer?' Babs stepped inside, careful to pull the blackout curtain down behind her. 'I didn't wanna stick me nose in and disturb you two honeymooners but I couldn't help wondering how yer were. It's been such a long time.'

'Come in.'

Babs followed Evie along the dark passage to the front room of the flat that took up the ground floor of the three-storey house on the Mile End Road.

'This is nice,' Babs said, looking round at the jumble of ill-matched furniture with its tatty, worn upholstery that Queenie had given them.

'Don't tell lies,' said Evie, lowering herself into a battered armchair by the gas fire.

'You all right?'

'Yeah, fine. You know me.'

Babs stood by Evie's armchair. 'Shall I make us a cuppa?'

'Have one if yer like. But don't do nothing for me. Everything I have makes me feel sick.'

'I won't bother either then. I've gotta get home soon anyway, to get Dad's tea. He's on shift later tonight.'

Evie didn't say anything.

Babs sat down in the wobbly armchair opposite Evie.

A silence fell between them but it wasn't like the comfortable, companionable times when they'd been at home in Darnfield Street, when it didn't matter if neither of them spoke for hours on end; this was different, uneasy, as though there were things that were being left unsaid, making a barrier between them.

'So long as you're all right, then,' Babs said eventually, standing up. 'I'd better be off.'

'Yeah.' Evie stretched out her hand and absent-mindedly stroked Flash's sleek back. 'I won't get up. I need me rest, see.'

'Course, you stay where you are. I'll let meself out.'

As Babs ran along the Mile End Road, the tears streamed down her cheeks. What had happened to them? What was going to happen to Evie? And as for the baby when it was born, she couldn't bring herself to think about it.

Back in the flat, Evie stayed where she was in the armchair until the first of the evening's air raid warnings went, then she heaved herself up from the armchair and went into the kitchen, pulling Flash behind her. She still wasn't that big – she might have been nearly six months pregnant but she was hardly eating anything – but her body felt unbalanced somehow, as though it wasn't anything to do with her any more, and she couldn't control how it moved.

'Come on, Flash,' she urged the reluctant dog, pulling its lead, trying to make it join her in the steel-framed Morrison shelter that Chas had brought round for them as his idea of a wedding present. 'I know yer don't like it, nor do I, but we've gotta get in here 'cos of the bombs.' She shook her head. 'You daft cow,' she admonished herself, 'just listen to yerself, yer talking to a bloody dog.' She gave Flash one last tug and got her safely inside. 'Still, if it wasn't for you, Flash, I'd wind up talking to meself and we can't have that, can we? Me going bonkers.'

The raid was long and loud but Evie must have eventually fallen asleep because the next thing she knew was Flash licking her face and the sound of heavy footsteps stumbling along the passage towards the kitchen. She hauled herself up onto her knees and pushed open the heavy netting door of the shelter. Flash bounded out and went straight over to her water bowl in the corner.

As Evie pulled herself upright, Albie came staggering into the kitchen. His eyes looked out of focus and his clothes were rumpled.

'Where've you been again?' Evie asked, going over to the sink to fill the kettle. She looked at the little clock on the shelf by the sink. It was nearly half past eight. She lifted the corner of the window curtain; the thin wintery sunlight made her blink. So, it was morning.

'Shut up, can't yer?' Albie slurred. 'Where's me tea?'

'Flash had it last night. Baked up to hell it was.'

Albie opened the food cupboard. 'Where's all the grub?' He turned on her. His eyes were bloodshot and puffy. 'What d'yer do with all the dough I give yer if yer don't buy any grub?'

'It's been hard. You ain't gimme much money this week.'

Albie grabbed the cupboard door to steady himself. 'Ain't I?'

'No.' Evie set the kettle down on the stove and took a step towards him. 'Albie, where yer been?' She spoke softly, not wanting to antagonise him. 'I ain't moaning or nothing, but I'm lonely, stuck in here all day. Yer don't seem to care no more.'

Albie curled his lip in distaste. 'Shut up and pull that dressing gown round yer. What do you look like?'

'Albie.' Evie moved closer and reached out to kiss him, but then she lurched backwards. 'You rotten bastard. You stink of scent. Where've yer been, eh? Albie? You answer me. Where yer been?'

Evie didn't see him raise his hand to her; she just felt the impact of the blow and the sting of his palm swiping across her cheek.

Flash leapt forward at Albie, snarling and snapping. Albie lashed out at her with his boot but lost his balance and went crashing sideways into the stone sink. Evie grabbed at Flash's collar, dragging her away from him.

'Don't you ever raise yer hand to me again.' Her breath was coming in short, shuddering gasps. 'Or touch that dog. 'Cos if yer do, I swear, I'll kill yer stone dead.'

Albie steadied himself against the sink. 'Aw yeah?' he sneered. 'You and whose army?' He looked her up and down with disgust. 'Look at yer. Look at the state of yer.' He turned his head and did his best to focus on the door and then staggered out to the passage.

'Look at the state of me?' she screamed after him. 'How about this place? Where's the lovely home you promised me, Albie? Albie?' There was the sound of the front door opening. 'Albie, don't you walk out on me. Albie. Albie.' She ran out into the passage just as he slammed the door behind him. 'Come back. It'll all be all right again. I promise.' Evie fell to her knees and covered her face with her hands. 'I promise,' she sobbed.

Flash nuzzled into her neck, whining softly.

Evie spent the rest of the day frantically cleaning, scrubbing and tidying the flat, doing what she could to make the rooms more homely. Then she washed and made herself up, careful to put a thick layer of powder over the ugly bruise that was spreading across her cheekbone. It didn't actually hide it but she convinced herself that it made it look less obvious. Next she did her thick blonde hair as painstakingly as if she were going out for a night on the town, and then took off her dressing gown and slipped into one of the loose floral maternity dresses that she had sworn she would never use, but was now glad that Blanche had insisted she borrow 'just in case'. Eve looked at herself in the mirror over the fireplace in the front room, standing on tiptoes to try and get the full effect. She looked almost like she used to.

There was a knock on the door. She smiled at her reflection in the glass. 'That'll be Babs come to see us again,' she said, bending down to fondle Flash's ears. 'Wait till she sees how nice it all looks.'

As Evie opened the front door, the smile froze on her face. It wasn't Babs standing there at all, it was Albie's mum.

Queenie barged her way past Evie and marched through to the kitchen where she sat down and made herself comfortable at the Morrison shelter that doubled as a table.

Evie followed her into the kitchen and stood by the old but now sparklingly clean stove. 'Can I make yer a cup o' tea?' she asked flatly.

Queenie stared at the bruising on Evie's face. 'You ain't keeping this place very nice,' she said, her lips pursed to show her disapproval. 'My boy's used to a clean home and decent things round him. He won't be very pleased with all this.'

Evie could scarcely find the words. 'Your boy's used to a clean home and decent things?' She scratched her head in disbelief. 'For a start, you give us most of this old junk. And for another thing, your house is—'

'My house is *what*?' Queenie narrowed her eyes and fixed Evie with a stare that made her look just like Albie when he was in one of his tempers.

'Nothing.' Evie felt her heart racing as she busied herself with the kettle.

'I dunno what yer complaining about. Way that boy looks after you.' Queenie thumped the table top, making her bosom and her chins shake. 'He got you this Morrison shelter and everything.'

'He didn't actually.' Evie tried to keep her voice calm as she spooned two measures of tea into the cracked earthenware pot. 'Chas got us that, but I hate the bloody thing anyway, like being in a cage.'

'Oh, I'm so sorry,' Queenie said sarcastically. 'I forgot you was used to so much better.'

'At least I saw a bit of life when I sheltered in the Drum.'

'Aw yeah, yer've always liked a bit of life, haven't yer? All you Bells are the same.'

Evie spun round to face her, the kettle full of boiling water shaking in her hand. 'You old . . .'

Queenie stood up. She towered over Evie. 'Now you listen to me.' She jabbed her finger hard into Evie's shoulder, making her flinch with pain. 'My Albie come round my house this morning, before nine o'clock it was. And he was hungry. D'you hear me? Hungry. He'd been out all night, working hard to bring you in yer wages and there wasn't even a bit o' grub for him. I'm just here to warn yer that yer'd better sort yerself out and start behaving like a proper wife or—'

'Or what?' Evie slammed the kettle down on the top of the shelter.

'You little . . .' Queenie raised her hand.

Evie ducked her head, covering it with her arms. But she was saved from Queenie's blows by the sound of someone knocking at the front door.

'That'll be my Albie,' said Queenie, straightening herself up. She was breathing like a steam train. 'Go on, let him in. Let's hear what he's got to say about how yer talk to me.'

Evie was sure it wouldn't be Albie, not at six o'clock in the evening; as she walked towards the door, she prayed she was right.

She opened the door just a crack and peered out into the darkness. 'Babs. Thank gawd.' She pulled the door open wide and practically dragged her sister inside. 'Come in.'

Babs grinned. 'Yer pleased to see me then? Hope yer don't mind me coming again so soon,' she said as she closed the door. 'But I was so worried about yer yesterday. Yer seemed right down.'

Evie quickly finished draping the blackout curtain over the glass panel in the door and turned to face her sister.

Babs's mouth fell open. She reached out and touched the bruising on her twin's face. 'What the bloody hell happened to you?'

Queenie came storming along the passage and almost sent Babs flying as she shoved past her. 'Can't stop,' she barked. 'My Bernie'll be expecting me.' She pulled the door open and then twisted round to Evie. 'And you just remember what I said.'

Babs was about to say something to Queenie but Evie stopped her. 'No, Babs, yer don't know what's going on.'

'Leave off, I can see exactly what's been going on.'

Queenie stepped outside and slammed the door behind her, leaving them standing in the passage staring at each other.

'I don't need you starting, Babs.' Evie turned her head away. Suddenly she seemed to have clammed up on her sister.

'I ain't starting, Eve. I told yer, I'm worried about yer.' Babs nibbled her lip, trying to keep calm, but she couldn't take her eyes off the bruising on Evie's cheek. Seeing her twin suffer was just like being hurt herself. 'He did that to yer, didn't he?' Babs's voice was trembling with anger.

Evie laughed emptily. 'Don't be daft. I walked into the bloody door, didn't I? I went outside in the yard. For the lav. It was dark and I didn't have me torch. Yer know what this blackout's like.'

'Evie, what yer lying for? It's me, Babs, yer can't kid me. It *was* him, wasn't it?'

'Look, I'm a bit busy what with Christmas coming up and everything.' Eve pulled back the curtain again and opened the door. 'I've got a lot to do.'

'Well, if yer busy now, I'll come round tomorrow after work. We can have a chat then.'

'No. I'll drop round to number six in a day or so. When I've got a bit more time.'

★ ★ ★

It was nearly half past seven on Christmas Eve. Evie was standing in her kitchen, listlessly stirring a pot of soup for Albie's supper – at least soup didn't spoil when he came in late. Two weeks had gone by since she had seen Babs, but Evie still hadn't been to Darnfield Street.

Albie came in the kitchen with his arms full of brown paper parcels and dumped them on top of the Morrison shelter.

'Albie, what's all this? What's in 'em?' Evie put the wooden spoon on the draining board and smiled happily – he hadn't forgotten to buy her something after all.

Albie shrugged. 'Some of me "clients" reckoned they could get round me by giving me little "seasonal gifts",' he sneered. 'Bloody idiots. All I want's me dough off 'em. They can shove their bloody presents.'

He strode out of the kitchen and into the bedroom.

Evie followed him. 'I did me roots this afternoon,' she said, watching him as he stripped off his shirt and took a clean one from the drawer. 'So's I'd look nice if we went out tonight.' She paused. 'Being Christmas Eve and everything.'

'You mad?' Albie didn't even bother to look at her. He just got on with buttoning his shirt and fastening his cufflinks. 'What would I wanna be seen out with you for?'

Evie fought back her tears. 'If yer won't take me out, won't yer even stay indoors with me, Al? Just tonight? Please?'

'Aw, shut yer nagging.' Albie selected a tie and eased it under his collar.

'Go on then,' Eve shrieked, 'go out with yer fancy women. Yer no good, just like everybody told me.'

Albie said nothing. He coolly picked his jacket off the bed, slipped it on, turned to face Evie and then slammed his fist into her stomach, sending her reeling backwards and crashing into the wall.

303

As Evie ricocheted forward, her head jerked back; she opened her eyes and, in a blur, saw Albie disappearing through the door.

The next morning, Babs was in the kitchen at number six, doggedly cutting crosses into the stalks of Brussels sprouts. The last thing she felt like doing was celebrating Christmas when she knew, deep inside as only a twin could, that Evie was in trouble. But she also knew that she had to keep up appearances for her dad's sake. He was doing so well, settling into his new life at the fire station and, though he'd been so exhausted he'd not mentioned her so much the last few weeks – with Maudie. He still enjoyed a pint down the pub with his mates but he wasn't boozing to forget like he used to.

All that apart, Babs still couldn't settle. She kept looking up at the clock, wondering what Evie was doing, longing to go and fetch her, but knowing that the last thing her sister would want was for her to interfere.

She tossed the last of the sprouts into the pot and then opened the oven. The delicious smell of roasting pork filled the kitchen. And, despite her anxieties, she smiled as she thought of how proud her dad had been when he'd brought home the joint of meat, a gift from a grateful butcher whose shop Georgie and his pals had saved from being gutted by fire bombs.

She closed the oven and started setting the table for three – her, Georgie and Maud.

'Can't yer find room for a little one?' someone asked her.

Babs turned round. 'Evie!'

Eve ran her hands over her middle. 'Well, maybe not such a little one any more.'

Babs dropped the knives and forks and hugged her sister. 'Happy Christmas.'

'And you. Careful, yer'll squash me parcels.' Evie

dropped her packages on the table and then collapsed into Georgie's carver chair that still stood by the stove. 'Here, sort this lot out,' she sighed.

Babs went through the pile of bags. 'Oranges. Scotch! Where'd yer get this? Even Nellie ain't had none of this in for I dunno how long. And there's a . . . a . . . What *is* this?' Babs held a heavy, plucked bird up by its legs.

'It's a goose.' Evie winced as she spoke. 'Yer can cook it tomorrow.'

'Hark at me going on.' Babs knelt down by Evie's chair. 'And there's you, I've gotta say it, yer don't look well. What's wrong, you in pain?'

Evie tried to smile. 'I see that old photo of us in the passage still ain't got no glass on it.'

Babs stood up. 'All right, so you don't wanna tell me how you are, but I've been really concerned, yer know.' She went over to the sink and began collecting up the trimmings from the sprouts, wrapping them in half a sheet of old newspaper ready to give to Maudie for her hens. 'I wanted to come to see yer but I didn't feel that I was very welcome.'

'Where's Dad? He about?'

'No, he's gone to have a quick pint with Jim.'

'If he's on the sherbert again . . .' Evie began hauling herself up from the chair.

'No, yer all right, I really meant a quick pint. He's been as good as gold since he joined the service and since him and Maudie have been, you know, friends like.' She flicked her head towards the table. 'I've even laid a place for her. Dad's gonna knock and see if she wants dinner with us. He went along earlier but she must've already gone to church.' Babs looked up at the clock. It was a quarter past twelve. 'They'll be a while yet. Dad said they'd be here for one.' Babs squatted back down next to Evie's chair. 'Come on, why don't yer tell me what's up?'

'Me and Albie have had a few words. He went out last

night and he's been amongst the missing ever since.'

Babs did her best to sound cheerful and encouraging. 'He'll be round his mum's. Yer know what she's like, how she spoils him. He'll have stayed there the night.'

'Don't treat me like I'm stupid, Babs. You know as well as I do that he might well spend most days round there, but he wasn't round there last night.' Eve buried her face in her hands. 'He was off with some tart again. I know he was.'

'Eve, don't do this to yerself, yer can't carry on like this.'

'So you know all about being married, do yer? You ain't even seeing no one.'

'There's no need for that.'

'No. I'm sorry, Babs.'

'Don't let's have him spoil our Christmas. Come on, let's go down the Drum and see Dad. Have a drink with him. He'd like that.'

'How can I? Look at the state of me. Me face is all puffy and I look like a flaming barge.' As she stared up at Babs, Evie's eyes, with their purple smudges of exhaustion under them, looked huge in her pale, drawn face.

'It's up to you.' Babs shrugged. 'You sit there then and I'll finish clearing up.'

Babs busied herself with the dishcloth while Evie sat silently watching her.

It was nearly half past one when Georgie came in. Babs had already started dishing up the dinner.

She looked up from carving the pork. 'Hello, Dad,' she said, a broad smile on her face. 'Look who's here to see us.'

Evie hauled herself out of the chair and went over and kissed Georgie. 'Happy Christmas, Dad.'

Georgie hugged her to him. He stank of booze.

'Where's Maud, Dad?' Babs asked as she laid a thick slice of pork and a piece of crackling on each plate.

'She wasn't in.'

Eve flashed a glance at Babs. 'Must still be at church. Probably some special service for Christmas.'

'Yeah. Must be.'

Georgie hardly spoke during the meal, then he disappeared into the front room with the bottle of Scotch that Evie had brought.

'Shall I go and see if there's anything I can do?' Evie asked as Babs stacked the plates in the sink.

'What, interfere in someone else's private business, Evie? That's rich coming from you, Little Miss Secrets.'

'And how about you, Little Miss Perfect?'

'Aw, shut up.' Babs snatched the cloth from the draining board and began scrubbing furiously at the dirty pots and pans.

'No, *you* shut up. Do us all a favour.'

'Evie, here's a cup o' tea.'

As Evie stretched and yawned, the blanket that had been covering her legs fell to the floor. She sat up in the chair and blinked. 'What's going on? Where am I?'

'It's all right. Yer still here with me and Dad in Darnfield Street.'

'What time is it?' Evie rubbed her hands over her face. 'I feel like I've been asleep for hours.'

'You have. It's Boxing morning.'

'It's *what*?'

'Yer went out like a light last night. I tried to get you upstairs but I couldn't shift yer. And Dad was no help, he was out sparko and all.' Babs sighed loudly. 'Mind you, that was no wonder after the amount of Scotch he put away. Come on, drink yer tea.'

'I'll have to get going, Babs.' Evie tried to stand up, but her legs were numb from sleeping in the chair all night. 'I'll have to try and get a cab.'

'I dunno if there'll be any about this morning.'

'Well, I'll just have to walk, won't I? I'll drink this then I'll get going.' She took the cup from Babs and swallowed down the hot tea. 'I had a smashing time yesterday, Babs. Really smashing.'

Babs smiled ruefully. 'What, us two having a go at one another, then you sulking?'

'Yeah, just like it used to be.' Evie drew in her breath as she creaked her way over to the back door.

When she got back in from the lavatory, Babs was standing in the kitchen wearing her coat. She had Evie's coat over her arm.

'Where d'yer think you're going?

'With you.'

'No, Babs, thanks all the same, but it wouldn't help.' Evie let Babs help her on with her coat. 'I've gotta go.'

'Yeah, I suppose Albie will be wondering where yer got to. Will he be wild with yer?'

'Him?' Evie laughed off the idea. 'He won't mind. No.' Her fingers shook as she buttoned up her coat and picked up her handbag. 'He'll have got over our little tiff and he'll be nice as pie to me. No, it's, er, Flash I'm worried about. Yeah. Flash. See, I didn't mean to stay this long. The poor old girl'll have piddled herself by the time I get back home.'

'Can I come round and see yer in the week?'

Evie did her best to smile. 'I'd rather yer let me come and see you, Babs.'

'So long as yer promise.' She kissed Evie on the cheek.

'I promise.' Evie walked out into the passage and stopped by the door to the front room. 'I'll just go and say cheerio to Dad.'

'He ain't in there. He'd already gone out by the time I got up.'

Evie raised her eyebrows. 'D'yer reckon he's had words with Maud?'

Babs shrugged. 'I'm ain't sure, Eve, but something's

up. And I don't just mean with Dad neither.'

Evie sat in her kitchen shaking. She was on the edge of her seat, ready to jump up and get Albie his dinner the second she heard his key in the lock. She looked up at the clock, just as she had done every five minutes or so for the last hour. She knew that if Albie wasn't back soon, he wouldn't be coming in till much, much later. And when he did, he'd be drunk, foul-tempered and ready to hit her again at the slightest provocation, real or imagined.

She waited another hour then, caring less about the chance of an air raid than of Albie giving her a kicking, she made her way with Flash and her suitcase back to her old home in Darnfield Street. As she stumbled along the blacked-out streets, people kept bumping into her. It might have been still five hours until midnight, only just seven o'clock in the evening, but much to the annoyance of the wardens the streets were already full of people laughing and shouting, getting ready to see in the New Year as though there was no threat of bombs, no expectation of air raids, and no hangover to worry about in the morning.

'All right, all right,' shouted Babs, pulling open the door. 'Now what the hell's going on out here?' She took a moment to focus in the dark. 'Eve – what on earth are you doing here? And what was all that banging?'

Evie threw her bag into the passage. 'Sorry about that, but what with Flash and me suitcase, I couldn't get me key out. So I had to kick the door instead.'

Babs shut the door behind them and followed Evie into the kitchen.

'Sorry, Babs, I wasn't thinking. Look, yer all ready to go out,' said Eve, realising that her sister was dressed up to the nines. 'I can see I'm in the way.'

Babs led her sister over to the carver chair by the stove and sat her down, then she filled a bowl with water which she put down for Flash. 'Has that monkey bastard touched you?'

Evie tutted loudly. 'Don't be stupid, Babs. What sort of bloke'd hit a woman when she's six months' pregnant?'

'D'yer really want me to answer that?'

'I dunno what yer getting all wound up for, Babs. I just wanted to get out of the flat. I was so fed up with the bombing. It was that terrible raid the night before last that put the wind up me. You seen the papers? "Second fire of London" they're calling it.'

'Ne'mind all that old cobblers. Where's Albie? Why ain't he indoors with yer?'

Evie laughed unconvincingly. 'He's out on business, ain't he? Till all hours. Right busy he's been lately. So I thought, I ain't sitting here by meself all night waiting for them bombers to come over. I'll go and see Babs and Dad.'

Babs stared pointedly at the suitcase. 'I don't believe you, Evie. He's hurt yer, ain't he?'

'Leave off. As if I'd have anything to do with a bloke who hit me. And when have we ever kept secrets from one another?'

'You tell me.' Babs's expression was stony.

'I thought yer'd be pleased, seeing me for Old Year's night.'

'That ain't the point.'

'Look, Babs.' Evie's voice was wheedling, the voice she had always used since she was tiny when she wanted to get her own way with her twin. 'Albie's gonna be with his mum and dad, and yer wouldn't want me sitting round there in that dirty hole with them lot, would yer?'

'I thought yer said he was out on business.'

'Yeah, he is,' she said hurriedly. '*Then* he's going round his mum's.'

'That a fact?'

'Blimey, Babs, are yer gonna shut up and make me a

310

drink? Here.' Evie dug into her coat pocket and pulled out a big packet of tea.

'So that husband of your'n has got some uses then?' Babs said, slamming the kettle onto the stove.

'I had such a good time here on Christmas night.'

'So yer said. Yer've always liked a ruck.'

'I didn't mean that.'

'I dunno what yer do mean lately.'

'Dad on duty tonight?'

Babs shook her head as she took down cups and saucers from the shelf. 'No, he'll be back soon.'

'Good, I'll have a bit of company then.'

'I was gonna try and persuade him to come out with me.'

Eve gave the briefest of nods but, sulkily pushing out her bottom lip, she let her disappointment show.

'I'm only going down the Drum. It seems asking for it to go any further with how bad the bombing's been these last few nights. You come and all.'

'I don't think so.' Evie cocked her head at the sound of the front door opening and hauled herself out of her dad's carver chair. Ducking her head to catch her reflection in the little mirror by the sink, Evie pretended to be straightening her hair but was surreptitiously checking that there was no sign of the now almost faded bruising under the layers of powder. 'There's Dad now.'

Georgie looked exhausted. He had been on duty for seventy-two hours straight.

Evie smiled brightly at him. 'I've come to stay for a bit, Dad.'

He collapsed into the chair. 'I told yer, yer welcome to stay as long as yer want.'

'Fancy coming down the Drum?' Babs asked as she poured him a cup of tea. 'To see in the New Year.'

Georgie swallowed down the lukewarm tea. 'I'm too tired.' He closed his eyes and within moments was asleep.

Flash crept over to him and rested her muzzle on his leg.

Babs pulled down the corners of her mouth. 'I'm not going without you two.'

'I'll make us some fresh tea, shall I?' Evie didn't even bother to hide her pleasure that she had won and that they were both staying in with her after all.

'No thanks. I'm full up to me bloody ears with tea. I was hoping to have something proper to drink and a bit of a laugh.'

'Suit yerself, humpy. Tell yer what, I'll turn on the wireless, shall I?'

'If yer like. Might as well listen to the other lucky buggers enjoying 'emselves while I'm stuck in here.'

Evie made a great show of rubbing her back as she walked slowly towards the front room to go and turn on the wireless.

'Aw, leave off acting, Eve,' Babs snapped impatiently. 'Get out of me way and I'll do it.'

As she slipped past Evie and into the front room, the familiar wail of the air raid warning sirens filled the air.

'Well,' Babs said, turning to Evie with a broad grin. 'I never thought I'd be pleased to hear Moaning Minnie. Now we've gotta go down the Drum. And I've got me own way for once.'

Georgie appeared behind Evie with Flash straining on her lead. 'Come on then,' he said, his face haggard with fatigue. 'Let's be off.'

When they opened the door of the Drum, Nellie rushed over and practically dragged them into the bar. 'Hurry up and get down that cellar,' she grinned. 'Seeing you girls has proper made me night.' She winked at Georgie and took Flash's lead from him. 'And I reckon you being here's gonna make someone else's night and all.' She flicked her eyes over to where Maudie was standing by the bar, waiting to go down the steps into the cellar. 'That's all we've had out of her all night, Ringer:

312

"Does anyone know where George's been these last few days?'"

Despite her vanity about her size, Evie was soon thoroughly enjoying herself. She adored being back in company where she was fussed over and loved, and was delighted to find that being pregnant was far from the humiliation that Albie had forced her to feel; in fact, it was actually a bonus to her popularity. It didn't take long for her to be surrounded by admirers. She stood there, holding court, a sandwich in one hand, a drink in the other, determinedly working on coaxing Babs to join her in a sing-song.

Georgie was taking his pleasure a bit more warily. He stood by the bar, a makeshift arrangement of barrels and planks that Jim had set up earlier in the day, just in case, his forearms resting on the splintery surface, sipping slowly at a pint of best.

'Hello, George.'

He half turned and raised his glass to her. 'Maud.'

'Everyone's saying you're a hero.'

'I thought they was more interested in what my Evie was up to.'

Maudie looked over to where Evie had just persuaded Babs to join her in an effervescent rendition of 'Don't Sit Under The Apple Tree'. 'If that's true, George, she doesn't look too worried about it.'

Georgie twisted round and leant his back against the bar. 'If only she'd let me sort that Denham out. He'd never go near her again.' He took a long swallow of his beer. 'But I've gotta do what she wants, she's a grown woman now.'

'You're a good man, George.'

He looked at Maud, trying to figure her out. 'Drink?' he asked for want of something better to say.

'Thanks, a shandy'd be nice.'

'Nothing stronger?'

313

Maudie shook her head and Georgie beckoned to Jim.

He leant across the bar and watched Jim mixing the beer and lemonade while Maudie happily tapped her toe in time to the twins' song. But Evie suddenly stopped singing and shouted for silence. She held up her arm and pointed to her watch.

'Happy nineteen forty-one!' she yelled and threw her arms round Babs.

The room erupted into yells and whoops of good wishes and hopes for the New Year. Maudie touched Georgie gently on the back. As he turned round, she reached up and planted a kiss directly on his lips.

Georgie backed away, frowning.

Maudie's hand flew to her mouth. 'I'm sorry, George, I didn't mean anything. I let the moment get the better of me.'

'Don't be sorry, girl.' Georgie felt like a sixteen-year-old, his ears were burning and his heart thumped. 'Yer took me by surprise, that was all.'

They looked at each other, neither sure where it was all leading to, if anywhere.

They were saved from having to make any immediate decisions by Minnie, who dragged them away from the bar to join in with 'Auld Lang Syne'.

As their crossed arms pumped up and down to the rhythm of the familiar tune, Georgie ducked his head and whispered to Maud, 'Would yer think about letting me take yer out?'

'I'd be honoured.' Maudie had to yell into Georgie's ear to make herself heard.

At the end of the song it seemed that everyone was kissing or shaking hands with everyone else. Babs and Evie hugged their dad and wished him everything he would wish himself for the New Year.

'And you, darlings,' he said, letting his glance flick

across to Maudie who was being wished all the best by Blanche.

Babs nudged Evie. 'See that?' she mouthed.

Evie opened her eyes wide and nodded.

'Go and sing something, eh, girls? I fancy having a dance.'

The twins whispered conspiratorially to one another and made their way to the far end of the cellar where they began singing a series of smoochy love songs.

'Dance?' Georgie held out his hand to Maud and led her onto the crowded, makeshift dance floor.

As George held Maudie close to him, he felt a stirring that he hadn't felt for years; it made him want to weep at the waste of time that he had kidded himself could pass for a life.

'Maud.' His voice sounded husky as he whispered into her thick, sweet-smelling hair.

'Mmmm?'

'I want yer to know that I've had something on me mind lately.' George hesitated, not sure how to tell her about his confused feelings about the wedding dress she'd given Evie. At times he had almost convinced himself that she had got it from one of the women round the church but at other times . . . No, he didn't want to go over all that again, nor did he want to frighten her off by prying into what was, after all, private. If Maudie had been married and wanted to keep it a secret, then that was her business. 'This thing that's been worrying me, I wanted to sort it out, but I haven't known how. And it's been stopping me from doing what I really, deep down, want to do. But now I've come to a decision. I realise, I think, that at a time when people are risking everything and don't even know if there's gonna be a tomorrow, well, it just don't make sense to let it rule me and what I should be doing to make meself happy. I suppose.'

Maudie bent her head back and looked up at him. 'I

don't really understand what you mean, George. But I trust you and know you'll tell me about it when – if – you're ready. So I'll leave it at that.'

He nodded.

Evie and Babs finished their medley and took a break to have a drink. George ushered Maudie over to where their own drinks stood on the bar.

'I'm really pleased yer've asked me out, George,' she said quietly.

'Good.' He stared into his glass. 'So, what did yer do with yerself at Christmas?' He tried to keep his voice even.

Maudie took a little taste of her shandy. 'I went to church in the morning.' She looked up at him. 'I was hoping you might have come with me.'

'I . . .'

She held up her hand. 'No, George, I didn't mean for you to explain yourself to me. Well, one of the WVS came up to me after the service. She asked me if I'd be prepared to take in a family.' She put her glass down on the counter and slid it back and forth in a little puddle of beer. 'I *know* there's a lot of people who have lost their homes but I didn't really like the idea of strangers staying with me. It was a bit, well, frightening, I suppose. It was different when I asked the Jenners, I knew them. Anyway, she took me to the church hall and there were all these poor people, eating the Christmas dinner the WVS had made for them, doing their best to be cheerful.' She sighed loudly. 'What could I do? Say sorry, no room at the inn? So I said they should give me a week or so, so that I could organise beds and things.' She picked up her glass again. 'I'm expecting a family, the Dintons, to arrive at any time.'

'So that's where yer were.' It was a statement not a question.

Maudie looked at him quizzically.

'Me and the girls was hoping yer'd have yer Christmas dinner with us. We laid a place for yer and everything.'

She laid her hand on his arm and smiled up at him. 'Aw, George. If only I'd known.'

Georgie felt his heart racing at her touch. 'It's not right, you having strangers pushed on yer.'

She shrugged. 'It's not so bad.' She looked away, avoiding his eyes. 'And at least it'll make me feel a bit useful again. Because, well, since Evie's wedding, I've felt that something's happened, that there's been something wrong between us.'

Now it was Georgie's turn to look away. 'You've felt that, Maud?' His voice cracked as he spoke.

She nodded. 'Yes. I have. And it scares me. Because for a while, when I was helping Evie organise her wedding, I can honestly say I've never felt so much a part of things.' She hesitated. 'So much part of a family. I felt I was useful, needed. Wanted, even. I liked that feeling, George, and I didn't want to lose it.'

'That's why yer taking this family in?'

'Partly.' She lifted her eyes to look at him. 'And because I'm scared. I don't want to go back to the old days when I was just Miss Peters, the old spinster along the road that everyone felt sorry for.'

'No one feels sorry for yer, Maud.' He gnawed on his lip, then he looked at her and said, 'But yer mean widow, don't yer, Maud? Not spinster.'

Maudie frowned. 'I'm sorry? I don't—'

'It's nothing. Take no notice of me.' Georgie held up his glass, still almost half full of his first pint. 'It's the booze talking. Now, tell me about these lodgers.'

21

January 1941 brought with it even more bad weather and
also plenty for Alice to get her nose stuck into – and only
some of it was to do with the Bells. The gossip that Alice
was spreading to anyone in the market who cared to listen
was about Evie, who was still staying at number six
despite being pregnant and married to Albie Denham;
about Ringer, who had been seen, bold as brass and more
than once, with Maudie Peters on his arm walking along
the street for everyone to see; and about Babs, who
seemed to be permanently tired and in a foul mood most
of the time – pregnant maybe, Alice speculated, and
therefore no good, just like her mum and her sister. But
what really interested the vicious-tongued old bat was
what the Dintons, Maudie Peters's new lodgers, were
getting up to.

Alice had quickly established that the mother's name
was Tilly. Her marital status was left for others to guess at
and Alice to invent, but what was known for a fact, and
for once not just by Alice, was that she was a hard-faced,
brassy-looking type in her late thirties, not much older
than Blanche but looking years older with her heavy
layers of make-up and her rotten teeth and too tight
clothes. Her boy, Sonny, was thirteen. He seemed to
have the unnerving knack of appearing out of nowhere in
people's back yards and even, once or twice, in their back
kitchens, looking a picture of innocence but, more likely

than not, with his pockets stuffed to bulging with someone's prized possessions. Then there was Janette, Tilly's daughter. She was a good-looking girl of fourteen but, with the way she got herself up, she looked more like a twenty-one-year-old on the game than someone who had just left school. Blanche's daughter Mary, because of her fondness for, and proprietorial attitude towards Micky, Alice's grandson, shared the old gossip's immediate dislike of the flashy young girl. Much to Blanche's annoyance, for she didn't like that sort of talk, Mary let it be known that she suspected that Janette earned more from selling what she let the fellers get hold of than from what she had to sell on her counter in the Woolworth's at Aldgate.

Despite the local bad feeling that their presence was causing, Maudie did her best to make the Dintons welcome. She tried not to admit, even to herself, that she found them a truly awful bunch, because she had promised the WVS that she would help them. And Maudie wasn't one to break a promise if she could help it. So she really tried to put up with them and to ignore Tilly Dinton's moaning and her crafty ways and to forgive all the little things that went missing from the house and the complaints from Alice that she had seen young Janette sneaking soldiers into the house after the blackout.

By the February, Maudie had got into an odd sort of routine where, if she was going out for any length of time, she would lock anything of value in her wardrobe and, probably pointlessly, expressly forbid any of the Dintons to enter her bedroom. She didn't like doing it, but it was either that or throwing them out on the street. And she couldn't bring herself to do that, even though the streets were far safer than they'd been for months now that the big air raids, in London at least, seemed to be over. They would probably have found an abandoned place somewhere, but it was too cold to wish that even on the Dintons.

The alternative was to return the whole dreadful lot of them to the WVS with a strongly worded reprimand to the organiser about her thoughtlessness in landing her with such a family, but that would mean them living in the church hall until another mug – because that's what she now realised she was – could be found to take them in. And, as the war dragged on, those mugs were few and far between. For a whole month now it had been practically nonstop low cloud, rainy nights, freezing mist and fog, the sort of weather that both depressed you and made your very bones ache with the damp. Much as she felt like it at times, Maudie knew she couldn't inflict the privations of living in the barely heated church hall with its cold hard floors and its endless round of other bombed-out families on anybody. No, not even on the Dintons. So the Dintons had, in their insidious way, settled themselves very comfortably into number seven and into Maudie Peters's life.

Evie had also made herself comfortable in Darnfield Street. It was clear to Babs, and Georgie too if he'd ever admitted to thinking about such a thing, that Evie had made no attempt whatsoever to go back to her flat in the Mile End Road. But then Albie had made no attempt to come and fetch her. He hadn't even been to see her to talk things over.

Evie spent her time much as she had done in the flat, except that now she had someone other than Flash to complain to and to shelter with when the sirens started screeching their shrill warnings in the night.

Evie seemed happy to sit back while Babs went to work and looked after the house and Georgie, and her and the dog as well. She was beginning to get on Babs's nerves by playing on her 'condition', as she had taken to calling her pregnancy. She seemed to be happy to divide her time

321

into either moaning about her loss of freedom to go out and have a good time, or acting like a holy martyr rubbing various bits of her body, complaining about the aches and pains that she was having to endure for the sake of the unborn child.

It was nearly seven o' clock in the evening and Babs had only just stepped in the front door. She had been out since before half past six that morning; she was tired out and she was angry.

'If that's you, Babs, come in here and see to this fire,' Evie groaned pitifully from the front room.

'Can't it wait a minute?' Babs called back to her from the passage. She shivered as she took off her coat and slung it over the banister. 'I've just got in from work. I had to walk nearly all the way from Aldgate.'

'I thought yer was late. I was worried the fire'd go out.'

Evie's wheedling voice set Babs's teeth on edge. She took a deep breath and threw open the front room door. 'What's the matter with you doing it? Got yer fat arse stuck in the chair?'

Evie's lip quivered. 'Even you think I'm ugly now I'm pregnant,' she wailed, making a full dramatic production of shifting herself to a more comfortable position in the armchair by the hearth.

Babs controlled herself. 'No, Eve, I don't think yer ugly.' She knelt by the grate and raked through the cinders until they glowed, then she shook in some coal from the scuttle and hauled herself back to her feet.

'You don't seem in a very good mood,' Evie pouted. 'I was looking forward to having a bit of company when you got in, but yer've come home all humpy. Who's upset yer? That Ginny from work?'

Babs looked at her coal-blackened hands. 'What's for tea?' she asked over her shoulder as she walked out of the room.

'Charming. Don't bother to answer me, will yer?' Evie

got up and followed Babs into the kitchen. 'Thought we could have some sandwiches.' She smiled sweetly and looked down at her hands resting on her stomach. 'And that you wouldn't mind making 'em. 'Cos of me condition, like.'

Babs looked at her as if she had gone mad. 'Sandwiches? But Dad'll be in soon and he'll need some proper grub.' She jerked her thumb behind her. 'D'yer really think I'm gonna be able to make a meal for the three of us out of that miserable specimen of cheese?'

Evie's eyes grew wide. 'No hope of that,' she giggled, pointing to the table.

Babs turned round just in time to see Flash stealing the small piece of Cheddar cheese off the table. 'Aw wonderful, that was the whole bloody ration and all.'

Eve flopped down into the carver chair by the stove. 'It's all right, there's plenty more where that came from.'

Babs frowned. 'How d'yer mean, plenty more?'

Eve waved towards a cardboard box on the draining board. 'Chas was round here just now. He come to fetch all that stuff. Albie sent him with it.'

'So that's why he was here.'

'Eh?'

'I saw him when I was coming along. Up the top of the street, he was, trying to get a cab. Too stupid to walk along to Mile End to get one.' Babs went over to the sink and started sorting through the box for something to make a meal with. 'This arrangement seems to be suiting Albie,' she said, putting a tin of corned beef to one side. 'He don't seem to be missing you. Or the dog.'

'That's where yer wrong, clever dick,' Evie snorted. 'Why d'yer think he sent all this stuff round? 'Cos he cares for me. I'm here because he likes me having company while he's so tied up with his business, that's all. He's been really busy lately.'

Babs unhooked the string bag of potatoes from the nail

under the sink. 'Corned beef hash?' she asked.

Evie nodded sulkily.

Babs filled a saucepan with water and began peeling the potatoes into the sink. 'Why'd yer keep on kidding yerself, Eve? He's a no-good bastard and he couldn't care less about yer.'

'Yer just jealous, I've said it all along.'

'Look, Eve, we both know all about him being busy and what he gets up to.'

'What's that supposed to mean? Other women?'

'That and all, but you know exactly what I mean.' Babs looked over her shoulder at Evie and shook her head contemptuously. 'Business? Don't make me laugh. Ducking and diving, that's the only business Albie Denham's ever known. And don't look so hurt, Evie, you know full well what he's up to. He's making all this dough out of the war while people are suffering and going without.'

'I thought better of you, Babs. They're all stories and rumour-mongering. Yer no different to bloody Alice Clarke and her street-corner gossip if yer believe all that shit about my Albie.'

Babs dropped the knife into the sink and twisted round to face her sister. She stuck her fists into her waist. 'Aw yeah? Gossip? Well, let me tell yer some home truths about *your Albie*. When I saw Chas just now, the stupid sod thought he was impressing me showing off what he knows about your precious husband. He's hijacking lorries in the blackout, did yer know that? Fags, clothes, booze – you name it. Aw yeah, and the warehouse raids. That's another little line of his.'

Babs leant forward. Evie could feel her hot breath on her face as she spoke.

'Albie Denham is bribing dockers so that him and his cronies can nick food that should be on the tables of decent people like your own dad, Evie. And while blokes like Dad're risking their lives for the likes of him, that ponce is swanning around up West in and out of clubs with a different tart on his arm every night.'

She went over to the draining board and tossed the corned beef back into the box.

'I dunno what I was even thinking of, I'd rather starve than eat his filthy food. And so would Dad.'

Evie sat silently staring at the floor.

'Sending Chas round here with all this. Couldn't even face coming round here himself, could he? And that money, that's just to keep yer quiet. Bloody conscience money, that's what that is.'

'Money?' Evie asked. Her voice was tiny.

'Yeah, money.' Babs reached into the box, pulled out a handful of notes and waved them under Evie's nose. 'Yer'd better get used to it, Eve, he don't want nothing to do with yer. He's bought you off. And the sooner you realise it the better.'

A single tear rolled down Evie's cheek.

Babs bowed her head. 'Don't start crying, Eve,' she said, her anger spent. 'He ain't worth it.' She picked up the tea towel and wiped Evie's face with it. 'Me and my big mouth, I didn't mean to upset yer. I was just angry, that's all.'

'But it ain't you in this state,' Evie said, her voice flat and lifeless. 'So what you gotta be angry about?'

'Aw Evie, can't yer see? I'm angry 'cos of the way the rotten bastard's treating you. Yer me sister and I love yer, Evie.' Babs folded her arms round her twin and rocked her, letting her sob. 'And I'm fed up with this sodding cold weather,' she whispered, fighting back her own tears. 'And with this whole bloody, stinking, rotten war.'

22

'But yer can't have started, it ain't due for at least a couple of weeks.'

'I can't help that, Babs,' panted Evie, grasping at the sheets as though they were life-saving ropes keeping her secured to a mountainside.

'We've gotta get down the Drum.' Babs looked up at the ceiling as though it were transparent. 'The planes are already on their way over. Listen.' She threw Evie's coat onto the bed. 'It must be the warning that's brought you on early.'

Evie gritted her teeth. 'I don't care about no poxy air raids, Babs. They're hardly a surprise, are they? Now, for Christ's sake, *do something*.'

'I'll fetch Ethel, she usually helps out with babies, don't she?'

Evie wiped her damp hair back off her forehead. 'No, Babs, not Ethel, don't bring her.'

'Shall I go and fetch Blanche?'

'Yeah. Do that.'

Relieved to be doing something, Babs walked hurriedly out of the bedroom and was down the stairs in a moment. But before she had a chance to open the front door, Evie was calling down to her.

'Don't go, Babs. Don't leave me. I'm scared.'

Babs ran back upstairs. She leant over the big double bed and frowned down at her twin. She looked like a little girl, all wide-eyed with fear.

'What d'yer want me to do?'

Evie's face contorted as another wave of pain shuddered though her body.

Babs backed away. 'Look, I don't wanna leave yer, but it's only next door. I'll be one minute.'

Evie groaned.

Babs swallowed hard. 'I think it's best if I fetch Blanche.'

Babs bashed on Blanche's door. No reply. The sirens had stopped so perhaps they were already sheltering in the pub. She pulled her coat tighter round her and glanced up at the sky as she dashed across the street to the Drum. The searchlights picking up the suggestion of the outline of a plane in the cloudy night sky still gave her the creeps, even after all those months of bombing.

The bar was empty but she could hear the sounds of laughter and talking coming from the cellar. She almost smiled to herself as she pulled up the cellar door and picked her way down the wide, shallow steps; sheltering had become quite a popular event for some people.

'We wondered where yer were,' said Clara, the first to see her. 'Whatever's up, darling? Yer white as a sheet.'

'It's Evie, she's started. Please, Blanche, yer've gotta come. She's asking for yer.'

Blanche handed Janey to Mary and grabbed her coat. 'She indoors?'

Babs nodded frantically and practically dragged Blanche towards the cellar steps. 'She's in a bad way.'

'Don't worry, Babs,' Minnie called after them in her brash, warm-hearted way. 'She might as well be at home as in the laying-in ward. If it's like the hospital where me and Clara work, there ain't hardly nothing left, all the gear's been nicked for the forces. Everyone's saying so.'

Babs knew from the tone of Minnie's voice that she was

trying to be kind but she didn't take in a word of what she was saying. Nor did she respond to all the shouts of good wishes that followed. All she could think about was getting back to Evie.

Maudie stood up. 'Wait,' she said, pulling on her coat. 'I'll go with you.'

Nellie pointed at Terry. 'Youngster like you can run fast. D'you think you can go and see if Dr Land's in?'

Terry looked pleased to be included in the excitement; he liked the idea of being able to do something for Evie, but he knew what his mum was like. He glanced over to her for permission.

Blanche nodded. 'Go on.'

'And tell him I'm paying,' added Nellie. She held out her hand to Jim who immediately dug in his pocket. 'And you make sure yer watch yerself. If it's too bad out there, don't take no silly risks.'

Alice surprised everyone by saying to her grandson, 'You go with him, Micky. Keep an eye on him.' She looked round at the shocked faces. 'Well, it's a baby involved, ain't it?'

Terry and Micky disappeared along Grove Road in search of Dr Land, while Babs, Blanche and Maudie ran along Darnfield Street as fast as their legs would carry them, the metallic report of their shoes hitting the road sounding clear and sharp in the cold night air. But that sound could hardly compete with the droning of planes overhead, the staccato clatter of anti-aircraft guns coming from Victoria Park or with the blood pulsing in their ears.

'Door's on the jar,' Babs gasped, shoving it open to let the other two inside. 'Front bedroom.'

'Thank gawd yer back,' they heard Evie wail as they scrambled up the stairs. 'I thought yer'd left me.'

'I wouldn't leave yer.' Babs sat on the side of the bed and took Evie's hand.

Blanche stood at the end of the bed. 'Right, let's see

329

'what's going on here then,' she said brightly, peeling off her coat.

'I'm being ripped apart,' Eve panted, digging her nails into Babs's palm. 'That's what's going on.' She twisted her head sideways. 'I wish Dad was here,' she wailed.

'Don't think he'd be much use,' Blanche said with a little laugh as she rolled up her sleeves ready for action.

'I don't think I'm going to be much use either,' said Maudie from the doorway.

'Yer can boil a kettle, can't yer?' Blanche asked over her shoulder.

Evie looked horrified. 'What d'yer want boiling water for?'

Blanche went round the side of the bed and stroked Evie's forehead. 'To make us all a cuppa tea, yer daft hap'orth.'

'I'll be two ticks,' said Maudie, glad to have a job.

'Bring that lamp over here, Babs. Have yer got a clock?' She looked down at Evie. Her hair was soaked with sweat and her lips were drawn back over her teeth as she panted through another contraction. 'Don't suppose yer've been timing 'em or nothing, have yer?'

Babs shook her head and answered for her twin. 'I didn't think.'

Blanche smiled up at Babs. 'Don't fret. We'll get by. And anyway, this is all good practice for me. My Ruby's due next month. Yer should see her Davey's letters, he's been getting himself in a right state. Made me promise on me life to be there with her. As if I wouldn't.'

Blanche timed three contractions. They were close together, very close.

She looked into Evie's eyes; there was real terror in them. 'Got any draw sheets ready?' she asked, being careful to keep a cheery lift in her voice.

'Draw sheets?' Babs said blankly.

Evie looked imploringly at her sister, and then her face

330

crumpled in despair. 'I ain't got nothing, Blanche. I didn't think this was ever really gonna happen.' She started sobbing. 'I thought I'd wake up and it'd all be gone away.'

'Yer silly little thing,' Blanche said softly, stroking her hand. She felt choked for Evie, she looked so scared. She was no longer the noisy, boisterous young woman who'd stand up to anyone and do anything for a laugh, but a frightened little girl. 'Don't you worry yerself. We can make do for sheets.'

Maudie came back into the bedroom carrying a tin tray laden with a teapot, cups and milk. 'I've got plenty of linen indoors,' she offered, setting the tea things on the dressing table.

'Good.' Blanche was now all calm efficiency. 'And if yer've got any brown paper, fetch that and all. Or newspaper if yer ain't.'

Evie groaned again.

Babs gnawed at her bottom lip as she felt herself getting close to panic.

As Maudie put her coat back on, they all looked up at the ceiling as the sound of an aircraft engine grew louder and closer.

'One of ours,' said Blanche confidently.

'I don't like it, Blanche,' Evie shouted. She grasped the sides of the mattress, her knuckles white with the strain. 'Stop it hurting me. Please.'

'Ssshh,' Blanche soothed her. 'You wait till it's born, yer won't remember none of this. How yer feel for 'em takes all this away.'

Blanche continued chatting, trying to keep Babs's and Evie's spirits up, trying to remain calm while Babs grew paler by the minute and Evie became more and more distressed.

She soaked a flannel in a basin of cold water and put it gently on Evie's sweat-soaked forehead. 'They kind of become part of yer, kids. I miss my Lennie so much, yer know. Little sweetheart, he is. But that's what he had his little heart set on, going back to Cornwall. So I couldn't disappoint him, could I? Mind, bit of luck our Terry never got it in his head to go back there with him. Dunno what I'd have done. He's running that stall with Micky a treat, he is. Just like a proper little man.' She wrung the flannel out and resoaked it. 'He's always had an eye for you twins, yer know that Terry, young as he is.' She laughed. 'But then, what feller ain't?'

Evie's face twisted in pain.

'And my Archie, well, I miss him more than I can begin to tell yer. He writes regular but, I don't know, yer still worry about what might happen.'

A loud crash came from somewhere nearby. The dressing table shuddered and a sprinkling of plaster fell from the ceiling onto the bed.

'Listen to them bombs.'

Blanche couldn't quite keep the edge of fear from her voice. 'Maybe we should get you downstairs, darling.'

Evie screamed, then she began whimpering softly to herself; it was the sound of a frightened child. 'I don't wanna have it, Blanche. Blanche. Please. Help me.' She thrashed her head from side to side. 'Please. Please, make it stop.'

Blanche grabbed her hands. 'It's too late for that, darling.'

Babs looked ready to bolt as Evie screamed again.

'All right, all right.' Blanche's voice came in gasps from the pain of Evie sinking her nails into her arm. 'Now, calm down. There's a good girl.' Blanche looked over her shoulder at Babs. 'Tell yer what,' she said, desperately trying to keep smiling. 'I'm glad we never got them Anderson shelters down Darnfield. When they first come out, I was like Alice, right jealous. Wanted one for the kids, see. But now I've heard how they flood right out in this bad weather. Can you imagine? Horrible. All that mud. We're better off in the Drum, I'm telling yer.'

As she heard Maudie coming up the stairs, Blanche could have wept with relief that she was back – someone who wasn't panicking and who could give her a bit of help was just what she needed. But when Maudie appeared in the doorway, Blanche's relief melted away.

'Whatever's up, Maud? Yer look like yer've seen a ghost.'

'This is all I've got.' Maudie sounded stunned as she put a few sheets of paper, some big white towels and a set of sheets on the end of the bed. She looked round at Babs and then back to Blanche and Evie. 'I had something for you, Eve. Something I'd been saving for today. A lovely lace nightgown, it was.'

'Here, sit down.' Blanche stood up and put her arm round Maudie and guided her to the dressing table stool. 'Yer place ain't been hit, has it?'

'No. It's not that.' Maudie shook her head sadly. 'The Dintons, my lodgers. When I got back they'd disappeared. Been right though my wardrobe. Taken all the things that I kept in there. A whole pile of stuff. Things that I'll never be able to replace.' She swallowed back her tears. 'And the nightgown. Someone bought it for me years ago. It was lovely, Eve. And it was for you.'

'Yer know what they can do with the sodding nightgown, don't yer?' panted Evie. Her hair was stuck flat to her head, and her eyes were closed tight with pain. 'Same thing they can do with all sodding men. I hate bloody men. All of 'em. Every single, sodding rotten one of 'em. They can—' She let out an ear-piercing shriek. Her fingers dug deep into the mattress.

Blanche bent over her. 'Come on now, Eve,' she said briskly, knowing she had to keep her going, that she mustn't let her get hysterical. 'Yer nearly there. Just a few more pushes.'

'I can't.'

'Don't be silly. Come on,' she encouraged her. 'Just get on with it. Soon be over.'

Evie puffed and swore and grunted and cursed all men. Then she gave one almighty yell.

Blanche bent over her and then nodded to Maud to hand her the scissors.

'Hello, sweetheart.' Blanche no longer sounded cool and capable – she was cooing in a tone of voice that Maud knew could mean only one thing. 'Let's just snip this for yer, shall we? Then we're in business, ain't we? Yes, we are.'

When she straightened up, Blanche had a baby in her arms.

Blanche looked down into the tiny infant's screwed up little face. 'Right in the middle of all these bombs and you popped out, all perfect and beautiful, and right here in the front bedroom of yer grandad's house. Just wait till he sees you, you little angel.'

Babs stood there with her mouth open.

Maudie got up and rushed round to the head of the bed and plumped the pillows, making Evie as comfortable as she could, all thoughts of the Dintons banished from her mind. Like Babs, she was on the verge of tears.

Evie just looked dazed and exhausted.

The baby let out a lusty, lung-stretching screech as Blanche wiped its eyes, nose and mouth with a flannel. 'March the ninth, nineteen forty-one,' she said softly. 'It's your birthday today, darling. Yes, it is. Aw, you're so beautiful. Look at them little fingers and toes.'

Blanche carefully wrapped the baby in one of Maudie's towels and handed it to Evie. 'There y'are, darling. Yer've got a lovely little girl.'

Evie gingerly took the child in her arms. 'Betty,' she said, her voice hoarse from her exertions. She looked up through puffy, bloodshot eyes. 'After Betty Grable.'

334

Babs didn't know whether to laugh or cry.

A loud knocking made them all look up.

Maudie leant forward to get a closer look at the baby then said, 'I'll go down and see who it is.' She was no longer bothering to hold back her tears. 'And I'll make some more tea.'

Evie held the baby out for Blanche to take. 'Try and straighten me up a bit, Babs,' she said urgently. 'It might be Albie.'

Blanche took Betty reluctantly. 'Yer should be putting her to yer breast, yer know, to get the milk going.'

Evie looked up at Blanche as though she'd taken leave of her senses. 'It might be Albie, Blanche.'

Babs looked across the bed to Blanche, willing her to say something.

'I don't think so, Eve,' Blanche said. 'Albie won't know yet, will he?' She put the baby over her shoulder and patted its back. 'It's probably Dr Land. Terry and Micky went for him.'

Eve sank back into the pillows and closed her eyes. She made no attempt to take the baby back from Blanche.

Someone rapped on the frame of the bedroom door.

'Come in,' Babs said and did her best to shift out of the way in the already crowded room.

Dr Land came in and sat on the edge of the bed. He smiled down at Evie. 'You're Evie? Babs?'

'She's Evie,' said Babs.

Dr Land nodded. 'So, Evie. How did you do?'

'How d'yer think?' Evie said. She had a sad, distant look about her.

Blanche laughed pleasantly. 'It was fine, Doctor. I only had to catch the little mite.'

Evie said nothing.

'Evie, would you like them to wait outside while I check you over?'

335

Evie shrugged noncommittally. 'They can stay if they like.'

'We'll go if yer prefer,' Blanche said kindly. 'Leave you to a bit of privacy, eh? Coming, Babs?'

'Don't go. Please.' There was panic in Evie's voice. 'I don't wanna be by meself.'

Blanche grinned at Dr Land. 'Yer'll regret that in a day or two. You wait, yer'll be willing to do anything for a bit of peace. Why don't yer make the most of it?'

'I don't wanna "bit of peace".' Evie sounded hard. 'I don't wanna be quiet. I'm fed up with being quiet.'

'All right, Eve,' Babs reassured her. 'We'll stay here with yer.'

While Dr Land got on with his examination, Blanche handed Babs the baby, knelt down on the floor and set about improvising a cot from one of the dressing table drawers and the rest of Maudie's towels.

Babs sat down on the stool in front of the dressing table. She looked at the reflection of herself holding the baby, her niece, Albie Denham's daughter. 'Should I send a note round for Albie, Eve?' she asked.

'Terry'll go, if yer like,' Blanche said, lifting her head. 'If yer want him to, that is, Eve.'

'Yeah, send him a note, Babs. But to the flat. Not round to his mum's. I don't want that old cow Queenie coming round.'

Dr Land frowned. Albie? Queenie? Those names were familiar.

Maudie stood in the doorway with another tray of tea. 'I'll just bring this in.'

'I mean it, Babs, I don't want that old bag near me.'

'It's been quite a while since I've seen you, Evie, or your twin,' Dr Land said. 'I don't even know your married name.'

'Denham,' Evie said flatly. 'Mrs Albie Denham.'

Dr Land stood up and busied himself with washing his

336

hands in the basin on the bedside table. He wasn't a native East Ender but, like anyone who'd lived there for any time at all, he had learned to mind his own business and not to offer any opinions about people's way of life. And he knew all about the Denhams and certainly didn't fancy getting involved in their family squabbles. He'd make sure the girl and baby were all right – he wouldn't want to upset anyone – then he'd be off. As soon as possible.

'Promise me, Babs,' Evie pleaded. 'Keep her away. All she wants to do is poison Albie against me.'

The baby started crying.

'Now, you have to calm down,' Dr Land said firmly. 'You're absolutely fine, young lady but if you start getting yourself all worked up, you won't be able to feed her. And that's what she wants now. She's hungry.'

'Feed her?' Evie was horrified. 'I ain't feeding her. She can have a bottle.'

Dr Land looked exasperated.

Blanche took Evie's hand. 'What'll happen when you have to run down the shelter and there's no bottle there for the poor little love?'

Evie shuddered with disgust. 'Don't, Blanche. The thought of having to feed her, and in front of all them people in the Drum what's more, makes me feel sick. No, yer not gonna persuade me. She's having the bottle and that's final.'

Dr Land looked round the little room. He was beginning to get a headache. 'Have you got any bottles?'

'No.'

He turned to Blanche. He knew her to be a respectable sort. 'Mrs Simpkins?'

'Yeah, I've got some indoors, Doctor. From Janey.'

'Good. So, if you can organise that? And I'll leave you some Epsom Salts, Evie, to help dry you up.' He took a box out of his bag and handed it to Babs. 'You might be

337

best moving your sister downstairs when she feels strong enough,' he said, nodding at the box. 'So she can be near the lavatory.'

'Dry me up! Be near the lav?' Evie covered her face with her hands. 'How the hell did I get into all this?'

Almost as soon as the all clear sounded the next morning, Babs, Blanche and Maud were taking turns to let people into number six. Baby things were either in short supply or rationed, just like everything else, but the neighbours, even those who very publicly disapproved of Evie's way of life, raked round in their cupboards and drawers to 'sort out a few bits' for her and the little girl.

Nellie was one of the first to arrive. When she saw Betty she could hardly speak she was so choked up.

When she had finished the cup of tea that Maudie insisted on making for her, she sat by Evie and held the baby in her arms. 'If only me and my Jim had been as blessed,' she sighed. 'Even one kiddy like Rita and Bert had would have been a miracle. Still, mustn't get all humpy. It wasn't to be and that's that.' She stroked her finger tenderly across Betty's cheek. 'Will yer just look at her.' She held her out for Evie to take from her and reached into her handbag. She put a two shilling piece in the baby's tiny hand. 'There y'are, sweetheart,' she said, folding Betty's tiny fingers round the silver coin in the traditional East End way. 'You hold on to that and yer'll always have good luck and never want for nothing.' She looked at Evie. 'And here's a little present.' She held out a flat, leather-covered box.

Eve took it from her but just dropped it onto the bedcover without bothering to open it.

'Yer must be tired,' Nellie said. 'Here, let me.' She undid the catch and showed Evie what was inside. On a pad of pale cream velvet was a delicately entwined gold chain holding a heart-shaped locket. 'For when she's

338

older,' beamed Nellie, holding it for the baby to see. 'I've had it put by for a month or so now, just hoping it'd be a little girl. Couldn't resist it, could I, when one of the customers brought it in?' Nellie leant forward and kissed Evie on the cheek. 'I'll let yer get yer rest now.'

Evie nodded listlessly.

'Has Ringer seen her yet?' Nellie asked as she got up.

'No,' Babs said. 'Blanche's Terry took a message round the station early this morning but Dad's crew was still at a fire.'

'He'll be like a dog with two tails when he sees her. Tell him to pop in for a drop to wet the baby's head when he gets back.'

As Babs saw Nellie out, Rita from the baker's came along the street. She was pushing a big, old-fashioned pram.

'What's this?' Nellie grinned, poking Rita in the ribs. 'You ain't had a little surprise and all, have yer, Reet?'

Rita grinned back. 'No such luck, Nell. Putting jam in doughnuts is about all Bert can manage nowadays. This was my Bill's. I got it all cleaned up for Evie a while back. Didn't wanna bring it round till the baby was born though. I mean, yer don't wanna tempt fate, do yer?'

And so it went on, with people popping in and out of number six nearly all day. They brought gifts, offers of help and their best wishes. And Evie couldn't have cared less. If they had been coming to see her, she would have been pleased to see them, but all they could talk about was the baby, and it was getting on her nerves.

Babs put a soup dish down on the bedside table. 'Try a drop of this what Maud sent along for yer, Eve.'

'Sure the soup ain't for Betty?' Eve sniped, turning her head away.

'Don't be silly. Come on, yer've gotta eat something.'

Evie shifted onto her side and stared at the wall. 'I don't want it, Babs. Take it away.'

Babs picked up the dish and left the room.

Evie rolled onto her back and closed her eyes. It was a nightmare, that's what it was, it wasn't really happening to her at all. Here she was, not even nineteen and her life was over.

'Eve?'

She took a deep breath. 'Babs, I told yer. I don't want the poxy soup.'

'I know. Yer've got a visitor.'

'I've had enough visitors to last me a rotten lifetime. Tell 'em I'm too tired.'

'What? Too tired for me, darling?'

Evie's eyes flicked open. 'Albie!'

'I got this note from Babs.' He was standing over her. His big handsome face was smiling.

Evie smiled back at him.

'Yer looking better than I thought yer would,' he said.

He dropped down heavily onto the bed, and even though it jarred her sore and aching body, she didn't flinch. Albie didn't like people who were sick or under the weather and she didn't want him to get all upset and leave.

He chucked her under the chin. 'You'll have that figure of your'n back in no time, won't yer, babe? Then I'll take yer up West and show yer off again, all done up like my little platinum doll.'

Just as Evie put her arms round his neck and lifted her face to kiss him, Betty woke up and started to cry, making low whimpering sounds as she snuffled round for food.

Evie looked over Albie's shoulder and flashed her eyes at Babs, signalling urgently for her to do something.

Babs rolled her eyes and went over to the drawer at the bottom of the bed. She picked up the crying baby and took her outside onto the landing. As she jiggled Betty up and down over her shoulder, she could hear what Albie was saying to Eve, even over Betty's cries.

'Cor,' he complained. 'Does she make that racket all the time? And what's that smell in here? Sick?'

There was a pause then Albie spoke again; he had an impatient laugh in his voice. 'I think it'll be best,' he said, 'if you and the nipper stay here for a while. Till it gets a bit bigger. I mean, girl, that flat ain't no place for a kid, now is it?'

23

By the time Betty was six weeks old, Evie was back to her old self. At first, Babs was relieved that she'd got over the baby blues so quickly. She had her figure back, her dark roots had been freshly bleached and she was going out enjoying herself again. But when she showed no signs of any maternal interest in her daughter or even a touch of domesticity, Babs wasn't sure that she was so relieved after all. Especially as Evie didn't even think to ask her if she minded when she left her caring for Betty every night, while she divided her time between going out with Albie – when he deigned to see her – and doing the rounds of the local pubs. At least when Evie had been depressed she'd stayed indoors.

Babs threw her coat over the banister and hauled herself up the stairs to the front bedroom. Thursday night, she reminded herself, so only one more day at work before the weekend and the chance of having a rest. But no matter how tired she felt, she was still elated at the prospect of seeing her little niece, always the first thing she wanted to do when she got in from work.

She crept into the bedroom so as not to disturb her, but pulled up short in the doorway when she saw Evie sitting at the dressing table smoothing her long blonde hair into a careful roll round a twisted scarf that she had fastened to the back of her head.

Evie didn't greet her sister, she just looked at her

343

reflection and asked, 'So, what do yer think? It's all the go, this look.'

'I think yer taking the piss if yer going out again, Eve. That's what I think.' Babs bent over the drawer that stood on the ottoman at the bottom of the bed. The sight of her beautiful little niece, tucked up so cosily in the pale pink blanket that Blanche had given her, made her smile.

'I'll have to remember to take a rag out with me to wipe me legs,' sighed Eve, as she began applying the first layer of lipstick. 'There's mud and rubbish all over them bloody streets from the bombsites. Someone should do something about it.'

Babs straightened up and stuck her hands on her hips. 'Shut up about the mud a minute, Eve, and tell me where you think you're going.'

'Out.'

'Where?'

'Some feller I met the other night, his mate's got a boozer up Whitechapel way. He's asked me to sing a few songs in there tonight. Give all the soldier boys a bit of a treat while they're home on leave.' She smacked her lips together to blot the lipstick then grinned into the mirror. 'And they'll have all that lovely back pay to spend. It'll make a nice change enjoying meself.'

'Nice change? Yer out nearly every night of the week.'

Evie raised her eyebrows and shrugged.

'Ain't it about time yer thought about going back to yer flat? This room was crowded enough when it was just the two of us.'

Eve twisted round on the stool to face Babs. 'You saying me and the baby ain't welcome?'

'Course not, and keep yer voice down, yer'll wake her up. But it don't seem right, Betty not being with her dad. What must Albie think? You and the baby hardly ever see him.'

'Albie? Don't make me laugh.' She turned back to the

344

mirror and began dusting her face with powder. 'Why should I worry about him? He only ever turns up when he ain't got nothing better to do. Or he fancies a bit of how's yer father.' She grinned at Babs's reflection. 'Not that he's had any luck there for a while.'

Babs tried another tack. 'Don't yer wanna stay in, spend some time with the baby?'

'Here, you saying yer don't wanna look after her?' Evie countered.

'No. Yer know I'm not. It's just that you're her mum.'

'Yeah? So? I have her all day.' Evie spoke to Babs as if she were stupid. 'And you like being with her. So everyone's happy. So what's the problem?'

Evie had only been gone half an hour when yet another raid started. Babs was torn between making the dash along the street to the Drum in the chilly evening air with all the things needed to keep Betty fed and comfortable, or staying put and sheltering under the table. But, tired as she was, she knew she had to keep Betty safe. So she gathered up bottles and nappies, threw them in a basket, lifted Betty gently out of the drawer and wrapped her in a blanket.

'Let's just hope yer mum's safe, eh, sweetie?' Babs whispered to the baby, and made a run for it.

The next morning, bleary-eyed from spending yet another uncomfortable night sleeping on a makeshift bed and tending to Betty, Babs crawled back to number six. There was no sign of Evie.

She laid Betty in Rita's big old pram that almost took up the entire passageway and went into the kitchen. She put the kettle on to boil for tea, steeped the night's dirty nappies in the enamel bucket outside the back door and then, summoning what she felt was the very last of her energy, had a wash in cold water at the sink.

She peered up at the clock over the top of the towel.

345

Wherever Evie had got to, Babs hoped she'd hurry up; she had to leave for work in half an hour.

She was just finishing her second cup of tea, fighting her craving for her bed, when the street door opened.

She heard Evie swear angrily as she bashed into the pram.

'For gawd's sake, Eve,' she hissed, 'don't wake her up.'

Evie dropped down onto one of the kitchen chairs. 'Aw, stop moaning.' Her voice was slurred with drink.

'Where've you been?'

Evie grinned lopsidedly. 'Did singing in the pub. They loved me.' She closed one eye in an effort to focus on her sister's face. 'Then we went to get fish and taters but the warning . . .' She paused, trying to keep her thoughts on track. She nodded. 'Yeah. The warning went. So me and the boys, we went down the Underground. Right laugh, it was. Singing. Dancing. Drinking. Like a night club. Mind you, yer should have seen the lavs.' She screwed up her nose in distaste. Her elbow somehow slipped off the table, making her burst into a fit of hiccuping giggles.

Babs got to her feet and looked down at her sister. She wouldn't argue with her, she wouldn't waste her breath when she was like this, but she had to say something. 'It's all right for you staying out all night, but I've gotta get out to work.'

Evie clasped her hands to her chest in a pose of melodramatic shock, then she batted her lashes and said, in a mock posh voice, 'What, would yer rather your only sister risked her life by running through the streets in the middle of an air raid?'

'You ain't funny, Eve, yer a pig. Now just shut up. I should have knocked for Blanche five minutes ago.' She deliberately bashed into Evie as she stepped past her. 'I've fed and changed Betty, so she should sleep for a couple of hours yet, give you a chance to sober up before Dad gets in off shift.' She swept out of the room before

Evie had a chance to speak: she knew she would only try and persuade her to stay and look after the baby while she slept the day away.

Babs knocked impatiently on Blanche's street door. 'Come on, Blanche,' she muttered under her breath. 'We're late enough as it is.'

The door opened.

'Blanche!' Babs stepped forward and put her hand on Blanche's arm. 'Yer look terrible. It's not Archie, is it?'

'No.' Blanche pulled her coat on and shut the door behind her. 'I was over with our Ruby last night.'

'The baby still no better?' Babs glanced sideways at Blanche as they fell into step. Babs thought she herself looked rough after the hard night she had had, but Blanche looked totally drained.

'No. Poor little bugger. They're hoping for the best but it ain't doing very well. All we can do now is pray for a miracle.'

'I'm sorry, Blanche.'

'Yeah, we all are. Heartbroken, she is. No reason, just one of them things, the doctor said. Don't seem right, does it? She wants it so much. And there's your Evie, couldn't give a . . .' She stopped in her tracks. 'Sorry, Babs, I'm just a bit upset, that's all. There was no need for that.'

'No, you're right, she don't wanna know about Betty.'

'You still doing everything?'

'Just about. And, I can tell you, Blanche, it's tiring me out, but what choice have I got? I've gotta keep going, get on with it.'

'And hide it all from Ringer?'

'Yeah.'

'What a pair we are,' Blanche said. 'Come on, we'd better get going or we'll never get to work.' She linked arms with Babs.

They had only taken a couple of steps when this time

347

Babs stopped dead. Her head jerked round and she glared across the street to where Alice was pretending to clean her doorstep. Nobby was standing next to her, arms crossed and eyes narrowed, sucking on his pipe.

'What did you say, Alice?' Babs asked, striding across the street, arms swinging menacingly.

Blanche followed her.

Alice grabbed hold of the door frame and dragged herself to her feet. She folded her arms and looked contemptuously from Babs to Blanche. 'I was saying to my Nobby how I thought there was shocking goings on down this turning lately, what with young girls coming home at all hours, pissed as farts, when they should be indoors minding their kiddies. Neglect, that's what it is.' She turned to Nobby. 'Her old man should be in the forces and all,' she said.

Nobby knew his place, and he knew the price of disloyalty. He nodded his agreement, his stumpy pipe bobbing up and down in his mouth.

Babs went to speak, to give the vicious old bag a piece of her mind, but in that moment she knew she couldn't find the words that would silence Alice without bursting into tears and making a fool of herself. Because, deep down, she had to admit that Alice, cruel as she was, was right.

Blanche, however, didn't have any such problem. She shook her head, an expression of loathing darkening her usually generous, open face. 'There's a sodding war on, Alice.' She pointed angrily at the pile of rubble at the end of the street that had once been the Jenners's home. 'Innocent people are getting killed and maimed. Brave men are fighting to protect the likes of you. And all you can do with yer time is run young girls down when it's nothing to do with you. Nothing at all.' She prodded Alice in the chest. 'So why don't you just shut that trap of your'n, you interfering, miserable old bastard, and let

348

things alone that are none of your business?'

With that, Blanche took Babs by the arm and dragged her away.

'Charming!' snapped Alice. Then she shoved her scrubbing brush into the bewildered Nobby's hand and yelled furiously, 'Now get that bloody step finished. And do it right.'

Babs felt someone pushing her. 'What, what's up?'

'I'm so tired, Babs,' Evie moaned pathetically. 'You get up and feed her this morning. Please. I can't. Go on, it's Saturday, so you ain't even gotta go to work.'

Betty was crying softly in the brand new cot that, since yesterday afternoon, had stood at the bottom of the bed in place of the dressing table drawer.

'I never got a wink of sleep last night. I was so upset about that old cow coming round here yesterday. She must've known I'd be here by meself.'

As she lay there in the dark, Babs could just visualise Evie's lip trembling dramatically.

'I dunno what all the fuss is about. Queenie only come round to bring all that gear for Betty. I thought yer'd be pleased.'

Evie's tone immediately hardened to one of complaint. 'Well, she took her time coming round with it, didn't she? Fancy letting yer granddaughter kip in a drawer when yer've got all her money.'

'You hypocrite! It was you what didn't wanna see her.'

Evie returned to her whining. 'How can yer talk to me like that, Babs? Yer know all she really come round for was to have a go at me. Reckons I should be at home in that flat with her precious bloody Albie. If only she knew the half of it, it'd be him she was having a go at, not me.'

'I can imagine Queenie having a go at Albie. She thinks the sun shines out of his backside.' Babs paused, then added, 'Just like you used to.'

'Aw, shut up, Babs.'

Betty's whimpering started to get louder, closer to an all-out bawl, as she demanded her breakfast.

Babs sighed loudly. She knew she would be wasting her breath arguing with Eve; she'd still wind up feeding Betty even after they'd been rowing for half an hour, and by then Betty would have worked herself up into a real state and wouldn't be able to take her feed anyway. Babs threw back the covers, crawled out of bed and got on with it.

'This is the last time I do this today, Eve. And I mean it.'

Evie smiled to herself as she turned over and pulled the blankets up over her head.

As Babs sat with Betty suckling at her bottle contentedly on her lap in the peace of the little kitchen, she stared up at the sky though the window over the sink. It was a lovely spring morning, clear, bright and full of hope. And it was a Saturday.

She sighed, happily this time, as she looked down into the baby's wide blue eyes – she looked so much like her and Evie it was difficult to take in at times. Betty's little face puckered into a smile of recognition round the rubber teat that filled her tiny rosebud mouth.

'I dunno if that's wind or a real smile,' Babs said to her, as she put her over her shoulder and rubbed her back, 'but I reckon it makes yer look pretty as a little princess. Tell yer what, it's a nice day, I think we'll go for a walk down the Roman and show you off. You ain't been out much yet, have yer? Then we'll have a little turn round the park. How would that be?'

When Babs went upstairs to get herself and Betty dressed for their outing, Evie was still sound asleep.

As Babs wheeled Betty past the baker's on the corner, Rita came running out of her shop to have a peep at the baby, but her face fell when she saw the gleaming new, elegant black coach-built pram with its cream leather lining and satin coverlet.

'Morning, Reet.'

'Morning, Babs. That's a flash old get-up,' she said, nodding at the pram. 'Must have cost a bit.'

Babs blushed. 'Yeah. Don't think we ain't grateful for the one you give her, but Queenie, you know, Albie's mum, brought it round for her yesterday. Laden down like bloody Father Christmas, she was, according to Evie. This baby's got everything she's gonna need till she goes to school, I reckon.'

Rita wiped her hands down the front of her white, flour-sprinkled overall, leant over the pram and pulled down the edge of the cover to get a better look at the baby. 'Who can blame her for wanting the best for that little angel,' she smiled. 'I know I'd wanna give her everything if she was my granddaughter.' She straightened up. 'Evie having a rest, is she? It might be a long time ago but I still remember what it was like having to look after a new baby. I'll bet she's whacked out, ain't she, Babs?'

'Yer could say that, Reet.' Babs released the pram's brake and smiled. 'Gotta get on, we're off down the Roman.'

'But I ain't had a chance to tell you how well my Bill's doing,' Rita called after her. 'Right hero, he is.'

'Sorry,' Babs said over her shoulder. 'Tell me later.'

Babs had only got as far as looking over the first couple of stalls when she bumped into Percy Bennett.

'Hello,' he said. 'What's all this? I know I've been away a while, but you with a nipper?'

'She's Evie's.'

'Blimey!' Percy took off his forage cap and scratched his head. 'I always thought it'd be you first.'

'Yer know, Perce, so did I.'

Percy moved closer to Babs and said quietly out of the

351

corner of his mouth, 'Fancy a night out with a soldier, toots?'

Babs grinned at him. 'Yeah, why not. I'd love to.'

'Tonight?'

Babs waggled her hand from side to side. 'Maybe. I'll have to make sure that I can get someone to mind the baby first.'

Percy looked baffled. 'How about Evie?'

Babs widened her eyes. 'Evie?'

'Still a bit of a girl, is she?'

Babs laughed. 'Just a bit.'

'Tell yer what, I'm just off round me gran's to show meself off in me uniform . . .'

''Cos yer mum said?'

Perce grinned. 'Course. And so's Gran can feed me till I'm sick. But when she's finished with me, I'll pop into your'n to see if yer've sorted something out for tonight. How's that?'

'It should be all right.'

'Good, 'cos I wanna hear the full story of this little chavy. See yer about, what, six?'

'Sounds good to me, Perce.'

'Smashing.'

It was gone midnight when Percy walked Babs back home through the dark East End streets, but she didn't feel the least bit tired; in fact, she felt she could have stayed out all night.

'Yer know, Perce, in that pub, when we was dancing with all them people in that big circle, and with our arms all wrapped round each other and singing at the tops of our voices, I felt all the weariness and bad feeling that I moaned to you about just drain out of me.'

Percy laughed. 'So you enjoyed yerself then?'

She laughed back. 'Yeah, I had a really nice time, ta. It was just what I needed.' She glanced sideways and shone

352

the pale gleam of her torch at him. 'And I don't even care that Evie's gonna be sulking when I get in.'

'I'm glad yer happy.' Percy put his arm round her shoulders. 'Yer know I've always fancied yer, don't yer, Babs?'

Babs cuddled close to him. 'Yeah, I know, Perce.'

'I've been thinking. Can I write to yer when I go back?'

'If yer like.'

Percy stopped walking and turned her to face him. 'Don't yer want me to, Babs?'

'Course I do. I'd love to know how yer getting on, Perce, but I don't want yer to get the wrong idea or nothing. It wouldn't be fair.' Babs bowed her head; even though it was pitch dark, she still couldn't face him. 'Yer know how fond I am of yer, I always have been, but I've always thought of yer as me mate, Perce.'

'Yeah, I know, worse luck. Ne'mind. Perhaps next time I come back I'll be a sergeant and yer'll be right impressed with me, eh? Tell yer what, I'll send yer a postcard letting yer know when I get me first medal!'

Babs lifted her head. She concentrated hard, trying to make out his features in the darkness. Then she took his kind, trusting face between her hands and kissed him tenderly on the lips. 'Yeah, Perce, you do that, and who knows, yer might turn me head yet.'

'Stranger things have happened, Babs.'

24

Queenie sat in the stiflingly hot, grimy jumble of her front room studying one of the little black notebooks that she kept on her overcrowded table; the notebooks didn't actually hold much useful information, but Queenie knew that they made her look efficient, impressed the punters, and this particular customer owed her plenty; she wanted him impressed. Albie served a similar purpose as he stood there, almost filling the doorway, cleaning his nails with his pocket knife while he leant casually against the chipped paint of the frame. She swept her eyes slowly up and down the nervous-looking specimen before her. He was a fair size but, compared to her Albie, she knew there wasn't much chance that he'd be stupid enough to try and leave without paying his dues. But Queenie always thought it was a good idea to remind the punters who was in charge – and anyway, she enjoyed intimidating people.

'Well, Ronnie boy,' she said with a smile that cracked the thick layer of orange-tinged pancake make-up she applied at regular intervals throughout the day in the mistaken impression that it hid her wrinkles. 'You got it all?'

Ronnie nodded.

Queenie held out her hand. The lines on her palm were ingrained with dirt. 'Give it over then.'

Ronnie dropped his head and glanced sideways at

355

Albie. He had been thinking of maybe trying to sweet talk the old cow into giving him a bit more time, but with her bully boy of a son standing there like a bloody mountainside he knew he might as well save his breath. He reached inside his jacket and took out a wad of notes and began peeling them off slowly, one by one.

Albie levered himself away from the door. 'Good to see yer doing so well, Ron. I thought yer said something about times being hard.'

Ronnie felt the sweat break out on his top lip as Albie moved towards him. But he couldn't back away; he couldn't do anything, not with Albie looming over him.

Albie reached out and gently plucked the whole wad from Ronnie's clammy hand. He kept his eyes on Ronnie but held up the money so Queenie could see. 'That do yer, Mum?'

'I reckon,' Queenie said.

'Good. Now, don't be late with the next payment, will yer, Ron, 'cos yer know how I hate to see Mum upset and I know she'd be heartbroken if anything happened to them kids of your'n.'

Queenie sniggered, and her huge bosom wobbled like a badly constructed trifle. 'Yeah, heartbroken I'd be if anything happened to them little angels of your'n, and accidents do happen, Ron, don't they?'

Ronnie flashed a look of hatred at Queenie. Threaten his kids? How could she even call herself a woman? He felt like grabbing the old bastard by the throat and choking the life out of her. His breath was coming in short, fast bursts; he knew he stood no chance fighting her animal of a son but he could hurt him in other ways, could belittle him in front of his precious mother.

Ron walked over to the door and stood there for a moment, silently judging whether he had given himself enough of a start to have it away on his toes before Albie recovered from what he was about to say. He went to speak but his mouth was so dry he had to swallow a couple of times before any sound came out at all.

'Your missus is enjoying herself,' he said eventually. He wiped the back of his hand across his parched lips, his heart racing so fast he thought his chest might explode.

Albie cocked his head slightly and narrowed his eyes as though he was having trouble understanding.

'Lovely voice, she's got. All the geezers in the boozers round Whitechapel say so. She might have looked a bit the worse for wear when she left with a couple of fellers the other night. But she is one very popular lady. Yer must be very proud.'

Queenie heaved herself to her feet. Grasping the sides of the table for support, she ignored the pile of papers that fluttered onto the already littered floor. 'That blonde-haired little whore.'

She had said it very quietly but her venom made the hairs on Ron's neck prickle.

She jabbed her pudgy, dirty finger at her son. 'You gonna let her get away with making a show of yer? A show of yer family?'

Ron took his opportunity and legged it like a greyhound out into the cool evening air. He couldn't believe he'd just done that. He'd insulted Albie Denham's old woman and had made him look a fool in front of the old lady. He'd have to go amongst the missing, that was for sure.

There had been no major raids that night, just the odd shower of incendiaries, so all the pubs and illegal drinking clubs in Whitechapel had stayed open and remained busy. By the time Albie had dragged Chas in and out of just about every one of them, Albie could hardly stand. But Evie was nowhere to be found.

Chas tried to persuade him to give it a rest for the night but Albie would hear none of it.

'This is family business,' he yelled, swiping the air as he stumbled towards the Riley. 'Just drive me to her old man's gaff and then piss off. I'm going to sort that rotten little trollop out if it's the last thing I do.'

Babs could hardly believe it when she heard the knocking – she had only just got Betty settled after her midnight feed – Evie was too selfish even to remember her key. As Babs pulled on her dressing gown and stuck her feet in her slippers, she was boiling. She had just about had enough of it. With a quick glimpse into the cot to check that Betty was all right, she padded down the stairs, ready to give Evie a piece of her mind.

In her temper, Babs forgot that she shouldn't turn on the light in the passage before pulling the street door back on its hinges. 'Why don't you shut up, yer'll wake the ba—' Her mouth fell open.

'Chas? What the bloody hell do you want this time of night? It's nearly one o' clock in the morning.'

Chas jerked his thumb over his shoulder to where Albie was dragging himself unsteadily from the car.

'He's come to see Evie,' Chas said apologetically.

A voice that Babs immediately recognised as the grating tones of Frankie Morgan hollered at her from across the street, 'Put that bloody light out!'

It was Albie who replied. 'I'll put your bloody lights out if yer don't shut up.'

'You what?' Frankie was bristling. He adjusted his armband, picked up his pump and bucket and strode purposefully over to number six. But he pulled up short when he saw who had had the nerve to question his orders.

'In fact,' slurred Albie, gripping the car door for support, 'if yer don't shut yer trap I'll stick that stirrup pump of your'n right up your jacksy.'

Chas was at a loss; still harbouring the hope that he

might be in with some sort of a chance with Babs, he wanted to do something, anything to make him look as if he had at least some grasp of the situation.

'Look, Al,' he said, trying to sound friendly but firm, 'why don't we go and have a little drink somewhere?'

Albie lurched forward and threw his full weight against Chas's chest, sending him reeling backwards into the wall. 'Why don't you bugger off, yer useless cowson?' Albie righted himself and then slumped back against the wall, staring sideways, glassy-eyed, at Babs as he gradually slipped down to the ground. 'You ain't Evie,' he said accusingly.

'No,' said Babs. 'Thank gawd.'

She looked at Chas, who was still bent double from Albie's winding, and then at Frankie, who was muttering to himself about authority and respect. What had she done to deserve this?

'Now,' she hissed, hands on hips, 'I want yer to shut up, the lot of yer. The baby's asleep up there, and so's me dad. He's been on solid shift and he needs his rest.' She pointed at Frankie Morgan. 'You,' she said. 'You're so keen to do yer job.' She jerked her head towards number five where a chink of light had appeared at the corner of the Clarkes' blackout curtain. 'Yer wanna go over and tell Alice that she should turn her lights out before she starts nosing at the neighbours.'

Frankie was more than glad to cross the street to number five; anything to get away from Albie Denham. Alice might be a holy terror but at least he stood a reasonable chance of coming out alive if he had a set to with her.

Then Babs nodded to Chas. 'And you, you can get him back in that motor car of his and get him out of here. Out of my sight.'

Chas shook his head. 'I'm sorry, girl, I'd love to do it for yer, but I can't. Yer know what he's like usually, but he goes completely barmy when he's been drinking like this. He'd kill me stone dead in the morning.'

Babs nodded. 'Yeah. I suppose so.' She rolled up the sleeves of her dressing gown. 'Help me in with him, Chas, but then you'll have to clear off.' She grasped Albie by the sleeve and started pulling. 'Be quiet,' she warned Chas. 'And watch yer don't scratch that pram.'

As they half dragged and half marched Albie bodily along the passage, Flash shot out of the kitchen and started snapping and growling at him.

'They've even turned the bloody dog against me,' groaned Albie, leaning his head on Chas's shoulder.

Babs made sure that Albie was balanced against Chas and then grabbed Flash by the collar and shoved her into the front room, pulling the door firmly shut.

'Babs?' The voice came from the top of the back bedroom.

She closed her eyes and sighed. 'It's all right, Dad,' she called up to him, keeping her voice as steady as she could. 'It's only Frankie Morgan going on about the blackout again. He's set the dog off, that's all.'

She waited, listening for the familiar creak of the bed springs from her dad's bedroom as Georgie settled himself back to sleep.

'Right, Chas, along here to the kitchen.'

Despite her anger, Babs couldn't help but be impressed as Chas hoisted Albie single-handedly into the carver chair.

'Can I do anything else?' he asked. His face was red from exertion and as eager as a little boy's.

Babs shook her head. 'Just take the car and clear off, Chas. He'll be in no fit state to drive the thing till the morning and I want him gone long before then.'

'Can't I wait with him?'

'No. There's been enough of a performance here tonight as it is. I don't want him starting on you for gawd knows what as soon as he starts sobering up.'

'I'm sorry I couldn't take him with me.' Chas dropped his head and walked out of the kitchen.

'Chas. Wait.'

Chas spun round. 'Yeah?'

'Thanks. I appreciate it. You know.'

Chas grinned. 'Any time, darling. Just wish I could do more.'

If he wasn't Albie's stooge he might be a halfway decent bloke, she thought sadly as she closed the door behind him. Albie Denham had a lot to answer for. But worrying about Chas definitely wasn't at the top of her list, not for now anyway. What she had to worry about was getting Albie sober enough to talk some sense into him, tell him some sort of a tale and get him out of the house and into a cab before Evie came back.

'Come on, Albie, drink it.' Babs held another cup of tea to his lips as though he were an invalid.

'Don't want any more,' Albie complained, swatting it away. 'I wanna piss.'

He lurched forward out of the chair and tried to focus on the back door. Babs nipped round him and hurriedly unlocked it. He had had four cups of tea; the last thing she needed was for him to wet himself.

Albie stumbled out into the yard and into the lavatory. The cold air hit him and rapidly took effect: his head swam and he vomited violently.

While he was outside, Babs put the kettle on again and nervously looked up at the clock. Twenty to two. She could only hope that Evie wouldn't be back until the morning.

By the time Albie eventually came back into the kitchen, it was nearly two o'clock. He was feeling like death but he was almost sober.

He lowered himself gingerly into the carver chair and

361

shakily accepted the tea that Babs handed to him.

'Where is she?' he asked, looking at Babs over the brim of the cup.

'She's not here.'

'I didn't ask that.'

Babs leant back against the draining board and shrugged. 'Look, this is nothing to do with me. She's not here. That's all I know.'

Albie didn't look as though he thought that was a satisfactory answer either.

'Look, Albie, don't start nothing. The baby's asleep and I don't want her upset, do you understand me?'

Albie rose unsteadily to his feet. 'Yer've got guts. I like that in a bird.' He moved towards her.

'So's Evie,' Babs said warily.

'Yeah, but she's only interested in herself, ain't she? You're speaking up for the nipper. That's what I like. Shows you ain't a selfish bitch like her.'

Babs tried to flatten herself as he pinned her against the sink.

Albie stroked his finger slowly down her cheek. His hand reeked with the sour taint of vomit.

'Yer know, things would have worked out different if Evie had been more like you, Babs.' He lowered his head and lifted her chin with his finger. He stared directly into her eyes. 'I've always thought you was the one I should have married.' He was suddenly all over her, pressing hard against her, rubbing his hands roughly over her breasts and forcing her lips open with his tongue.

Babs gagged. The taste of sick on his breath was even worse than the stench on his hands. She struggled and kicked, trying to escape his touch and his kisses, trying to force him off her, trying to break free.

'You bastard! You just wait, you no good stinking bastard!' Evie's incensed and only partly coherent screams rang through the kitchen. It wasn't just her yelling that made her words unclear; from the look of her, all flushed and dishevelled, she had been drinking as well.

Albie sprang away from Babs as though someone had thrown a switch.

Babs blundered her way out into the yard, threw her head back and took great gulping lungfuls of air trying to get the stench of Albie out of her mouth and her nostrils.

Inside the kitchen, Evie was pummelling her fists into Albie's chest, sobbing over and over again, 'Bastard. You bastard.'

Albie grabbed hold of a handful of the blonde hair he had once admired so much and pulled her head up so she had to face him.

His face was contorted with contempt. 'You stupid slut,' he sneered and pushed her off him.

Evie stumbled backwards and went crashing into the kitchen table but she felt no pain. And she no longer felt drunk. She knew what she had to do. Albie faced the sink and turned on the tap; he bent forward, and scooped handfuls of the icy water over his face and neck, splashing it all over the floor. She kept her eyes fixed on him while she reached one hand behind her. There it was. The bread knife.

'Albie!' she screeched. 'Look at me, you bastard.'

As he spun round, he lost his footing on the wet floor and fell to his knees. With the pointed blade raised above her head, Evie launched herself at him with an animal-like howl of rage. She threw herself across his back, grabbed a handful of his hair in her left hand and with her right held the knife to his throat.

'I'll show you, pulling hair. You've had it now.'

Out in the yard, Babs could hear them fighting. She wanted to go in and do something but she was shaking all over and felt as if she were rooted to the spot by legs made of lead. But the moment she heard Betty's screams, she found the energy to shift herself and she burst in the kitchen ready to protect her little niece against anything and anyone.

She took in the scene in a single, horrified glance: Georgie was standing in the doorway, dressed only in his vest and underpants; in his arms he held Betty who had worked herself up into a red-faced rage. The expression on Georgie's face as he looked down at Evie straddling Albie's back and holding the bread knife at his throat, was one of disbelieving but mounting fury.

'If you've touched either of my girls . . .' Georgie's breath was coming in short, hard gasps.

Even with a knife at his throat, Albie was sneering and mouthy. 'What'll you do about it, yer pathetic old lush?'

'I'll show yer, shall I?' Georgie shoved Betty into Babs's arms.

'Shut up!' Babs shouted, putting herself between the two men. 'All of you. Can't yer see what yer doing to the baby?'

Georgie took a step back, he opened and closed his fists, barely able to contain himself.

'Now, please, be quiet. All of yer.' She held Betty over her shoulder and gently patted her back, trying to calm her. 'Evie, get up.'

She shook her head. Her hair was damp with sweat.

'I mean it, Evie. Yer've got to. Can't yer see what he's doing to yer?'

Albie laughed.

'I'd keep me gob shut if I was you,' Babs said calmly. 'Now come on, Eve. Get up to bed. I'll sort all this out.'

Babs handed Betty back to George; the baby was still crying, but she was less hysterical now.

Babs knelt down next to Albie and held out her hand to Evie. 'Gimme the knife, Eve.'

Evie looked at her twin. 'I can't take all this, Babs,' she whispered, the tears spilling from her eyes.

'I know, come on.'

Babs peeled Evie's fingers back one by one, took the knife from her hand and led her to the door. 'Up yer go. I'll be up later.'

When Babs turned round, Albie was standing up.

She spoke to Georgie over her shoulder. 'Take the baby in the front room, Dad. Please. Just till he's gone. We've had enough trouble here tonight.'

'All right. But I'm doing this for the baby, not for that no good whoreson.'

'I know, Dad.'

Babs turned back to Albie. He had ducked his head and was looking at himself in the mirror, straightening his hair, preening himself like a strutting, fluffed-up racing pigeon.

'Yer've gotta go,' she said firmly. 'I know there's a lot that's gotta be said and a lot to be sorted out, but that'll have to wait till the morning.'

'I thought it already was the morning. She's been out all bastard night, ain't she?'

'Always got an answer, ain't yer? Think yer know everything but yer know nothing.' Babs shook her head sadly. 'Yer don't impress me, Albie Denham. I think yer should go now.'

Albie twisted round and stuck his finger almost in Babs's face. 'Yer a stupid mare, d'you know that? You actually stood a chance with me. I could have shown you a really good time. The big time.' He looked contemptuously round the little kitchen. 'But it'd be wasted on a twat like you.'

'Come back later when everyone's calmed down.'

'I'll be back later all right, don't you worry about that.' He shoved her roughly out of the way and stormed out of the room.

She waited for the street door to slam and then went into the front room.

365

Georgie was still doing his best to comfort Betty, but his anger and tension had communicated themselves to the bawling infant.

'I should've socked that bastard right on the bloody chin,' Georgie spat the words through gritted teeth, 'the first time he showed his stinking face in this house.' He hardly noticed as Babs took Betty from him.

'Go up to bed, Dad. I'll stay down here and try her with a feed.'

This time when the knocking started, Babs really thought she must be dreaming. She switched on the lamp and peered at her watch. Half past six. She'd been asleep for less than two hours.

By her side in the double bed, Evie was on her back, sound asleep, snoring like a pig.

Babs staggered down the stairs praying that it wasn't Albie back for a return match.

She pulled open the door and blinked at the cold dawn light.

'Blanche?'

Blanche took her hand. 'We'd better go inside and yer'd better call Evie down. I've got some bad news, Babs.'

It took some doing, but Babs eventually got Evie out of bed and into the kitchen.

Evie had come down the stairs with her eyes closed and her head thumping, nursing what promised to be the makings of a violent hangover.

Blanche looked at the twins then bowed her head and fiddled with the buttons of the coat that she had thrown over her nightgown, no longer having the courage to launch straight in to what she had to say. 'My Terry come running home just now,' she eventually began. 'Him and Micky Clarke was out getting the stall set up when one of the market traders told him.'

Evie lit a cigarette. 'This had better be good,' she said, blowing out a stream of smoke and breaking into a loud racking cough. 'Me head's splitting.'

Babs frowned, she had never seen Evie smoke before. But then, she had to admit, there was a lot she didn't know about her sister lately.

Blanche reached out and took one of Evie's cigarettes from the packet on the table. She lit it slowly, making a performance out of striking the match and blowing it out. It was clear that she was stalling. She took a long drag and then blurted out: 'Albie. He's been killed.'

'What?' Babs thought she'd misheard.

'Who did it?' Evie asked coolly. She closed her eyes and rubbed her temples with her thumbs. 'Someone's old man who caught him at it?'

Blanche lowered her gaze. 'He got trampled to death, Eve.'

'What?' Babs said again.

Evie flapped her hand at Babs. 'Shut up, can't yer, Babs? "*What? What?*" Yer sound just like a sodding parrot.'

Blanche took another long draw at her cigarette. 'A shower of incendiaries fell on Dixon's haulage yard. Direct hit on the stables. The horses went crackers. They broke out of the yard and bolted, right into the street. Albie never stood a chance in the blackout.'

'Aw, Christ. No.' Babs buried her face in her hands and began to cry softly. 'It's my fault. I shouldn't have thrown him out like that.'

Blanche stubbed out her cigarette. She stood up and put her arm round Babs. 'You mustn't blame yerself, darling.'

Evie laughed mirthlessly. 'No. Yer should be proud of yerself, girl. Yer've probably done me a favour.'

Blanche stared at Evie. She had always been one of the first to make excuses for her wild behaviour whenever anyone criticised her, putting it down to Violet running off like that, but this was definitely out of order. 'As much as I disliked the man, Eve – everyone knows he was no good – I think you could show a bit of respect. The man's dead, and he was Betty's dad, after all.'

Evie lit another cigarette from the butt of the one she had just finished. 'So, he was her dad, was he? I never noticed.' She crossed her legs and jiggled her foot impatiently up and down. 'Good riddance to him, that's what I say. And there's no need to look at me like that. Why should I be sorry? In fact, d'yer know what? I'm really glad he's dead. Chuffed as hell. Perhaps now I can go out and have a bit of fun.'

Babs lifted her head and said quietly through her tears, 'I thought that's what you'd been doing anyway.'

Evie leant back in her chair and stretched her legs out in front of her. 'I ain't even started yet.'

25

Just a week after Albie's funeral, Evie had moved all her possessions back into Darnfield Street. By two weeks after the funeral, it was as though she had forgotten that Albie had ever been her husband, and she treated Betty's existence at number six with as little interest as she did Flash's presence in the household.

It was Saturday, 3 May, a bright, sunny morning full of the promise of a lovely spring day. Babs was washing up after a late breakfast while Evie sat at the kitchen table drinking her way through the pot of tea and flicking idly through the morning paper.

She took a long drag of her cigarette and then balanced it on the edge of her saucer. 'Can't you shut that bloody kid up?' she said without looking up.

Babs dropped a plate into the bowl of lukewarm water and took a moment to compose herself. Then she went out to the passage and cooed and rocked the pram until Betty settled.

'It's not for you, you know,' she said, getting on with the dishes. 'I don't want Dad upsetting, that's all. He needs his rest, he's been working that hard lately.'

'Hark at Saint bleed'n Babs of Bow,' sneered Evie and sucked hard on her cigarette.

Babs put the final dish to drain on the side and emptied the greasy water down the sink. She wiped her hands on the tea towel and sat at the table next to Evie.

Evie continued to glance indifferently at the newspaper stories of bombings and death that had become an everyday part of the Blitz.

Babs poured herself some tea. 'I can't believe how hard you've got, Evie. You've changed so much.'

'Me? Changed? Yeah, I reckon I have with all I've had to put up with. And I mean to keep changing and all. But before yer start, yer wanna look at yerself. How *you've* changed. When was the last time you went out with a feller? You've got like a bloody old woman, staying in all the time.'

'Go out with a feller? Chance'd be a fine thing. Who'd look after Betty while you're out enjoying yerself?'

'There's no need to talk to me like that.'

Babs laughed in amazement. 'No need?'

Evie closed the paper, folded it in half and then looked earnestly into her sister's eyes. 'Look, Babs, yer don't understand. I have to get out. I'm stuck in here all day by meself while you're out at work. I'd go mad if I didn't see a bit of life sometimes.' She lowered her eyes. 'Please. Don't be wild with me. Yer do understand, don't yer, Babs?'

'I understand all right. Yer a selfish, conniving mare. And I'm pissed off with the way yer carrying on.'

Evie's expression and mood changed in a flash. 'Aw, shut up, Babs. Who'd yer think you are, telling me what to do? How d'yer think I feel, eh? I'll tell yer, I feel really pissed off and all. Pissed off with yer going on at me all the time.' Evie turned away and opened the paper again.

Babs stood up and snatched the paper from Evie's hands and slammed it down on the table. 'Yer don't get pissed off with me looking after the baby though, do yer?'

They stared hard at each other, both knowing that things could easily be said that would be very difficult, maybe too difficult, ever to heal.

Babs swallowed the remains of her tea and poured

herself another cup. She sighed loudly. 'I don't want bad feelings, Eve. I know it ain't been easy for yer.'

Evie shrugged.

'Anything happened about the flat?'

Evie seemed to brighten up. 'Yeah. I had a real result there. Got rid of the dump easy as pie.'

'I suppose there's plenty need homes at the minute.'

'Yeah, and willing to pay good money to get 'em and all.'

Babs frowned. 'So yer've got some money for yerself and the baby then?'

'Only a bit,' she said hurriedly.

'What did Albie's mum have to say about yer getting rid of it?'

Evie poured herself more tea, draining the pot without offering more to Babs even though it was nearly the end of the ration. 'Who cares? Don't want nothing to do with that family.'

'They're Betty's family as well, Eve. You must have some sort of responsibility to 'em.'

'Look, Babs – not that it's anything to do with you – but I went to the funeral to do the grieving wife act, and I let the old bag see the baby, if it's convenient, so what more do yer want me to do?'

Babs didn't say what she really felt; instead she said, 'There is something yer could do. Yer could try and get some food for Flash. I'm having real trouble getting enough grub for her.'

Evie shook her head disbelievingly. 'What, it's the dog now is it? I really don't think you're happy unless yer moaning. Honest, Babs, yer getting right on my nerves.'

'And Flash whining and scratching at the door 'cos she's hungry, that don't get on yer nerves?'

Evie rolled her eyes. 'If it'll make you happy, Babs,' she said sarcastically, 'I'll sort something out when I pop out later on. How about that?'

'Where yer going?'

Evie looked over her shoulder to the little window by the sink. 'It's such a nice morning I thought I'd have a walk down the Roman.'

Babs nodded and smiled. 'Yeah. I'll come with yer.' She poked Evie in the ribs, just like she used to, her face glowing with a happy grin. 'And I can watch Betty for yer when yer go in the butcher's shop for the dog's meat.'

Evie stood up and wrapped her dressing gown tightly round her. 'I hadn't planned on taking the pram. Yer know how crowded it gets of a Saturday. So you stay here with her, eh, Babs?' It wasn't actually a question.

Outside the butcher's, Evie smoothed down the powder-blue dress which she knew set off her eyes so well, flicked her long, waved blonde hair over her shoulder, straightened her back and sashayed into the shop, a picture of fresh healthy beauty. Inside, the smell of clean sawdust sprinkled over the floor made her wrinkle her pert little nose, giving her a young, innocent look.

The elderly butcher, his striped navy and white apron stretched tight round his broad middle, raised his straw boater to her in appreciative greeting. 'And what can I do you for, twin?' he asked with a wink.

As Evie smiled back and breathed her requests for 'a bit extra' in sultry, intimate undertones, two stern-looking women, waiting for the youthful assistant to wrap their meat, stood with arms folded aggressively across their bosoms, discussing what they called Evie's performance.

'Just look at her, will yer,' said the grey-haired one. 'Not a coupon'll change hands and she'll get all the gear she wants. Just you mark my words.'

'Yeah,' said her friend, a big woman with a dingy-looking turban and dull brown eyes. 'And I'll bet the butcher'll be getting what he wants and all later on.'

'Dirty cow.'

'Just like her mother.'

'Yer right there,' the first woman said knowingly. 'Violet was always out more than she was in, and I don't mean standing chatting on her street doorstep neither. That place was like a tip while she went out with her fancy fellers. The old man took to drink, yer know.'

'Yer'd think she'd be in black,' said the other one, adjusting the knot on her turban.

'Not even an armband.'

Evie thanked the butcher, piled her parcels into her basket and turned round from the counter. She smiled serenely at the two gossips and said quietly so that the butcher couldn't hear her, 'Why don't yer both get stuffed, yer nosy old bastards?' Then, with a friendly wave and a cute little shrug at the happily smiling butcher, she went out to have a look at the stalls.

While Evie was flirting her way along the Roman Road market, Babs was trying to cope with Queenie, who had turned up completely unexpectedly. It wasn't like her to be even dressed before lunchtime.

Finding the street door wedged open to let in the fresh spring air, she had walked into the kitchen unannounced. Babs had jumped back in alarm at the sight of her, big as she was, clad from head to foot in black and without her usual layers of make-up, looking ghostly pale and drawn. Even her hair looked less of a startling orange than normal, more of a dreary, subdued copper. She was carrying two bulging bags, piled high with yet more things for her granddaughter.

Babs had taken her through to the front room, where they had sat on the matching armchairs, facing each other warily from opposite sides of the hearth.

'So, what's she doing for money?' Queenie's voice was cold but quiet, so as not to wake Betty who she was holding in her arms.

373

'Me and Dad're seeing her all right.' Babs studied her hands as she spoke.

'I wondered how she was managing.'

Babs glanced up at her. 'What d'yer mean by that? What d'yer think she's doing for money?'

'That flat must have fetched something.'

Babs blushed. 'A bit. Not much.'

Queenie shook her head and snorted derisively. 'I can't see that one getting caught.' She ran her hand tenderly over Betty's soft, down-covered head. 'Anyway, that don't matter, so long as the baby's not wanting for nothing.'

'She's fine.' Babs tried to hide her surprise. Concern was the last thing she had expected from Queenie Denham. 'Especially with all that gear yer've fetched again for her, she's got more than enough stuff.'

Betty stirred and Queenie shifted her to a more comfortable position on her lap. 'Right, we've got all the old flannel out of the way, now let's get down to business.'

'Sorry?'

Queenie's expression hardened. 'Don't come the little Miss Innocent with me, girl.'

'But—'

'And there's no use even thinking about trying to cover up for her. I ain't come straight off the boat, yer know. I know all about her gallivanting. And I don't like it.' She waved a ring-encrusted hand. 'It's all right for blokes, it's in 'em to be like that, I should know. But not for women. It ain't right. And now she's got my granddaughter here to look after. I ain't having it, my little Betty suffering.'

'But, Mrs Denham, you can see how well Betty's doing. She's smashing. Yer've only gotta look at her. I don't understand what yer on about.'

'We'll have to see, won't we? All I'm gonna say is that I ain't very happy with the arrangements. And that if

374

things don't change, she'll have me to reckon with.' Queenie held Betty to one side as she pulled her handkerchief from her sleeve. She dabbed at her red-rimmed eyes. 'Yer do know she ain't been near nor by that cemetery since the funeral?'

Babs was beginning to feel irritated; she didn't like Queenie as it was, but her criticising Evie was getting on her nerves. 'What d'you expect? He was only buried just over a week ago. D'yer want her there every day? I thought yer wanted her here with the baby just now.'

Queenie jabbed her finger at Babs. 'Don't you get lippy with me, yer little madam.'

Babs bit her tongue. The last thing she wanted was Queenie finding excuses or, worse still, genuine reasons to try and take Betty away. She determined to try and keep polite. 'Look, Mrs Denham,' she said with a smile, 'yer can see for yerself how well Betty is. She's a really happy little thing. Honest. And I know how upsetting a time it is for yer.' Babs stood up. 'Tell yer what, I'll go in the kitchen and make us both a nice cup of tea.'

As Babs boiled the kettle and got the cups and saucers ready, she cursed Evie and her selfishness. But by the time Evie got back from the market, Queenie Denham had departed and Babs had calmed down a bit, but Evie was furious when Babs told her she'd been there.

'The interfering old cow,' Evie fumed, dumping her bags on the table.

'Eve, don't. Stay calm. I've tried to explain to yer, yer really have got to watch yerself with that mother-in-law of your'n.'

'I ain't stupid, Babs, but no one talks about me like that.' Evie dragged her coat off the back of the kitchen chair where she had only just thrown it. 'I'll have her,' she shouted as she marched out into the hall.

'Where yer going now?' Babs called after her. 'Betty'll want feeding again in half an hour.'

'Keep yer hair on,' Evie answered her, pulling open the street door. 'I won't be long.'

Evie knocked on the faded and peeling paint of the narrow door that had been cut into the high wooden entry gates which opened onto the haphazard cluster of stables and sheds used by the local rag and bone men.

A stooped little man of indeterminate age and equally indeterminate layers of clothing peered round the door.

He grinned, showing an odd assortment of stumps and broken, tobacco-stained teeth. 'Hello, twin,' he said, first raising his battered bowler hat and then wiping his nose on the greyish green sleeve of what might once have been a raincoat. 'What can I do for yer, darling?'

'Hello, Tots, just the feller I was hoping to see.' Evie gave him a thin smile, trying not to flinch at the stench wafting towards her. 'I was just wondering if I could have a word.'

'Sure, darling, come in, come in.'

He beckoned her in and Evie stepped gingerly through the doorway, doing her best to avoid the steaming piles of dung that punctuated the slippery surface of the uneven cobbled junk yard.

'So, how yer doing?'

'Lovely, darling,' he cackled. 'We're all respectable suddenly, ain't we? Salvage workers, we are now. And how's yer family?'

'Well, thank you.'

He put his head on one side. 'This ain't no social visit, is it?'

'No, I can't tell a lie, Tots, it ain't.' Evie opened her bag and took out a crisp ten shilling note. She held it out to him. 'You don't like Queenie Denham, do yer?'

'No, I bleed'n don't, girl. Nor do hundreds of others,' he said, keeping his eye on the money. 'Ain't got time for no money lenders, but she's a really hard cow, that one.

Sits there in the boozer like she owns the bloody place, letting everyone buy her drinks no matter how short they are. And everyone knows she's got bags of money. And all made out of poor sods like me.'

'Thought so.' Evie paused. She tapped the note against her chin. 'If I give yer five bob for yer trouble and five bob for the load, Tots, d'yer think yer could deliver something for me tonight? Late, it'd have to be.'

'Course, darling. Anything for the Bells. You just name it.'

'I want a load of horse's muck from yer stable. As a surprise for Queenie's back yard.'

'But they ain't even got window boxes in them gaffs on Bow Common.'

Evie gave a broad exaggerated wink. 'No. I know. But she's thinking of digging for victory, ain't she?' She grinned, making her cheek pucker into its deep, captivating dimple.

A slow look of understanding spread across the man's lined and weather-battered features. 'A surprise, eh?' he said. 'I get it.'

Evie dug into her bag again. 'Tell yer what, Tots, we don't want her having to lug it too far, do we? So, take this extra half a dollar for yerself and make sure yer put the, you know, the business right up close to her front door. In fact, right on her street doorstep would be nice.'

Tots took the ten shilling note and the half-crown coin from Evie. Then he lifted her hand and slapped the money back into her open palm. 'You keep yer money, sweetheart,' he said sincerely. 'Think of this as me war work.'

26

It was Saturday, a week after Queenie had received her anonymous and definitely unappreciated gift of horse muck. The morning had dawned cold and clear and Georgie was half asleep and shivering as he made his way home from the fire station.

'Ringer!'

Georgie yawned loudly as he looked across to where Jim was calling to him from the doorway of the pub.

'Glad I caught yer. I've been keeping an eye out for yer while I was bottling up.'

Georgie raised his chin in greeting. 'Morning, Jim. What can I do for yer?' He scratched at the soot-sprinkled stubble on his chin.

'Thought yer might be able to use this.' Jim crossed over to where Georgie was standing almost asleep on his feet by his street door. 'Feller in the pub last night was flogging 'em and I thought a brave feller like you deserved one.'

Georgie blinked rapidly as he stared down at the piece of paper that Jim was handing him. It was a ticket for that afternoon's game at Wembley, the Cup Final between Arsenal and Preston North End.

'Ain't too tired, are yer?'

'Too tired?' he said, suddenly wide awake. 'Leave off, this is bloody fantastic, Jim. I can't believe me luck.'

'Well, see if yer mate Vic can believe his,' said Jim. He

handed Georgie another ticket and clapped him across the shoulder. 'Couldn't have yer screaming yer head off on the terraces all by yerself, now could I?'

By three o'clock Georgie and Vic were standing among sixty thousand other football supporters roaring and cheering on their teams. The war had been forgotten for the afternoon: the battle on the pitch was the only confrontation that anybody there was interested in.

But the mood of elation wasn't to last. As they made their way out of the ground, Georgie tore his ticket into bits and let the pieces flutter away on the breeze. 'D'yer fancy calling in the Drum for a swift half, Vic?' He sounded fed up.

'Yeah, might as well, and I'd like to say ta to Jim, even if the silly buggers could only manage a one all draw.'

'Compton did his best,' said Georgie mournfully. 'But with no back-up what can one player do?'

Vic kicked viciously at a lump of rubble as they passed yet another bombed-out house. 'I knew it was too good to be true, getting a ticket *and* getting the day off to see the match.'

Georgie and Vic walked into the Drum to be greeted by Jim shaking his head in commiseration. 'Arsenal? Call 'emselves a team? Like a load of big girls. Yer wanna support a decent side like me.'

Georgie managed a smile. 'All right, Jim, yer don't have to rub it in.'

Vic rested his forearms on the bar and stared sorrowfully at the pumps. 'I wouldn't be surprised if Hitler hadn't put something in Arsenal's drinking water, yer know. Trying to get at us, like. Break our morale.'

'Blimey, I wish I'd never given yer the bloody things,' said Jim, with a broad grin.

'Sorry, Jim.' Vic looked ashamed. 'Thanks for the ticket anyway.'

'Come on,' Jim said. 'Let me buy yer both a drink. Cheer yer up, eh?'

By eight o'clock, the three men had had a drink together, had discussed the football, insulted the Nazis and generally put the world to rights. There was still no sign of a raid and Minnie and Clara had come in for their usual couple of milk stouts as though it was any normal evening before war had broken out.

'Ringer. How yer doing, mate?' Minnie patted him on the back. She was obviously pleased to see him. 'Ain't seen enough of yer lately, what yer been doing with yerself?'

'Been working, Min. Them bleed'n Luftwaffe have been keeping us at it all hours.'

'Quiet tonight though.'

Vic lifted his gaze to the ceiling. 'Yeah, thank gawd.'

Georgie stuck his hand in his pocket. 'Put yer money away, Clara, I'll get these for yer.'

Minnie and Clara raised their glasses in thanks before sipping at their drinks.

'I bet the girls worry 'emselves sick about yer, Ringer,' Clara said as they settled themselves at a table close to the bar. 'It's such dangerous work yer do.'

'I don't think Evie notices or worries about no one, to be honest, Clara. Well, no one but herself.'

Vic puffed on his pipe. 'Worry, ain't they, kids?'

'I wouldn't mind that sort of worry,' said Nellie, wiping the counter briskly with a dish rag.

'D'you hear about Blanche's young sister, Nell?' Minnie asked. 'Lost her little kiddy after all, didn't she, poor little love.'

Nellie wrung the rag into the drips tray. 'Life ain't fair, is it?'

'No,' Minnie agreed. 'It ain't. In fact it's a right bugger at times.'

Vic tapped his pipe thoughtfully against the ashtray

that Nellie had pushed towards him. 'Yer'll have me crying in me beer in a minute, you mob. Give us another round, Nell, and maybe we should count our blessings for once, eh?'

Georgie shook his head. 'Blessings? I feel like throttling that Evie of mine at times. She's been driving me potty.'

'Ringer, yer shouldn't talk like that. Vic's right.' Nellie panted slightly as she pulled on the pump, filling the glasses with foaming beer. 'I know she can be a bit of a handful, but yer've got plenty to be grateful for. That granddaughter of your'n for instance.' She slipped the glass across the bar. 'Awww, I could eat her right up, I could.'

Georgie smiled. 'Yeah, she's a smasher all right.'

'It'll be hard for her growing up and not having a dad,' said Minnie, not yet into the optimistic spirit of things. 'I know Albie Denham was a waster but it's still easier to bring up a kiddie when there's someone bringing a wage in.'

'She'll be all right with me and Babs looking out for her, Min,' George said firmly.

Nellie agreed. 'Course she will. Couldn't go wrong with you two, could she? You love her to bits and work all hours, and that Babs, she's a real little diamond.'

'And don't I know it. I'm a lucky man having a kid like her. That Babs'd run from here to China if you asked her. And even though the other one's a right little mare, yer right, I should be grateful. Yer know, she don't half make me laugh at times.' Georgie took a swallow of his beer, wiped the back of his hand across his mouth and smiled. 'D'you hear what happened to old Queenie last Saturday night?'

'What,' asked Jim, 'with the horse shit, yer mean?'

Nellie flicked her husband with the drying up cloth. 'Language, Jim!'

Jim rolled his eyes at his wife's reprimand. 'I don't suppose that had nothing to do with your Evie, did it, Ringer?'

Georgie laughed. 'I'm shocked yer could even think that, Jim.'

A few minutes passed in companionable silence, then Minnie and Clara stood up.

'About time we was off, everyone,' Minnie said, helping Clara get her bag from under the table. 'Let's hope that the rest of the night's as quiet as this, eh? Dunno about the rest of yer, but I know I could do with a night's kip that ain't interrupted by them bloody sirens.'

'Yeah, yer right there,' said Vic, raising his glass in farewell.

'Night, night, ladies, mind how yer go,' called Nellie.

Jim called time but winked at Georgie and Vic to stay behind. When he had seen the last of his reluctant customers off the premises and had shut and bolted the doors, Jim ducked down behind the bar and reappeared with a bottle of Scotch.

'Have a nip of this before yer leave, lads. Reckon you deserve it and all, after having to watch Arsenal all afternoon.'

It was getting on for half past eleven when Jim offered them a refill, but Georgie put his hand over his glass.

'I'll stick at the one thanks, Jim. I've already had a pint and a half of ale, ain't I?'

'Go on. You ain't on duty again for a couple of days, are yer?'

'We ain't meant to be,' said Vic, cottoning on to what Georgie was thinking. 'But listen to them planes.'

They waited for a moment while Jim listened.

'There's been no warnings,' Jim said with a frown.

'Not yet, there ain't. I reckon they're our lads we can hear, and by the sound of it, they're getting ready for something big.' Georgie jerked his head towards the door. 'Come on, Vic, I know yer knackered mate, but this sounds like it could be serious. We'd better get down the sub-station a bit sharpish.'

By the morning, Georgie had been proved right. London had taken one of the worst beatings of the war. Factories, schools, homes and even the Houses of Parliament and Westminster Abbey had been hit. The destruction was so catastrophic in places that deaths and casualties were difficult even to begin to estimate.

But during the next few weeks, it seemed that that terrible night had, at last, marked the end of the Blitz, and Londoners took the chance to catch their breath, to begin the long job of clearing up all the damage and even to relax a little.

There were one or two moments of excitement, such as Hess landing in Scotland, which immediately caused rumours to fly that he was being fed on all the best while Londoners were doing without. And then the *Bismarck* was sunk, which gave an excuse for a much-needed celebration after all the dark days of gloom, which had temporarily returned to London when Arsenal lost the replay of the Cup Final to Preston. Then summer started with a sudden, glorious heatwave. It was only June, but it was sweltering. And with the new double summertime, the evenings were really light with the blackout not starting until eleven o'clock at night. Londoners made the most of it and spent hours sitting in the street outside their houses, watching children, mending and knitting, drinking tea, smoking and endlessly discussing the war. Roughly painted 'V for victory' signs on walls and fences became as familiar to Londoners as the taste of pilchards and sardines.

But when it really did seem that, for civilians on the home front at least, the war was all over, there was a massive raid. On the last Sunday night in July, a landmine was dropped in Poplar, destroying a brick surface shelter. The rumour machine sprang into action again and pubs all over the East End were full of people arguing as to how many were killed and injured. For a while, people were back on their guard, but then things quietened down again and got back to what, during the autumn and winter of 1941, passed for normality in the wartime East End of London.

27

Maudie clapped her hands together and stamped her feet while she waited for someone to answer the door, trying to get some feeling back into her freezing fingers and toes.

Finally the door opened. 'Hello, Maud,' Georgie said, smiling at his unexpected visitor, his breath making steamy clouds in the cold air. He jerked his thumb over his shoulder towards the passage. 'Sorry I was so long but I was just getting Betty settled down for her afternoon sleep.'

He stepped back and held out his hand, ushering Maudie inside. He shut the door and she followed him through to the kitchen.

'Evie had to pop out,' George explained, pulling out a chair for Maud from under the table and putting it near the stove so she could warm herself. 'That's why I'm minding the little'un.'

Maudie nodded understandingly.

Georgie sat down beside her. 'She goes out more than ever lately. All the time really. Well, whenever she can get someone to sit with Betty.' He rubbed his hand through his hair distractedly. 'She's trying to avoid Queenie – so she says. But Queenie don't come round that often.' He sighed loudly. 'I ain't sure what to do about it, to tell yer the truth.' Georgie stopped abruptly and stared down at the lino. 'Hark at me rambling on.

Must sound like a right old woman.'

'I don't think you do, George,' Maudie said sincerely. 'I think you sound like a man who's worried about his daughter. And there's nothing wrong with that.'

'Maybe.' George shrugged. 'That's enough about me. What can I do for you, Maud?'

She stood up, lifted her basket onto the table and took out a parcel wrapped in newspaper. 'I'd been round to the church early this morning to deliver some clothing. You know, for the bombed-out families. And I saw a sign in the fishmongers, the one just along from the vicarage. "Mackerel in at two o'clock, bring your own paper" it said. The thought of something different to eat was just too tempting to pass up. So I went along at midday and queued for some.' She nibbled at her lip and looked up at him shyly through her lashes.

George blushed.

'I hope you don't mind – I got enough for you and the girls as well.'

He smiled soppily. 'That's really good of yer, Maud. I appreciate it.'

She smiled back. 'You know me, George, always looking for something to do. I try to be of use, when I see everyone else doing so much. There don't seem to be many ways I can contribute – except with my vegetables and knitting and odd bits and pieces round at the church. I wish I could do something more.' She looked down at the parcel of fish. 'I don't want to sound too pushy, but I wondered if I could cook this for you and the girls. If you wanted me to, that is.'

'That'd be smashing, Maud. I'd like that a lot.' He laughed. 'And it's bound to be better than whatever Evie was gonna chuck in the pot five minutes before poor old Babs got in from work. If she even remembers, that is.'

'I'm not sure if that's a compliment or not, George, but

I'm really pleased to do it. I even brought some vegetables over just in case.' She looked up at the clock. 'Perhaps I could start cleaning the fish now.'

'Sure.'

Georgie took Maudie's coat out to the passage to hang it over the banister while she got stuck in at the sink, cleaning and gutting the fish and peeling the vegetables.

When she heard him come back into the kitchen, Maudie asked over her shoulder, 'I don't suppose you've got any mustard, have you, George?'

He thought for a moment. 'Yeah, I think so. I'll have a look in the cupboard. What d'yer want it for? To soak yer feet?'

Maudie laughed. 'No. To make mustard sauce. It goes really well with mackerel.'

'Aw, blimey.' George raised his eyebrows. 'That sounds posh. Mustard sauce, eh? The only sauce I've ever had is liquor with me pie 'n' mash.'

'I'm sorry, George. I didn't mean to be . . .' Maudie turned back to the sink. She sounded flustered. 'If yer'd rather I just left the fish plain – I'm sorry.'

'Sorry? Don't be daft, girl, it'll be a real treat. Fancy grub's just not something I'm used to in this house, that's all.'

He found the little tub of mustard powder and put it on the windowsill in front of her.

'Yer know yer said yer was always looking for things to do? Useful things, like.'

'Mmmm.' Maudie was concentrating on lifting the central bone from one of the fish without leaving all the little sharp bits behind.

'Well, I know something yer could do.'

'There!' She turned round to him with a triumphant smile, holding the bone aloft in her hand.

'Yer can come and work down the sub-station with me.'

Maudie immediately turned back to the sink and got on with the fish. 'With you at the fire station, George? I don't think so.'

'Sorry, I didn't think.' Now it was George who sounded flustered, and hurt. He sat down at the table. 'Yer probably don't wanna spend even more time with me.'

Maudie dropped the knife and the fish into the sink and sat down at the table next to him. 'Nothing could be further from the truth,' she said. 'Don't ever think that. I really look forward to the time we spend together.'

'So what's the problem then? Yer could work on the phones. I know they're right short of staff now so many of the younger girls are doing munitions work. They're even having to *conscript* single women for war work now, the chief said – everyone from eighteen to thirty. And they definitely need someone in the watch room. It's interesting work and all, Maud. They have to take incoming messages and send out orders to the other sub-stations – where to send the pumps and that. There's all these maps and charts and things.' He tapped the side of his head with his finger. 'Right up your street, it'd be, Maud, 'cos you have to be able to use yer noddle, see.'

'I'm very flattered you should think of me, George, but there's a problem. I'm a little bit older than thirty.'

'Not much.'

'Enough.'

'Yer making excuses.'

'George, I'm . . . I'm in my forties.'

'Never. Yer must be a good five years younger than me.'

'I don't want to make myself look silly.'

'It'll be all right, you see. I'll have a word with Sub-officer Smith. He's a good old boy, retired regular fireman. Been around since the Great Fire of London by the look of him – he'll think yer a slip of a gel, a bit of a kid, you wait.'

'But George . . .'

He shook his head. 'I won't hear another word about it.' He winked at her. 'Now come on, woman, back to the kitchen sink.'

Maudie stood nervously outside the sub-station looking up at the sign that once had proudly proclaimed the name of the school but had now been painted out. 'Are you sure he said he'd see me, George?'

'Yes.'

Maudie fiddled with her hat pin. 'And I really do look all right?'

'Yes.' George took her arm to lead her through the gates, but she wouldn't budge.

'He's going to laugh at me, George.'

'I thought you said you wanted to do something useful.'

'I do.'

'Well, here's yer chance.'

Maudie took a deep breath and marched through the gate and into the playground. It was full of men busily doing things with complicated-looking pieces of equipment.

As Maudie passed them, one of the men let out a low whistle. 'Hello, darling, want any fires putting out?'

'Oi, Burns, watch it, she's with me,' said Georgie proprietorially.

'Sorry, Ringer,' said Burns.

'How about, "sorry Miss Peters"?' demanded Maudie, pulling her handbag further up her arm.

'Sorry,' muttered Burns.

Georgie bit on his lip to stop himself laughing at Burns's sorrowful expression and went into the mess room for a cup of tea, satisfied that Maudie could look after herself as she went in to see Sub-officer Smith in what, before the war, had been the headmistress's office.

Maudie handed Smith her completed form and waited

while he glanced at the details she had filled in. As she stared at the top of his bowed head across the big oak desk, she felt an almost hysterical urge to laugh. She knew it must be nerves, but she really did feel like a little schoolgirl who had been hauled in for pulling someone's pigtails in the classroom.

'This part of the form appears somewhat smudged,' said Smith with a sceptical flick of his eyebrows. 'Can't quite make it out.'

'Oh?' she said innocently.

He nodded. 'The part about your date of birth. So, I have to ask you. How old are you exactly?'

Maudie looked directly ahead. 'Thirty,' she said boldly.

Smith raised his eyebrows again. 'Thirty?'

'Yes.'

'Any experience of this type of work? On a telephone switchboard, for instance.'

Remembering what George had told her, she said without any hesitation, 'Of course. Although probably on a different system to the one you have here.'

Sub-officer Smith leant back in his chair and looked at Maudie. She didn't dare move or show any sign of emotion.

'Right,' he said suddenly. Then he leant forward, stamped the form and handed it back to her. 'Beggars can't be choosers,' he said, sighing wearily. 'Now get yourself over to the watch room. Someone there will explain the necessary.'

'Yes, sir,' said Maudie smartly and left the office as fast as she thought was decent.

Before going to the watch room, she found the mess room. She popped her head round the door and gave Georgie a double thumbs up.

Georgie strode over to her. '"Beggars can't be choosers"?'

392

She grinned and nodded.

Georgie bowed with mock solemnity and kissed her hand. 'Welcome to the fun palace, Auxiliary Firewoman Peters.' He held out his arm. 'Can I escort yer somewhere, miss?'

Maudie curtsied. 'The watch room, please, my man.'

'My pleasure.'

Maudie might have sounded confident when she was fooling around with Georgie, but once he had left her at the door to the watch room with a whispered, 'Good luck!' she was shaking. Then when she peered round the door and got her first look at the room, she froze. What she saw was a harshly lit space hazy with cigarette smoke. There was no natural light as the windows were bricked up. Along one wall was a bank of lights and levers, presumably the switchboard. The other walls were covered with boards and maps dotted with pins and discs. In the centre was a long table loaded with apparently haphazard piles of papers and several telephones. The one welcoming looking thing in the whole room was a battered armchair with stuffing spilling from its seat that stood incongruously in the corner by a dull green filing cabinet. Maudie wanted to run all the way home to Darnfield Street. And she would have done, had Flossie, the fearsome-looking operator sitting at the table, given her the chance.

'You the new girl Smith promised me?'

'Yes.'

'Thank gawd they've sent me some help,' Flossie said, winding her thick, wiry brown hair round her hand and securing it on top of her head with a pencil. 'I dunno how much longer I could have coped by myself. Have you ever seen so much bloody paper?' She waved one of the sheets at Maudie by way of demonstration. 'The other girl who used to do this shift with me got it in her head to train as a despatch rider. Silly cow. Two weeks' training she done down the speedway on that motorbike of hers and she *still* falls off the bloody thing every five minutes. Right menace, she is. The messenger boys hate it when she's driving them around. Every single bomb crater she gets near, the poor sods are off on their arses.'

Maudie wasn't sure what response was expected of her to all this information, so she just smiled.

'Right,' said Flossie, pointing to the swivel chair next to hers. 'Let's get down to business. Now, there's *usually* two AFS girls – Auxiliary Fire Service girls – that's you and me, and a mobilizing officer, that's Ernie for us; on each shift. Well, as I say, that's the idea.'

She scooted across the floor on her swivel chair and picked up a pad.

'We write down any details or requests that come in over the phones on one of these. Anything from Central maybe. Then there's the despatch riders, they bring in the reports and we use them to sort out who does what. What pump goes where, which crews are available, pinpointing fires. You know. Ernie thinks he's in charge but yer know what fellers are like. We do all the sorting and organising and he gets in a panic.'

Maudie smiled again.

'Right, that's in here. That's us – control. Then, outside, we've got twenty maybe twenty-five firemen on duty at a time in this particular station. This is the usual, you understand. Or the ideal, I should say. What actually happens is more like flipping bedlam. We have to work with what crews are available in all the surrounding stations. Fires don't run to time, yer see. Anyway, when the fellers are not on call-out, they're either seeing to the equipment or resting.'

Maudie gestured vaguely in what she remembered to be the direction of the playground. 'I think I saw them outside. Unrolling and scrubbing the hoses.'

'Give you any lip or whistles or anything?'

Maudie smiled, sincerely this time. 'Yes.'

'That'll be them.' She rolled her eyes. 'Our brave boys. They're all right once yer get used to 'em. They have to check all the equipment, see, test it and dry it. I mean, there's no good getting to a fire and it's not working. They depend on that equipment as much as they depend on us doing our job right. They might like having a laugh, but this ain't a game. There's lives at stake.'

Maudie looked a bit daunted.

'Don't worry, it ain't all bad. There's a kitchen in the mess room.' She wrinkled her nose. 'The rations are all right. Not that tasty but plenty of 'em, which is something nowadays. And we've been talking about starting a pig club. Mind you, it's usually so full of soaking wet uniforms drying out on the pipes, it's more like a laundry than a mess. And then there's the dormitory. Not very posh but the fellers could sleep standing up, they get that tired out. And last but not least, there's the recreation room. We've had a few laughs in there.'

'George mentioned that.'

'George?'

'George Bell.'

'Aw, Ringer, yer mean?'

Maudie nodded.

Flossie looked her up and down. 'So you're the one he goes on about. I wondered why it was him brought you over.' She frowned. 'Yer different to what I thought. Older. Quite a bit older actually. Here, I hope you ain't got a job here just 'cos he knows yer. Yer'd better pull yer weight.'

Maudie was a bit nonplussed; she wasn't used to such blunt speaking and had to stifle a nervous giggle that was building up in her throat. She opened her mouth without really having any idea what she was going to say, but one of the telephones rang and Flossie held up her hand to silence her.

Flossie spoke rapidly into the receiver, jotted down some details and then ran over to a switch on the wall. There was a sudden, piercing clatter of bells.

'Down go the bells!' Flossie yelled, and shoved her swivel chair across the room to the switchboard. 'Ever seen Hell break loose?' she asked.

Outside in the yard there was what looked like a totally disorganised mad scramble.

Ernie, the mobilizing officer, rushed into the watch room. In one hand he held a sandwich and in the other his glasses. 'Right,' he said, twisting the arms of his glasses round his ears. 'Let's be having yer.'

He stuck the sandwich in his mouth and snatched the note from Flossie, sat himself down at the table and picked up one of the telephones. Before he dialled he pointed at Maudie with the receiver and said to Flossie, 'Who's this?'

Florrie shrugged. 'Beggars can't be choosers. And we do need someone.'

'We'll see how she goes.'

Maudie stared at the switchboard. It had lit up like a shop window before the blackout. She was rapt with a paralysing mixture of excitement and fear.

'Go on, get that headset on,' Flossie instructed her. 'Just follow me. Yer in at the deep end, girl. Can't waste time gawping.'

Maudie pulled off her hat, sat down and did as she was told. At first she was totally baffled about what she was meant to do. Firemen ran in and out buttoning up their tunics, grabbing pieces of paper and shouting at the tops of their voices about exactly what routes to take to which fires. And then the AFS motorcycle despatch riders came in and the place turned into a madhouse.

She watched as they shoved the report forms they had brought at Ernie, the mobilizing officer, who scribbled something on each and then stabbed them onto a spike, ready for them to be dealt with in turn. Then the riders looked to Maudie and Flossie, urging them to hurry if they wanted any messages taking as they had better things to do than stand around or be polite. The adrenaline was rushing through the riders' veins as they strained to get back on their bikes and speed from incident to incident through the smoke and rubble of the streets to collect the on-site reports from the wardens and the police and then race them back to control. They definitely weren't prepared to stand around while Maudie dithered. She had to respond.

Following Flossie's example, Maudie threw herself into what emerged as a sort of lunatic routine that involved doing countless things at once. They were expected to answer the switchboard and take brief but accurate notes; grab the piles of reports that Ernie had scribbled on and transmit his instructions to other stations about which pumps and units to send where, while at the same time plotting the locality of fires on the large wall maps of their and the adjacent sub-stations' areas and mark on chalkboards the location of each fire and which unit was dealing with it. All that, as well as coping with the impatient and very noisy despatch riders.

While all that was going on, there was the faint but all too clear droning of planes passing overhead just loud enough to be impossible to ignore.

Suddenly, Maudie slammed down her pencil. 'Listen to me,' she shouted into the mouthpiece. 'Central says to get there now! No, all our appliances are out. Just do it, all right?'

Flossie spun her chair round and opened her eyes wide at Ernie.

'She'll do,' Ernie said, his mouth full of sandwich.

Almost as suddenly as the surge of activity had begun, it was over.

Flossie leant back in her chair and studied Maudie for a

moment. 'Yer did all right,' she said.

Maudie smiled proudly.

'Don't get too carried away,' Florrie warned her. 'Ernie'll tell yer, that was an easy introduction. Couple of stray incendiary raids like that are a piece of cake. Yer should have been here during the Blitz. Like being in the flipping monkeyhouse at the zoo, that was.'

Maudie felt intimidated. 'That must have been something to see.'

'It was.' Flossie stood up and held her hands out. Her tough expression softened into a half-smile. 'Looks like yer staying, so yer might as well take yer coat off.'

Maudie stood up, pulled off her coat and stretched. She felt as if she'd been on a ten-mile run.

'What did yer say yer name was?' Flossie asked, hanging Maudie's coat on the stand.

'Maud. Maudie Peters.'

'Right, Maudie Peters, now yer know what that armchair's for.'

Exhausted, Maudie collapsed into the chair and closed her eyes.

The next thing she knew, someone was touching her gently on the shoulder.

She opened her eyes. It took her a moment to recognise that it was Florrie standing over her.

'Here y'are,' she said with surprising softness. 'Nice cup o' tea and a slice of toast with a big dollop of jam. One of the shopkeepers sent it back with the lads.'

Maudie sat up. 'They're back already?'

Flossie grinned. 'Yeah, Ringer and all. He's fine.'

As if on cue, Georgie walked into the watch room, his eyes screwed up against the glare of light. He was black from head to foot.

'But you weren't on duty,' said Maudie, pulling herself out of the chair.

'Nor were you,' Georgie said. As he smiled, white

creases in the soot appeared around his eyes and mouth. 'But I heard you couldn't let this mob try and get by without yer either.'

Maudie ran her hands through her hair. 'I must look a sight. What's the time?'

'Ten to two.'

'In the morning?'

'Yeah, you went out like a light, according to yer mate here,' George said, nodding at Flossie.

Two freshly made-up, efficient looking young women came into the watch room, laughing and joking.

'Here's our relief,' Flossie said, pulling on her coat. 'Thank gawd for that.'

'Watcha, Ringer,' said one of the girls, settling herself at the table and flicking briskly through Ernie's notes.

'All right?' said the other one, sitting down at the switchboard and putting on the headset.

Maudie looked bewildered. 'I think this might all have been a mistake, George. I'm not sure if I'm going to be able to cope with the fire service.'

'Well, I hope you can,' said Georgie. He looked at the two girls who had just come in, then leant closer to Maudie and whispered, 'I've just told Smith I've decided to sign up to be a proper fulltime fireman.'

Maudie blinked. 'You've what?'

Georgie looked at her so intensely she felt as though he were trying to read her mind.

'I thought it might be a good idea,' he said. 'So's I'll have a decent trade to turn to. When this war's over.'

28

In the front room of her house, Blanche was sitting with Babs and Evie on the newspaper-strewn floor making Christmas decorations. Blanche was painting eggshell halves and fir cones to hang on the tree; Babs was dressing up a clothes peg as a fairy and a scouring powder tin as Father Christmas; and Evie was glueing blue strips cut from old sugar bags to make paper chains.

'I can't believe it's nearly Christmas again,' said Babs, fiddling with the cottonwool beard she was trying to stick onto the odd-looking Santa's chin. 'I must be getting old – they say time goes quicker the older yer get.'

'Hark at you,' said Blanche, squinting at the paint-splattered eggshell she was holding at arm's length. 'You ain't even twenty yet. Wait till yer my age.'

'What? Hundred and four, yer mean?' grinned Eve.

'More like hundred and five, how tired I feel.'

'Yer know, I reckon it's better making yer own decorations,' said Babs. 'More Christmassy like.'

'I'd rather nip down Woolworth's and buy 'em, if they had any,' said Blanche. 'But they ain't, and I don't want the kids to go without, so hand me another fir cone.'

When little Janey saw Babs reach over to the basket full of cones that they'd collected over the park and hand one to Blanche, she toddled over, tipped the rest of the cones onto the floor and began carefully putting them back, one by one.

'Is your Ruby coming over to have dinner with yer?' Babs asked.

Blanche looked at Janey playing happily on the floor, totally absorbed in her new game, and at Betty who was lying on her back cooing contentedly at the wooden spoon she was waving in the air above her. 'No. No, she won't. Can't bear being with the kids,' she said. 'Chokes her too much.'

'Still in a bad way since, you know, the business with the baby?'

'Yeah. Poor little cow. Don't seem to be getting over it at all. Right down, she is.'

'Has her Davey got leave yet?' Evie asked over her shoulder as she climbed onto a chair and fixed one end of the paper chain to the picture rail with a drawing pin.

'No, worse luck. They've tried, but his ship's still gawd knows where. He ain't expected home for at least another month, I think it is.' Blanche hesitated. 'Anyway, Ruby's gonna stay over at Mum's for Christmas. It's for the best really.'

Evie twisted the paper chain into loops and fixed the other end to the far side of the room. 'There.' She stood back to admire her handiwork. When she turned round to get the reaction of the other two, she took one look at Blanche and ran over to her.

'Don't upset yerself, Blanche. Yer've done everything yer could.' Evie knelt down on the floor next to her and put her arm round her. 'Come on, cheer up, yer'll upset little Janey.'

'I'm sorry, I can't help it,' sniffed Blanche. 'It's just that everything's . . .' She buried her face into her handkerchief and started crying.

'I ain't having this,' said Evie. She jumped to her feet, lifted Betty off the floor and handed her to Babs. Then, before anyone realised what she was up to, Evie had tucked her dress in her knickers, had flipped forward and was standing on her hands, giving a panting, strangulated rendition of 'A Bicycle Made For Two'.

Janey clapped her hands with delight. 'Look at Evie!' she shouted. 'Look!'

'Come on, Babs,' puffed Evie, still staggering around upside down. 'Join in.'

'Fat chance of that,' Babs grinned with a shake of her head. 'Yer barmy you are, Evie. I always said so.'

Evie dropped back onto her feet. 'Yeah, but I make yer laugh, don't I?'

Blanche blew her nose loudly. 'You could make anyone laugh, Evie Bell.'

'And I know someone who's making Dad laugh,' Evie said, straightening her dress and going cross-eyed at the giggling Janey. 'Ain't never seen him so happy.'

'No, and I think it's smashing,' said Babs, putting Betty back on the floor and getting on with making her Father Christmas.

'Maudie, yer mean?' asked Blanche, stuffing her hankie back up her sleeve.

Babs nodded. 'Yeah. Closer than ever they are. Giggling away like a pair of school kids half the time. It's really nice to see them happy like that. Maud's coming in for her Christmas dinner with us and everything.'

'I wonder if they're, you know, serious?' mused Blanche. She threaded a piece of cotton through a hole in one of the eggshells. 'I mean, they don't seem bothered about anyone seeing 'em when they go out together, do they?'

Evie flung herself into the armchair that stood by the window, her hands dangling limply over the sides. 'I wish I was going out with someone,' she whined, her mood suddenly melodramatic. 'Someone who'd really love me and wanna do all sorts of exciting things. Someone handsome like Clark Gable.' She picked distractedly at

403

the chair's brocade upholstered arm. 'Maybe I should get meself an airman.'

'What,' said Babs, 'someone like Rita's Bill?'

'No fear,' said Evie indignantly. 'He might be a hero, but I'd want someone like a pilot. Someone with a little moustache and a posh voice.'

Babs looked at Blanche and stifled a giggle. 'Queenie'd love that.'

'Stuff Queenie.' Evie let out an exaggerated sigh and looked out of the window at the rapidly fading winter light. 'Don't you wanna *do* something, Babs? Something different? Go somewhere with someone exciting?'

'Course I do.'

'I don't,' said Blanche.

'It's different for you, Blanche. You're a married woman.'

Babs wanted to say that that had never stopped Evie when Albie was around. In fact, she was sorely tempted to say being recently widowed hadn't stopped her either but, not wanting to cause a row in Blanche's, she changed her mind. Then a thought came to her. 'I know what we could do,' she said brightly. 'Me and you can go to that New Year's dance next week. The one Maudie told us about. You know, that the WVS are putting on.'

'Blimey, you youngsters. It's only Christmas Eve and yer already making plans for New Year.'

'I bloody ain't,' Evie sneered. 'Sounds right exciting that does. WVS? It'll be all spotty-faced kids with bum-fluff and no money who just want a quick grope before they leave for the war. No thanks.'

Babs looked deflated. 'Please yerself. I was thinking of going with Lou anyway. I only asked you to do you a favour.'

'Well, I hope you enjoy yerself.'

'I will.'

'Good.' Evie stuck her tongue out.

'Ugly,' countered Babs.

'Fat bum.'

Blanche stood up and stuck her hands on her hips. 'Will you listen to yerselves? Yer like a pair of five-year-olds.'

The twins looked at each other and burst into uncontrollable laughter.

'I still ain't going,' spluttered Eve, tears running down her cheeks.

Babs hugged her sides. 'Good!' she screamed.

'Mad, the pair of yer,' said Blanche with a shake of her head and started dabbing spots on another eggshell.

Blanche looked up at the big clock on the workshop wall. 'Fancy coming up to the canteen now, Babs?' she asked wearily.

Babs stopped her machine. 'Bit early, ain't it?'

Blanche shrugged. 'It's being back at work, I suppose. I shouldn't have taken that time off over Christmas, it's made me all fidgety.' She drummed her fingers on the work bench and then began fiddling around absent-mindedly with the spool of thread on her machine. 'Seems daft. It wasn't that long ago that even the idea of coming out to work gave me a thrill. But now, I dunno, I feel right cheesed off. I feel like I can't be bothered with nothing.'

'Still feeling down over Ruby?'

Blanche hesitated then said, 'It ain't just that, Babs. It's Archie. Him not being with us over Christmas. Way I feel now, it's like we're never gonna be together again. I love the kids and they've been really good, a real help, especially Terry, but, aw, I dunno, I'm fed up with managing without my Archie. And, yeah, the business with my poor Ruby still don't seem no better. She's like she's in another world when yer try and talk to her. Like she ain't there.'

'Come on. Get yer bag. Let's go up and see what poison they've cooked up for us today.' Babs leaned back in her chair and called along the row: 'Coming up with us, Lou?'

As they waited in the canteen for the cook to open the hatch, Blanche, Babs and Lou sat on the edge of one of the long refectory tables swinging their legs backwards and forwards.

'Yer should have come to that New Year's dance, Babs,' said Lou. 'Right good it was. And there was loads of fellers. I had partners all night. Didn't miss one dance.'

'Sounds good,' said Babs. 'I was looking forward to it.'

'So why didn't yer come with me?'

Babs wrinkled her nose. 'Evie wanted me to go to the Drum with her.'

'So you went with her? Just like that?'

Babs shrugged. 'Dad was working, so I couldn't leave her, could I?'

'Aw, what, like she's never left you, yer mean?'

Babs didn't answer.

'Honestly, Babs, I dunno how you put up with her. I know she's family and everything, but—'

'Leave it, eh, Lou?' Babs snapped.

Lou went to say something but Blanche shook her head. 'Leave it.'

The three of them sat and waited in silence, listening to the wireless playing over the loudspeakers that Mr Silver had had wired up throughout the factory as part of the air raid precautions.

'I wish Workers' Playtime'd come here,' said Blanche out of the blue. 'I'd love to see 'em. Might cheer me up.'

'I know what'd cheer me up,' said Lou longingly. 'A few more rations. D'yer know I actually have dreams about lamb chops.'

'Roast beef and all the trimmings, that's what I'd love.' As Babs spoke she had a faraway look on her face.

Blanche closed her eyes. 'Pork crackling and apple sauce.'

'Don't,' Lou groaned. 'Yer making me belly think me throat's been cut.' She looked at the still firmly closed serving hatch without much hope. 'Wonder what we'll be having today.'

'Bound to be something delicious,' said Babs sarcastically.

'I think we've got more chance of having Workers' Playtime turn up.' The corners of Blanche's mouth drooped despondently. 'I'm sick and tired of this sodding war.'

Babs picked up a spoon from the table and held it as though it were a microphone. 'By special request for the lady with the hump. A special edition of Workers' Playtime, from Styleways of Aldgate!' she proclaimed and, holding on to Lou's shoulder for support, she climbed onto one of the metal canteen chairs and began to sing, swaying to and fro in time to the tune: '*A cigarette that bears lipstick traces . . .*'

Blanche smiled at Lou and sniffled happily, 'Her and that sister of hers, what a pair.'

While Babs continued with her song, the rest of the girls from the workroom and the men from the warehouse in the basement filed into the canteen and formed a straggling queue by the serving hatch.

'Go on, Babs,' shouted the man everyone knew as Old Dick. 'Lovely little number that one. Sing it, girl.'

'Yer've put me off now, Dick. I was getting all romantic then.' Babs clambered down from the chair. 'Tell yer what, how about this one?' She dragged Lou to her feet and made her stand behind her. '*Horsey, horsey, don't you stop*,' she began. 'Come on, you lot, join in.'

She soon had a line formed behind her, all singing along and joining in the actions: '. . . *and the wheels go round. Giiiiddy up! We're homeward bound.*'

'Yer'd better not be homeward bound,' came a stern voice from the canteen doorway. 'There's plenty of work to finish downstairs if you've got time to waste. I don't know what's happening to this firm. It's getting more like a variety palace than a clothing factory.'

'Don't be mean, Mr Silver.' Babs walked over to the doorway, flashed her dimples and peered up at him through her lashes. 'It's dinner time, ain't it? And we was only having a lark. And yer know what they say about keeping the workers happy.'

Mr Silver smiled. 'You. You could charm the sparrows from the trees if you wanted. Now, enjoy your meal and get back to work.'

The queue re-formed behind Ginny and Joan, neither of whom had joined in with the singing.

'I'd love to sing like her, Gin,' said Joan wistfully as she took the plate of grey, gristly meat and pale watery vegetables from the cook and followed Ginny to the table where they sat down opposite each other. 'She could be another Vera Lynn if she wanted.'

'Think she can sing?' sneered Ginny. 'I don't call that singing. More like a ruddy cat's chorus. Only reason old Silver and anyone else puts up with her is 'cos she's got a pretty face. Imagine if I'd talked to him like that. He'd have had a right go.'

Joan shrugged and concentrated on piling more food onto her fork.

'And have you heard about that sister of hers, that Evie?' Ginny shook her head disdainfully. 'They reckon yer have to see her to believe it. All cased up and going out every single night, she is. And her a widow with a baby and everything. Everyone's talking about it. It was the same when she was working here. Yer could see where all her wages went – straight on her back. Done up like a bleed'n fashion plate, she was.'

'I always thought she looked smashing,' Joan dared to say.

Ginny ignored her. 'Even with clothing coupons she still gets all the gear she wants. And I bet I know how and all. Right old scrubber.'

Lou tapped Ginny on the back. 'I'd watch that gob of your'n if I was you, Ginny. 'Cos if Babs hears yer, she'll have yer head right off yer shoulders. Just change the subject, eh?'

Lou sat down next to Ginny and pulled out a chair for Babs. Maria and Blanche sat down opposite.

'This looks terrible,' said Maria, pushing the food around her plate. 'If my mum could see me eating this . . .'

'I suppose you Eyties are used to better,' sneered Ginny. 'Some hopes.' Then she whispered something to Joan, who giggled nervously.

Maria didn't respond to her taunting, instead she turned to Babs. 'I've got to get some things down the Lane after dinner. Fancy coming with me?'

'Yeah.'

'I'll come and all,' said Lou.

Ginny slammed down her fork. 'Oi, Axis. I was talking to you. Ain't you bloody Eyties got no manners?'

'Shut yer mouth, Ginny.' Babs spoke quite calmly as she laid her knife and fork across her plate.

Ginny shoved Joan. 'Go on, say it,' she hissed.

Joan bowed her head and said softly, 'Italians are all cowards and spies, ain't they?' There was silence. She looked round uncomfortably. 'Well, that's what people say.'

'That's what *who* says?' Babs demanded. 'No. Let me guess. Ginny?'

Ginny curled her lip contemptuously at Babs.

'You spiteful big-mouthed cow. And you, Joan, I know yer stupid, but even you should know better. You know what it's like having people have a go at yer all the time.' Babs pushed back her chair and stood up. 'I dunno about you, Maria, but I've lost me appetite all of a sudden, must be the stink in here. How about us going down the Lane now? I could do with the fresh air.'

'I'll come and all,' said Blanche.

As the four of them walked from the room, Ginny turned to Joan and said disdainfully, 'That Babs is a bit sensitive, ain't she? Must be having an old brass for a sister and mixing with bloody Eyties.'

Tiddler, who had been sitting quietly on one of the other tables with the warehouse staff, slammed down his knife and fork and shouted across to Ginny, 'Why don't you shut up, you wicked-tongued bitch?'

'Hark at him!' Ginny burst into outraged laughter. 'Here, yer don't reckon *you've* got a chance with that Babs, do yer, Tiddler? I know them Bells'll go with anything in trousers but I don't think even she'd look at a little runt like you.' She turned to Joan and sniggered. 'Not that I wanna hurt yer feelings, you understand.'

Tiddler got unsteadily to his feet and drew himself proudly up to his full four feet ten inches. 'I wouldn't expect someone like you to know the first thing about feelings. But, for your information, it ain't Babs I'm interested in.'

29

It was 9 March 1942, Betty's first birthday, and Babs had eventually managed to persuade Evie that they should have a special tea party to celebrate the event. The sisters were standing at the kitchen table making sandwiches, Babs humming away happily to herself while Evie puffed and cursed at every bit of effort required to cut and fill the bread. In fact, everything and anything seemed to be getting on her nerves, especially Flash, who was doing her best to creep up and steal food from the table.

'If you don't get down,' Evie hollered, nudging the dog away with her knee, 'I'm gonna wallop yer. And I mean it this time.'

'Yer don't have to shout at her like that, Eve. I'll put her outside.' Babs grabbed the dog by her collar and tried to drag her over to the back door, but the scent of the food was too much. Flash lunged at the table and knocked the three precious slices of ham that had been tantalising her to the floor and wolfed them down before anyone could stop her.

Babs practically threw Flash out into the yard and slammed the door shut behind her.

That wasn't enough for Evie, she was furious. 'That's it, I've had enough. Even the bloody dog's got it in for me. I *was* gonna enjoy that ham.' She threw down the butter knife and pointed accusingly at the toppling pile of unappetising-looking sandwiches. 'And just look at the state of them. They look horrible. I hate this rotten grey bread we have now. And if I have to even look at one more pilchard, let alone eat one—'

'Don't start, Eve,' Babs pleaded. 'Yer know yer only wound up 'cos Queenie's coming round. I told yer, just ignore her, don't let her get to yer.'

'How can I ignore her? You know as well as I do what she's like. She'll sit there like the flaming Queen of Sheba – right name she's got herself and all, ain't it, "Queenie"? She'll expect us to wait on her and be looking down her nose at everything we do. I wouldn't mind if she was used to better, but she ain't. She's a filthy, soapy mare. And I hate her.'

Babs knew it was no good arguing with her twin, she was too stubborn for one thing and for another, even though she wouldn't admit it out loud, Babs agreed with her completely – about Queenie Denham anyway.

Although it was getting on for a year since Albie had been killed, when Queenie turned up for the tea party at number six, she was dressed from head to foot in deepest mourning.

Babs showed her into the front room where Minnie, Clara, Maud and Blanche were already sitting drinking tea and nibbling their way, without much conviction, through the pile of pilchard sandwiches which sat threateningly on the small, drop-sided table under the window.

Betty, the centre of attention, was working her way round the room supporting her staggering attempts at her newly acquired skill of walking by grasping hold of the furniture or the nearest person's legs, while Blanche's little girl Janey was sitting on Minnie's lap enjoying being admired as the 'big girl'.

Queenie lowered her bulk into one of the armchairs which stood either side of the fireplace.

'Hello,' Minnie greeted her, with her usual pleasant

smile. 'How are you doing these days, Mrs Denham?'

'How d'yer think?' said Queenie, unknotting her black scarf and stuffing it in her pocket. 'Me boy's dead. How d'yer expect me to be? Celebrating?'

The room went very quiet.

'I'll go and fetch yer a cup,' Babs said, glad for an excuse to escape into the kitchen.

When she got there, she was furious to see that Evie was still sitting, stern-faced, by the stove in the big carver chair, flicking listlessly through the newspaper.

'If I have to,' said Babs, checking along the shelf to find the least chipped cup and a matching saucer, 'I'm gonna drag you into that front room.'

Evie turned to the next page. 'It's nothing to do with me. It was all your idea.'

'And it's your baby's first birthday.'

Evie lifted her head and the sisters glared at one another for a long resentment-filled moment.

Babs was the first to give in. 'Please,' she said, lowering her eyes.

Evie closed the newspaper and said slowly, 'I'll come in there with you if you'll do me a favour later on.'

'Yeah, all right,' Babs hurriedly agreed and handed Evie the cup and saucer. 'But only if you go in and pour Queenie's tea for her.'

'Aw, ta. What a treat.' Evie stuck her nose in the air and followed Babs into the front room.

From the look on everyone's face, Babs knew immediately that the atmosphere hadn't improved in the slightest.

'Well,' said Evie scowling at Babs, 'wasn't this a smashing idea having people round.' She went over to the table, poured Queenie's tea and shoved the cup towards her. 'Here.'

Babs forced a smile to her lips. 'Dad should be here soon. He had to pop out to get something.'

413

'Aw, good,' sneered Evie, sitting down on one of the hard, high-backed dining chairs. 'I can't wait.'

'More tea anyone?' asked Babs, hoping for another excuse to leave the room. She pointed to the table. 'Or another sandwich?'

Queenie glowered at the table, her face full of disgust. 'No thanks.'

Clara held out her cup. 'I wouldn't mind a drop more tea, Babs. If it's no trouble.'

'I'll go and freshen the pot,' she said.

There was a knock at the street door.

Babs put the pot back on the table. 'Sorry, Clara, I'll get it in a minute. It's probably Dad.'

'I'll get it,' said Evie, jumping up.

'No. Yer all right, I'll get it.' Babs dived from the room.

'Tell yer what,' Evie said to Clara, 'I'll fetch the tea.'

'So long as it's no trouble.'

When Babs opened the door, it was not her dad standing there, but Nellie. She practically dragged her inside. 'Nellie, am I glad to see you,' she whispered. 'It's like a bloody funeral in there. Evie's got a gob on her like a wet weekend and Queenie's doing her best to start a fight.'

'Good job I'm here then to sort out the old bag,' fumed Nellie. 'And on that little angel's birthday and all.'

She strode into the front room with a determinedly friendly grin on her face. 'Hello, all.' She crouched down by Betty. 'Look what Auntie Nellie's fetched for yer, sweetheart.' She kissed the baby on her head and put a big oblong box on the floor next to her.

Janey clambered down from Minnie's lap and rushed to help Betty open it.

When the two little ones saw the brightly coloured wooden building bricks, they promptly tipped the lot onto the floor and got on with playing with the box.

414

'So much for that present,' sneered Queenie.

'Typical, bless 'em,' laughed Nellie. 'Right, that's the kids. Now for something for us bigger girls.' Nellie produced a bottle of port from her voluminous handbag just as Evie came back into the room with the tea.

'That looks just what the doctor ordered, Nell,' she said, putting the pot on the table.

'We ain't got enough glasses, I don't think,' said Babs. 'All right if I just rinse the cups up, everyone?'

Everyone except Queenie smiled their approval at the idea, but Evie snatched Queenie's cup from her anyway and handed it to Babs.

Babs soon returned from the kitchen with a tray of damp cups and Nellie, her face set in a rigid I'm-going-to-be-happy-if-it-kills-me grin, poured them all a generous measure of the thick, dark port.

Minnie took a sip of her drink and then handed her cup to Clara to hold for her. 'I think it's present time,' she cooed at Betty. She handed Evie a parcel roughly wrapped in brown paper. 'Me and Clara thought this might come in handy for her, Eve.'

Evie opened it and held up a pale pink hand-knitted cardigan. 'It's lovely, Min. And thanks, thanks to the both of yer. It's just the job. I'll put it on her now, shall I?'

'No, don't disturb her,' said Minnie, obviously pleased with Evie's reaction. 'Let her finish her game.'

'Looks a bit small to me,' Queenie grumbled. 'Would have done better a few sizes bigger, but I don't suppose you lot round here know how to get the wool.'

Clara shook her head and touched Minnie's arm to silence her.

Babs went to the sideboard and opened one of the drawers. 'I got this done for her birthday.' She took out a framed photograph of Betty and gave it to Evie. 'It's as much for you as for Betty, really.'

Evie smiled at the lovely image in the picture, a miniature version of her and Babs. 'When d'yer have this taken?'

'I had it done the other Saturday, in that studio near Chrisp Street. I'd gone in with that old photo of us from the passage, to have the glass put back. It was about time, and all; it was getting all faded from the light.'

'Was it broke then?' Evie asked, her face a picture of innocence.

Babs nudged her playfully. 'Yer know very well it was.'

'I've got loads of photos of my Albie,' Queenie said flatly. 'He was such a lovely, handsome boy.' She stared at Evie. 'Everyone said so. No one had a bad word to say about him. But it ain't much comfort to a mother, looking at pictures. Not when yer flesh and blood's been taken from yer.'

The room fell into another uneasy silence. Then the door opened and everyone looked round, glad for the distraction. It was Georgie.

Betty squealed with pleasure when she saw her grand-dad. He scooped her into the air and then kissed her. 'This is nice,' he said, putting her back down next to Janey, 'seeing all you girls together and enjoying yer-selves. Having a right old natter, I bet.'

Maudie put her hand to her face and pulled a face at him, trying to signal that he could be on very dodgy ground if he continued in that vein.

But Georgie either didn't understand her message or he had chosen to ignore it. 'Right little tea party this, ain't it? But I can smell that ain't tea yer drinking.' He winked broadly at Clara who hurriedly looked away and stared wide-eyed into her cup, wishing fervently that she was a million miles away from both Evie and Queenie Denham.

'Nellie fetched it.' Babs held up the bottle of port. 'Fancy a drop, Dad?'

Georgie shook his head. 'Too sweet for me. But I know

416

something that could never be too sweet. This beautiful little darling of mine.' He reached into his coat and pulled out a little wooden fire engine. He squatted close to Betty and put the toy in her hand. Betty looked at it for a moment and then stuck it in her mouth and started gnawing it.

Georgie looked over his shoulder at Evie. 'I got Vic Johnson to carve it for me. He's so clever with his hands, that feller.'

Queenie snorted. 'Homemade cardigans and boys' toys. Whatever next? This is a more suitable present for a girl.' She held out a tissue-covered packet, waiting for Evie to take it from her.

Evie stared at her, not moving until she had no choice in the matter because Babs had shoved her forward.

'It's a gold bracelet,' said Queenie, watching as Evie let it dangle from her fingers.

'I ain't blind.'

'Hallmarked, it is. Good quality eighteen carat.'

'She's too young for it.' Evie wrapped the bracelet back in its tissue and threw it carelessly onto the mantelpiece.

'It's to put away for her till she's older. Bit of security. And mind you don't wear it in the meantime. It's for me granddaughter, not for you.'

Evie shook her head in wonder and said loudly to Babs, 'I don't believe her.'

Queenie didn't even blink. 'I noticed you ain't wearing the pearls my boy gave yer.'

Evie looked her mother-in-law straight in the eye. 'Didn't like the memories, did I? So I pawned 'em.'

Queenie half rose from her chair. 'You little . . .'

Georgie stepped over to the hearth, placing himself between Evie and Queenie. 'You heard the news, Maud, about women up to forty being conscripted for work now?' His laughter sounded hollow. 'Yer nearly legal at last, girl.'

Maudie tried a little laugh in return, but it sounded equally unconvincing.

Georgie rolled his eyes at Maudie and mouthed, 'Say something.'

In desperation, Maudie turned to Blanche. 'You've been very quiet this afternoon, Blanche. How are things going with you and your family?'

As Blanche sighed and shrugged, Babs buried her face in her hands. Of all the people to ask at a time like this.

'I'm worried about my Archie.' There was a dull resignation in Blanche's voice. 'There's still been no word from him.'

'Oh,' said Maudie, a frown forming on her forehead. 'I didn't think, I'm sorry . . .'

'And my sister, Ruby,' Blanche continued. 'She's the one whose kiddie died. She seems a bit better now she's gone back to work but she still won't talk about it or come to visit me. It's all so sad. And then there's our Len, down in Cornwall. He wrote to me and he said even though the raids have stopped, he still don't wanna come home. Not yet, anyway. Not while his dad's still away.' Blanche's bottom lip trembled and she brushed at her eyes with her fist. 'I miss 'em, to tell yer the truth, Maud. I miss 'em all.'

'We all have our suffering to bear,' intoned Queenie.

'Well,' said Evie, her voice dripping sarcasm. 'As nice as this is, I'm gonna have to love yer and leave yer, everybody.' She walked over to the door.

'Hang on.' Babs jumped up and put her hand over Evie's to stop her turning the door handle. 'Where d'yer think yer going?'

Evie craned her neck to look round Babs and stared challengingly at Queenie. 'Didn't I tell yer? I'm going to a dance. And you're coming with me, Babs. We've gotta be out in half an hour and it'll take me that long to get me face on.'

418

'This is news to me. What makes yer think I'm going?'

'Remember that little favour yer promised me earlier?'

'That's not fair.'

'I think it is. And I also think yer'll never find yerself a feller while yer stuck indoors all the time.' She kept her eyes fixed on Queenie. 'Yer've gotta be like me. Make an effort. And anyway, yer've gotta come 'cos yer making up the foursome.'

'You make me laugh. When I wanted you to go out with me to that dance on New Year's Eve, yer wouldn't hear of it.'

Evie turned her gaze onto her twin. 'These are men, not boys,' she said deliberately.

'Have you two finished?' Georgie demanded.

'I've never heard such talk from a widow in all my life. My Albie'd turn in his grave if he could see how his baby's being dragged up.' Queenie's face was scarlet.

Babs grabbed Evie's arm. 'Leave it,' she hissed.

'I think we'd better be going.' Minnie stood up and nodded at Clara to do the same.

'And I'll have to be opening up soon,' said Nellie briskly. 'That Jim's useless without me.' She bent down and kissed Betty. 'Happy birthday, angel.'

The twins stood back to let Nellie out of the room. She was quickly followed by Minnie and Clara and then Blanche carrying the protesting Janey in her arms.

'I'll see our guests out.' Georgie shook his head angrily at his daughters and went to open the street door.

'I got this for Betty,' said Maudie, standing up and taking a book of nursery rhymes from her bag. 'If you're going out tonight, maybe I could read them to her – if you'd like me to look after her, I mean.'

Evie smiled. 'Yer've got no excuses now, Babs.'

'Why don't you leave off, Evie?'

They heard the street door close.

Maudie bit her lip. 'I didn't mean to interfere. I just

419

thought I could help, that was all.'

Babs shook her head. 'It's all right, Maud, it ain't your fault.'

Georgie came back into the room; he looked ready to boil over with anger.

Maudie touched him gently on the arm. 'I'm keeping an eye on Betty tonight, George, while the girls go out for a few hours.'

Babs frowned. 'But I never . . .'

George's expression softened. 'That's kind of yer, Maud.'

'I'm glad to be of help.'

'I'm not on duty tonight. Maybe we could share a bit of supper?'

Evie turned to Babs and smiled triumphantly. 'That'll be nice for Dad, won't it?'

Babs looked away, not trusting herself to say anything.

Queenie heaved herself to her feet. 'That child won't know who her mother is.' She pulled her black scarf from her pocket, stuck it on her head and stormed out of the house without saying another word.

Evie giggled. 'What's got up her kilt?'

Within twenty minutes, the twins were powdered, rouged and dabbed all over with Evening in Paris. They had drawn seams up the back of their legs with eyebrow pencil and had brushed their hair into smooth waves.

Babs stood up from the dressing table stool and put on her coat. 'Well, that's me ready. Come on, if yer coming. We might as well get this over with.'

'No need to sound so bored. We're gonna really have a good time tonight, you wait and see.' Evie lifted her chin, admiring her profile in the mirror. 'With my figure, I reckon I could be a pin-up girl, yer know.'

Babs shoved her out of the way and checked her own image in the glass as she adjusted her hat. 'I dunno why I put up with you, Evie.'

'Course yer do,' she beamed. 'It's 'cos yer love me.'

'You promise yer'll tell us when we get to our stop, won't yer?' Evie smiled winningly up at the fresh-faced young bus conductor. 'I mean, yer never know where yer might wind up these days, what with the windows being blacked out and everything.'

'I'll make sure you don't miss it, darlings. I'd hate to think of two beauties like you lost out there in the dark.'

Evie flashed a giggling glance at Babs. 'Makes a change to see a nice feller like yourself, thought it was all girls on the buses now.'

'Well, I'm waiting to do me bit, ain't I? Just waiting for me papers to come through then I'm off to the front to be a hero.'

'Aw, bless him,' Evie cooed, tweeking his cheek. 'Didn't realise you was such a little lamb.'

The conductor, glowing from being in contact with two such stunners, made a big deal of personally helping them off the bus at their stop in Stratford High Road.

As the bus pulled away, Evie waved to him and blew him a kiss.

'Yer terrible, you,' Babs admonished her. 'D'you have to be at it all the time?'

'Good practice,' said Eve with a wink and linked arms with her. 'This dance is in the function rooms over the Oak, but Harry and Alf said they'd be waiting for us in the saloon bar downstairs.'

When the twins entered the crowded, smoky bar, they drew the usual admiring glances from all the men present and sneering, resentful comments about their flashy obviousness from most of the women.

Babs followed Evie as she wiggled her way over to the bar.

'Babs, this is Harry, and this is his mate Alf.'

Babs smiled at the two tall, handsome young men. Evie

421

hadn't been kidding, they were both really good-looking.

When they all had drinks in their hands, Babs said, 'So, what do you two chaps do then?'

'We're both on leave from the Engineers,' said the dark-haired one, the one Babs preferred. 'Alf here,' he continued, nodding towards his fair-haired friend, 'is from the west country, Bristol way, but me, I'm an East Ender like you girls. From Plaistow, I am.'

Babs flashed her dimples. 'I like to mix with me own.'

Harry held out his arm to Babs and then said to Evie and Alf, 'We'll go up and see what this dance is like then, shall we?'

Upstairs, the big function room that took up the whole middle floor of the pub had been decorated with streamers and balloons to make it festive. There was a bar at one end of the hall and a band playing dance tunes on the little stage at the other end. There were chairs and tables dotted round the sides of the floor which was crowded with couples dancing closely together. Some of the women and most of the men – Harry and Alf included – were in uniform.

Babs didn't hesitate when Harry nodded towards the packed dance floor; she let him take her in his arms and was soon gliding into a smooth, easy quickstep.

Evie and Alf joined them. The twins were in their element, as both men were happy to dance to every single tune. The girls swapped partners a couple of times but by the time the lights were raised and the band had stopped for their break, Babs had made sure that she was back in Harry's arms for three out of the last four tunes.

'Same again, girls?' asked Alf, holding his hand up in a mime of drinking from a glass.

They both nodded. 'Please.'

'Let's nip down to the bar downstairs,' Alf suggested to Harry. 'We'll never get served up here.'

While the men went to fetch the drinks, the twins went

into the Ladies to check their hair and make-up.

'Glad yer come?' asked Evie, shoving her way to the front of the huddle of young women all vying for a space in front of the single mirror over the sink.

'Yeah. I've gotta admit it, Eve, I am enjoying meself.'

Evie took her comb from her bag and handed it over her shoulder to Babs. 'Do the back of me hair for me.'

As Babs smoothed down the thick blonde waves, she smiled at Evie's reflection. 'It's just like it used to be, ain't it?'

Evie looked down her nose at a short, skinny girl who was trying to push in front of her. 'Yeah,' she said haughtily. 'All the fellers gawping at us and all the girls dying of jealousy. I dunno why they bother. They can hardly compete with the Bell twins, can they?'

The short skinny girl cringed back into the crowd.

Babs stopped combing and frowned into the mirror. 'Bell? What's all this then? Ain't you a Denham no more?'

Evie waggled her left hand. There was no sign of her wedding ring. 'Seeing Queenie this afternoon decided it for me. If I never saw that old bag again it'd be too soon.'

Babs nodded, the thought of Queenie's performance was all the explanation that she needed. Then she said, 'About these two fellers, Eve. I can't really figure it out.' She handed Evie the comb and turned round so that she could have her own hair tidied up. 'You with either one of them specially like? As a couple or anything, I mean.'

'No.' Evie ran the comb briefly through her sister's hair and then put it back in her bag. 'Why?'

'No reason.'

'Babs?'

'Well, I think Harry seems quite nice.'

'Do yer?' Evie grinned.

'Yeah, and Alf,' she added quickly, for she knew what a tease her sister could be. 'They both seem really nice.'

423

Evie's grin widened. 'Yeah, right dishy, ain't they? I told yer they was all right. So, let's get back to 'em, shall we?' She looked at the group of young women pushing and shoving around her. 'Excuse me,' she said bossily and, with a lift of her chin, she made her way gracefully from the lavatory and back to the hall as though she was strolling through the lobby of an exclusive hotel rather than a dingy corridor in an East End pub.

Harry and Alf beckoned to them from the table they had bagged.

While they sipped their drinks, the four of them laughed and chatted away as though they had known each other for years and Babs was filled with a happy, easy warmth that she had almost forgotten.

The band returned to the stage and the lights were dimmed again. Babs held out her hand to Harry and jerked her head towards the floor. 'What d'yer reckon?' she said with a happy smile.

'I reckon I'd love to,' he smiled back and took her in his arms.

But the music didn't begin immediately. First the trumpeter made an announcement: the next dance was to be a 'blackout special', which everyone knew meant that the lighting would be turned down until it was almost pitch dark and there would be far more kissing and cuddling going on than dancing.

When the lights went out and the band struck up the first potent notes of 'I'm Always Chasing Rainbows', Babs drew in her breath as she felt Harry pull her even closer to him and covered her mouth with his in the tenderest of kisses.

He was kissing her just as she had hoped he would. He wasn't rough or all over her but was sensitive and caring, his lips soft and gentle.

When the lights came on again, she blinked and smiled up at him shyly. 'I'm having a really good time, Harry.'

He leant back and looked down at her, his eyes searching hers. 'I'm glad.' He smiled and drew her close to him.

She rested her head on his shoulder as the music began again and whispered into his chest, 'It's like I've forgotten everything else, even the war, and I'm just here with you.'

Babs was pulled from her reverie when Evie cut in again. Babs had the next couple of dances with Alf but she made sure that she had the last waltz with Harry, even though it meant her tapping Evie on the shoulder and insisting firmly, albeit in a bright and playful voice, that they should swap partners for the final tune.

As they stepped from the warmth of the crowded pub and into the street, Babs shivered; the icy wind made it feel more like December than March, but she was soon glowing when Harry put his arm round her and pulled her to him.

'How are you girls getting home?' asked Alf, pressing Evie against the wall and leering suggestively at her. 'If you've got too far to go, we could always go back to the boarding house where I'm staying. I'm sure I could find room for a little cracker like you.'

'Cheeky bugger,' said Evie and pushed him away from her. She took a cigarette from her bag, turned to Harry and waved it in the air, waiting for him to light it for her.

Harry let go of Babs, took his matches from his pocket, cupped his hands and struck one. As the yellow light flared in the blackout it illuminated his dark, handsome face. Evie moved close to him, keeping her eyes fixed on his as he held the flame to her cigarette.

When Alf saw what Evie was up to, he didn't lose any time; he sidled up to Babs and put his arm round her instead.

Babs didn't object, she was too preoccupied trying to figure out what Evie was up to.

'Ta,' said Evie, when her cigarette had caught. She was still staring up into Harry's big brown eyes as she blew a stream of smoke from the corner of her mouth. 'Yer on leave for a week, didn't yer say?'

Harry nodded and smiled down at her. 'That's right.'

'Fancy coming round to our place tomorrow?' Evie didn't shift her gaze for a moment. 'Come for tea if yer like. You can meet Babs's little girl. I look after her while Babs is at work.'

Babs blinked in bewilderment. 'What?' She was too taken aback to notice how quickly Alf had dropped his arm from round her shoulder.

'It's ever so sad,' Evie went on. 'Her husband was taken prisoner. He's in one of them camps. Terrible it is. She goes to work to take her mind off it.'

Alf did up the top button of his overcoat. 'Blimey, that the time?' he muttered. In his mind there loomed the horrific prospect of getting stuck with some poor sod's wife and kid. 'I'd better be off, mate. See yer.' And with that, he was gone.

'He left a bit sharpish,' Evie said innocently. 'What was up with him?'

Harry jerked his head towards Babs. 'Don't fancy being beat up by someone's old man, even if he is locked up. These tales have a habit of getting back to women's husbands.' He shook his head at Babs. 'He didn't mean nothing personal, love.'

'Babs wouldn't be unfaithful to her Ron, would yer, Babs?'

'Evie!' Babs was pale with anger.

'Look, I hate to leave yer like this, Eve, but I'd better get after him, he ain't got a clue about finding his way round London. Give us yer address and I'll see yer tomorrow, eh?'

He took Evie's hastily scribbled note and disappeared along the street after Alf.

Evie pulled her coat collar up round her neck and said, as though nothing had happened, 'Yer coming, Babs?'

'Am I coming? What the bloody hell d'yer think you're playing at, telling all them lies about me?'

Evie looked surprised. 'What's it to you?'

'You're Betty's mother, that's what.'

'Having a kid ain't gonna cramp my style.'

'And another thing.' Babs was now too angry to notice the cold. 'I thought you said that you didn't care which one of them you wound up with.'

'I didn't.' Evie looked confused by her sister's rage. 'I just thought Harry was a bit better looking, that's all. Never really fancied fair blokes that much. And now I'm a blonde I think I look better next to someone with dark hair, shows me off more.'

'I honestly don't believe you.'

'What? Here, yer didn't fancy Harry or something yerself, did yer? Yer should have said.'

Babs swallowed hard and stared down at her feet. 'Would it have made any difference if I had?'

'Dunno,' said Evie with a bored shrug. 'Didn't really give it a thought. Anyway, I've had enough of all this. Come on, I'm freezing. Let's get the bus.'

The next morning, at the sub-station, Georgie and Maud were working alongside the other firemen and women assembling wireless equipment in one of the converted classrooms. There had been hardly any major raids for several months but they were keeping themselves busy, whilst at the same time doing their bit for the war effort.

Georgie dropped his screwdriver down on the bench and rubbed his eyes hard with his knuckles. 'I know this is all for a good cause, Maud, but do you fancy coming out and doing a bit more work on the vegetables? I'm going boss-eyed doing these screws and wires. And these great big hands of mine definitely ain't cut out for fiddly jobs like this.'

'I think going outside's a really good idea, George.'

Vic Johnson laughed. 'You two must be potty. Going out in all that mud when yer could be sitting in here in the warm.' He shivered. 'No thanks.'

Maudie gave him a friendly pat on the back. 'Well, I'm still a country girl at heart, Vic. I love a bit of digging in the mud. Does me the power of good and blows away all the cobwebs.'

'You're welcome, girl.'

Georgie followed Maudie outside to the patch of ground that had once been the school garden. He opened up the little shed that Vic had built with timbers they had collected from the bombsites and took out the tools. He offered Maud the hoe, but she refused with a grin and took the less delicate, long-handled spade from him instead.

'It was good of yer looking after the little'un with me last night.' Georgie rested the hoe against the shed while he rolled up his sleeves. 'She's right fond of yer, yer know.'

Maudie picked her way carefully along the rows of vegetables. 'I'm glad,' she said, stooping to examine the leaves of a cabbage. 'I'm very fond of her.'

Georgie began poking the hoe gingerly at the weeds that had sprouted between the plants – the memory of his 'weeding out' a whole row of recently planted onions was fresh in his mind and was making him particularly cautious. 'Did you ever want kids of your own?' he asked matter-of-factly.

Maud, who was still bent double, looked through her legs at him. 'Yes,' she said, and then straightened up to face him. 'But it wasn't to be, was it? Not for an old spinster like me.' She shrugged. 'So, I've had to accept it.'

Georgie pulled at a ferny looking leaf, hesitated, then tugged a bit harder. The whole plant came clean out of the ground and he held the resulting prize up for Maudie's inspection. 'Weed?' he asked hopefully.

She laughed. 'This time, yes. But be careful. I don't want you destroying any more crops.'

He tossed the plant onto the gravel path. 'Yer good at this, gardening.'

'I suppose it's because I enjoy it so much.' She moved further along the rows, looking critically at the plants and their development.

'Yer said something earlier to Vic. It made me think.'

'What was that?'

'About being a country girl.'

Maudie stopped at the end of the rows by a section of bare earth that had been marked out with pegs and string. 'I did live in the country for a while.' She plunged her spade deep into the ground and panted from the exertion of turning the heavy clay soil.

'I always knew you wasn't from round here.'

Maudie didn't say anything, she just moved forward, stuck the spade in again and repeated digging and turning the sodden earth.

'So, how did you turn up here then? In the East End.'

Maudie rested her forearm on the handle of the shovel. 'That's a long story, George. A very long story.' She returned to her digging. 'With enough elbow grease, we'll turn this place into a right little farmyard before the summer comes. I've thought about maybe getting a few hens.'

From his experience of previous attempts at finding out more about Maudie's past, Georgie knew that that was the end of the matter – for now at least.

That evening, when Georgie arrived home at number six, Harry was just leaving the house.

'You must be Mr Bell,' Harry said, stretching out his hand. 'They're three lovely ladies yer've got indoors.'

'Glad you approve, son,' Georgie answered, his pride momentarily overcoming his curiosity. He shook Harry by the hand.

'I'll be back later on tonight, to take Evie out. If that's all right with you.'

Georgie frowned. 'Yer don't mean Babs?'

Harry frowned back at him. 'Evie is the blonde one, ain't she?'

'Yeah, that's right. That's Evie.'

Harry relaxed. 'Yeah, that's what I thought.'

Georgie let himself indoors. He could hear Babs and Evie talking in the kitchen. It sounded as if they were rowing again.

He stood in the kitchen doorway a moment, trying to figure out what was going on this time. 'Evening,' he said.

They both looked round. Neither of them spoke.

'I met that young feller in the street, Eve.'

'What, Harry? Did yer?' She glanced sideways at Babs.

'Yeah. He seemed all right. Polite enough.'

'Aw, he's that all right.' Babs folded her arms and tapped her foot impatiently on the dull red lino.

'Look, Eve,' Georgie said. 'I know things ain't been easy for yer, but you mind what yer letting yerself in for, eh, getting mixed up with another feller so soon.'

'Yeah, and try and keep Harry from getting too confused with all the lies yer telling him and all,' snapped Babs.

'I don't know what's going on between you two,' Georgie said. 'But I don't think I like coming home to all this bad feeling. All right?' He looked first at one daughter then the other. 'I said, all right?'

Evie bowed her head. 'Yes, Dad.'

'Babs?'

Babs shook her head furiously. 'Why don't you all just

leave me alone?' she shouted and ran from the room and up to the bedroom she now hated sharing with her sister.

Harry came back to the house that evening as he had promised, and every other day and evening for nearly a week. Then his leave was almost up and it was his last few hours of freedom before he had to go back to camp. He arrived at number six with his arms full of flowers and a bottle of scent that he had paid ridiculously over the odds for on the black market.

After an evening at the pictures, Evie told him she wanted to go straight home because she had a headache. When they got back to the house, she wouldn't let him past the street doorstep.

She smiled up at him wistfully. 'Go now, Harry,' she said, lowering her eyes. 'I'm finding this really hard.'

He touched her gently on the cheek. 'So am I.'

'Go on, please,' she said, looking away. 'I'll start crying in a minute.'

He kissed her tenderly on the forehead, turned, paused and then strode off down the street.

Evie closed the door behind him, went into the kitchen, dropped down into the carver chair and kicked off her shoes.

'Thank gawd for that,' she sighed. 'He was like a flipping leech, that bloke. I didn't think I'd ever get rid of him.' She turned to Babs who was sitting at the table darning Georgie's socks. 'Any tea in that pot, Babs? I'm gasping.'

Babs let the mending fall into her lap. 'What did you say?' She raised her hand. 'And no, I don't mean about the tea.'

'I'm glad to see the back of him. All right? Blimey, I invited him round the once but I didn't think he'd be here every five minutes. I thought he'd never go. It was worse than being married.'

'I don't think I know you any more, Eve.'

'What you on about now?'

'You, you're so hard.'

'Can yer blame me? What do I wanna waste me time with a no-hoper like him for when there's all these blokes coming over from America?' She looked up at the ceiling with a dreamy look in her eyes. 'GIs . . . sounds great, dunnit? I'll bet they're just like yer see in the films.'

'So you ain't interested in Harry no more?'

Evie folded her arms, leant back in the chair and closed her eyes. 'Who?'

30

'How d'yer think I look in this, Babs? Good, eh?' Evie dropped her chin and put her head on one side to show her twin the new black chenille snood in which she had piled her thick blonde hair.

'It's all right,' Babs said without much interest. She leant back against the sink. 'What have yer done us for tea tonight, then? I'm starving.'

'Gawd, you're in a lovely mood, ain't yer?' Evie sat down on one of the wooden kitchen chairs and pulled the snood from her head. Then a smile spread slowly across her lips. 'I know what's up with you. Yer've got the hump about this letter, haven't yer?'

'What letter?' Babs folded her arms.

'The one yer've been staring at for the last ten minutes – ever since yer got in from work, in fact.' Evie jerked her head towards the letter that had been left carelessly on the kitchen table, half in, half out of its envelope.

Babs concentrated on brushing an imaginary piece of fluff from the sleeve of her dress. 'Why should I care about a letter what's addressed to you?'

Evie's smile became broader. 'I see, so yer've noticed it's addressed to me, have yer?'

Babs raked her fingers through her hair. 'I just guessed, that's all.'

'What, like yer guessed about every other letter he's sent me these past few months?'

'Look, Eve, it's nothing to do with me if Harry wants to write to yer.'

'Aw, that's interesting, so yer know who it's from as well. Yer a really good guesser, ain't yer?'

'Shut up, can't yer? Yer've always got a bloody answer, you.' Babs pushed herself away from the sink and strode angrily across to the kitchen door.

'Sausages,' Evie said.

Babs stopped in the doorway and sighed. 'What you on about now?'

'Sausages. It's what we're having for tea. They won't be a minute.'

'I know your minutes,' Babs said coldly. 'Call me when they're ready. I'm going up to see Betty.'

Nearly half an hour later Babs heard her name being hollered up the stairway from the passage below.

'Babs!' Evie shouted again. 'Yer tea's on the table. Now.'

Babs stepped out onto the landing. She closed the bedroom door gently behind her. 'Ssshhh. Keep it down, can't yer, yer'll wake Betty.'

In the kitchen, Evie had indeed put the tea on the table. On the bare wooden surface stood two plates, each boasting two almost incinerated sausages, a limp pile of anaemic looking chips and a slice of badly cut, dry, grey bread.

'This looks smashing,' said Babs sarcastically. 'Now, which one's mine?' She pulled out a chair from under the table. 'This one, I hope,' she said, pointing to one of the equally horrible looking meals.

Evie rolled her eyes, tutted loudly and sat down next to her sister. 'What d'yer bloody expect, Babs, tea at the Ritz? There is a war on, yer know.'

'Well, bugger me, and I hadn't even noticed. Good job yer told me.'

'Salt?' Evie slammed the cellar down hard on the table,

making Flash run for cover into the passage.

'No thanks. Even the dog's turned her nose up,' said Babs, disgustedly pushing the plate away from her.

'I dunno what yer complaining about.' Evie took a bite of sausage and promptly screwed up her face at the revolting taste. 'Yeughhh!' She rubbed the back of her hand across her lips. 'I can't eat that muck.' She, too, shoved her plate away from her. 'Fancy coming out tonight?'

'Where yer going?'

'Up West.'

'How about Betty?'

'Dad'll be in about eight. He can mind her.'

Babs got up from the table. 'Flash,' she called, slapping her thigh with her hand. 'Here, girl.'

The dog trotted into the kitchen, her tongue lolling from the side of her mouth.

Babs scraped all the food onto one plate and, with a click of her tongue to encourage Flash to follow, opened the back door and tipped the lot into the yard.

Flash sniffed and circled it suspiciously, then overcoming her fastidiousness, guzzled the lot.

'I'd like to see yer run round a track with that lot inside yer,' said Babs, closing the back door. Then she put the plates in the sink and sat back down at the table. 'So, what is it yer doing tonight? I wouldn't mind going to a dance or something.'

'We ain't going to a dance, we're going on a pub crawl. Me and this girl Gina who I met the other night. She knows all the best places where all the GIs go.'

Babs winced and shook her head. 'GIs? No thanks.'

'Please yerself but yer don't know what yer missing.'

'And you don't know what yer getting yerself into.'

Evie laughed disparagingly. 'You're such a moaner, Babs. Every time I've even mentioned Americans, you've gone potty. Go on, come with us, yer'll have a really good time, I promise. And yer'll love Gina, she'll really make yer laugh. Does anything for a lark, that one.'

'Well, that should suit you right down to the ground, shouldn't it – anything for a lark.'

Evie ignored her. 'And the GIs, they're a scream and all.' She smiled. 'They make yer die, honestly, Babs. Like, you ought to hear 'em complain about the damp. I said to this feller the other night, I said, this is flaming summer, mate, if you wanna see damp then you ought to be here in February! He couldn't get over it. And then they go on about how they can't get a glass of cold milk, and they hate the beer. And as for Brussels sprouts, well . . . See, they're missing the good life what they have over there in America, so they need someone who can show 'em the ropes a bit. But, best of all, they miss having a bit of company.' Evie winked saucily. 'And *that* is where me and Gina – and you if yer've got any sense – come into the picture. I'll bet you that if yer come out with us tonight, yer'll have the best time yer've ever had in your life.'

'Will you hark at yerself, Eve. Tell me what's so bloody special about Americans.'

'For a start, yer've never seen so much money being flashed about.'

'Yer used to say that about Albie Denham.'

'Don't talk about him, if yer don't mind, Babs.' Evie waved her hand dismissively. 'And yer know how they're saying that they're overpaid, over-sexed and over here? Well, I say, flipping good job! I mean it, you ought to meet some of 'em, Babs. Them uniforms make 'em look like real dreamboats. All the girls are saying it. Yer can give me a doughboy rather than a Tommy any day.'

'Yeah and the clap and more unwanted babies and all, I suppose.'

Evie jumped up from her seat and jabbed her finger at

Babs's face. 'Oi, you. Yer might be me sister but I ain't having that, not from no one.'

Babs stood up as well. She moved very close to her sister. 'D'you know what I heard someone say about you the other day, Evie?' she asked in a low, controlled voice.

'No. What? What did they say?'

'They said have you heard about that Evie, she's wearing them new utility drawers – one yank and they're down.'

Evie pressed her lips tightly together, then she took a long, deep breath. 'Wouldn't have been that Ginny, I suppose? That loud-mouthed bitch at Styleways?'

Babs shrugged. 'Does it matter who said it?'

'Well, whoever it was, I hope you told their sodding fortune for 'em.' She stared at Babs, her expression hard as nails. 'Well, did yer?'

'D'yer need to ask?' Babs dropped down onto her chair. 'Course I did. Yer know I wouldn't let anyone get away with that. And if yer must know, it *was* Ginny and I would have given her a good hiding and all if Lou hadn't have pulled me off her.' She rubbed her hand over her eyes. 'But whoever says it, it still hurts to hear that sort of thing being said about yer own sister.'

Evie sat down as well. 'So I suppose this means yer don't fancy coming out tonight.'

'Nothing gets past you, does it, Evie?'

'Shut up, Babs.'

They sat there for a moment, both lost in their thoughts.

'So, are you writing to him?' Babs asked eventually.

'Who? President Roosevelt to ask him to send over some more GIs so's I don't run out of fellers?'

'Why don't you stop it, Eve, being clever all the time? Everything ain't a joke.' Babs picked up the letter from the table and waved it in Evie's face. 'You know who I mean. Harry.'

Evie went over to the mantelpiece to fetch her cigarettes. 'What would I wanna be bothered writing to him for?' She lit her cigarette and sat down again.

'Because he writes to you. Really kind, friendly, lovely letters and he deserves a reply. Even if it's to tell him to get lost.'

'I *knew* you'd been reading 'em! Get 'em out of the bin, did yer?'

'Shut up.' Babs hesitated. 'I think you're really cruel.'

Evie picked a piece of loose tobacco from her lip. 'If you're so keen, why don't you write to him?'

'Me? But it's you he's interested in.'

'Is it?' Evie opened her big blue eyes as wide as she could. 'Is it really? I don't think so. It was the *single* one he was interested in, if yer remember. The one without the husband and the baby. Anyway, I dunno what difference it makes who writes to him. If it's "Evie" he wants, just write to him and sign that name. Pretend you're me. Pretend you're the person he *thinks* is Evie.' She laughed. 'Complicated, innit? He thinks that I'm the single one and that you're married. But you're really single and I'm a widow. I mean, neither of us has actually got a husband.'

'Let alone one in a prison camp called Ron,' Babs muttered to herself.

'And he thinks that Betty is the married one's little girl, but . . .' Evie stopped short, having lost track as well as interest; she flapped her hand to show she was bored with the whole thing and then took another drag at her cigarette. 'Aw, I dunno, do what yer like, I don't give a toss. It's no skin off my nose either way.'

'Evie, how can yer treat him like this?'

'Like what? Look, I don't understand why it's such a big deal with this bloke. We've pretended to plenty of fellers before.'

'But Harry's really nice.'

'Aw, it's up to you. Write to him if yer like, if not, chuck the letter in the bin like all the rest.' Evie stood up. 'I'm going up to get ready. If you definitely ain't coming, you can look after Betty and I can go out a bit earlier.'

Babs also stood up. She walked slowly over to the sink. 'Yeah, you go,' she said without looking round.

As she filled the kettle to boil water for the washing up, she heard Evie run up the stairs. Babs stared into the flame as she lit the gas and wondered whether she should, or even if she dared, do what Evie had suggested. Could she really write to Harry pretending to be the make-believe version of Evie Bell that her twin had created – an unmarried young woman without a child? A young woman, in fact, exactly like her except for the bleached blonde hair. And, if she did pretend to be the person he believed Evie to be, could she keep up the pretence, and what should she say to him? I love getting your letters? Please don't write again? Or, worst of all, the truth, and risk him feeling that he had been made such a fool of that he wouldn't want anything more to do with either of them?

Even for November it was an especially dark and gloomy afternoon in the Roman Road. The market traders, many of whom had disappeared from their usual pitches since the war, hated this sort of weather, as people preferred to stay at home round their firesides and keep warm rather than stroll among the stalls.

'Great to hear them old bells ringing again, wasn't it, eh, Art?' said Wally, a fat, elderly man whose stall held nothing but potatoes and carrots. 'Cheered me right up, they did.'

Art, a dealer in secondhand clothes, puffed his chest out proudly. 'My boy was there, yer know, Wally.'

'What, El Alamein?'

'Yup.'

439

'Well, I never knew he was out there, Art. Yer must've been right chuffed when the news about the victory broke.'

Art smiled with pleasure. 'Me and the missus was pleased as punch, I can tell yer. And, d'yer know, when them old bells started ringing to celebrate, it was like being a bit closer to him. Know what I mean?'

'Talking about bells, here's another Bell what's always welcome.' Wally pointed to Babs who was walking towards his stall. 'Hello, love, how are yer?' He turned to Art. 'Look at them dimples. She can even brighten up a rotten November day like this with that smile of hers. If I was a few years younger, girl!'

'Yeah, and if yer wife wasn't working in the pie 'n' mash shop right behind yer, eh, Wally?' laughed Babs. She put her string bag and basket on the ground, balancing them carefully between her feet.

Art nudged the young boy who helped him on the stall. 'See that smile of hers, and how she's all glowing, like? Know what that means?'

The boy shook his head.

'Means she's found herself a chap.'

Babs tutted. 'You and Wally are as bad as each other, Art.'

'Does it?' the boy asked, with a soppy, crooked grin that made his face look lopsided.

'Here,' said Art, poking his young helper in the ribs. 'It ain't you she's sweet on, is it, kiddo?'

The boy blushed crimson from the teasing. 'Leave off, Art. Course it ain't me.'

'It could be.' Babs smiled kindly at the lad and ruffled his hair. She leaned closer to him and whispered, 'Just ignore these two old sods. You give it a while and yer'll be breaking all the girls' hearts round here, just you see. Them two are jealous 'cos they're past it.'

440

The young lad, made confident by Babs's words, repaid her with a wink.

The two elderly traders laughed noisily at the boy's audacity, both enjoying the chance for a bit of a chuckle on a miserable winter's afternoon.

'And how's that gorgeous blonde twin of your'n?' asked Wally.

'Still putting herself about with all the blokes, is she?' the newly self-assured but still very naive youngster asked.

Art and Wally exchanged horrified looks.

Before the boy realised that he had said anything even remotely wrong, Babs had caught him a stinging wallop round his ear. 'Don't you be so bloody cheeky, you rotten little bugger.'

'He didn't mean no offence to yer, darling,' said Art, trying to placate her. 'Did yer, yer big-mouthed little tyke?'

'No,' the boy said, a scowl on his face. 'I didn't mean *you* was like it. I just meant yer sister what's knocking around with all them Yanks.'

This time, Babs didn't have to clout him. Art and Wally did it for her.

'Oi,' the boy yelled, covering his stinging ears with his hands. 'That bloody hurt, that did.'

'Good,' snapped Babs. 'Perhaps yer'll remember it, and it'll learn yer some manners.'

'Want some potatoes and carrots, Babs?' Wally asked, shaking his head in wonder at the boy's stupidity.

Babs shook her head; she couldn't answer, her eyes were brimming with tears.

'Don't upset yerself 'cos of yer sister,' Wally said, putting his short, fat little arm round her shoulder. 'She ain't worth it.'

Babs shoved his arm away. 'Why don't you piss off, the lot of yer? And yer know what yer can do with yer bloody carrots.'

'But I didn't mean—'

'I know exactly what yer meant.'

Wally dropped his arms to his side and lifted his face to the sky. 'Keep yer gob shut, Wally,' he told himself. 'Aw no,' he said, feeling the first spots of rain on his upturned face. 'That's all we need.'

'Good,' sniped Babs. 'I hope yer all get soaked putting yer stalls away.' With that she gathered up her things and stomped off back towards Grove Road.

When she eventually got to Darnfield Street, it was she who was soaked. Her hair was plastered flat to her head and her arms were aching from carrying the shopping. The final straw was when she got to number six and pushed sideways at the door to find it was shut tight. She couldn't believe it.

She didn't want to put the shopping on the ground in the pouring rain, so while she tried to find her key, she juggled the bags from one hand to the other. But it was no good, it wasn't in either pocket, or in any of the bags. She shouted loudly for Evie to open up, but no one came. As a last resort she kicked the door as hard as she could. 'You'd better be in, Evie Bell,' she muttered, looking up at the sky that had now turned a deep leaden grey.

The door opened unexpectedly and Evie was standing there with, of all things, an apron over her dress. 'Look at yer,' she said, 'yer soaked.'

'Yeah. I know. I've been out to get the shopping in the rain, ain't I. And then I couldn't get in me own house and I've been standing here shouting like a flipping nutcase.'

'Well, why don't yer come in then, yer silly mare? Here, let me take them off yer.'

Babs threw her bags on the floor.

'I had to shut the door 'cos Betty was running in and out.'

'Aw.'

'I've made us a nice hot casserole for our tea, from that chicken Maudie give us.'

'Aw.'

'Is that all yer gonna do, stand here in the passage dripping all over the place and saying "aw"?'

'It's just that you surprise me sometimes, Eve.'

'I hope so. I do me best.' Evie picked up the bags and carried them through to the kitchen.

Babs followed her. 'No, I ain't messing around, Eve. I . . . I forget how nice yer can be when yer want to.'

Evie sighed as she heaved the bags onto the draining board. 'Look, Babs, I know yer think I'm a selfish cow, but I really don't mean to be. It's just that I've got so many other things on me mind most of the time.' She looked down at Betty who was sitting under the table totally absorbed in playing with her bricks. 'I sometimes wonder how I got into all this. Being a widow and having a kid. And I don't feel much more than a kid meself half the time.'

Babs put her arms out to Evie and hugged her. 'I know it ain't been easy for yer. And I know yer think I'm a moaner at times, but I don't mean to be ratty with yer. I just worry about yer so much, that's all.'

Evie pulled a face as she lifted Babs's wet hair from her cheek. 'What, worry about me? Don't waste yer time, girl. I'm a survivor, me.'

'Yeah. I know you are.'

Betty looked up. When she realised that Babs was home she clambered up from the floor and grabbed her round the legs. 'Babs!' she yelled, delighted to see her.

Babs bent down and kissed her. 'I can't pick you up, tuppence. I'm all wet, look at me.'

Evie went over to the sink and threw her a towel. 'You get dried off and I'll dish us up some of the casserole.'

Babs wrapped her hair in the towel and went out to the passage to hang up her wet coat. When she came back in, she sat down at the table, lifted Betty onto her lap and started reading a letter that she had brought in with her.

Evie looked round from the stove. 'What's that yer've got there?'

'Nothing.'

'It's that letter that come this morning, ain't it? I bet it's from him again, that Harry.'

'What if it is?' Babs shifted Betty to a more comfortable position.

'Blimey, that's how many months yer've been writing to each other now?'

Babs shrugged. 'A few,' she said nonchalantly.

'A few?' snorted Evie, as she poured ladlefuls of the chicken into two big bowls for her and Babs and a small one for Betty. 'More like six months, I'd say. At least.' She put the rest of the food back in the oven for Georgie and wiped her hands on the apron. 'Come on, let's have a look. Is it full of soppy stuff?'

Babs smiled coyly. 'Might be.'

'It is, innit?'

'Well, the letters have got a bit sort of loving lately.'

Betty, bored with the adults' conversation, scrambled down from her Auntie Babs's lap and returned to her game under the table.

'How d'yer mean, loving?'

'It says all sorts of nice things.' Babs glanced at the letter. 'I really look forward to getting them, more than I can tell yer.'

'Blimey, they must be good. Let's have a look.'

'No.'

'Come on, it's addressed to me, ain't it?'

'Evie, I said no.'

Evie ignored her; she reached out and grabbed the letter from Babs's hand. 'Right, let's see.'

'Evie, I mean it. Give it here. Give it back.'

'No. And look, it *is* addressed to me.'

'You know it's not.'

'But it is, look, it says so. Evie Bell. You're still pretending to be me, ain't yer?'

'I'm pretending that my name is Evie, that's all. You're the one who did all the other pretending. Now give it to me!'

Evie wasn't going to give in so easily, not when she had her mind set on something. She skipped backwards and leapt onto a chair, holding the letter high in the air.

Betty crawled out from under the table and jumped up and down with pleasure at the new game.

Evie's eyes widened as, with head tipped back, she began reading the letter out loud: '"You are being faithful to me, aren't you, Evie?"' she read. '"You are still my girl?" Blimey!' She looked down at Babs and giggled. Babs didn't share Evie's amusement.

'"How's yer sister getting on? Let me know if she's heard any more news of her husband yet. I've been asking around when anyone mentions prisoners of war, yer never know, I might hear something out here."' Evie's mouth fell open. 'Look,' she squealed, holding the letter out of Babs's reach. 'He's done a little drawing of stars and the moon to go with the next bit. Here, he ain't a bad artist, is he?' She winked. 'I've always liked artistic types.'

'Eve, if you don't give me that letter—'

'Sssshhh,' Evie put her finger to her lips. 'Don't shout, yer'll upset Betty.' She returned to her reading. 'This is the bit that goes with the drawing. "Every night at ten o'clock, I want you to go out and look at the stars and I'll be doing the same. Even though we can't be together we'll know that we are looking at the same sky. You know, Eve, lots of fellers get married after only a weekend together." Married, he said! "And I know how they feel. It's like everything's urgent, important. It makes you realise how important it is to have something

445

and someone stable in yer life. I hate to think of you so far away. And I wish you was in the country somewhere instead of in the East End. But I bet Babs is grateful to have you with her and helping her with her little girl. I really do hope she's had good news about her husband. Wish I could explain how important it is to get the letters from you. I'd like to be able to tell you all about what it's like out here. Not to scare you or nothing, but to share it with you. And I'd like you to meet all my mates one day. Good blokes, they are. Tell you what, send me a picture of yourself so I can show them all my blonde bombshell!"' Evie began to giggle. 'Bloody hell, Babs, just you watch him run when he finds out he's fallen in love with a lie!' She dropped her hand to her side and shook her head in wonder. 'What an idiot that bloke must be.'

Babs took her chance to snatch the letter back. 'I hate you sometimes, Evie Bell,' she sobbed and ran out into the passage.

Evie shrugged as she climbed down from the chair. 'Yer always saying that,' she called after her. 'Now come back in here and get this chicken soup down yer. Yer'll soon forget all about it.'

'No, Eve, I won't, not this time,' Babs shouted back as she ran, crying her heart out, up the stairs.

31

Babs pushed open the door to the baker's shop.

'Me!' squealed Betty, pointing up to the brass chime that hung, jangling, behind the door.

Babs lifted her little niece in her arms for her to reach the shiny bell.

'I bet Auntie Rita's got something special for this little girl,' said Rita coming from behind the counter with a glossy topped bun. She held it out for Betty to take.

'Cake!' Betty shouted happily.

'Ssshhh. Uncle Bert made that just for you, don't tell no one,' she whispered.

'Say "ta",' said Babs, lifting Betty onto the chair that stood by the counter.

'Ta,' she echoed as she wriggled backwards to get comfortable and then began busily tackling the sticky treat.

'Dunno about the little'un having a sitdown,' said Rita, glancing critically at Babs's pale complexion. She stepped back behind the counter. 'Looks to me like you could do with a seat.'

'I'm all right, Reet. Bit tired, that's all.'

'It'll be this miserable weather getting yer down. Ne'mind, spring'll soon be here and that always puts a bit of colour in yer cheeks.'

'I hope so.' Babs smiled wearily. 'Got a loaf for us, please, Reet?'

Rita selected the crustiest one from the blackened metal tray that stood on the wide wooden shelf behind her and put it on the counter in front of Babs. 'And there's some birthdays coming up soon if I've got me dates right, ain't there, Babs? That'll be something to look forward to and all.'

'Yeah.' Babs bent down and wiped some cake crumbs from the front of Betty's coat. 'Betty's two on the ninth of March.'

'Betty's!' said Betty gleefully. 'What Betty's?'

'Betty's lovely,' Rita smiled at her.

Satisfied with the admiration, Betty got on with her bun.

'That's this Tuesday, innit?'

'Yeah,' said Babs, straightening up.

'Two, eh? Don't time fly?'

Babs looked at Betty and sighed. 'Yeah, it's unbelievable sometimes. And so's the fact that it's only a couple of months till me and Evie's twenty-first.'

'Smashing! Now that really *is* something to celebrate.'

'D'yer reckon? I don't feel like I've got much to be happy about.'

'The war's getting everyone down, love, don't let it make yer miserable. It don't help, yer know.'

'I know it sounds selfish when people like your Bill are being so brave, but it ain't just the war, Reet, or the weather that's getting me down.' She turned her back to Betty. 'It's Eve, if yer must know. I'm totally knackered and Evie's carrying on like . . . Well, like she always has and I'm just about sick and tired of it.'

'Sick!' repeated Betty.

'Ears like bats, ain't they?' said Rita with a smile. She came from round the otherside of the counter and put her hand gently on Babs's shoulder. 'Look, darling, it's none of my business, and I don't know what's happened between you girls, but I couldn't help but notice the bad

448

feelings between the pair of yer – no one could. But yer shouldn't have bad feelings, especially not in a family. It don't do no one no good. It can only lead to heartache.'

Babs dropped her chin and stared down at the scrubbed tiled floor. 'Since, you know, the way I see her ignoring the little one,' Babs whispered and nodded towards Betty, 'I've really had it with her. I feel like I'm more of a mum than . . .' Babs's words petered out as the shop door opened with a jangle of the bell. 'Hello, Ethel,' she said.

Rita stepped back behind the counter. 'Don't usually see you this early on a Saturday, Ett. Whatever's up with yer? Yer look like yer've had a kick up the bum.'

Babs lifted Betty off the seat and stood her in the corner with the remains of her cake while Ethel Morgan sat herself down on the chair.

'I ain't slept all night,' she said gravely. 'It's my Frankie.'

Rita's hand flew to her mouth. 'Aw no, Ett, he ain't . . .?'

Ethel shook her head and laughed mirthlessly. 'No, I'll never get shot of the dozy old bugger that easy. He's like a bad penny, that one, he'll never come to no harm. No, it was what he told me when he got in last night that's upset me.'

'What?'

'You heard about that terrible business down the Tube at Bethnal Green, didn't yer, Reet?'

'What, that happened a couple of nights ago to them people what was sheltering?'

Ethel nodded.

Rita looked at Babs. 'Did you hear about it? Awful it was. A bomb rolled down the steps and killed every single one of them.'

'No, it wasn't a bomb, not according to the warden what told my Frankie about it.' Ethel shook her head in disbelief as though she couldn't comprehend what she was about to tell them. 'This feller who was telling him, like, he reckons it was getting on for about half past eight, in the evening like. All pitch dark. And they went and let off these new guns they've got in Victoria Park. Massive great things he said they are. Special anti-aircraft, like. Well, the noise carried and them people over in Bethnal Green panicked. Thought it was Jerry bombs gonna fall on 'em. So they all started running for cover, didn't they?' Ethel took out her handkerchief from her bag and wiped the palms of her hands. 'Yer know the station there at Bethnal Green's the main shelter for them parts?'

Babs and Rita nodded.

'So, it was the obvious place to go, wasn't it? And that's where they headed.' She paused again to wipe her hands. 'But the shelter's only got the one entrance, see? Down them steep stone steps. It only took one to stumble.' She bowed her head. 'Frankie said there was a hundred and seventy-three killed.' She looked from Babs to Rita then back to the floor. 'A hundred and seventy-three. Can you even start to think about it? Plus gawd knows how many badly hurt.'

Rita leant against the counter. 'Just up the road really, ain't it, Bethnal Green? I ain't never heard nothing like it. Everyone who's come in the shop's been sure it was a bomb.' She hugged herself and rubbed her arms as though she was cold, sending little puffs of flour dust floating off into the warm air. 'So how comes it's only out now about what really happened?'

Ethel shrugged. 'I asked my Frankie the selfsame question. He just said, they can't just tell us the truth, can they? They're too worried about people getting down-hearted if they knew all that was going on all the time.'

'Getting downhearted,' said Rita scornfully. 'That's a good word for it.' She paused. 'But I suppose they're right in a way. I mean, this bloody war's getting to all of us as it is, without having news like that, that we're all so sodding scared it don't even need bombs to kill us.'

'Yeah,' said Babs. She spoke so quietly that Ethel had to lean forward in her chair to hear her. 'But when yer don't know the real truth about something, that's when yer get all these rumours starting, don't yer? And that hurts people even more. Lies never help.'

Ethel looked up at Babs. 'The truth can hurt and all, girl,' she said. 'And you of all people should know that, coming from your family.'

Babs bristled. 'I think yer'd better explain what yer mean, Ethel.'

Rita drew in her breath and said quickly, 'Poor buggers. Terrible, terrible thing to happen.'

'Yeah,' Babs agreed, keeping her stare fixed on Ethel. 'And it makes silly little family worries seem a bit pathetic, don't it?'

Ethel narrowed her eyes. 'Not when they're family worries about your own sister and her carryings on.'

Babs turned to Rita. 'Sounds like Alice Clarke's been opening her big gob again.' She grabbed her loaf from the counter and stuck it in her string bag. 'Come on, Betty. Time we was getting home to do Granddad's breakfast. I mean, we stand here gassing instead of getting on with our jobs and yer don't know what rumours might get started about us.'

As Babs slammed the shop door behind her, Rita folded her arms and said to Ethel, 'That wasn't called for, Ett.'

Ethel stood up and tucked her handkerchief in her pocket. 'I was only speaking the truth. No harm in that.'

'After all you just said about being careful with telling the truth? And about making people downhearted?'

Ethel curled her lip contemptuously.

'And anyway, you hardly get the truth by listening to Alice Clarke.'

'I ain't had to listen to no one,' Ethel said, striding over to the door. 'I've got the evidence of me own eyes. I live next door to the little whore, remember. I see all her carryings on for meself, thank you very much.'

It was a lovely early June evening, a week after the twins' twenty-first birthday, and Evie was doing her best to work her old trick, perfected over the years, of charming Babs into being friends because she wanted something from her. But it wasn't going very well. Babs hadn't been such an easy touch lately, and it was beginning to get on Evie's nerves; she wasn't used to not getting her own way.

Like most of their neighbours in Darnfield Street, the sisters were sitting out on the pavement on kitchen chairs, making the most of the sunshine. Betty and Janey were playing happily on the step with Betty's building bricks, and the front window of number six was pushed up so they could hear the music on the wireless while they ate the strawberries that Evie had somehow procured, with the sole intent of using them to ingratiate herself with Babs when she got in from work hot and tired.

'It's only for a couple of hours, I promise,' said Evie, sorting through the colander for the darkest red fruits she could find and handing them to her sister. 'And I'll be back well before eleven. And if I can't go, it'll be rotten because there's no way I can get in touch with Gina to tell her, and she'll be left standing there like a right peanut.'

Babs nibbled thoughtfully on one of the luscious berries, licking her lips to savour every last drop of juice. 'How come you said yer'd go out with her in the first place if yer didn't have no one to mind Betty?'

For a brief moment, Evie forgot that she was trying to persuade Babs by being charming, and snapped angrily at her, 'I didn't *say* I would go. Weren't you listening?'

Babs calmly raised her eyebrows at Evie, then bent sideways to put another handful of strawberries onto the plate the children were eating from as they carried on with their building game.

Evie exhaled slowly. 'Sorry. I didn't mean to shout. All right?' She raked her fingers dramatically through her blonde hair. 'It must be the strain of being stuck at home all day that's making me so edgy.'

'Stuck at home? You?' Babs suppressed an incredulous laugh. 'So – you were explaining about Gina.'

'Aw yeah. Gina. Well, she pushed this note through the letter box—'

'You were out, you mean? Not stuck at home?'

'I have to go out sometimes.' She gestured agitatedly at the fruit. 'How d'yer think I got them?'

'I was wondering that. Where did yer manage to get 'em?'

Evie knew when she was on dicey ground and she hurriedly changed the subject back to one that suited her. 'Anyway, this note. It said how I should meet her. Tonight. And 'cos I was cooking yer tea I didn't have a chance to go round and tell her I couldn't go, did I?'

'Let's see.'

'What?'

'The note.'

Evie hesitated. 'I can't remember what I did with it.'

'There's a surprise.' Babs held up a strawberry. 'And this is me tea, I suppose?'

Evie dismissed Babs's cynicism with a shrug and a little wrinkle of her nose. Then she tried a different approach. 'Listen to that,' she said pointing to the open window. '"Besame Mucho" your favourite.'

'Is it?' Babs looked surprised.

'Yeah, yer know yer love it. Come on, let's have a dance.'

'What, out here in the street?'

'Why not?'

Evie got up from her chair and pulled Babs after her into the road. 'I'll lead,' Evie said with a wink. And spun Babs round by the arm and into a rhythmic Latin two-step. She knew that music was one thing that Babs could never resist.

Janey and Betty watched the adults from their seat on the step, and clapped with delight at grown-ups acting so daft.

'Blimey, will yer look at them, Clara,' Minnie called out from across the street. 'It's Fred and Ginger!'

Evie tossed her head back as she and Babs swayed past them. 'Come and join in, girls.'

Minnie grabbed Clara by her hand and the big, buxom women were soon pirouetting around like a pair of youngsters less than half their age.

When the song finished, Minnie and Clara were puffing, their big bosoms heaving from the effort.

'Fancy a few strawberries?' offered Evie, banking on Babs being more amenable if they had company.

Minnie and Clara both nodded.

'Lovely,' said Clara politely, patting her chest as she tried to steady her breathing.

'Not half,' said Minnie, shoving Clara forward.

'We'll fetch yer chairs over for yer,' said Evie, beckoning Babs to help her.

The four of them settled down by the step outside number six, where the children had returned to their game.

Minnie bit into a strawberry. 'Mmmmm,' she murmured approvingly. 'The last time I had these was when me and Clara went fruit picking down in Kent. Before the war, it was. Stayed the whole summer and then for the hop picking. Happy days.' She gestured with the hull end of the berry at Janey. 'How's the little one's mum getting on?' she mouthed. 'She any happier lately?'

Babs leant forward. She checked that Janey was absorbed in her game and then whispered, 'Blanche is still hoping for news, but there's been nothing. She's hardly eating and she looks worn out all the time.'

Minnie turned to Clara. 'We ain't seen nothing of her lately, have we, Clara? We asked her a week or so back if there was anything she wanted, or that we could do to help, like, but she said no.'

Clara nodded. 'Yeah, yer wanna help but yer don't wanna stick yer nose in where it's not wanted.'

'So long as she knows we're here if she does need help.'

'She knows, Min,' said Babs. 'And Mary and Terry are good kids for her. They're doing what they can.'

'But it don't make up for not knowing where Archie is, does it?' said Clara sadly.

Babs shook her head. 'No, Clara, it don't. And she's started taking loads of time off work and all. Staying at home brooding like that can't be no good to her.'

'Yer right,' said Evie, seeing her cue. 'It ain't no good to no one staying at home by yerself all the time.'

Neither Minnie nor Clara had any idea that Evie was trying to bring the subject round to her own problems. Minnie was completely spoiling her plan by continuing to ask about Blanche Simpkins.

'How about the army, can't they help her?' she asked, keeping an eye on Janey in case she realised what they were talking about.

Babs shook her head again. 'Not so far. She says they've gone through the lists of prisoners being held in North Africa but he ain't on any of them. When she's being a bit hopeful she admits they ain't got details of everyone and he still might be being held somewhere. But at other times, yer know, when she's really down, she don't actually say it, but yer can tell she reckons he might be, you know . . .'

'It ain't right,' Evie suddenly piped up, doing her best to turn the conversation back to her. 'Decent people getting killed.'

Minnie and Clara nodded their agreement, but Babs narrowed her eyes suspiciously.

'Then there's that old bag, Albie's mother, who's never done a good turn for no one in her entire life and she's as fit as a fiddle and as strong as a bloody horse. And, you watch, she'll be going strong for bleed'n years. I hate her. She's round here every five minutes when I'm indoors by meself all day, won't sodding leave me alone. Drives me barmy. I wish she'd copped it with her no-good son.'

'Yer shouldn't speak like that, Eve. Not about no one, but especially not about her. She's a nasty bit of work. Yer wanna try and keep on the right side of her.'

'It's all right for you to say that, but you ain't stuck at home having to put up with her coming round and having a go at yer all the time, are yer? Yer should hear her telling me what to do with Betty all the time. I really need a break from it all, Babs. She really is driving me barmy.'

'She's Betty's nan, Eve. And if yer ain't careful, she's gonna really start throwing her weight around. Yer know what she's like.'

Evie was getting angry with Babs; she just wouldn't take the bait and now she had the cheek to have a go at her about bloody Queenie – it'd be a different matter if it was Babs having to listen to her nonstop complaints. 'Course I know what she's like. It's you what ain't got a clue.'

Babs turned her head. 'Have another strawberry, Min, Clara,' she said.

As Clara took another strawberry, the scrawny figure of Alice appeared behind her chair. 'They look nice,' she said with an artful sigh. 'I've been sitting across the road watching yer all enjoying yerselves dancing and eating.

And I thought how lovely it must be having something nice and tasty for a change.'

Evie snatched the colander from Babs and held it up to Alice without a word.

Alice stuck in her bony fingers and pulled out a handful. 'I mean,' she said, her mouth stuffed full of fruit. 'Yer just don't know what to cook from one day to the next. There ain't nothing in the shops, is there?'

'Yer right there,' Minnie said with as friendly a smile as she could manage when looking at Alice Clarke. 'What yer doing for tea tonight?'

Alice popped in another strawberry. 'Stuffed hearts,' she mumbled, her usually sunken cheeks bulging.

Minnie shuddered. 'We can't bear them, can we, Clara?'

Clara shook her head. 'No!'

'See, they remind us of the hospital. That's all they seem to cook for the poor sods in there, and when yer cleaning of a morning yer can smell 'em from the night before, mixed with that horrible stench yer get in the hospital anyway.' She held her nose to demonstrate her distaste.

'But we mustn't complain too much though, eh, Min?' Clara said. 'Since a lot of the firms where we was charring up the City got bombed out, we've lost a lot of our regulars.'

'She's right,' Minnie admitted. 'I never thought we'd say it, but we're really glad of the cleaning work down the hospital lately.'

Evie was not only not very happy with the way things were going, but now she was bored as well. She sucked a final strawberry into her mouth and tipped the rest of the fruit onto the children's plate.

Alice screwed up her mean little face in anger. 'Oi, I wouldn't have minded a few more of them.'

'Tough,' said Evie.

'I dunno,' fumed Alice, shaking her tiny fists with temper at being spoken to like that. 'There's you two old girls working all hours God sends and there's this young madam here sitting around on her arse all day with nothing better to do than upset her elders.'

Minnie and Clara looked mortified to be brought into Alice's ravings, but it didn't seem to bother Evie. She folded her arms and, putting her head to one side, said, 'You talking about me, Alice?'

'If the cap fits,' grumbled Alice, staring at the two little ones tucking into the strawberries.

'Well, yer wrong then, ain't yer,' she said, with a satisfied smirk on her face. ''Cos I won't have time to sit around on me arse, as you put it so charmingly.'

'Eh?' Babs said, suddenly interested.

'You know,' said Evie, flashing a signal with her eyes for Babs to agree. 'Betty starts going to the nursery in Olga Street first thing in the morning and I go back to me old job at Styleways making uniforms.' She smiled sweetly. 'We all have to do our bit for the soldiers, don't we, Alice?'

Alice opened and closed her mouth like a stranded fish and then stormed back across the road to take her frustration out on the long-suffering Nobby.

Babs curled her lip and shook her head at this new wonder. 'I never knew about all this.'

'Never knew meself,' grinned Evie, 'not until I said it just now, anyway.' She stood up and stretched. 'I'll just nip in and get meself tidied up. Gina'll be waiting if I don't move meself.'

'But I never said—'

'She's a real good'un this sister of mine, ain't she, girls?' Evie said to Minnie and Clara, then kissed Babs loudly on the cheek and ran indoors.

'A real idiot, yer mean, don't yer?' Babs said to herself.

The next morning, Monday, Maria had been in the workroom at Styleways for less than five minutes when Ginny started on her.

'Heard any news from Mussolini recently, Axis? He ain't doing very well at the minute, they reckon. Even the flaming Jerries ain't got no time for him no more. I bet you and your mob don't like that very much, do they, eh?' Ginny shoved Joan in the ribs. 'These Eyties stick together, see? They have to, 'cos no one else can stand the sight of 'em, or the stink.'

Maria settled herself in her seat and picked up the first jacket from the pile ready for finishing.

'Oi, Axis,' Ginny shouted. 'I'm talking to you. You ain't deaf as well as stupid, are yer?'

Maria bit off a length of khaki button thread and began lining it up with the eye of her needle. 'Don't waste yer time talking to me, Ginny, 'cos I ain't listening to yer.'

Ginny's mouth fell open. 'Will you listen to her? Cheeky Eytie mare! *She* won't listen to *me*?'

'Have a nice weekend, Maria?' Babs called along to her from her end of the row.

'Yes thanks, Babs,' Maria called back. 'You?'

'Charming,' fumed Ginny. 'She'll talk to the old tart's sister but she won't talk to a decent person like me.'

The double doors at the end of the workshop swung open and Evie wiggled her way in. 'You still stirring it, Ginny?' she asked, waving and grinning at Lou and Maria.

Ginny's mouth fell open. 'What you doing here?'

'I work here. Why? Is it a problem or something?' Evie pulled out the chair next to Babs. 'This where Blanche usually sits, ain't it?'

Babs nodded.

'Good, 'cos Silver said I was to work here for now, till he knows what she's gonna do.'

'What else did he say?' Babs asked.

'The usual.' Evie shrugged and began to intone what the governor had said to her, counting the points off on her fingers. 'Yer a good little worker, Evie. I could do with another pair of hands while Blanche is taking all this time off. I'm glad yer got the nursery to agree to take yer kid, but yer've gotta behave yerself or yer out. All that.' She winked at Babs. 'Aw yeah, I forgot, he also said I was looking as beautiful as ever, much better than me boss-eyed, knock-kneed twin.'

Babs threw a reel of cotton at her.

Evie ducked. 'But if he reckons I'm gonna stay here all night fire watching, he's got another think coming. He thought I'd jump at it. Cheek. He must be mad. Who'd wanna stay here in the dark for three bob a night? Let him do it if he's so bloody keen.'

Ginny threw back her head, sucked in her cheeks and looked at Evie down her nose. 'We should all do our bit, Evie.' She twisted round in her chair and said to Joan, 'But I suppose she's too busy doing her bit for the Yankee soldiers.'

Evie pushed her chair back from the bench. 'Did I hear you right?'

'Dunno. What d'yer think I said? You know what yer up to.'

'Right, that's it.' Evie was on her feet.

Babs grabbed her arms and held her.

'Ignore her, Eve,' Maria said, with a shake of her head. 'The only reason she likes to do the fire watching is so that she can look through all the papers in the office – she's desperate to find out something bad about me.'

'And so she can nick bits of cloth,' Lou reminded her.

'Aw yeah,' said Maria, 'that and all.'

Evie laughed and Babs let her go. She sat back down at the work bench. 'I'm glad I'm back, I missed all this friendliness.'

'I'm glad you're back as well, Eve.'

'Thanks, Maria.'

Maria stared hard at Ginny. 'The more decent people like you that work here, Eve,' she said, 'the easier it is for me to bear having poisonous witches like her around the place.'

Ginny stood up, very slowly. 'What did you say, you rotten, Eytie mare?'

Evie calmly began sewing a button onto a soldier's tunic.

'Oi, deafy, I spoke to you. What did you say?'

Evie stabbed her finger towards Ginny. 'You heard what she said.'

Ginny lunged across the work bench at Maria and grabbed her by the collar of her blouse, but she had hardly touched her before Evie had hold of her by the hair.

Ginny squealed like a pig. 'Let go! Let go of me!'

The double doors flew open. 'Girls, girls.' Mr Silver stood in the doorway with his hand to his forehead. 'Evie. I might have known – back two minutes and there's trouble.'

Evie let go of Ginny's hair and stood up. She smoothed her skirt down over her thighs. 'Only having a laugh, Mr Silver,' she pouted. 'All the girls are so glad to see me.'

Lou said, 'That's right. Delighted, we are.'

Mr Silver relaxed. 'Go on back to work,' he said, and went back to his office.

Ginny's face was twisted with hatred. 'I'll have you, yer rotten Italian cow,' she hissed.

Evie smiled cheekily at Babs. 'I dunno,' she said, her dimples appearing deep in her cheeks. 'What a welcome back, eh. Yer know, I feel like I've never been away. Nothing changes, does it?'

'It don't seem to, where you're concerned,' said Babs.

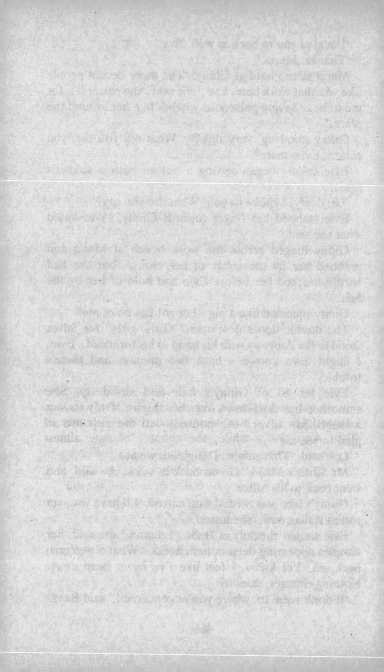

32

On the 3rd of September 1943, as summer faded into yet another autumn, people all over the country marked the fourth anniversary of the outbreak of the war. But it was no time for celebrations. There was still no sign of it coming to an end, and now when people said that surely it couldn't go on for much longer, they sounded as though they didn't really mean it; there was no longer any confidence in their words as they reassured one another that it would soon be at an end and that life would return to normal.

There were, as always, brief moments of relief, such as when Italy capitulated, and again when, at the end of September, services were held on Battle of Britain Sunday in remembrance of the RAF's victories over the Luftwaffe in what now seemed the distant summer of 1940. And, for a while, the country became almost enthusiastic about the war again when rumours began to circulate that the Allies were going to go over to France and give the Germans what for, once and for all. But, by November, gloom had settled in once more, and the thought of starting yet another New Year with the country still at war was beginning to seem like some terrible nightmare that, even with the coming of the early morning light, would not go away.

But, difficult as life was for everyone, Georgie Bell was a man who still had much to be grateful for. Even though

Evie was causing the usual ructions at home and Babs had taken to shouting at her even more than usual, at least his family were fit and well, and his little granddaughter was wonderful, his pride and joy. He had a job that made him feel like a man again and not just some useless drunk who people sneered at or pitied. He had good mates at work who really seemed to like him and enjoy his company. And then, to crown it all, there was his relationship with Maudie Peters.

Since they had started seeing each other and Maudie had taken the post at the sub-station, Georgie had watched her open like a flower that had been put in the sunshine after having been starved of light. He had been afraid to admit it at first, after the pain and loss he had suffered when Violet had left him, but now, whenever he looked at her shining like a freshly polished penny, Georgie was absolutely sure that he was in love with Maudie.

He checked his watch: one minute to six, right on time. He straightened his tie and rapped his knuckles on the door of number seven.

As Maudie opened it, she smiled up at him. 'George, come in, I'm nearly ready.'

Georgie stepped into the dark passageway and waited for her to adjust the blackout curtain across the doorway before she turned on the light.

'I won't be a moment, I'll go up and fetch my coat.' She paused on the second stair, her hand on the banister rail. When she looked over her shoulder at him, she was smiling shyly, the smile that Georgie thought made her look like a young girl. 'I wish you'd tell me where we're going. I've no idea if I've dressed properly.'

'You could wear a potato sack and yer'd still look just the job,' Georgie said. 'And I mean that, Maud. Yer a beautiful woman.'

Maudie blushed. 'I'll just go and fetch my coat.'

As they stepped from the theatre into the sharp cold of the November night, Maudie looked up at Georgie, her eyes sparkling. 'Oh, George, I enjoyed that so much, it was a wonderful surprise. Irving Berlin's music *and* going to the Palladium. What a treat. I'll be singing those tunes in my head for days.'

'Did yer really enjoy yerself?' George asked as he placed himself protectively between her and the crowd that was now pouring out of the theatre.

She nodded. 'I really did. Thanks.'

'Thanks for coming with me.' Suddenly he was frowning. 'I'm standing here rabbiting and you're shivering. I'll get us a cab. There'll be plenty in Regent Street.'

'I'd like to stretch my legs, if that's all right. Do you mind if we walk for a bit?'

'Course not. Whatever suits you.' He jerked his head sideways. 'It's this way.'

Maudie pointed in the opposite direction. 'But isn't the Underground that way?'

Georgie looked sheepish. 'There's another little bit to the surprise. I've got us a table in a little place what Vic Johnson told me about. For our supper like. He took his missus there on their anniversary once.' George concentrated on looking at the wall over Maudie's shoulder. 'Said it was right romantic. Candles and that. And music. Dancing. You know.'

Maudie tucked her arm through his. 'It sounds perfect.'

Georgie felt that he was going to burst with happiness as they strode along in the dark, cold air, with Maudie snuggling into his side to keep warm.

'It must be about three years, you know, since I started to realise what I was feeling.' He laughed at himself. 'Three years. I ain't a very fast worker, am I?'

'Your feelings about what, George?'

465

'About . . .' He hesitated. 'About . . .' Then he came to a complete halt.

'Is the restaurant far?' Maudie asked, sensing his awkwardness.

'No, not too far.' He gulped. 'I wanted to tell yer that . . .'

'Listen, George, I'm not sure if the restaurant's a very good idea.'

Georgie looked crushed. 'If yer'd rather I took yer home straight away . . .'

Maudie shook her head. 'No. Listen.'

He realised what she meant and listened: there was the unmistakable drone of planes approaching and it was growing louder all the time.

'Wonder if they're ours or if they've broken through,' Georgie said, squinting up at the searchlights crisscrossing the black night sky.

'There's your answer,' said Maudie as the sound of an incendiary shower whistling down was quickly followed by the flash and fizz of one of the bombs falling almost at their feet.

Maudie kicked it hard with the side of her shoe and sent the metal canister sputtering into the gutter.

Georgie laughed in amazement. 'You're game for a little'un,' he said admiringly.

'What do you expect from an auxiliary fire woman?' she demanded with a grin and grabbed his hand. 'Come on, let's make a run for it. We can shelter in the Underground.'

'Looks like it's gonna be a bit of bread and scrape when we get home for our supper,' he said. 'I'd really like to have taken yer to the restaurant and all.'

'Bread and scrape sounds wonderful, George.' Maud was panting as they ran along. 'I don't mind what it is so long as it's with you.'

Georgie stopped abruptly, pulled Maudie close to him

and kissed her hard on the mouth.

'I've been waiting so long for you to do that,' Maudie said, looking up at him.

As another incendiary shower came clattering down, they were both laughing so loudly they could hardly move, let alone run.

Maud and Georgie were happier than either of them had been in years, but they were also very cautious and, even though neither of them actually said it in so many words, they didn't want to tell anybody about their feelings about each other – although most people had guessed long ago that they were far more than friendly neighbours. But the unspoken agreement between them was that they would wait and see what the new year would bring and how the war would develop.

When 1944 began, it brought with it bitterly cold winds and snow showers but also a spate of renewed, optimistic rumours that the war was finally coming to a close. But just as with previous moments of confidence, the rumours disappeared as rapidly as they had circulated. It soon became clear that it was to be another New Year of disappointments. Dreams of peace became less frequent and were replaced for many by dreams of more ordinary things such as having a decent plate of food to put on the table – anything rather than powdered egg or whale meat – or maybe a new coat to replace the shabby one that wouldn't see out another winter but might yet have to.

There were intermittent raids, like those towards the end of January, so violent that they led to fears of another Blitz on the East End. But by March, everything on the home front had quietened down again and the only things that marked the month of March for the residents of Darnfield Street were Betty's third birthday, the loud rows and tearful reunions that went on between the Bell twins, and Blanche's further decline into depression.

But with the brighter, longer days of spring came new hope and the murmurings began again that the Allies meant business at last and the Germans would be stopped once and for all. And this time it was not so easy to dismiss the rumours; the Cockneys who had suffered so much and for so long had the evidence of their own eyes to tell them they had something to be genuinely hopeful about. The increased troop movements through London and the spate of furious activity down at the docks told a more convincing story than any rumour in any corner shop or pub could. In fact, almost everyone was now certain that as soon as the weather improved, this would be it – the Allied invasion of Europe, the beginning of the end, the road to peace.

Over the weeks the atmosphere of there being some impending, momentous event intensified, and when in the first week of June the Fifth Army entered Rome, the belief that something closer to home was about to happen reached almost fever pitch.

It was Monday morning and Babs and Evie were meant to be on their way to work but they were still standing at the bus stop in the Mile End Road. The traffic was crawling at slower than walking pace.

'Look at all these rotten lorries holding everything up,' said Babs miserably as she stood on her toes trying to see if their bus was anywhere in sight. 'We're gonna be really late.'

'Silver can't blame it on us this time,' reasoned Evie as she took a cigarette from her bag. 'It ain't our fault half the British forces are passing through London.'

'Wonder if it's true, what everyone's saying about them going to France. D'yer reckon it is?'

Evie tossed her spent match into the gutter. 'I know I've never seen so many soldiers and sailors in me whole life.'

The traffic ground to a complete halt and a handsome

young soldier hung out of the window of his truck. 'Well, what have we here?' he called to the twins in a broad Scottish accent. 'Two little darlings for the price of one. I dunno which one to choose, the blonde or the brunette.'

'Watcha, Jock!' Evie called back to him. 'Give us a lift to work in that motor of your'n and you can take yer pick.'

'I'd love to, sweetheart, but I don't think the army'd let me.'

'Where you off to then?'

'Nowhere by the look of this traffic,' he laughed.

'I'll give yer a lift,' shouted a pink-cheeked young lad driving a delivery van.

Evie shoved Babs hard in the ribs. 'Blimey,' she laughed. 'Don't fancy yours much.'

When Babs saw the unfortunate youngster flush scarlet, she glared at Evie then smiled at him. 'No, thanks all the same,' she shouted back. 'Me and big-mouth here are gonna walk to work. It'll do her good to get some of that weight off her bum.' With that Babs sprinted off along the street in the direction of Aldgate with Evie hot on her heels.

If Babs and Evie, like most other Londoners, had not been sleeping during the early hours of the next morning, they would have been able to see where the soldier had been heading with his truck: to the docks, where ship after ship set off down the Thames. This was it at last, D-Day had come. The Allies were headed for the Normandy beaches.

'Turn the gas stove down a bit, girls. We can have our dinner later on this afternoon.' Georgie held up the Sunday paper; it was full of the successes of the Normandy landings and promises that a swift Allied victory was in sight. 'I think this little lot deserves a bit of a celebration, don't you? Come on, let's go over the Drum.

469

Nellie won't mind if we take Betty in, not on a special day like this.'

Evie had her apron untied almost before Georgie had finished speaking.

'One to keep, this is,' he said as he carefully folded the paper. 'I'll nip along and see if Maudie wants to come.'

'And shall I knock for Blanche?'

'Yeah, good idea, Babs,' said Georgie, disappearing into the passage.

'Leave off,' said Evie, checking her face in the over-mantel mirror. 'I wanna enjoy meself, not listen to her moaning.'

'Don't be horrible, Eve,' said Babs, sitting Betty on the kitchen table and wiping her face with the flannel. 'She's been good to us. You remember that.'

Evie sighed with grudging resignation. 'Aw, go on then.'

Babs pecked Evie on the cheek. 'And it'll give Micky and Blanche's Mary a chance for a bit of a cuddle in private. He's off to training camp tomorrow.'

'Little Micky?'

Babs laughed. '*Little* Micky? I'm surprised you ain't noticed, he's all grown up now. Quite a looker.'

'Blimey.' Evie blotted her lipstick on her handkerchief. 'Makes yer feel old, don't it?'

'Right, I'm going for Blanche. Mind Betty with that stove while yer busy titivating, won't yer?'

Evie turned round from the mirror. 'Babs,' she whined. 'Can't you take her?'

Babs held her hand out to her little niece. 'Come on, sweetheart, come with yer Auntie Babs.'

When Babs knocked next door, it took her and Mary some time to persuade Blanche to go over to the Drum, but they had only been in the bar for a couple of minutes when Blanche left again, spoiling Mary's intentions of

470

giving Micky a leaving present he wouldn't forget in a hurry.

What had sent Blanche running out of the pub, pale-faced and ready to be sick, was Frankie Morgan and another of his catastrophic stories.

'Have you heard?' he broadcast, as he sipped at his pint. 'We've got our very own local hero from Normandy.'

'Aw yeah, Frank,' said Jim. 'Who's that then?'

'Young Percy Bennett from round the corner. Died real brave, they tell me. Won a medal and everything.'

'Dead? Young Percy?' Jim shook his head sadly. 'What a waste.'

Babs didn't notice Blanche leave. She sat there, staring into space, with Betty on one side of her and Evie on the other and Maudie and her dad sitting opposite. 'He won a medal,' she said quietly. 'Just like he said he would. Back in – when was it?' She thought for a moment. 'Some time in 1941 it must have been. Before the Blitz ended.'

'You all right, Babs, love?' Nellie came round from the bar and stood behind Georgie's chair.

Babs shook her head. 'No.'

'What's up with her, Ringer?'

Georgie rubbed his hand over his chin. 'It's Percy, innit? She used to see him at one time. You know, a few years back.'

Nellie gathered Betty up into her arms. 'Jim,' she said, striding back to the bar. 'Take that girl a brandy.'

Brandy was getting to be a rare commodity but Jim immediately poured a generous measure from the bottle he kept for himself under the counter.

'Here y'are,' he said gently, pushing the tumbler towards Babs. 'Get that down yer, love.'

'We used to write to each other now and again, yer know. He reckoned that when he got home I'd marry him. Poor old Perce. I never would have married him.

471

But I liked him. I liked him a real lot. He was decent. His poor mum was so proud of him.' She winced as she took a gulp of the brandy. 'I'll have to take his letters round to show her. I've got some photos and all what he sent me.'

Georgie reached across and touched her hand. 'You do a lot of writing, don't yer, darling?'

Babs looked up at her dad. 'What?'

'Them letters yer write to that other soldier. In the Engineers in Africa or something, didn't yer say?'

'You what?' Evie looked stunned. 'You ain't still writing to old Harry boy, are yer?'

Babs took another drink. This time she didn't flinch, in fact her expression was stony. 'What if I am?' she said flatly.

Evie leant forward, fascinated. 'Does he still think it's me – or the me I made up – what's writing to him? Does he, Babs? Eh?'

Maudie tapped Georgie on the leg.

'Shut up, Eve,' Georgie said, instantly understanding Maudie's signal to break up whatever was going on between his daughters, even though the nature of their dispute was, as usual, a total mystery to him.

Evie pouted and lit herself a cigarette.

Babs sipped at her drink, wide-eyed and lost in some distant place in her mind.

Georgie exhaled slowly and shook his head at Maud. 'Sorry I got yer into this, girl,' he said. 'I thought we was coming over to celebrate.'

Maudie smiled reassuringly and squeezed his hand under the table.

The bar door opened again and Alice Clarke stepped into the pub, closely followed by her husband Nobby.

'What's up with you lot?' Alice asked in her penetrating, scratchy snivel of a voice. 'Someone died?'

'Yes, someone has, actually,' said Evie, putting her arm protectively round Babs – it was all right for her to

472

upset her twin, but woe betide anyone else who dared do such a thing. 'And me sister's upset about it and all, so you watch yer trap, Alice.'

Georgie stood up and looked imploringly at Maud. 'Say something,' he urged her. 'I'll fetch some more drinks.'

'Even with this terrible news about young Percy Bennett—' Maudie began.

'Percy Bennett?' shrieked Alice, never one for discretion. 'That's who's dead, is it? Here, weren't he sweet on you at one time, twin? How'd he die then?'

Georgie sat down defeated, but Maudie ploughed gamely on. 'We shouldn't be downhearted. We should be feeling proud and hopeful. We're really winning now. There's really light at the end of the tunnel this time.'

Frankie Morgan strolled over to the table and shook his head wisely. 'No,' he said. 'It don't do to get too excited. Everyone's going bonkers over this bit of luck we had in France. They wanna think on, or they'll be laughing on the other side of their faces before the week's out, you mark my words. I'm telling yer, I've seen it all before. Yer laughing one minute then yer crying. Yer never know what horrible news is waiting for yer just around the corner.' He took a long pull at his beer. 'Light at the end of the tunnel? Aw yeah, there's that all right, and it's a sodding train that's coming steaming towards yer, that's what it is.'

'Leave off, Frankie,' Ethel Morgan growled at her husband. 'Yer as bad as Nobby Clarke.'

'No one's as bad as my Nobby,' said Alice, bristling with competitive indignation.

Ethel glared at Alice then turned her attention to her hapless husband. 'Well, I reckon we should be able to accept a bit of good news for once without it being spoilt by something horrible going wrong. D'you hear me, Frankie? All right, Percy Bennett's dead, and it's very sad for his mother, but the war's gonna be over soon, and I reckon we should all be glad. Not bloody moaning.'

'Not moaning? Yer wrong, Ethel, I told yer. I tell yer all the time,' Frankie corrected his wife authoritatively. 'It's no good going around with a grin on yer bloody chops 'cos life ain't like that.' Then he lowered his head and muttered to Nobby Clarke out of the side of his mouth, 'And I should bloody well know, I've been married to Ethel for forty years.'

33

The next day, sad as the news about Percy had made her, Babs still couldn't help but be infected by the new atmosphere of light-heartedness and hope for the future that was all around her at work. The successes in France seemed to have convinced them all at Styleways that not only was London actually safe to live and work in at last, but that the war was almost over and life would soon return to normal. And even though it was a Monday morning, everyone was chirpy and making jokes; Ginny was only a bit horrible to Maria, and Mr Silver brought in a tray of cake he had managed to get from somewhere which he shared out during their afternoon tea break by way of celebration. With such a buoyant atmosphere, it was easy to dismiss the isolated pessimists like Frankie Morgan as being out-of-touch doom merchants. But, before the next day had fully dawned, it was to be Frankie Morgan, not the exuberant optimists, who was to be proved correct.

It was almost sunrise, not quite half past four on Tuesday morning. The date was the 13 June: *the thirteenth*, an unlucky day as Frankie was later continually to impress on everyone.

Betty, who now slept in the double bed in the front bedroom of number six with her mum and her aunt, sat up and began to shake Babs's arm.

'Flash, Babs. Flash,' she pleaded insistently.

Babs sat up beside her. She yawned and rubbed her hands over her eyes. 'What, darling?' she asked, her voice thick with sleep. 'D'yer want a wee-wee?'

Betty shook her head, making her thick dark curls bounce round her face. 'Flash. She's sad.'

Babs blinked. She was waking up now. 'I dunno about sad, she's going flaming barmy.' She threw back the covers. 'Move over here next to yer mummy, babe, and let me get out.'

'Wanna come with you.'

'What's up?' Evie pushed herself up on her elbows and opened one eye. 'It's the bloody middle of the night, what's going on?'

Babs was standing by the bed putting on her dressing gown. 'Flash. There's something the matter with her. I'm going down to see.'

Evie groaned, turned over and pulled the covers up over her head.

'I won't be a minute, precious. You stay here with Mummy.'

Betty pouted but did as she was told.

Babs padded barefoot down the stairs and into the kitchen. She screwed up her eyes from the glare as she turned on the light. 'Now, madam,' she said softly, trying to calm the distraught animal. 'What's all this fuss about? Wanna go out, do yer?' Babs opened the back door and Flash dived out into the yard like a mad thing. She sniffed the air and then threw back her head and began howling pitifully.

'For gawd's sake,' hissed Babs, dragging her back by the collar. 'Yer'll have the whole bleed'n street awake.'

Flash wouldn't be held; she pulled away from Babs, leapt at the back wall and started baying loudly.

Next door, someone slammed the upstairs window right up on its sash making the frame shake and the panes rattle. 'What's all that sodding row down there,' hollered

Frankie. 'I'm on lates, fire watching from tonight, and if you don't stop that bloody hound's noise, I'll come down there and—'

'Shut up, Frank,' shouted Babs.

Frankie's mouth dropped open. He looked more carefully; it *was* the dark twin and not the saucy blonde one. 'Cheeky little mare.' Frankie turned round and called into the bedroom, 'Ethel, can you hear the way she's speaking to me? And it ain't the blondie neither.' He stuck his head back outside and scowled at her. 'I've told Ethel,' he said, as though that settled everything.

'Frankie, please,' Babs insisted. 'Shut up, I mean it. Just listen, will yer?'

Reluctantly, Frankie listened. There was a strange sound in the distance, not quite like an aeroplane but not quite like anything else either. It grew louder. Now it sounded more like a revved up motorbike engine. Then, quite suddenly, it stopped.

'I ain't got no time for this,' Frankie scolded her. 'I've gotta get me rest, I'm on bloody duty later.'

Babs gasped and pointed to the end of the yard. A huge dark shape was whistling down from the sky.

'What the hell?' shouted Frankie. 'Blimey, it's a plane coming down. I'll have to—'

Frankie was silenced again, but this time it wasn't by Babs, it was by a terrible explosion followed moments later by an unbelievably powerful blast.

Frankie held his hands over his eyes to protect them from the grit. 'Christ Almighty, that couldn't have been no plane,' he hollered, squinting through the dust. 'But whatever it was, it looks like it's come down by the railway bridge in Grove Road. We've gotta go and help.' As he finished speaking he disappeared inside, leaving the bedroom curtains flapping out of the open window.

By the time Babs managed to drag the now almost hysterical Flash indoors, Georgie was in the kitchen pulling on his trousers over his pyjamas and Evie was helping Betty put her coat on over her nightie.

'I told Eve, you girls get yerselves and that baby over the Drum,' he instructed Babs over his shoulder and strode into the passage. 'And barmy as its howling's driving me,' he called from the street door, 'yer might as well take that flaming dog and all. I'm gonna go and see what's happening.'

When the twins followed Georgie outside, they coughed and spluttered in the dirt and dust from the explosion that had turned the dawn light into a hazy dusk. The street was full of activity. Maudie, with a first-aid kit tucked under her arm, was almost at the top of the turning where it joined Grove Road, and Georgie had broken into a run to catch up with her; Frankie was on his step trying to make himself ready for action by adjusting the strap of his warden's helmet, but was being hampered by Ethel's insistent supervision; Alice and Nobby Clarke were standing at the street door of number five with cups of tea in their hands looking for all the world as if they were spectators at a sporting event, while upstairs Minnie and Clara were leaning out of their window trying to find out what was happening by Minnie shouting questions down to Terry Simpkins, his sister Mary and Jim Walker from the pub, who were standing in the middle of the road.

'Honest, Min, we dunno what it was,' Terry shouted back with a shrug. 'But Jim's called the fire brigade and they're on their way with the rescue people, so we should know something soon.'

Bert and Rita from the baker's came up to the little group and stood next to Mary who looked as if she was about to cry. They both looked dazed and there was a thin trickle of blood coming from Bert's nose. 'What's happening?' Bert sounded odd, half asleep. 'I was doing the loaves down in the bakehouse and it started shaking

478

about, like we was on a ride at the fair or something. When we come upstairs, all the windows was blown out.'

Nellie came striding over. 'Come on, Reet, and you, Bert. Girls,' Nellie jerked her thumb at the twins, 'get yerselves down my cellar. Yer never know, there might be another one of them things on the way.' She beckoned to Mary who had started softly weeping. 'And you fetch yer little sister and try and get that Blanche over here and all, Mary.'

'I can fetch Janey over,' Mary sniffled and shuddered through her tears. 'But I can't make Mum get out of bed, Nell. She won't move.'

Nellie put her arm round Mary's shoulders. 'You go in the pub with the twins. Go on. And I'll go in yours and fetch Janey. And I'll see what I can do with yer mum.'

Mary nodded and let Babs lead her away.

Nellie twisted round and pointed to the upstairs of number five. 'Minnie, why don't you and Clara go in the pub and all? Go on, yer dunno if that thing's gonna go off again. And you two, come on,' she said briskly, nodding at Alice and Nobby. 'And tell Ethel while yer at it. I'm sure I saw her go back indoors.'

'Any more orders?' muttered Nobby.

'No, that's all,' said Nell and made her way smartly over to number four.

While all that was going on in Darnfield Street, at the top of the turning and just round the corner – where the thing, whatever it was, had fallen – Grove Road was in total confusion.

Maudie and George just gave each other one look and got stuck straight in, doing what they could. Maudie rolled up her sleeves and set to work with the ambulance crews, putting to good use the first-aid training she was now grateful to have done at work, while Georgie, who recognised some of the men from the sub-station, helped them shift the timbers and rubble away from the trapped and injured victims, in the race to release them before the ruptured gas mains blew.

'I ain't never seen no bomb damage like this before,' puffed Georgie as he helped heave a massive lump of plaster-covered brickwork to one side.

'Nor me, mate,' said the gasping grey-haired man who was working with him.

'And why's there so many law about?' he asked as the two of them somehow flipped what had once been a section of internal wall onto its side, exposing a tangle of wooden roofing rafters lying at weird angles in the remains of the front parlour of what, only fifteen minutes ago, had been a three-storey home housing two peacefully sleeping families.

'There's talk it was a Jerry plane what crashed,' groaned the grey-haired man as he braced himself against a pile of rubble and tried to wrench out one of the beams. 'They're here searching, in case there's a pilot what bailed out.'

Georgie took a deep breath and helped the man dislodge the timber; his palms were stabbed with splinters as his hands rasped along the shattered edges. 'What, yer reckon a plane could make a crater this big? Cause this much damage?' He sounded more than a little sceptical when he eventually managed to get the words out.

'No, mate,' the man replied in gasps. 'I don't reckon I do. To tell yer the truth, I dunno what could have done this kind of damage. Look, the WVS are here, let's get a cuppa. I've gotta have a break.'

'What's the reckoning so far?' Georgie asked a rather elderly-looking police officer who joined them at the mobile canteen.

The constable lowered his head and let out a long, slow breath. 'They've counted six dead so far.' His voice was flat, expressionless from shock. 'At least thirty badly injured. And just for good measure the feller over there reckons there's gonna be a good couple of hundred people left homeless and all.'

The grey-haired man wiped the back of his grimy hand across his grit-covered mouth. 'I don't understand why there weren't no warning.'

The policeman took off his helmet and hooked it over the wing mirror of the WVS truck. 'That's why they're saying it must have been a Jerry plane what copped it.'

Georgie shook his head. 'No. That weren't no plane. Me and this bloke here've been digging in that lot and we've both been on sites where planes have crashed. We ain't seen no sign of no airman, no bits of plane. Nothing like that at all.'

The police officer put his empty cup on the fold-down counter and nodded his thanks to the volunteers. 'So what was it then?' he asked, unhooking his helmet from the mirror. 'What was it caused all that damage?'

During the next three days, people all over the capital were asking the same question – just what was causing these terrible blasts? Whatever it was, they were happening at a reported rate of up to seventy-three a day. There weren't the huge fires afterwards as there had been during the Blitz, but the immense explosive power was causing devastating numbers of deaths and appalling destruction. Worst of all, some said, was that there was no accurate warning; the sirens would stop and start and stop again, bringing consternation and confusion. But what really caused panic was when the terrifying noise, a distant humming that became louder and louder and more and more threatening as it got closer, suddenly cut out. That was the moment of real terror, the appalling interval of silence when you waited for it to strike, not knowing where it would hit until the impact finally came, followed by the tremendous explosion.

After three days of this nightmare of not knowing, it

was at last admitted in an official statement that London was under attack from a new weapon: the V-1 rocket. *That* was what had hit the houses by the railway bridge in Grove Road.

And so, with the coming of what was soon to be known as the doodlebug or flying bomb, a new chapter of war began; a new threat to the lives of the East Enders who had put up with so much already, and a new wave of exhaustingly hard work for the fire service which, with the rescue and search services, the ambulance crews and civil defence workers, had to cope with the horrifying consequences of the new weapon.

After five years of war, it was as if London had been smacked in the face; it wasn't nearly over after all, and by the time the long summer days were stretching into July, the doodlebugs were targeting London both night and day.

On one of those bright summer mornings, Babs and Evie were taking Betty to the nursery before they went on to work. As they stood on the kerb waiting to cross Grove Road, they saw Minnie and Clara walking towards them on their way back from their early morning cleaning jobs.

'Morning, Min, Clara,' Babs called with a little wave. 'You're back early today, ain't yer? It ain't half past seven yet.'

As the two grey-haired women got closer, the twins could see from the stunned look on their ashen faces that something was wrong.

Babs scooped Betty protectively into her arms.

'Clara, what's up?' Evie asked steadily. 'Min? Talk to me.'

Clara covered her face with her hands.

'It's the hospital,' Minnie said, waving her hand feebly in the direction of Mile End. 'It's been hit by a doodle-bug.'

Evie's hand flew to her mouth. 'Aw gawd, Min. You all right?'

Minnie shook her head. 'No. No, I ain't. I don't feel that well, to tell yer the truth.'

Evie flashed a look at Babs and then took the women's bags and gently steered them towards Darnfield Street. 'Come on, ladies, me and Babs'll take yer in the baker's and Rita'll make yer a nice cup o' tea.'

Evie knocked on the shop's recently replaced glass door with her knuckles. 'Hurry up,' she urged, peering into the unlit interior of the shop. She stepped back. 'Here's Rita.'

Rita's head appeared at the top of the narrow stairway that led down to the kitchens in the basement. She was red-faced from the heat of the ovens and didn't look best pleased at being dragged upstairs, but she took one look at the four women and little Betty standing outside in the street and rushed over to open the door.

'What's up?' she asked, pulling the door back on its hinges. She gestured with her head for them to come inside.

Babs put Betty on the floor and whispered to Rita, 'There's been one of them sodding doodlebugs at the hospital, while Minnie and Clara was working.'

Rita stared at Minnie and Clara's colourless cheeks. 'I put the chairs out the back in the storeroom while I was cleaning,' she said to the twins. 'Yer know where they are. And mind yer don't slip, I've only just mopped the floors up here.'

Evie and Babs ducked behind the counter to fetch them.

Rita patted first Minnie's hand then Clara's. 'I'll go downstairs to Bert and tell him to put the kettle on. I'll only be a minute.' She held out her hand to Betty. 'You come down with me to see yer Uncle Bert, eh, darling? I'll bet he's got something nice for yer to eat.'

Evie and Babs returned from the storeroom and the two grey-haired woman sat down gratefully on the seats.

Rita reappeared from the stairwell and bent forward to take the tray of tea that Bert was handing up to her.

'Did someone at the hospital have a look at you two?' Rita asked them gently as she put the tray on the counter and poured the tea. 'Shock can be nasty, yer know.'

'No. See, they was ever so busy, Reet.' As Minnie spoke she was looking out of the window, but her eyes were glazed, unfocused. 'There was people there what got hurt, real bad some of 'em. And they was ill already and all. Poor sods.'

'So we come home.' Clara's voice was so quiet they could barely hear her. 'We didn't know what else to do.'

Rita tried to give her her cup, but Clara's hands were trembling so badly she couldn't hold it. 'I'm gonna fetch Dr Land,' Rita said.

Clara looked up. 'Please don't bother him, Reet, we're all right.'

Rita bit her lip. 'Well, at least let me go over to Nellie's to get yer both a drop of brandy,' she said. 'Look at yer, yer shivering.'

'You stay here,' said Babs, walking over to the door. 'I'll go.'

Clara was getting on for sixty but as she glanced up at Rita the look in her eyes made her seem like a frightened little girl. 'I've been scared before, Reet,' she said. 'Lots of times. But this time . . . this time . . . Aw, I'm *really* scared. And Minnie looks real bad. Look at her.'

'Please, Clara. Don't upset yerself.' Evie knelt down beside her chair and held her hand.

Clara sniffed. 'I'm beginning to believe them stories you hear.'

'What stories are they then, Clara?' Evie asked her quietly.

'That these flying bomb things know how to find yer.'

Now Clara was weeping openly. ''Cos I'm sure they're after us. First Grove Road, then the hospital.'

The sight of the two fine, big women reduced to tears almost had Rita and Evie crying with them.

'Look, here's Babs,' Rita said, trying to sound cheerful.

Babs handed Rita a bottle of brandy. 'Nellie said she wishes yer both well and she'll pop down and see yer later on. And yer to have as much as yer want of that 'cos it's only Jim's, so she don't care.'

Rita smiled and tipped a good measure of the spirit into Minnie's and Clara's cups but their hands were still shaking so much that she and Babs had to help them hold the cups to their lips.

'You'll get used to these rotten doodlebug things,' Evie said brightly. 'You just see. Yer'll be like me soon. If Babs here hadn't woke me up, I'd have slept right through all that bloody row the night that first one fell in Grove Road.'

'That's right,' said Babs, smiling encouragingly. 'She would have and all.'

'It's like that old Mrs Meacher,' said Evie, with an equally determined smile. 'D'yer know her? Funny-looking old girl from down Bolldover Road way. I saw her down the Roman when we was queuing for spuds the other day.'

Babs looked at Evie questioningly. 'Who?' she said.

Evie winked. 'You know, Babs. Nose like a beetroot and ear'ole like a cauliflower.'

Babs nodded. 'Aw yeah,' she said, realising that this was one of Evie's tales. 'Her.'

'Well anyway, this Mrs Wheeler—'

'Meacher,' Babs reminded her.

'Yeah,' Evie said. 'That's what I mean. Well, she only woke up to find all her windows blown out, didn't she. A doodlebug had crashed into the very next street and she didn't know a thing about it. Slept right through the whole lot. Bad as me. And yer'll never guess what, when someone from the newspaper come round to talk to her, to ask her about it, like, if the bombs scared her and that, do you know what she said? She said, I look at it this way: when the bloody thing's got as far as England, then it's gotta find London, ain't it? Then after that it's gotta find its way down to the East End. And then it's gotta find its way here to Bow. And however it'd sort out Bolldover Road from all the rest, I don't know. And after all that it's still gotta find its way to number fourteen. And even if it did, if yer knew me and my Lukey, yer'd know the chances are that me and him'd be down the Earl of Aberdeen anyway!'

'You're a girl, Evie,' Rita said, and she and Babs started laughing. Then, despite everything, Minnie and Clara joined in.

'Blimey,' said Evie, 'that brandy must be a bit cooshty, making you pair laugh. Here, give us a drop.'

'You stick to tea, girl,' Babs warned her, picking up her cup. 'We don't wanna give Mr Silver no more reasons to threaten yer with the push.'

Evie tutted loudly and rolled her eyes, making Minnie and Clara start laughing again.

Babs sipped at her tea and then said, 'I'm not sure what yer think of this idea, but Maudie Peters was saying the other day how the vicar had told her about some rest place the church has got in Gloucestershire somewhere. She mentioned it 'cos of Blanche, but shall I say that you two might be interested in having a little break away from all this?'

'That's a good idea,' said Rita. 'Here, and hopping starts in about six weeks, don't it? Yer could do worse than go down there for a couple of weeks.'

Clara clasped Minnie's hand and looked at her imploringly. 'Aw, Min, I don't think I wanna leave here. Not even for a little while.' She looked at the twins, then at Rita and then back at Minnie. Her lip was quivering. 'I wanna stay here with me friends, where there's people we know we can depend on.'

'We ain't gotta go nowhere,' Minnie reassured her. 'Babs and Rita only wondered if we wanted a little holiday.'

'Course we did,' Babs promised her.

Rita took their cups and put them on the tray. 'Let me make some more tea.'

'Not for us, ta,' said Babs holding up her hand.

'It's all right, yer welcome. I've got plenty. Bert got some off a feller he knows – swapsies, it was, for a tray of pie.' She laughed. 'Don't ask what was in the pie, yer don't wanna know.'

'No, it ain't that, Reet, honest, and we know we're welcome, but we've gotta be off to get Betty to nursery.' She looked at her watch. 'And if we don't hurry ourselves we're gonna be late for work.'

Evie winked at Clara. 'Old Silver, that's our governor, he's a good bloke but he can be worse than any flipping doodlebug when he gets going. Gets right excited, he does.'

Clara smiled weakly.

'Look, why don't yer let Betty stay with me today?' Rita suggested. 'It won't hurt, will it? And I bet she'd enjoy herself. She's no trouble, love her little heart.'

'Suits me,' said Evie, looking at Babs.

'Smashing, Reet, but someone'd have to drop a note round the nursery to let 'em know, like. They worry if yer don't come in, 'cos of,' she pointed to the ceiling, 'you know, in case something's happened.'

'I'll make sure they get a note, girls. Don't you worry. You just get yerselves off to work.' Rita ushered them to the shop door. 'Thanks for bothering to bring Minnie and Clara in,' she whispered.

'Daft,' said Babs. 'How's that a bother?'

'Well, I reckon it was thoughtful. They was in a right state.'

Babs shrugged. 'It was a pleasure.'

Rita kissed each of them on the cheek and then looked up at the bright blue summer sky. 'Now, you two look after yerselves, won't yer. Yer never know when them bastard things are coming over.'

'Don't worry about us, Reet,' grinned Evie. 'We're as tough as old boots, us Bells.'

Evie tossed another greatcoat sleeve to one side and looked up at the clock. 'Quarter to five.' She sighed. 'Blimey, this afternoon ain't half dragged. And I'm hungry.'

Babs turned to Lou and smiled. 'Hark at her.'

'Going out tonight, Eve?' Babs asked.

'Probably,' Evie said wearily. 'Me mate Gina mentioned something.'

'That's a shame,' said Babs, winking at Lou. ''Cos Lou said she was gonna ask us round hers tonight, 'cos they're having roast beef and Yorkshire pudden for their tea. Ne'mind.'

Evie threw a sleeve at Babs's head and squealed, 'You liar.'

Babs threw the sleeve back. 'No I'm not,' she giggled.

'Are!' Evie shouted back and soon the sisters were in a laughing, wrestling heap on the floor, flapping at each other with khaki overcoat sleeves.

'Just look at them,' sneered Ginny. 'What a disgrace.'

'No sense of humour, some people,' Lou said to Maria.

'And some people have got no sense of loyalty to their own country, talking to Eyties,' fumed Ginny.

Maria stood up. 'I've just about had it with you and your snidey comments, Ginny.' She took a step towards Ginny and suddenly she felt as though the world had been turned upside down. There was a massive explosion, the windows buckled and then the glass came crashing down on her. Maria was thrown right across the room in a tumbling heap of cloth, chairs and boxes.

'Bloody hell!' yelled Evie and rolled herself into a ball.

When the thundering sound stopped, she lifted her hands gingerly from her head and got herself onto her knees. She peered around her; the air was thick with dust.

'Blimey,' she said. 'This place looks like a bomb's hit it.'

'Yer scatty, mare,' she heard Babs say. 'Of course it looks like a bomb's hit it. One just flaming did.'

'Babs?' Evie coughed and spluttered, trying to rid her throat of the grit. 'Babs? You all right? Where are yer?'

'Here. I'm stuck down here under the work bench.'

'Stuck? Aw, Christ.' Evie crawled towards her. 'D'yer think yer can move without me hurting yer?'

'Yeah. I don't think I'm injured or nothing, it's just this flaming machine in the way.'

Evie took a deep breath, grabbed the heavy industrial machine in both hands and wrenched it free with one enormous pull.

'You been eating yer greens?' Babs grinned up at her as she crawled out on her belly from under the work bench. She rolled over on her back and lay there, eyes closed, trying to get her breath.

Evie dropped to her haunches. 'Yer sure yer all right?'

'Bit bruised and a few cuts, that's all.' Babs laughed. 'You was right this morning, weren't yer? When yer told Rita that us Bells are as tough as old boots.'

Evie grinned and ruffled her twin's filthy hair. 'Yer might be tough, but yer look lousy. Yer should see yer face. Looks like yer've been doing a coal round.'

Babs opened her eyes. 'Yer don't look so good yerself. And yer sleeve's all ripped and all.' Babs patted her hair primly. 'I dunno if I wanna be seen on the bus with you tonight,' she teased.

'Saucy mare.' Evie held up her tattered sleeve. 'I did that pulling out that machine. You can get me a flipping new frock for that. I want all your coupons. Every one of 'em.'

Babs smiled up at her. 'Typical. I might have known yer wouldn't save me life for nothing.'

Suddenly serious, Evie bent forward and kissed her. 'So long as yer all right, Babs, I wouldn't care if I didn't have another new frock ever again.'

'Will someone help me?' The sound of Joan snivelling made Evie turn round. 'I've got glass in me corsets,' she whined. 'And I'm frightened to take 'em off in case I cut meself.'

Evie pulled herself to her feet. 'Hang on, Joan. I'll just see to Babs.' She went and got her coat from the stand. 'I think this is about the cleanest thing in here,' she said, shaking it violently back and forward. Then she propped it under Babs's head. 'Don't you dare bleed on that,' she said, wagging her finger at her twin. Then she took Joan by the arm. 'Come on, you. Let's go in the lav and I'll sort yer out.'

Joan limped along pathetically beside her. As they got to the double doors at the end of the room, Mr Silver and the warehouse workers came rushing in.

'Careful, you,' Evie shouted at Mr Silver. 'Joan here's leaning all her weight against me and I can hardly support her as it is, without you lot bashing into me.'

'Sorry, Eve. Go on, through you go.' Mr Silver ushered them past him. 'Everyone else accounted for up here?'

Babs looked up at him from her makeshift bed on the floor. 'I ain't sure, but I think I just heard a noise coming from under the bench here.'

Lou knelt down and peered into the jumble of chairs, bench legs, machinery and broken glass. 'I think it's

Ginny. But I can't get through there to see properly.'

Maria knelt down beside her. 'I reckon I can get in there,' she said and started squeezing her way into the tiny gap, edging her way forward inch by inch.

'I think we should wait for the rescue squad,' Mr Silver said nervously.

'It is Ginny,' Maria called to them. 'I can see her. She's wedged sideways. I can't tell how bad she's been hurt though.'

Mr Silver went over to the glassless window and looked out. 'There's chaos out there. No sign of the rescue people.'

'I'll have to do something.' Maria sounded serious.

Mr Silver thought for a moment. 'Well, for God's sake be careful, Maria.'

After a few tense moments, Maria called out again. 'This stuff keeps slipping when I try and move her. I need another pair of hands in here.'

'I'm little,' said a male voice from behind Mr Silver. 'I can get in there next to yer.'

'Tiddler?' Mr Silver frowned. 'I'm not sure.'

But Tiddler wasn't listening to his governor's reservations. Ducking down, he began wriggling his way forward. After much panting and puffing, he reached Maria.

'Hold that bit to one side for me,' Maria said, 'so's it don't fall and I can get this chair shifted. It's digging right in her back. That's it, Steve. Hold it there.'

'What did you say?' Ginny's voice was faint.

'Don't worry yerself, Ginny, Maria said gently, 'it don't look like the chair's damaged yer or nothing. It's just the legs are blocking yer in.'

'I don't mean about the bloody chair,' Ginny snapped impatiently, her voice more like her usual whine.

'What?' Maria said.

'I heard you call him "Steve".'

'Well,' the now fascinated machinists and warehouse

workers heard Maria reply, 'when me boy friend's name is Steven, what d'yer think I should call him, Cyril?'

'No,' they heard Ginny answer. '"Tiddler", just like everyone else.'

There was a pause and then they heard Maria speak again. 'Shall I let this chair fall back on her, Steve?'

'No!' Babs shouted insistently. 'Don't do that, Maria. I wanna see the look on her face when yer drag her out.'

Unaware that his daughters were waiting at the factory for their turn to be checked over by the ambulance crew, Georgie had just gone into the watch room at the sub-station to sign on for the evening shift.

When he had handed the completed duty book back to Sub-officer Smith, Flossie touched him gently on the shoulder. 'There's already a couple of incidents on the report sheets from this afternoon, Ringer.'

He smiled over at Maudie who was sitting by the switchboard. 'We could be in for another busy night, then.'

'One of them was Aldgate way,' Flossie said.

He swallowed hard. 'Blimey, I hope the girls are all right.'

'I thought you'd want to know.'

'Yeah, ta, Floss.' But Georgie didn't have much time to worry.

Within minutes the reports were coming in again and he had no choice but to put his daughters to the back of his mind and concentrate on driving his crew.

When Georgie eventually got back to the sub-station, dawn was breaking.

Yawning loudly, he dragged himself into the watch room where he knew, even though her shift was over, Maudie would be sitting waiting for him.

'Bought yer a present,' he said, kissing her on the top of her head.

He stuck his filth-engrained hand into his tunic pocket and took out a slab of grey, bone dry cake wrapped in his hankie.

Maudie fluttered her eyelashes. 'You old romantic,' she said.

'An old girl come out with it from one of the houses opposite where we was working. "Get yer laughing gear round that," she said. "Used me last few currants in that, I did."'

Maud took it from him and looked at it closely.

Georgie winked at her. '"I'm giving this to me girl," I told her, and that's what I've done.'

'Aw, ain't he sweet,' said Flossie from the battered old armchair in the corner.

'You still here as well, Floss?'

'Yeah, we can't sleep till all our boys are home, can we, Maud?'

'Well, they're here now, so bugger off,' one of the girls from the other shift said. 'Go on, go and get some kip.'

Outside in the playground, Georgie said to Maud, 'Yer ain't really gonna eat that horrible cake, are yer?'

'Not if you promise you won't be offended. But it does seem ungrateful when the woman's used her last currants and everything.'

'I didn't wanna take it off her, but she really wanted me to have it.' Then Georgie grinned. 'I know someone who'll really enjoy it.'

He led Maud over to the pen the firemen had built for the pig club sow, took the cake from her and threw it to the fat pink creature who snuffled it up in one appreciative gulp. Then he put his arm round Maudie's shoulder and started to laugh loudly.

'What's tickling you?'

'I just thought about a stroke that Albie Denham pulled. He was a rogue, that one. Know what he did? Went to all these restaurants up West, pretending he was collecting swill for pigs. The restaurants was only too glad to let him have the stuff, specially when he offered 'em a nice little monthly payment and all. Well, he told 'em they had to supply their own drums, right, told 'em to use old oil drums 'cos they was the right size and everything. And what does he do? He goes round and collects 'em all, dumps the swill and then sells the drums for scrap. What a character.' Georgie shook his head. 'But yer know, Maud, wicked as it sounds, and I wouldn't wish anyone dead, I have to admit that there's part of me that's relieved that he ain't around to bother our Evie no more. She can be a right little mare at times, I know that, but at other times she's a different character altogether. She can be a really good kid. Kind and caring. Yer know, before I came on shift, Rita was telling me how she'd gone and looked after Minnie and Clara this morning.'

'Yesterday morning, you mean,' said Maudie looking up at the now brilliantly blue sky.

George rubbed his hand over his stubbly chin. 'Yeah, yesterday morning. Come on. Let's get home.'

They walked along slowly, enjoying the fresh, early morning air.

'I often wonder, yer know, what would have happened if Evie had landed herself a decent bloke and not got herself hiked up with Denham. Someone steady like, who would have kept her in order a bit. I ain't saying it was all his fault. I mean, she don't need much encouragement, that one. She can be a right little madam, I can tell yer. And that temper.'

Maudie nodded. 'You should have heard her the other day, going on about Albie's mother.'

'Her. Hard old cow. Babs is always saying how she's Betty's nan and we should make allowances, but when all's said and done, she's bad news, that one. Real bad news. I don't trust her. Wouldn't trust no one what makes a living out of other people's trouble and misery.'

494

Maudie grabbed hold of his arm and pulled him up short. 'Queenie Denham might be bad news, George, but look there. There's definitely a bit of good news.' She pointed excitedly to the headlines on the newspaper stand. 'Someone's tried to assassinate Hitler!'

34

It was a warm summer evening in August, almost a month since the factory had been hit, and Babs and Evie were still shocked enough by the fact that one of them might have been injured or even killed to still be in a reasonable state of truce in their dealings with one another. It hadn't, however, stopped them from carrying on with their usual, everyday needling of each other.

As she stepped into the front bedroom, Babs's hand flew to her mouth. 'Gawd help us, Eve,' she said, screwing up her nose at the overpowering scent of Evening in Paris. 'It stinks like a tart's parlour in here. How much of that stuff have you put on yerself?'

'Enough to do its job, I hope,' said Evie with a saucy wink. She carefully replaced the lid on the bottle of Cutex varnish then started flapping her hands and blowing on her nails to dry them.

Babs fell back onto the bed and closed her eyes. 'I'm too tired to go out tonight. Tell Dad that I'll have Betty, and him and Maudie can go out for a drink or something.'

'Well, if you wanna stay in on a Friday, it's up to you. But I think yer must be mad.'

Babs opened her eyes and stared up at the ceiling. 'It's not as if I had anything much planned really. Lou mentioned going to the flicks, but she wasn't that keen. She's broke again and wants to save her dough for when we go out tomorrow night.' Babs levered herself up onto her elbows. 'Where you going then? Somewhere good?'

Evie twisted round on the dressing table stool and struck a fashion-plate pose with her hands cupped beneath her chin. 'I, my dear,' she said in a mock posh voice, 'am going with Gina to Rainbow Corner.'

Babs yawned. 'What's that then?'

'Don't yer know nothing?' Evie sounded scandalised. 'Blimey, Babs, I think the world passes you by. I wonder if it's even worth talking to yer sometimes.'

Babs flopped back onto the pillows. 'All right, if that's how yer feel, don't tell me.'

Evie tutted dramatically. 'Calm down. It's a club in the West End, all right? It's been set up special like, for American servicemen.'

Babs yawned again. 'Aw yeah?'

'Yeah, it's on the corner of Shaftesbury Avenue and Piccadilly. You know, where Del Monico's and Lyon's Corner House used to be.'

Babs sat up. 'How the hell would I know about places like that, Eve? I wasn't married to Albie Denham, was I? I never went out gallivanting all over the West End. Now name any pie shop in Bow and I'm yer girl.'

'Oooo,' Evie teased her. 'You know how to enjoy yerself, don't yer?'

Babs got off the bed and went and sat on the stool next to Evie. 'Good, is it?' she asked. 'This Rainbow place.'

Eve turned back to face the mirror. 'Dunno. I ain't never been there. But Gina goes mad about it. A lot of girls do.' Evie took the top of her pancake stick and stroked streaks of the thick, pinky beige make-up onto her cheeks and forehead. 'Do you know, she had to put me name down *forty-eight hours* ago to say that I was gonna be this bloke Ray's guest? That's how hard it is to get in there.'

Babs wasn't sure how Evie expected her to respond.

'Well, fancy that,' she said, for want of something better to say.

Evie finished smoothing the foundation over her skin and then liberally dusted her face with powder. Then she held up a deep red lipstick. 'See this,' she said, nodding at the scrap of lipstick protruding from the end of the tube. 'I'm gonna use all of it. It'll be a good investment.'

Babs frowned. 'I hope so, 'cos that lipstick's bloody mine.'

Evie waved her hand dismissively. 'Don't worry about it. According to Gina, the Yanks have got loads of everything in this place. Even more than they usually have. And yer can imagine what that means. She says they've got as much lipstick as yer can carry. And they're right free with it and all. Tell yer what, I'll bring yer home a few tubes, if yer like.'

'Aw yeah. Lovely,' Babs said sarcastically. 'But don't go putting yerself out, will yer? Just a plummy sort of colour and a pillar box red'll do me.'

'You can laugh, Babs,' Evie said primly. 'But Gina says they've got everything.' She thought for a moment. 'Meat they've got. Real meat, I mean, no stinking snook or Woolton pie for them. And, well, everything.' She looked at herself dreamily in the mirror, and began carefully applying the colour to her mouth. 'All it takes,' she said through stretched lips, 'is a ride on a number fifteen bus and yer in Paradise.' She tossed the empty lipstick tube onto the dressing table. 'Right, that's me done.' She turned to Babs for her to get the full effect. 'Gorgeous, eh?' she said blowing a pouting kiss.

'Eve.' Babs touched her gently on the arm.

Evie drummed her fingers impatiently. 'Yeah, I know,' she said evenly. 'Be careful.'

'Actually, I was gonna say have a nice time.'

Evie's expression softened. 'I will, Babs,' she said, running her hand down her sister's cheek. 'Ta.'

As Evie left the drab greyness of the wartime London street and stepped inside the doors of Rainbow Corner, it was as though the world had suddenly been painted with Technicolor. Her mouth fell open.

'It's just like yer said,' she whispered to Gina. 'It *is* Paradise.'

Gina laughed. 'That's how it takes all the girls when they first come here.'

'And Ray . . .' Evie rolled her eyes and clicked her tongue. 'He is so handsome.'

'My Eddy ain't bad either, is he?'

'He's gorgeous.'

'Yeah. And I mean to hang on to this one.'

'What are you girls whispering about?' asked Eddy, draping his arm round Gina.

Gina smiled up at him. 'We were just having a bit of girl talk.' She pointed to one of the many doorways. 'Come on, Eve, we'll get rid of our hats and jackets over there and check our faces.' She winked at Eddy. 'Then we can talk about these two in peace.'

As Gina led her over to the Ladies, Evie stared about her at the brilliantly colourful posters and pictures of America that covered all the walls, and gawped at all the activities that were going on, and at all the things like Coca-Cola machines which she had only ever seen in the films.

'I don't think I can take all this in.' Evie stared at herself in the sparkling mirror over the sink as she handed the lipstick back that Gina had lent her. 'I've been out with plenty of GIs since they've been over here, but I ain't never seen nothing like this place.'

'Glad yer like it.' Gina twisted round to check the seams of her stockings in one of the elegant full-length mirrors.

'And I wanna remember every bit of it all to tell Babs.'

'You'll remember it,' Gina said. 'Now come on, Ray and Eddy'll be getting fed up waiting out there.'

When she and Gina closed the door of the Ladies behind them, Evie didn't need to turn on her dimpled smile as Ray and Eddy came towards them; she was smiling fit to burst already. She thought Ray was quite the most dazzling man she had ever seen. Not quite as tall as Albie had been, but still much taller than she was, he had thick, dark brown hair, eyes as blue as her own and teeth that were so gleaming white they could have doubled as a warning in the blackout.

Eddy nudged Ray and nodded to Gina and Eve. 'Worth the wait, huh, feller?'

Ray nodded back enthusiastically. 'Worth every moment,' he agreed.

Gina and Evie took their partners by the arm. As they walked through the bright corridors, crowded with GIs and their girls, Evie and Ray told each other about themselves while Ray pointed out to her the various rooms and the different things they could do. There were films to see, sports to watch or play, two sitdown restaurants and a cafe that sold a bewildering range of unfamiliar, exotic-looking items; there were quiet places to sit, music to listen or dance to, and everywhere there were delicious, unidentifiable scents and aromas – perfume maybe, Evie thought at times, or perhaps some sort of food, but whatever they were, they made her feel as though she had tumbled into a giant Aladdin's cave.

'That's about it,' Ray said. 'End of tour.'

'It's . . . smashing,' Evie said.

Ray smiled happily at Eddy. '"Smashing", hear that?' He looked at Evie. 'You like it then, huh?'

She nodded.

'Good. How about a little dancing?'

Evie smiled excitedly – she loved the way he spoke – and turned to Gina to see what she should say.

Gina grinned. 'Smashing,' she said.

Evie nodded. 'Smashing.'

'In here then, ma'am.' Ray ushered them through another door. It led into a bustling, boisterous dance hall. In the middle of the ceiling was a spinning mirrored ball that sent out sparkling rainbows of light over the band and the dancers gyrating below.

Eve turned to Ray, barely able to contain herself. 'I love it here,' she said.

'Can you jitterbug?' Ray asked her.

'Can she jitterbug?' Gina began, intending to brag about her friend's dancing skills, but Evie silenced her with a coy smile.

'I can try, Ray,' she said demurely. 'If you'll show me. I'm a quick learner.'

Gina laughed as Eddy swept her away in his arms. 'Yeah, she's a real quick learner, that one.'

After their first dance together, Ray was stunned. 'Honey, you're terrific. A natural. I never saw anyone dance the jitterbug so good.'

'I've gotta be truthful with yer,' Evie said shyly, looking up into his big, deep blue eyes. 'I didn't pick it up just like that. It was me sister, the one I told yer about. With the baby, you know.'

Ray nodded.

'See, she was seeing a GI for a while and he taught her how to do it. And she showed me.'

Ray laughed. 'Beautiful and honest. I've hit the jackpot!'

Evie flashed her dimples. She lowered her lashes and peered up at him, coyly nibbling at her bottom lip. 'I can sing too. In fact, some people reckon I can sing better than I can dance.'

'Wow! You should be on the stage.'

'I could sing now if they'd let me.'

'Let you?' Ray guided Evie over to the band.

'What's happening?' Eddy asked Gina.

'Wait and see,' she laughed and shook her head. 'Them Bell twins, can't stop 'em if there's a bit of music.'

'You said twins? She's a twin?'

'Yes, Ed, she's a twin.' Gina folded her arms. 'But don't you get no ideas.'

Eddy smiled and kissed Gina on the cheek. 'Why should I want hamburger when I've got steak?'

'Yer a smooth talker, Ed. Come on, we might as well get up the front and cheer her on.'

By the time they had pushed their way forward, Evie had already launched into an achingly sweet rendition of 'A Nightingale Sang In Berkeley Square'.

As the final notes died away, Evie closed her eyes and gave a little bobbing curtsey and the room exploded into applause. She opened her eyes and beamed at the saxophone player who grinned back in reply and immediately burst into a rousing swing version of 'Yes, My Darling Daughter'.

Evie had them eating out of her hand.

When she had finished, Ray proudly swung her off the stage while everyone around them clapped and whistled and frantically shouted for more.

'Jeez,' Ray said. 'Is there nothing you can't do?'

'I dunno, Ray.' Eve looked up at him, a picture of girlish innocence. 'Depends what yer've got in mind, don't it?'

Ray knew exactly what he had in mind but he didn't have the chance to tell her. Any suggestions he was about to voice were interrupted by a young GI who came careering into the ballroom, shoved his way through the crowd and launched himself with a great leap onto the stage. He grabbed the microphone and yelled at the top of his voice, 'Paris just got itself liberated!'

And the whole place went wild.

★ ★ ★

It was almost half past eight on Saturday morning when Evie eventually got home.

Babs was in the kitchen cooking fried bread and tomatoes for breakfast while Betty sat in the big tin bath, chatting away to herself as she played with the soap and flannel.

Babs looked up from the frying pan. 'Yer home then?'

Evie ruffled Betty's hair absent-mindedly, dropped onto one of the kitchen chairs and hugged herself. 'Yeah,' she sighed happily. 'And yer'll never guess what.'

'Yer've met a bloke yer really like.'

Evie frowned. 'How d'you know?'

'Lucky guess. Get Betty dried, will yer? This'll be ready for her in a minute.' Babs pointed the fish slice at the fried bread. 'Want some?'

Evie shook her head and yawned. 'No thanks, Babs, I couldn't eat a thing.' She got up, took the towel off the table and lifted Betty from the bath.

'Blimey, yer must be in love. I've never known you refuse grub.'

'It ain't that,' said Eve, standing Betty on the chair to towel her dry. 'I had so much to eat last night, I'm still full up.'

Babs turned the two slices of bread and the single, sliced tomato. 'Nice was it, the food?'

'Unbelievable. They've got these two dining rooms. Two. And yer can't imagine the food. And then there's a snack bar where they do these waffle things. And you can get hamburgers. They're great, full of all bits and pieces and mincemeat made into little rissole things. And sandwiches – well, that's what they call 'em, but I ain't never seen sandwiches like 'em.' She held Betty's knickers out for her to step into them, then pulled her vest over her head. 'And there's this machine, it makes doughnuts with holes in the middle. And yer can get Coca-Cola. You'd like that, Babs.'

'Me?' said Betty.

'Yes, you'd like it and all,' Evie said. She buttoned up the back of Betty's dress and lifted her down to the floor.

'This don't look much, does it? Not now yer've said all that.' Babs dished a slice of fried bread and a few slices of tomato onto two plates and put them on the table for her and Betty.

'Looks all right,' said Evie unconvincingly.

Betty clambered back onto the chair and got stuck into her breakfast.

'What's he like then?' asked Babs, sprinkling salt over her food to try and make it a bit more interesting. 'This soldier boy of your'n?'

'Ray? He's dreamy. He's ground crew with the, let me get it right, USAAF.' She said the letters slowly, with a meaningful rise of her eyebrow. 'Been here a few months now, he has. And I think he really likes me. When I wanted something to drink, he just gave his mate, that's Ed, a handful of money and said, "There y'are. Take it out of that." And his voice, Babs, yer should hear it, really deep and sexy it is. And he called me Honey, and Sugar and Doll Face.'

Babs pushed her plate away from her. She had hardly touched her food. 'How about making us a cuppa then, Doll Face?'

'Doll Face,' mimicked Betty with a little laugh.

Babs could hardly believe her eyes as Evie got up and filled the kettle without a murmur of protest.

'Yer know,' she said as she swilled hot water round in the pot, 'I reckon this might be me big chance at last.'

Babs reached across and wiped a dribble of tomato from Betty's chin with the hem of her apron. 'How d'yer mean?'

Evie giggled. 'It's obvious, ain't it? Soon as the war's over, I'll go to the States and get into films. I've got the looks and yer know I've got the voice. The Yanks loved me, Babs. All of 'em. And I'll bet Ray knows all sorts of people what can help me get on over there. I could be a star, Babs.'

'Is that tea ready?'

Evie brought the tea to the table. 'I'll have to see if Ray can get you into Rainbow Corner with us one night. Yer'd love it. Yer know, even Glenn Miller's played there. *The* Glenn Miller.' She pushed Babs's cup towards her. 'Well, ain't yer got nothing to say?'

Babs slowly stirred her tea. 'Yeah, I've got something to say. Does he know about . . .' She nodded towards Betty. 'This one?'

Eve pulled a surprised face. 'Who, Glenn Miller? I shouldn't think so.'

'Don't be clever, Eve,' Babs snapped at her. 'You ain't showing off to some bloke. It's me, yer twin, yer talking to.'

Evie didn't answer, she just picked up her bag and stomped upstairs to the bedroom.

'Evie's cross,' said Betty quietly.

Babs drew in her breath. 'Yer mustn't call yer mummy that, Betty. *Mummy* yer have to call her. *Mummy*.'

That evening Evie went out with Ray again, and the next day, Sunday, she was full of excitement because not only did Ray want to see her yet again, he was actually coming to the house to collect her.

'These Yanks, Babs,' she giggled, as she studied her profile with her hair piled up and then with it left loose around her shoulders. 'They think places like this dump are cute. Cute. Can yer imagine? And full of history, Ray says. Bloody barmy, if yer ask me. Still, who cares, eh?'

'Not you, Eve,' said Babs as she put the ironing away in the dressing table drawers. 'That's for sure.'

'Yer know, I was gonna hide where I come from, but he'll love it.'

'If he gets in here.'

'Eh?'

'Ain't yer noticed? Dad's down in the front room staring out the window like a dock copper at the gates. He don't seem very happy about a Yank coming round for yer.'

'Sod it.' Evie's voice was hard. 'If he dares spoil things for me . . .'

She crashed down the stairs and into the front room. 'Dad, I wanna talk to you.'

Georgie ignored her. He was standing at the window with the net curtain pulled back. Ray had just arrived at the door and was about to knock.

'I don't like the look of him,' said Georgie. 'Look how he's standing there. Can't he even keep his back up straight?'

'He's smarter than a Tommy any day.'

'Huh.'

'And they know how to treat a girl. He said I was beautiful enough to be a spy.'

Georgie turned on her. 'What sort of stupid talk is that? Full of shit, the lot of them.' He almost ripped down the curtain as he pulled it back in place. 'I'm going on duty.' He strode furiously out into the passage, flung open the street door, and barged past Ray who was standing patiently on the step.

Georgie was halfway past the Simpkins's house next door when he stopped in his tracks, turned and looked Ray up and down.

Ray straightened up smartly. 'Good evening, sir.'

Georgie shook his head and snarled by way of response and stormed off along the street.

'Ignore him,' said Evie with a flap of her hand.

Ray shrugged. 'He's a protective father. I'd be the same if I had a beautiful daughter like you.'

Evie sighed contentedly. 'Yer say the nicest things.'

She lifted her jacket off the banister, linked her arm though his and called over her shoulder, 'See yer then, Babs. Don't wait up.'

Later that evening, while Babs was getting Betty ready for bed, someone banged loudly on the street door.

'Hang on, babe,' Babs said, sitting Betty on the edge of the bed. 'You wait there and I'll go down and see who it is.'

As she skipped down the stairs, she thought to herself, 'I'll bet that's Evie. She's had a row and come home with her tail between her legs. She's always the same, always mad about the latest and then, five minutes later, fed up with 'em.'

When she opened the door, Babs was really surprised to see that it was Queenie standing there.

'I've brought some stuff for Betty,' she said. Then she paused, and stared challengingly at Babs. 'And I've decided to take her out for a bit.'

Babs frowned. 'This time of night?'

Queenie jerked her head towards the car that was standing by the kerb. 'Chas fetched me round here in the car. She won't be outside in the night air.'

Babs kept a firm grip on the edge of the door and stood her ground on the step, making sure she was blocking the passageway. 'Yer can't.'

'You what?' Queenie leaned close to Babs and stuck her finger nearly in her face. 'You listen to me. I wanna see my granddaughter now. And I mean to take her with me. I've had just about enough of the carryings on in this place. Now fetch her.'

Babs swallowed hard; her mouth was dry. 'I can't,' she said. 'She's out.'

Queenie's face was distorted with rage and disbelief. 'She's out. Who the hell with?'

'With her mum of course, who else?'

'You lying little mare. I thought you at least was a bit

decent, but I might have known. You Bells, yer all the same. No better than yer whore of a mother and no better than that little scrubber of a sister of your'n.'

Babs blinked. 'What did you say?'

'I've heard all about that little tart. Hanging around with all them Yanks. And I ain't having it. It's no way to bring a child up. Especially my grandchild. And I mean to do something about it.'

Babs took a deep breath and then very quietly and slowly said to Queenie, 'Now listen here, you. What Evie does is none of your business. And if you think you can come round here saying what yer like about her, well, yer've got another think coming. It's only 'cos she feels sorry for yer that she lets yer see Betty at all. So I'd be careful if I was you.'

Queenie laughed in her face, a dry mirthless sneer. 'It's you what wants to be careful, darling. Yer wanna mind yer tongue, 'cos I ain't very happy. I don't like the thought of my granddaughter living in this knocking shop. And yer can tell yer little brass of a sister that from me.' She gestured over her shoulder towards Chas. 'I know a lot of people, some right hard nuts who are only too pleased to do me favours when I ask 'em. And if things don't change sharpish, you and yer sister are in for a very nasty surprise. I'll have that baby off yer so fast yer won't know what's hit yer, you see if I don't.' She looked round at Chas and nodded for him to open the car door for her. Then she turned slowly back to Babs. 'I'll be back and I'll be keeping an eye on what's going on round here,' she said in a low, menacing growl. 'Don't you worry about that. But next time I might not be so nice.'

As Babs watched the car pull out of the street, she felt sick, unable to move.

'That was Albie Denham's mother, wasn't it?' Alice called across from her doorstep where she was sitting knitting in the late evening sun.

509

Babs didn't answer.

Alice dropped her knitting onto the pavement beside her chair and trotted over to Babs. 'Oi, I asked you a question.'

'Go away, Alice,' said Babs, trying to close the door.

'Don't you talk to me like that, you trumped up little madam,' she said, sticking her bony foot in the door. 'I'm having to take a tonic for my nerves as it is, what with that dog of your'n barking night and day and that sister of your'n keeping me up all hours.'

Babs looked down at Alice's foot then raised her eyes to the woman's mean little face. 'Yer've got a choice,' Babs said. 'You either move that foot of your'n or I stamp on it.'

Alice stepped back. 'Well!' she puffed, but her indignation was wasted, Babs had closed the door in her face.

It was gone midnight when Babs was woken by the strange sound of some sort of a vehicle pulling up outside the house. She peered through a crack in the blackout curtain. There was an American jeep outside and Evie was giggling loudly as she stumbled out onto the pavement.

When she eventually made it indoors, Babs was waiting for her in the passage.

'Eve, I've got to talk to yer. I'm worried about Queenie.'

Evie tutted. 'Queenie? Leave off, Babs. Can't whatever it is wait till the morning? I'm really tired.'

Babs stepped back. 'Your breath. Yer've been drinking, haven't yer?'

Evie giggled. 'Bourbon!'

'Look at the state of yer. Yer lucky Dad's still on duty.'

'I'm going up.' Eve grasped the banister and heaved herself onto the first step.

Babs shook her head and stared at the floor. 'Well, don't wake Betty,' she said quietly.

The next morning, Babs took Betty down to the kitchen for her breakfast earlier than usual so that she could have a private talk upstairs with Evie.

Babs sat on the side of the bed and as calmly as she could manage said, 'Listen, Eve, I've gotta tell you. Albie's Mum was here last night.' She nibbled her lip, determined that she wouldn't cry. 'Eve, I'm scared she's gonna try and take Betty away from us.'

'Leave off, Babs.' Eve snuggled down into the bed. 'You know what's she's like. Silly old bag.'

'Eve! I'm talking to you. This is serious.' Babs pulled the covers off her. 'Will you listen to me? It ain't the first time I've felt this. I'm really worried.'

Eve opened her eyes and stared threateningly at Babs. 'Look, I'm tired and my head aches. Just go away.'

'In case yer've forgotten,' hissed Babs, 'it's Monday morning. How about work?'

'How about it?' Eve closed her eyes and turned over.

Babs went downstairs, took Betty to the nursery, then made her way to work alone.

That evening when she got in she went into the kitchen and looked at the cold, empty stove. Evie was sitting on a chair out in the back yard while Betty played at throwing a ball for Flash.

Babs leant against the back door. 'I thought you might have made us something to eat while yer've been home all day, Eve.'

Her sister didn't bother to turn round to speak to her. 'I've been busy doing me roots.'

'I really don't understand you lately.'

'Look, whether you like it or not, Babs, I'm going out to see Ray tonight, so I wanted to look me best. And you can have sandwiches or something, can't yer? Blimey, Babs, it is flaming summer. What d'yer want, a meat pudden? And Ray's gotta go back to his base tomorrow so I wanna see him. Right down in Essex it is.' Eve

511

looked over her shoulder and smiled. 'He's asked if I can get down there. What d'yer think of that?'

Babs rubbed her hands over her face.

Evie threw her hands up in exasperation. 'And don't look at me like that, Babs. What d'yer expect me to do? I've got a choice, ain't I? There's this,' she pointed inside to the cramped little kitchen, 'a rotten dismal hole with rationing, the blackout and no fun. Or there's his way of life. Bright, loads of everything and full of fun. Which would you choose, eh?' She took a Lucky Strike from her pocket and lit it, blowing a slow stream of smoke up into the air. 'And he's teaching me how to talk Yank like him,' she said in a purring, American accent.

Babs spun round and paced across the kitchen room. Then she stopped and pointed her finger at Evie. 'You reckon you can get round anyone, don't yer?' She snapped her fingers. 'Just like that. Make 'em laugh or flutter yer eyelashes and yer've got 'em. Well, let me tell you, Evie, yer've come unstuck this time. I've had enough. I've really had it with you.'

Evie tapped the ash from the end of her cigarette and trod it into the dusty ground. 'What's got up your nose all of a sudden?'

Babs could hardly keep herself from going over to her sister and slapping the smile off her face. 'Not that yer'd have noticed,' she said, pointing to the end of the yard where Betty was happily rolling around on the ground with Flash, 'but Betty don't even call you Mummy half the time lately.'

Evie took another puff of her cigarette. 'Silly cow, course I've noticed. It was me what told her not to.'

35

In a complete contradiction of the government's claim that 'except for a last few shots the Battle of London is over', October 1944 brought with it a new threat to the capital. People over a wide area of London were reporting hearing incredibly loud explosions that were almost immediately followed by a second, equally devastating blast. Each of the double bangs was so loud that, even if they occurred up to ten miles away, it sounded as though they were really close by. Other things marked the explosions: there was a reddish flash followed by a huge plume of black smoke, and the damage they did was even more devastating than that done by the doodlebugs, destroying whole terraces of houses with a single hit, and they didn't make any sound before they fell.

As had happened at first with the V–1s, nobody was saying what these new, mysterious bombs were so, as usual, rumours flew as to what they might be. Londoners were stunned when they eventually found out that the new terror weapons were V–2 rockets, that the ack-ack and barrage balloon defences were useless against them, and that they had been misled once again about the Allies having beaten Germany.

To add to the gloom, there had been a series of military setbacks in Europe, including the dreadful events at Arnhem, which had resulted in the death of thousands more Allied troops. So it was, on the whole, a depressed and demoralised London that was suffering the latest attacks. Evie, however, with her relationship with Ray Bennington coming along very nicely, was definitely not depressed or demoralised in any way at all; in fact she was positively chirpy.

It was late on an October Friday afternoon and Evie and Babs had just brought Betty home from the nursery on their way back from work. Babs had taken Betty with her into the kitchen to put the kettle on, while Evie, singing away happily to herself, was going upstairs to put away their coats.

Someone knocked on the door.

'I'll get it,' Evie called from halfway up the stairs and skipped back down to the passage.

'You're being a right little angel,' Babs called to her from the kitchen. 'What you after, Evie?'

'Shut up, yer sour old bag,' Evie called back to her twin goodnaturedly. She threw the coats over her shoulder and opened the door.

'Blimey, Chas. I ain't see you for years. How are yer?'

Chas took off his hat and dropped his gaze. 'All right,' he said quietly.

'Babs said you brought Queenie round a couple of weeks back.'

'That's right.'

'I'd like to say I was sorry I missed yer but Babs said yer wasn't very nice that night.'

Chas shuffled uncomfortably and Evie let him squirm for a while.

'So?' she said eventually.

'I've got some bad news, Eve.'

Despite her earlier anger, Evie reached out and took his hand. 'You all right, Chas? Yer've gone ever so pale. Wanna come in for a cuppa or something?'

He shook his head. 'No, I've gotta get off straightaway, ta. It's Albie's dad, see.'

'Bernie?'

'Yeah, he's been put away for running a black market racket.'

Eve's eyes widened. 'Christ. He won't be very happy. I thought he had all the law round his way straightened out. How come—'

Chas shook his head to silence her. 'That ain't all, Eve. When they took him away, Queenie had a stroke. Shock, they reckon.'

Evie turned round and chucked the coats carelessly over the banister. She paused, then said, 'And so how is the old cow?'

Chas scratched at the back of his neck. He looked awkward standing there, almost filling the doorway, like an overgrown child. 'She's dead, Eve. I'm just on me way to tell Bernie. That's why I can't stay.' He shrugged. 'I thought I ought to let yer know. There's no one else left, except you and the little'un.'

'Right.' Evie nodded. 'Thanks for coming round to tell us, Chas.'

'It's nothing.' He put his hat back on. 'Take care, won't yer. And give me love to that sister of your'n.'

'I will, but I dunno if she'll be very impressed.'

'Well, it wasn't my idea coming round that time, yer know what she was like.'

Eve nodded. 'I know.'

'If there's anything either of yer ever need, let me know, won't yer?'

'Ta, Chas.'

Evie waited until he had walked as far as the Drum where he had left his car, and then she closed the door and went into the kitchen to Babs. 'Guess who that was?'

'I could hear it was a feller.'

'It was Chas.'

Babs glanced anxiously at Betty who was sitting on the floor feeding Flash with pieces she was picking from the

515

end of a loaf. 'He ain't brought Queenie round with him, has he?' she whispered.

'Hardly,' Evie said, pouring herself a cup from the pot of tea that Babs had just made. 'She's gone and dropped dead, ain't she.'

'She's what?'

Evie sat down at the table. 'Bernie got his collar felt and she snuffed it. Just like that. Who'd have thought that old trout could have been killed off so easy?' She sipped at her tea.

'Don't be like that, Eve. And keep yer voice down. That's Betty's nan and granddad yer talking about, remember.'

Eve drank more of her tea. 'And don't I know it,' she said, looking at Babs across the rim of her cup. 'I had more than a bellyful of the pair of 'em.'

Babs opened her mouth to protest.

Evie wouldn't be silenced. 'Look, Babs, don't come all angelic with me, you hated them as much as I did. And I thought you'd be pleased she was out of the way.'

Babs bowed her head. 'I suppose so.'

Evie smiled. 'Still that's all in the past now, eh? It's long gone, and I'm glad and all. I'm living for today, Babs. While I've got the chance.'

'We back to that, are we?' said Babs wearily as she refilled her cup.

'Yes, we are. I'm fed up with how that lot treated me. I'm starting fresh, a new life. And that's why I'm gonna ask yer to do me a little favour.'

Babs looked suspiciously at her twin. 'How does this affect me?'

'Ray's fixed it so that I can go down to Brighton for the weekend with him.'

'Yeah?'

'And I was wondering if you could, you know,' she nodded at Betty, 'have her for me.'

'And if I said no?'

Evie put her cup down. 'Aw, Babs, don't,' she whined. 'Yer know I've always wanted to go there. And it weren't easy for him to fix, neither. He had to promise this feller all sorts, he did. See, civilians ain't really meant to travel down that way, not without special permission.'

'When's not having permission ever stopped you from doing anything?'

'Babs,' she pleaded.

Babs fiddled around with her cup and then looked at Betty.

'What's the matter with you, Babs? Yer've been a right miserable cow these last few weeks.'

Babs shrugged. 'You'd only laugh, or make sarky comments if I told yer.'

'As if I would. Why d'you always think the worst of me?' Evie smiled sadly at her twin.

Babs traced her finger round and round the rim of her cup. She didn't look at Eve when she spoke. 'I ain't heard from Harry for a while.'

Evie grinned. 'You mean I ain't heard from Harry for a while.'

'There, I knew I shouldn't have told yer.'

Evie lifted her hands in a gesture of surrender. 'Sorry, sorry.' She put her head on one side and smiled, sweetly this time. 'Now, are yer gonna have her for me or not?'

'Maybe.'

'Well, hurry up and make up yer mind, I've gotta lot to sort out. I'm meeting him tomorrow dinnertime.'

'*This* weekend, yer mean?'

Evie gulped down the remains of her tea. 'What, didn't I say?'

Evie cuddled into Ray's shoulder and pecked him on the cheek, ignoring the contemptuous glares of the middle-aged woman who was sitting opposite them.

'I love these little six-person compartments on your trains,' Ray said, kissing her gently on the head. 'And the blackout blinds. So romantic. Shame we've got company, eh Honey?'

The woman tutted prudishly.

Evie looked up at him. 'I'm really excited, Ray. I've always wanted to go to Brighton.'

Ray winked. 'Not exactly a sensible choice in October and in wartime, but whatever pleases you.'

Evie smiled happily to herself, basking in Ray's attention and the admiration of the other servicemen who were crowded into the little compartment. When she was sure that no one else was looking, she went cross-eyed and poked out her tongue at the now scarlet-faced woman opposite. When they got to the pub where Ray's contact had booked them a room, they had something to eat and then Evie insisted on going out for a walk.

Ray agreed reluctantly.

'This is some – what did you call it? – prom they've got here.' Ray shivered and pulled his collar up round his ears. 'All you can see in the dark is the glint of the barbed wire. And it is so cold.'

Evie twirled round in front of him, her arms stretched wide. 'I don't care. I think it's wonderful. Ignore the barbed wire, just look at that moon.'

Ray laughed. 'You're a great kid,' he said.

She grabbed hold of his hand. 'Tell me again, Ray, what's it like in America?'

'Well, back home, girls like you are always in the beauty parlour – you know, hairdressers you call them – getting fixed up some way.'

'I've thought about going to one of them smart hairdressers up West. I never did though.'

'I'll pay for you to go if you want.'

'Would yer?' Her smile faded. 'Does my hair look bad then?'

'No. It's perfect.'

'Tell me some more about America.'

'The sunshine ain't on ration for one thing.' He thought for a moment. 'It's difficult to describe.' He shrugged and pulled her close to him. 'Let's just say that it ain't like this in California, that's for sure.'

Evie kissed him. 'Let's go back to our room,' she whispered.

While Evie and Ray were finding their way back to the pub, Babs was making a final cup of tea before she went up to bed.

She wasn't sure at first but she thought she heard someone at the street door and Flash had pricked up her ears. Babs listened; it definitely wasn't the knocker she had heard.

She looked at the clock. It was gone eleven. Surely it couldn't be anyone calling this late on a Saturday night, but there it was again, the gentle rapping. She grabbed hold of Flash's collar and went into the front room and picked up the poker. Then she walked slowly along the passage towards the street door.

'Who is it?' she called, leaning close to the door so she could hear.

'It's me, Harry, Harry Taylor. Evie's friend.'

'Harry?' Babs could hardly believe it. She pulled the door open. 'Come in,' she said, holding the poker and Flash's collar in one hand and dragging her dressing gown round her with the other.

'Expecting trouble?' said Harry, taking off his forage cap and following her along the passage.

'It is late.' Babs was so dazed to see him she barely knew what to say.

'Yeah, I'm sorry about that.'

She let Flash go and the dog trotted back to the

kitchen.'You have to be quiet,' said Babs, putting her finger to her lips and then gesturing vaguely upstairs. 'Betty's asleep.'

Harry nodded and tiptoed along behind her like an oversized ballerina.

'I am sorry it's so late,' he whispered. 'But I just got off the train at Waterloo a little while ago. And when I changed to the Underground to go home to Plaistow, to go to me mum's, I got as far as Mile End and I had to get off and come and see Evie.'

Babs turned her head away.

'Sorry,' he whispered again. 'It was a stupid idea coming this late.'

'No it wasn't. Come in the kitchen.'

He sat down at the table and Babs shut the kitchen door behind them. 'There, we can talk normally now.' She pointed to the teapot. 'I've just made some to take up to bed. It's a bit weak, but fancy a cup?'

'Please.'

She handed him his tea. 'What happened to your face?'

Harry automatically put his hand up to cover the jagged scar that ran from his ear right across his cheek. 'I got this at Arnhem. It's why I haven't written to Evie for a while. And my leg got broken.' He touched his face again.

Babs's mouth went dry at the thought of him getting hurt. 'Bad, was it?'

'Bad enough. But I'm all right now. Well, apart from a bit of a limp and the scar. They've sent me home on extended leave, after the convalescence in the hospital.'

'I'm glad yer all right.'

'Is Evie in bed?'

Babs wanted to say that she probably was but she didn't. Instead she said, 'She's gone to see a friend. For the weekend.'

'Shame I've missed her.'

Harry reached inside his greatcoat and pulled out a little wooden duck on wheels. 'I made this for your little girl. Hope yer don't mind. I carved it when I was in the convalescent place.'

He smiled at her, the scar making his features look rakishly lopsided.

Babs took the toy and returned his smile and spontaneously kissed him on the cheek. The minute she'd done so, she jumped back as if she'd been scalded. 'Sorry.'

'What have you got to be sorry for?'

She pulled the dressing gown tighter. 'I must look a right state.'

'I think yer look lovely.' He looked down at the floor. 'Sorry, I had no right to say that. It's being with blokes most of the time, yer forget how to behave. The nurses was always telling us off.'

'That's all right.'

'Evie's always writing to me about Betty, telling me how she's getting on. She's right proud of her little niece, yer know.'

Babs had no idea what to say. She gulped at her tea, almost choking herself. Harry jumped up and patted her back. She nodded her thanks.

Minutes passed without a word between them. Harry didn't look as though it felt difficult for him, but Babs's mind was whirling with what she had got herself into.

When Harry eventually spoke, she nearly choked on her tea again.

'Look, Babs,' he said, 'I know yer a married woman and everything, but seeing as Evie's away, can I take yer out for a drink or something tomorrow? Maybe something to eat?'

It was the last thing she had expected. 'Well,' she stammered, 'it ain't that easy.'

'Sorry, I dunno what I'm saying. I'm making a right idiot of meself. It must be 'cos I'm tired.'

'No. No, I'd love to. It's just that I'll have to make sure that Dad can look after Betty, that's all. But I know he will. He's off duty for the next three days and he loves being with her.'

'Good. That's really good.' He stood up. 'Look, if yer think I've overstepped the mark . . .'

'Course not.'

'I'd better be off now, or Mum won't let me in. She'll think I'm a burglar, or a German paratrooper.'

Babs saw him out and shut the door behind him. Then she leant back against the wall in the dark passage and sighed loudly, wondering to herself just how she was going to keep up the deceit that it was her and not Evie who had been writing to him, but knowing that she wanted to see him so badly, she was prepared to lie through her teeth.

'You sure yer don't mind having Betty, then, Dad?'

'Course I don't. You go and enjoy yerself. Makes a change for you to go out. But yer will watch yerself, won't yer, darling? I've seen so much with these bloody rockets lately.'

'I'll be careful, I promise.'

When Babs got to Mile End Station, Harry was standing waiting for her.

'I thought we could go up West.'

'Smashing.'

'Have something to eat. Then maybe go to the pictures. Or for a drink.'

'D'yer mind if we go for a drink? I'd like to sit and talk.'

'Me too. Yer know, yer real easy to talk to, Babs.'

Babs smiled up at him.

'And you've got a beautiful smile.'

'Thank you.'

'Your husband's a lucky man.'

Babs looked away. She felt sick.

At the end of their evening together, Harry took her back to Darnfield Street. As they stood by the street door, Babs didn't know whether to laugh out loud with happiness or collapse into tears of despair.

'Goodnight, Harry,' she said brightly, trying to keep her voice from giving her away. 'I had such a good time.'

'I'm glad.' Harry's voice was husky. 'Me too.'

'Yer know, that scar makes yer look really handsome. Like a proper hero.'

Harry opened his mouth to say something then looked away instead. He held out his hand to her.

She shook it warmly, holding it for a brief moment longer than she needed to. 'Night, night, Harry,' she breathed.

Then she turned and opened the street door and, against all her body and heart were telling her, went inside alone.

She went upstairs and peered round the door of the back bedroom. Her dad was sound asleep, snoring softly on his back. Then she crept quietly into the front bedroom where Betty lay, curled in a contentedly sleeping ball, her dark curls spread on the white pillowcase.

Babs took off her shoes. She knew she had no hope of sleeping. She sat on the end of the bed and buried her face in her hands. She was in love with Harry and she didn't know how to tell him, or even if she would ever be able to tell him. What would he think if she told him the truth, that she was the one who had been writing to him and that Evie was Betty's mother, not her? What was worse was that it was all her own fault. Why hadn't she explained right away? Why had she listened to Evie's harebrained scheme? What had she done?

Babs looked at the clock. She had been sitting there for nearly two hours and was still wide awake. She stood up, made sure that Betty was settled and crept back downstairs. As she reached the bottom step, she heard someone running along the street. The sound stopped. Whoever it was was outside. She could hear their laboured breathing.

She paused for just a moment then opened the door. She squinted out into the dark. 'Eve, is that you?'

'No, it's me. Harry.'

She stepped back for him to come in. As he brushed past her, she could feel that he was shaking violently. She took his hand and led him into the front room and sat him down in one of the armchairs.

When she turned on the standard lamp in the corner, she saw that his face was grey and his eyes were staring.

'Mum's house.' He said it quietly in a dull monotone. 'It's gone. The whole street's gone. A rocket attack while we was out. Me mum's dead, Babs.'

He bowed his head and began weeping softly into his hands. Babs went over to him, took him in her arms and held him to her.

She held him like that, cradled in her arms, until his whole body shuddered and he stopped crying.

She got up and went over to the sideboard and took out one of Evie's bottles of bourbon and two glasses.

Babs sipped at her one drink while Harry drank his way through the rest of the bottle and told her all about his mum and how she brought him up single-handed and what a good woman she was.

'You'd have loved her, Babs,' he said, staring into the hearth. 'And she'd have loved you.' Then he closed his eyes and the glass dropped from his hand.

Babs went upstairs and fetched a blanket.

Before she covered him over, she put a cushion under his head and pulled off his boots. As he lay there, asleep in the chair, she looked down at the little curls of hair that twisted in tight tendrils on the back of his big, strong neck. Despite his size, they made him look so vulnerable.

She bent forward and kissed him softly on the scar on his cheek, wanting above everything to make him feel better, to take away all the pain.

She didn't go up to bed; she sat in the armchair opposite and watched him sleep. He might wake up and need her.

The sky was only just beginning to lighten when she heard Blanche's voice calling her through the letter box. She jumped up to open the door before Blanche woke the whole house up.

'Blanche, what's up?' she whispered.

Blanche was grinning all over her face. 'It might be a grey Monday morning in October, Babs, but this is the best day of my life. I've heard from Archie, love. He's all right. He's alive!'

'I'm chuffed for yer, Blanche. Come in, but keep yer voice down, Dad and Betty are still asleep.'

Blanche could barely contain herself; she definitely couldn't sit at the kitchen table. She paced around the little room. 'He's injured but he's coming home. Look, this is the telegram from the hospital. I've read it two hundred times, I reckon.' She put her hand over her mouth to stifle her laughter. 'He's in Cornwall, of all places. Not far from our Len.' She waved the telegram form excitedly. 'He got one of the nurses to send it. He'd been in some camp or something with these other blokes. And it was in North Africa after all.'

Babs nodded, she knew all about camps. Wasn't she meant to have a husband in one?

'Well, they escaped. Four of them, there was. Then they all got split up. Apparently Archie got a bash on the head somehow and the silly bugger couldn't remember who he was.' Blanche started crying and laughing at the same time. 'Silly bugger. Trust him. He's a bloody hero, and when they found him he didn't even know his name.' She blew her nose and then stuffed her hankie in her

525

cardigan pocket. 'He's being transferred to a London hospital today.'

Babs tried a little smile, but she wasn't very convincing.

Blanche sniffed and peered at her friend. 'What's up, Babs? Yer look peaky.'

'Nothing, I'm tired that's all.' Babs was suddenly very alert. There was the sound of a key in the front door. Flash barked and Babs grabbed her roughly and almost hurled her out into the back yard.

Blanche frowned at her in surprise.

'They're asleep,' Babs said sheepishly, pointing to the ceiling.

The kitchen door opened and Evie shimmied in; she was singing 'Someone's Rocking My Dreamboat' and waving packets of nylons around as if she were a child waving flags at a street party.

Blanche greeted her with a grin. 'You sound happy.'

'I am, Blanche. Very. I danced at the Regent to Syd Dean and his band. I—'

'Please, Eve, keep it down. They're still asleep.'

Evie tossed the nylons on the table, took Babs's face in her hands and kissed her on the tip of her nose. 'Anything for you, Babs,' she whispered. 'But I am so happy. And what more could a girl ask for than that?'

'I'll tell yer,' said Blanche. 'A girl could hear how her husband's safe and sound, that's what.'

'Blanche!' Evie looked at Babs and put her finger to her lips. 'That's the best news!'

Babs wearily went over and closed the kitchen door then slumped down into the carver chair.

'Yeah, I know. I'm going to see him at the hospital this afternoon, I hope.'

'There, take them.' Evie handed Blanche a pair of stockings. 'Wear them when yer visit Archie. Give him a treat. Better than cold tea or gravy browning on yer legs any day, eh, Blanche?'

526

'You ain't kidding. Where d'yer get them?'

Eve giggled. 'I won 'em in a poker game.'

'You what? Poker?'

'Yeah, Ray taught me. He's me new chap. And cop a load of that.' She held out her wrist.

'Gawd, you smell lovely. What scent is it, Eve?'

'That ain't no scent, that is perfume. French perfume. Here.' She snapped open her handbag and dabbed a spot of the fragrance behind each of Blanche's ears. 'That'll perk your Archie up a bit.'

'Just wait till I see him.' Blanche closed her eyes and hugged herself. 'I'm gonna cuddle him till he squeaks.' She opened her eyes and giggled like a teenager. 'I'd better be off, I've only got about six hours to get ready!'

Babs went to the door with her to make sure that she didn't slam it. Before she went back to Evie, she peeped nervously into the front room. Harry was still out like a light.

She took a deep breath and walked, chin up, into the kitchen, making sure that the door was tightly shut behind her.

'Sit down,' said Evie, pulling one of the chairs from under the table. 'I've got some good news too.'

Babs sat down; anything to keep her sister occupied while she tried to figure out what to do about Harry.

'Wait there, I'm gonna call Dad so he can hear about it and all.'

'No.' Babs jumped up. 'I'll go up and get him.'

'All right,' said Eve. 'Calm down. You get him. I don't care.'

Babs glanced up at the clock. It was nearly eight. Betty would definitely be awake soon. And then there was work to think about . . . She ran her fingers distractedly through her hair. 'And please, keep yer voice down, Eve, I don't wanna wake Betty. She didn't have a very good night.'

527

Babs led Georgie warily past the closed front room door as though he were a blind man needing guidance in a strange house.

'This had better be good,' he said menacingly as he sat himself down in the carver chair. 'This is supposed to be one of me rest days, Eve.'

Evie stood before her dad and her twin with her hands clasped primly in front of her. 'I,' she announced, 'am going to become Mrs Ray Bennington.'

'Did I hear her right?' Georgie looked at Babs, and raked his finger round in his ear.

'You did,' Eve said. 'I'm gonna be a proper American wife and Ray's gonna teach me to drive and everything.'

Babs and Georgie just sat there.

'Well?' Evie looked hurt. 'Aren't you gonna congratulate me? Dad? Babs?'

Georgie stood up slowly from his chair and took a single step towards her. He spoke calmly at first; he looked a bit bewildered, but that was all. 'What exactly do you think you're playing at, Eve?' he asked. 'And how about Betty? She ain't even met this bloke yet, so far as I know.'

Evie sat down. She had a stubborn, hard expression on her face. She crossed her legs and began jiggling her foot up and down. 'I knew yer'd try and spoil it for me.'

'Eve. Will you use yer loaf for just one minute? I know it don't come easy to yer but try.' Georgie was getting louder. 'You reckon yer gonna be an American wife, do yer? Well, I reckon he's a moody merchant just like the rest of them Yanks. Them and their tales about big houses and flash motors. I bet he ain't got a pot.'

'Do you know something?' Evie stood up. This time she took a step towards him. 'I never thought I'd say this, but I don't care if he ain't, Dad. I don't care if he ain't got a bean. See, I really love him. He's the only man I've ever loved.' She suddenly giggled. 'I can't believe I'm saying it

528

but I don't give a toss if he's broke.'

'You . . .' Georgie held up both his hands. 'I don't know what to call yer.' He slumped back into his chair. 'Well, I ain't signing no papers or giving no permission. And that's final.'

Eve stood there with her mouth open.

'And I know that I have to for you to go. One of the blokes down the station, his niece just went through it all. So don't think I don't know what I'm talking about.'

Eve stared down at him. 'There'll be a way round it.'

'Well, I'll make sure there ain't. You just wait and see if I don't.'

Evie's hands balled into fists and she exploded. 'How can yer do this to me?' she screamed. 'How can yer?'

Babs grabbed hold of her to try and stop her, but she was possessed.

'You should know what it's like to be hurt,' she shrieked. 'When Mum run off it nearly killed yer. Yer jealous, that's your trouble. And you always have been, any time anyone's got a chance of a bit of happiness.'

Georgie leapt from the chair and raised his hand. He just stopped himself from smacking it across her face. 'Don't you understand,' he hissed at her through his clenched jaws. 'Yer stupid little mare. I'm trying to protect yer. Look at the state yer got in last time.'

'But this is *different*.' Evie's hollering started Flash off barking at the back door.

Babs was frantic. They wouldn't stop yelling, and now the dog was going mad as well.

Georgie was breathing faster and faster as he tried to get control of himself. 'Look, I don't wanna upset you, Eve, I just don't want yer getting a knock back from this geezer, whoever he is. I don't wanna see yer breaking yer heart over some bloke yer know nothing about.'

'Please,' Babs begged them. 'Stop it.' She had to shut them up before Harry heard them.

It was too late. Just as Georgie grabbed hold of Eve and shouted, 'What's the matter with you, Evie? How can you even think of going away to America?' the kitchen door opened and Harry was standing there, holding his head with one hand and his boots in the other.

'Going away to America, Eve? But all those letters you sent me. I don't understand.'

Evie and Georgie both shut up and turned to stare at the intruder.

'What?' said Evie, her face screwed up in confusion.

'Who are you?' Georgie demanded. 'What the hell are you doing here in my house?'

Babs went over to the doorway and touched him on the arm. 'This is Harry, remember?'

'Eve?' Harry implored her.

'Look, please, everyone sit down.' Babs was shaking. 'I'm gonna run Betty next door, then I'll explain everything.'

Babs was gone for barely a couple of minutes and, as soon as she returned, she tried to explain herself to Harry as she had promised.

'So you're telling me that Betty ain't yours?' Harry stared at Babs's mouth as though she was speaking in a foreign language of which he only grasped one or two words.

Babs swallowed hard. 'That's right. Betty ain't my daughter. She's Evie's. And I'm not even married, Harry, let alone to a husband in a prisoner-of-war camp.'

'And it was *you* I've been writing to, not Evie?'

Babs nodded. 'I just signed meself Evie, that was all.'

'That's all?' He shook his head in disbelief. 'But what made yer do it?'

'That was my fault in some ways,' said Evie casually. 'I was the one who pretended that I was single and everything, 'cos I fancied yer and wanted to make sure yer wasn't interested in Babs. But it turned out that she was the one who liked yer best after all, 'cos when yer started writing to me, I was seeing someone else. But Babs didn't wanna have yer disappointed, and said I should write. But I couldn't be bothered, so she did it instead. I think it was quite nice of her, really. I dunno what yer so upset about.'

'Yer dunno why I'm so upset? I don't understand this. Yer tell me yer a married woman, or a widow, I should say, with a baby. And just because yer fancied a few nights out with me, yer tell all these lies. And now yer talking calmly about going off to America?' Harry shook his head in disbelief. 'I pity that kid of yours. She'll be dragged from pillar to post, I can just see it.'

Evie shrugged. 'Maybe she don't have to go with me.'

'I don't think I understand this either.' Georgie stood up and walked over to the back door. 'I need some air.'

'I'm disgusted with yer.' Harry bent down to pull on his boots.

'I feel sick.' Babs stared at the dull red lino; her head was swimming.

Evie nodded towards Babs. 'Why don't yer give her a chance, Harry, eh?' she urged him, flashing her best smile.

'Leave me alone, the pair of yer.' Harry stood up and walked out, slamming the street door behind him.

'Now look what yer've done,' Babs sobbed and ran upstairs to the bedroom.

Georgie didn't turn to face Evie when he spoke; he didn't trust himself to. He just said quietly, 'Go up to her. See if yer can make up for some of the trouble yer've caused her.'

'I ain't had no sleep since yesterday,' she complained, and dragged herself up the stairs.

She went in the bedroom. Babs was sprawled out on the unmade bed sobbing. Quietly Evie sat down next to her.

'I've got something to say, Babs,' she began. 'And I want yer to listen to me.' She took a deep breath. 'I ain't cut out for this motherhood lark. You have to understand that. Well, yer don't have to, but I'd like yer to. I love Betty, course I do, but like a little sister, not like she was me own child. I'm gonna marry Ray whatever anyone says. No one's gonna stand in me way, not even Betty.'

Babs was still sobbing, her face buried in the pillow.

'I know you love her different to how I ever could. I just can't feel that way for her. I dunno. You're the one who's been bringing her up, I just never got attached to her in the same way that you did.' She went over to the dressing table and searched through the top drawer for a packet of cigarettes. She tapped one on the back of her hand and then lit it. 'Don't hate me, Babs.'

Babs pulled herself up and sat on the edge of the bed. 'How could you even think of leaving her behind, Eve? Tell me. I love Betty and I can't bear the thought of yer taking her away from me, but she's *yours*, Eve. Your child.' She shook her head, trying to clear her thoughts. 'I can't believe yer saying these things.'

Evie inhaled deeply on her cigarette and slowly blew the smoke from her nostrils. 'And I can't believe how much I love Ray. The thought of him going back to America without me, I can't stand it.'

'Why can't you take Betty with yer?'

'No. I can't. I'm going to start again. Forget all this.'

'Forget? Listen to me, Eve, yer know I'd keep her, willingly. I love her more than I can explain. But you're her mother. You'd regret it for the rest of yer life.'

'You reckon, do yer?'

'Yeah. Think of what Mum did to us. How we felt when she run off with that bloke.'

Evie shook her head slowly. 'Don't try and make me feel guilty, Babs.'

'Look, don't you get the feeling, the feeling that yer

there to protect her and that yer'd do anything, give up everything for her?'

'No.'

'No? Just no?'

'I wanna make something of meself.'

Babs wiped her eyes on her sleeve. 'You'll never learn, will yer, Eve? They were dreams we had as kids at the pictures. It's not real. No one really comes along and sweeps yer off yer feet.'

Evie ground out the cigarette in the glass tray on the dressing table. 'I wasn't cut out to have kids, Babs, and that's that.'

'That's that? But you've had her now, she's a living, breathing child.'

'Babs, don't. Don't do this to me.'

'Don't do this to you? How about *me*? How about *my* problems? How about Betty? And Dad?'

Evie looked at her lap and shrugged. 'I don't care, Babs. I don't care about no one and nothing but being with Ray. And I don't care how long it takes to get all this sorted out, but I'm going with him. I'm gonna marry him and be his wife in America. And I'm sorry if it don't suit yer, but that's all there is to it.'

36

It was three o'clock in the afternoon, and Maudie was in number six, sitting at the table in the front room with the Bell family, looking at the remains of the Christmas dinner. But it could hardly have been called a celebration meal, as the food had hardly been touched. Since Evie had made her announcement in October about marrying Ray and going off to America, things had gone from bad to worse, and now the atmosphere in the house was so tense that practically every time the twins spoke to each other, yet another row began.

Maud was doing her best to make some sort of conversation but she was running out of topics.

'Have you heard the news about Terry Simpkins?' she asked. 'It looks as if he might be called up soon. Blanche is really worried. She says it's bad enough having Mary fretting over Micky being in the army, without having something else to worry about.'

'She should think herself lucky if that's all she's got to worry about,' said Evie, pushing the Brussels sprouts round her plate with her knife. She sighed dramatically. 'Christmas! I should be happy, not miserable like this. Just because I've got the pluck to try and better meself, none of yer can stand it, can yer? None of yer. And you all want me to be miserable.'

Georgie got up and threw some more wood on the fire. 'You're not the only one who's suffering, Eve,' he said.

535

'Yeah,' agreed Babs. 'How about me?'

'Aw gawd,' wailed Eve. 'You ain't still going on about that Harry Taylor, are yer?'

Babs didn't answer her twin, instead she looked at Maudie. 'I've been thinking about joining the Land Army, Maud.'

'Oh,' said Maudie, defeated in her search for a more suitable reply.

Evie didn't have that problem. 'Don't talk so stupid,' she sneered. 'What would you do in the Land Army? I can just see yer milking cows and making hay. I know what your game is, yer just saying that so yer can get out of having Betty 'cos yer think it'll stop me going to America with Ray. Yer pathetic, all of yer.'

Betty watched Evie run out of the room and go stomping up the stairs. 'Evie's cross,' she said, her eyes wide and serious. She clambered down from the table, sat on the mat in front of the fire, and proudly showed Flash the dolly that Maudie had given her for her Christmas present.

Georgie rubbed his hands over his face. 'It ain't right,' he said, 'that baby keep hearing all these rows.'

Maudie stood up and began stacking the plates. 'Come on, George. Help me with the washing up.'

Babs stood up to help.

'No, Babs,' Maudie said. 'It's all right, you sit down. We can do it. It was a lovely meal. Thank you.'

In the kitchen, Maudie put the dirty plates on the table, took down the apron from the hook behind the door and put it on over her dress. 'I want to speak to you, George,' she said. 'And I want you to listen to me without getting yourself all upset. All right?'

'All right.'

'Things aren't always straightforward, George.' She filled the kettle at the sink.

'You don't have to tell me that, I live with them two, remember.'

'Some women just can't feel motherly towards a child. And you mustn't blame Evie for being like that. I'm sure that there are reasons for the way she's acting with Betty, and I'm also sure that she wished she knew what they were. But try not to judge her, George. She really is suffering. Anyone can see that.'

Georgie scraped the leftovers onto an enamel plate and whistled for Flash to come and get the scraps. The dog came lolloping into the kitchen. Georgie opened the back door to put the food down for her in the yard. A bitter wind whipped round his legs. He shivered. 'That snow's falling again.' He pulled Flash back inside and put her plate down in the corner. 'Yer might as well eat it in here, girl,' he said, running his hand down the dog's silky back. 'No point us all suffering.'

'You're right, George,' Maudie said, lifting the kettle from the stove and filling the bowl. 'There isn't. There's enough suffering in this world without us adding to it. And, especially at a time like this, we should all try and make the best of things. Try and make something good out of what could so easily turn sour.'

Georgie handed Maud the plates.

'We have to grab happiness where we can, George. Surely that's something that these terrible wars have taught us. Surely.'

Georgie took his tobacco from his pocket and rolled himself a cigarette. 'I know you've always had a soft spot for my girls, Maud, but I don't know how yer can keep yer temper with 'em lately. I feel like I could strangle the pair of 'em.'

Maud smiled at him over her shoulder. 'You wouldn't be human if you didn't. But why don't you give them a chance? They've had a hard time, George. They've grown up without a mother, and lived through this war when they should have been young and fancy free.'

Babs coughed. She was standing in the kitchen doorway with Betty. 'I thought I'd go up to see if Evie's all right. I brought Betty in here 'cos I didn't wanna leave her with the fire.'

Georgie held out his arms to his little granddaughter. 'You'll be all right with us, won't yer, babe?'

Upstairs in the front bedroom, Babs found Evie sprawled across the bed, crying bitterly into the pillow.

Babs sat down next to her and gently stroked her hair. 'I've never had it from yer straight, Evie, but Albie used to hit yer didn't he?'

She pushed Babs's hand away. 'Leave me alone, I don't wanna talk about the no-good bastard. I wouldn't be in this mess now if it wasn't for him.'

'I know,' Babs soothed her. 'I know. But he did, didn't he? When yer used to make up them stories about how yer hurt yerself, that was him doing it to yer all the time, wasn't it?'

Evie sat up. 'Yeah.' She looked at Babs, her lovely face blotchy from weeping. 'I was a mug and I let the useless, bullying bastard belt the living daylights out of me. Satisfied?'

'I ain't having a go at yer, Eve, I'm trying to understand.' Babs looked down at her hands. 'Maybe if Betty hadn't been Albie's?'

A great, gulping, shuddering sob racked Evie's body. 'I've wondered that. Maybe if she hadn't have been anything to do with him, then I could have felt different about her. Closer.' She licked away the tears that were trickling into her mouth. 'I meant it when I said I love her, yer know, Babs. I really do, but not like, not like a mum should.' The tears ran faster down her cheeks. 'Babs.'

'Yeah?' She dabbed at Evie's face with her hankie.

'D'yer think I've taken after Mum and that I'm just no good?'

Babs wrapped her arms round her twin and held her close. 'Course I don't, daft. How could I ever think that?'

Evie shuddered again and then said quietly, 'Once, while I was carrying her, I can't remember how many months I was, anyway, he hit me in the stomach. I felt sure that I was gonna lose her. I had these terrible pains. And I was so scared, Babs, 'cos I didn't wanna lose her. I loved her, even before she was born.' She threw back her head. 'But not in the way I was supposed to. What's wrong with me, Babs? Why can't I love her like I should?'

'Ssshhh, don't upset yerself, we all have to love in our own way, Evie. We can't all be the same.'

'Ray loves me, Babs.'

'I know. I know.' Babs rocked her gently, trying to still her tears. 'Maybe I should meet him, eh,' she said. 'I mean, he must be really special if he loves a scatty cow like you, Evie Bell.'

Evie leant back. She was trying to smile through her tears. 'D'yer mean it? Yer'd really like to meet him?'

'Yeah, course I would.'

Evie hugged her tight. 'Aw, Babs, I can't tell yer what it'd mean to me.'

'But I ain't making no promises about nothing else.'

They both knew that she meant about caring for Betty but neither of them said it; they knew it would only reopen the wound that they had just that moment healed. Any decisions about Betty's future would have to wait.

Evie blew her nose loudly and stood up. 'Come on, let's go down and have a drink to celebrate. It is meant to be Christmas after all.'

Babs nodded. 'You go and pour 'em out and I'll follow yer down in a minute.'

She sat on the end of the bed and listened to Evie calling excitedly to Maud and Georgie to go in the front room and have a drink with her.

539

Babs looked at herself in the dressing table mirror and sighed. 'You might as well have a life, Eve,' she said to her reflection as she got up to join them. 'Why should both of us be unhappy?'

George led Maudie and Betty into the front room.

'Yer've cheered up,' he said, sitting in one of the armchairs and lifting Betty onto his knee.

Evie's hand was shaking as she took out the bottle of champagne from the sideboard. She handed it to Georgie. 'Ray gave me this for us to have today but I didn't feel much like drinking it. But I do now. Babs said she wants to meet him.'

'Good idea,' Georgie said, putting Betty down and glancing over to Maud, who gave him an encouraging nod. 'I was thinking, perhaps you should bring this Ray feller to see us. So we can all meet him. Proper like.' He stood up and looked quizzically at the champagne bottle, not at all sure how to tackle opening it.

Maud took it from him. 'Let me.' She smiled at Evie. '*I've* done this before.'

Georgie frowned. 'Have yer?'

Maudie didn't answer him, she bent down to get the glasses from the sideboard.

Evie walked over to her dad. She had to bite her lip to stop herself from crying again. 'I love you, Dad. D'yer know that?'

'I know.'

'I ain't always been the best of daughters, but I usually mean well.'

'There's an admission,' said Babs as she walked in. 'You *usually* mean well.'

'We can't all be flipping angels,' Evie laughed as she turned to face her. 'Now, how about if I write to Ray and say that me and you wanna go down to Essex to see him, on one of his evening passes? And when we're down there we can make arrangements for him to come up on his next long pass to see Dad and Maud. Furlough, they call it.'

'That's nice,' said Maud, obviously delighted to be included as part of the family. 'I'd enjoy meeting him.'

'But warn him not to expect too much of a welcome,' said Georgie, watching Maud as she lifted the wire cage off the top of the champagne bottle. 'He'll have to take us as he finds us. We ain't used to stuff like this every day in Darnfield Street.'

Maud pulled the cork from the bottle with a loud pop and poured the foaming wine into the glasses.

Evie was grinning from ear to ear. 'Don't worry, Dad, he loves warm brown ale. He thinks it's really English and neat.'

'Happy Christmas,' said Maud, raising her glass.

'Christmas!' shouted Betty happily and threw herself at Babs who picked her up in her arms, kissed her, then put her down again.

George sat in his armchair and Betty scrambled onto his lap. 'Come on, girls,' he said, jiggling Betty up and down on his knee. 'Why don't you two give us a little song.'

Babs shook her head. She wanted to be happy for Evie, but she couldn't get her own unhappiness out of her mind. She'd lost Harry, that was all there was to it. She knew that she wouldn't be able to sing without bursting into tears. 'I've got a bit of a sore throat, Dad,' she said quietly.

Georgie frowned. 'You are looking a bit pale. Here, I hope you ain't got that 'flu what's going round.'

'No, it's nothing. Just a bit off colour.'

'Well, I'll have to do a solo then, won't I?' Evie said.

Georgie laughed. 'Yer might be a twin, but yer've been like a solo act most of yer life, you.'

Evie put her glass on the sideboard, curtseyed and then began singing, '*I'm dreaming of a white Christmas . . .*'

541

That was as far as she had got when Babs stood up, mumbled her excuses about feeling unwell and ran upstairs to the bedroom.

It was the first week of January 1945 and Evie and Babs were getting ready for the journey down to Essex to meet Ray. Georgie was fussing about Babs's health, fretting about them travelling in the snow and ice and worrying himself sick about them being out at all when the V–2 rockets were coming more frequently than ever.

'Look, Dad,' Evie said, sticking her pin through the crown of her hat, 'there might be 'flu, bombs, six years of war, even earthquakes coming for all we know, but I promise yer, I couldn't be happier than I am today. Please don't spoil it with all yer nagging.'

'I ain't nagging,' he said solemnly. 'I'm just concerned, that's all. I'm allowed, I'm yer dad.'

Evie kissed him on the cheek.

'Yer both look a picture,' he said. 'I'm proud of the pair of yer.'

Babs kissed him on the other cheek and then opened the street door.

Georgie and Betty stood on the step waving goodbye until the cold drove them back indoors.

As the sisters reached the end of the Darnfield Street, Babs stopped dead. 'That's Harry,' she said, pointing to a figure walking briskly along Grove Road towards them.

'Come on. I ain't hanging around,' Evie insisted, grabbing her arm. 'We ain't got time for this, Babs. D'you wanna come with me to meet Ray or not?'

Babs pulled away. 'I've gotta talk to him, Eve. I can't just walk past him.'

Evie tutted impatiently. 'I'll wait at the corner of Burdett Road for ten minutes, then I'm off or I'll miss me connections from Mile End,' she said and strode off as quickly as she was able in high heels in the snow.

Harry ignored Evie as she passed him by; his eyes were fixed on Babs. He stopped in front of her. 'Hello, Babs.'

Babs smiled shyly. 'The leg looks like it's mending. How's it coming along?'

'It's a lot better, ta. I should be fit enough for work again soon, I reckon. Probably not good enough to go abroad again for a while, but I'm getting there.'

'That's good, Harry, I'm really pleased for yer,' she said.

They stood there in the snow, not noticing the cold, just looking at one another.

'So, what did you do over Christmas?' she asked eventually.

'Not much. No one to do much with. I stayed in the hostel place they fixed me up with and saw a few mates who were at home, but they wanted to be with their own families most of the time.' He shrugged. 'Obvious, ain't it, that people wanna be with them what they love this time of year. Not strangers.'

'Yeah.' Babs nodded again. 'So what yer doing round this way then?'

Harry shuffled his foot from side to side, making a little mound of snow. 'I was coming to see you, as a matter of fact, Babs.'

'Me?'

'Yeah. Makes yer think all sorts of things, Christmas time does.' He looked over Babs's shoulder, off into the distance. 'And all I could think about was you.'

'Me?'

He nodded. 'I wondered if yer'd consider coming out with me tonight. See if we can start again.'

'I don't know what to say, Harry. I was meant to be going with Evie . . .'

Harry nodded again, his lips tight. 'Fair enough. Maybe I should have been less pig-headed and asked you earlier. Should have swallowed me stupid pride.' He pulled his collar up round his neck. 'See yer around sometime then, eh?' And he started to walk away.

'No, Harry,' she called after him. 'Hang on a minute. I'm gonna do what I wanna do for once, not what Evie wants.'

He turned round.

'Please. Wait there.'

Harry nodded.

'Yer promise?'

'Yeah. I won't move.'

Babs ran along Grove Road, slipping and sliding on the snowy pavement, the icy air freezing her lungs. When she got to the corner of Burdett Road, she was gasping for breath.

'Eve,' she panted. 'I've made a decision. I'm making a life for meself just like you are.'

'Eh?'

She put her hand to her chest and took a deep breath. 'I ain't sure how it's all gonna work out yet, but I know that I want Betty and I'll take care of her like she was me own. But you, Eve, yer gonna have to start growing up a bit and realise that other people ain't always gonna be there to run after yer. Yer gonna have to start looking after yerself.'

'What?'

'I want happiness as well, Eve.'

'You ain't coming to Essex with me, are yer?' She wrinkled her nose and giggled. 'Yer staying here with Harry.'

Babs grinned. 'Yeah, I am.'

Evie shook her head. 'Go on. Yer can meet Ray when he comes up to meet Dad and Maud.' She threw her arms round Babs and squeezed her tight. 'No matter what, Babs,' she whispered in her ear, 'no matter what's happened between us, we've always been best friends as well as sisters, haven't we?'

544

'Course we have. Now stop it, or yer'll make me cry.'

'Go on,' Evie called with a wave as she walked briskly away towards the station. 'Grab yer happiness while yer can.'

Babs waved back to her sister. 'Give him my love,' she shouted after her.

'Give who yer love?' she heard Harry call from behind her.

She turned round and saw that he was running towards her.

'The bloke that I think's gonna be me new brother-in-law,' she said with a smile as he came to a skidding halt beside her.

'So long as it ain't yer boy friend.'

'I ain't got a boy friend at the minute,' she said demurely.

'Good,' he gasped, his breath forming into little clouds in the freezing air. 'I had to run after yer. I was scared yer wouldn't come back. And I couldn't let yer go, Babs.'

Babs looked up into his eyes. 'Couldn't yer?' she whispered.

He slowly shook his head. 'Not the way I feel about you, no,' he said. He took her in his arms and kissed her, a long, breathless kiss that left her in no doubt as to exactly how he felt. 'And I ain't never letting yer go again.'

Babs rested her head on his chest. 'I'm glad, Harry,' she said. 'Real glad.'

'But I dunno what I would have done,' he laughed, 'if yer really had been married with a baby.'

Babs took his hand. 'Let's go and get a drink somewhere, eh? I think we've got some talking to do.'

37

It was over a month before Ray finally came to London to meet Georgie and Maud.

He stood in the front room, his hands behind his back like a schoolboy waiting to be given a dressing down by the headmaster.

Georgie, who had been sitting at the table with Maud, stood up and held out his hand. 'So, we get to meet yer at last.' He smiled as he spoke, but it was a wary, hesitant smile, with little warmth in it.

Ray shook his hand. 'Mr Bell,' he said.

'George, or Ringer,' he replied firmly. 'It's all the same to me.'

Ray smiled.

Georgie sat down again and pointed at a chair for Ray to do the same. 'So. Ray. What d'yer do then? What're yer prospects as a provider for my Evie?'

'Dad!' Evie rolled her eyes.

Maudie stood up and signalled to Babs with a brief nod. 'Shall we go out to the kitchen to make some tea?'

Babs jumped up. 'Good idea.'

But Georgie motioned for Maud and Babs to sit down again. 'Got no secrets that these two can't hear, have yer, lad?'

'I don't believe this.' Evie was fuming. 'He's doing it on purpose.'

'No, Evie,' Ray said, keeping his gaze fixed on

Georgie. 'It's OK. Your father has a right to know all about me.'

Evie slumped, defeated, into one of the armchairs.

'Yer a millionaire, I suppose,' Georgie said cynically. 'Like all the other Yanks you hear about.'

'No, sir. Not me. I'm just a regular guy. But I'm a hard worker. And I've got plans to get on in my field.'

'Aw, so yer a farmer, are yer?'

'No, sir. I didn't mean that sort of field, I meant—'

Evie almost leapt out of her armchair. She threw her hands up in despair. 'He is, he's doing it deliberately. He's torturing me.'

Babs went over to her sister and shoved her hard in the ribs. 'Sit down,' she hissed at her.

'It was a joke,' Georgie said flatly. 'I was trying to be friendly.'

Ray immediately smiled; his even white teeth gleamed. 'I'm a trained electrical engineer. And after the war I hope to make my career in Philadelphia, working on a new type of machine they've been developing there.'

'What sort of a machine's that then?'

'It's called a number integrator and computer, sir.'

Babs looked wide-eyed at Evie.

Evie shrugged and whispered, 'Don't ask me. I just know I'm gonna marry him.'

'Sounds complicated,' said Georgie. He shifted on his chair, reached into his waistcoat pocket and took out his tobacco pouch.

'I guess it is, sir,' answered Ray, offering Georgie a cigarette from the packet he produced from the breast pocket of his uniform.

'Thanks, Ray.' Georgie took the offered smoke and tapped the cigarette on the back of his hand. 'I'm not sure what yer talking about with this machine of your'n, but yer think there's a living to be made in working with it, do yer?'

'Yes, sir. I do.'

Georgie stuck the cigarette in the corner of his mouth. 'Babs, Evie, go and make us all a cuppa tea.' He looked at Ray. 'Tea all right?'

'Thank you, sir.

'I'll come and help you,' said Maud, hurrying after the twins.

Ray stood up while the women left the room then held out his lighter to Georgie, who bent his head forward to catch the flame. Ray sat down again.

'It's going to be a very important machine, sir. A machine that will probably change a lot of things in the future.'

Georgie took a drag on his cigarette, blowing the smoke out of his nostrils. 'Changes for the better, I hope.'

'Of course, sir.'

'Ringer.'

'Ringer,' smiled Ray.

Someone knocked on the front room door. It was Evie. She poked her head into the room. 'Dad, I thought I ought to say something while Babs and Maud are in the kitchen.'

Ray stood up and guided her into the room.

'Just so things are straight, Dad.' She bowed her head.

Ray took her hand in his and smiled encouragingly.

'I've told Ray about Albie Denham,' she said.

'Everything?' asked Georgie.

She nodded.

'I know he was a crook, sir. That he beat her.' Ray squeezed Evie's hand. 'And I know about Betty.'

Evie raised her chin a little and gazed at Georgie, trying to gauge his reaction.

His face showed no sign of what he was thinking.

'That's why Babs took Betty into Blanche earlier this afternoon, Dad,' she said quietly. 'So we could talk to yer about it without her hearing.'

549

Georgie flicked the end of his cigarette into the hearth and watched it until it had burnt away to nothing. He kept his eyes on the flames and said, 'And it don't make no difference to how yer feel about her, Ray?'

Ray also paused before he spoke. 'It was hard to understand at first,' he said eventually. 'That Eve could feel that way about her own child.' Another pause. 'It nearly broke us up when she told me back in January.'

George looked at him. 'So that's why it took so long for yer to come and see us?'

Ray nodded. 'I think we both needed time. But, in the end, I knew that I wanted Evie more than I wanted anything else in the world. And that accepting her for what she is was part of that; it wasn't about trying to change her into some person I'd prefer her to be.'

Evie had to bite hard on her bottom lip to stop herself from crying.

'And I know she loves Betty in her own way. She just can't help it that she doesn't love her the way Babs does, the way she should.'

'Should?' repeated Georgie carefully.

'Sure, I'd be a liar if I didn't find it difficult. But she was honest with me and that counts for a lot. And we've worked it through between us. And everything's going to be just fine.'

Georgie stood up and put his hand on Ray's shoulder. 'I hope so, son,' he said. 'I really do.' He chucked Evie gently under the chin. ''Cos this little girl of mine's been hurt enough. And I'd kill anyone who hurt her again.'

'There's something else, Dad.'

'Well?'

'Ray's found a room for me, down near the base. I'm going back with him tonight. Babs knows already.' She covered her face with her hands. 'It'll help Betty get used to me not being here,' she whispered and bolted from the room.

The two men stood in silence as they listened to her run up the stairs and slam the bedroom door.

Evie and Ray had left for Essex and Babs had gone next door to fetch Betty. Maud and Georgie were sitting in the front room. The wireless was on, Georgie was staring into the fire, and Maud was darning a sock.

Without looking up from her sewing, she said, 'Why don't you have a glass of that bourbon that Ray brought for you, George?'

He got up with a sigh. 'Good idea. Want anything?'

Maudie shook her head. 'No thanks.'

He poured his drink, sat down and took a sip of the whisky. 'Babs is a long time,' he said.

Maudie put her darning down on the arm of the chair. 'Blanche'll be showing her that letter again.'

Georgie nodded grimly. 'Yeah, she's happy as Larry that young Len's coming home.'

'She really thought she'd lost him to the farming life,' smiled Maudie.

'It's funny with kids. Yer can never tell how they'll turn out.' Georgie bent forward, unhooked the poker from the companion set and raked it through the hot coals, sending sparks dancing up the chimney. 'Won't be having too many more fires now the weather's improving,' he said, staring unseeingly into the flames. 'I'll have to see about getting this lot swept. Ain't been done for a couple of years.'

Maudie returned to her darning. 'I'm glad you got on with Ray, George.'

He put the poker back on the stand. 'Yeah,' he said vaguely. 'That was a surprise, wasn't it? I'd built meself up to dislike the feller without ever having met him.' He drank some more whisky. 'I can't pretend I understand him accepting about Evie and Betty though. It hurts me to think of that girl moving down to live in lodgings in

Essex and leaving her baby here. Just like her mum, when yer come down to it.'

'There's more to it than that, George.'

'Yeah, I suppose so. She ain't a bad girl, not heartless like her mother was. Still, what do I know about women? Yer all a right bloody puzzle, if you ask me.'

Maudie smiled to herself, pulling the heel of the sock tight over the wooden darning mushroom. 'I think Ray will do her good, George. Make her happy.'

'I hope yer right. He seemed decent enough. Clever and all.' He lifted his glass. 'Mind you, that bottle of bourbon he brought helped.'

'And the soap. And the shaving cream. And the tinned fruit. You've got enough to feed the whole street.'

'I already have with half the last lot he sent up for Eve.'

Maudie smiled. 'I sometimes think you're too generous for your own good, Georgie Bell.'

'No I'm not, I'm just a feller who realises he's well off and wants to share it about a bit.'

'That's a good thing to say, George. There's not many people realise when they are well off, you know.'

'I've got two beautiful, healthy daughters that any man would be proud of. I've got an angel of a granddaughter. A job that makes me feel like I'm worth something. A roof over me head.' He sipped at his drink and studied Maud across the rim of his glass. 'And now I've got you for company and all, haven't I?'

Maudie put her mending down again. 'Do you think I could have a glass of that now?'

'Course.'

She took the glass from him and gulped down a mouthful of the bourbon. Her eyes watered and she started coughing as it hit the back of her throat.

Georgie took the glass from her. 'All right?'

'Not used to it,' she gasped, patting her chest. 'That's better. I'll take it a bit slower next time.'

Georgie handed the glass back to her.

'I'm going to say this outright, George. There's no point me beating about the bush or messing around. And I know you'll think I'm being a bit forward. And I know I'm no spring chicken.'

Georgie laughed, the first time he had done so all day. 'Come on then, spit it out.'

Maudie stared at the half-moon rug in front of the hearth.

'Do you think the two of us might make a go of it, George?'

'What d'yer mean? Me and you, proper like?'

'Why not?' Maudie took another big gulp of the whisky, and this time she didn't notice the effects. 'I only thought . . .' she began, then ran out of words.

'Blimey,' Georgie said.

Maudie took a deep breath and stood up. 'Look, George,' she said firmly. 'Maybe you'll think I'm terrible but I've gone too far to stop now. I thought that you could move in with me and leave this place for Babs and Harry.'

'Babs and Harry?'

Maudie grimaced. 'Don't tell me you hadn't realised? I've really put my foot in it now, haven't I?'

Georgie ran his fingers through his dark, wavy hair. 'I knew they were seeing each other, but I didn't realise they was serious.' He shook his head slowly. 'Yer know, I think I must be half daft sometimes.'

Maud looked at him expectantly. 'Well?' she said.

'Well what?'

'George!'

'There's a problem.' Georgie swallowed the remains of his bourbon. 'I'm still married.'

'I know.'

Georgie's chin dropped. 'What? And yer don't mind? You being a churchgoer and everything?'

'I'd rather you were free, but it can't be helped. The war's made me see a lot of things very differently.'

'Yer full of surprises, you.'

'I hope so, George.' Maud got up, walked over to him, took his face in her hands and kissed him gently on the lips.

Georgie stood up too. 'Before anything else's said, would you tell me something, Maud?'

She smiled gently. 'Anything.'

'It's something that I ain't been able to get off me mind. About that frock.'

'Frock?'

'The one you gave to our Evie to get married in. Did you ever wear it?'

Maudie sat down and nodded for him to do the same. 'I did wear it,' she said. 'But only to have it fitted by the dressmaker.' There was a faraway look in her eyes as she spoke. 'I was engaged to a young man. Richard, his name was.'

Georgie went over to her, sat on the arm of her chair and took her hand in his. 'I'm sorry, Maud, I didn't mean to pry.'

'No, you should know. But where do I begin?' Maudie took out her handkerchief and twisted it round and round her fingers. 'The old couple I lived with here in Darnfield Street, George. They weren't my parents. They were Richard's.'

'Well, there's a turn-up; everyone round here just presumed they was yours. So how about yer own mum and dad?'

Maudie hesitated.

'Sorry, Maud.' George stared up at the ceiling. 'Me and my big mouth. I didn't mean to poke me nose in.'

'No, you're not doing that, George. It's just that I haven't spoken about my parents for so many years. Although I still think about them. All the time.' She stuffed the hankie up her sleeve and drained the whisky glass. 'They were musicians,' she began. 'There were times when we didn't have much money, but the house where we lived was full of love and there were always lots of people laughing and singing. Your girls would have loved it.'

'Where was that then?'

'London. Bloomsbury.'

'I always knew you wasn't from round these parts.'

Maudie smiled.

'What happened to them?'

Maudie studied her hands for a moment. 'They died, both of them. Some sort of fever. It happened so quickly. I wasn't quite twelve years old, much too young to look after myself, so I was sent to live with an elderly aunt in the country. In a tiny village in Wiltshire.' Maudie's face clouded. 'She didn't take to me, George. She'd never had any interest in children. I was so unhappy.'

Georgie wanted to take her in his arms to comfort her, but he knew he had to let her speak.

'But then I was rescued. When I was almost fourteen, Richard's parents took me in. The idea was that his mother, who ran a free school in the village, needed a helper, and that I could also teach the piano there. It was nonsense of course, she didn't need any help. But they had plenty of money from their business, so paying a young girl wasn't a hardship for them. I was more than glad to accept, and my aunt was just as happy to be rid of me.'

'Would yer like another drink?' he asked softly.

'No, thank you.' Maudie shook her head and put her hand over the top of her glass. 'Well, let's see, what happened next? Richard fell in love with me, I suppose. And it was just taken for granted that I loved him. He was a handsome young man with excellent prospects – why would anyone have doubted that I loved him? Then the war broke out and Richard volunteered. Before he went away he asked me to marry him. It was as a sort of promise, I suppose, that I'd wait for him.'

'And you said yes?'

She nodded. 'I was seventeen years old, had no family except my aunt who didn't want me, and I was grateful to his parents for taking me in. We planned to be married on his first leave. The dress was made and the ceremony planned. But instead of him coming back, there was a telegram. He died at Ypres. His parents were heartbroken, and I was distraught. But I want you to know, George, I never loved him. I never loved anyone, not in that way, not until I met you.'

Georgie rubbed his hand thoughtfully over his chin. 'Yer being honest with me, Maud,' he said. 'I appreciate that. And so I'm gonna be the same with you. Much as I hate to think of that poor bloke getting killed and everything, and even though I'm hardly a kid any more, I can't pretend I ain't pleased to hear yer say yer never loved him.'

'We stayed in the village and life went on. But then, it must be what, nearly fifteen years ago, the family business went broke and they lost everything including their home. It was nothing of great importance to anyone else, the firm was just another victim of those hard times, and there were plenty who suffered worse. But they'd never really recovered from losing Richard, and the firm folding was like a final blow, it just broke their spirit. Almost overnight they became old, frail and vulnerable. That was when we moved here. The vicar at St Dorothea's was a family friend and he got them the house here in Darnfield Street. I cared for them until they died, loved them as though they were my own parents.'

'Yer know, I'm trying to picture 'em. But I just can't remember what they looked like.'

'They stayed indoors most of the time. This was a

strange world for them. And anyway, let's face it, George, you had more than enough problems of your own at that time.'

Georgie nodded grimly to himself, thinking about how his struggles to bring up his daughters had so nearly failed because he had let himself sink into becoming a self-pitying drunk.

'They were wonderful people, George, Richard's parents. They loved me just as much as they would have loved any daughter of their own.' She looked directly at him. 'Just as much as Babs loves Betty,' she said. 'And I never felt that I missed out because they weren't my own parents.'

Georgie couldn't sit there any longer. He got up, took her hand and pulled her to him. 'I'm glad you trusted me enough to tell me, Maud,' he whispered into her hair. 'It helps explain all sorts of things. I feel I really know yer now. That I understand yer.'

She rested her head against his chest. 'And I'm glad I told you. Perhaps it'll help you understand other things as well, about the twins and Betty. I know we sometimes have to just take what life gives us, but at other times we have to take a chance, grab something special when it comes along. Try not to blame Eve, George.'

He stepped away from her and put the fire guard round the hearth. 'Let's go over to your place, Maud,' he said, holding his hand out to her. 'I think I should see where I'm gonna be sleeping.'

38

Maud and Georgie were sitting in the cosy little front room of number seven Darnfield Street, the home they now shared. They had finished their evening meal and were listening to the wireless, waiting to hear the broadcast that would tell them that, this time, their hopes for peace were no longer wishful thinking and that the war was officially over. And, with the way things had been going for the last six weeks, they had every right to be optimistic. It certainly didn't seem likely, or even possible, that the news could be otherwise.

But when, at six o'clock, the announcer said that Mr Churchill would not be making a statement that night, Georgie and Maud, like many other Londoners, were disappointed and more than a bit puzzled.

Georgie got up and turned the set off, and he and Maud sat there for a while in silence. Then they began going over and over all the possibilities as to why the Prime Minister hadn't spoken, and trying to work out what might have happened or gone wrong. But, for all their efforts, they were still none the wiser.

'Aw well,' said Georgie. 'Might as well do what we always do at times like this – I'll go and make us a nice cuppa tea.'

He was just bringing the tea through to the front room when there was a terrific banging on the front door and the sound of Babs shouting at him through the letter box to open up and let her in.

'Hang on,' he called. He chuckled to himself as he put the cups down on the stairs. 'Can't you youngsters wait for anything?'

As he opened the door, Babs burst into the passage.

'Did you hear it, Dad?' she shouted. Her eyes were shining and she was grinning fit to burst.

'Hear what?'

Maudie appeared in the passage behind George. She stood on tiptoes and looked over his shoulder. 'What's happened?'

'On the wireless, just now. Tomorrow and the next day are national holidays.' Babs paused for them both to take it in. 'It's all over, Dad. Maud. The war's finished. It's true.'

Maudie's hand flew to her mouth. 'It really is all over?'

Georgie stepped out onto the pavement, picked up Babs and swung her round. 'And we're alive to tell the tale!'

Maudie closed her eyes and threw back her head. 'Just think, I'll be able to fill up that bath and have a proper soak without having to worry about doodlebugs landing on me.'

'Be able to get a decent bit of grub,' grinned Georgie.

'New clothes, more like,' giggled Babs. 'Get yer priorities right, you two.'

All along the street front doors and windows were being flung open as the neighbours stuck their heads out to share the good news with their friends.

'Go over and fetch Harry, Babs. We're going down the Drum to start our celebrations right now.'

The next day dawned grey and wild. And, just as nearly six years ago the last night of peace had been marked by violent, electric storms, so the early hours of V-E Day were marked by a torrential downpour.

But not even hangovers or bad weather could dampen

the spirits of the residents of Darnfield Street. Everyone got up early regardless; they were determined that after six years of war they were going to have a party that everyone would remember.

Babs and Blanche enlisted Harry, Georgie and Blanche's young Len to help them decorate the street. They had strings of fairy lights that Maudie had produced from a dusty old box under her stairs and yards and yards of bunting that Babs and Blanche, like the other girls at Styleways, had been making for the past two weeks in preparation for the big day they had all been praying for, Mr Silver being only too pleased, in the circumstances, to turn a blind eye to their clandestine efforts.

Frankie Morgan brought out a whole collection of Union Jacks that he and Nobby draped over the trestle tables that Bert and Jim had set up along the middle of the street.

Everyone mucked in to do something. And, by the afternoon, when the weather had cleared up, everyone was outside and ready. The tables were laden with whatever food the neighbours had found in their cupboards and Rita and Bert had donated their whole day's baking; there was plenty of beer and lemonade, partly bought from the proceeds of the street's whip-round and the rest supplied by Jim and Nellie from the Drum's cellar.

By three o'clock, everyone had dressed in their best clothes, steps had been scrubbed and windows washed. The street had put on its finest.

'Ready?' called Frankie and blew two loud blasts on his warden's whistle.

Windows were opened wide and wireless sets were turned up full and the whole street gathered together to listen to the Prime Minister's announcement. This time Churchill did speak as promised and, when he had finished, there was wild cheering and the party in Darnfield Street began.

At first it was quite a refined affair with people handing one another plates and offering round sandwiches and drinks, but that wasn't good enough for Nellie; she definitely wasn't impressed by such sedate behaviour.

She stood, hands on hips, at the end of the tables and bellowed, 'What's this meant to be, a bloody Mothers' Meeting? We're supposed to be enjoying ourselves. Maud, the fellers are dragging me piano out of the bar up there,' she said, jerking her thumb towards the top of the turning. 'I've told 'em to fetch it down here a bit. And you'd better start playing right away 'cos that Nobby's had his eye on it, and I ain't having him bashing away on the poor bloody thing.'

'Can't have that, can we?' Georgie said to Maud with a wink.

'And you, Babs,' said Nellie, pointing along the table to where Babs was sitting with Harry and Betty. 'You can give us a song. Come on, get this mob dancing.'

Maud and Babs did as they were told and soon the party had turned into a proper old-fashioned knees-up. They danced and sang to all the old favourites and hardly noticed when the daylight faded and lights began shining all around the neighbourhood.

'Mum. Mum.'

'Excuse me a minute, Bert,' said Blanche. She turned round to see who was tugging at her sleeve, leaving the baker to do a solo dance in the middle of the street.

It was Len.

'What, darling?'

'I think we'd better get that fire lit soon,' he said eagerly, nodding his head towards the bonfire he had been building so busily for the past fortnight on the waste ground that had once been the Jenners's house.

Blanche ruffled her youngest son's hair affectionately. 'Yer desperate to get them matches to it, ain't yer, mate?'

'Please, Mum, let me light it now. I've nicked all them

tarry blocks from round the corner. They'll go right up. Lovely.'

Blanche smiled happily. 'And to think I was worried about you turning into a little carrot cruncher down there in Cornwall.'

'Mum,' he whined.

'Yer'll have to ask yer dad.'

'Ask Dad? I'm nearly fifteen.'

'Go on then,' said Blanche, chucking him under the chin. 'But mind yer eyes with them stones spitting out of the blocks.'

'Yes, Mum.'

''Cos if you get yerself hurt, yer dad'll kill me.'

Len soon had the bonfire roaring, and the sight of the flames leaping high into the night sky drew everyone to it like a magnet.

Georgie and Maud stood next to Harry who was giving Betty a flying angel ride so that she could see what was going on all around her.

'Did yer make sure Flash was shut in, babe?' Harry asked Babs, shielding his eyes with his hand from the heat and the brilliant light. 'Yer know her. She won't like this very much.'

'Yer right. I'd better go and check,' said Babs. She reached up to lift Betty down from his shoulders. 'And I'll take this young lady in at the same time. She should have been in bed a long time ago.'

'No,' Betty grizzled. 'I wanna stay with Nanna.'

Babs smiled at Maud and explained. 'I thought she was entitled to have a nanna. Every little girl is.'

Maudie bit her lip to stop herself from bursting into tears. 'Well, in that case,' she gulped, 'I'd better be the one to put my little girl to bed then, hadn't I?'

Betty reached down to Maudie.

'Are you coming with Betty and her nanna, Grand-dad?' Maud asked Georgie proudly.

He nodded. He kissed Babs on the cheek. 'This is turning out to be one of the best days, girl.'

If Ethel and Alice were impressed with the proceedings, they weren't letting on.

'Look at that old fool,' said Ethel to Alice with a contemptuous shake of her head as her husband, Frankie, helped young Len throw another big piece of timber into the flames.

The sparks flew into the air and Frankie whooped and laughed like a child.

'Bloody men,' grumbled Alice. 'Never grow up. My Nobby's exactly the same.'

'You just watch yerself, Frankie,' shouted Ethel. 'Yer'll set light to yer bleed'n trousers at that rate, and I ain't putting 'em out for yer.'

'No fear,' said Alice, with a shudder. 'Dunno where they've been.'

Harry put his arm round Babs. 'You all right?' he asked. 'Not too hot?'

Babs shook her head. 'I'm fine.' She nestled closer to Harry. 'I wonder what Evie's doing? D'yer think maybe she'll try and get up from Essex to see us soon?'

'Don't bank on it, will yer Babs,' Harry said and kissed her gently on the top of her head. 'She'll be too busy getting all her gear ready to take to the States.'

'I know yer just trying to make me feel better,' said Babs sadly. 'Yer a kind bloke, Harry Taylor.'

'Course I am!' He pulled Babs back as a stone spat from the now blazing bonfire. 'Oi, watch it, Len, or we'll have to get Ringer out with the hoses if you ain't careful.'

'Frankie!' hollered Ethel. 'Will you behave your stupid self?'

'Can we go over there and get a drink or something?' Babs asked quietly.

'Course.' Harry took her hand and led her away.

When they got to the tables, Babs bowed her head and started weeping bitterly.

Harry looked aghast. 'Babs, don't. What's the matter?'

'Harry,' she wailed. 'I'm so worried about her.' She clung on to him and sobbed into his shoulder.

'Oi, you.' Someone tapped Harry on the back. 'You making my sister cry?'

Babs spun round. 'Eve! What you doing here?' She wiped her tears away with the back of her hand.

Evie lifted the glamorous sequin-dotted veil from her face and folded it back over the crown of her hat. She opened her bag and handed Babs an expensive-looking lacy handkerchief. 'I ain't stopping,' she said. 'I just dropped in on me way back to Essex. Been up West to the officers' club.' She turned to Harry. 'My Ray's been promoted again.' Evie closed her eyes. 'Yer should see it, that club. It's terrific.' She opened her eyes again. 'And the West End! There's lights on *everywhere*. The whole place is just lit up like a Christmas tree. And honestly you can hardly push yer way through all the crowds 'cos of the singing and dancing.' She laughed, throwing her head back and showing her white even teeth to perfection against her expertly made-up face. 'There was people swinging from lampposts. Truth. And spilling out of all the pubs onto the streets. All linking arms with one another. All in love with being alive and with whoever happened to be on their arm.' She sighed longingly. 'Everyone was kissing everyone else. Here, yer'll never guess who I saw up there? Lou, from the factory, with an airman, she was. Having a right good time and all. Yer should have gone up there with her instead of staying round this dump.'

Babs blinked away the last of her tears. 'You finished?' she asked.

'Eh? Finished what?'

Babs looked into her twin's eyes, the eyes that had

once been indistinguishable from her own but were now so different. Now they were hard, glittering in response to something that Babs could no longer understand. 'Finished showing off,' she said. 'Some of us didn't wanna go up West.' She held out Evie's handkerchief to her. 'Like me, for instance. I wanted to stay here in Darnfield Street. With people I care about.'

Evie brushed away the hankie and laughed dismissively. 'You always did want to stay here. Even as a kid.'

'Yeah. Maybe I did.'

Evie took her gloves from her bag and began easing them onto her hands over her scarlet-painted nails. 'Well, I can't stop. I just wanted to say goodbye. We're leaving next week.'

'Yer mean you ain't coming back? Yer not coming to see—'

'No,' Evie interrupted her quickly. 'No,' she said again. Then she kissed Babs firmly on both cheeks and waved her fingers at Harry. 'Gotta be going. Ray's waiting for me in a cab round the corner. Give my love to Dad and Maud, won't yer.'

The twins looked at each other for a long, silent moment.

'And to Betty,' Evie added, with a tight little smile. Then she turned on her heel and ran off along the street.

Babs stared down at the ground. 'I wonder how she'll manage without me, Harry?' she whispered.

Harry held her close to him and stroked her hair. 'Like she always does, babe. With a saucy smile and more cheek than a barrowload of monkeys. Gawd help that Ray, Babs, that's all I can say. I just hope he knows what he's let himself in for.'

'The dog's fine,' said Maud, coming over to them. She still held Betty in her arms. 'But look who wouldn't go to sleep.' When Maudie saw the expression on Babs's face, her smile disappeared. 'Babs, have you been crying?'

'I'll tell you later, Maud,' sniffed Babs, smiling at Betty. 'Come on, let's get some drinks and go over and warm ourselves by the fire.'

As Babs was about to pour Georgie a glass of beer, Alice Clarke came over and slipped herself between Babs and the table. 'Ethel's told me that she thought she saw your Evie just now.'

Maud and Georgie both looked at Babs.

'Did she?' Babs said with a little shrug and reached round Alice's skinny frame for a bottle of pale ale.

'Gonna marry a Yank's what I hear.'

Babs slammed down the bottle and glowered at Alice. 'So?'

'Must be mad. Everyone knows they've all got wives and kids back home.'

George shook his head angrily. 'Come on, Maud,' he said. 'Let's get the baby away from her.' Then he leant very close to Alice's face and said, 'We can go and chuck something on the bonfire. That's what they used to do with old witches, yer know.'

'I only speak as I find,' Alice said through her mean, pursed lips. 'And fancy going off and leaving her kiddie like that.'

Maud looked at Georgie. 'I think Betty and I'll leave you to it, George.' She glanced at Babs. 'Coming with us?'

'No. I'll wait with Dad and Harry, if yer don't mind.'

When Maud and his granddaughter were safely out of earshot, Georgie said, as calmly as he was able, 'I know yer a silly old woman, Alice. And I don't think yer can even help it half the time. But yer'd better shut yer trap, 'cos that's my daughter yer talking about.'

Archie came swinging over on the crutches he still needed to get around on, with Blanche and Mary on either side of him. 'What's all this then, Ringer?' he asked. 'This old bag spreading her poison as usual?'

Alice bristled, playing for time as she tried to think of something spiteful to say about the Simpkinses.

'All right, Arch,' said Georgie, still glaring at Alice. 'Sit yerself down, mate, and Babs'll pour yer a pint.'

Archie lowered himself gingerly onto one of the chairs.

Blanche winked at Harry. 'Ignore the wicked old bastard,' she whispered. 'She's always like it. Never did like the Bells.' She laughed. 'Never liked no one really.'

'What did you say?' hissed Alice.

Blanche smiled pleasantly at Alice. 'I was just telling Harry, him being a neighbour now like, that we heard from our Terry yesterday. And how I wish he was here with us. 'Cos I know how much he'd enjoy the company. Specially yours, Alice. Yer such a little ray of sunshine.'

Mary sighed. 'I wish Micky was home and all.'

Alice tutted extravagantly and poked her scraggy finger almost up Mary's nose. 'And yer can leave my grandson alone and all, yer saucy little madam.'

Mary opened her eyes wide and stared challengingly at Alice. 'I was gonna keep it a secret till Micky came home on leave. But it seems a shame not to share it with yer on such a happy day as this, Alice. Your grandson, *my* Micky, proposed to me in his last letter. And I think I'm gonna say yes.'

Alice's eyes bulged.

'Blimey, Alice,' said Archie, spluttering his beer all over her. 'That means me and Blanche'll be related to you and Nobby.'

'That made yer laugh, Babs,' said Harry, patting her back to try and stop her from choking.

'You won't need yer jacket, Maud,' said Georgie, looking out of the bedroom window. 'It's a beautiful day out there.'

He turned round and watched her smoothing the creases from the eiderdown where'd she been sitting on the bed putting on her shoes.

'Yer a lovely woman, Maud. Lovely.'

She looked over her shoulder at him and smiled her thanks. 'Ready?'

At the bottom of the stairs, she stood back for Georgie to open the street door for her.

'Wait a minute,' he said. He reached up and straightened the four photographs that he had put up in the passageway since he had moved in with Maudie. There was a copy of the old one of the twins as cute, apparently inseparable, five-year-olds; the one of Betty that Babs had had taken to mark her niece's first birthday; a more recent group photograph of two couples and a little girl: Georgie and Maud, Babs and Harry and Betty – Betty in a pink satin bridesmaid's dress and Babs holding a bridal bouquet. And then the most recent picture of all: Evie in a frothy white wedding gown and Ray in his officer's uniform standing outside a white clapboard church in a beautiful green landscape that looked like it could have been a million miles from Bow.

'Quite a family, the Bells,' Georgie said to himself as he opened the street door. 'Quite a family.'

Across the street, Babs was sitting outside number six on a kitchen chair, Harry standing protectively by her side as she laughed happily at Betty trying to play the skipping games with Janey Simpkins and her friends.

'Not joining in this time, you two?' Babs called across to Minnie and Clara.

'No, we don't know these new songs,' chuckled Clara.

'Sing up, kids,' called Minnie. 'See if me and Clara can learn the words and then we'll show yer how to skip.'

The girls obliged gladly and sang at the top of their voices:

Vote, vote, vote for dear old Atlee,
Punch old Churchill in the eye,

                    If it wasn't for the king,
                    We would do the bastard in,
                    And we wouldn't go voting any more!

'Didn't expect them words, did yer, Clara?' said Georgie
with a wink as he and Maudie crossed over the street to
number six.

Babs stood up, but Harry anxiously persuaded her to
sit back down again.

'Ain't yer coming to the polling station with us, you
two?'

'Sorry, Ringer. Babs's feeling a bit dicky,' Harry
explained. 'So we'll have to go along later, when she's not
so queasy like.' He put his arm proudly round her
·shoulder. 'We've gotta be careful, see, what with her
condition and everything.'

'*You!*' Babs smiled shyly and jabbed Harry in the side
with her elbow. 'I was gonna tell 'em meself.'

Georgie's mouth dropped open. 'What? Yer don't
mean?' He scratched his head. 'No. You're not?'

'I think she is,' laughed Maud.

'I am.' Babs nodded and her smile broadened into a
grin. 'I'm having a little playmate for our Betty.'

Maudie kissed Babs on the cheek. 'That's wonderful,
darling. You take care of yourself. If you need anything,
anything at all . . .'

'Blimey, she'll be knitting by this afternoon.' Georgie
rolled his eyes at Harry. 'But there'll be plenty of time for
all that, Maud. Come on, Nan, we've got another grandchild's future to think about now. We'd better go and
vote for this new Britain they're all promising us.'

Maud slipped her arm through Georgie's and smiled up
at him. 'I've already got everything I want, George.'

'So have I, girl,' he said, patting her arm. 'So have I.'

Dream On

For Tanja Howarth

As with all my previous novels, *Dream On* is set in a real place during a real time, but I have created the characters and some of the street names especially for the story.

Book One

Book One

Chapter 1

1945

'Ginny? Gin? It's only me.'

Dilys Chivers was shouting at the top of her voice as she barged, uninvited, through the open street door and along the narrow passageway of number 18 Bailey Street.

'Come on, you lot,' she went on, throwing her coat over the end of the banisters, 'if you don't get a move on, you know what'll happen. That greedy mare from number 20 will have stuffed all the grub. She'll be dancing with all the fellers. And you'll all still be—'

As she stuck her head round the kitchen doorway, Dilys quite uncharacteristically shut her mouth and stood stock still in puzzled silence.

Sitting in the kitchen, hunched over the little scrubbed table, nursing a cup of tea, was a miserable-looking middle-aged woman. 'All right, Dilys?' she muttered.

'Whatever's the matter, Nellie?' Dilys, recovering her composure, pulled out a chair and sat herself down opposite the woman. It looked as though there might be a story to glean here and, young and pretty as she was, Dilys was as partial to a bit of gossip as any of the elderly battleaxes of Bailey Street.

'Honest, Nell,' she went on, pulling off her hat and tossing it on to the table between them, 'you look just like you wanna go for a' – she flashed her eyebrows – '*you know*. But you've gone and lost the key to the lavatory door.'

'It's this party, ain't it?' Nellie answered, her lips pursing in self-pitying anger. 'I can't go, can I?' She tilted

3

her head to one side and stared sorrowfully into the middle distance over Dilys's shoulder. 'And after surviving all them years of war an' all. Putting up with the Blitz, and what with the doodlebugs . . .'

Dilys might have relished a bit of scandal, but putting up with Nellie Martin's tale of woe was a price she wasn't prepared to pay. Dilys had never been a patient sort of person, and while she wanted the full story, she didn't fancy the boring moaning bits that looked like going with it.

'You just forget all about them bad memories, Nell,' Dilys said briskly, slapping her palms on the table. 'You just tell me what this is all about.' She paused, then added firmly: 'Briefly, like.'

Nellie's lips twitched. 'It's her, ain't it?'

It took Dilys a moment. 'D'you mean Ginny?'

'Yeah,' spat Nellie, unable even to speak her daughter-in-law's name.

'What on earth's she done to get you into this state?' Dilys's forehead pleated into a frown; this was getting really confusing.

While there wasn't exactly any great love lost between Nellie and Ginny, they usually managed to rub along well enough together. With Ginny keeping her mouth shut and doing as she was told by her husband – Nellie's son – and with Nellie not giving a bugger about anyone but herself, in its way, the household functioned. So all this upset, especially on a day like today, well, it just didn't make sense.

'If you must know, she's shut herself in the bloody front bedroom and won't come down, that's what.' Nellie spread her hands in wretched supplication. 'How am I meant to go to the party by myself, Dilys, eh? You tell me that. I'll be a laughing stock. Everyone'll have their

4

families with them – except me. And I can just see that Florrie Robins . . .'

Nellie paused for a moment, visualising the woman who was her oldest friend and, therefore, her oldest rival. 'I know her. She'll be sitting round there at her daughter's street party in St Stephen's Road, with all her grandchildren round her, acting like flaming Lady Muck, while they all wait on her, and fuss over her, and make sure the old cow's got everything she wants.'

Nellie's face puckered in on itself until she looked exactly as though she was sucking a lemon. 'And you know what everyone'll be saying, don't you? I can just hear 'em. But I swear on my life, Dilys, he never so much as touched—'

'Hang on, Nell,' Dilys interrupted, 'why're you so worried about Ginny not going with you? You can go with your Ted, can't you?'

'Him!' sneered Nellie, astonishing Dilys by showering her son's name with almost as much venom as she would probably have trowelled on to her daughter-in-law's – had she allowed her name to pass her lips. 'You wanna ask *her* about *him*.'

Nellie lifted her chin and stabbed her thumb ceilingwards. It was a gesture reminiscent of the one that the minister from the local evangelical hall used when he admonished the sinners, telling them they should be listening with their hearts to the Lord of Heaven, and not with their throats to the landlord of the Prince Albert. But it would have been obvious, even to the unbeliever, that Nellie's reference was not exactly reverential.

'Go on,' she hissed, 'you go up and see if you can get any sense outta the snivelling little mare, 'cos I'll be buggered if I can.'

'Gin. Gin, it's only me, babe.' Dilys's voice was tender

and wheedling as she tapped gently on the door. 'Come on, girl, let me in, eh?'

A muffled sob came from inside the bedroom.

Dilys stuck her ear to the door. 'What was that?'

There was another low whimper.

'What?' Dilys knelt down and squinted through the keyhole, as though it would help her hear more clearly. 'Speak up, Gin. I mean, I can't help you if I can't hear you, now can I?'

Ginny blew her nose loudly, then croaked in a tear-sodden voice: 'Leave me alone, Dil, please. Just leave me.'

'As if I'd do that, you dopey cow.' Discarding the softly-softly approach, Dilys gave the doorknob a good rattle. 'Now you either open this door, Ginny Martin, or I'm gonna go along to Tommy Fowler's and borrow his ladders. And then I'll stick 'em up against your front wall and I'll climb in through the bloody bedroom window. How'd you fancy that!'

She paused, listening for a response. 'I mean it, Ginny. You know me.'

Ginny did indeed know Dilys – for as long as either of them could remember, in fact – and Ginny also knew that once Dilys Chivers had made up her mind about something, there was no stopping her. And Ginny didn't much relish the idea of having her clambering up the outside of the house and messing up all her VE-Day decorations. Especially not in full view of the neighbours, who had all been out in the drizzle-slicked cobbled street getting the party ready since first light.

With weary resignation, Ginny decided she had no choice. 'Hang on, Dil,' she sniffled, 'I'm coming.'

'I knew you would.' Dilys grinned in self-satisfied triumph as she straightened up from the keyhole. She smoothed the silky fabric of her new dress down over

6

her thighs, tossed her head and patted her dark, shiny, permanently waved hair back into place with a little sigh of contentment.

The bedroom door opened and Ginny stood there, her head bowed and her arms dangling loosely by her sides.

'Blimey, Gin, will you just look at yourself,' chirped Dilys without a trace of compassion in her voice. 'You look worse than Nellie and that's saying something. Whatever's got into the pair of you?'

Without even pausing for a reply Dilys executed a neat little pirouette on the tiny lino-covered landing, flung out her arms in best pin-up style, dropped her chin and peered seductively through her lashes. 'Well?' she demanded. 'Ain't you gonna say nothing about me new frock, then?'

Before Ginny had the chance even to wonder how Dilys had managed to get something as expensive-looking as that – when they both knew she'd used up all her clothing coupons ages ago – Dilys was shoving her back into the bedroom.

'So,' she whispered conspiratorially, rolling her eyes and jerking her head towards the door in the general direction of the stairs, where Dilys presumed Nellie would be standing earwigging – just as she would have been doing in her position – 'what's been going on with her down there, then?'

Ginny slumped on to the double bed she shared with her husband and started picking at a loose quilting stitch on the pink satin eiderdown.

'Come on, Gin, you know you can tell me.'

Ginny shrugged. 'I dunno, Dil, do I.' She shook her head, making her soft blonde curls bounce around her face. 'I really don't.'

'For Gawd's sake, Ginny, pull yourself together girl. You're like looking at a bleed'n' wet weekend. Even

Violet Varney's making more effort than you.' Dilys gestured dramatically towards the window and the street beyond. 'That woman was out there last night till all hours doing up her front with a bit o' bunting.'

'So was I.'

Dilys huffed dismissively. 'Yeah, but her old man's in a bloody prisoner of war camp.'

Ginny looked up at her pitifully. 'At least she knows her Bert'll be home soon.'

'Whatever you on about now?'

Ginny turned her head so that Dilys couldn't see her tears. 'Look, Dilys, I know how much Nellie's looking forward to the party and I really hate letting her down, 'cos I know it ain't her fault, it's mine. And I feel terrible. But I can't go out there. I just can't.'

'Why not?'

A sob shuddered through her body. 'It's Ted. He's not been home.'

'He's *what*?' Dilys sprang up from the bed and stuck her fists into her waist. 'The rotten, stinking, swivel-eyed, no-good cowson of a . . .' Her fury got the better of her tongue and Dilys ran out of insults.

Ginny covered her face with her hands. 'Don't say them things, Dil. Like I said, it's my fault. No one else's. I must have upset him somehow. But I've been sitting here racking me brains—'

'I'll kill him,' Dilys fumed. 'I'll bloody well kill him.'

Ginny dropped her hands and looked up at her friend. 'You're a good mate, but it's down to me to sort it out.'

She turned her head away again and said in a voice so small that Dilys could only just make out the words: 'You and your mum are really important to me, Dilys, you know that, but since losing my own mum and dad . . .' Her shoulders shook as she rubbed the tears roughly from her cheeks with the back of her hand. '. . . Ted and

8

Nellie are all the family I've got. And I just don't know what I'd do if Ted left me. I do try to make him happy, but sometimes I just seem to get on his nerves. He gets so wild with me. Now he's started staying out all night. What am I gonna do?'

'That's it. I've heard enough.' Dilys took Ginny firmly by the arm and pulled her over to the polished walnut dressing-table, which took up almost the whole wall beneath the window of the cramped front bedroom in the little terraced house.

'Now you listen to me, Ginny Martin. You sit yourself down on that stool. Go on. Do as you're told. And you get your war-paint on. You're going to this sodding party whether you want to or not. We'll show bloody Ted Martin that he can't get away with this; he'd better start watching his step or he's gonna be in for a nasty surprise, a very nasty surprise indeed. 'Cos if he ain't careful, the bastard's gonna have me to deal with.'

As Ginny reluctantly stepped out of number 18, with the help of a push from Nellie and a shove from Dilys, she actually found herself smiling – she would have had a hard heart not to – because, just like every other ordinary little turning in the East End, Bailey Street in Bow had resolved to put on its finest for its VE-Day party. And, in the watery afternoon sunshine, despite the debris left from the bomb damage where the rocket had fallen in nearby Grove Road, and the houses that were boarded up, and the tarpaulin-covered roofs, Ginny saw a street where the residents had done themselves proud.

Each one of the remaining terraced houses was festooned in every conceivable shade of red, white and blue. They were draped with swags of home-made bunting; handwritten banners declaring Britain's greatness and the East End's allegiance to the King; and strung up high, right across the street, on cords stretched between upstairs windows, were tattered but loyal Union Jacks, flapping in the still damp, but now warmer, afternoon breeze.

Along the middle of the road stood a line of ill-matched kitchen tables, transformed by a covering of assorted patched and darned bedsheets into a single long dining-table. Although letting your neighbours have a close-up look at your repaired sheets certainly wasn't what most people in Bailey Street would have considered proper behaviour, it didn't matter today, because it was a day unlike any other. All that was important was the mountain of food piled on top of them; food which despite the rationing had been victoriously, if rather mysteriously, procured for the great event.

There were plates of sandwiches – none, it had been agreed by common consent, made with the usually unavoidable tinned pilchards – trays of pies and tarts, bowls of trifle, dishes of jellied eels, mounds of winkles and cockles, jugs of orange and lemon squash and, stacked next to a gleaming urn that someone had managed to 'borrow' from the church hall, tottering stacks of cups and saucers.

As if all that wasn't enough, outside the Prince Albert, the pub on the corner of the street, there was a row of beer barrels, topped with a double layer of crates of light and brown ale, ready and waiting for the festivities to begin. And there was certainly plenty to feel festive about.

There would be no more bombs and no more rockets; dragging yourself out of bed and down to the shelter was a thing of the past; and, with a bit of luck, rationing would soon be nothing but another bad memory – just like the Blitz and Utility underwear. The East End was ready to celebrate all right and no one would be able to accuse the families who lived in Bailey Street of not doing their best to show everyone how it should be done.

'Over here!' Pearl Chivers shouted from across the street, waving both arms at Nellie, Ginny and Dilys.

Pearl, Dilys's mum, was standing outside her house, number 11, supervising her husband, George, and her two teenaged sons, Sid and Micky, as they battled with her beloved piano, trying to manoeuvre it out of the house, over the doorstep and into the street without damaging it.

'Come and help me organise this idle mob, will you? Just look at 'em.'

She turned to point at the impromptu removal crew. 'Oi! Watch my walls, you dozy lot. That passage was only decorated last year.'

'I know, sweetheart. Sorry,' replied George good-naturedly. He knew better than to try and argue with his wife. He loved Pearl with all his heart, and everyone knew she was a genuinely good woman – as Ginny would have been the first to testify – but she was also the possessor of what George described as a 'strong type of personality' and had more energy than a dozen normal people. Like her daughter, Dilys, Pearl Chivers wasn't one to be messed around with.

'I was the one what painted and papered the flaming thing,' George added under his breath.

'Oi! I heard that!' Pearl grinned. 'Tell you what, girls, let's leave the fellers to it and go and help with the food instead. By the looks of it, they need some sorting out up there or it'll never get finished. Just look at 'em. You'd think they was doing it for a guv'nor instead of for 'emselves.'

She turned back to her husband and sons. 'And no

slacking, you three, I've got eyes in the back of this head of mine, remember.'

'As if we could forget,' Sid muttered.

'And I've got ears like a bat.' She chuckled, nudging her son in the side. 'So you wanna watch it, my lad. You might be nearly six foot in your stockinged feet, but you're still not too big for a wallop with the copper stick.'

Pearl didn't wait for Sid to reply, she just linked arms with Nellie and guided Dilys and Ginny forward in front of them towards the knot of women milling about at the business end of the tables, where yet more sandwiches were being made.

When he judged the women, or more specifically Pearl, to be out of earshot, George gave up the unequal contest and surrendered to the piano, leaving it perched on the street doorstep, hanging half in and half out of number 11 like an indecisive visitor.

Nodding for his sons to do likewise, George relaxed back against the door jamb, took a packet of Capstan Full Strength from his waistcoat pocket and offered them to the boys.

'And for Gawd's sake don't let your mother see,' he said, striking a match for them.

Micky inhaled deeply, his eyes narrowing against the smoke. 'Sixteen years old and she still treats me like I was a little kid,' he complained.

'Less of the "she", thank you, Micky.'

'Sorry, Dad.'

'You can talk,' sneered Sid. 'How d'you think I feel? If this war hadn't have ended just before I was old enough to bloody join up, she'd have *had* to have started treating me like an adult.'

'Pipe down, will you? I'm sick of the pair of you sulking and moping about. You don't know you're

12

sodding born, either of you. You should have had the life I had, when I was your age.'

George took a long drag on his cigarette, then lifted his chin towards Ginny. She was standing to one side of the other women with a sad, far-away look in her eyes.

'Or the worries that poor little cow's got; then you'd know what trouble was all about. Look at her. Left all alone with Nellie again while he's out and about, and up to Gawd alone knows what.'

Sid shook his head in wonder. 'Honest, Dad, I reckon Ted Martin's gotta be off his head. I mean, you'd have to be mad wouldn't you, leaving a lovely bit of stuff like Ginny at a loose end?'

Micky snorted, his youthful imagination painting glorious visions of Ginny in his mind. 'I wouldn't leave her at any sort of end. I'd—'

Sid punched his younger brother in the shoulder. 'Shut up you, you little squirt.' He rolled his eyes at his dad in a gesture of mature male solidarity, to demonstrate that he was obviously above such smut. 'Typical of him though. I reckon he gets away with murder, that Ted Martin.'

'You're right there,' agreed George with a sigh. 'Must be one of the fittest young fellers in the street. And what is he, twenty-five, twenty-six? But did he do the decent thing and join up? Do me a favour. Bad chest, he reckoned. I've never heard so much old fanny. If he's got a bad chest, then I'm—'

'Here we go,' murmured Micky.

Sid punched him in the arm again. 'Shut up, mouthy.'

'Come on.' George flicked his half-smoked cigarette into the gutter and straightened his cap. 'You've had your break. Let's get this finished before the foreman catches us.'

*

'Least the weather's cleared up, eh, Ginny love,' Pearl said gently. 'You know, I was surprised our bedroom ceiling never come down on top of us when that thunderbolt dropped last night. Right overhead it was. I thought we was back in the Blitz for a minute.'

She put down her butter-knife and smiled at Ginny, trying to encourage her to join in. Pearl knew it was no use leaving it to Nellie to look after the poor little thing, it wouldn't even occur to her. She might, on a very rare occasion, consider her son, Ted, whom, Pearl was sure, Nellie loved in her own peculiar way; but it would be very seldom that she would put even his needs before her own. And apart from that, well, she had no mind for anyone but herself; even on that terrible night in 1941, which Pearl supposed the inconsiderate old trout probably wouldn't even remember.

But Pearl would never forget that night.

Ted and Ginny had been together, on and off, for almost two years by then; far more off than on, as anyone but the starry-eyed Ginny would have admitted, but a kid as innocent and trusting as her had stood no chance against the smooth ways of a handsome charmer like Ted Martin. After spotting the newly blossoming, pretty little blonde going into number 11 to see Dilys, Ted had homed in on her like a rocket launcher.

The night that stuck in Pearl's mind was one of the occasions when Ted had actually turned up to take Ginny out as he had promised, and after an evening spent up West, he was taking her back to her house in Antill Road.

They were later than they'd said they'd be and Ginny was expecting a right rucking, but, instead of finding her mum and dad sitting up waiting for them in the back kitchen, all they had found was a pile of bombed-out rubble.

It was strange, the sort of thing that made the hairs

14

stand up on the back of Pearl's neck just to think about it, but Ginny had said afterwards that before she and Ted had even turned out of Grove Road and into her street, she had known there was something wrong. She could feel it somewhere deep inside, as surely as if someone was speaking to her.

Ginny had let go of Ted's arm and stumbled along in the black-out, tripping and sliding on the debris and the sand spilling from the ripped and shredded sacking bags, ignoring the firemen, policemen and wardens who tried to stop her. She cared nothing for their shouts and warnings, nothing for her own safety, all she wanted to do was reach her house and her family. She had to get to them.

As she finally skidded to halt on the pavement, her heart was racing and her blood pounding in her ears.

But she was too late.

Her mum, her dad, and her five little brothers and sisters – all seven members of her family – were dead. Gone together in a single hit.

Ted had held her to him, stroking her back and rocking her as if she were a child with a grazed knee that he could make better with a kiss. He'd breathed into her hair, telling her not to cry, soothing her. But there was no need. Ginny couldn't cry, she was too numb; tears had no purpose or meaning.

Ted had walked her back to his house in Bailey Street, whispering gently to her that everything would be all right; she would stay with him and his mum for the night, and he would sort everything out in the morning.

But when they reached his house, they couldn't get in. Nellie had locked up the place hours ago, having cleared off to the shelter in the cellar of the Drum and Monkey, a pub on the corner of nearby Darnfield Street. She had paused, it had to be said, for a brief moment to think

15

about her son as she had locked the door against potential looters; but had then blithely presumed that, being like her – a twenty-four-carat survivor – her boy Ted would have made his own arrangements and had proceeded to untie the key from its string behind the letter-box and pop it into her pocket.

And so it was, with the flash and the flare of bombs and shells lighting up the black, moonless sky, and with the stink of fires and explosives souring the night air, that Pearl had taken the pair of them into her home.

They were lucky to have found her in. Pearl and her husband had intended taking the children down to the underground station at Mile End to shelter, but at the last minute their plans had changed. George had been asked to cover a fire-watching shift for a sick mate and Pearl hadn't fancied packing up all the gear and organising the kids by herself – the boys were at the age when they would start a row if one of them even thought that his brother was looking at him a bit sideways – so she'd decided to stay home instead.

She and the children had spent an uncomfortable and chilly night crammed under the kitchen table; not that a few inches of scrubbed deal would have made any difference if a bomb had fallen on them, but Pearl was a home-loving woman and her kitchen, and its table, made her feel safe.

Ted Martin was also lucky on another count: ordinarily, Pearl would never have let him across her doorstep. Unusually for a woman as generous and loving as her, she'd always found it difficult to take to him. She'd watched him grow up in the house right across the street and had seen a spiteful, selfish streak in him even as a little boy – probably not surprising with a mother like his – and she had been happy to avoid having anything to do with him. But when she'd opened her front door that night and had seen him with his arm folded round Ginny's shoulders, Pearl couldn't turn him away. She wouldn't have seen a dog left out on a night like that. And then later, when he'd told her what had happened, Pearl had actually been quite impressed by how well he was handling young Ginny's terrible shock. She resolved to try to see the good in him from then on and Ted had pleasantly surprised her – for a while.

But the occasions on which Ted Martin showed his decent side were becoming rarer and rarer and, try as she might for Ginny's sake, Pearl found it harder and harder to find excuses for his behaviour. It broke her heart to see the way Ted was turning out, and as for the way that Nellie was treating her daughter-in-law, sometimes it beggared belief that Ginny could put up with it. Maybe if she hadn't been put through so much, if she hadn't been left feeling so completely alone, maybe then she might not have been so quick to marry into such a family. But although Pearl had come to have feelings for Ginny that were almost as special as those she had for her own children, Pearl wasn't an interfering woman and it was really none of her business what went on behind the street door of number 18. She'd leave meddling to the likes of Florrie Robins. It would be an entirely different matter, of course, if Ginny ever came asking for help, then Pearl would be over there like a shot; or even if it was her Dilys who'd got herself hiked up to the no-good so-and-so. But her daughter wasn't even married. More was the pity. With so many young men lost, whatever would happen to girls like Dilys?

Pearl sighed and shook her head at the thought of it, but common sense, past experience and bloody awful, grinding necessity told her that it was no good fretting about things like that. She wasn't the sort to dream, she was the sort who pulled herself together and got on with

17

the job at hand, no matter what it was. And, right there and then, Pearl's job was spreading marge.

'Dilys, you and Ginny take these ones what I've done on the trays and start dishing them out on to them dinner-plates.' Pearl waved her knife to show where she meant.

The two young women did as they were told, Ginny silently and Dilys with eyes rolling and tongue clucking in complaint. Dilys would much rather have been helping the men. Especially the couple in uniform, who were staying along the street in the Albert with their Aunt Martha and Uncle Bob. Dilys had been dying to talk to them since she'd first set eyes on them that morning. It was driving her mad having to waste her time hanging around with all the old girls.

'That's that done, thank Gawd,' said Dilys, shoving the pile of empty trays under the table.

'Don't leave them there, Dil.' Ginny bent down to retrieve them from beneath the layers of sheeting. 'Someone might hurt themselves.'

Dilys made no effort to help her. 'Fancy going along to the Albert to see if we can do anything for Martha?'

'You go, I'll just take these trays back to Pearl.'

'Suit yourself.' Dilys shrugged, then flicked back her thick dark hair and wiggled her way along the street towards the pub, targeting the two young servicemen as surely as a darts player eyeing up the bull.

The party turned out to be a real success. Everyone was in just the mood to celebrate: looking forward to the dawning of the wonderful new world where families would be reunited, where there would be plenty of every-thing for everyone and, as soon as Japan was sorted out, fighting would be at an end for ever.

Everyone was in the mood, that is, except Ginny.

As she leaned back against the soot-blackened wall of the terrace, watching the now drunken dancers whirl around outside the pub in the flickering light of the bonfire burning on the bomb-site opposite, Ginny had none of their optimism. All she could feel was disappointment.

Plenty of others had had their own share of disappointment, of course: loved ones still abroad and fighting in the East; husbands and sons still being held in camps; or, worst of all, no loved ones left, just black-crêpe-swathed photographs on the sideboard that would have to take their place for ever.

But Ginny's disappointment was different. She had married Ted Martin and that didn't get her sympathy so much as pity. After all, her husband was not abroad fighting and he was still, as far as she knew, very much alive – or at least he had been when he'd left home yesterday morning on 'a bit of business', whatever that was supposed to mean. But with the pain he was causing, he might as well have been amongst the missing. Ted Martin had let her down yet again. Increasingly, he made his own rules, deciding what was or wasn't important and, unfortunately, Ginny seemed to come very low down on his list of priorities lately. But even though he thought only about himself and did exactly as he wanted, the trouble was, Ginny still loved him, loved him with all her heart. He was all she had, he was her life. That's why it was so hard for her to bear. She had had so many hopes for their future together; now it began to seem as though they were nothing more than a handful of girlish dreams. But they were dreams she had to hold on to. What else was there?

'Come and have a dance with us, Gin,' slurred Dilys, weaving towards her, a half-empty glass of something slopping about tipsily in her hand. 'I'd rather dance with a feller.' She grinned as she flopped back against the wall next to her. 'But there ain't too many of them about here tonight, are there?'

She waved her glass in the direction of the pub. 'There's a flipping queue up there for them two soldier boys. And when you start talking to 'em, you know what? You realise that's all they are: bloody boys. Give me a man every time, I say. Fellers more in their sort of mid-twenties. Like your Ted. They're more my cuppa tea. Men with a bit of experience.'

Ginny said nothing.

'There'll be plenty of 'em around soon enough though, won't there?' Dilys went on, oblivious of the tears that had started to spill slowly down Ginny's cheeks. 'Soon as they get this demob lark sorted out, there'll be plenty for everyone. And add in a few of them GIs for good measure and it'll be flipping paradise.'

She nudged Ginny in the side and giggled. 'Till then, Gin, I'll have to make do with you for me partner. Come on.'

'Leave me alone, Dilys.'

'What's up with you this time, humpy? Even bloody Nellie's smiling.' Dilys sniggered wickedly. 'Reckon she's forgot all about seeing something nasty in the black-out, eh, Gin?'

Ginny couldn't help herself; she turned on Dilys. 'It's not funny, Dilys. I know everyone's having a good time and I don't wanna spoil it or nothing, but how can I join in, while he's off Gawd knows where? Look at me, I'm only twenty-two years of age, a married woman, but I might as well be an old maid.'

'You ain't gonna start going on about Ted again, are you? Why don't you give it a bloody rest?'

Ginny shrugged wretchedly. 'How can I?'

'Leave off, Gin. You know what blokes are like when they get going.' Dilys waved her arms about expansively as though the street were packed full of men, all standing there just waiting to illustrate her theory. 'The silly buggers have about ten pints too many and wind up drunk in a gutter somewhere.'

'Some blokes, maybe.'

'Well, to be honest, Gin, if you can't let a feller celebrate tonight, then when can you, eh? I mean, who wants a man what's tied to your apron strings? You wait and see, he'll sober up and be back home before you know it, with a head on him like a sore bear and not the foggiest about what happened to him.'

Satisfied that her words of wisdom had had the desired effect, Dilys grabbed Ginny by the arm and began hauling her along towards the pub. 'Come on, we'll get a few drinks inside you, we'll have a bit of a dance and then, you trust your Auntie Dilys, you won't know yourself.'

Just as they reached the pale pool of light coming from the street's single lamp-post, with three doors still between them and the tantalising draw of the Albert, Ginny pulled away from her friend. 'No, Dilys, I can't. I'm going back indoors.'

'You're *what*?'

'I wanna be there when Ted gets back.'

'Eh?'

'Look, I don't wanna upset him again by being out here at the party, all right? And we've gotta get up for work tomorrow, remember.'

'Work? Work?' Dilys looked horrified. 'I do not know what gets into you half the time, Ginny Martin. You must be mad, it's the only answer. You wanna be like me, girl. Start living for today. Forget tomorrow, forget yesterday. Just live for today.'

'It's not as easy as that.'

'It could be if you bloody well tried.' Dilys's knees wobbled and she grabbed at the lamp-post for support, shaking her head in despair at her friend's obvious insanity. 'Know the trouble with you? I'll tell you. You're always sodding mooning about. It's like you and that bloody old film.' She paused for a moment, doing her best to gather her drink-befuddled thoughts into something approximating sense. 'You know. That load of old rubbish.'

'Dilys . . .'

'*Gone With the Wind*.' She sneered with distaste as she remembered. 'That's the one. You go on and on about that Scarlett tart, or whatever her name is. I wouldn't mind, but anyone with any brain in their head could tell you it's that other dopey mare what you're a dead ringer for. That bleed'n' goody-goody.'

'Melanie.'

'That's her!'

'I thought you said it was a bloody old film and to forget the past. But you seem to know enough about it.'

'Are you surprised?' Dilys let go of the lamp-post, swallowed the rest of her drink and took a long moment to balance the empty glass on the window-ledge behind Ginny. 'We might have seen the flipping thing right at the beginning of the bloody war – flaming years ago – but you've gone on about it so much, I know the bleeder off by heart.'

Ginny was on the defensive. 'Well, it's a good story. And I like the clothes, and the house, and . . .' She paused. 'I know Scarlett's everything I'm not, but—'

'Who but you would care about old-fashioned toot like that?' Dilys butted in. 'And anyway she didn't even get the bloke.'

'You don't know that. Not for sure. It's like at the end she's still kept her dream, and—'

Dilys poked her finger close to Ginny's nose, her aim as shaky as her inebriated logic. 'I tell you, you wanna be like me and stick with the modern stuff. *Brief Encounter*. Now *that's* a film. None of that old fanny you go on about. Just a proper good story about fancying having a bit of how's your father when your old man ain't about.'

Dilys tried to wink, but the drink had not only loosened her tongue and ruined her aim, it had also made her eye co-ordination a bit haphazard, so she contented herself with a lopsided grin instead.

'Mind you,' she continued, her face suddenly serious, 'when you think about it, she didn't get the bloke either in the end. I don't understand that, Gin.' She shook her head in bewilderment. 'I'd have left my old man like a shot and gone off and, you know, *done it*, with me fancy piece. Bugger all that being noble lark. Gimme a bit of adventure every time.'

Ted stretched back on the pillows, yawned and released a rumbling, smelly fart.

'Oi, Ted, d'you mind?' she wailed. 'D'you have to be so rude?'

Ted rolled over, trapping her beneath his muscled forearm. 'I'll show you rude.'

'You're a dirty pig,' she said, pushing him away with an unconvincing shove.

He flopped on to his back and grinned drunkenly up at the ceiling, still half cut despite the pubs having closed hours ago. 'That's me all right, darling. *Dirty*.' Then, smacking the sagging mattress, he sat up and rubbed his face, drawing his fingers slowly down his stubble-covered cheeks. 'Better be off, I s'pose.'

She sat up next to him. 'But Ted, you promised you'd stay with me all night. You said we'd celebrate together.'

Leaning back and taking his weight on his elbows, Ted considered her prettily pouting mouth. 'Maybe I could stay just a bit longer,' he drawled, in a passable imitation of Clark Gable, which immediately had her giggling. 'But you'd have to be extra nice to me, of course. I was meant to be taking me old woman to a party tonight, so when I say extra nice—'

The podgy young redhead, who, for the life of him, Ted couldn't remember taking back to this room wherever it was, didn't let him finish speaking; instead, she threw herself at him and began covering his face with kisses. She wasn't going to let him get away that easily, not after the amount of money she'd seen him pull out of his back pocket while they were in the boozer. He must be good for at least another fiver.

A couple of hours later, Ted lifted the gently snoring girl's plump arm from across his chest, threw back the blankets and carefully swung his legs out of the bed and on to the grubby rug.

'What is it?' the girl mumbled in her sleep.

'Ssssh, it's all right,' he soothed her, as he scrabbled round in the darkness for his clothes. The room was so gloomy it was almost as though the black-out was still on, but it wasn't a few yards of cloth that was obscuring the light from the gas lamp in the street outside, it was the layers of grime and soot which caked the unwashed window-panes.

He had been in some bugholes in his time, but this was something special. The place didn't want fumigating, it wanted burning down. It made him sick to the stomach to see how some of these toms lived and he didn't exactly feel proud of himself for winding up in such a dump. He must have had a real skinful.

Finally dressed, and with the two pounds he had given the girl earlier tucked safely back in his pocket with the rest of his money, Ted started for the door, creeping away from the bed with the practised guile of a stray dog nicking sausages from the butcher's shop.

But this time he just wasn't careful enough. As he reached for the handle, a floor-board creaked and a wail went up from behind him. 'Ted! Where you going? You promised me you'd stay.'

Slowly, he turned round to face her. 'Shut your noise,' he said calmly, his face creased with disgust.

'But Ted, you did, you said—'

'I said, shut it.'

'Yeah but—'

He moved so fast that she didn't even see him raise his fist; the first thing she knew was the pain of her front teeth shattering beneath the full force of his punch and the metallic taste of blood filling her mouth.

Dilys sat up in bed with a start. It sounded just as though someone was rattling the letter-box. But who'd be doing that in the early hours of the morning? Definitely neither of the soldier boys; they'd cleared off with two sorts she'd never even laid eyes on before. But they weren't much of a loss, they were a right pair of drips.

Maybe it was the wind, or she'd been dreaming. She dropped back on to her pillow and pulled the covers up to her chin.

It could have been a drunk. There were still plenty of those left sitting outside on the kerb when she'd come in to bed and that was the sort of prank that would probably amuse them. But that was hours ago. Surely they'd all have gone home to sleep it off by now?

Dilys closed her eyes.

There it was again.

It was definitely the letter-box. And it was getting on her nerves.

She slipped out of bed, pulled on her dressing-gown and tiptoed across the room, so as not to disturb the rest of the house.

Lifting the corner of the curtain, she peered down into the street.

Hardly able to believe what she was seeing, Dilys dragged back the rest of the curtain, raised the window as quietly as she could, leaned out and waved her arms frantically at the person below. 'Stop it, for Christ's sake!' she spluttered. 'You'll have the whole flaming street awake!'

'Well, come down and let me in, then.'

Dilys flew down the stairs with barely a sound, wrenched open the street door and dragged Ted inside. Looking up to the landing to make sure no one had heard them, she closed the door gently behind him.

'What the hell d'you think you're up to?' she whispered.

Ted grinned and grabbed roughly at her breast. 'Quite a lot, I hope, darling.'

'Ssssh!' she warned him, brushing away his hand. 'You'll have them all out of bed. You *know* you're meant to tell me when you're coming over. If anyone hears you—'

Quite suddenly, she stopped speaking and shrank back against the wall. 'Whatever's that you've got on you?'

Her mouth dropped open like a trapdoor as she realised what it was. 'Ted,' she gasped. 'It's blood. There's blood all over your hands. And on your shirt. Look at you.'

'You know me, Dilys.' Ted waggled his eyebrows and

pulled her back to him. 'I can't help it if I'm irresistible. I have a few drinks in a pub and wind up fighting, don't I? Blokes get jealous of the way their girlfriends look at me and start having a pop. What am I meant to do? Ignore 'em?'

He touched his lips gently to hers. 'You can't blame them, can you? Handsome bloke like me goes in a place. I drive women wild, don't I?' He kissed her again, harder this time.

'I know you drive me wild, Ted,' Dilys breathed, her hand sliding down his chest, over his taut belly and coming to rest on his groin, where she began opening his fly buttons with practised ease.

Ted jerked his head towards the stairs. 'We going up then, or what?'

Dilys didn't answer straight away. She stopped fondling him and ran her hands through her hair, watching his eyes staring into hers. It was always exciting smuggling Ted up to her room in the early hours when everyone else in the street was in bed – including her own family upstairs – it made what they did even better. But Dilys was still annoyed with him for spending most of the night somewhere else; he'd promised her he'd be at the street party. If he was playing away from home, then Dilys wanted it to be with her, and only her, not with some little tart, or worse still with some glamorous sort he'd met up West in one of the clubs he was so fond of.

'You do love me, Ted, don't you?'

'Course I do.'

'I wore the frock you got me for the party. And I was right disappointed that you weren't there to see me in it. You said—'

'Look, Dilys, do us both a favour, just shut your noise

and get up them stairs, there's a good girl. Or I might
get bored and have to go over home to Ginny instead.'

Chapter 2

Ted flapped his hand in her face, trying to brush her off, as she kissed him tenderly on the forehead.

'Leave off, Dilys, for Christ's sake. You know I hate all that sloppy stuff of a morning.'

'Sorry, Ted. I wanted to wake you up nice and gentle, that's all.'

He rubbed his knuckles into his eyes and stifled a yawn. 'What time is it?'

'Nearly a quarter to six. Dad'll be getting up in about ten minutes, so I—'

'It's what?' Ted just stopped himself from shouting. That would have been all he needed, having her dad and brothers bursting in to give him a working over.

As he threw back the covers and started pulling on his clothes, Ted felt as if he'd gone ten rounds with Joe Louis. He was worn out. What he wouldn't have given just to have rolled over and gone back to sleep, but he knew he had to get a move on. He might have been getting pretty good at dishing out the kicks and punches, but Ted was definitely against the idea of anyone laying so much as a single finger on him. And in the sober morning light, he didn't have an ounce of the courage left that his drunken self had had, when he'd thrown his weight about under the coward's cover of darkness.

Ducking his head to look in the mirror that stood on Dilys's chest of drawers, Ted ran his fingers through his hair and barked his orders. 'Go and see if the coast's clear.'

29

Dilys did as she was told: clambering across the narrow single bed and poking her head out of the door of her little box-room, which stood at the top of the stairs.

From there she could see that the two other doors – the one to her parents' room and the one to the room shared by her brothers – were both still closed. It was a routine to which she was accustomed.

'You're all right. There's no sign of them.'

Ted snatched up his jacket, tucked his shoes under his arm and then, pushing past her with a conspiratorial wink and a grin, took the stairs two at a time in his stockinged feet.

Dilys stood on the landing and watched until he disappeared through the street door, then rushed back inside her room, scrambled across the bed and over to the window and looked out at him as he made the short journey across the cobbled street to the house he shared with his wife and mother.

Even though the Chivers' street door was on the jar, Ginny waited politely for someone to answer her knock.

George, Dilys's dad, welcomed her with a baffled smile. 'I'm sure I shut that door last night,' he said, scratching at his head so that his greying hair, which had until then been oiled into flattened submission, stood up in an untidy fan. He was wearing his usual outfit for that time of the morning: collarless shirt, open and showing his vest; shiny trousers resting on his increasingly round pot-belly; and braces dangling to his knees.

'Must have had more to drink last night than I realised. That or I'm going a bit doolally.' George chuckled to himself as he stood aside to let Ginny in. 'Go through, love.'

'Dilys still in bed then, Mr Chivers?' she enquired

matter-of-factly as she walked along the passage towards the back kitchen.

Although Ginny was in front, George Chivers shook his head as though she could see him – he was used to women having eyes in the back of their heads; he was married to Pearl, after all. 'No girl, she ain't. Believe it or not, our Dilys was up and about this morning, singing like a flipping skylark, before her mum or me was even dressed.'

Now it was Ginny's turn to be baffled. She stood in the kitchen doorway and gawped. Dilys was indeed up and about; there she was, admiring herself in the flower-etched mirror on the chimney-breast, fiddling about with her compact, tipping her head this way and that, as she considered the effect of the finishing touches she was adding to her make-up.

George stepped round Ginny, took the couple of steps it needed to cross the little kitchen, and let himself out of the back door and into the yard without another word. Three women chattering away nineteen to the dozen was more than he could take at that time of the morning, especially after the amount of ale he had sunk at the VE do the night before. A visit to the sanctuary of the outside lav was just what the doctor ordered.

'Morning, Gin.' Dilys greeted Ginny's bewildered reflection with a cheery wave of her powder-puff. 'I was right, wasn't I? Told you he'd be back.'

'Eh?' was all Ginny could manage in reply. She was genuinely confused by this strange turn of events. It was part of their regular morning routine – always – that Ginny came over half an hour before they actually needed to leave. She then spent a frustrating twenty-five minutes coaxing and persuading her friend to get a move on, so that they could get to the clothing factory off the

Whitechapel Road where they worked, without being too outrageously late for clocking in.

Dilys never, ever, got up without a fight, yet here she was, looking as though being out of bed was a pleasure she wouldn't have missed for the world.

'Blimey, Gin, pull yourself together girl, for Gawd's sake,' Dilys said, snapping the lid off her lipstick. 'I'm talking about Ted. I said he'd be back, didn't I?'

'Cup o' tea, Ginny?' Pearl asked, flashing a warning look at her daughter to both mind her manners and to keep off the subject of Ted Martin. 'I think the boys left some in the pot.'

Dilys finished painting her mouth and then sat herself down at the table to straighten the seams of her stockings. 'They looked as gormless as you, Gin, when they went out just now. You should have seen 'em. Talk about wreck of the flaming Hesperus! But at least they had an excuse, they must have drunk that Albert dry between the pair of 'em.'

'I didn't get much sleep last night,' Ginny said quietly. 'I tried to keep awake for Ted.'

'It bloody shows.'

'We all got to bed late last night,' Pearl said sternly, narrowing her eyes at her daughter. Then, turning to Ginny she held up the teapot. 'You having one then, sweetheart?'

'I'd love a cup, please, Pearl.' Ginny sat down opposite Dilys. 'How d'you know he was back then?'

'Nosy, ain't I?' chirped Dilys. 'I woke up early see, and I heard a noise down in the street. So I looked out and I saw him going indoors. Lovely bright morning it was,' she added with, for her, unusually sweet wistfulness. 'Really lovely.'

Ginny nodded at Dilys's explanation, as she took the cup that Pearl was shoving towards her across the oilcloth-covered table. 'You was right about where he was and all, you know, Dil. He hadn't stayed out 'cos he had the hump with me at all. It was like you said, he'd just had a few drinks too many. He met these fellers in some pub over Bethnal Green way and, before he knew what was happening, he was out cold in one of their mum's armchairs. I dunno if you noticed,' she added with a sheepish, almost guilty, glimmer of a smile, 'but he'd had a bit of a fight and all by the look of him. His shirt's got all sorts on it. I dunno how I'm gonna get it white again.'

'Can't say as I did notice, actually,' Dilys said hurriedly. 'I mean, I was only looking out of me bedroom window. I didn't say I had flaming binoculars, now did I?'

She reached behind her and picked up her handbag off the green-painted dresser. 'Come on,' she said, taking the still half-full cup from Ginny's hand. 'We don't wanna be late, do we?'

Pearl frowned as she watched her daughter almost skip out of the kitchen. What on earth had got into the girl? Whatever it was, Pearl wasn't sure she liked it. In her experience of her daughter's moods, this was probably just the lull before a very nasty storm.

As they stepped out of the house, Dilys linked her arm through Ginny's and took a deep breath of morning air. 'What a smashing day,' she sighed.

'Yeah, you're right, Dilys, it is a smashing day.'

Ginny looked up and down the street and smiled, a smile which came more easily this time, as she took in the signs of last night's party, still evident all around them. From the empty bottles and crushed paper hats littering the gutter, to the now slightly drooping swags of flags and ribbons draped across the soot-ingrained

33

terraced houses, anyone could see that Bailey Street had had a good time.

'I know I get a bit down now and then, Dilys, but you know how it is. No one said being married was easy, did they? Still, I should have listened to you, shouldn't I? Ted came home, and he came home to me.' She squeezed Dilys's arm. 'And on mornings like this I'm counting me blessings, 'cos I don't half love him, you know, despite our little ups and downs. And he was so sweet when he got in. Right sorry he was that he'd got himself tanked up and missed the party and everything. I've promised meself I'm gonna be extra nice to him to show him I understand and that it's all all right.'

Ginny lowered her chin and added quietly. "Cos if he ever did get fed up with me, I dunno what I'd do without him, Dilys, d'you know that? Soon as I was old enough to realise what fancying a bloke was all about, I started thinking what it'd be like to be Ted's wife. What it'd be like to set up home together. And then, when me mum and dad—'

'All right. Leave off, can't you?' Dilys snapped, pulling her arm away from Ginny's. 'There's no need to go on. Just leave it, will you?'

Ginny shut up immediately and automatically. She had been married to Ted for three years now and, despite keeping hold of her romantic dreams, she was also learning the self-protective habit of doing as she was told.

'Well, come on, if you're coming.' Dilys straightened the collar of her jacket and began walking along towards the end of the street with Ginny following obediently behind.

As they came to the Varneys' house, the last one before the pub on the corner, they saw Violet balancing on the

34

top of a set of steps, unhooking the bunting from the upstairs window-ledge.

When Ginny stopped to talk to her, Dilys folded her arms and tutted with impatience. 'You've got one minute!' she said to Ginny without further explanation.

'Don't take them down yet, Vi. Leave them up a bit longer,' Ginny urged her.

'No,' said Violet flatly without looking at her. 'I'm taking them down now.'

'Go on, be a devil. Everyone else is. Makes the street look right cheerful.'

'I said, no.' Violet pulled out a drawing-pin from the window-ledge and dropped it into the pocket of her cross-over apron.

'But why d'you—'

'I've had a telegram. This morning. It's my Bert. He's dead.'

Carefully and slowly, Violet wound the bunting round her arm as though it were a skein of wool.

'Funny, ain't it?' she said, as much to herself as to Ginny. 'I was celebrating yesterday 'cos the war's meant to be over. And my Bert goes and cops it. And I never knew. Dancing and drinking I was, like I didn't have a care in the world. Don't make no sense, does it? Don't make no sense at all.'

She let the flags drop on to the pavement and buried her face in her hands. 'The kids don't know yet. I couldn't bring myself to tell the poor little sods.' Her shoulders shook as she began to sob.

'Violet, I'm so sorry. Is there anything I can do?'

Dilys, with a look of contemptuous distaste at such a public display of grief, tugged at Ginny's sleeve. 'Come on, Gin.'

'Hang on, Dilys.'

'She don't want us. And we can't do nothing anyway.'

'But—'

'Look, me mum'll be popping out for her errands in a minute. She'll see to her. You know what Mum's like.'

Ginny might have learned not to put up a fight, but she still felt ashamed of herself as she allowed Dilys to drag her away. In fact, she felt so guilty at her own weakness that as they came to the corner of Bailey Street she twisted round and called to Violet, 'I'll pop in after work, Vi. I promise.'

Violet didn't reply.

Ginny and Dilys turned into Grove Road and headed for the busy junction with the Mile End Road, walking past the debris left by the rocket attack on the railway bridge that, like bomb-sites all over London, was now blooming with all kinds of gloriously colourful wild flowers.

As usual, the sight of the pinks and mauves and yellows bursting triumphantly through the rubble brought a smile to Ginny's face, but they could have been rare orchids and Dilys still wouldn't have given a damn. 'D'you know what, Gin,' she said as they dodged across the broad thoroughfare to the bus-stop by the tube station, 'you've right got on my nerves, you have. I was in a proper good mood this morning and now you've gone and upset me. First you keep going on about Ted, then you wanna hang around with bloody Violet Varney and make us late for work. What's up with you?'

'I'm sorry,' Ginny apologised, steering her friend carefully to the back of the queue to prevent her from trying her usual embarrassing trick of pushing to the front. 'But that poor woman, she must be—'

'For Christ's sake, Ginny! No wonder Ted stayed out all night. The way you go on, it's a wonder he bothered to come home at all.'

They completed their journey to work in silence, with

Ginny wondering how she could find ways of being nicer to Ted so that he would spend more time with her, and Dilys thinking exactly the same.

By the time they were ready for their midday break, Dilys had at last calmed down. Even though all the girls in the workroom, except Ginny, had been at parties till the early hours, they had all worked flat out on their sewing machines. They were on piece work and if they wanted a decent wage packet on Friday they knew they had no choice but to get stuck in.

But nobody really minded, especially today. The war was over and boyfriends, husbands and brothers would soon be home; everything would be wonderful again. And the nurses' uniforms they were making were definitely a lot easier on the fingers than the greatcoats and battledresses they had been sewing for the last few years. The money wasn't quite so good with the medical clothing, but it was certainly quicker and more pleasant working with the lighter-weight fabrics.

'Where we going, then?' Dilys shouted over the whine of the machines and the blaring of the wireless, as she tossed another completed tunic on to the pile by her chair. 'Canteen? Or down the Lane?'

Ginny allowed herself a little smile of relief; it wasn't in her nature to like being in anyone's bad books, but she particularly hated upsetting Ted or Dilys. Along with Pearl, they were the people who mattered most in her life and it really worried Ginny when either of them was wild with her. Sometimes she didn't even know why they were angry, they just were; it must have been something about her she supposed. She had that effect on Nellie as well at times. She only wished she could figure out what it was that set them off.

'I don't mind, Dil,' she hollered back. 'Wherever you fancy.'

'Down the Lane,' Dilys decided for them. 'I could do with buying a few bits to cheer myself up.'

'That's good,' Ginny agreed happily. 'I'll be able to pick up some veg and that'll save Nellie having to lug it home from the Roman Road tomorrow.'

Dilys said nothing, she just rolled her eyes at Ginny's totally aggravating saintliness.

After walking through the grim, bomb-damaged streets, with their high-walled, soot-impregnated warehouses and sweatshops, stepping into Petticoat Lane – the local name for the market area around Middlesex Street and Wentworth Street – was like entering a fairground. Stall after colourful stall lined the roadsides of the shop-filled streets, their owners calling a running commentary of jokes and invitations to passers-by to come and look at their wares, be they dark-green, curly-leafed cabbages, or enormous salmon-pink satin corsets.

Competing with their shouts were the street-corner beigel and herring sellers. Draped from neck to foot in swathes of stained white cotton aprons, their feet in big rubber boots and their sleeves rolled up to show their reddened arms, they dipped into their brine-filled barrels and held up the pickled fish for the customers' inspection. Then, their sale made, they slapped them into a cone of paper with a couple of the shiny, sweet bread rolls they'd hooked off the tall wooden pegs balanced precariously against the kerb.

Then there were the less vocal vendors: the sharp-suited men with goods that had somehow been liberated from locked and guarded warehouses, and from the backs of tarpaulin-sheeted lorries. A nudge and a whispered offer to examine their wares was a temptation that few resisted. Even the supposedly upright citizens, those who worked for respectable companies in the nearby City offices and banks, crowded round eagerly to bargain for the illicit contents of the spivs' battered suitcases and from inside the depths of their lairy jackets.

But none of these attracted Dilys; she was more interested in a stall selling sewing notions: the ribbons, bows and buttons of the haberdasher.

'What d'you think of these then, Gin? Big enough to go on the front of me new cream swagger jacket, d'you reckon? I don't like them bone ones on it, they're too dull.' She shoved a card of silver-coloured button backs in Ginny's face for inspection. 'I could take them in to the Ugly Sisters and get them made up, if I can find a bit of black velvet,' she said, jerking her head towards the little shop behind the stall. 'That'll look the business that will. Black and cream.'

'Don't be rotten,' Ginny scolded her, as she visualised the two elderly spinsters who spent their days covering buttons for the steady stream of customers, most of whom were just as uncomplimentary about their looks as Dilys.

The Ugly Sisters might have been skilled and inexpensive workers, but they were certainly no beauties and had earned their unfortunate nicknames when they had been little more than plain, skinny girls learning their trade at the knee of their surprisingly pretty mother.

'You're such a bloody hypocrite, Ginny. You know they're ugly.' Dilys threw down the buttons, bored with the thought of having to go to the trouble of finding material suitable for covering them.

'Yeah, but it don't mean you have to be nasty about them.'

'I don't *have* to be nasty about no one,' Dilys said

casually, as she strolled along to the next stall, 'I just like to be.'

'Morning, Mum,' Ted yawned. He rubbed his hands over his unshaven face, sat himself down at the kitchen table and opened the paper. 'What's for breakfast then?' he asked without moving his eyes from the story on the inside page about the intensifying official outrage over the black market.

'Breakfast?' sniffed Nellie. She was standing at the butler sink, up to her elbows in an enamel basin of soapy water. 'More like sodding dinner, you lazy bugger.'

'What time's it then?'

'Gone half past twelve, ain't it.'

'It's *what*?' Ted leapt to his feet, sending his chair skidding across the lino-covered floor. He might have been only twenty-five but sometimes he thought he was getting too old for all this carrying on with birds lark. He must have gone out like a light when he eventually got into bed with Ginny.

He ignored the now overturned chair, reached round Nellie and tipped her bowl of sudsy water straight down the plughole.

'Oi you, that was me hand washing I was putting in to soak.'

'Ne'mind your bloody laundry, Mum. I'm late and I need a shave.'

Ted was washed, dressed and out of the house within minutes; with his hair freshly oiled and his gleaming white collar held neatly in place with a discreetly striped tie, his hat in his hand and his overcoat slung over his arm, Ted Martin looked a picture of well-presented prosperity. And within less than an hour, he was sitting in a pub not five minutes' walk from the market where Ginny was doing her best not to aggravate Dilys by taking too long over buying her vegetables.

'So, what's your best price then, Joe?' Ted asked, pushing a pint along the bar to the middle-aged man by his side.

Joe half emptied his glass in a single swallow, brushed the foam from his moustache with a delicate flick of his forefinger and thought for a moment. 'It's a lovely little runner, Ted. Whoever owned it took good care of it. Very good care.'

'I didn't ask that.' It really got on Ted's nerves when someone he was trying to do business with jerked him around like some bloody mug punter. If he hadn't wanted to do this deal with Joe he'd have told him where he could stick it. But although Ted had a temper, he wasn't stupid; he knew that Joe had the cheapest cars anywhere north of the river, which wasn't surprising, considering his finely tuned system for acquiring them.

Joe would nick the motor, get it back to his workshop under the arches in Bow Common Lane, have the numbers changed and any distinguishing marks wiped out, all within a couple of hours; then come up to this discreet little City pub to flog it off to the so-called respectable types – the respectable types with a few quid in their pockets, that is – the ones who made their living pushing pieces of paper back and forward across their big, polished desks, the same ones who flocked around the spivs in the Lane.

He was a real craftsman, was Joe; Ted admired that.

Joe knocked back the rest of his pint and stared down at the empty glass. 'Now let's see.' He screwed up his face and scratched the side of his head. 'Got a fag?'

Ted tossed his cigarettes on to the bar. 'Stop pissing about, Joe. You ain't dealing with a know-nothing knob of a shipping clerk. This is me, Ted Martin. The bloke what's seen you right for the last few years.' He lowered his voice. 'The one what's got you all them lovely petrol coupons. Remember?'

Joe stuck one cigarette in his mouth and another behind his ear. 'Buy us another pint; get us another couple of bottles of that Scotch. The good stuff mind, you can keep the old shit for the mugs. And it's yours for a oner.'

A flicker of a smile passed across Ted's lips as he slapped palms with Joe. An almost brand-new Talbot for a hundred quid! 'You've got a deal, my son.'

Ted walked out of the pub with his chin in the air and a swagger in his step, every trace of tiredness forgotten. Now he had a decent motor he'd be well away.

He'd been doing all right up until now, of course, but now there'd be no stopping him. Things were really going to look up. Ted Martin had plans, big plans.

He was going to be a face to be reckoned with.

Chapter 3

During the next few months there were many changes for families in the East End and those who lived in the area around Bailey Street were no exception.

They experienced home-comings, as husbands, fathers and sons returned from abroad and were demobbed; and departures, as young women married boyfriends newly back from the war and went to live in what were, to them, alien neighbourhoods. The girls were, in reality, moving just a few streets away, but might as well have been going to try their luck at surviving in the depths of the Amazon jungle, such were the ties that cockneys had with their own tight-knit communities.

Most of the home-comings were, of course, joyful: moments to be photographed, treasured and remembered, but it wasn't the same for everyone. After the exhilaration of the victory in Europe and then in Japan, the longed-for pleasures of being back home and returning to what had once been normality, had more than their share of pressures and frustrations. Six years of war had changed people. Women had learned to control their own lives, to be the bosses in their own homes; they had earned wages and made decisions and now their men – who, to their children, were sometimes little more than a vague memory and a faded, sepia-toned snap on the mantelpiece – were expecting to take charge again and the women didn't always appreciate it.

It wasn't always easy for the men either. While they weren't exactly sorry to be away from the danger and the dying, they certainly missed their mates, the routine, the excitement even, and, as they were beginning to realise, they were missing out on a lot of other things as well. The land fit for heroes that they had been promised now all seemed to be a bit of a con. Instead of getting what they had all looked forward to: good homes, decent food and sharing a few pints down the local with the lads, they had come home instead to bomb-sites, queuing and ration books, and wives who seemed more interested in going out to work than in fetching them a cup of tea while they toasted their toes in front of the fire and listened to the Light Programme on the wireless.

Some of the older residents of Bailey Street weren't at all surprised by the younger men's disillusionment and were only too keen to say so, adding dire warnings about the newly elected Labour government for good measure. It wasn't so much that they didn't approve of what they were being offered by this Labour lot – who but a fool would refuse the promise of a bright new Britain for all, and most had actually voted for them – it was just that they couldn't help but think how it was all so reminiscent of what had happened to them after the Great War.

Promises had been made then too. And they had all been broken, dissolving in front of their eyes like the foam in a wet beer glass. The so-called boom had quickly turned to dust and the brave new world had sunk into the horrors of the 1930s and the Depression. How could they not be wary when their dreams were still haunted by nightmare visions of the workhouse and the shame of being visited by the despised Relieving Officer?

Sometimes, when Ginny stopped to pass the time of day with one or other of her elderly neighbours, she found herself sympathising all too readily with their fears about the way the world seemed to be heading, especially when Ted was being difficult – as he seemed to be more and more lately. But she knew that no matter how down she felt at times, it was always best to try and put on a brave face, to keep her chin up and to look cheerful. That way she didn't upset things even more and it also helped her convince herself that everything would turn out all right in the end. Although it wasn't always easy to be positive, especially when Dilys was working herself up into a mood.

'I just don't see why you ain't bloody furious like I am,' Dilys fumed, as they waited at the bus-stop on the corner by Aldgate East station. 'Anyone'd think you'd had a win on the dogs instead of getting the flaming sack.'

'But we've not had the sack, Dil, have we? Not really. It's more like we've lost our jobs.' Ginny stamped her feet to warm them against the damp autumn chill. 'I mean, you can't blame old Mr Bloom for retiring, now can you? He must be eighty if he's a day. And what with the last of the uniform work going . . .'

'Can't blame him?' Dilys shook her head in amazement.

'Anyway, this might be just the chance we could both do with. You've always said you fancied going on the buses.'

Dilys's mood, always unpredictable, took a swing away from gloom and touched on almost optimistic interest. She pouted and swung her shoulders, as she visualised herself in a conductress's uniform being chatted up by a bus stuffed full of men, all eager to show her a good time.

Ginny dropped her chin and continued shyly, 'And what with Ted doing so well, it's probably as good a time as any for me to start thinking about staying at home and having a baby. I've—'

Shocked back to reality by such treacherous talk, Dilys almost exploded. 'You wanna get *pregnant*? By *Ted*?'

A large, middle-aged woman standing in front of them in the queue looked over her shoulder at Dilys and stared in scandalised reproach. 'That's nice talk for a young girl, I don't think. In my day, we didn't even know the meaning of the word.'

In reply, Dilys poked out her tongue and the woman looked away with a loud huff.

'Of course by Ted,' Ginny hissed, her fair cheeks flushing as pink as a stick of candy-floss. 'Who d'you think I wanna do it with, the bloody coalman?'

'You take my word for it, Al, I'm telling you, if you can show her you've got plenty o' dough, then any bird you fancy, she's yours for the taking. You don't even have to spend that much on 'em. Just flash it about a bit. They ain't got a lot of brains see, birds ain't.' Ted tossed back the last of his drink and weighed his empty glass in his hand.

'Like another one in there?' asked Al, rising from his chair.

'Why not? And you can get us a chaser an' all this time.'

At barely eighteen years of age, and not usually much of a drinker, Al was not exactly sure what sort of a drink a chaser was, but he would find out and Ted would have one if that was what he wanted. Al was determined to impress this new-found friend of his, because while he might not have known much about boozing, Al knew something very clearly: he definitely did not like the idea of being conscripted, especially now there wasn't even a war to fight. And Ted, whom Al had met only a couple of hours ago – when he had tipped him the wink that he had better put his suitcase full of nylons back in his boot

46

as a copper was heading his way – had been telling him all sorts of fascinating things.

Ted had told him, for instance, that there were plenty of ways to avoid being called up and had even gone so far as to slip him a piece of paper with a doctor's address on it, with the promise that it would come in more than useful when the dreaded buff envelope arrived. He'd told him, as easy as that, and just to repay him for his help in avoiding being collared by the law!

After a few rounds of drinks, all paid for by Al, Ted had gone on to tell him that he too could earn enough money to have a flash motor and sharp-looking suits. But probably most important of all for a reluctant virgin such as Al, Ted had been generous enough to share with him the benefit of his experience with women.

Ted had said, quite matter-of-factly, that after the cheapest of nights out, he should definitely expect a whole lot more than a quick fumble inside their blouses.

This was music to Al's ears. He wouldn't have admitted it to someone as sophisticated as Ted, of course, but he had often spent the best part of the week's wages he earned at his clerking job and had not even got as far as a serious kind of kiss, let alone a real bit of how's your father.

But then, according to Ted, the way that Al earned his living showed what a mug he was. In Ted's book, anyone who worked for a governor was no better than a fool.

Al put down the three drinks, his own half pint, Ted's pint and a tot of whisky – the barmaid had been very helpful in explaining chasers, especially after Al had bought her a drink as well – and sat himself down next to Ted. 'So, Ted,' he said, raising his glass in salutation, 'you was saying about this, what was it, working the tweedle? How does it go again?'

Ted grinned; it was a while since he'd met a kid as

47

innocent-looking and as trusting as this one. He was a real one-off. Particularly around the East End. He must have been brought up wrapped in cotton wool.

Ted studied him across the rim of his glass. Maybe he could be of further service some time. All right, so he wasn't exactly Brains Trust material, but a look-out with an honest face was always useful when you were on the creep around a warehouse. And anyway, it amused Ted to see the kid hanging on to his every word. He enjoyed a bit of respect.

Patiently Ted explained the con one more time.

'I get it!' A flash of understanding at last lit up Al's baby face. 'You have *two* rings. A real one and a fake one. And when you go back, you sell the jeweller the schneid!'

'Right. That's it.' Ted winked at the lad, then asked his usual question whenever he met anyone under the age of thirty. 'Now, tell me about yourself; you got any sisters, son?'

'No, only brothers.'

Ted paused. No sisters. Well, you couldn't have everything. Then another thought struck him. 'So how old's your mum then?'

'Dunno.' Al grimaced. 'Just old, I suppose, like all mums.'

Ted didn't let his disappointment show. 'Where's this office o' your'n? Up the City?'

'No, down the docks. I do the paperwork for the bonded warehouses.'

Ted could feel the happiness spreading through his body like warm treacle dribbling over a spotted dick.

When their bus finally arrived, Ginny was, for once, delighted to see that it was really crowded and that she had to sit by herself. She had been shown up quite enough for one day by Dilys and her big mouth.

Dilys, on the other hand, wasn't very happy at all, though her increased displeasure had nothing to do with losing her job or how many people were on the bus. It was the idea that Ginny was thinking about having a baby that had *really* upset her. That was the last thing she wanted to happen, because Dilys had been thinking very seriously about her future with Ted. Despite all the servicemen being demobbed, good-looking blokes with a few bob in their pockets were still very thin on the ground and Dilys wasn't getting any younger. She was nearly twenty-three, for goodness sake, and Ted was getting to be a bit of a last resort. All right, he was already married, but the papers were full of stories about people getting divorced. Once it had been something only the rich and famous could do, but nowadays it seemed as though every Tom, Dick and Harry could get shot of his wife if he wanted to. All you had to do was spend a couple of days down in Brighton with some willing tart or other, have a quick snapshot taken leaving your love nest, and Bob appeared to be your uncle. So why not Ted? Well, maybe it was a bit more complicated than that, but if Ginny went and got herself up the duff, it probably wouldn't matter anyway, as Dilys had seen how funny blokes could get when their wives got pregnant.

They came over all stupid and loyal, and started staying in and holding their old women's hands and talking about whether it would be a boy or a girl, and if they should name it after Auntie Flo or Uncle Harold. No, Ginny getting herself pregnant was definitely not a very good idea, not a very good idea at all. Dilys had to get the thought right out of Ginny's stupid, curly blonde head, and she had to do it soon, before it got out of hand and Ted got to like the idea of becoming a daddy. And a little thing like the three rows of people sitting between her and Ginny certainly wasn't going to deter Dilys from putting her plan into action.

To Ginny's alarmed embarrassment – but to the obvious interest of the press of passengers surrounding them – the moment she sat down, Dilys started firing a barrage of questions at her. 'Oi, Ginny! So what's Ted got to say about all this baby lark then?'

Ginny took a deep breath, twisted round in her seat and mouthed very quietly, 'I haven't mentioned it to him yet, Dilys.'

That wasn't exactly true; she had tried to raise the subject once or twice, but Ted wouldn't even discuss it. In fact, he had forbidden her to talk about it. But now she had no job and the war was over, maybe he'd feel differently. She would have to be careful how she brought it up, of course, as she didn't want to aggravate him, and Dilys opening her big gob certainly wouldn't help matters.

'And I'd appreciate you not mentioning it either, Dilys.'

Dilys could have kissed the silly cow. She hadn't even talked to him about it. Perfect!

Suppressing the urge to burst into laughter, Dilys carried on – her face now arranged into a concerned frown. 'Well, he won't like it, you know.'

'I don't agree.'

'I'm telling you.'

'Dilys, please, d'you mind?' Ginny pulled her coat collar tighter around her throat and tried to shrink down into her seat.

'And how about Nellie? What's she gonna say?'

'I'm sure Nellie would love a grandchild.'

'What, Nellie? Are you sure? With all that screaming and crying keeping her awake all night? Clothes-horses full of wet nappies all over the place. She'd go barmy.

50

And you know Ted can't stand fat birds,' she added with a sudden flash of inspiration. 'And with your legs and figure, you'd blow up like a barrage balloon. You do know that, don't you, Ginny? You'd be like a right flipping elephant. Stuck in a chair, day in day out, with just Nellie for company. You'd hate it. I'm telling you.'

'That's what happened to me,' chipped in a sharp-nosed woman in a peculiar brown felt hat, who was sitting across the aisle from Ginny. 'Didn't it, Charlie?'

Charlie nodded. 'It did. Just like an elephant she was. And her legs . . . You've never seen nothing like 'em.' He winced at the memory. 'Went all veiny and horrible, they did. And her ankles! Swollen up like a pair o' prize marrows they was. Months she was like that. Couldn't get a pair o' slippers near her feet, let alone a decent pair o' shoes on her. And as for her guts . . .' He shuddered. 'Talk abouf taking over the Bile Beans factory. She must have swallowed a hundred boxes of the bloody things. But nothing worked her. Bunged up like a bottle with a cork, she was.'

Dilys was triumphant. 'See! Can you just imagine what Ted would have to say if he had to put up with all that for nine months?'

That was enough for Ginny. *She knew* Ted could be difficult and that Nellie wasn't exactly a loving mother-in-law, but Dilys didn't have to let the whole bloody bus know. She stood up and jerked the string above her head to ring the bell.

'Excuse me,' she muttered to the woman next to her, 'I wanna get off.'

'Where you going?' Dilys bellowed, as Ginny shuffled sideways along the aisle towards the back of the bus.

'Home. But I've decided to walk. All right?'

Dilys raised her eyebrows in surprise, then turned to

face the steamed-up window. 'Suit yourself. But you must be garrety, it's started pouring down out there.'

By the time Ginny eventually got back to Bailey Street she was cold, wet through and thoroughly miserable; but even though all she felt like doing was going indoors, slipping into a warm dressing-gown and sitting in front of the fire with a nice, hot cup of tea, she couldn't bring herself to walk past Violet Varney's without at least knocking on her door to see how she was getting on.

In the four months since the poor woman had heard of her husband's death, Ginny had called on her most evenings, although Violet usually found a reason not to let her over the street doorstep. It was obvious, even from the brief glimpses Ginny had of her, that she was not doing very well.

Ginny rapped on the glass panel in the door. 'Violet? You there?'

Violet's youngest, a skinny, hollow-eyed child of about ten, opened the door just wide enough to peer through the crack. 'Who is it?'

'It's me, babe. Ginny, from over the road.'

The little girl opened the door wider. 'Me mum's in the kitchen,' she said, nodding along the passage.

'You sure it's all right if I come in? Mummy usually talks to me out here.'

'Mum only said I was to say she wasn't in if it was the rent man, or the bloke for the tally money. She never said nothing about you.'

Ginny nodded, but she wasn't actually listening to what the child was saying, she was far too preoccupied with the look of her. There had been talk that Violet was neglecting the kids, giving them a beating even – something that nobody would ever have thought of accusing her of before – and here, right in front of Ginny seemed to be proof that the gossips were right for once. The child's cheek had a series of wounds across it that certainly hadn't come from any playground rough and tumble; she had been cut with something a lot sharper than a stone or a hopscotch marker.

As soon as she noticed Ginny looking at the red, angry slashes, the little girl instinctively raised her hand to her face and dropped her chin, making Ginny flinch at her victim's shame.

'She's in the scullery,' the child muttered, then turned on her heel and fled.

It tore at Ginny's heart as she watched the poor, scrawny mite disappear up the unlit stairway. She felt as though she could cry out loud with pain, but not only for the desperate youngster.

Ginny had seen herself reflected in the look that had clouded the child's pale, careworn little features. It was a look that Ginny sometimes glimpsed lately, when she sat in front of the mirror. No matter how she tried to deny it – to brush it away, refuse to acknowledge it – it was a look that had stained, and that told anyone who chose to see that Ginny was a woman who knew what it was like to have her dreams shattered.

When Ginny eventually went home she found Ted sitting at the kitchen table eating his tea, with the evening paper propped up in front of him against the sugar bowl.

'Where d'you think you've been?' he asked, flicking over the page.

Ginny took off her sopping wet coat, draped it over the back of one of the chairs and stood it in front of the gas stove to dry. 'I popped in to see Violet Varney, on me way back from work,' she said shaking out her hat and combing back her damp hair with her fingers. 'She wasn't very happy at first that her little one had let me in.'

Ted looked up at her with disgust. 'Well, while you was over there chatting, me mum had to do me tea for me. And now she's so whacked out, she's had to go up and have a lay down. Satisfied, are you?'

Ginny thought about her spoilt, idle mother-in-law snoring her head off upstairs, and she thought about how exhausted Violet Varney looked and how skinny and unhealthy the child had been.

She would have liked to have gone up and dragged Nellie out of bed and across the street to see what being whacked out really meant. She'd have liked to have rubbed her self-regarding nose in it, and she'd have liked to have told the lazy old bugger – and Ted – exactly how she felt.

Instead, Ginny said nothing. She knew there were lines she shouldn't cross, so, as always, she acted the appeaser. 'I wasn't chatting, Ted,' she said defensively, as she filled the kettle at the sink. 'And I only meant to go in for a couple of minutes. You know, to see if there was anything I could do. But when I saw the state she was in—'

'What state d'you expect her to be in?' Ted interrupted. He tore a chunk of bread from the loaf, mopped up the gravy from his plate and shoved it in his mouth.

Ginny didn't reply immediately. She lit the gas and sat down at the table to wait for the water to boil. Ted liked to have a cup of tea after he had finished his meal. She herself had no appetite after what she had seen across the road, but even if she had, she knew it would have been pointless to ask if Nellie had made anything for her to eat.

'I didn't expect her to be as bad as she is, to tell you the truth, Ted,' she said eventually. 'She was going on about all sorts. Kind of rambling. She was talking about this place, Southern Rhodesia, wherever that is. A welfare lady went round to see her the other day and said they

54

was offering places at some college over there. And parents who ain't managing very well can send their kids. Their older ones like. It's because they need more people in their country or something. I didn't really understand what Violet was going on about, but she reckoned it sounded like a good thing.' Ginny sighed loudly. 'Can you imagine being that desperate that you'd let some stranger take your child?'

She waited a moment to see if Ted had anything to say about such a terrible decision for someone to make. When he said nothing, she continued with her story. 'You see, this welfare lady turned up because of the school.' Ginny got up and warmed the pot and began slowly spooning in measures of tea. 'They was worried Violet's been beating the kids. Not giving them a smack, I don't mean, but really hurting them. She's been driven off her head I reckon, since she heard about her Bert.'

Ginny filled the pot with the boiling water and carried it back to the table. 'I think she's gonna do it, you know, Ted. See, she's really in trouble.'

Ted snorted derisively and forked in another mouthful. 'What, one of her punters put her in the club, has he?'

Ginny almost dropped the teapot. 'You *know* what she's been up to?'

'Don't everyone? She's been hanging around outside the billiard hall down Chris Street for months now, waiting for customers.'

Ginny shook her head. 'I never knew. In fact, I didn't even know whether to believe her when she was telling me just now. It's not like her to say much at all, especially about personal things. So when all that came pouring out, well . . . I didn't know what to say. But she said it was a relief to have someone to talk to about it.'

She poured Ted's tea, added sugar and milk and automatically stirred it for him, before setting it down next to his plate.

'And d'you know what else she told me?' she continued in a low voice. 'She thinks she's got a dose.' Ginny shuddered. 'VD. Can you imagine? Said she's been going with all sorts of men, just to get a few bob for the kids. She was so scared they'd put them in a home if she wasn't feeding them right and dressing them decent. But the poor little devils was more at risk in their own flipping house. She was so upset when she saw how one of the blokes she brought home the other night looked at her youngest that she went sort of barmy.'

Ginny took a gulp of her scalding hot tea as Violet's horrific words replayed in her head. 'She held her down and cut her little face. With the bread knife. Said she was trying to make her look ugly.'

'Silly whore.' Ted threw down his knife and fork, and shoved his plate away from him.

'I don't understand it either, Ted. I can't imagine how desperate you'd have to be to go and do something like that. How anyone could sell their body . . .' Ginny shuddered again. 'But at least she's gonna try and do her best for the kids. She's gonna send the oldest two to this Rhodesia place. And the others are gonna live with her sister. Until she can find a way to get herself straight. She feels so guilty about what's been happening. But I said to her, it's not your fault, I said. Well, what else could I say? But honestly, Ted, fancy doing that. It's horrible. If only she'd have said something. If only she'd have let people help her.'

Ginny picked up Ted's plate and carried it to the sink. She turned on the tap and looked over her shoulder. 'I suppose it'll be easier to understand when we've got kids of our own.'

Ginny winced as she realised, too late, that she'd gone

and blurted it out. Instead of preparing him gently as she had intended, of speaking to him about her dreams of them having a baby, a proper family of their own, and getting him used to the idea, she'd just gone and said it. She could have bitten her tongue off. She'd mucked it up. She was *so* stupid.

Ted picked up the paper and folded it neatly. 'What did you say?'

'I never meant—'

'Look. You've got on me nerves enough tonight already. Now what did I tell you?'

'I'm sorry, Ted, I—'

'Don't sorry me.' Slowly, he rose to his feet and walked over to her. 'I asked you a question. What did I tell you?'

Her mouth was so dry she could barely get the words out and the cold, hard edge of the sink was digging into her back. 'Not to talk about having kids.'

'And what did you just do?'

'I didn't mean—'

'You didn't *what*?' Ted grabbed hold of a handful of her hair and jerked her head back.

'I didn't mean anything,' she gasped through the pain, desperate not to let the plate slip between her fingers and drop to the floor. That would only make him angrier.

Ted drew back his fist and slammed it full into her cheek. 'I told you last time. Why don't you just keep that mouth o' your'n shut? That's another black eye you've made me give you.' He stared at her already swelling face and blinked rapidly as though he couldn't quite believe what he was seeing. 'Look what you've made me do, you stupid cow.'

Ginny opened her mouth to apologise, but said nothing when he yanked her hair even harder.

'Now, you ain't gonna start making no noise and wake me mother up an' all, are you?'

Ginny gave a tiny shake of her head. Why *was* she so stupid? She felt so ashamed of herself. She'd done it again. Why did she have to go upsetting him all the time?

Careful not to pull away from him, she stretched her arm behind her and put the plate gently on to the wooden draining board. Then, biting her lip to stop herself screaming out in agony, she let him drag her out of the room and up the stairs by her hair.

Chapter 4
1946

'Ted . . .'

'Yeah?' He sounded bored. He could never see the point in talking after sex.

'Have you read about them GI brides?' Her voice was soft and cajoling.

'What about 'em?' Ted stretched his arms above his head and drummed his knuckles rhythmically on the headboard. Here we go.

'They're going to special camps to learn about what it's gonna be like in America. Before they leave to go over to be with their new husbands.' She sighed longingly. 'Can you imagine what it must be like? Fancy having to learn about a whole new way of life because it's so different from this rotten hole. They've got everything over there. Just like you see in the films. It must be smashing.'

'You got something to complain about, then?'

She gasped at the stupidity of his question. 'Are you kidding? With this new rationing lark it's as bad as it was during the sodding war. It's freezing cold out; there's no coal; and I'm telling you, I'm sick and tired of bloody queuing for every single thing I want. And at least when the war was on there was a bit of fun.'

A slow smile spread over Ted's face. 'I thought we just had a bit of fun.'

Dilys snuggled up to him. 'We did, but . . .'

'But you want some more little presents?'

'Well . . .'

Ted threw off the covers and, unselfconsciously naked, he walked over to the wardrobe he shared with Ginny and pulled open the door.

'There's no rationing when you're with me, darling. Help yourself.'

He picked up his jacket from the floor and patted the pockets to find his cigarettes and matches. 'But don't be too greedy, eh?'

Ted hadn't even finished speaking when Dilys, also naked, was beside him on her knees, raking through the pile of things that had been half hidden by the hems of her supposedly best friend's dresses.

'These are lovely, Ted,' murmured Dilys, tearing open a packet of stockings and draping the shiny lengths of nylon over her arm. 'Really lovely.'

Carefully she put them to one side and dived back into the treasure store.

Her face was glowing with covetousness as she reappeared with a square-shouldered bottle of scent. 'Is this really the proper gear?' she breathed.

'What else would you expect me to have?' he asked, flopping back on to the tangle of bedclothes. 'Dig a bit deeper, there's some chocolates in there and all.'

Dilys was in heaven. Sitting there, rooting through the packets and cartons, she was the picture of a spoilt child on Christmas morning, unwilling to share her booty with her less pushy brothers and sisters.

'Oi, Dilys! Watch how you handle them boxes,' Ted warned her, his eyes narrowed against the smoke from his cigarete. 'I've gotta sell that lot.'

She flashed a worried look at him over her shoulder. 'Not all of it?'

He laughed, recognising his own greed in hers. 'No. But don't go too mad. I've got a living to make, remember.'

60

Dilys held up the nylons again, admiring their sheen against the pale March sunlight that was filtering through the freshly laundered lace curtains – the same lace curtains that, only a few days before, she had stood on her street doorstep watching Ginny rehang after she had washed them and cleaned the windows.

She touched the nylon to her cheek and gave a little moan. She loved nice things. She deserved them. And she would have them, no matter what the price.

With her lids half lowered and her lips pressed into a sultry pout, Dilys crawled over to the bed on all fours. She then slinked her way across the bed until her naked body was draped across Ted's. Slowly she ran her fingertips up and down the inside of his thigh. 'Ted,' she murmured into his ear, 'will you take me to a club tonight? So's I can wear me new stockings and that lovely scent?'

Ted rolled her off him, propped himself up on his elbows and looked down at her flushed, eager face. He reached across her and ground out the stub of his cigarette in the pink cut-glass pin tray that had pride of place on Ginny's dressing-table. 'D'you think I'm made of money?'

'Well, ain't you?'

'No.' He dropped back on to the pillows. 'Anyway, how about you earning some money for a change? You ain't done a day's work since you lost your job last year.'

'What? D'you really want me to go out all day like Ginny?' She sounded horrified.

'At least Ginny's bringing home wages.' He clasped his hands behind his head. 'That girl's done all kinds of jobs since Bloom's closed.'

Dilys was having trouble keeping up with this new turn of events. 'But, Ted, who'd keep you company?'

He grinned up at the ceiling. 'There's that to it, I suppose.'

This was more like it. He was obviously having a joke with her. 'This is my job now.' She giggled, crawling back on top of him and grabbing him between the legs.

'That's enough of that, Dilys,' he said, lifting her hand away.

'But, Ted—'

'You've gotta go, I've got business to see to.'

'But—'

'Don't start whining, Dilys. Anyway, Ginny'll be back from work soon.'

'She'll think I've been over here helping Nellie for you, like she always does. And Nellie won't give us away. You know she likes me better than Ginny. We have a laugh. And I don't walk around the place with a face like a kite and keep tidying up round her all the time.'

'Ginny don't bribe her with a bottle of the hard stuff every couple of days you mean.'

'You give me the bloody stuff to give her!' Dilys fumed.

'Look, Dilys, I reckon even Ginny'd be suspicious if she finds us both up here stark bollock naked. Now come on.'

'But why d'you even bother with her, Ted? Why—'

'Look, don't give me earache about it again, Dilys. She's me old woman. Right? And while it suits me to have her live here, have me shirts washed, the place kept nice and be looked after—'

'But if you got rid of Ginny, I'd look after you.'

'Yeah. Right. Course you would.' Ted snorted in contemptuous disbelief. 'You can't even look after yourself. Now, come on, Dilys. Play the game, girl. Get yourself dressed and get moving.'

What Ted didn't add was that he wanted her out of there before her brothers got in from work. Sid and Micky might have been a good ten years younger than Ted, but they had earned themselves reputations for being a tough pair of bastards and Ted wasn't about to start messing with them.

They now both worked in the docks, with George, their dad, who had managed to wangle them in there. And the boys couldn't have been happier. The physical work suited the pair of them well; not only were they built like a pair of muscled-up oxen, but doing dock work had meant that they could avoid the threat of conscription – something that preoccupied most young men and their families now that the war was over and joining up all seemed such a complete waste of time.

No, Ted definitely wasn't interested in upsetting those two. He always liked the odds to be very much in his favour whenever he got a bit rough with someone. So he wasn't going to start advertising the fact that he was knocking off their big sister. Especially as the arrangement suited him so very well just the way it was.

Ted was a man who had developed quite a need for women. Not a liking for them, definitely not that, but a real need to have them do as he said, a need to have them submit to him. He was only interested in women who kept very much in their place – and that could be the bedroom, or the kitchen, he didn't mind which – and Dilys popping over of an afternoon suited him very nicely. For the moment at least. He got his end away whenever he fancied it – which was most of the time – and his old mum got a bit of help round the house. Not much help, it had to be said, but enough to keep her quiet until Ginny got in of a night.

Ted reached out for his jacket again and fumbled around until he had found his wallet. He slipped two pounds from a fat wad of notes and handed them to Dilys, who took them without protest. 'Now will you shut up and get dressed? And take *one* pair of stockings and *one* bottle of scent. And then get your arse down them stairs and peel the spuds for me mum, or whatever it was you was meant to have been doing all afternoon. And then bugger off and be indoors when your family gets in like a good little girl.'

Dilys scowled sulkily. Peeling spuds! She'd have to get things better organised than this or he'd have her scrubbing the bloody floors next.

As Ginny turned into Bailey Street, the sight she always dreaded confronted her. There, in a pool of light from the gas lamp, she saw Ted, all booted and suited and rubbing the early evening dampness off his windscreen. He was going out again. And it was Friday. She'd be lucky if she saw him again before Monday morning. And that was being optimistic. If only she could handle him a bit better. Make him care more for her. Make him less angry with her. Try and get him to share her dreams . . .

She pinned on a smile and broke into a trot. He hated her to be miserable and was likely to accuse her of nagging if she wasn't grinning from ear to ear whenever he saw her. If she could at least have a quick word with him, maybe he'd stay in.

Maybe.

'Ted!' she called with a cheery wave.

'All right?' he said, straightening up. He tossed the cloth he had been using into the passenger side of the car and wiped his hands on his handkerchief.

'Sorry I'm a bit late,' she puffed, 'but I've been doing that bit of overtime, because I know Nellie's had her heart set on a new wireless. So I went and put a deposit on one. For her birthday.'

Ted looked at her for a long moment. Sometimes he really wondered if she was taking the piss with all her kind little thoughts and all her concern for Nellie. Surely she must have known that his mum now felt nothing more than contempt for the pathetic doormat she had let herself become.

But who cared, so long as she kept the place nice and did as she was told? And, it had to be said, she wasn't too bad at the other, considering she was his wife. Good little figure. Pretty face. And a lovely pair of pins. If he wasn't in such a hurry . . .

'Ted? Is something wrong? You're staring.'

'Eh?'

She looked into his eyes and lifted her gloved hand to her cheek as though she was using him as a looking-glass to reflect the blemish she was sure he was staring at. 'Have I got a smudge or something?'

'No.' Ted walked round to the driver's side and got in. 'Don't wait up,' he said, then slammed the door and drove off.

Ted whistled softly, a short, high note followed by a lower, longer one – the prearranged signal for Al to let him in.

'Hurry up, Al,' he grumbled, as the young man fiddled around with the locked gate. 'It's brass monkeys out here.'

'I'm sorry, Ted. You know me. I'm nervous,' was all that Al could offer by way of defence.

'You're what?' Ted tutted irritably. 'We've been doing this for how many months now? And you're still acting like some bloody big girl.' Ted reached through the bars of the gate and held out his hand. 'Give it here. Come on. Or we'll have the sodding dock coppers on our backs.'

With practised ease, Ted held the torch in his mouth and slipped the key into the lock, then switched off the torch and swung the gate open without a sound, just enough to let him edge through.

The experience Ted had gained going on the creep during the war – breaking and entering houses and shops that might, or might not, be occupied – had stood him in good stead, and not just for sliding into Dilys's bedroom without disturbing her mum and dad. Ted's skills had equipped him to manage in all sorts of delicate situations.

He shoved Al in the direction of the deserted office. 'Move yourself, for Gawd's sake.'

Inside, Al pulled down the old black-out blinds that nobody had bothered to remove, checked that the door was locked securely, then turned on the green-shaded clerk's lamp on his desk.

Ted sat himself down in the battered, high-backed leather chair and leaned back with his fingers linked across his taut, muscled stomach. 'What you got for me tonight then, Al? Something tasty?'

Al went over to the window and lifted the edge of the blind, a nervous checking that the dock police hadn't suddenly taken it into their minds to alter their nightly routine patrol.

Ted was losing patience. 'Look, Al, I don't need all this. This ain't the only dock office with a bit of bent gear to sell. I'm flaming freezing, I want a drink and I ain't got all night. Okay? So are you gonna show me what you've got or shall I take myself off down the road and see what's on offer down there?'

'Sorry, Ted. It's all that stuff they've had in the papers about the black market. They've been having all these checks.'

Ted sat up straight. 'When?'

'Earlier.'

'They catch anyone?'

'Yeah, Arthur Waters.'

'What, red-headed Arthur?'

Al nodded miserably.

'Don't look so worried, Al. That's good news.'

'Is it?' Al didn't sound very convinced.

'Course it is.' Ted broke into a broad grin and tapped his temple with his forefinger. 'Use your loaf, Al. They won't be looking for any thieves tonight, now will they? They'll think that everyone'll have the wind up and'll be lying low. I mean, who'd be stupid enough to go nicking when someone's just had his collar felt?'

Disarmed by such logic and bolstered by Ted's apparent lack of concern, Al did his best to impress him with his own confidence. 'I was only being cautious, Ted, I wasn't really worried.'

Ted stood up and slapped him matily on the back. 'Course you wasn't, son. Course you wasn't. Now, let's see what you've got for me, shall we?'

When they had finished ferrying the final cartons of illicit goods through the dock gates, and round to a dimly lit street where the Talbot was parked in the shadows of a tall, bomb-damaged warehouse, Ted slipped Al a tight roll of notes. 'Good work, son,' he said with a wink. 'Now, how about a little celebration?'

Al nodded readily. He savoured the excitement of going for a drink with Ted Martin after their deals almost more than he enjoyed the money Ted gave him. Being a clerk might have brought him the kind of respect that his mum and dad approved of, but Al craved respect of a different sort: the sort that had birds ready to jump into bed with you and blokes wanting to shake your hand and be your mate. And going into a pub with Ted Martin gave Al a much-savoured glimpse of what that felt like. He scared him a bit too, if he was honest, but that was part of the thrill.

Al waited for Ted to get in the car and then did the same. He sat there, silently watching in the shadows as Ted checked the angle of his hat in the rear-view mirror.

'Tell you what,' said Ted, turning and flashing him one of his devastating smiles as he fired the engine into life, 'I know of a couple of right dirty sorts who'd just love to keep us company tonight. Fancy having a few drinks with them and then . . .' Another one of his smiles. 'Well, who knows?'

Al nodded again. He hadn't even been with a bird when he first met Ted, but he had certainly got the taste for them since.

The 'sorts' turned out to be two flashily clothed, over-made-up girls of about twenty, who were drinking in a dodgy-looking Limehouse pub on the edges of what remained of Blitz-ravaged Chinatown. They were standing up at the bar with two tall, well-dressed men, but the moment one of the girls spotted Ted coming in with Al she nudged her friend, pointed at Ted and whispered something to her.

The other girl cast a a worried look over to where she was pointing. Her friend nudged her again, harder this time, and she immediately replaced her frown with the broadest smile she could summon up. Without another word between them, the two young women abandoned their erstwhile companions and began to push their way through the smoke-filled fug of the bar towards the door.

'Teddy!' squealed Lilly, the shapelier of the two girls, the one who had first spotted them. 'I've really missed you. I ain't seen you for weeks.' She threw her arms round his neck and, much to the amusement of all the other drinkers – barring the two men who had just been dumped – kissed Ted full on the lips.

In response, Ted ran his hand up her skirt and grabbed

the top of her thigh, where her stocking-top dug into her flesh.

'If you're gonna give her one, Ted, let's all watch!' hollered a big, pug-nosed man playing darts in the corner of the pub. 'I could do with a bit of a laugh!'

Lilly swung round to the man, her fists stuck into her waist. 'That's no way to talk in front of ladies!'

'We all know that,' Ted joined in, squeezing her leg even harder. 'But he wasn't talking in front of no ladies, now was he? He was talking in front of you and Marge.'

To Al's surprise, rather than being offended by Ted's lack of gallantry, Lilly gave every impression of being really pleased with such treatment and, with only the merest hint of a glance at her friend Marge, she gave him another full-on-the-mouth smacker by way of reward. She then linked her arm through his and nodded at a table at the far end of the room. 'Let's go over there and sit down,' she suggested, without so much as a glance back at the two men who were still standing, tight-lipped with hostility, at the bar.

'Come on, Marge,' she prompted her friend, flashing her eyes for emphasis, 'come and sit with us. And bring that little cutie-pie with you. He's a real little smasher, ain't he? Where d'you find him then, Ted?'

As Lilly sashayed over to the table with Ted's hand clamped firmly over her buttock, Al felt his neck and then his face flame red, but it wasn't Ted's crude behaviour, or even Lilly's teasing that was making him blush, it was the strangeness of the situation. While Ted might have been happy to go and sit down in the corner, Al definitely wasn't. In fact, he didn't want to be in the pub at all. He couldn't see the sense in staying in a place where you'd just taken two women away from a pair of blokes who had probably been buying them drinks all night. Novice as Al was at this sort of thing, it seemed to be asking for trouble.

As Al followed Ted across the room to the table, he leaned forward and spoke to him in a tone so low that it was just about audible. 'Don't you feel a bit awkward?'

Ted looked round at him in surprise. 'No. Why should I?'

Al jerked his head over to the bar where the two men were watching them with unmistakable resentment. 'How about them?'

Ted threw his head back and laughed loudly. 'Here, you ain't one of them nancy-boys, are you, Al? You don't fancy them instead of the girls, do you?'

'Blimey, I hope he don't!' Marge shrieked in a voice so shrill it sounded more like that of a puppet than a fully grown woman.

'But if he *is*,' Lilly screeched back at her, 'you'll soon be able to show him better ways, won't you, Marge?'

'Course I will! You know me, Lilly, always glad to oblige!'

'So I can see,' muttered one of the two disgruntled men. 'Drink up, Johnno, and we'll be on our way. I don't like the stink what's come up in here.'

With that, both men drained their glasses, snatched up their hats and topcoats from their bar-stools and barged their way out of the pub, followed by hoots of derisive glee from Ted. 'I think you've upset your friends, girls,' he hollered after them.

'They ain't no friends of ours,' Marge said, wriggling her body closer to Al's. 'We ain't never set eyes on 'em before, have we, Lil?'

Lil shook her head dismissively. 'No, never.'

When the door was slammed firmly shut behind them, Ted turned to the darts player in the corner. 'So who were the pair of charmers then, Puggy?' he called.

'Dunno mate. I'm as much in the dark as the girls.'

That was good enough for Ted. They weren't locals, just visitors. And it wasn't as though he'd enticed the girls away, they had come over to him by choice. And anyway, blokes didn't get into fights over birds like Lilly and Marge. They were disposable, interchangeable, the sort you used and then dumped. Within Ted's logic, everything was just fine.

He banished the two men from his mind and set about really enjoying the rest of the evening. And he had every reason to celebrate: he'd done a good deal down at the docks – more than a good deal, actually, as Al was still wet behind the ears when it came to asking a fair price for the knocked-off gear he passed on to him – and now he had a pint in his hand and a warm and willing woman pressing herself against him, just asking for those chubby thighs of hers to be groped. Yes, Ted had every reason to be a happy man.

Marge watched Ted and Lilly fondling and kissing one another with growing nervousness. She was doing her best to get Al in the mood, but he didn't seem to want to know, and she was worried that, being Ted's mate, Ted would get angry with her for failing to get the kid's interest. She knew Ted. The trouble was, Al seemed less concerned with putting his tongue down Marge's throat than in pouring booze down his own gullet. And he kept looking over at the door as though he was waiting for the other two blokes to come back. Maybe it wasn't a joke after all, maybe he was a bit the other way. Marge hoped not. That was all she needed. Still, she could only do her best . . .

When the four of them eventually staggered out of the pub – Lilly clinging gingerly to Ted as though he were an over-inflated life jacket that was liable to explode in

71

her face at any moment and Marge with the now paralytic Al draped round her like a fur stole – the cold night air hit them like a wall.

'Bloody hell, Ted,' gasped Lilly, pulling her thin woollen coat tighter around her neck, 'I'm gonna freeze me tits off if we don't get inside soon.'

'I've got the motor, ain't I?' Ted grinned, towing her across the street towards the Talbot. 'We'll soon warm up, with the four of us all going at it at once in there.'

'What? All in there together? That'll be cosy, won't it, Al?' giggled Marge, rolling her eyes suggestively at him, in what, she promised herself, was her final attempt to arouse his interest.

It should have been clear, even to Marge, that Al was now so drunk, a whole harem of girls, hand-picked to suit every taste and with fairy lights hanging from every digit, would have been hard pressed to have gained even a glimmer of appreciation or response from his semi-conscious form.

Being about as used to drink as he was to women, Al, in his efforts to make himself feel better about the two men, had drunk himself almost senseless. If he hadn't had quite so much to drink he would have realised what Ted had in mind and wouldn't even have contemplated letting Marge drag him over to the car. Al was only just getting used to the idea that he could engage in the straightforward type of liaisons with women. In any other, even slightly more sober, circumstances, the thought of all four of them being together in the car would have terrified the life out of him and he would have had it away on his toes, back to his mum's and dad's place as though the dock coppers themselves were after him. But Al was not only drunk, he was now what could only be described as totally rat-arsed.

Marge looked at him with resigned weariness and frustration. She just hoped he'd liven his ideas up a bit before they got down to it, or she was really going to have to put on some sort of act so that Ted wouldn't realise what was going on. If that was the case, she could only keep her fingers crossed that Lilly was in good enough form to keep his interest from straying to what she and Al were supposedly up to.

She pulled Al's arm more firmly round her shoulder and hauled him over to the car, where Lilly was pawing Ted in a show of increasingly revved-up anticipation. 'Hurry up, Ted,' she was urging him in a breathy little voice.

'All right, all right,' Ted snapped. 'I know you can't keep your hands off me, Lil, but let me find the bloody keys, will you? And stop pulling at me coat.'

The pulling stopped, but was immediately replaced by a hand gripping Ted's shoulder. It felt like a vice being tightened against his collar-bone.

'What the fuck?' Ted demanded and spun round to confront her for daring to do such a thing. His face was contorted with anger at her presumption. But it wasn't Lilly who had grabbed him.

The next thing Ted knew was a knee slamming into his groin. As he crumpled to the frosty cobbled ground, cupping his testicles in an effort to protect himself from further agony, he squinted up through his pain to see one of the men who had been drinking with the girls at the bar.

'Billy Saunders,' said the man, raising his hat in a parody of polite introduction. 'Don't forget the name, will you. You'll be hearing it a lot round here. I've decided Limehouse might just be the place to start up a little business.'

He turned, raised his hat once more and smiled magnificently at the two now ashen-faced girls. He pointed at Lilly and jerked his head towards where Ted was still squirming on the damp ground. 'What's his name?'

She didn't answer, but Billy noted that the girl shot an urgent, warning look at her friend.

'Scared of him, eh?' said Billy with a disgusted shake of his head. 'I wondered why you both went running over to the flash little bleeder.'

Billy took a cigarette out of his case and waited for the other slightly taller man to light it for him, then he strolled the few steps over to Ted. 'You fucking coward,' he said simply, gave him another vicious kick and turned back to Lilly and Marge. He raised his hat again. 'Ladies. Let me wish you both a very good night.' With that, the man and his companion strode off into the shadows.

The girls exchanged a terrified glance. What the hell were they meant to do? It was bad enough being stuck with a nutter like Ted Martin when he wasn't even upset, but now . . .

Lilly took a deep breath, put her handbag on the kerb and linked her arm through Ted's. It was just a shame he wasn't as pissed as the stupid kid he'd brought with him, then she and Marge could have cleared off and left them both to the dippers and cosh gangs from Chinatown and neither of them would have been any the wiser that the girls had abandoned them. Still, it was no good wishing; good things just didn't seem to happen to the likes of Lilly. 'Help us then, Marge,' she gasped.

Between them, the girls somehow managed to haul Ted to his feet. He staggered backwards and slumped against the car.

'Billy Saunders,' Ted panted. 'I won't forget you, you bastard.'

Al dropped down on to the kerb next to Lilly's handbag and stared at the three people in front of him. Even with all the alcohol fuddling his brain he was able to see that the girls were as scared of Ted as he suddenly realised himself to be.

There was something in Ted's expression, a strange, distant look in his eyes as though he were seeing something that was only visible to him. Something that Al felt genuinely relieved he couldn't see, or even begin to understand.

He had seen Ted turn to violence before, going berserk over the merest slight; smashing his fist into a woman's face for just looking at him the wrong way; or giving a real whacking to an old night-watchman at one of the bonded warehouses, who had simply asked him what he wanted. In fact, in the months since Al had first met him, Ted Martin had proved himself to be a really vicious sort of bloke, especially where women were concerned, but Al had never seen that look before. And it really frightened him. Drunk as he was, Al knew that he was well out of his depth.

He picked up Lilly's handbag, clasped it to him like a comforter and vomited all over it.

Chapter 5

When Ginny woke up the next morning she was saddened, but not surprised, to find that the covers on Ted's side of the bed were undisturbed and that his pillow had not been slept on again. She might have become accustomed to him staying out all night, sometimes for days on end, but she would never feel happy about it.

Sleeping alone and being scared to open her mouth when Ted actually deigned to be there: it wasn't how Ginny had expected things to turn out.

Early on in their marriage, Ted had been nothing like he was now, or so she had thought. Maybe love, or grief for the loss of her family, had blinded her to the truth, but even though she had heard rumours about Ted she had put them down to jealous gossip; there was always plenty of that in the neighbourhood for those who chose to listen. All right, she knew he had a reputation for having a bit of a temper, so did a lot of blokes his age, but Ted himself had never given her any reason to believe that they wouldn't be leading a happy, ordinary married life together. She had pictured it so many times: the war would be over – she was right about that, at least – and Ted would be going off to work every morning, doing a normal sort of job. Something like Dilys's dad and brothers did down at the docks maybe, where he would graft hard, but honestly, not ducking and diving and pulling the Lord alone knew what sort of strokes. And he would come home every evening and greet her and their children with hugs and kisses, scooping them high

76

into the air, making them giggle and shriek with happy laughter that would ring around their picture-book, perfect home. Then she would put on a pretty flowery apron to keep her dress nice and dish up their tea, and afterwards Ted would help her put the little ones to bed, and . . .

She rubbed her hands roughly over her eyes, refusing to cry at the cruelly taunting images in her mind.

Children. Would they only ever be a dream?

She rolled on to her side and slapped angrily at Ted's untouched pillowslip. Dreams *did* sometimes come true and her dreams were the one thing she wouldn't ever let anyone take away from her.

She *would* dream about having children; about Ted changing into the sort of man she'd believed she'd married; and – her latest fantasy – about Nellie vanishing from number 18 and leaving her and Ted alone in the house for ever. Ginny didn't know why, but her mother-in-law was treating her more and more like an unwanted lodger lately and Ginny honestly, if guiltily, wished her gone.

She had a glorious vision of her disappearing in a puff of red smoke, just like the wicked witch in the films, leaving behind only a pair of steaming carpet slippers and a smouldering cigarette end dangling in mid-air like the smile of the Cheshire cat.

Ginny too was smiling – at the picture she had conjured – although she felt no happiness. What she felt was a desperate, intense, gut-wrenching loneliness: a woman imprisoned by her own girlish dreams.

But if anyone had seen her, on that bright but chilly mid-March morning, as she drew back the curtains and looked down on to Bailey Street from her bedroom window, they would never have been able to guess at her sadness. Instead of weeping and wailing and making a fuss, as many others would have done, Ginny simply took Nellie her morning cup of tea and got on with the chores. Just as she did every weekend.

Nellie could, of course, have done a lot of the jobs during the week while Ginny was out at work and, up until about a year ago, she had at least made some pretence at helping. But that was all in the past. Now Nellie did nothing, except for the odd times when she cooked something for Ted.

The only time Ginny had been foolish enough to ask her to lend a hand more recently, Nellie had looked at her as though she had taken leave of her senses and had gone straight to Ted, accusing Ginny of being a slave driver. She had ranted and raved like a mad thing, screaming and shouting about the hard time her lazy good-for-nothing daughter-in-law was giving her. Her, a woman in her fifties! And why she should be expected to work her fingers to the bone while Ginny, a bit of a girl, sat around doing nothing, she couldn't imagine.

Ted had been furious with Ginny and given her such a slap that one of her back teeth had come loose. She had been in agony for days.

Ginny had not made that mistake twice. She held her tongue and got on with things, just as she was doing that Saturday morning. At least since Dilys had been out of work, she had taken to popping over to do a few bits and pieces to help Ginny out, peeling a few spuds or chopping a cabbage. But it made very little dent in her workload; there was still so much to do.

Before Nellie had even shifted herself from her bed that morning, Ginny had scrubbed and whitened the street doorstep; she had stripped the linen from her and Ted's bed; had put the washing in to soak, while the copper heated up ready for the weekly boil; and had gone on to sweep and dust, and mangle and peg, and scour and rub, and wax and polish, until she was all but exhausted.

By then Nellie had roused herself and had found her way down to the kitchen. That was the cue for Ginny to take a break from the housework; not to sit down, but to make a pot of tea and a plate of toast and dripping: a rushed lunch for her and a leisurely breakfast for Nellie.

After downing a quick cup of tea and swallowing a few mouthfuls of bread, Ginny went out to the backyard to bring in the still damp washing for ironing and airing. Although it was a fine, early-spring morning, the air still had the damp feel of winter about it and the laundry would get no drier hanging outside.

While Ginny stood at the table ironing, Nellie sat by the blazing kitchen fire scorching her legs to a mottled, corned-beef red and finishing off the rest of the tea and toast, actually shifting herself at one point to shoot another shovel of coal on the fire.

Ginny had it on the tip of her tongue to ask her mother-in-law to be a bit more careful with their precious fuel, because although Ted usually turned up with a few sacks he had managed to get from somewhere – rationing seemed to have no meaning for him – Ginny knew she couldn't depend on him remembering. And if they ran out of coal and they had another cold snap like last week, Nellie would really get her moaning hat on. Ginny had enough on her plate without the thought of her leading off about her poor old frozen feet and the agonies she was suffering with her chilblains.

But Ginny had seen Nellie in action too many times of late to dare comment about being wasteful. Her mother-in-law had changed so much. She could now take it into her head, for no reason other than causing mischief it seemed, deliberately to misinterpret the most innocuous of Ginny's remarks as being the most cutting criticism.

And she would throw even more coal on the fire just for spite.

Tired, anxious and fed up as she felt, Ginny had no choice but to try and keep Nellie in a good mood. 'I'm really glad I've got this new job, you know, Nell. But who'd have thought I'd be working in an electrics factory, eh?' Ginny allowed herself a little smile as she thought about the deposit she had taken from her week's wages to put on the wireless the day before. With her staff discount she had chosen a model that was really top of the range. Even Nellie couldn't help but be pleased when she saw it.

'I'd prefer to be doing machining still, of course, but at least I'm earning until something more suitable comes up. And I can get plenty of overtime at this place.'

'Overtime? Is that what you call it? Well I call it staying out all hours. You're never sodding here when I need you.'

Ginny flinched at Nellie's tone. 'You've got Dilys to help you,' she replied cautiously.

She draped the final shirt over the clothes-horse and put the iron outside the back door to cool down. 'She told me she's been doing all sorts over here,' she said, straightening up and kneading her knuckles into the small of her aching back.

'You could say that,' Nellie snorted.

Ginny refilled the kettle at the sink. Nellie put away more tea than anyone Ginny had ever known; and Ginny was expected to keep her well supplied. 'So,' she said, lighting the gas stove, 'what gossip have you got for me then, Nell? I haven't had much of a chance to catch up, what with all the extra hours I'm putting in.'

Nellie paused for a moment, torn between pointedly ignoring Ginny's attempts at pleasantness on the one hand and, on the other, the pleasure she would gain in passing on a story that would wind up the silly little cow like a watch spring.

Nellie's new-found fondness for malice against her dozy daughter-in-law won. But it was her own fault, Nellie reasoned; if only the girl had shown some spirit, Nellie would probably have left her alone – she might even have tried discouraging Dilys a bit – but Ginny was just too easy a target to resist.

At one time, she had tolerated Ginny – just – but over the years she had started wearing down her patience more and more, and Nellie was beginning to wonder whether she should really start working on her and perhaps she'd bugger off and let Dilys move in. Not that Nellie was that struck with Dilys. But at least she made her laugh. Plus she was generous with the booze; and Nellie seemed to get through the hard stuff faster and faster these days. She'd have hated that little source of pleasure to dry up.

'You heard what happened to that stupid mare over the road yesterday, I suppose?'

'What, Dilys?' Ginny asked over her shoulder as she rinsed out the teapot.

Nellie was sorely tempted to say yes, that's right, Dilys. She's been over here schtupping your old man while you've been grafting all the hours God sends. That'd wipe the stupid smile off her face. It would do her good to hear a few home truths. But she didn't. Not because she cared for her daughter-in-law's feelings, of course, but because Ted wouldn't have liked it if she'd grassed on him. Nellie had never really figured out why, but her boy seemed to like keeping her around the place, flapping about with her bloody dusters and irons. The more Ted had a pop at the soppy tart, the more she tried to keep the house looking like a flaming palace. It drove Nellie to distraction.

Nellie looked her up and down as she walked back to the table, folded the ironing blanket and stuck it away in the bottom of the dresser. At least she had a decent figure, Nellie supposed, and her Ted liked that in a woman. So maybe she was good for something.

'I was talking to Pearl earlier,' Ginny said amiably, 'while we was both out scrubbing the street doorsteps. And she never said nothing about Dilys.'

Nellie sighed theatrically. Huh! Pearl Chivers. Dilys's flaming perfect mother and Ginny's *special friend, who was always there if Ginny needed her.* She made Nellie sick. She was another one always cleaning and polishing. But at least Pearl could have a row and had a mouth on her like a docker when she let go. Nellie had to hand that to her: she wasn't a mouse. Not like Dolly Day-dream, who didn't seem to know what day of the week it was half the time, let alone how to stand up for herself.

'I don't mean Dilys, do I?' Nellie rolled her eyes and tutted. 'And if you'd just keep your trap shut for a couple o' minutes, and let me get a flaming word in edgeways, I'd bloody well be able to tell you who I mean.'

'Sorry, Nellie.'

'I should think so.'

'Well?' Ginny asked, her voice small and coaxing.

'I was talking about Violet Varney.'

'What, she's turned up, has she?' Ginny asked hopefully, as she returned to the sink and filled a blue-rimmed white enamel bowl ready to peel the potatoes for teatime.

'Yeah. She's turned up all right.'

'Thank Gawd for that.' Ginny bent down and took a string bag full of potatoes and some old newspapers from under the sink, and carried them and the basin of water over to the table. 'You know, Nellie, I reckon it broke Violet's heart having to send them kids away.

When she went amongst the missing last week, I really thought, that's it, she's gone off her head, she's had it away 'cos she can't stand it no more.'

Nellie folded her arms triumphantly across her aproned bosom. This was going to shock the dopey little madam. 'If you must know, you was right. She did go off her head.'

'How d'you mean?' Ginny let a long thin curl of peel drop on to the paper she had spread out on the table.

'The stupid tart's gone and topped herself.'

'She's *what*?' The knife and the half-peeled potato fell from Ginny's hands into the bowl with a messy splash.

Nellie stared critically at the spilt water. 'Left this really miserable note, didn't she? Her Bert found it propped up on the front room mantelpiece. Went screaming along the street to Bobby and Martha at the Prince Albert, just like a man possessed. I'm surprised Pearl never mentioned it to you. She must have heard him. And what with you two being so *friendly*.'

She said the last word as though it were a nasty, contagious affliction that might infect the incautious at any moment.

Ginny could only stare, as Nellie paused to search the pockets of her cross-over apron for her Woodbines. Having found them, she stuck one in the corner of her mouth, lit it and tossed the spent match carelessly into the hearth.

Picking a stray strand of tobacco from her lip, Nellie continued as casually as if she had been discussing nothing more interesting than the price of cod. 'That kettle's boiling,' she said with a lift of her chin. She made no attempt to get up.

Automatically, Ginny went over and switched off the gas. She twisted round to face Nellie with a puzzled frown. 'Look, Nellie, am I missing something here? You

83

did say Bert, didn't you? Bert Varney? How could Bert find the note? He's dead.'

'No he ain't. It's Violet what's dead. Mind you, when he finds out Violet was on the sodding game, I bet he'll wish he was a goner.' Nellie screwed up her nose and shuddered with revulsion. 'And wait till he finds out about her getting a dose ... What a show-up! A right win double!'

Ginny dropped down on to her chair and rubbed her hands over her face, trying to make sense of it all. 'I know I must sound stupid, Nell, but start again, will you? You're saying Violet's dead, but Bert Varney ain't?'

'Blimey, you got cloth ears or something?' She puffed irritably on her cigarette. '*Yes*, Violet's Uncle Ned. And *no*, Bert ain't. Got it? It was all a mistake. He was in a camp, wasn't he. In Japan or somewhere.'

Ginny could hardly take it in. 'But that Japan business was all over more than six months ago. How could he—'

Nellie threw up her hands in exasperation. 'I *know*, but he was sick or something, wasn't he. Got transferred to some hospital. With some nuns ...'

'How d'you mean?'

Nellie shrugged nonchalantly. 'I dunno, do I. He had this fever thing. Didn't know his arse from his elbow, let alone who he was, or what his name was. But when he got better they sent him home.' She shook her head contemptuously. 'Bet they were glad to get rid of him, with all his moaning. You know what he's like.'

'So how did—'

'And *then*,' she continued, not best pleased at being interrupted – conversations were always more monologues than dialogues as far as Nellie was concerned – 'when he found out that Violet had mullered herself and she'd sent his oldest kids to the other side of the world to that Africa place, and that his youngest had gone to live with Vi's sister down in Yalding. Well, he led off alarming, didn't he. Bobby got him straight out of the pub and on to the first train down to Kent. Best place for him, if you ask me: surrounded by hop gardens and sheep, and with a bunch of bloody carrot crunchers for neighbours. They won't know no better if he goes dool-ally, will they? 'Cos they're all a bit funny down there anyway.'

Nellie shifted her bosom with the back of her hand. 'Must be all that fresh air.' She wrinkled her nose with distaste. 'Can't do you no good, can it?'

'Nobody should have to sink as low as she did.' Ginny dropped her chin and stared down at the floor. 'I should have done more to help her. But you know what she was like. She was so private—'

'Private?' Nellie spluttered. 'She was bloody ashamed! Filthy trollop.'

Ginny shook her head in disbelief that so much tragedy could visit just one family. 'That poor feller.'

'Who's a poor feller?' someone asked.

Ginny looked up to see Ted standing in the kitchen doorway, leaning against the jamb.

'Ted!' Ginny leapt up from the table and ran across the kitchen to him, but he held up his hands to make sure she kept her distance.

'Mind off, you dozy cow. Can't you see I'm in pain?'

She winced, not at his harsh words, but at the unmis-takable, if faint, whiff of scent. She swallowed hard, determined to keep her voice steady, then asked softly, 'What's wrong, Ted?'

'I slipped, didn't I? Last night. On the wet stones down the docks. While I was having a trade. I hurt me leg.'

She frowned as she watched Ted hobble over to the table and carefully lower himself on to one of the hard kitchen chairs. It didn't look as though it was his leg that was hurting.

Carelessly, he shoved the bowl, potatoes and peelings to one side and rested his elbows in their place. 'I couldn't drive, could I. So I had to stay the night with a bloke I was doing the bit of business with.'

She felt relief flood through her. He had stayed at a friend's house. The scent must have been from his wife. Ginny was a past master at convincing herself of anything where Ted was concerned.

'And have you brought anything home from the docks for your poor old mum?' Nellie asked pathetically.

Gingerly, Ted, shifted his weight and eased his hand into his trouser pocket. He held out his car keys to Ginny. 'Go out to the car. There's some bananas on the back seat.'

'Bananas!' Ginny ran out to the car to fetch them.

Nellie wasn't so impressed. 'I'd rather have a few quid. Or a nice leg o' pork.'

Ted snorted at his mother's ingratitude. 'I bring you the first bananas this country's seen since bloody 1939 and you don't even say thank you.'

'Well, can you sodding well blame me?' Nellie no longer sounded pathetic, she sounded put out, very put out, and very loud. 'D'you know what they had in the paper yesterday?'

Ted didn't answer.

'Oi! I'm talking to you. A bloody recipe for Squirrel Pie. That's what. That's what the sodding government's telling us to eat.' Nellie was getting into her stride – it didn't take much. 'We're going to have a lovely time, ain't we? Squirrels and pissing bananas. I'm not getting no younger, Ted. I need a bit of comfort in me old age.'

Ginny had heard her mother-in-law's hollering from outside in the street, but she was determined not to let

Nellie upset her. Ted was home and that was all that mattered.

She came back into the kitchen and took the bananas from under her apron – although she was sure that all the neighbours knew what Ted was up to, she didn't like to advertise the fact – and, with a careful smile, put them on the table in front of Ted.

Ted ripped one off the bunch and tossed it to Nellie.

Grudgingly she peeled off the skin.

'Don't get a gob on you, Mum,' he sighed. 'What sort of a son do you think I am? You know you won't have to go eating no squirrels while I'm around.'

Nellie shrugged, unable to speak with all the fruit she had crammed in her mouth.

'We've got plenty.' Ted jerked his head at Ginny. 'Go up and get some of them boxes down, Gin. Show the old girl what I've got up there. When I flog that little lot, we'll be rolling in it. And there's plenty more where they come from an' all.'

As Ginny knelt in front of the wardrobe, she heard someone come into the room behind her.

She looked warily over her shoulder – she would never get used to Ted's 'business' – but it was all right, it was Ted.

He limped slowly towards her. 'Leave that for now,' he said, his lips stretched with pain. 'I wanna bit of peace. I'm going to bed.'

Ginny stood up. 'Shall I get in with you?' she whispered.

'Leave off.' Ted climbed on to the bed and rolled over on to his side, clutching himself in agony. Billy Saunders, he fumed to himself. I swear, I'll find you, and I'll have you, you bastard . . .

*

It was Saturday morning, two weeks after Ted had been attacked, and Ginny hadn't seen hide nor hair of him since the night before.

He could now walk around without clasping himself in agony, but his improved health hadn't done anything to improve his mood. Whenever he did condescend to come home – which wasn't very often – he always seemed to be angry with Ginny about something or other. Anything could get him going: from the food on his plate suddenly not being to his liking, to Ginny singing quietly to herself as she washed up after him. It was like living with a time bomb that was ticking away, just waiting to go off in her face.

Any other Saturday, Ginny might have kidded herself that she was pleased Ted wasn't there to get in her way while she did the housework, but today was 30 March, Nellie's birthday and she had expected her son to be there with her. So Nellie wasn't very happy.

She had carried on at Ginny as though it was all her fault that he had stayed out all night again, and instead of being grateful, or even pleased, with the wireless that Ginny had bought her, Nellie looked at it with about as much interest as if she'd been given a pair of size fifteen football boots without any laces.

It wasn't that Nellie didn't like Ginny's gift – she loved it, although it would have killed her to say so – no, it was the fact that she wanted her Ted there, fussing over her, giving her presents, treating her like the queen she believed herself to be. Her son had gained himself quite a reputation around the East End for being a black marketeer, a real spiv, and Nellie basked in his notoriety as the bloke who could get you anything. It gave her a feeling of superiority to know that people were beholden to her boy for all the little things that were so difficult to get unless you had 'contacts'.

No matter how they pretended to be good, law-abiding citizens, it seemed that nearly everyone was involved in some sort of fiddle: buying a bit of this and a bit of that from any source they could find. And it wasn't only luxuries that were hard to come by. Everyday food items were still in short supply and anything that could help stretch the rations – that were now even meaner than during the worst of the war years – could be sold for a good profit. As to where the stuff actually came from . . . Well, that didn't seem to be much of a cause for concern for all the eager customers.

Nellie had longed to see her Ted walk through the kitchen door with his arms full of gear that her neighbours could only dream about and say, 'Here you are, Mum, happy birthday.' But he hadn't, and she had gone on and on about it. She went on so much, in fact, that when Pearl and George came over to take Nellie down to the Albert for a lunch-time celebration port and lemon – Pearl's all-seeing eyes hadn't missed Ginny's predicament – Ginny put her hands together in gratitude. It seemed almost like a treat to be left in peace to get on with the housework.

Ginny had just finished scouring the wooden draining board when the back door flew back on its hinges and Ted burst into the kitchen. 'Get upstairs,' he snapped. 'Now.'

Ginny's heart leapt: Ted might not have expressed himself very romantically, but she was so relieved that he was still interested in her, she treasured his words as though they'd come written on a card with a dozen long-stemmed roses.

It had been two weeks since they'd last been to bed together and she'd been seriously worried that he'd finally gone off her. And she couldn't have stood that.

Despite everything, Ginny just couldn't contemplate life without him; couldn't stand the thought of being completely alone. The past fortnight had been terrible. Whenever Ted had been home, he'd made her sleep downstairs on the armchair in the front room. She knew it was because he was in so much pain, but she would have happily slept on the bedroom floor – if he would have let her.

'I've missed you, Ted. I've really—' she began, walking towards him.

'You can get that idea right out of your head,' he sneered, barging past her and out into the passage. 'Now come on. Move yourself. We've gotta get all that gear out of the wardrobe.'

'What, have you got a customer for the whole lot?' she asked, running up the stairs after him. Someone must have a few bob to spare. That should put him in a good mood.

'Just help me shift it out to the motor.'

'The motor?'

He spun round on the landing and glared at her. 'What are you? A fucking parrot?' he snarled. 'Just do it. Unless you wanna get me nicked.'

Ted jumped into his car with a muttered warning that, if Ginny knew what was good for her, she was to keep her trap well and truly shut, except for what he had told her she could say. He was going to lie low for a while and he didn't want her blabbing her big mouth off to anyone. Not to Nellie, Dilys, Pearl, no one. Then, with his car full of gear, Ted disappeared out of Bailey Street with a screech of rubber.

Less than ten minutes later there was a loud rapping on the front door of number 18. Ginny took a deep breath, nervously patted her hair into place and walked slowly

90

along the passage. Ted had told her what to say; all she had to do was remember it. She could only pray that she got it right. Thank Gawd Nellie was down the Albert. She would just have got herself hysterical and made matters worse.

Pinning a neat smile on her face, Ginny opened the door.

As she had expected, it was the police. There was a black squad car parked outside and in the driver's seat sat a uniformed officer. But what she hadn't expected were the two smartly dressed men confronting her on her doorstep. From the little she knew about coppers, Ginny assumed they were detectives of some kind. And if they were, then this was no casual warning about selling bent gear, this was serious.

She licked her lips. Her mouth was so dry, it felt as though she had been eating uncooked porridge. 'Can I help you, gentlemen?' she eventually managed to say.

'Mrs Martin?' asked the taller of the two men, taking off his trilby.

She nodded.

'Perhaps we could step inside for a moment?'

Ginny nodded again and stood back to let them in, ushering them towards the front room. 'Won't you sit down?'

As she stepped inside the room and gestured towards the matching over-stuffed armchairs standing either side of the fireplace, Ginny hoped they didn't notice her hand was trembling.

'We'll be all right standing, thank you,' said the man who had spoken before.

'Cup o' tea?'

'No thanks.'

Ginny blinked slowly. She felt as though she were watching a film. Take deep breaths, she told herself.

You've got nothing to worry about. Ted's shifted everything.

Before anyone had the chance to say anything else, the street door was sent crashing back on its hinges and Nellie came hurtling into the room like a lunatic. 'What's happened?' she yelled, grabbing the smaller of the two men by the lapels. 'Has my boy been hurt?'

The taller man spoke. 'Mrs Martin senior?'

Nellie ignored him. 'I asked you a question!' She spat the words into the shorter man's face. 'Someone runs into the Albert and tells me there's a law car outside my house and you stand there asking me my sodding name!'

Surprisingly delicately, the man unpeeled Nellie's fingers from his coat and brushed her hand away. 'No, Mrs Martin, your son hasn't been hurt.' He paused and exchanged a brief, smug grin with his colleague. 'Not yet. But someone's got it in for him. I think you ought to know that, so you can pass that little message on to him. And whoever it was didn't mess about. They went straight to the top. Tipped off the Ministry of Food.'

The other man nodded at him to indicate that he would take it from there. 'I'm sure you've heard about the Ministry's campaign against the black market. Well, we're co-operating with them. There's road blocks going up all around London. We're searching lorries, vans, cars. You name it. Shops and restaurants, they're all being raided.' He flashed another look at his associate. 'Aw yeah, I forgot. And houses. They're being searched too. So if you don't mind, Mrs Martin – either Mrs Martin will do – I'd like you to show us around the place.'

Two hours later the house was in a shambles and the two men were putting on their hats ready to leave.

'Satisfied now you've upset an old lady?' wailed Nellie.

'Not really,' said the tall one casually. Then, turning to Ginny, he added, 'You will remember to tell your husband that someone's got it in for him, won't you, Mrs Martin? The word is that he's upset one of the big boys. And I reckon they're right. So I'd watch out if I was you. See, they're not too fussy how they go about paying someone back, especially when it's just a little two-bob spiv they've got the hump with. They'll pick on wives, mothers . . . Anyone.'

With that, he raised his hat and treated both Ginny and Nellie to a bright, sunny smile. 'Cheerio then, ladies. I'm sure the Detective Constable and myself will be seeing you again soon.'

At thirty-eight years of age, Billy Saunders was a man in the prime of his life. He was tall, dark, powerfully built, and had a self-assured manner that convinced everyone he was handsome, despite the fact that, on closer inspection, he was more striking, in a rough, almost threatening sort of way, rather than conventionally good-looking.

He and Johnno, the minder who had been with him on the night he had given Ted a kicking as a reward for his bad manners, were paying an afternoon call on the same dodgy Limehouse pub where it had happened.

As they walked through the door, a few people looked up, but most of the customers got on with what they were doing: drinking, playing cards, or just staring into their beer. People in that area, so close to the docks and what remained of the bomb-damaged but still secretive world of Chinatown, knew to mind their own business.

That attitude – as well as the possibility of buying up cheap property – was one of the reasons Saunders was interested in the area.

Two of the people who did take notice of Saunders and his sidekick were Lilly and Marge, the girls who had inadvertently been the cause of Saunders giving Ted the beating.

The pair exchanged a nervous glance and hurriedly grabbed their handbags from the bar. The last thing they wanted was trouble; it was hard enough finding pubs that weren't complete bugholes, where they'd tolerate girls plying their trade. As it was they had to give the landlord his cut. Causing fights could only put his price up even more.

Billy Saunders, with his most charming smile, took off his hat and walked over to them. 'Not leaving already, are you, ladies?'

'Er, yeah, we've gotta be going, ain't we, Marge?'

'That's right. We've got an appointment,' she agreed.

'Shame,' Saunders said. 'I was going to make you both a nice little offer and all, wasn't I, Johnno?'

Johnno stretched his lips tight across his teeth in regret. 'He was.'

Marge immediately put her handbag back on the beer-stained counter. She wasn't going to let a chance like this slip by. These two looked much cleaner and better off than their usual punters and they might even take them to a decent hotel, instead of expecting to have a quick knee-trembler under one of the slimy, dripping railway arches. She grabbed Lilly's arm, holding her back. 'What sort of offer would that be then, darling?'

'I was going to offer you a job.'

Marge's face dropped. A job! What was he, barmy?

Lilly looked relieved. 'Come on, Marge.'

'I don't think you understand.' Saunders turned to Johnno. 'Fetch a round of drinks and bring them over to that table,' he said, walking over to the corner of the pub.

The girls followed him. They weren't stupid, they knew when they had to do as they were told; there was no one in the pub who would take a tom's side in the general run of things, never mind against these two big buggers, and especially not after what they'd done to Ted.

There were two men already sitting at the table that Saunders had chosen. 'You don't mind chaps, do you? Only me and the ladies want a bit of privacy.' He winked and slipped a ten-shilling note into the nearest man's hand.

Without a word, the men moved.

Saunders sat down on the bench seat that ran along the wall and gestured for the two girls to sit opposite on the rickety, splintered little stools.

He shrugged out of his camel coat and folded it carefully, setting it beside him as though it were a pampered pet cat being bedded down for the night.

He looked across at the girls, fixing them with his unusually pale blue eyes. 'I'm expanding my interests.'

'Aw yeah,' said Marge warily. 'What sort of interests would they be then? Painting and decorating?'

He laughed at her cheek. People didn't usually give him that sort of backchat, nervously or otherwise. 'Business interests. Property. Clubs. Mostly clubs at the minute.'

He paused while Johnno put down a tray of drinks. Beer and chasers for him and Saunders, and gin and orange for the girls.

'Up West, they are,' Saunders went on. 'But I fancy setting up one or two out this way, and in a few other spots round the East End. Shoreditch maybe. From the sort of deals I've heard are going on round here, and with all the money I've seen change hands, I reckon there's plenty of people with spare dough to chuck about on having a good time. And that's where you two come in.'

Lilly and Marge sipped at their drinks, listening in watchful silence.

'I'm looking for pretty girls like you. Girls who know their way round the sort of punters you get in these parts. And that's why you're gonna work for me.'

Lilly's eyes opened wide and she mouthed something to Marge.

'If it's that twat Ted Martin you're worried about, you can forget him. He won't worry you while I'm around.' Saunders took a long swallow of beer and grinned at Johnno across the rim of his glass. 'Even a no-mark like him's got the sense to keep his head down when he knows he's in Billy Saunders's bad books.'

It wasn't even six o'clock in the evening, but as Lilly climbed, or rather stumbled, up the bleak, unlit staircase to the top floor of the grubby Stepney boarding-house where she had her miserable little room, her head was spinning as though she'd been out all night.

Billy Saunders was generous with the gin, she'd give him that. And he wasn't mean in other ways either. He had told Johnno to see them home as if they were proper ladies or something. Lilly had protested at first, not liking too many people to know where she lived. She'd never been one to work from home unless she couldn't help it, as you never knew with punters, some of them could be right nasty buggers. But, in the end, she was glad she'd given in. She could never have shifted Marge once the booze got the better of her and she'd passed out on the corner of Salmon Lane. But it was no trouble for Johnno. He'd just hoisted her up on his shoulder as though she were a bag of nutty slack and had carried her all the way home to her flat.

Lilly smiled drunkenly to herself, as she thought what Marge would say when she told her how she had been carted through the streets like a parcel. And as for the look on her landlady's face! That was something to behold.

But after the walk back from Marge's, having to persuade Johnno that she'd be just fine and then the further effort of getting to the top of her stairs, Lilly was now feeling really groggy.

She paused in the gloom for a moment, taking deep breaths of cabbage-stinking air, trying to get her balance. Pushing open the door – she never bothered locking it, she had nothing worth nicking – Lilly called huskily into the darkness, 'Ted. You awake yet?'

A groan came from the single bed that took up more than half of the mean little space.

She staggered across the room in the direction of the sound. 'Ted. Come on. You've gotta get up. It's gone tea-time.'

'So?'

'You've gotta go,' she slurred. 'You can't stay here no more.'

Ted sprang from the bed as though it were on fire and slapped her hard across the face. '*What* did you say, you dirty little whore?'

It must have been the drink that made her so brave. Swaying slightly, Lilly took aim, then stabbed her finger hard into his chest. 'I wouldn't do that again if I was you, Ted Martin. I've got someone looking out for me now.' She took another step forward. 'And his minder's downstairs waiting for me to throw you out,' she lied recklessly, half wishing that Johnno was still down there.

After a fortnight of putting up with Ted's increasingly unpredictable temper, the idea of being shot of him definitely appealed to her, although she still felt bad about chucking him out without any notice. She knew what it was like to have nowhere to go. But he *was* married –

97

weren't they all – let him go back to his old woman. 'I mean it Ted. You've gotta go. Now.'

Ted raised his hand. 'You stinking, little—'

Lilly lurched back towards the door, out of his reach. 'I'll do you a favour. I'll go down and say I'm giving you a couple of hours. A chance to sort yourself out. Then I'll go along to the coffee shop and wait for you to clear off. But I'm telling you, Ted, if you ain't gone by the time I get back, I won't be responsible.'

Holding on to the jamb, she paused, stared down at the faded lino and muttered that there was some grub in the cupboard and a fresh bottle of milk in the sink, then, somehow, she found her way back down the stairs.

Ginny dipped her chin and yawned loudly. She wanted to put up her hand to cover her mouth, but couldn't because she was so loaded down with shopping bags. As well as going out to work, keeping the house clean and doing all the washing, Ginny was now responsible for doing every bit of shopping as well. She felt worn out and cold. The evening sky might have been clear and bright, but there was a chill in the air that made her shiver.

When she had worked near the Lane she had often brought home a few bits and pieces during the week, but it wasn't so easy now she was working in the factory at Stratford. And getting the bags home on the bus was bloody murder. She would have made do with a sandwich but Nellie always wanted a proper dinner, which was easier said than done since Ted hadn't been around for the past few weeks, and what with all the queuing and rationing ...

Ginny thought with longing about having a proper dinner hour when she could sit down with a cup of tea and the paper instead of standing with a bunch of women all moaning-about the price of mince. Sometimes she wondered what things would've been like if Britain had lost the war instead of winning it. They couldn't have been much worse.

If only Nellie would try to help a bit, no matter how small the effort, at least it would have been a gesture. But there was less chance than ever of that now. Since Ted had gone into hiding from the police, Nellie had been even more of a pain to live with and had taken to going to bed for most of the day. She hadn't even roused herself for Violet Varney's funeral.

Ginny shuddered as she thought what had happened to Violet. How she'd wound up a disease-ridden tom, just like the women who hung around the street corners in Whitechapel. Bad as things might be, Ginny would never let her life get out of hand like that, she'd take an oath on it. She'd never give up, not like Violet.

Poor, sad Violet.

Her funeral had been a terrible affair. Martha had organised a collection in the Albert so there had at least been a few flowers, but apart from the neighbours who had turned out to show their respects for Bert's sake – the man was a war hero when all was said and done – the church was almost empty. And when the undertakers lowered the coffin into the cold, damp earth, Bert had cried silently to himself, doing his best to keep a bit of dignity, but it was obvious that he knew what people were thinking: however had Violet let herself stoop so low?

Ginny sighed. There must have been another way, surely.

Violet really must have lost her mind. There was no other explanation.

Nellie didn't even have that as an excuse. She was just a selfish, idle old trout, and her not bothering to go to the funeral hadn't surprised Ginny in the least. In fact, there wasn't much about Nellie that could surprise her any more. During the four years Ginny had been married to Ted, any illusions she had had about Nellie becoming a mother to her had slowly, but surely, worn away.

Ginny could only think herself lucky that she was fortunate enough to have someone like Pearl to go to; not that she did very often. Pearl had enough to worry about with her own family. Dilys had always been a handful, Ginny knew that, but now the boys as well – both girl mad, like any young fellers of their age – were causing Pearl aggravation of their own. She certainly didn't need Ginny bothering her as well. But it was still comforting to know that she was there. A sort of safety net, a last resort if Ginny couldn't cope any more.

At last Ginny reached the corner of Bailey Street. She turned out of Grove Road and crossed the street, heading straight for number 18. She had almost reached her front door, when she heard Dilys calling her name.

Dumping her bags on the step, Ginny turned round. 'All right, Dilys?' she greeted her.

'Come over for a minute, will you, Gin?' whined Dilys. 'There's something I've gotta ask you.'

'Dilys, I can't. Really. I've just got home and there's Nellie wanting her tea, and—'

'But, Ginny, I've been waiting for you for ages,' moaned Dilys.

'Hang on.' Wearily, Ginny reached inside the letter-box, pulled out the key on the length of string and undid the door. She put her shopping bags inside the passage and called out, 'It's only me, Nell. I'll be in to do your tea in a minute, but I've just gotta pop over the road first to see Dilys.'

She dragged herself back across the street to number

11, preferring not to wait for what she rightly suspected would be Nellie's sarcastic reply.

'D'you know how long I've been waiting for you?' Dilys demanded, pulling the door to behind her, so that nobody inside could hear them.

'Sorry, Dil, but what with Ted being away still, I'm having to do even more hours. Nellie might have the hump but it don't stop her eating like a flipping horse. And I've gotta get the money for grub from somewhere.'

Ginny didn't know how, but Dilys, as usual, had managed to make her apologise even though she had nothing to apologise for. It was one of the knacks she had.

Dilys folded her arms. 'I reckon I quite fancy a job there,' she said carelessly. 'Anything going, is there?'

'Well, they're always looking for more workers on the conveyor belt.'

Dilys looked shocked. 'Why didn't you tell me?'

'I didn't think you'd be interested.'

'I've got no choice, have I?' Dilys kicked viciously at a bit of slate, sending it spinning into the gutter. 'I've gotta be interested. Me mum and dad'll throw me out if I don't start bringing in some money soon.'

'Pearl and George wouldn't do that to you. Anyway,' Ginny grinned, shoving her supposed friend playfully in the ribs, 'how about that feller of yours you're always going on about? You said he was keeping you.'

Dilys nibbled her lip as she thought of how much she was missing Ted and, more importantly, how much she was missing the money he gave her.

'Well?' Ginny urged her.

'He's working away, ain't he?' Dilys snapped.

As Ginny lay in bed that night, she thought about Dilys's chap. He might have been working away but at least

Dilys knew where he was. She knew it was wrong to be envious, but she couldn't help thinking how fortunate Dilys was.

She wished she knew where Ted was hiding himself.

Ginny wasn't exactly angry with him for going away, she knew he had no choice, she was more worried. He'd been gone for weeks now and it was dangerous out there. The police were really after black marketeers. And, it was no good wrapping it up in any other words, that's what her husband was.

Still, he never did anyone any harm. So why did this bloke, whoever he was, have it in for him?

Something else for her to worry about. She sighed out loud and rolled on to her side, staring at the shadows cast on the wall from the street lamp outside her window.

It was bad enough being concerned about money – Nellie just wouldn't get it into her head that with Ted away there wasn't as much coming in as usual – but thinking that Ted might be in danger was far worse.

If only her mum and dad were still around, they'd know what to do. She missed them and her brothers and sisters so much.

She felt so alone.

Ginny swallowed hard, trying to sniff back the tears, but it was too late, she could already feel them gathering in the corners of her eyes. She rolled on to her back and stared up at the ceiling as they spilt down on to her cheeks, then slowly found their way into her ears.

The sound of a car turning into the street and a pattern of headlights criss-crossing on the ceiling made her turn over and stare at the curtained window.

That would be Sid from over the road. He'd just bought himself a little motor and was really proud of it. She even managed a brief smile as she thought of how Pearl had warned him over and over again to be careful, and how Sid had snapped back that he could hardly go speeding with the amount of juice the bloody government allowed you.

If only all *she* had to fret about was the petrol ration. Things were so simple when you were free and single.

Suddenly she sat up.

It was the street door.

She jumped out of bed and ran on to the landing. It wasn't Sid's car, it was Ted's! Ted was home!

Ted rolled off her, turned on to his side and closed his eyes. It was good to be back in his own bed. That tart Lilly he'd been shacked up with the past couple of weeks had really started getting on his nerves. All that old toffee about minders and him having to get out. What would minders have to do with the likes of her? Any idiot would have realised she was spinning him a line. She probably had someone waiting downstairs who was gonna slip her a few quid rent to use her bed while she was out whoring.

He only wished he'd given her a few more hidings. The mouthy cow certainly deserved them.

Ted couldn't stand lippy women like her. Mind you, he put up with Dilys's old bunny often enough, but that was only because it amused him to be having his wife's mate as his bit on the side. It added a bit of spice and he liked that. In fact, if he didn't think they'd both give him earache about it, he'd often thought it'd be nice to get them together some time . . .

A slow smile eased its way over his lips. Now there *was* a lovely thought.

It surprised him, but he'd quite missed Dilys. Come to think of it, he wouldn't mind nipping over the road to her now. She'd be as pleased to see him as Ginny had been and she always got all excited when everyone else was in the house.

But could he really be buggered getting up and going out again? He knew the answer to that: no, he couldn't.

Instead, he rolled over to face Ginny and grabbed her breast. She'd do again for now.

'Ted,' she said softly.

'What?' he grunted, annoyed at being interrupted. He hated it when women started chatting while he was doing the business.

'Please, wait just a minute, there's something worrying me. Something I've gotta tell you. When the police came—'

He levered himself up on to his elbow. 'This had better be bloody good, Ginny.'

She pulled the sheet up to her chin and nibbled nervously at her lip. How could she put it without upsetting him? 'It's something they said.'

'For Christ's sake spit it out, will you? I've been away for a fortnight and—'

'Ted, they weren't just looking for gear, there was something else. They'd come here to sort of warn you.'

'What?'

She let the sheet drop and ran her fingers distractedly through her hair. 'Well, not warn you exactly. But they said you – we – should be careful. They said someone grassed on you. Someone who's got the needle. Someone who's out to get you.'

'They *what*?'

Ted threw back the covers and grabbed his trousers.

It was that fucking Saunders! He just knew it. Everywhere he bloody turned it was fucking Saunders. Everywhere he'd been during the last few weeks, every face in the East End was talking about pissing Saunders. How he was gonna do this, and do that. Now he couldn't even be in bed with his bloody wife without the bastard haunting him. And, now he came to think about it, maybe Lilly was telling the truth. Maybe he'd even got to her . . .

'Ted, where you going?' Ginny was standing beside him, not daring to touch him, but willing him not to go.

'Shut it, Ginny.'

'Ted, please.'

'I'm going out.'

'No, Ted, please. Promise me you won't go out again. You have the bed. I'll go and sleep downstairs.'

Ted replied with his fist, hitting Ginny so hard in the stomach that she collapsed into a heap on the floor.

He stepped over her and wrenched open the bedroom door.

Lilly. He'd show her where messing about with the likes of Saunders would get her.

But not just yet. Ted wasn't stupid, he'd bide his time. For now he'd just have to take his frustrations out on Dilys.

As Ginny heard the street door slam, her tears began to flow once more. It had all been going right: Ted had come home to her, made love, even stroked her hair the way he used to, and then she'd gone and opened her big mouth.

She'd got it all wrong again.

Why didn't she ever learn?

Chapter 6

July 1946

'My Alf took me to see that new Joan Crawford picture last night, Gin.'

'No good talking to her, Mavis,' said Dilys, lounging lazily on her high-backed stool, watching the electrical circuits pass slowly by on the conveyor belt, as though they had nothing to do with her. 'You might as well try talking to the lavvy wall as trying to get any sense out of that one.'

Dilys bent forward and poked Ginny in the arm. 'In a right bloody dream lately, ain't you, Gin?'

Ginny kept her eyes firmly on her soldering iron as she guided the molten drops towards their target. 'Sorry?'

'Nothing.' Dilys flopped back in her chair and rolled her eyes in wonder at the paragon sitting between her and Mavis. 'You just keep working, girl. All the less for us to do in this bloody heatwave.'

Dilys leaned forward again and spoke to Mavis across Ginny as though she wasn't there. 'So what was it like then, Mave, her new film?'

'*Mildred Pierce* it was called.' Mavis sat up straight and arched her eyebrows Joan Crawford style. 'All about this woman and her right little tart of a daughter. What a cow! Smashing it was.'

'She's good, Joan Crawford.' Dilys folded her arms and settled back comfortably in her seat.

'Yeah, but she played a different sort in this film to what she usually does. I mean, I do a lot for my kids – I even put up with their bleed'n' father, and that's something a bloody saint'd say no to – but what she put up with from that little madam. I'd have wound up wringing her flaming neck for her, long before she—'

'Don't spoil it for me!' squealed Dilys, leaning across Ginny and slapping Mavis on the hand. 'Oops! Sorry, Gin.' Dilys pulled a mock-sorry face as she saw that she'd knocked Ginny's arm, making her spoil the fiddly bit of soldering she'd been doing so conscientiously.

Ginny shook her head. 'It's all right, it'll clean off.'

'Hark at you.' Mavis tutted. 'You sound just like Mildred flipping Pierce. Putting up with all her old fanny all the time. Have a go at her, Gin. Go on, have her!'

'She wouldn't do nothing like that to me. I'm her best mate, ain't I?' Dilys grinned, flapping her hand dismissively. 'And talk about saints; she's Saint bleed'n' Ginny of Bow, ain't you, girl?'

Ginny shrugged, but said nothing; she just got on with her work.

Dilys didn't seem at all put out or embarrassed by Ginny's silence. 'Come on, hands up,' she chirped, looking along the assembly line, 'who's going out at dinner-time then?'

A babble of replies came from either side of her.

'Count me in and all, girls.' Mavis sighed dramatically. 'My bleed'n' larder's empty again for a change.'

She leaned back and had a quick look along to the glass partition that sectioned off the foreman's tiny cubicle of an office from the rest of the workshop. Satisfied that he wasn't there, she took out her cigarettes and lit one, holding it discreetly down by her knees between puffs.

'I dunno about the papers going on about sodding bread riots in France,' she went on, somehow managing to blow smoke from her nostrils as she spoke, 'but I tell you, there's gonna be bread riots in bleed'n' Stratford if I can't get hold of a loaf this dinner-time. My old man's going mad not having nothing to take with him for his sandwiches. And he hates that canteen grub.'

She chuckled happily to herself. 'Reckons they cook even worse than me, and that's saying something.'

Mavis blew out her cheeks and stared wistfully at her work-roughened hands. 'You know, I wish the war was still on sometimes and that the ungrateful bleeder had stayed in bloody India or wherever he was. Gets right on me tits, he does. It's like having another kid around the place, getting under me feet all the time and expecting to be waited on.'

'Watch it, Mave!' someone hissed along the line. 'It's Himself!'

As the big double doors at the far end of the workshop closed, and Stan the foreman began walking slowly towards the line, Mavis made her cigarette disappear with all the cunning of a skilled prestidigitator and, like the rest of the women in the room, suddenly became fascinated by the work in front of her.

Stan came to a halt by Ginny. 'What's the chance of you staying late for me tonight, Ginny love?' he asked ingratiatingly. 'Only I'm right backed up with orders. I've been down in Dispatch and they're going barmy down there. Like raving lunatics they are. And I really wanna get off home.'

He stood there, his fingers linked across his belly, beaming down at Ginny. He was a friendly, elderly man, but he was carrying far too much weight for his height and was really suffering in the summer heat. Just the thought of spending another hour in the oppressively stifling atmosphere of the factory, when he could have been out in his backyard in Plaistow training his latest brood of young pigeons, was more than he could bear to contemplate.

He knew that if Ginny agreed to stay, he'd be able

to get away with going home at knocking-off time –
something he hadn't had the opportunity to do for
months now. Since the war had been over, it seemed that
everyone had gone mad for buying things. Any sort of
things. And what with all the rationing on clothes and
food still, anything else they could get hold of was
snatched up as though spending your money was in
danger of going out of fashion.

Stan had been pleased at first, very pleased. It was
always good to have a bit of overtime to take home to
the missus, but lately it was getting out of hand,
especially with the choking summer heat. And then there
was the racing season. His pigeons were the first youngsters he'd been able to raise since before the war and he
was already well behind with them. They wouldn't stand
a chance unless he managed to get them into training
really soon. But, if he went home, he needed someone to
keep an eye on things at the factory, and that was where
Ginny came in.

Ginny was not only a good worker, but, if Stan asked
her to, she always covered for him if he wasn't around
when the governor decided to come down from upstairs
and stick his nose in. And also if Stan asked her, he knew
he could trust her to make sure that no liberties were
taken by any of the others who stayed on.

There was no doubt about it, Ginny Martin was a good
kid, and pretty too, which made it all the harder to see
her putting up with whoever the bastard was who gave
her the regular hidings that the poor little cow was so
ashamed of. She'd invented more far-fetched stories than
Scheherazade to explain how she got her black eyes, fat
lips and split cheeks. She was too soft for her own good,
that one. She could do with standing up for herself more.
But then she'd probably had all the fight knocked out of
her. Stan had seen it all, in his years supervising at the

factory, and had become an unlikely authority on women. But it still made him wild to see how some of them lived: girls working their fingers to the bone all week, then their old men pissing their wages straight up the wall on a Friday night and leaving nothing for their wife and babies. The thing was, it never happened to the likes of Dilys Chivers, only to good-hearted kids like young Ginny.

Still, at this particular moment, and from Stan's point of view, Ginny's good nature was something to play on, not to sympathise with.

He put on what he thought was a winning sort of smile and, just for good measure, added a conspiratorial wink. 'I'd see you all right, Gin. You know that, don't you, ducks. And I know you said you could do with the extra money.'

'I know, Stan, and I'd love to help you out—'

Stan's face dropped with disappointment. 'But?'

Ginny rubbed the back of her hand across her sweat-soaked forehead and pushed back her chair, leaving the other women on the assembly line to get on with their jobs of checking and soldering the electrical circuits that passed before them in a never-ending stream. 'You know I wouldn't let you down unless I had a good reason.'

'I know.' He looked like a big, sad baby.

'You could ask Mavis. Or Dilys.' She lifted her chin to indicate the overalled figure of her friend slumped sullenly over the conveyor belt.

Stan opened his eyes wide and let out a huff of incredulity at such an idea. 'Don't be silly, Gin. Even if I could persuade either of them two not to dash out of here the second the hooter goes, could you really imagine me trusting that pair to keep an eye on things for me? And I could just imagine what old Larkin would have to say, if he came down from upstairs and found either of them in charge.'

He put his big, beefy arm around her shoulders. 'You sure you won't change your mind, babe? Like I said, I'd make it worth your while.'

'To be truthful, Stan,' she whispered, making sure that the others couldn't hear, 'I really wanna get straight home myself. I ain't feeling very well.'

Stan released his hold on her and backed away slightly. 'Nothing catching I hope.'

Ginny smiled ruefully. 'I don't think so.'

'There's only a few minutes to go.' Stan took another step backwards. That's all he wanted, bloody head-cold germs to pass on to his birds. 'If you ain't well, Ginny, you'd better get yourself off right away.'

'I'll go with her,' volunteered Dilys almost falling over her own feet in her hurry to leave the line.

Outside the factory gates, there seemed to be even less air than there was inside. At least inside there had been the breeze blowing through the open skylights. Outside there was nothing but traffic, fumes and noise, and crowds of people making their way home from work in the sultry afternoon heat.

The prospect of having to walk up to Stratford High Street, getting on to a bus full of sweaty bodies and travelling with them all the way back to Mile End – never mind the slog along Grove Road to Bailey Street at the other end of the journey – was making Ginny feel bilious.

She leaned back against the rough brick of the factory wall, oblivious of the mass of her fellow workers now coming towards her, all as eager to leave the place as Dilys. Any moment they would come surging through the gates and whisk her along in their wake like a twig being washed along in the gutter.

'Blimey, Gin, shift yourself!' Dilys grabbed her by the arm. 'Unless you wanna get dragged along to bloody West Ham with that crew from Loading. And you know how I hate them. Shifty-looking bleeders.'

Ginny closed her eyes. 'You go on, Dil. I don't feel too good.'

'Don't you really?' Dilys sounded surprised. She peered at Ginny more closely, turning down the corners of her mouth at what she saw. 'Come to mention it, you don't look all that.'

'Why d'you think I came out early?'

'To be honest, I really thought you was swinging the lead for once. I was quite impressed. I mean, it's usually me what gives Stan the old flannel, not you.' Dilys cocked her head on one side. 'So what's up?'

Ginny sucked in a lungful of air, trying to clear her head. She immediately wished she hadn't. It tasted foul, just like the stench from the stinking clouds that wafted along from the smoking chimneys and boilers of the factories in nearby Carpenters Road.

Now her head really was swimming.

She buried her face in her hands and took little gasping breaths, as the sweat broke out on her top lip. 'D'you think we could go and get a drink somewhere?'

'Anything to get away from this mob.' Dilys wrinkled her nose in disgust at the press of bodies pouring through the gates and swirling around them.

'Oi! Watch yourself, you!' Dilys yelled, as she elbowed a tall, skinny lad who had dared to brush against her, shoving him out of the way. 'Come on, Gin.' She pouted through daintily pursed lips. 'Let's nip over the Railway away from these bloody hooligans. I could do with a nice cold shandy.'

Ginny was relieved to see that apart from a few grumpy-looking old men – dressed, despite the heat, in the regulation cockney uniform for males of their age: collarless shirt, stock, braces, waistcoat, watch chain and flat cap – the pub was almost empty. Too early for the evening crowds, she supposed, and too late for afternoon drinkers, who had better things to do than hang around pubs at tea-time.

At least that was one problem out of the way. It was going to be difficult enough as it was to make up her mind about just how much she would tell Dilys, but if the pub had been crowded with eavesdroppers, it would have been impossible to tell her anything at all. She felt so ashamed.

'You go and sit down there, Gin,' ordered Dilys, pointing to a table by the propped-open door, 'and I'll fetch the drinks over.'

Dilys wasn't feeling uncharacteristically thoughtful in taking it on herself to go to the bar, it was that, by the look of her, Ginny couldn't stand up much longer and Dilys had never really seen herself as being the nursing type. For one thing, it took far too much sympathy and understanding, and for another, Dilys didn't fancy having to scoop Ginny up off the floor if she passed out. It was far too hot for that sort of lark.

'Just a plain soda water for me thanks, Dil,' Ginny said, her voice wobbling with the effort of speaking.

Then she did as Dilys had told her and went and sat down, more than grateful for the breeze blowing through the open doorway and the opportunity to take the weight off her feet.

Although Dilys returned almost immediately with the drinks, Ginny had had enough time to decide that she was going to tell Dilys all about it. Well, not *all*, exactly, just the most immediate of her worries. Dilys was her best friend after all.

Ginny took a big gulp of the luke-warm, bubbly water that Dilys had handed her. The salty taste made her want to gag. But then most things seemed to have that effect on her lately.

Taking a deep breath to steady herself, Ginny closed her eyes, opened her mouth and out came the words. 'Dil,' she said, 'I'm expecting.' There, she had said it out loud. The words that made it true.

Dilys almost choked on her shandy; she felt her cheeks colour and a pulse begin to drum in her temple. 'But you *said* . . .' she spluttered. '*We* said that Ted wouldn't—'

Ginny shook her head and grabbed at Dilys's hand. 'Ted doesn't know nothing about this, Dil. And he ain't gonna know. Promise me you won't say nothing. Please.'

Dilys scraped her chair closer to the table. Her face a picture of suppressed fury as, with her forehead almost touching Ginny's, she stared across at her. 'It ain't exactly something you're gonna be able to keep a secret, now is it, you daft mare?'

'Look, Dil, you're me best mate. If I tell you something, will you promise me you won't breathe a word?'

Dilys leaned back in her chair and puffed sarcastically. 'You've already told me quite a lot, I should think. What more could there be? Someone else's, is it? Not a China-man's or nothing?'

Ginny was used to Dilys's taunts and didn't rise to them. Anyway, this was more important than that. 'You know how long I've wanted a baby.' Her voice was cracked and sad. 'It's something I've dreamed about. But I'd never really got it settled with Ted.'

Dilys shrugged non-committally as though she had little thought on the matter, but her mind was working nineteen to the dozen: Ted didn't know yet. That meant she must be quite early on. Or maybe she was mistaken. False alarms happened all the time. Dilys had had enough frights of her own to know that only too well. You got all wound up and then you woke up one morning and found you were fretting over nothing. That's what this would be. Nothing.

But even if it was a false alarm, Dilys decided, it would still be best if Ted was kept in the dark. The last thing she wanted was for him to start getting broody. She would have to play her cards very close to her chest on this one. It could go in any number of directions. And, if she wasn't careful, it might go exactly opposite to the way she wanted.

'Well, Ginny, all I can say is, I hope you're wrong, girl. I mean, I've said it often enough, Ted'd go spare if you ever did get yourself knocked up.'

'It's not that, Dil, it's ...' Ginny turned her head slightly, her gaze flicking nervously about the dull little bar. 'I've decided ...'

'What? What have you decided?' Dilys snapped. Although she was sure she could control the situation and was convinced that she wasn't going to let Saint bloody Ginny the martyr spoil things between her and Ted, Dilys still wasn't going to make it easy for her. Just the pathetic look on her pretty little face made Dilys want to slap her. 'Well?' she demanded.

'I've decided that now ain't the right time.'

Dilys took a gulp of her shandy. 'When would be the right time? He ain't gonna be pleased whenever you tell him. You know that, don't you? He's gonna go—'

'Dilys, I ain't talking about that. I mean it ain't the right time for me to have ...' She lowered her chin until it was almost touching her chest. 'You know.'

'Do *what*?'

'Please, Dil. Don't shout. My head's splitting and I don't want everyone in the pub earwigging.' She sipped the soda water and shuddered. 'I've thought about it,' she went on, unable to meet her friend's gaze. 'In fact, I've thought about nothing else these last few weeks. Not only do I feel really ill, but I can't afford to give up my job.'

She paused, getting a grip on the tears that were threatening to spill down her cheeks before she could continue. 'You see,' she sniffed, 'since Ted's got himself involved—'

'Who with?' Dilys demanded. She was wide-eyed with alarm. 'Who's he involved with?'

'It's nothing like that. There's no other woman.' Ginny shook her head, dismissing the very idea. 'He's got involved in something dodgy.' Slowly she raised her eyes until she was looking at Dilys. 'You know when the law came round, a few months back?'

Dilys nodded dumbly. Silly cow, what was so new about that? Surely she realised everyone knew how Ted earned his living? He was a spiv.

'Well' – Ginny's voice was now so small it was barely audible – 'he ain't only selling bits and pieces no more. He's fencing big stuff. Expensive gear from down the docks. And he's sort of in trouble.'

'Blimey, Gin.' Dilys did her best to sound shocked, reckoning that there was no point letting on to the miserable-looking little mare. 'That's a bit of a turn-up for the book, ain't it, girl? Your Ted fencing, eh? Who'd have thought it?'

Dilys glugged down the rest of her shandy and stood up, marvelling at the close shave she'd just had. Just for the moment she had really been convinced that Ginny had either found out about her and Ted, or that the rat had gone and found himself an extra bit on the side. 'I'm gonna get another drink,' she said, holding up her empty glass to Ginny by way of invitation.

Ginny shook her head. 'No thanks, Dil,' she murmured. 'I'm fine with this.'

While Dilys was up at the bar, Ginny went over and over in her mind why she wouldn't have the child she was carrying. Why she really, honestly couldn't.

It had almost broken her, coming to that terrible decision, but she couldn't go through with it. She couldn't have a baby. Not yet. She just couldn't.

Deep in her heart, Ginny knew Ted was a violent, womanising, selfish bastard. But even when she was explaining away yet another cut or bruise, she had always told herself that he acted that way because he was worried, or had been working too hard, or, more often than not, that it was her fault, because she had irritated him through her own thoughtless stupidity.

Ginny had become an expert at lying to herself.

But there were some things even she couldn't pretend weren't happening: Ted was away more than ever and it was down to her to earn the wages. Okay, when Ted was around they might have chops, or sausages, or steak even – twice on the trot the other week – but then he'd be gone for days on end, leaving them without a word, without a penny. On the run from the latest police raids, or so he reckoned when he came back. But whatever the real reason he chose to be away, it could have occurred to him that Ginny and his mum still had to live when he wasn't there.

By the time Ginny had paid the rent man, put money in the gas, had paid her fares to work and had given Nellie enough to take her off to the Albert for her now regular nightly guzzle, the few bob that were left barely bought enough grub to satisfy Nellie's hungry guts, let alone to feed the pair of them something decent every night. It didn't bear thinking about what would happen if she had to give up her job. And if there was another mouth to feed . . .

But maybe Ted would change if they had a child.

And maybe they'd ask her to star in the next Joan Crawford film and buy her a sable coat to wear for the première in Hollywood.

Ginny knew she had no choice. And, much as she disliked her mother-in-law, it wasn't in Ginny's nature to let anyone, even Nellie, suffer. She knew what she would have thought if her own mum and dad, God rest their souls, had needed to depend on someone and they had been let down.

And then there was this bloke, whoever he was, the one the police said had it in for Ted. Even if she didn't have money worries, how could she bring a child into the world knowing that was going on?

'I *said*, so, what you gonna do then?'

'Sorry?' Ginny lifted her chin and frowned at her friend as though she was surprised to see her there.

'Blimey, Gin, you're in a right dream. I go up and get myself a drink, have a quick piddle and come back to find you've turned into a flipping zombie.'

'I'm gonna find someone to get rid of it.' Ginny said the words in a flat, conversational tone as though she was discussing something of no more significance than how she would get rid of the beer stains on the rickety little table which stood between them.

Dilys managed to suppress her smile as she reached out and took Ginny's hands in hers. 'I'll help you find someone, darling,' she cooed. "Cos you know I'll always be there to help you, don't you, Gin?'

Although it was barely five o'clock on a bright summer's afternoon, Marge was dressed up to the nines, looking more suited to doing a turn on the stage than to wandering about in the shabby back-streets of the East End.

She stopped outside a soot-covered, derelict-looking warehouse – one of the few buildings in the grubby little turning off the Bethnal Green Road that hadn't been damaged in the Blitz – and pushed open the faded, nondescript door.

Once inside, hampered by the tightness of her skirt, the height of her heels and her bad temper, Marge tutted and wiggled her way up the narrow, uncarpeted flight of stairs that lead to the top floor of the building.

She was going in to work nearly three hours early and she wasn't very happy. If it hadn't been for one of Billy Saunders's men turning up at her flat to tell her that she was wanted, she could still have been snoring her head off in the blissful, solitary comfort of her bed.

She just hoped Saunders hadn't arranged a private party. That was all she felt like, being nice to some mug punter, with her make-up running in the heat and her drawers sticking to her with sweat.

With a bored sigh, Marge dragged her handbag up her arm and rapped her knuckles on the plain, black-painted door at the top of the stairway.

A small spyhole opened at eye level. 'Who is it?' asked a gruff voice from behind the door.

'The Old Bill. Who d'you think it is, you great daft sod? Now come on, Phil, open up.'

The door was opened immediately and Marge brushed past Phil, a huge, cauliflower-eared goon, without so much as a glance.

Phil and the other minders were useful if any of the customers started getting too friendly without coughing up enough for drinks, but other than that, Marge ignored them. She had enough trouble with the men she was paid to be nice to, so she was buggered if she'd be nice to any of them just for the sake of it.

'Mr Saunders about yet?' she asked nonchalantly, staring at herself in one of the dingy mirrored panels lining the walls.

She leaned forward and concentrated, dabbing the tip of her little finger at a streak of scarlet bleeding from her lipstick. There were definitely more lines around her mouth than there had been yesterday, she was sure of it. She would have to start getting a few decent nights' sleep a week or she'd wind up looking like the battered old bags who plied their trade along the Mile End Waste.

'Well?' she repeated impatiently, peering closely at the deepening crow's feet around her eyes. 'Is he or isn't he?'

'I'm here, Marge.'

She spun round. 'Sorry,' she stammered. 'I thought—'

'It doesn't matter.' Saunders jerked his head towards one of the spindly legged tables dotted around the room. 'Sit down.'

Marge did as she was told. What the hell was this about?

Saunders sat opposite her. He looked enormous, perched on the little chair. 'I hear your mate Lilly ain't been in to work for the last five days.'

Marge frowned. 'She ain't been feeling too well, Mr Saunders.'

Saunders leaned forward. 'If she's been working a foreigner—'

'No. No, she ain't. Honest, Mr Saunders, I'd stake my life on it. Me and Lil ain't ever been so well looked after as we have here. We love it. We'd never go behind your back. Never.'

'Do me a favour, Marge. I don't like being messed about. She might only be a brass but I still expect loyalty in my staff. And if my girls start getting the reputation for being street whores, then they know what they can do. I wanna start getting a bit o' class in my clubs. I've had it up to here with old scrubbers.'

'Honest—'

'Just listen to me, Marge, I took you two on 'cos I

wanted to start up here with girls who knew the ropes round these parts. But now there's plenty more working here I don't need you if you ain't gonna behave yourselves.' Saunders's voice was low, threatening.

Marge licked her lips nervously. She could feel the sweat trickling down her back. 'You've got it wrong, Mr Saunders. Honest. As true as I'm sitting here.'

'Look, if Lilly wants to go independent, that's fine by me. We all know you toms ain't the most reliable of workers; you come and go like sodding Christmas. But *not* on my patch. And I ain't having her coming in here and making private arrangements. Got it? You knew from the outset the cut you'd get. And you knew the rules.' Slowly he rose to his feet. He towered over her. 'Go on, Marge. Out. And don't come back.'

Marge also stood up, far more unsteadily than Saunders. 'Please, Mr Saunders, give us a chance. If I go and get her right now, you'll see.'

'See what?'

'Please, just give me a quarter of an hour.'

'Marge, I can't.' Lilly's lips were so swollen, she could hardly speak. 'Look at the state of me.'

'It don't matter what you look like,' Marge wheedled. 'Well, it does, I suppose. It's a good thing. He'll be able to see why you ain't been in.'

Lilly lifted her hand and cautiously ran her fingers along the cuts and bruises on her cheek. 'No. Not like this. I feel ashamed. Stupid.'

'You'll feel even more stupid if we wind up back down the docks, going with seaman under the arches who're too pissed or too tight-fisted to go to the dearer girls working in the case houses.'

*

'Lift your head up, Lil,' Marge urged her friend. 'Go on, show him. Show Mr Saunders why you couldn't—'

'That's enough from the gallery, thanks, darling,' Saunders snapped. 'Get yourself over to the bar and tell Phil I said to give you a drink.'

Marge went to say something, but, for once, she had the good judgement to keep her mouth shut and to do as she was told.

She flashed a look of helpless apology at Lilly. Fancy dragging her here for this. Lilly would skin her when they got outside, or rather, when they were chucked outside by one of the minders.

Nodding dumbly at Saunders, Marge slid her way along the cracked leather seat of the booth and disappeared over to the bar, leaving Lilly to learn their fate from Saunders all by herself.

Saunders took out his cigarettes and offered one to Lilly.

With a trembling hand she took one, wincing with pain as she opened her mouth to put it between her lips.

As though he had nothing else in the world on his mind, Saunders took his time and lit first Lilly's cigarette, then his own. He blew out the match and dropped it carefully into the glass ashtray he had positioned on the table between them. 'So,' he began, lifting his chin to indicate her injuries. 'What's the S.P. on all this, then?'

Lilly blew a plume of lavender smoke down her nostrils, wishing she could stop her hands from shaking. 'I fell down the steps,' she whispered. Why the hell had she let Marge talk her into doing this?

Saunders threw back his head and laughed. 'Yeah,' he said amiably, 'and you and the rest of the girls are all gonna give up the game and start working for a living.'

Lilly almost joined in with a little laugh of her own – anything to keep on his good side and to save herself another hiding – but she counted herself lucky she hadn't: in a split second his expression had changed to one of fury.

He leaned forward and smacked the table so hard the ashtray rattled around like a spun coin in a game of pitch and toss. 'Give me some credit, Lil, for fuck's sake. Now, let's have a bit of truth, shall we? Number one – Marge swears you ain't working a foreigner.'

'I ain't—'

'So it wasn't a pimp or some punter you picked up what did it?'

Lilly swallowed hard. What she wouldn't have given for a large scotch. 'It was a punter,' she said carefully. 'But one I took home from the club. He liked a bit of rough stuff.'

He held out his hand. 'So where's my cut?'

Lilly dropped her gaze and stared at the table. 'I never got no money off him.'

Saunders narrowed his eyes. He didn't appreciate being treated like a mug. 'So who was he, this bloke what gave you a slap and never even paid you for it? Never paid *you* mind, which means *I* don't get paid either.'

'I don't know his name.' Lilly's voice was barely audible, as she shrank back in her chair like a terrified child.

Saunders ground out his almost unsmoked cigarette. He was really losing patience. He had better things to do with his time than spend it arguing with toms, but he had to show that he could keep discipline or they'd all be working foreigners.

'You know the rules,' he snarled. 'No one takes home no one they don't know. Then I don't risk losing my cut 'cos you've been tucked up by some con man, now do I?'

Lilly let out a little shuddering sigh. 'I'm sorry,' she sniffed.

'Don't bother with the old flannel, Lil. Just tell me who it is. And don't bother to lie to me. I'll find out one way or another.'

'I can't. I'm too scared.'

'Look, Lil, I might be a nasty bugger at times, but you know I'd never raise a hand to a woman.'

'It ain't you I'm scared of,' she said, lying through her teeth – any tom with any sense of self-preservation learned to be scared of all men from very early on in their careers; too many men thought they could treat them like punch-bags.

'I'll protect you from whoever it is, all right? Now I can't say fairer than that, can I? But I mean it, Lil, I wanna know. 'Cos I ain't having no one taking liberties with no one who works for me. It's a piss take and I ain't having that. I ain't gonna stand for that from no one. And that includes you.'

Dropping her chin, Lilly closed her eyes and began to talk quickly. She wanted to get it over with. 'All right, I'll tell you. I did know him. He wasn't a punter. That's why I never told no one. I wasn't trying to keep your cut, Mr Saunders. I swear, on my mother's life.' She lifted her chin and looked directly into his eyes. Pleading with him to believe her. Marge was right, just the thought of going back on the streets was too much even to contemplate and maybe, with a bit of luck, Saunders wouldn't smack her one.

'It started out all right,' she went on. ''Cos I took him back to my room as a favour, see. Not to do business. His wife had chucked him out and he had nowhere else to go. She's a rotten old cow, Mr Saunders, he's had to put up with murder off her for years and—'

'Lilly.' Saunders's voice was menacingly calm. 'Would you do me a favour and stop all this old shit and just tell me the truth? Would you just explain what any of this has got to do with the state of your boat?'

She took a long drag on her cigarette, pulling the smoke deep into her lungs, then shrugged and stared down at her lap. 'I knew we was gonna do it, I suppose.' It was as though she was talking to herself. 'But there was never any question of money being involved. It weren't like that.'

'So, you've been giving it away for free, eh, Lil? That ain't very bright, now is it? At least if you was working a foreigner there'd be a bit of sense in it.' He shook his head as though unable to believe the stupidity of what he was hearing. 'Go on,' he said wearily.

'He's always been a bit on the handy side, ever since I've known him. He'd only have to get a bit upset over something and he'd give me a little slap.'

'A little slap!' Saunders's voice was incredulous.

Lilly looked up at him and began to cry. 'He just sort of went raving mad. Kicking me and punching me, and then he . . .' She shook her head, unable to go on, unable to describe the humiliating things he had put her through.

Saunders was shaking with temper, he felt ready to rip someone's head from their shoulders. Someone had had the gall to interfere with his business. To keep one of his girls off work and lose him money. To damage his property. *His* property. He'd kill the bastard slag when he got hold of him.

'Think carefully, Lil,' he warned the now sobbing woman. His voice was even, measured. 'Tell me his name, there's a good girl.'

'Ted,' she sobbed. 'Ted Martin.'

Chapter 7

It was six o'clock on a hot July afternoon, less than a week since Ginny had sat in the Railway Arms, confiding in her supposed friend, Dilys Chivers.

Jeannie Thompson was standing waiting in her kitchen doorway, picking her teeth with a broken matchstick, staring into the middle distance and thinking hateful thoughts. Jeannie couldn't bear waiting.

She was forty-one years old, but, with a good light, she could just about pass for fifty. She was what could best be described as frazzled-looking. Her mass of matted hair – bleached a startling, unnatural orangy yellow – contrasted starkly with the dark brown of her roots and of her tobacco-stained teeth. And with the red of her mottled, vein-threaded skin, she looked a more than sorry sight. Jeannie was a hardened drinker by anyone's standards and it showed. Just as the squalor in which she lived showed her not to be a student of the school of good housekeeping.

'Well,' she said to the manky ginger cat that was threading a path in and out of her bare legs, 'if the silly tart don't turn up soon, she can forget it. I've got better things to do with my time than standing about waiting.'

She bent down and picked up the mangy creature, cradling it to her well-upholstered bosom. It emitted a desultory purr.

'Mind you, if she don't turn up, Twinks, you can forget your fish supper. It'll be scraps again for you, my little pet.'

She planted a loud, wet kiss on the animal's head, which had the immediate effect of driving it into a frenzy of flat-eared, stiff-tailed anger. Escaping from her grip with a wild-eyed leap, the cat spat and hissed its way to the floor, leaving Jeannie's front smothered in ginger hairs.

It then shot out of the kitchen and, with dead-eyed accuracy, darted through the open street door, along the weed-infested path and between Dilys's splayed legs to feline freedom.

'Bloody, rotten, flea-bitten moggy!' Dilys yelled, aiming her toe at the creature's rear. 'Nearly had me off me sodding feet!'

Ginny clung to the gatepost. She had felt sick all day, but now, looking at this terrible place, she felt worse than sick, she felt completely disgusted. The house not only looked repulsive, but, even from the street, it smelt absolutely rank. Her twitching nostrils were filled with a sickly sweet stench, like the inside of a rubbish bucket that had been left to fester and moulder. There was a smell of stale cabbage about it, and something Ginny couldn't begin to describe, let alone name.

She grabbed hold of the post more urgently, anchoring herself as firmly as a barnacle stuck to a Thames barge at high tide. How could she even have considered doing this? It was madness. She would go home, tell Ted and everything would be okay.

It would just have to be.

'I can't do it, Dilys.' She shook her head determinedly. 'I can't. I can't go in there.'

Dilys gripped Ginny's arm and tugged her roughly. 'Look, Ginny,' she said through gritted teeth, 'you either do it this way, or you go home, dose yourself up with slippery elm, stick a knitting needle up your fanny and probably wind up with blood poisoning – if you don't bleed to death first. So what are you gonna do?'

Ginny screwed her eyes tight and began weeping silently.

'At least this way you know you'll be safe,' Dilys reasoned. 'Only uses best yellow soap, does Mrs Thompson. She's well known for it. Never uses none of that old—'

Realising what sort of an impression she was giving, Dilys added hurriedly: 'Not that I know anything about it, of course, but it's what everyone says. And she's got a proper rubber syringe and everything. None of that scraping and digging about.'

Ginny felt the sweat breaking out on her top lip. 'No, Dilys. Please.'

'Now you listen to me, Ginny Martin. It's a bit late to start acting up now.' Dilys was growing angrier and more desperate; surely the stupid cow wasn't going to change her mind and go through with having the bloody kid? That'd really mess things up. 'If you'd had any sense in the first place, you'd have got yourself some Rendell's—'

'Please, Dilys. Don't.'

'Well, it's you what got yourself in this state, innit?' Dilys paused as something occurred to her and then, with an even more callous lack of sympathy than usual, she actually started giggling. 'Here, d'you know old dozy-drawers in Dispatch? That Mary whatever her name is? Well, on her wedding night, she only thought she had to swallow the Rendell's, didn't she? Instead of ...' Dilys raised an eyebrow and nodded downwards. 'Sticking 'em up her you-know-what. Must have been foaming at the mouth like a sodding mad dog. Still it worked. She went bright green from the vile taste of it and spent the night with her head down the lav. Put her old man right off his stroke, that did. Never got up the duff that night, though, did she!'

All the talk about douches and scraping and swallowing Rendell's pessaries made Ginny feel worse than ever. 'Dilys,' she wailed, 'I feel so sick. Please, I wanna go home.'

Before Dilys could reply, Jeannie Thompson threw the street door wide open and stood there, looking like a gorgon. 'What the bleed'n' hell's going on out here?' she bellowed.

'We've come to see you, Mrs Thompson,' Dilys explained sweetly, shoving Ginny in front of her. 'Sorry we're a bit late like, but me friend missed her bus, didn't she. I've been waiting for her for ages and was just giving her a right telling off for leaving me standing here on me Jack.' Dilys treated Jeannie to a charming little smile. 'Right inconsiderate some people, ain't they?'

The back kitchen of the house was worse than Ginny could possibly have imagined, and so was what Jeannie Thompson did to her.

During the next few weeks Ginny suffered. She suffered more than when Ted had beaten her; more than when she was lying awake at night, pretending to herself that he wasn't off somewhere with another woman; more even than when she had lost her family in the Blitz. This time she was experiencing a new type of pain: that of knowing she was no longer carrying the child she had dreamed for years of holding in her arms. The child she had decided she could not have.

Although Dilys had been there with her on the day, and it was Dilys who had taken her to that awful woman's house, in the end it was she, Ginny, who had made the decision that her life was in too much of a mess to bring a child into the world to share it.

And that knowledge haunted her.

The first few days after Ginny's visit to Jeannie Thompson's were a nightmare of physical pain: the result of the wild-haired woman's rough and unhygienic attentions. But she was right when she told Ginny, as she had ushered her and Dilys out of her house, that a strong young girl like her would soon recover from a *little bit of discomfort*, as she had put it. Before long, Ginny was as fit as ever, but that wasn't the end of it, it was only the beginning. The distress she had felt very quickly spiralled down into a dark, frightening despair, and she realised she would never be – or feel – the same again.

At least Ted wasn't around – which, for once, was a relief – but Nellie, unfortunately, was.

In an effort to conceal what was really wrong, Ginny pretended she'd eaten something that had upset her, made her so ill, in fact, that she could hardly get out of bed, never mind go to work. But that wasn't good enough for Nellie. Night and day she nagged her to get back to the factory, griping and groaning about her daughter-in-law's idleness and how she, an old woman, was having to go without.

Not that she actually *was* going without, Pearl had seen to that, because, unlike Nellie, Pearl guessed right away what was wrong with Ginny and her heart had gone out to her.

Like so many others, Pearl had learned, with a combination of fear, guilt and overwhelming relief, of the women who would 'help you out' if you were in trouble. During the hard times of the 1930s, having to feed and clothe the family they already had was difficult enough for most mothers and plenty found themselves paying discreet visits to their local equivalents of Jeannie Thompson. So Pearl could just imagine what young Ginny was suffering and was glad to do whatever she could to make things a bit easier for her.

But despite their neighbour's generosity, Nellie wasn't satisfied with being supplied with money for food and light. No, she wanted more. She wanted money to pour down her throat at the Albert.

When Pearl had just laughed at her request for a few extra bob for a drop of something to calm her nerves, Nellie had played her usual trump. She had gone along to the pub with her empty purse and played the old soldier, trying to mump drinks from Bobby's and Martha's more well-oiled customers. But this time it hadn't worked.

Nellie couldn't understand what was going on and said so. She wished she hadn't. It was pointed out to her, very clearly, that the reason she wasn't exactly welcome in the Albert was all down to her precious son. Using his black-market profits as a float, Ted had widened his 'business' interests to include money lending. A lot of people now owed him money, many of whom could ill afford his sort of interest rates, but they were so terrified by his growing reputation for resorting to violence over the least little thing, that they found ways, desperate ways, to meet his outrageous demands. Nellie was no longer another old moaner who wasn't particularly liked, but who was tolerated and treated to an occasional nip of the hard stuff; she had become, by association with such scum, an unwelcome ponce.

She had stormed out of the pub and back to the house, her mood fouler than ever, and even more determined to make Ginny's life a misery.

Ginny could only be grateful that she had a friend as good as Pearl to turn to.

'Ginny, love. You there?' Pearl stood in the hallway, a plate covered with a tea-towel in each hand, calling up the stairs. 'I've brought a bit of supper over for you and Nellie. How about coming down and seeing if you fancy it?' She rested her broad forearm on the banister and added, 'And don't worry, the coast's clear; I've given in and slipped Nellie a few bob to go and have a drink. Mind you, I think she's giving the Albert a miss for some reason, she was heading for the Aberdeen according to my George.'

Ginny sat at the kitchen table, picked up her knife and fork, and stared down at the boiled bacon and pease pudding. 'D'you mind if I eat it later, Pearl?'

'Course not. I'll put it in the stove with Nellie's.' Pearl covered the plate with an enamel dish and bent down to undo the cooker door. 'So, how're you feeling?' she asked over her shoulder.

Ginny stared down into her lap and began weeping softly.

'Don't upset yourself, Ginny, love.'

'You wouldn't be so kind if you knew what I've done.'

Slowly Pearl closed the oven, straightened up and said quietly. 'Don't be daft.'

'But I ain't really been ill, Pearl.' She swallowed hard. 'It was all a lie. I was expecting, and I . . .'

'I know.'

'I couldn't have it.' Ginny buried her face in her hands.

'Ssssh. There, there, darling.' Pearl wrapped her arms round Ginny and held her close. 'It's all right.'

Ginny pulled away. 'No it's not. It's not all right. Nothing's all right. Not doing that, not living here with Ted . . .' Ginny lifted her chin and looked up into Pearl's concerned, motherly face. 'And it's probably not right talking about my own husband, either, but I've gotta tell someone.' A shuddering sob ran through her body. 'Pearl, Ted's not being very good to me lately.'

Pearl bit her tongue. Not being very good? The bloke was being a first-class bastard.

'And when I found out I was . . . you know, I tried to think how I could keep it. I tried so hard. I even thought about getting a divorce. But how could I bring up . . . Not on me own. And I couldn't have it adopted. I couldn't give . . . If I still had me mum, maybe I could've had . . .'

'Ginny, listen, you musn't punish yourself like this.'

'But I—'

'But nothing. It's like poor Violet Varney—'

Ginny's eyes widened with horror. 'I've never done nothing like Violet did.'

'Ssssh. Calm down, sweetheart.' Pearl pulled out one of the chairs and sat down next to her. 'I'm not saying you did. What I'm saying is you ain't a criminal, you're a bloody victim. You've lived a life that would have driven anyone to breaking point. But you've survived, and now you've gotta start thinking about yourself for a change, not waste any more time doing what other people tell you. Throw the sodding monkeys off your back; stop letting them push you this way and then shoving you back the other. You're a grown woman, Ginny, not a servant or a kid to be ordered about.'

Ginny blew her nose noisily as her tears began to flow again. 'It's easy for you, Pearl, you're lucky, you're strong and you've got your family round you, and . . . and, what have I got?'

'You've got me for what it's worth.' With surprising tenderness, Pearl took Ginny's hand in hers. 'But I dunno how you reckon I'm lucky. Look at me, I'm in me fifties and I look a right wrinkled old bat—'

'No, you don't.'

'Yes I do! I see myself in the flipping glass of a morning. But you're beautiful, Ginny. And you've got youth on your side. You've got time to be strong, but even a lorry-load of Pond's wouldn't help me. Here, know what my mum used to say? If you didn't die from it, it made you stronger; whatever "it" was when it was at home.'

Ginny managed a weak smile through her tears. 'You're my "it", Pearl, you make me feel stronger.'

Pearl touched her on the cheek. 'I'm glad, but I want you to promise me you're gonna start standing up for yourself a bit more.'

Ginny swiped away her tears with the back of her hand. 'I know you're right. I mean, look where being a doormat's got me.' She twisted the soggy handkerchief around in her fingers. 'And I've gotta stop kidding myself that everything's all right. Gotta stop making excuses.'

Nellie appeared in the kitchen doorway and glared at Pearl. 'What're you still doing here at this time of night?'

Ginny stood up and answered for her. 'Pearl's been giving me some very good advice, Nell. And I've decided to go back to work.'

'About time too. I could've starved if it—'

'No, Nellie, you don't understand, I ain't going back so's I can give you more money to piss away up the pub,' Ginny told her now slack-jawed mother-in-law. 'I'm going back to the factory to get away from your moaning.'

Now Pearl was also on her feet, she was enjoying Nellie's pop-eyed reaction to the worm so suddenly turning, but there was concern in her voice as she spoke to Ginny. 'Are you sure you're strong enough to go back, love?'

'She's only had a bit of food poisoning.'

Pearl ignored her. 'Take another week off, eh?'

'No, Pearl, I've decided. You know, I'll never forget what you've done for me. One day I'll pay you back for all your kindness. I swear I will.'

Nellie rolled her eyes in disgust at such a display.

134

'The only paying back you'll do, Ginny love, is looking after yourself. Now you eat up that dinner I brought over and I'll see you in the morning.' Pearl turned to Nellie. 'There's a plate made up for you an' all, Nell. I stuck it in the oven.'

Nellie dropped down on to one of the kitchen chairs. 'Get it out for me, Ginny.'

'No, Nell, you get it, I'm seeing Pearl out.'

Pearl bit her lip to stop herself from laughing and followed Ginny out along the passage. 'That gave her a bit of a shock, Gin!'

Ginny pulled open the street door and stood aside to let Pearl pass. 'Yeah, but the crafty old cow knows I'll still look after her.'

'You're a good girl, Ginny, one of the best.'

'Hark who's talking. You've stood by me, Pearl, and I can't tell you how grateful I am. But I meant what I said, I'll find a way to make it up to you. I'm gonna help *you* one day.'

It wasn't long before Ginny had the opportunity to do exactly that.

'But, Dilys, you can't be.' Ginny looked from Dilys to Pearl and back again. She felt as though someone had whacked her in the guts. She'd only come over to collect Dilys for work, but instead of the usual morning performance of getting her friend moving she'd been presented with this.

'Pearl,' Ginny said, trusting her to have a sensible explanation for what her daughter had just come out with, 'has she gone mad or something?'

Pearl didn't say anything, she just sat there at the kitchen table, her hands folded in her lap and her head bowed.

'Pearl?' Ginny said again, more loudly this time. 'Tell her she can't be.'

'You're right,' Pearl eventually answered. Her voice came out low and flat, as she stared down at the scrubbed wooden table top. 'She can't be.' She gave a mirthless little laugh. 'I mean, she ain't even got a regular feller, has she?'

Ginny nodded in urgent agreement. 'That's right, Pearl. She ain't.' She turned to Dilys. 'You must have made a mistake.'

Dilys shoved the last of her toast into her mouth and shrugged. 'You can say I ain't; and you can say I can't be; and you can both say it till you're blue in the face. But I am and that's the strength of it.'

Still chewing on her breakfast, Dilys stood up and walked over to the back door. Standing sideways on to it, she squinted thoughtfully at her outline reflected in the gleaming glass panels that made up its upper half. 'Will you just look at the size of me,' she marvelled, smoothing down her skirt to reveal what the other two couldn't deny was a definitely swollen middle. 'I'm like a flaming barrage balloon.'

Pearl leapt to her feet. '*Look at the size of you? Look at the bloody size of you?* That's the least of your flaming worries,' she hollered. 'It's hard enough bringing up kids when there's two of you. However d'you think you'll manage by yourself?' Pearl threw up her hands and appealed to Ginny with tears pouring unchecked down her cheeks. 'Whatever's her dad gonna say, Gin?'

At that totally inopportune moment, George walked into the kitchen. 'Whatever am I gonna say about what?' he asked with his usual pleasant smile.

'What are you doing here?' gasped Pearl, turning away and hurriedly drying her eyes on the hem of her apron.

'Flipping charming, ain't it, girl,' George grinned,

winking at Ginny, 'when a man ain't even welcome in his own home.' He sat at the table and opened his paper.

'Why ain't you at work?'

'Blimey, Pearl, I'm sorry if I've come in and messed up your mothers' meeting for you.'

Pearl flinched at the irony of her husband's words.

Completely unaware, George closed his paper and carried on. 'Didn't get picked off the stones again today. Weren't nothing for me. Still, our Sid and Micky both got picked. That's a blessing.' He lifted his chin with pride. 'Them boys of our'n, Pearl, they're built like a couple of brick . . .' George checked himself. He was a traditional old East Ender in that way and hated it when men used bad language or off-colour talk in front of the ladies. '. . . warehouses,' he continued primly. 'Strong as lions, the pair of 'em. A ganger'd have to be mad not to pick our lads for his crew.'

To Pearl's dismay, George folded his arms across his chest and leant back in his chair. He was obviously warming to his subject and was keen to share his thoughts on it.

'You know, I reckon they think I'm a bit too long in the tooth to pick me out these days,' he continued, oblivious of the increasingly tense atmosphere in the cramped little room. 'They either have to have a mountain of work on, or be desperate, to pick an old boy like me.' He smiled good-naturedly at Ginny who tried, but failed to smile back at him.

'I'll be retiring soon, won't I. Be a gentleman of leisure. And I can't say I'll mind too much neither, especially not on a lovely August morning like this, when I could be along the road having a natter with my old mates and then popping in to see Bob for a swift one.'

He lifted the teapot and weighed it in his hand to see if there was any left. 'I dunno, girls, it don't seem like no time at all since I first started down them docks. Hardly five minutes ago, if I was truthful. Funny, ain't it, how time flies by as you get older? I was a cheeky little so-and-so then, but when I went there on that first day with me old dad, God rest his soul, terrified I was.' He shook his head. 'Seems just like yesterday. But before you know it, that'll be me, finished.'

To George's astonishment, Pearl snatched the teapot from her husband's hand. 'Well you ain't no gentleman of leisure yet, George Chivers,' she snapped. 'And if you ain't got nothing better to do with your time, you can get yourself down the Roman and get me some potatoes and greens.'

George blinked in surprise at his wife's outburst. 'Do what?'

'Potatoes and greens,' Pearl hissed through her teeth.

A look of realisation came over George's face. Thinking that his wife was trying to get him out of the house because there was something up with Ginny again – the poor kid had had so many problems with her useless waste-of-space of an old man over the years that George was used to the sight of her crying in his back kitchen – he leapt from his chair as though he'd been scalded. If there were women's problems going to be discussed, George didn't want any part of it.

He grabbed his cap and pulled it firmly on to his head; it might have been over seventy degrees outside, but George would have felt naked going out without his cheese-cutter – and he was definitely going out.

He strode hurriedly over to the kitchen door, but then paused and turned round to snatch a surreptitious look at Ginny for signs of bruises. He could see it now: she looked upset about something all right, but there were no obvious cuts or anything. Not on the poor little love's face anyway.

He switched his attention to Pearl. 'Righto then, darling,' he said, with a brief nod and the barest hint of a wink, 'I'll go and get the spuds and that for you. But don't expect me back right away. I've got a feller I've gotta see about a dog, so I'll be a while.'

The three women stood in silence as they waited for George to leave. The moment they heard him call a cheery goodbye and the sound of him pulling the street door shut behind him, the crying, recriminations and disbelief began all over again.

'You must have made a mistake, Dilys. You must have. You can't be expecting.' Pearl was shaking her head as she spoke, as though denying it would make it all go away. Then, in complete contradiction she added, 'You know when your dad finds out he'll go stark raving mad. He'll bloody well kill you.'

Ginny couldn't take it in, all she could think of was what had happened to her in Jeannie Thompson's disgusting house. And what she had let that woman do to her. And all the blood . . .

'I've decided I'm gonna keep it,' Dilys announced blithely.

Ginny's head snapped up in amazement. 'But how can you?' she gasped.

It wasn't something that she would be proud of later, but at that moment Ginny felt outraged, betrayed even, that Dilys – her best friend – could even think about keeping her child after what she had seen Ginny go through at that woman's hands.

Dilys misunderstood Ginny's question. She opened her eyes wide and stuck out her bottom lip in a casual gesture of speculation. 'The father'll have to give me money, won't he?'

'What, you mean—' Ginny shut her mouth as if it were a trapdoor. She was about to say: What, you mean the

139

married feller you told me's been keeping you on and off for the last few years? But I wasn't talking about money, Dilys. I mean how can you do this *to me*? But Ginny didn't say anything of the sort. The last thing she wanted to do was hurt Pearl.

There was a long moment's silence, then Pearl, in a voice husky with tears, asked flatly, 'What feller, Dilys?'

Dilys stared brazenly at Ginny. 'I met a GI. In a club.' She was rather pleased with herself for coming up with that so quickly.

Ginny frowned. It was the first she'd heard about any GI.

'Up West it was,' Dilys offered without prompting. 'Lovely place. Makes round here look a right slum.' She sniffed haughtily. 'But then that's what it is round here, ain't it? A slum.'

'A GI.' Pearl uttered the words in a monotone.

'That's right,' said Dilys brightly, 'a GI.'

What Dilys didn't say was that although she had indeed met an American soldier, it had been only about a month ago – far too recent to account for her current condition of being almost five months pregnant. And the meeting had hardly been intimate.

It had happened one evening when Dilys had gone to meet Ted outside Leicester Square tube station. As usual, she hadn't wanted to risk Ted getting there first, becoming bored and leaving before she arrived, so she had turned up almost fifteen minutes early. As she had crossed the Charing Cross Road, she was more than surprised to see him standing there already. And that he wasn't alone.

But, for once, he wasn't chatting up another woman, he was talking to a good-looking, broad-shouldered man, made even more handsome by his stylishly cut American military uniform. Dilys was quite excited by the thought of being introduced to the man with the movie-star looks, as she'd always rather fancied the idea of going out with an American, but any such hopes were dashed. Ted was doing business.

After a brief, low-volume exchange of words, then a nod, a firm shake of hands and the passing over of a tight roll of banknotes, the serviceman flashed her a quick salute, then disappeared into the West End's Saturday evening crowds.

So, Dilys *had* met a GI and it wasn't too much of a lie for her to claim she'd met the man in a club, because Ted had taken her to a sort of club that very night. It was actually more of a drinking den, and it was a good half-hour after the soldier had left them, but she'd really enjoyed herself. Even though it wasn't much like the glamorous cocktail lounges she'd seen in the films, it was still a club. And there had been a GI. Sort of. It all suited her very nicely.

Just as being pregnant suited her; just as did taking Ginny to see Jeannie Thompson. Dilys knew what she wanted and she knew exactly how she was going to get it. If her plans continued to fall into place as neatly as they seemed to be doing up until now, then she would be very happy indeed.

Pearl heaved herself up from the table and went to the sink to fill the kettle. 'So, where is he now then? This GI?'

'He's had to go back to America. But he's promised he'll look after me. Gonna send me all the money I need, he is.'

'You know if he don't, and if your dad takes against you, you'll have to go into a mother and baby home, don't you?'

Dilys snorted with contempt. 'Don't you worry about me; I won't have to go into no home.'

Pearl put down the kettle on the wooden draining board. It was as though she didn't have the energy or the will to carry it over to the gas stove. 'I'll do me best for you, Dilys. But you know how your dad feels about girls getting into trouble. I'm telling you, this'll kill him. You know you've always been his baby girl.'

Gripping the side of the butler sink, Pearl started to cry again. 'But he'll wanna wring your neck for you when he finds out.'

Dilys sighed irritably. 'No he won't.'

'Maybe not,' sniffed Pearl, 'but when your brothers find out they'll bloody well wanna kill the bastard. No matter who, or where, he is.'

It was one of those miserable November days when night seemed to have fallen before it had ever really got light; rain had been bucketing down solidly for a week and Ted was just about pissed off.

A wet Wednesday night in Upton Park. Definitely not his idea of a good time. There he was with a suitcase full of gear to flog, but every pub he's been in was almost empty. At this rate, he'd be going home before closing time with less in his pockets than he'd come out with.

He leaned miserably against the polished mahogany bar of the Boleyn, nursing his almost empty glass, debating whether to have another scotch, when he felt a tap on his shoulder.

'Ted Martin?'

He stuck a smile to his lips and twisted round to see who wanted him. With a bit of luck, it might be a customer just wetting himself to buy a caseload of bent watches, or wanting a nice fat loan.

'Who wants to know, mate?' he asked, the perfect image of the chirpy spiv.

'Names don't matter, but you can call me ... Let's see. Charlie. Yeah, you can call me Charlie.'

'Charlie' was big, very big. In all directions. He was wearing a dark-blue overcoat that was, Ted noted, of the best quality – the feller obviously had a few bob – but it was so massive it could have served as a tent for a whole boy scout troop and still have had room for the Akala. And he wasn't alone. The man standing with him was almost as big as he was. Both of them had on snap-brim trilby hats pulled down hard so that their faces were in shadow, although Ted could still see that Charlie sported a cauliflower ear that would have won first prize in any sort of contest.

Ted nodded with a grin. Very nice. It sounded like he was about to do a bit of business with Charlie and his mate. Probably not a loan, but definitely some sort of a trade.

Charlie jerked his chin towards the door. 'Let's step outside, eh?' It was an instruction rather than a question.

Charlie picked up Ted's case and started to walk away. In his great meat plate of a hand the bag looked more like a small portmanteau than a full-sized suitcase.

Ted downed the last of his drink and hurried off after his potential customers.

'Down here,' said Charlie, tipping his head towards a narrow, unlit pathway that ran alongside the pub and through to the back of the shops. 'We don't want no one to see us, now do we?'

'You're right there,' agreed Ted, stumbling his way along the pitch-dark alley. 'They all love a bit of bent gear, but only if it's them what's buying it. If some other bloke's got a few quid to spend, they come over all moral on you and wind up getting on the trumpet to the law.'

Ted tripped again, this time barking his shin against a pile of crates. 'Shit!' He sucked his teeth as he bent down and rubbed his leg. 'Here, you'll need to see what I've got. Either of you two got a torch?'

'I don't think we need a torch for what we've got in mind,' Charlie said.

'How d'you mean?'

The men moved very close to him and Ted, realising too late that he had actually been mug enough to go down an unlit alley with a pair of gorillas he had never set eyes on before, flattened himself against the slimy brick wall.

Dark as it was, Ted saw the outline of Charlie's leather-gloved fist quite clearly as it drove towards his solar plexus. 'Christ!' he gasped, doubling over with pain.

'We've been waiting quite a while for an opportunity to bump into you on our travels, Mr Martin,' Charlie sneered. 'And I mean waiting, 'cos let's face it, we didn't wanna waste our energy actually looking for someone as unimportant as you, when we knew we'd see you crawling out from under some rock sooner or later.'

Still bent forward, and with his arms shielding his head, Ted whimpered pitifully, 'I don't understand. I ain't done nothing.'

'No?' Charlie's voice dripped with sarcasm. 'I don't suppose you have, a piece o' crap like you. But think about it, you slippery little bastard. Something you done to a little lady?'

'That kid's nothing to do with me. I swear. Dilys is a fucking liar. You ask—'

'Dilys? Who the hell's Dilys?' Charlie looked at his silent mate who just shrugged. Then he grabbed hold of Ted by the collar. 'What, give a good hiding to more than one, have you?'

Ted tried a conspiratorial laugh – a man dealing with his equals. 'You chaps know how it is. You have to shut their gobs for 'em sometimes, or they start taking liberties.'

When they didn't join in with his laughter, Ted shut up.

'Lilly ring any bells?' asked Charlie.

'Lilly? I ain't seen her for months.'

'Five months, actually. It was July if you recall.'

Ted shrugged. 'You don't expect me to keep tabs on all the old sorts I knock about with, do you?'

'Knock about? You said it, moosh. But she weren't yours to knock about, now was she?'

Two hours later Ted came to. He was lying in a puddle of filthy, icy cold water, on a bomb-site off the Ratcliffe Highway near St Katherine's dock, in the shadow of Tower Bridge. But with his eyes puffed up to slits from the beating he had taken, he had no idea where he was. And, with the pains in his head befuddling his thinking, he had only vague memories of how he had got there.

What he did know, as he dragged himself towards the road, was that he vowed, if it was the last thing he did, he would get his own back on Lilly, the filthy little whore who had grassed him. He'd make her suffer until she begged him to finish her off.

When he eventually got back to Bailey Street it was nearly five o'clock in the morning and still pouring with rain.

It took all his effort to bang on the street door.

Ginny was down the stairs in a matter of moments. She hardly ever slept well when Ted was away. Not that she worried about what might be happening to him any more – she was past all that. She now worried about herself, about what he might do to her if he did decide to come home in the early hours.

But when she opened the street door, instead of finding

Ted loud-mouthed, roaring with drink and ready to pick a fight as she had expected, he was soaking wet, bleeding and, by the look of him, totally exhausted.

Automatically, she reached out to steady him as he fell into the pssage. 'Ted, whatever's happened?'

He lifted his head and glared at her through cut and swollen eyelids. 'What d'you think's happened, you brainless mare? I've been to a ball and tripped over me partner's dance frock.'

Ginny stiffened. She never knew how to handle Ted at the best of times, but when he was already in a temper he was capable of anything. But despite her resolve to look out for herself she couldn't just abandon him, not in the state he was in.

'What can I do?' she asked quietly as he staggered towards the kitchen.

'Get me a drink, and a basin of hot water and a flannel to clean myself up. And then you can piss off out of it and leave me alone.'

Ginny went over to the corner cupboard and took out what was left of Nellie's scotch and a glass, which she wiped with the tea-towel before filling it. She wasn't taking any chances, something as inconsequential as a smeared glass had, in the past, been enough to get her a cracked rib.

As she took the drink over to Ted, her hand shaking, Ginny's imagination was working overtime. Thoughts and fears spun and twisted around in her mind. For Ted to have had such a beating he must have really upset someone. The man the coppers had warned her about that time maybe, the man who had it in for him. Or someone's husband.

She put the drink down carefully in front of him, went over to the sink and filled the kettle. Her heart was pounding. All she wanted to do was go back to bed, pull the covers up over her head and pray that Nellie had left enough whisky to knock Ted into oblivion before he too made it upstairs. But she wasn't banking on it. She was a woman with few illusions left and knew that things didn't work out that easily. Well, not for her they didn't.

As she searched under the sink for the disinfectant to clean Ted's wounds, Ginny was startled by a frenzied banging on the street door. She straightened up and flicked a quick look at the clock on the dresser. Ten past five. It was either the police, or – God forbid – whoever it was who had jumped Ted had decided to come round and finish the job properly.

'What shall I do?' she breathed, as the banging grew more insistent.

'Get rid of 'em,' spat Ted, stumbling to his feet and lurching towards the back door.

Ginny ran out into the hall, pulling her dressing-gown around her.

Upstairs, Nellie was yelling, 'What's all that noise down there?'

Ginny closed her eyes. Nellie starting; that was all she needed. 'It's all right, Nell,' she called up to her. 'I'm getting it. You go back to sleep.'

'Some bloody chance I've got of that.'

Ginny closed her ears to the rest of her mother-in-law's ranting, took a deep breath, swallowed hard and grasped the door handle with both hands.

When she saw who was outside she could have kissed them with relief.

Standing there in the gloom of the early morning – without coats, hats or even shirts, and with the freezing rain soaking through their vests – looking for some inexplicable reason as though they were about to pass out, were Sid and Micky, Dilys's two younger, but now enormous brothers.

'Thank Gawd you've woke up,' gasped Sid, grabbing her by the arm. 'You've gotta come over and help Mum, Gin. Please. Dad's gone for the doctor, but I think he's gonna be too late.'

All thoughts of Ted shivering and bleeding out in the lavvy in the backyard were immediately forgotten. Pearl needed her.

Pulling away from Sid's huge paw was impossible, but Ginny managed to stretch back just far enough to grab her coat off the end of the banister.

'How long's Pearl been ill?' she asked, throwing the coat over her head to protect her from the rain.

'It ain't Mum,' Micky quavered. 'It's our Dilys. She's only having the baby, ain't she.'

Ginny rushed through the Chivers' open door and took the stairs two at a time up to Dilys's back bedroom where the panic-stricken brothers had directed her.

They needn't have bothered, the sounds of Dilys screaming and hollering were signal enough for even the dimmest of wits to follow.

The brothers themselves were more than happy to have been relegated by Ginny to the kitchen to boil water – she wasn't sure they needed any, but at least it would keep them busy and away from under her and Pearl's feet.

Ginny paused on the landing. If the truth were known, she was just as scared as the boys were. This was the moment she had been dreading: Dilys having her baby. For no matter how well Ginny had managed during her waking hours to shake off any jealous or resentful thoughts about Dilys, her dreams were a different matter. Those she couldn't control. Over and over again, they came to taunt her, always the same: spiteful visions of cradling her new-born baby in her arms. Sometimes it

148

was blonde like her, other times it was dark like Ted. But whatever it looked like, it was her baby. Hers. The images were so real that in her first waking moments she would be puzzled at not seeing her baby's crib at the end of the bed. Then she would remember, and she would weep at the unfairness of it all.

She was the one who was married – even if it was to Ted Martin – and she was the one who should be having a baby. Not Dilys. And seeing Dilys, as she bloomed with approaching motherhood, had been a daily torment for Ginny. If she hadn't gone to Jeannie Thompson's, she would be almost eight months gone by now. Ironically, almost the same as Dilys.

Almost eight months?

Ginny frowned. It hadn't occurred to her until now that there might be a problem. Babies, or rather, healthy babies, weren't meant to come into the world so soon.

Warily, she pushed open the bedroom door and focused on the scene inside.

Lit by the stark glare of the overhead light, rather than the soft glow of the bedside lamp, Dilys's bedroom was no longer the cheerful place where she and Ginny had spent so much of their girlhood gossiping and giggling, practising dance steps and trying on each other's clothes and make-up. It had been transformed into an unfamiliar place, with the smell of fear hanging thick in the air.

Pearl was kneeling down next to the bed with her back to the door, wiping Dilys's forehead with a flannel.

Dilys looked terrible. Her thick dark hair, usually her pride and joy, was plastered to her head with sweat, despite the freezing damp of the early morning, and her face was deathly pale and contorted as she thrashed about, tangling the bedclothes around her legs.

Ginny knew that Dilys had never been much of a heroine – George had always joked that whenever his daughter had said she was unwell, he never knew whether to call the doctor or a drama critic – but this time it was obvious that Dilys wasn't crying wolf. She was really suffering; the anguish on her face was, for once, genuine.

Pearl, whispering reassurances to her daughter, pulled herself up off her knees, did her best to straighten the sheets and turned round. She let out a little gasp of surprise to see Ginny standing there in the doorway.

'Hello, love,' she said, fixing an encouraging smile to her lips and doing her best to block Dilys from Ginny's view. 'What you doing over here?'

'The boys asked me to come and help,' Ginny managed to mutter.

Pearl felt like going downstairs and braining her pair of lummocking great blockheads of sons. As if she didn't have enough on her plate seeing to Dilys. How was she meant to cope with Ginny as well? The poor little thing hadn't got over her own trouble yet. Still, she sighed to herself, they weren't to know. Fellers didn't know much at the best of times, let alone at a time like this.

She put her arm round Ginny's shoulder and said gently, 'You sure you wanna stay, love? I'll understand if you'd rather go home.'

Ginny hesitated, then nodded. 'I'd like to stay if it's all right.'

'Course it is. Now you roll up those sleeves and give your hands a good scrub in that basin; then you can mop her forehead to cool her down, while I have a look at the business end of things.'

'Mum!' Dilys screamed.

'And I think I'd better be quick about it.'

As Pearl pulled back the covers she saw the look on Ginny's face. It was obvious that Dilys wasn't the only one in pain.

Pearl did her best to sound calm as she encouraged her alternately furious and then terrified daughter to push and to breathe through the final stages of her labour, but she too felt like screaming – at the complete, bloody injustice of it all. What was wrong with the world when . . .

All thoughts of unfairness were forgotten. 'Here we go!' Pearl urged her daughter. 'One last time, darling!'

Dilys grunted and heaved and yelled like a banshee, as she made her final effort, clasping Ginny's hand as though she were the last lifebelt on a sinking ship. 'I ain't never, ever,' she hollered, 'going near no bloke, not ever again.'

A few moments later Pearl straightened up and stared at her daughter. 'Dilys,' she breathed. 'You've done it.'

Ginny backed away from the bed, dropped down on to the dressing-table stool and covered her face with her hands.

For a baby born so early, Dilys's little girl was surprisingly lusty.

'Hello, darling,' cooed Pearl as she held the bawling infant in her arms. 'Today's your birthday, my sweetheart. November the twentieth, 1946. The most special day in my life.' She kissed the warm, down-covered head. 'You go to your mum, while me and your Auntie Ginny here clear up a bit.'

She bent forward to hand Dilys her child, but Dilys shook her head pathetically. 'I can't,' she wailed. 'I'm so tired and I can't stand all that noise.'

'You'll have to soon,' Pearl warned her. 'She'll need to go to your breast, love.'

Dilys shuddered with horror. 'You're having a laugh, ain't you? She can have a bottle and like it.'

Pearl turned her head away from her daughter so that

she wouldn't see the look of disappointment that had clouded her face. 'Good job I got some in then, eh?' she said, her voice light and comforting.

'Can I hold her?' Ginny whispered. 'If you don't mind.'

Pearl nodded. 'Course you can.'

As she placed the little bundle into Ginny's arms, Pearl saw the tears brimming in her eyes and felt fit to weep along with her. It wasn't the right thing for a mother even to think, Pearl knew that, but it would have been clear to anyone that her daughter wasn't exactly the type to take to all this, whereas Ginny looked like a natural.

Pearl watched her, stroking the baby's face with her fingertip and smiling so lovingly as its crying gradually eased, and wondered again why things hadn't turned out differently, why it hadn't been Ginny's child she had just delivered.

Pearl could only imagine what the poor kid was going through as she rocked and whispered to the baby. The thought of what that bastard had done to her, what he'd driven her to, made Pearl's usually generous heart turn to ice as far as Ted Martin was concerned. He was the one man she would gladly have seen disappear from the earth – and preferably in as unpleasant a way as possible . . .

'Mum!' Dilys wailed. 'Do something. I feel terrible.'

'You'll be all right soon, love,' Pearl said cheerfully. 'At least me and Ginny delivering the little mite saved us the six quid we'd have had to have paid the doctor.'

Pearl puffed as she bent down to parcel up the newspaper and the soiled draw sheet that she had taken off the bed. 'I've had it put by in the dressing-table for weeks now,' she explained. 'Been saving a few shillings every week, I have. From the very first day you told us you was expecting. So, I tell you what, I'll give it to you to spend on yourself. When you're up and about you can treat yourself to something nice to wear.'

'I don't think I'll ever be able to fit in nothing nice again neither.'

'You'll feel better once you've had a nice cup o' tea. I'll just sort this out first.'

'Shall I go down and make it, Pearl?' Ginny asked.

'If you don't mind, darling. Then I can get this finished up here.' Pearl wiped her hands down her apron and reached out for the baby. 'Let me take this little angel off you and I'll get her settled down next to Dilys.'

Just as Ginny was about to open the bedroom door, she pulled back in alarm at the sound of someone crashing up the stairs and coming to a skidding halt outside on the landing mat.

'Pearl?' It was George on the other side of the door; he sounded frantic. 'I found the doctor for you. But he's gonna be at least another hour. What shall I do?'

'Why don't you come in for a start?' Pearl answered him.

'You sure?' he asked warily.

'Course I am, love. All the worst is over now.'

Dilys was about to say speak for yourself, but the look on her dad's face as he stepped gingerly into the room and had his first glimpse of his grandchild was enough to silence even her mean mouth.

George, a great lumbering docker who had spent all his working life heaving weights up to shoulder height that most men would barely have been able to lift, tiptoed over to his wife and grandchild with the lightness of a gossamer-shod ballerina.

Tears streamed down his weather-beaten cheeks as he looked down at the tiny infant in his wife's arms.

'Here's your granddaughter, George. Here's Susan Elizabeth.'

The expression of love, pride and wonder on her mum's and dad's faces – never mind the sheep's eyes on Ginny – cheered up Dilys considerably. It wasn't her own maternal love and pride that was being uplifted, it was the fact that she now knew she had no worries whatsoever about being thrown out and no problems at all with having someone to mind the baby.

With a bit of luck she'd be back to normal and out on the town again with Ted before anyone even realised it, or, from the soppy look on their faces, before they even cared.

Dilys had great hopes for Susan Elizabeth: she was going to be a very useful claim on Ted Martin and a very convenient distraction.

Chapter 8

July 1948

It had been a glorious summer's day and Dilys had been sitting on a kitchen chair outside number 11 all afternoon, waiting for Pearl to come back from the Roman Road. It was now getting on for six o'clock and her mum was still not back from the market. She'd told Dilys that she was only going for a few veg and a bit of fruit and maybe to pick up something pretty for the little one, and yet she'd been gone for hours – since just before dinner-time, now she came to think about it.

Dilys was not very happy, in fact she was becoming really agitated. If her mum didn't get back soon, she wouldn't be able to get away; Ted would be left waiting for her by Mile End station, then he'd think she wasn't coming and clear off without her. Her whole evening would be ruined.

Dilys folded her arms and tutted indignantly to herself. It just wasn't good enough. Where the hell was she? It wouldn't have been so bad if her dad had been around to give her a hand with Susan, but he was off with his mates as usual. That's all he seemed to be interested in now he'd retired: hanging around talking to the other old boys about flipping football, and pigeons, and grey-hounds. Everyone was so flaming selfish; it really got on Dilys's nerves.

Susan, who was now twenty months old, had also grown impatient with waiting. She liked to toddle around on the floor and play, but Dilys, not wanting to be bothered with keeping an eye on her, had had different ideas and had strapped her firmly into the big carriage-built pram that Sid and Micky had bought for her when she'd been born. With nothing more to amuse her than a crust of bread and the fringing round the hood, Susan had dropped off to sleep.

Before finally giving up and closing her eyes, she had made a feeble attempt at whining for attention, but, young as she was, Susan had already learned that it wasn't easy to get a reaction from her mummy. Her nanny and Auntie Ginny were a very different matter, they were always ready to pick her up, to talk to her and play with her, but they weren't here. So sleep had been her refuge.

It might have been better if Dilys had also had a nap, maybe then she wouldn't have been in such a foul temper. As it was, she was fuming. She was so angry that she was actually about to get off her backside and do something for herself for once. She was going to go indoors and fetch her coat, and start walking round to the Roman Road to see if she could find Pearl. But she hadn't even stood up, when her salvation appeared on the corner of the street – Ginny Martin, striding along on her way home from work, a bag of shopping swinging from each hand.

Dilys leapt to her feet and waved frantically; she would have shouted but she didn't want to wake Susan. Not that Dilys was worried about her daughter's rest being disturbed, it was just easier when she wasn't wanting attention all the time. That could wait until someone else was looking after her.

Within a matter of minutes Dilys was indoors washing and primping herself, and Ginny, delighted that her friend was going out for a few hours with her new mystery boyfriend again – the GI was still sending money over from America apparently, but that didn't stop Dilys from needing company – was only too pleased to keep an eye on Susan for her.

Ginny had popped over home first to let her mother-in-law know she was back from work and to give her the ham she had had freshly sliced off the bone for her tea. Nellie hadn't been very impressed by the idea that she was expected to boil herself a few potatoes and wash her own lettuce, and had gone on and on about her daughter-in-law's terrible behaviour. Ginny, as she usually did now, just ignored her and got on with putting away the rest of the shopping.

Being bold enough to deal firmly with Nellie wasn't the only thing about Ginny that had changed; since Susan had been born, her life had been turned around. She now felt content, complete almost, in a way she would never have imagined possible. Susan was, after all, the child of a friend, not even related to her, but the fact that Dilys was Susan's mother didn't seem to matter somehow. Ginny and Pearl spent far more time with the child than Dilys ever did and it seemed to suit them all.

Ginny smiled to herself at the thought of the happy hours and some of the unforgettable moments that she had spent with Pearl and Susan: the day the little one's first tooth had finally come through after miserable days of fretting; the first excited steps she had taken when she had tottered across the kitchen to be scooped up in her proud grandmother's outstretched arms; the wonderful feeling Ginny experienced as Susan relaxed into sleep in her arms, as she and Pearl shared a pot of tea and an afternoon's easygoing chatter about whatever came into their heads.

It was as though Ginny, who had had so much taken away from her, was being given a second chance to be part of a proper family once more. Sid and Micky often teased her, as they rushed in after work to get ready to go out with their latest girlfriends, that she spent more time in number 11 than they did and they were probably right.

Ginny almost couldn't have been happier. She no longer hungered for the crumbs of affection that Ted might let fall from his table to nourish her. She had no need of such condescension. Even the fact that he had been missing again was almost of no consequence. Maybe he was still up to his old tricks. But so what? She now had Susan to fill her time and her thoughts; a little girl she loved and who Ginny knew loved her in return.

While Dilys was indoors getting ready, Ginny sat outside the house in the fading evening light, with Susan no longer in her pram but settled comfortably on her lap, watching the children from Bailey Street and their mates from the surrounding neighbourhood playing at being in the Olympics. With all the wireless and newspaper coverage about the run-up to the great event that was to happen in August when the games were coming to London, 'playing Olympics' was all that most of the kids in the East End had been interested in for weeks.

Ginny smiled and nodded at the enthusiastic sprinters, jumpers and relay racers as they tore up and down the road. They were without the skills or the equipment of their adult idols, it had to be said, as most were dressed in ill-fitting home knits and patched and darned hand-me-downs, but they had as much passion as any internationally renowned athlete. Ginny would usually have cheered them on, willing them on towards the winning tape – a rough chalk line sketched between the pub and the bomb-site – but this evening she restricted her support to silent nods and encouraging smiles, as Susan was still fast asleep.

But the little girl's peaceful slumbers were rudely shattered as a great holler of incensed protest went up from the far end of the turning.

The older boys, using all kinds of ingenious items 'borrowed' from backyards and kitchens, had just added the triumphant finishing touches to a makeshift hurdle track, when Sid had come charging round the corner from Grove Road as if he were being chased by Old Nick himself, scattering supports, and cross bars flying in all directions.

'Oi you! You've spoilt our game, you rotten bleeder!' was one of the more polite hollers from the chorus that echoed after Sid as he skidded through the wreckage of their course.

Susan opened her eyes with a start and let out a whimper of fright at all the noise.

Sid seemed not to hear or even notice the protesters as he continued his wild flight along the street, crashing towards Ginny and Susan like an out-of-control steam engine.

Ginny stood up, hugging Susan to her shoulder, ready to give Sid a piece of her mind, but he didn't even slow down; he just ran straight past her and into the house, nearly knocking her off her feet, and Susan with her.

Clinging to the banister rail, trying to get his breath back, Sid shouted up the stairs, 'Dilys. I know you're up there. Where's Dad? I've gotta find Dad.'

'Shut your mouth, you,' Dilys yelled back at him from upstairs. 'You'll wake the bloody baby.'

Ginny was now right behind Sid. She stood on tiptoe and shouted in his ear. 'She's already awake, Dil. No thanks to this big lump. Half frightened her out of her little wits, he has.'

Sid turned around, still panting, and reached out to

159

ruffle his little niece's shiny dark hair. 'Sorry, sweetheart,' he breathed. 'Uncle Sid didn't mean to scare you.'

Ginny frowned disapprovingly and held Susan closer. 'I dunno what's got into you, Sid. First you go upsetting all them kids out there, and now—'

'Look, Gin, do us a favour, just tell me where me dad is.'

'No good asking me,' she said primly. 'He wasn't about when I got in from work and that must have been a good half-hour ago.'

Sid bowed his head. 'I've gotta find him, Gin. I dunno what to do.'

Ginny set Susan down on the floor. 'Go and see if your dolly's in the kitchen, babe,' she said gently, guiding the serious-faced toddler in the right direction, then she straightened up and turned back to Sid. 'Are you in trouble, Sid Chivers?'

He didn't reply, he just kept staring down at the floor.

'Dilys,' Ginny called up to her. 'Come down here. Just for a minute.'

'Leave off, Ginny. Can't you see I'm getting ready?' Dilys appeared on the landing at the top of the stairs, waving her mascara brush in the air by way of proof. She was just about to step back into her room, when Sid called after her to stop.

'You'd better come down, Dil,' he said flatly. 'It's Mum, she's been knocked down by a trolleybus in Grove Road.'

Dilys was down the stairs in a flash. 'Where is she?'

'They took her away in an ambulance.'

'They what?' Dilys rolled her eyes in enraged disbelief. 'If she's in the hospital, then who's gonna sit with the baby?'

She shoved her brother to one side so that she could see Ginny. 'You ain't gotta go home just yet, have you, Gin?' she wheedled.

Before Ginny could answer, Sid grabbed Dilys by the shoulders. 'You'd better sit down, Dil,' he said, pushing her on to the stairs. 'Mum ain't in the hospital. She's in the mortuary.'

Ginny shook her head in disbelief and pulled Sid round so that he was facing her. 'No. You're wrong. She can't be. It must be someone else. It must . . .' Ginny suddenly felt unbearably cold; the blood drained from her face and, as if she were a rubber balloon being deflated, she crumpled slowly to the floor.

'He wants to watch himself,' snapped a miserable-looking old woman, as George Chivers accidently brushed her arm as he edged past her on the way back from the bar. 'He might have just buried his wife, but that ain't no excuse to go knocking people's drinks out of their hands.'

'You're right there, Florrie,' agreed Nellie, who was standing with her. 'Ignorant as shit, some people.'

If George heard the women's complaints he certainly didn't show it. He kept his eyes lowered and his head down as he made his way back to the table in the corner of the Prince Albert, the base from which he had plied backwards and forwards to and from the bar, gradually getting more and more drunk, but still feeling stone-cold sober.

He had no need to fetch his own drinks, there were more than enough of the mourners – some genuine, some, like Nellie's elderly companion Florrie Robins, only there for the free food and drink – who would have been more than willing to fetch them for him, but George hadn't listened or said a word to anyone since the funeral cars had come to the house that morning.

He plonked down onto the bench seat and knocked

back the scotch he had in one hand, then downed half of the pint of bitter he had in the other in a single swallow.

'George.' Ginny, her eyes puffy and red-rimmed from weeping, touched his arm gently. 'Can I get you a sandwich or something? You should eat just a little bit, you know.'

George said nothing, he just stared unseeingly at the floor as though watching some distant episode playing in his head.

Sid came up behind Ginny, tapped her on the shoulder and whispered quietly into her ear, asking her if she'd help him start getting people to make a move so that he could get his dad home before he drank himself into a stupor.

Ginny nodded and went to find Ted, who had actually turned up for the funeral just as she had asked him.

She found Ted at the other end of the pub. He was sitting next to Dilys. He had her child on his lap and was singing to her, a happy little nonsense ditty that he seemed to be making up as he went along. It was about a pretty canary bird called Susan, and he was smiling blissfully.

Ginny stood there watching him, not caring that she was being buffeted about by the crowds of increasingly drink-enlivened mourners.

As he continued with his song, Ted was so entranced by the beaming toddler that he was completely oblivious of Ginny's presence.

The tender intimacy she was witnessing felt like a knife in Ginny's guts. Could this sensitive, affectionate man really be the same one who had refused even to discuss having a child? The same one who had kicked her in the stomach as she lay on the floor begging him to stop just because she'd mentioned it?

'Ted.' Ginny's voice sounded strange even to her.

Ted looked up, the enchanted smile still on his handsome face; an expression he hadn't deigned to share with his wife in a very long time.

The moment he realised who had spoken to him his smile melted away like snow on top of a chimney pot.

'I didn't realise you even knew Dilys had a baby,' Ginny said quietly. 'Let alone that you knew her name.'

'Here, Dilys,' he said wearily. 'You take her.'

Ginny flinched as she saw how he handled the little girl: not clumsily, but in an experienced, easy sort of way, as though he cherished the very bones of her.

Ginny tried to stop herself even beginning to think it, but her thoughts were galloping ahead of reason. Ted and Dilys? Surely even Ted wouldn't do that to her?

He stood up. 'You ain't gonna start, are you, Ginny?'

'No, Ted,' she said, her voice flat. 'I'm not starting. I've just come to tell you that Sid and Micky asked if we'd all start making a move. George is getting slaughtered and they wanna get him home.'

'Shouldn't a man expect to get pissed at his wife's funeral?' someone behind her asked.

Ginny closed her eyes and groaned inwardly. It was George. She hadn't realised he was standing there.

She twisted round, ready to apologise, but George wouldn't let her. He held up his hand and shook his head. 'It's all right, Gin, I ain't blaming you,' he slurred. 'I heard what Sid said to you. But just leave me be, eh?'

With that, he shoved his way back towards the throng at the bar, leaving her standing there, red-faced and more distraught than ever.

She turned back to Ted.

He stared levelly at her. 'Me mother's not got a drink,' he said, sitting down next to Dilys again and taking Susan back on to his lap. 'You'd better go and get her one. Go on.'

Ginny said nothing. It wouldn't be right starting anything, not on a day such as this. So, as she had so often done in the past, she just did as she was told.

'All right, Nellie,' Ginny said by way of impassive greeting, as she handed her mother-in-law a glass of port and lemon.

'How about Florrie?' Nellie barked. 'How about one for her?'

Ginny didn't rise to Nellie's nastiness. Not only did she not want to row in front of everyone, but she was too distracted by the image of Ted and little Susan to bother.

'I'll get her one, Nellie, and I tell you what, I'll even fetch you a few rounds of sandwiches an' all. That do you, will it?'

'We don't want nothing hard mind,' Nellie called after her. 'Florrie's had all her teeth pulled out like me and she ain't got used to her false ones yet neither.'

Ginny was fed up with hearing about Nellie's new National Health choppers. Yes, she had agreed, over and over again, it was a wonderful thing that such luxuries could be had by anybody now, and for free, but if she'd to express her amazement at the sight of the bloody things once more she'd grab them from the old trout's mouth and dance up and down on them until they crumbled away like a stick of stale seaside rock.

And not only was she sick of Nellie's sodding teeth, if she or Flo said one more word about their made-to-measure Health Service glasses and how they beat the ones you bought lucky-dip style from the counter at Woolworths, Ginny would not be responsible for her actions.

She could feel herself coming very close to the edge and Nellie was just the person who could push her over.

Taking a deep breath, Ginny carried on towards the buffet table at the far end of the counter, keeping her chin in the air and her eyes fixed in front of her so that she didn't have to look at Ted and Dilys who were still sitting together in the corner right opposite the food.

With a weary sigh, Ginny began piling up a plate with anything and everything even vaguely soft-looking. Maybe if the old bats had their gobs full of food they'd give everyone a bit of peace for five minutes.

Ginny was just about to carry her load back to Nellie and Flo when someone rammed into her back with such force that the loaded plate was sent flying from her hand. It sailed through the air like one of the lethal tin-lid discuses the mums had barred the kids from playing with in their Bailey Street Olympics and landed with a resounding crash against the edge of the polished counter top, sending the sandwiches arcing across the bar in the direction of Martha, who had her head down pulling a pint of best.

'What the bloody hell?' yelped the landlady, as a slice of bread, butter-side first, landed with a slap on the side of her rouged and powdered cheek and slowly slipped down towards her bosom.

Ginny spun around to confront the idiot who had pushed her, her mouth open ready to ask the clumsy so-and-so what exactly he thought he was up to. But when she saw George standing there, swaying alarmingly from side to side, she was more concerned than angry.

He was jabbing his finger at Dilys and muttering furiously to himself, 'It was her what killed you, Pearl. Her. The shame of it. Bringing trouble home like some little tart.'

Dilys ignored him and carried on talking to Ted.

'Come on, George,' Ginny coaxed him, 'it's time we was all going home.'

George twisted round and tried to focus on Ginny. 'Pearl?'

Ginny swallowed hard. 'No, George, it's me. Ginny. Ginny Martin.'

'Ginny?' George stared at her as though he was trying to make sure that it really wasn't his wife.

'Yeah, that's right, George.'

George's lip trembled and his head lolled forward. 'Well maybe you can tell me what Dilys is doing with your old man. Ain't she in enough trouble with blokes?'

Ginny closed her eyes and bit back the tears that were threatening to start again. 'Come on, George,' she said, doing her best to keep her voice under control, 'let's be off, eh?'

'But look at her encouraging him,' George persisted. 'She's letting him sniff around her like a bloody bitch on heat.'

'Please, George.' Ginny grabbed his arm. 'Don't. Don't do this.'

George lifted his chin. Looking at Ginny as though he were seeing her for the first time, he nodded meekly and let her lead him through the mass of mourners towards the door.

Dilys watched their slow progress with unconcealed venom, sneering as people stopped him to pledge their promises of help and support.

'Just look at 'em,' she hissed. 'All fussing around him. They ain't got a clue how I'm suffering.'

She altered her tone to a pitiful whine. 'It's terrible indoors, Ted. Really terrible. Him and the boys sitting around with faces like fiddles, with not a thought of what I'm going through now I've got no one to help me. I hate it living there with them. Really hate it. I told Dad I should have the big bedroom now, but he wouldn't even hear of it. And you should hear the things he says to me.

And you can't imagine what it's like, Ted, having to push that bloody pram in and out of the passage with Dad's bike to get past.'

'You finished moaning?' Ted asked, smiling down at Susan as he chucked her under the chin, making her giggle happily.

Dilys shrugged. 'You do want me to be happy, don't you, Ted?' She sipped her drink daintily. 'Just look at him.' She jerked her thumb towards her dad, whom Ginny had propped against the wall while she opened the door. 'Fancy having to live with that. I can't stand it no more, Ted. I really can't.'

She grimaced with revulsion as Sid looped his arm affectionately round his dad's shoulders. 'Pathetic.' She dropped her chin and made miserable little sniffling noises. 'You've gotta do something, Ted. You've just gotta.'

Slowly she raised her eyes and blinked pitifully at him. 'If not for me, then for this poor little love.'

'Thanks, Gin,' Sid said, letting the pub door close with a slam behind them. 'Me and Micky'll see to him. And I'm sorry about what he said just now.'

'It's all right. I know he's had too much to drink.' Ginny stepped aside to let the two burly young men take over.

'What did he say to you then, Gin?' Micky asked, as he took George's weight against his shoulder.

Sid flashed a look of warning at his younger brother. 'Can't you keep your gob shut just for once, Micky?'

'What? I never heard what he said, that's all.'

'I didn't mean to upset you, Ginny love,' George slurred. 'I never meant nothing.'

'What you upset about then, Gin?' Micky asked.

'Micky, are you gonna belt up?'

Ginny could see the anger flaring in Sid's face. She laid her hand gently on his chest and said quietly, 'Leave him alone, Sid. I don't want no rows started on my part. Just get George off home, eh?'

'All right. Thanks.'

Sid and his brother stood one on either side of their now weeping father and gently guided him along the street, leaving Ginny in the doorway, watching them make their way back to the emptiness of number 11.

Without warning, George stopped dead in his tracks, threw back his head and a great shuddering sob shook through his body. 'It *was* her getting herself into trouble what caused all this. My Pearl wouldn't be laying in that cold ground if it wasn't for her.'

Sid squeezed his arm, encouraging him to start moving again. 'It was an accident, Dad, you know that.'

George shook his head, as he reluctantly shuffled forward between his sons. 'Your mum never said nothing to no one, but I could tell. I knew what she was thinking. She had it on her mind all the time. Every minute of the day. Day in day out. She wasn't concentrating when she crossed that road. I'm telling you, it would never have happened otherwise.'

He flicked his tongue at the trail of snot that dripped from his moustache. 'If I ever find the bastard what got that girl pregnant I'll kill him. I swear on my Pearl's grave, I will.'

Micky's chin was set with fury. One way or another, whoever it was who had made his dad cry – his dad whom he had never seen shed so much as a single tear – was going to pay. 'You don't have to worry yourself about that, Dad,' he said through gritted teeth. 'Me and Sid'll sort the whoreson out good and proper.'

If they hadn't been holding up their dad between them, Sid would have grabbed Micky by the throat and shaken the silly little sod till his teeth rattled. 'Think before you open that cakehole o' your'n for once, can't you, Micky?'

It wasn't the first time that Sid had felt like thumping his little brother. Micky was so hot-headed, Sid was sure it would land him in real schtuck one day. All right, so they'd discussed between them, plenty of times, what they'd do to the lousy no-good who'd dumped their sister – and Sid was growing more and more convinced that he knew who the bastard was, and it wasn't some American soldier – but mouthing off about it in front of their dad, especially just a couple of hours after their mum had been laid to rest, well, that was just about the last thing any of them needed.

Sid would bide his time and he just hoped that Micky would do the same.

'So it's like this see, now I'm getting this new motor, I won't be needing this one no more.' Ted patted the bonnet of the Talbot as though it were a much-loved family pet. 'And I thought, I know, it might come in handy as a runabout for Mr Roberts and his good lady. You are a married man, aren't you, Mr Roberts?'

The man in the cheap-looking brown suit rubbed his sweaty palms dry on the seat of his trousers, leaving a greasy slick on the already shiny cloth. 'I am indeed, Mr Martin. And am proud to be the father of two lovely little girls into the bargain.'

Ted smiled beatifically and slapped the man on his skinny shoulder. 'Two little girls, eh? You are a man truly blessed. And, I'm sure you have to agree, this here vehicle could only add to those blessings.'

Mr Roberts looked warily over his shoulder. They might have been standing well away from the street light, in a rain-slicked, deserted back-street in Hoxton, but a man in his position, a council officer, could not be too careful. Everyone in the town hall knew that everyone else was on the make, ready to take a bung or a backhander for all sorts of little favours, it was common knowledge, but proving it was another matter and there was no point in handing it to them on a plate.

He licked his lips anxiously, his wet tongue flicking around his narrow mouth in a curiously obscene display of intimate bright-pink flesh. He knew what he had to ask next, but how to phrase it?

'What sort of cost would that entail then, Mr Martin? Buying a fine motor vehicle such as this? Probably out of my sort of price range, I shouldn't wonder. But who knows, eh? Trouble is, a chap like me might have excellent job security and a fine pension plan – a very fine pension plan, in fact – but I'm afraid the actual wages are a very different matter.'

Ted flashed him one of his specials, a real winner of a smile that made the sides of his eyes crinkle as though he really meant it. 'Look here, Mr Roberts, I am going to sell this motor, because I am now fortunate enough to own an MG.'

Mr Roberts cooed in appreciation at such bounty.

'And you know me from our previous dealings,' Ted went on. 'I like to spread me good fortune about a bit.'

Mr Roberts was practically wetting himself at the thought that he might soon be driving around in a Talbot! It would take a bit of explaining to his colleagues, of course, but maybe he could invent an aged uncle. Of Ellen's, of course, not of his. He would be called Bernard, Uncle Bernard, and he would have left the Talbot to them in his will. Perfect!

Mr Roberts couldn't resist a little smirk at his own guileful inventiveness.

'Spread your good fortune, Mr Martin? So how would that relate to this instance, then?'

'Well, Mr Roberts, let's see.' Ted clapped the man matily around the shoulder. 'You know the old saying, you scratch my back . . .'

'I do indeed.' Here it comes, thought Roberts, just about able to stop himself from drooling.

'Now, I have this friend, a young lady. Tragic story, Mr Roberts. Her fiancé, the father of her little kiddie, her only child I might add, was killed in the most terrible accident. Just two weeks before the wedding. In the RAF he was. Testing one o' them new secret bombing planes. You know, the ones what're gonna keep us all safe so we never have to have another world war again.' Ted took off his hat to show respect for the non-existent hero, shaking his head in sadness at such misfortune. 'I don't have to explain to a man such as yourself, Mr Roberts, that it was all kept very hush-hush.' Ted tapped his index finger on the side of his nose. 'Walls have ears, as they say.'

Roberts arranged his face into a suitably sombre expression. 'They have indeed.'

'Well,' Ted wrapped his arm round Roberts's shoulders, 'what I was wondering like, was how you'd be disposed to finding the little lady, this good friend of my family's, some sort of a place to live? She wouldn't be expecting no Butlin's holiday camp, just something nice. So's I can visit her privately, to offer me sympathy without anyone knowing what a charitable man I am.'

Ted winked and dangled the car key tantalisingly in front of Roberts's eyes, twirling it between his fingers so that it glittered and flashed in the light from the street lamp. 'And without getting no bugs while I'm there. If you catch me drift.'

Ginny unknotted her headscarf, stuffed it in her pocket

and threw her coat across the end of the banister. 'It's only me, Nell,' she called.

'Mum ain't in.'

Ginny stood in the kitchen doorway, her eyebrows raised in surprise. 'I didn't expect to see you here.'

'No?' Ted flipped the *Evening News* shut and tossed it to one side. 'Who was you expecting then? The milkman? The landlord? The coalman?'

'Leave off, Ted.' Ginny heaved her bag on to the draining board and began unpacking the shopping. 'Where's Nelly got to, then?'

'She went round Dilys's.'

Ginny twisted round to look at him, a loaf still in her hand. He was leaning back easily in his chair, with his hands linked across his firm, muscled stomach, staring at her.

She couldn't deny it, he could still make the blood thump in her ears. He was a good-looking man all right. In fact, at getting on for thirty years old Ted Martin was more handsome than ever. If she didn't know him better, she might almost be tempted to believe that he would still change . . .

With a quick swallow and a little shake of her head to clear her mind, Ginny said hurriedly, 'No, I don't think she is. There was no lights on across the street when I come along just now. And you know Dilys, she always turns 'em on full pelt, even at this time of evening.'

Ted yawned loudly, leaned forward and rested his elbows on the table. 'Dilys ain't over the road no more.'

'How d'you mean?'

'Her and the little 'un have been given a prefab. Down Stepney. The bloke come round to tell her today.'

'A prefab?'

'You ain't gonna start that bleed'n' parrot lark, are you?'

'But—'

'Now I'm here, I might as well have a bit of something for me tea. What we got then?'

Ginny turned back to the shopping bags and carried on the unpacking. 'I've got some corned beef. I was gonna make a hash.' Her voice was flat, dull with shock.

Ted opened up the paper again. 'That'll do.'

Ginny was no longer listening to him. All she could think was that Susan, her lovely little Susan, was no longer just across the street waiting with chubby, out-stretched arms for Ginny to lift her high into the air and to cover her soft baby face with kisses.

What was wrong with her; what had she done that was so bad that meant every bit of happiness, every dream she ever had, was always snatched away from her?

Her family. Her hopes for her marriage to Ted. Then Pearl. Now Susan . . . How much more could she take?

It was a golden autumn evening and Ted was enjoying himself. He had the slanting rays of the last of the sun warming his back; he was being admired; and he was lapping up every single bit of attention, every envious or appreciative glance, as he drove along the busy streets with the top of his MG rolled back, showing him and his motor off in all their handsome glory.

Ted especially relished the attention from the girls, of course, many of whom seemed prepared to do every-thing short of throwing themselves in front of his wheels for the chance of a ride with a man like him in a car like his.

At first, however, the car hadn't proved to be such an asset. In fact, it had been a bloody millstone and Ted had seriously considered getting rid of it.

First there was the law. He had had no more trouble

from the plain-clothes mob – Saunders had obviously moved on to making someone else's life a misery and had called off his grasses – but every time Ted drove past a uniformed copper, anywhere around his usual manor, they were on him like a ton of bricks. How could he afford such a vehicle, him with no apparent means of support? They had always ignored the Talbot, but the flashy lines of the MG just seemed to get to them for some reason. But, in the end, coppers were only human and were as keen on getting their hands on a bit of steak and a few luxuries for the old woman as anyone else. And after a few weeks he had given a little sweetener to just about every Old Bill from Plaistow to the Aldgate pump. That was one problem off his back.

But then there was Dilys. Ted had just about had enough of her. Every time he went round to the prefab she wanted to go out in the car with him and would lead off alarming if he dared refuse her. If it wasn't for Susan – who, he didn't know why but he couldn't help it, had really got under his skin – he wouldn't have gone within a mile of Dilys and her bloody prefab. He wished he'd never set eyes on the silly tart.

He was on his way to Dilys's now and was dreading her starting again. He had almost not bothered, but someone he'd done a deal with the night before had quite unexpectedly presented him with the prettiest china doll he had ever seen. The bloke had meant it as a gift for Ted's wife, a little extra to thank him for his 'custom'. It was the sort of thing that birds liked to sit on their beds as a decoration, he had said. But the moment Ted had seen it he knew he had to give it to his little Susan. He could just imagine the expression on her face when she saw the dolly, almost as tall as her; and with its pretty dress and lacy bonnet she'd go mad for it.

He was just turning off the Mile End Road and into

Stepney Green when a particularly shapely backside wiggling along in the same direction caught his eye. The girl was balanced on such high heels and her dress was so tight that she could just about walk.

He slowed down to a crawl and drove along behind her, waiting for her to realise she was being followed and to turn round so he could see what sort of a boat went with such an appealing chassis. If he approved, he'd give her the full treatment: the smile, the chat, the whole bit. He could always take the dolly round another day.

It didn't take long for the woman to cotton on. She stopped, paused and slowly swivelled round.

As she did so, Ted eased on his brake.

At the moment their eyes met it would have been difficult to guess who was the most surprised.

'Lilly!'

'Ted!'

Ted was out of the car in a flash and grasping her arm. 'It is you, ain't it, you little whore?'

'Let go of me.' Lilly tried to pull away from him, but Ted was much stronger than her and had the advantage of not being balanced on top of a pair of almost four-inch heels.

'D'you know what you did to me?'

'Nothing. I ain't done nothing.'

'Nothing?' Ted's fingers pinched into the soft flesh inside her upper arm. 'Is that what you call it? That arsehole Saunders tells two of his bastards to give me a good hiding. They beat me black and blue and leave me to fucking freeze to death. But you reckon it's nothing?'

Lilly didn't even try to hide the contempt she felt. '*You* got beaten black and blue? Poor you.'

'Don't you get lippy with me, you filthy little trollop.'

'I ain't scared o' you, Ted Martin. Mr Saunders is looking after me.'

'Well you should be scared, darling. 'Cos d'you know what, because of you grassing me to that shit I had to shift me business interests away from that bastard's turf – *my* turf I should say – and I ain't very happy about it.'

'Ain't you? Aw, poor little baby.' Lilly stuck her chin defiantly in the air. She could feel her blood pumping round her body as though she'd run all the way to the West End and back, but she knew she had to try and keep some sort of control of the situation. No one was going to stop and help her if Ted started, not in an area like this where respectable families going about their business looked down on the likes of her. Even though some of the husbands were probably amongst her customers, if one of her sort got a whacking, they'd all look the other way or come over all moral and say it was what they deserved. If only she hadn't promised to come and get Marge on the way to work this would never have happened. The lazy cow would just have to get herself up and ready for the club in future.

Ted pushed his face close to hers. 'You ain't learned to shut that smart mouth of yours then?'

'Let go of me, Ted. 'Cos if you even touch me, I swear—'

He shook his head in disbelief. 'You really ain't got it, have you?'

'Got what?'

He dragged her across the pavement and threw her roughly into the car. She landed awkwardly and knocked the china doll that had been propped on the passenger seat crashing to the floor.

'You stupid bitch!' he breathed. 'Now you've really got me upset.'

*

'Hun at three o'clock!'

Young Tom Copley, a scrawny, scabby-kneed boy, with thick-lensed National Health glasses wound tightly round his ears, held both arms out wide, as he flew around the bomb-site near his house in Wapping with his best pal, Charlie Tillotson. Every shot they fired, at any German fool enough to dare invade their air space, hit home with deadly accuracy. They were the heroes of the RAF. The fad with the Olympics already forgotten, the boys, just like their comic-book favourites, had returned to their all-absorbing passion of Playing War.

'Nnnnneeeeowwww!' Tom whined down his nose as he swerved in a wide ark to confront the enemy.

Charlie, his plane imitation momentarily forgotten, pulled the pin on an invisible hand grenade and lobbed it into a German dug-out. 'Cop that, Fritzy!' he yelled, throwing himself to the ground and covering his head to protect himself from the explosion.

'Here, Charlie,' Tom called, 'come and have a look at this.' Tom held up the remains of a china doll and waved it in the air like a trophy. 'It ain't even broken or nothing. Well, not much.'

Charlie scrambled over the rubble-strewn remains of what had once been Ethel Briggs's outside lavatory to reach his friend. 'Show us here, Tom.'

'The arm's a bit cracked and one of its legs has come off, but I reckon we could fix it.'

Charlie raised his eyebrows in astonishment. 'What'd we wanna fix a doll for?'

Tom rolled his eyes and tutted at his mate's stupidity. 'So's we can sell it or something.'

'Right! Here, let's look for more treasure.'

'No,' Tom said authoritatively, 'there won't be nothing else. We've gone over this debris hundreds of times and never found it before. Someone must have dumped it last night.'

Charlie looked disappointed. 'I don't reckon you could mend it anyway.' He sulked. 'Look at the state of its hair.' Suddenly his expression changed. 'Tell you what'd be good,' he beamed, 'let's go and throw it in the river, see if it floats.'

Tom grinned back at his friend and, as if a starting pistol had just been fired, they both began running full pelt towards the lighterman's steps that led down to the Thames.

Little did the boys realise how fortunate they were not to have searched any further, or they might have found something that would have haunted them for ever: part of the left arm and the right foot of poor dead Lilly.

The rest of her, unrecognisable from the beating she had taken, was scattered about the bomb-sites of London like so much unwanted rubbish.

Book Two

Chapter 9

May 1951

'All right, Gin?' Micky Chivers called, as he closed the street door of number 11 firmly behind him.

Ginny, parking her bags on the step of number 18, looked over her shoulder and called back across the street, 'Yeah. Fine. You all right, Mick?'

Micky checked that the door was shut, stuck his hands deep into his pockets and wandered over to her, his shoulders stooped in a self-deprecating slump. Like plenty of other lads in the neighbourhood, Micky had fancied Ginny since he had been tall enough – just – to peer surreptitiously down the front of her blouse. She was a fair bit older than him of course, and she certainly wasn't like the strong-minded sort of girls he usually went for – in fact she was probably too quiet for her own good – but she was a kind, smashing-looking bird and she definitely deserved a whole lot better than the deal she got from being married to Ted Martin.

Micky had often talked to Sid about the pair of them getting hold of the no-good bastard and sorting him out once and for all, and on a couple of occasions – soon after their mum's funeral being one Micky particularly remembered – his brother had very nearly agreed. But then Sid had, as usual, calmed down and made Micky see sense, stressing what their mother had always taught them: it wasn't right to go interfering in other people's business, not unless they asked for your help and especially when it was your own sister's best mate who

181

was involved. But with Micky's temperament, it wasn't always easy for him to bite his tongue.

'So you're doing all right then, Gin?' he said with a lift of his chin.

'Yeah, not so bad, Mick.' She shrugged. 'You know.'

Micky stood next to her, leaning back against the sooty brick wall trying to look casual. He folded his arms and crossed one leg in front of the other. 'I ain't seen much of your Ted lately. Been busy, has he?'

'Yeah. He's been out and about all over the place.' She dipped her chin, hoping to conceal her flaming red cheeks. 'You know what he's like.'

'I know.'

'How's that brother of your'n getting on with his new girlfriend then?' she asked, hurriedly changing the subject.

'Dunno, Gin. Ain't seen much of him neither. As a matter of fact I don't seem to see much of no one lately. Dad's always down the Albert, or with his pals – he ain't really got over Mum yet. I don't suppose he ever will.' He hesitated, staring down at his boots. 'Nothing's really been the same indoors since . . . You know.'

'I know.' Ginny smiled ruefully as she echoed Micky's words. 'We're a right pair o' Billy-No-mates, ain't we?'

Micky nodded in superficially amused agreement. He had plenty of mates, but Ginny, she didn't seem to have anyone except Dilys, and *she* was as selfish as they come. If only he could find the words; this could be a real opportunity. Ginny might have been in her late twenties – probably even getting on for thirty if he was honest – but she was still a terrific looker, and here she was: lonely, obviously fed up and, he would lay money on it, at a loose end on a Friday night. He liked the girl he was seeing at the minute – a feisty little redhead from down the market, just his cup of tea – but surely it wouldn't hurt to put her off for just this once . . .

'So you ain't seen Dilys neither, then?' she said, interrupting his thoughts. She ran her fingers through her mop of dark-blonde curls in an easy, yet unconsciously disturbing gesture that had Micky squirming.

'No,' was all he managed.

'I'll have to try popping round the prefab again,' she said, bending down to pick up her bags in a movement that allowed him one of the tantalising glimpses down her blouse. 'I ain't seen her for nearly a fortnight and I've got some lovely little bits I bought down the Roman for Susan and all. If I don't get the chance to give them to her soon, she'll have grown out of them.'

'I've been meaning to go round to see the little 'un myself,' Micky said in a sudden moment of inspiration. 'It ain't always easy though, what with work and that. But tell you what, I could go with you now if you like. I was only on me way to have a few jars with some of the lads from down Eric Street,' he lied. 'I'm sure they won't miss me.'

Ginny heaved the shopping further up her arm and sighed the sigh of a woman whose time was not her own. 'That'd have been smashing, Mick, but if I don't get indoors and do you-know-who's tea, there'll be murders. And I've got a few jobs to do an' all. I dunno when I could get away.'

'I heard that!' came a gruff holler from the other side of the door of number 18. 'You leave me in here starving to bloody death, while you're out there sodding gabbing about going to see your mates. What're things coming to in this house, eh? You tell me that.'

Ginny rolled her eyes. 'All right, Nell, I'm coming.'

She flashed Micky a radiant smile that had his hopes rising and his toes curling. 'I'll have to go, Mick. Even though the old trout knows I've queued up all me bloody dinner hour to get her tea for her, she still ain't grateful.' She chuckled wearily. 'But what's a girl to do, eh? If I don't look after her, who will?'

Micky shook his head in bemused admiration. 'You put up with too much I reckon, Gin.'

She shrugged. 'Not really, I just like a quiet life. Look, I'm gonna try and nip round Dilys's later on, when I've finished seeing to Nellie and that. I dunno when that'll be. But give her and Susan my love, will you, Mick? And tell them I'll be round later.'

'Look, Gin, come to think of it, I'd better not go now. It's my mates, see. They'll be expecting me, won't they?'

'You go and enjoy yourself, Mick. Go on.' She leaned forward and gave him a conspiratorial wink. 'But you know, I reckon even I deserve a bit of time off for good behaviour. So maybe you can be me gallant escort round there some other time, eh?'

Micky grinned at her like a fool. 'Yeah?'

She smiled and ruffled his hair as though he was still a little kid, completely unaware of the effect of her touch on him. 'It's a date.'

Levering himself away from the wall, Micky strode along Bailey Street towards Grove Road, whistling away as if he'd just won the coconut.

'Dilys?' Ginny shielded her eyes with her hand and peered through the prefab window, then she stretched across and rapped hard on the door frame with her knuckles.

She knew that nine o'clock in the evening wasn't the usual time that Dilys would expect her to call, but surely not even Dilys, a woman who could sleep perched on a clothes-line without so much as a dolly peg to keep her

184

attached, would be asleep at this time of night. And Ginny was sure she could hear the wireless playing.

After what felt like a good ten minutes of calling and knocking, the door suddenly opened.

It was Susan. She stood there in her grubby little nightdress, with her hair in tangles, clutching the teddy bear that Ginny had bought her last Christmas. She looked as though she had been crying. Was that the noise Ginny had heard?

'Hello, Auntie Gin,' she said, her tone unusually wary.

'Hello, babe!' Ginny bent down and scooped the four-year-old up in her arms, trying not to sound worried. 'Let me have a good look at my best girl.'

Susan's bottom lip quivered as she peered at Ginny through tear-dampened lashes. 'Mummy said I wasn't to open the door while she was out. I didn't know what to do.'

Ginny frowned. 'Mummy's out?'

Before Susan had the chance to explain, Ginny felt someone poke her hard on the shoulder. She spun round, expecting to see Dilys standing there, holding a pint of milk she'd gone and borrowed from a neighbour, or maybe a packet of fags from the pub up by Stepney Green station, but instead she saw a stern-looking woman in her forties dressed in the housewife's uniform of cross-over apron and cotton headscarf tightly knotted into a turban.

'I've seen you round here before,' the woman said sharply. 'Friend of her'n, are you?'

Ginny simulated a smile for the hatchet-faced woman. 'I'm sorry,' she said politely, hugging Susan to her shoulder, 'do I know you?'

'I'm her neighbour, ain't I.' The woman said the word 'her' as though it were an insult of the worst kind. 'I'm Milly Barrington. She might have mentioned me.'

'No. I don't think so.'

'In my day women cared for their kiddies. They didn't only give 'em a wash when they was expecting visitors. And they certainly didn't go gallivanting around clubs in cocktail frocks every night of the bloody week.'

'Look here, Mrs Ba—' Ginny tried to interject, but the woman was in full flight.

'And all that old toffee about her old man copping it out East in the war.' She snorted disdainfully. 'I ain't never heard so much old fanny in all my life. She ain't never even had no old man, if you ask me. I know a trollop when I see one. And I know a married man when I see one an' all.'

She flashed a look over her shoulder as though checking for eavesdroppers, then nodded knowingly at Ginny, narrowing her eyes for emphasis. 'There's this one feller what comes round here at all sorts of funny hours. I've seen him. And I know his sort and all, believe you me. Dark-haired, really good-looking type of a bloke he is. Always got nice ironed shirts – that's a sure sign they're married. And drives a right flashy car an' all. If I wasn't a decent sort of a woman, I'm telling you, I'd . . .'

The woman was still droning on and on but Ginny was no longer listening. A sensation of sickness had flooded her throat. Dark-haired, she'd said. Good-looking. Flash car. No. She'd been through all this in her mind a hundred times before. It was just jealousy making her think the worst. It had to be. Ted not being around most of the time and her having to try to make ends meet and putting up with Nelly, it had driven her to thinking all sorts of crazy things. After all, there must be plenty of good-looking blokes with flashy cars. Of course it wasn't him. But if she didn't pull herself together she'd end up going round the bloody bend and winding up in Banstead.

'Look, Mrs Barrington,' Ginny broke abruptly into the woman's monologue, 'I dunno why you think any of this is your business, but I'm here to look after Susan now, so if you don't mind I'll take her inside and get her into bed.'

With that, Ginny stepped inside the prefab, with Susan held tightly against her, and shut the door firmly in Milly Barrington's flabbergasted face.

Ginny smoothed the eiderdown under Susan's chin, kissed the sleeping child gently on the forehead and tiptoed from the bedroom.

By the time she had moved the few feet along the hall and into the front room, she was trembling with rage. If Dilys had been there, she would happily have throttled her with her bare hands. Whatever had got into her, leaving Susan alone like that? And in such a state. The poor little love was filthy.

After Ginny had washed and changed her; it had taken her almost two hours to reassure her that she wasn't going to be abandoned again.

But from what she had gathered from Dilys's big-mouthed, nosy parker of a neighbour, it was no wonder she was nervous – it obviously wasn't the first time she had been shut in the prefab all alone with nothing but her teddy for company and a warning not to answer the door. Dilys was lucky no one had called the welfare people out.

Why hadn't she asked her to sit with Susan? She knew Ginny was always only too pleased to spend time with her – well, whenever she could get away she was. But then again, if that Barrington woman was telling the truth, it sounded as though Dilys was up to all sorts and probably wanted to keep her gallivanting to herself.

Guilt and anger rose up in Ginny's throat until it nearly choked her; she thought of herself back in Bailey Street, pandering to Nellie just so she could have a bit of peace and quiet from her moaning, while all the time little Susan was here, huddled up in her bed, alone and terrified. She'd have to try and find a way to see her more; Nellie would just have to lump it.

Ginny felt the tears prick her eyes. If it wasn't for her, Susan probably wouldn't know what being loved was all about.

She flopped down on to one of the burgundy uncut-moquette armchairs that one of Dilys's mysterious 'friends' had come up with – part of a three-piece suite that made Ginny's furniture look as shabby and drab as the gear they'd made do with down in the air-raid shelters – lit herself a cigarette and sat smoking in the darkness, waiting for Dilys to come home.

She stifled a yawn and reached, yet again, for her cigarettes.

At least it was a Friday night and she wouldn't have to get up for work in the morning, she thought to herself, as she watched the shadows of people walking home from the local pubs flickering past the windows. It must be chucking-out time, but there was still no sign of bloody Dilys. Where the hell was she? She was going to give her a piece of her mind when she eventually decided to show her face. Not that she'd take any notice.

Dilys never took notice of anyone; even when they'd been kids at school she'd always got her own way, and whenever she'd caused trouble it was always someone else who got blamed by the teacher. Maybe if Dilys had been brought up in number 18 Nellie would have been a match for her . . .

Nellie. Going home to face her was another bloody nightmare to look forward to. Despite the fact that Ginny now tried to ignore her as far as was humanly possible, the thought of the ear-bashing she knew she had to look forward to when she eventually got back to Bailey Street made her groan out loud. And if Ted had decided to come home for once she'd really be in for it.

From the look of things, she wouldn't be getting back there this side of midnight. That was if Dilys actually condescended to come home at all.

Ginny was shocked out of her musings by what sounded like someone trying to break in. She was immediately on the alert, her protective instincts towards Susan making her grab the poker from the companion set and stand there poised, ready to strike any intruder fool enough to try and invade the home of the child she was there to protect.

The tautness in Ginny's body relaxed, and she let out a relieved sigh, as she recognised the voice cursing the stupidity of the street doorkey and the even stupider lock.

Ginny made a dash for the hall to put a stop to all the noise before it woke Susan. 'Dilys!' Ginny hissed through the letter-box. 'That *is* you?'

'Who the fuck d'you think it is?' Dilys hissed back. 'Sodding Lady Docker?'

As Ginny straightened up she winced; while Dilys might never have had what could be called a dainty mouth, her language lately would have made a sailor blush.

There was more fumbling and rattling.

'Here, Ginny,' Dilys said, more loudly this time. 'What

you doing round here this time of night? And why ain't you got the poxy light on? I can't see a bastard—'

Ginny jumped clear as the door flew back on its hinges, the lights suddenly blazed and Dilys fell into the hall at her feet.

The combined stench of booze, stale cigarette smoke and too much expensive French perfume was stifling.

Ginny had planned to have a go at Dilys, to demand to know exactly what she thought she was up to, but she decided that could wait until later; for now, the best course of action was to humour her. Much as she wanted to bring up the subject of Susan being left alone, the last thing she wanted was for Dilys to start hollering and hooting – she had a voice on her like a foghorn in a peasouper at the best of times, never mind when she was half cut. And Susan had already had more than enough upset for one day without hearing her mother's drunken screeching.

'Your neighbour said you'd had to pop out,' Ginny said, following Dilys as she staggered her faltering way into the sitting-room.

'Neighbour?' asked Dilys, clinging to the sideboard for support as she twisted round to confront Ginny through puffy, red-rimmed eyes. 'What sodding neighbour?'

'Milly Barrington.'

'Her, the nosy bastard.' There was real venom in Dilys's voice. 'If she didn't have a face like the back of a trolleybus maybe she'd have a bit of a life of her own and stop sticking her oar in where it's not wanted.'

Dilys's attention, never having much in the way of a span at the best of times, wandered from her neighbour to the more immediate, and therefore more graspable, question of Ginny. 'Did I ask you round or something?' she asked, dropping down on to the sofa.

Ginny shook her head sheepishly and perched herself

on the edge of one of the armchairs. 'No . . .' she said slowly. 'Not exactly. See, I was just . . .'

This was ridiculous. Dilys always did this to her: *she* wasn't the one who was in the wrong, yet here she was, ready to apologise. Well, she was damned if she was going to, not this time.

'Look, Dilys, I think you've gotta start thinking about other people.' She nearly said 'thinking about Susan' but immediately thought better of it; the point of this wasn't to provoke a row. 'See, while *you* might be all right – and I'm pleased for you that you are – you probably haven't noticed, but things haven't been exactly easy for most of the rest of us.'

Dilys didn't appear to be getting the point at all, so Ginny decided to elaborate – but still without actually mentioning her worries about Susan being left alone and her fears that she was a little girl growing up without knowing a mother's love.

'Out there,' Ginny began cautiously, waving vaguely towards the window, as she stalled for time, trying to think out what she should be saying. 'In the real world like.'

Dilys nodded towards Ginny's cigarettes and wordlessly held out her hand.

Ginny took one for herself then threw the packet and her box of matches into Dilys's lap.

Dilys lit one and settled back on the sofa to study the smoke as she blew it down her nostrils.

'You see, Dil, the thing is, there's a lot of problems for everyone at the minute. What with the meat ration being cut again. And all the shortages and everything. And the terrible weather we had all winter, and the price of coal and coke. I mean, blimey, it's enough to get anyone down. And that's without all this stuff you hear on the wireless about what's going on with this Korea lark. I mean, that's enough to scare the pants off you, innit? Especially with these bombs they've got now. So it's obvious we all need a bit of fun.'

'That it? You finished?' Dilys picked a strand of tobacco from her lip, examined it, then flicked it on to the half-moon-shaped hearthrug.

'I suppose so.'

'Well, Ginny,' she said, with a loud yawn, 'I ain't got a sodding clue what you're on about, except that last bit, that bit about needing a bit of fun.' Resting her elbow on the arm of the sofa, she fluffed her fingers through her thick, dark, wavy hair and frowned from the effort of thinking straight. 'So why don't *you* shut your moaning gob, go out and have a few laughs and stop coming round here and giving me sodding earache?'

Ginny gulped. *Stop coming round here.* That's what she'd said. If Dilys had meant it, then she wouldn't be able to see Susan. And Dilys could be so pig-headed; once she'd made up her mind about something there was no shifting her. Ginny had to put it right before it was too late.

'You're right as usual, Dil,' she said, pasting on a smile. 'I always did take things too seriously. You always said so. Tell you what, I was thinking about going over the river, to see that Festival of Britain thing. Everyone's saying how good it is. Fancy coming?'

Dilys opened her eyes wide and puffed in astonishment. 'You trying to have a laugh? No thanks. I've got better things to do with me time than hanging around poxy concert halls.'

'But there's a lot more to see than that. There's—'

'You ain't got a clue, Gin.' She belched loudly. 'You understand nothing. My feller likes me always to be here.' She stabbed her finger towards the floor. 'Ready and waiting. Available like. And I ain't gonna go upsetting a bloke what keeps me so nice, now am I? I mean, look at this place. It's a little palace.' She took in the messy, but well-furnished room, with a sweep of her arm. 'So if he wants to go out, I'm here, all done up, ready to hook my arm through his and make him proud of me.'

Ginny leapt in: 'You know I'll always come round to mind the little 'un, don't you, Dil? I know how hard it must be, to be on your own with a kiddie.'

Dilys curled her lip in an unattractive snarl. 'Aw yeah? And how would you know what it's like to have a kid? You threw away your chance of being a mother. Round Jeannie Thompson's. Remember?'

Ginny lowered her chin. She took a deep breath to swallow away the pain, then said in a low monotone. 'I could take Susan to the Festival if you like. I bet she'd love the Pleasure Gardens.'

Dilys didn't answer, instead she rose shakily to her feet and stumbled across the room, her tight dress and her unsteady gait accentuating her sensuous curves. 'Fancy a drink? I've got a few bottles in the kitchen.'

Biting back what she wanted to say, Ginny said quietly, 'Just a small one. Ta.'

Dilys paused in the doorway and twisted round to face Ginny. 'Me boyfriend gets the booze for me,' she said, then added with a flash of her eyebrows and her voice heavy with innuendo, 'he gets me all sorts.'

She wobbled out of the room, intending to go to the kitchen but somehow, losing her train of thought, she wound up in the lavatory.

She pulled down her expensive imported silk knickers and sat down on the wooden seat – the novelty of having a warm, indoor, fully-plumbed-in bathroom forgotten already – and thought about Ginny's offer to look after Susan while she went out.

As far as Dilys was concerned, the more chances she had to be shot of the demanding little madam, the better; she was always wanting something. A drink, or food, or clean clothes. It drove Dilys to distraction. She was four and a half years old and was still as much of a nuisance as she'd been when she was a baby. But, despite her drunken state, Dilys could still focus on why she had to resist the temptation of having someone looking after the kid for her: Susan was getting older, she was seeing things. Noticing things. Asking questions. Dilys couldn't risk her blowing the gaff. She'd already had to threaten her not to open her whining gob to Ted about being left at home by herself, and to say that nice Auntie Milly was coming round to sit with her. What he'd have to say if he knew Susan was alone, or worse still, that she was being left alone with Ginny, Dilys could only imagine. He'd warned her enough times: if Ginny was there, Dilys had to be there too, to mind what the kid said, because he'd told her, if Susan ever let on to Ginny about him always being round at the prefab . . .

Dilys pulled the chain and sighed. If it was up to her, she would have told Ginny about her and Ted *herself*, and let her stick that in her pipe and smoke it, but she knew Ted wouldn't have it. He still wanted her around the place to look after Nellie. And if she ever did find out about Ted and her, Dilys reckoned that even a right mug like Ginny would be off like a shot.

Because that's all she was, a bloody mug. Ted didn't even bother to give her any money any more, let alone presents like he used to. She worked her fingers to the bone in that shitty factory all day, then ran round after a mother-in-law who couldn't give a toss about her. Dilys wouldn't put up with that sort of bollocks from anyone. Well, from anyone but Ted. He was different, he was worth it. He treated her all right – most of the time – but she knew just how far she could go with him; and what she'd get if she started upsetting things.

She stood up, smoothed down her skirt, belched once again, then started giggling. Living in Bailey Street with Nellie wasn't exactly the life that that dozy mare Ginny had dreamed about when they were a pair of wide-eyed, open-mouthed kids sitting in the front row of the pictures. Some flipping Scarlett O'Hara she'd turned out to be!

In the sitting-room, Ginny heard the lavatory cistern flush and, a few minutes later, she watched Dilys return with two glasses and an almost full bottle of port.

'Well, what d'you think?' Ginny asked pleasantly.

'Eh?'

'About me taking Susan to the Festival.'

Dilys shook her head. 'No. I don't think so.'

The look of disappointment on Ginny's face actually made Dilys feel a bit sorry for her. Ginny really didn't have much of a life now, not if all she had to excite her was the thought of taking a kid out for the day.

And to think Dilys had once actually been jealous of her and her pretty blonde looks. Now she was as dingy and as badly dressed as all the other idiots who didn't know how to get hold of a bit of gear, or who had no one interested enough to buy it for them.

'Why don't you ask Nellie to go with you?' she asked, more out of pity than as a genuine suggestion, as she handed Ginny the glasses and poured them both a full measure of the dark ruby wine.

Ginny stared up at Dilys as though she'd gone stark raving mad. 'Have you taken leave of your senses, Dil? I'd rather go with old Florrie's bulldog, and you know how that bugger stinks.'

Dilys threw back her head and burst into loud, drunken laughter.

Despite her earlier anger, Ginny couldn't help joining in with her. In fact her whole body shook with great sobs and gulps of laughter. It was as though she was releasing herself from all her pain, from all her loneliness and from her unspoken fear that life was rapidly passing her by.

Dilys, her moment of guilt about her supposed friend's plight forgotten as suddenly as it had arrived, smirked as Ginny wiped the tears of almost hysterical laughter from her eyes.

She chucked Ginny roughly under the chin. 'We don't have to worry about you, do we, Gin? You can go on your own. I mean, you should be used to it by now.'

Ginny turned her head; she didn't want Dilys to see the now bitter tears spilling down her cheeks.

They were right, Ginny decided: the Festival of Britain, with its pavilions and halls sparkling and gleaming on the South Bank site, where, just a short time before, a mass of Blitz-blown rubble had stuck out like an ugly scar, was indeed a miracle of achievement. A genuine, there-it-was-in-front-of-your-face miracle. Dreams really did come true.

Despite her disappointment at not having been allowed to bring Susan, Ginny was completely caught up in the wonders surrounding her. She felt just like Dorothy in *The Wizard of Oz*; as though she had left behind the black-and-white existence of the past and had entered the future, a world of glorious Technicolor. Never before had she seen anything like it.

She walked around the Festival, amongst the bustling crowds, her every sense aroused. Even the jostling was part of the fun. She smiled at other people's happy chatter, joined in with their gasps of astonishment and echoed their exclamations of delight. She marvelled with them at the Dome of Discovery; shared their appreciative laughter every time she heard the same old joke that the amazing Skylon symbol hovering high in the air was 'like Britain, because it had no visible means of support'; and even felt a genuine, if surrogate, pleasure as she watched dewy-eyed couples dancing in the open air as though they were part of a film made in a far sunnier place than England.

Although she had no partner to dance with, Ginny didn't feel so alone any longer, she was part of something big and important. It felt like being a child caught up in the wonder of Christmas and towards the end of her day at the Festival she determined that somehow, no matter what it took, she would persuade Dilys to let her bring Susan along to see it all. She had to share this with her.

Then, as she was taking one last look at her favourite part of the whole Festival, she heard someone say something so shocking, it threatened to bring it all tumbling down around her. She felt as though she'd been smacked full in the face with a wet kipper.

There she was, in the pavilion designed to show 'contemporary living created by and for the British family of today' – contemporary! that was the style she wanted, what a wonderful word! – admiring the fantastic kitchen that made even Dilys's smart little prefab look dowdy, when she overheard the most astonishing conversation.

'Honestly, Shirley, will you just look at it,' sighed a tall, slim, elegant woman who, despite the warm May afternoon was wearing a luxuriously thick fur wrap draped around the shoulders of her beautifully cut emerald-green shantung two-piece costume. 'They should be ashamed of themselves, trying to fool people into thinking that these goods are something special.'

'Well, Leila,' her similarly elegant, though slightly less

glamorous, companion sighed back in an equally bored tone, 'I suppose some people aren't used to the finer things of life.'

Ginny was furious. She hated snobs at the best of times, but ones who didn't seem to care if they spoiled what had been the best day she could remember in years were enough to raise her usually mild temperament dangerously close to boiling point.

'Excuse me,' she said as politely as her dry mouth would allow, 'but I think you're wrong. I think this kitchen's lovely. It's all right for the likes of you. You can probably have anything you want, whenever you want it. But people like me dream about having something like this one day.'

The woman who had been referred to as Leila looked Ginny up and down with an unashamedly appraising eye, taking in every inch of her from her neatly polished but shabby shoes to her naturally pretty but home-trimmed hair. 'So could you, sweetie, if you knew how to go about it,' she said with an amused lift to her smoothly cultured voice.

'Leila!' her friend hissed. 'You're not going to start, are you?'

'Don't be such a fusspot, Shirley.' Leila smiled at Ginny, showing white, even teeth. 'The name's Harvey,' she said, extending her gloved hand. 'Leila Harvey. And this miserable person is my friend, Shirley Truman. Fancy a little drink?'

Ginny, completely taken aback to be asked to accompany such stylish, well-to-do women, didn't know how to reply.

'My treat, darling,' purred Leila, 'and you can tell me all about these dreams of yours.'

Ginny was mesmerised by the woman's easy, confident manner. She thought for another moment then, almost before she realised what she was doing, replied impulsively, 'I'd really love one. In fact, I'm gasping. And as for a sit-down, well, I could murder one of them an' all. Me feet are steaming like saveloys in an urn. But I dunno what the chances are.'

Shirley's eyes rolled at the vulgar turn of phrase, but Ginny didn't notice, she was too busy trying to control the urge to ask Leila where she got her handbag from – it was real crocodile, Ginny would have laid money on it, just like the ones Ted had brought home that time, beautifully made and reeking of quality. He had unloaded them up West in no time, probably to husbands or boyfriends of women just like Leila.

She could see the bags now, as Ted stuffed them into the gloryhole under the stairs in Bailey Street. He had offered Ginny one for herself, said she *deserved* a little treat, but she had refused, thinking it far too nice for the likes of her. She could even remember the day; it was less than a month after all her family had been buried and Ted was still being really nice to her, and somehow crocodile bags had always made her feel cared for, loved. It was a feeling she missed.

She suddenly realised that Leila was staring at her in expectation. Her cheeks flamed.

'I'm not quite with you, sweetie. Would you like to join us for a drink? Or not?' Leila asked.

'Yeah, but, you see,' Ginny stammered, stabbing her thumb over her shoulder in the direction of the exotic Regency Tea Pavilion, 'I tried getting in for a cuppa just now, before I started making me way home like, thought I could do with a bit of a reviver, but there was queues like you'd never believe.'

Leila turned to Shirley and grinned broadly. 'Isn't she a poppet!'

Twisting back to face Ginny, she flashed her expertly

made-up eyes. 'I meant a proper drink. For God's sake, it must be six o'clock soon, I feel like I've been here for absolutely hours. So. Time for cocktails, don't you think?'

Riding in the taxi back across the river with Leila and Shirley made Ginny think again about how it had once been with Ted. He had sometimes hailed taxis for them after they'd been out for the evening, had enjoyed splashing his money about. But that was a long time ago; a time when she hadn't had to fret constantly about making ends meet. She'd never experienced quite the style of these two of course, but she certainly hadn't had to worry about things in the way she did now.

Ginny's stomach lurched and her hand went to the run in her stocking, as the taxi drew to a halt outside an impressive-looking, white stucco hotel, hidden away at the end of a quiet Mayfair side-street.

'I've never been round here before,' whispered Ginny as they sat down at a highly polished table, the feet of which were sunk deep into the thick pile of a sumptuous dark-blue carpet. She wasn't sure why she was whispering but it seemed appropriate; maybe it was because the church in Limehouse where she and Ted had been married, and the picture palace in the Commercial Road, were the only similarly opulent places she had ever visited – and in those places you had to keep your voice down.

'Haven't you, sweetie?' said Leila, dropping her wrap carelessly over the back of her chair. 'I'm thinking about buying myself a little flat near here, actually. Security for my old age.'

Deliberately ignoring Shirley's desperate signals to keep quiet, Leila took a cigarette from her handbag and screwed it into what Ginny was sure was a real gold holder.

As Ginny watched, fascinated by the poise of her every movement, she was suddenly distracted by the appearance of a dark-suited man behind Shirley's chair.

'Good evening, mesdames,' the softly spoken man said, with a bob of his head. 'May I fetch you something?'

Conscious of how dowdy she must have looked compared with the other two, Ginny screwed herself down into her seat, trying to hide her threadbare skirt and tatty stockings under the table.

'Three champagne cocktails, Richard,' Leila said without even consulting the other two. She lifted her chin, treated him to a flap of her lashes and a dazzling smile, then turned her beam on Ginny. 'How about a little bite of something?'

Ginny was in shock at the thought of champagne cocktails. How could she think about food? But she had to say something, she couldn't just sit there like a dummy in a shop window. She was scared of how her voice was going to sound. Coughing loudly into her hand to fill the silence, she nodded vigorously and peered wide-eyed at her hostess through her fingers. 'Can I have some crisps?' she eventually managed to croak. 'If that's all right.'

Leila laughed delightedly and addressed the waiter without turning to face him. 'You can arrange some crisps for the lady, can't you, Richard?'

'Of course, madam.'

'Good. And some smoked-salmon sandwiches. Enough for three.'

For some reason, no matter how Ginny wrestled with the crisp packet, the blue twist of salt would not come out of the corner of the bag, but now she had started trying to salvage the damned thing she couldn't show herself up by giving in.

'Here, let me.'

Ginny watched, horrified, as Leila dipped her flawlessly manicured finger into the contaminating grease of the fried potatoes and hooked out the little blue twist for her.

Handing the crisps back to Ginny, she wiped her fingers delicately on a lace-trimmed handkerchief, took a sip from her drink and smiled. 'So, tell me, what do you do?' She half closed her eyes and regarded Ginny closely. 'Don't tell me. You stay at home and look after some man?'

'No. Well, yes, I do.' When he's there, she thought but didn't say. Despite his neglect and cruelty, Ginny still couldn't bring herself to be disloyal to Ted. 'But I work as well.'

Leila flashed an amused eyebrow at Shirley, as much as to say, you're not the only one, dear. Shirley frowned with disapproval and gave a barely perceptible shake of her head.

Leila smiled reassuringly at her companion, pushed the plate of untouched sandwiches towards her, then returned her attention to Ginny. 'Now what sort of work do you do, I wonder.'

'I work in a factory. On the assembly line.'

Shirley rolled her eyes in boredom, lifted her glass to her lips and knocked her cocktail back in a single hit. 'Fancy another?' she asked resignedly.

Leila nodded. 'Thank you. I don't mind if I do.'

While Shirley spoke to the waiter and silently drank her way through several refills, Leila concentrated on finding out more about Ginny Martin.

It took her less than half an hour, and a few little

snippets about herself thrown in by way of reward, to gain a pretty accurate picture of Ginny's life.

She studied Ginny's flushed cheeks as she drained yet another glass.

Ginny was feeling wonderful. 'So you come here all the time then,' she chirped. 'I can't imagine what that must be like.' She shook her head in wonder.

It was a big mistake; unused to drinking very much, and definitely unused to knocking back four champagne cocktails one after the other, Ginny came over quite giddy.

Holding on to the edge of the table she levered herself to her feet. 'I've just gotta go to the lav,' she explained.

Leila pointed to a door in the corner. 'Over there, sweetie.'

As Ginny made her way across the room, Shirley leaned across the table. 'For Christ's sake, Leila, she'll get us thrown out.'

Leila sighed theatrically and took her time preparing another cigarette before replying, 'Stop going on, Shirley.'

'But why're you doing this? I know you and how bored you get, and that you like to amuse yourself, but why her? Why risk it?'

'She reminds me of me a few years ago.'

'You?'

'I'm telling you. She's one of us. She wants something more than she's got and it's killing her. You can just smell it on her.'

'Don't be ridiculous. All she is, is a quiet little drudge working in some God-awful factory, with no past, no future, no nothing. Except some old hag of a mother-in-law to torture her.'

'You're wrong. I can spot it a mile off.' Leila blew a cloud of lavender smoke above Shirley's head and watched as it curled up towards the elaborately decorated plaster-work ceiling. 'And you know the governor's always ready to pay a bonus for introducing new girls, especially if they're as pretty as her. And if they've got a brain as well, then—'

'Brain? Her? All right, I grant you, she's got a decent sort of face, but—'

Leila's face grew dark. 'Not jealous of her because she's younger than you, are you, Shirley?'

'Young? From what she said, she's got to be in her late twenties.'

'I'm sure you're right. But even you have got to admit she doesn't look it. Her skin's perfect. And with that body I'd lay money she's never had a child. And, if she works on it, she's got that sophisticated look that the foreign punters really go for. And with those big eyes. Come on, be honest, what do you really think? Am I right?'

Before Shirley could reply, Leila hissed through her teeth, 'That's enough, Shirley, there's a good girl. She's coming back.'

As Ginny slipped back into her seat Leila was all smiles again. 'Everything all right?'

'Yeah, not half. I had a bit of a wash and now I'm smashing.' She shielded her mouth with her hand and confided, 'You should see that lav. I ain't never seen nothing like it, even in the films. Imagine having a place like that to use whenever you fancied.'

'You could have a nice place, Ginny. If you wanted it badly enough.' Leila flashed a look at Shirley, warning her to keep her mouth shut.

Ginny's face puckered into a shy smile. 'You mustn't laugh, but I have this dream when I've got this really lovely place, with this great big staircase.' She dropped her chin. 'You'll think I'm daft.'

'No we won't, will we, Shirley?'

'No,' said Shirley flatly.

'It's just like Scarlett's house: Tara, from—'

'*Gone With the Wind*,' Leila finished for her.

'That's right!'

Leila acknowledged Ginny's admiration with a little shrug. 'So, where do you live now?'

Ginny turned her head away. 'You won't have heard of it.'

'Don't be so sure.' Leila giggled girlishly for Ginny's benefit, as she peered with steely resolve at Shirley across the top of her glass.

'I come', Ginny said with slow deliberation, 'from a place called Bailey Street.'

'Near the Roman eh, darling?' Leila grinned. 'Know it well.'

The difference in Leila's accent – from West End to East End in a single sentence – had Ginny boggling. 'But the way you were talking about the kitchen back at the Festival. And the way you're dressed '

'I have to admit', Leila said, her accent slipping effortlessly back to her previously haughty tones, 'I was saying those things for effect.' She lowered her voice to a breathy whisper as she leaned closer to Ginny. 'Did you notice that posh old chap standing behind Shirley? The one with the RAF moustaches? The one who was pretending to look at the electric gadgets?'

Ginny thought for a moment, then nodded.

'Well, I knew different. I knew exactly what he was looking at. In fact, I thought he was going to explode, the way his eyes were bulging as he was clocking my tits!'

Ginny suppressed a gasp. She was going mad.

Leila draped herself back into her chair. 'But I did mean what I said back there at the Festival. There are better kitchens than that to be had. Much better. That stuff's meant for the plebs. I've been in places that'd make you cry they're so beautiful. And I intend to have a place just like them.' As she spoke, Leila's eyes shone. 'The place I've got now is already quite something, but when I get *my* Swedish kitchen put in the flat I'm going to buy, it's going to be hand-made. Custom-built. Exquisite. Just for me. And as for the way I'm dressed, well, it's exactly the same. You just have to know the right places. Good shops. Good dressmakers.' She paused for effect, smoothing her hands down her emerald-silk-covered thighs. 'And you need a bit of style and a right sort of shape to go with it, of course. That's how you interest the right sort of gentlemen.'

She looked at the tiny face of her gold watch, reached out and tapped Ginny playfully on the end of the nose, then picked up her bag. 'Come on, sweetie, let's find ourselves a taxi, and while we're driving you home, I'm going to tell you a story.'

'So that's it, that's all there is to tell.' Leila ducked her head to catch a fleeting glimpse through the taxi window of the tall, shadowy buildings of the London Hospital – the hospital that could have saved her mother; the hospital that had been just around the corner from the slum where her mother had died giving birth to her, because she couldn't afford the few shillings for the local handy-woman, never mind the three quid for the quack doctor who earned his gin money 'seeing to' the local working girls. That was a part of her story, like so many others, that no one would ever know.

'The top and the bottom of it, Ginny, is that I was poor once,' she went on, 'and now I'm not. And, believe me, not is better. Don't look so shocked. What's the difference between what we do and in you being nice to the coalman for a sack of nutty slack when your old man

206

hasn't bothered to leave you any money to heat the house again?'

Ginny's head felt fuzzy with drink. She couldn't remember telling this woman anything about Ted. But she must have done. 'I'm not shocked—'

'No?' Shirley interjected.

'No. And whatever I said about Ted I never had to be nice to no coalman.'

'I'm not saying you did. But whatever you said about Ted was the truth, wasn't it?' Leila coaxed her. 'He's left you and his mother in the lurch.'

'Well, yeah, sort of. But I've never been with no one else. Never. Not even in the war.'

'Who said anything about "going" with anybody?' Leila, quick to recover the ground she'd nearly lost, squeezed Ginny's arm reassuringly. 'Silly girl. I was simply giving an example about keeping someone company.' She laughed brightly. 'You make it sound as though we're on the game!'

Ginny clambered out of the cab on the corner of Grove Road. She was sure that was where she was, because she could make out the lights and the outline of what definitely looked like Mile End station.

'You've got the address?' Leila called to her through the open window.

Ginny nodded dumbly and, by way of proof, waved the piece of paper that Leila had given her. As she did so, she wondered at the strange, yet magical, day she had spent, but also how on earth she was going to set about cooking Nellie's tea when she could barely see straight.

She was still waving feebly as the taxi pulled away from the kerb.

Shirley fell back into her seat in a heap; her lips pursed

as though she'd been sucking lemons. 'I thought you said she was one of us.'

'She will be,' said Leila, checking her face in her compact mirror. 'As soon as she puts on a bit of slap and a bit more colour in that hair of hers. Really blondes it up – platinum would look good with her eyes. And when she learns how to speak a bit more softly in front of the clients, of course. As though she's got a bit of class rather than being just another little tart on the make.'

Shirley sighed; she felt exhausted, definitely not ready for the night's work she had in front of her. Wrapping one silk-stockinged leg over the other, she eyed her ankles with despair. She was sure they were getting thicker by the day. It wasn't fair, she didn't feel a day older than when, as an *almost* innocent seventeen-year-old, she had found herself alone and hungry in Greek Street and had let a nice man buy her dinner. Yet here she was, what felt like barely two minutes later, with a head full of grey hair that had to be tinted every single week and a body that seemed determined to give out on her. And with bloody younger women muscling in on her patch. It was a bit of luck the clubs were so dingily lit, and that she had her few special talents, or she wouldn't have stood a chance.

Leila snapped her compact shut. 'When she turns up—'

'*If* she turns up,' Shirley snarled.

'When she turns up,' Leila repeated without a blink. 'I'll talk to her about her hair and make-up.'

'It's going to take a bit more than a bottle of Hiltone to get that one working,' Shirley spat nastily.

Leila, noticing the driver ogling her in his rear-view mirror, smiled seductively. 'Don't you be too sure,' she said. Then, deliberately dropping her compact, she bent down and whispered up to Shirley from the taxi floor, 'Play our cards right, girl, and this cab ride's for free.'

Chapter 10

Ginny stared at her reflection in the little mirror over the sink. It was a long time since she'd done more than swipe a quick stroke of lipstick across her mouth and she was worried that the mascara, powder and rouge she'd put on were a bit too much.

She let out a long, slow breath and glanced at the clock – five to nine. Damn! Well, it was too late to worry about make-up now, if she didn't leave soon she probably never would, and anyway, looking on the bright side, maybe her sooty eyes and peachy pink cheeks would take the attention away from the old-fashioned floral frock that, after a thorough search of her meagre wardrobe, was the best she could come up with.

With far more determination than she actually felt, Ginny twisted round and offered Nellie a bright, confident smile – anything to stop her mother-in-law asking any more of the awkward questions she'd been firing at her all day. 'So, Nell, like I said, as it's the first time I've done this late shift, I ain't sure what time I'll be back exactly.'

Nellie stared at Ginny through narrowed eyes. 'You're a bit done up, ain't you?'

'How d'you mean?'

'For the factory. You look more like you're going on the stage.'

Ginny gave a brittle, unconvincingly carefree laugh. 'I had to make a bit of effort, Nell, didn't I? I'll be working with all new girls and I don't wanna scare 'em.'

'And how come you're on this late shift all of a sudden? You never even mentioned it till this morning.'

Ginny's patience with Nellie's cross-examination was wearing very thin and her nerve was threatening to give out. 'I told you: lates pay a lot more than the day or evening shifts. So we'll have more money to spend on ourselves.'

'How much more?'

Ginny shrugged and puffed out her cheeks as she fished around for a likely answer. 'Awwwww . . .' she finally came up with, 'plenty, I reckon.' Another false laugh. 'Enough to buy us both fags and to take you down the Albert for a few, anyway.'

Nellie digested the information in silence.

'Well, I'll better be off, or I'll be getting the push on me first night. And that wouldn't do now, would it? So I'll see you later, Nell, and don't bother to waste the electric, leaving the light on for me.'

With that, Ginny bobbed her head and kissed Nellie's crêpey cheek, grabbed her bag from the table and made a dash for the street door before her nerve really did give out and she changed her mind.

Nellie listened for her to shut the door behind her. 'That's funny, you working nights,' she said to herself, as she rubbed her face free of every trace of her daughter-in-law's kiss. 'According to Florrie's girl, they don't let women work no later than the twilight shift at your place. And that don't start at ten; that's when it finishes.' She sniffed loudly. 'Never try and kid a kidder, you stupid little cow.'

When Ginny arrived at the address Leila had given her – a place in Frith Street, a busy thoroughfare in the heart of Soho, linking Shaftesbury Avenue with Soho Square itself – she was trembling. But she wasn't cold. She was shaking from the ordeal of having walked along streets where she'd been propositioned by men in doorways, had been insulted by foul-mouthed women accusing her of intruding on their pitches and alarmed by wild-eyed, tangle-haired drunks thrusting filthy hands at her, begging for spare change.

She swallowed hard. Squinting in the dim light coming from the single red bulb glowing above her head, she read the hand-written 'Members Only' notice that was attached to the black-painted door with a rusty drawing-pin.

What on earth was she doing outside a place like this? She could have kicked herself. Even someone as naive as she was should have been aware that although the address was in the West End, it was also bang in the middle of the red-light district. A place as threatening and dangerous as any of the roughest of the dock-side neighbourhoods in the East End, places where Ginny would never have dreamed of going.

Leila had seemed so plausible when she described the club: that it was a place where tired and lonely businessmen, who wanted a quiet drink and a bit of pleasant company, could go after a hard day's work. Men who were prepared to pay good money for such a haven. Okay, Leila had admitted that some of the girls made private arrangements with the customers, but that was life, wasn't it? Ginny couldn't disagree with that; you found that sort of thing going on everywhere. But Leila had assured her that the club itself was all above board, a good place to earn a good wage for not doing very much. And, also according to Leila, Ginny wouldn't be doing very much at all, just carrying a tray of cigarettes around to the customers and maybe helping out with a bit of waitressing if things got busy.

Ginny covered her face with her hands. Had she really been *that* drunk?

No. What she had been was desperate. Desperate to have just a taste of the life that she had once had, when there had always been money in her purse and a meal on the table good enough to satisfy even Nellie's demanding appetite.

'If you're not going in, get out of me way, will you.' A tall, bosomy redhead, dressed in a Persian lamb swing coat that showed her high-heeled, sheer-black-stockinged legs right up to mid-knee, shoved Ginny unceremoniously to one side, pushed open the door and teetered into the dimly lit interior.

Ginny watched the woman as she paused half-way up the flight of stairs at the end of the hall and threw up her arms in what looked to Ginny like intense indignation.

Ginny was right.

'For Christ's sake,' she hollered over her shoulder, 'the minder don't come on for at least half an hour. If you're coming in, then come in. If not, then shut that bloody door. We don't want every tramp in the flaming street walking in and pissing on the carpet.'

With that, she pulled her collar huffily up to her throat and flounced up the rest of the stairs.

Ginny hesitated for barely a moment, took a deep breath and stepped inside. Even as she heard the door slam behind her, she wasn't sure what had made her do it – maybe the realisation that the redhead's coat probably cost more than Ginny managed to earn in six whole months of eye-straining tedium at the electrics factory. Or maybe because she knew that if she didn't at least try to make a better life for herself, she would more than likely go out of her mind with the worry of it all. She had to find a way to end the scrimping and scraping, the darning of stockings and the humiliation of queuing outside the butcher's, only to be able to afford the cheapest cuts when her turn finally came, while – she was sure of it – the neighbours gloated at her downfall. She was, after all, married to Ted Martin.

As Ginny reached the top of the stairs and stood in the doorway, looking at the barn-like, shabby room before her, its every dusty corner and grimy crevice picked out in the harsh overhead lights, she almost turned on her heel and fled.

When Leila had told her about working there, Ginny hadn't had a very clear picture of what she was expecting the club to be like, but she certainly hadn't even begun to imagine that it would look quite so depressing as this.

The run-down room was empty, apart from a man who was standing behind a shabby semicircular bar with his back to her. He appeared to be engaged in an unequal struggle with one of the drinks optics and was muttering angrily to himself.

Ginny coughed politely and the man turned round to face her.

The first thing that struck Ginny about him was that he was holding a whisky bottle in mid-air, as though he were a rather bored magician who hadn't been in the least surprised to have produced it from out of a top hat, and the second was that his eyebrows had been plucked into perfect Joan Crawford half-moons.

He looked her up and down, taking in every inch of her old-fashioned outfit with conspicuous distaste. 'Mmmm? Can I help you?' he asked in a camp, slightly northern lisp.

'I'm looking for Miss Harvey.'

He sucked in his cheeks and shook his head. 'Sorry, not with you, dearie.'

'Harvey?' she repeated. 'Leila Harvey?'

'Aw, Leila. You should have said.' He returned his attention to the bottle and the disobliging optic. 'She's not here.'

'But she told me to come tonight.'

He sighed wearily and jerked his head to one side without looking round. 'Ask that lot out the back.'

'Out the back' turned out to be a dressing-room of sorts. It was a cramped, not very clean space, with a single chipped sink in one corner, a selection of mismatched chairs and a couple of mirrors propped up on rickety tables, amongst piles of cosmetics, over-spilling ashtrays and cheap, thick china teacups.

Six women, dressed in a variety of eye-poppingly low-cut dresses, were fighting for elbow-room in front of the mirrors. They were primping and preening themselves with various articles of make-up, which, by the look of their astonishingly brightly painted faces, they had plucked at random with their eyes closed from the heaps on the tables.

'Hello,' Ginny ventured, her voice tiny. 'Does anyone knew where I can find Leila?'

'Who's asking?' the tall redhead wanted to know. She was sitting in a prime position right in front of one of the mirrors, plastering yet more Panchromatic on to her already deep-orange face.

'Ginny. Ginny Martin. Leila said I was to come here tonight. To work.'

Six pairs of eyes were turned on her.

'Aw yeah, the new cigarette girl.' The redhead sniffed inelegantly and rubbed at a lipstick smudge on her teeth with a nicotine-stained finger. 'I thought you'd be older from what Shirley said.'

Ginny ignored the Shirley remark. 'Cigarette girl.

That's right,' she said politely. 'Could you tell me who's in charge, please?'

'I don't think the governor's in tonight. Well, not till much later.'

'Could you tell me what to do then?'

The redhead rolled her eyes. 'You really are fresh off the boat, ain't you, darling?'

'If you could just—'

'Look, your costume's over there in the wardrobe,' she said, flicking a scarlet-painted finger-nail towards a curtain-covered recess by the sink. 'And the cigarette tray's kept behind the bar. Gloria's in charge when the governor isn't here. She'll give it to you and explain.'

'Gloria?' Ginny looked expectantly from face to face.

'Don't look at us, darling,' one of the women said, with an amused snigger. 'Gloria's the old queen out there behind the bar. The one who probably wants to scratch your eyes out 'cos you've got better legs than he has.'

The women laughed raucously as Ginny mumbled her thanks and backed hurriedly out of the room.

With the main lights dimmed and the pink-shaded table lamps glowing, the three-piece band playing soft, easy jazz tunes in the background, and the room crowded with customers and the six girls from the dressing-room – plus about another dozen who had turned up in a giggling waft of scent and cigarette smoke – Ginny felt strangely exhilarated. The club now seemed much more like the ones she had seen on the films. While it might not have had quite the sophistication of the place where Rita Hayworth had sung and danced and twirled her long satin glove provocatively above her head – while Glen Ford's eyes stood out on stalks, poor man – it was definitely much more like it.

And the work wasn't too bad either. All she had to do

was walk around the room with the tray round her neck, selling cigarettes, chocolates and fluffy dogs. It was almost like being an usherette at the pictures, selling cartons of Kia-ora and Lyons Maid lollies during the interval. Admittedly, her uniform was a bit briefer than the cinema's regulation overalls, in fact, there wasn't much more to it than a sparkly bathing costume with a frilly skating skirt attached, but it wasn't too bad. And the men didn't bother her much either, which was a relief.

They were more interested in the girls – the hostesses, as she had to learn to call them – who were sitting staring admiringly into the men's eyes, listening to them while they paid a fortune to drink cheap booze and for the girls to sip drinks that were actually plain tonic water, so they could keep their wits about them. In fact, the men barely looked up at Ginny as they handed her crisp, unfolded fivers for items off her goody tray to impress their chosen girl for the evening. Their chosen girl who, in a few hours' time, would return the ridiculously over-priced cigarettes, toys or chocolates to the tray, on the promise of earning herself an extra pound in her wage packet every time she did so.

She also had to deliver drinks from the bar to the tables when Gloria was too busy, or overwrought – which seemed to be most of the time – but Ginny didn't mind that either. He wasn't exactly friendly, but he fascinated her with his outrageously rude manner and his camp affectation as he nagged incessantly and minced about behind his bar complaining and sighing like Bette Davis on overtime.

But although the work wasn't that hard, it was tiring. Ginny wasn't used to wearing such high heels and the effort of smiling the whole time was making the muscles in her face ache; so she was more than glad when, at ten past three the next morning, Gloria said it was time to pack up for the night.

She was surprised, however, when the redhead – who had been sitting wrapped around a man in one of the darker corners of the club all night – signalled to Ginny that she should go out the back with her.

'Come on. Let's stick our feet up for five minutes before you go,' said the redhead, plonking herself down in an ungainly sprawl across one of the chairs. She offered Ginny a cigarette.

Cautiously, Ginny took it – 'Ta' – but she didn't sit down. After the way they'd laughed at her earlier, she was a bit wary of what strings might be attached to this apparent overture of friendship.

'Come on,' the redhead coaxed her. 'Keep me company while I have a smoke. I hate being by myself. I've told lover boy out there that I had to go to the little girls' room.' She lit her own cigarette, then Ginny's. 'Silly bastards. They'll believe any old rubbish.' She patted the chair next to hers. 'Come on.'

'Me feet are aching a bit.' Ginny dropped down beside her, kicked off her shoes and rubbed her calves.

'There, that's better. Now, I'm Yvette.' She grinned saucily. 'Well, that's what I call meself. I daren't tell you me real handle. You'd never stop laughing.' She sucked in a lungful of smoke and exhaled slowly. 'What was your name again?'

'Ginny.'

'So what did you make of your first night then, Ginny?'

'Interesting.'

'Interesting!' Yvette laughed, not unkindly this time, but from genuine amusement. 'That's one way to describe it, I suppose.'

218

'Well,' Ginny said slightly defensively, 'it's just that there are so many different people out there. It's been a while since I've been out much, so, yeah, I do find it interesting. Just watching them. And it's been a while since I've seen anyone spending that sort of money an' all.'

'You just watch yourself,' Yvette warned her. 'Don't get carried away with all their flash acting. Some of them ain't got two bob to rub together. They're just spending money they should be using to pay their bills or to give their old woman for the housekeeping.'

Ginny frowned. 'What sort of people are they, then?'

Yvette waved her cigarette in the air. 'All sorts. Black marketeers. Genuine businessmen. Playboys even – well, sometimes. Servicemen. Posh blokes out slumming. Artistic sorts. You get a lot of them round here. Painters, writers, actors and that – they've never got a ha'penny to bless 'emselves with, but they're a good laugh if you ain't busy.'

Ginny smiled. 'See. I told you it was interesting.'

Yvette returned the smile. 'You seem a genuine sort of a girl, Ginny. Make sure you stay that way. Don't let none of this get to you.' She suddenly leaned forward and stubbed out her cigarette. 'Hark at me, I'm getting sentimental in me old age. But, seriously, there are one or two things you should know.'

'Yeah? Like what?'

'There's some hard men round these parts. Men who fight over every bit of turf. The men who run the betting, the protection and most of the girls out on the streets. Men who'd think nothing of smacking a good-looking sort like you into a pulp.'

Ginny hurriedly looked away for fear that Yvette would be able to see in her eyes that she knew exactly what she was talking about.

'They're the ones,' Yvette continued, seemingly not noticing Ginny's discomfort, 'who don't have to pay for anything when they come in here. We'll make sure you know who they are.'

The two women were sitting there, both locked into their private thoughts, when two of the other hostesses came barrelling into the dressing-room like children bursting out of the school gates at home time.

'I got a fair tip but I don't reckon Leila's gonna be very pleased,' squealed one of them, a black girl with a strange accent that was a cross between a South London drawl and a musical Caribbean lilt. 'He was off like a stuck pig when I told him we could go upstairs. Stupid sod. What's he come in here for if he don't wanna do nothing?'

She inhaled deeply on a hand-rolled cigarette, holding the smoke in her lungs until she sould stand it no longer. 'How about yours, Patty?' she asked in a gasp of expelled breath, handing the cigarette to her platinum-blonde companion. 'He on for it, is he?'

'Tell you the truth, Carmen,' Patty said in a low, guarded voice with a hint of Irish brogue just audible behind her flat London vowels. 'I don't think I fancy it. See, I reckon he's pissed himself. He stunk just like the bloody men's lav.'

Carmen went cross-eyed, stuck out her tongue and made a loud, gagging sound. 'How'd you get rid of him?'

'Told him I'd just got the curse.'

'Yeah, the curse of having to have it away with ugly bastards like him!'

They both burst into loud, uncontrolled laughter.

'Ginny,' said Yvette loudly enough to interrupt their hysterics. 'Let me introduce the comedy double act – Carmen and Patty. I'm always telling these two they should go on the stage.'

As if on cue, the girls linked arms and broke into

an impromptu routine of badly co-ordinated high kicks, until, with tears of laughter streaming down their faces, they collapsed on to a pile of coats that had been dumped in the corner of the room. 'But we can't dance!' Patty screeched.

'Shut your mouth, you,' giggled Carmen, shoving her friend in the ribs. 'I'm a lovely little mover.' She puckered her lips and blew Ginny a kiss. 'Pleased to meet you, Ginny love.'

'Likewise, I'm sure,' offered Patty in a mock-posh voice that had her and Carmen spluttering and snickering all over again.

'Much as I'd love to stay and enjoy the fun . . .' Yvette said with a resigned sigh, as she stood up and smoothed the wrinkles from her short sheath dress. 'Who's left out there?'

'Only one or two,' gasped Carmen, puffing from the exertion of propping herself up on her elbows. 'The others have either disappeared upstairs, or they've gone off for the night.'

'Ah well, no peace for the wicked, eh? I'd better get out there meself before my mark gets fed up and has it away on his toes.'

'That big feller with the moustache?' Patty asked, her nose wrinkling in distaste.

Yvette nodded gloomily. 'That's the one.'

Patty flapped her hand. 'Sit down for five more minutes, Yve, he won't know the difference. He didn't even know what time o' day it was by the look of him.'

Yvette didn't take much persuading; she dropped back on to her chair without a murmur of protest. 'You wanna stay away from these two, Ginny,' she said, throwing back her head and closing her eyes. 'They're bad influences. They could lead you astray.'

'Well I reckon it's smashing to see someone enjoying themselves so much,' Ginny said.

'See,' Carmen said, thumbing her nose at Yvette. 'She loves us.' Then, suddenly serious, she said, 'Anyway, it's Shirley she wants to stay away from. Spiteful bitch.'

'You're right there,' Patty agreed with a flash of her eyebrows.

'Don't start, you two,' sighed Yvette. 'You married, Ginny?' she asked, pointedly changing the subject.

Ginny shrugged. 'Sort of.'

'He left you,' Carmen said.

'Sort of.'

'It's all *sort of* with you, ain't it?'

'I suppose it is.' Ginny shrugged. 'I've had a bit of a bad time, see, and ...' She took a long, last drag on her cigarette before grinding it out in one of the over-spilling ashtrays. 'I can't explain it, but I always wanted more than what I seemed to wind up with. I don't mean just things, although I've always liked nice stuff, but ...' She ran her fingers distractedly through her hair, trying to find the words to explain. 'It's different for girls now, they can get an education. Make a living with their brains. But I've got to work with what I've got. I can work here at night and do another job during the day. And I'll be able to save enough to get out of—'

'Look,' Yvette said, signalling for the other two to stop laughing, 'we all say that, darling. And we mean it. But then we all stay in bed all day.'

'I won't. I'm going to work hard. *And* I'm going to get out of the mess I've wound up being stuck in.'

'We all say that an' all, darling.'

Patty folded her arms and leaned back against the wall. 'I was talking to this bloke the other day. He reckoned he could get me in the films. Be a starlet like. I might give it a go.'

Yvette gasped in disbelief. 'You're as bloody green as Ginny. At least she's new to the game. Look, we all dream about getting out of the business and becoming models and film stars, don't we? But how could you do anything else? You need a block and tackle to get you off your arse, you lazy cow. You don't even get out of bed before four o'clock in the afternoon.'

There was a tense silence as the girls thought about their lot, then Ginny said, 'Leila reckons I've got the real makings of something.'

'Leila?'

'Yeah. That's right. She said working here would be a good start for me. That I'd meet a lot of people who'd help me get on. Give me opportunities not just to earn good money, but to change my life.'

'If it's so good,' Carmen sniffed, 'why isn't she working here?'

Ginny frowned. 'She does, doesn't she?'

The girls laughed as though she'd just cracked the funniest joke they'd ever heard.

Yvette shook her head in amused wonder. 'Leila wouldn't lower herself to actually work here, darling. She's a bit more select. And a good friend of the governor, if you get me drift. She does a bit of this and that in some of the posher clubs, and sorts out the takings here and in some of the governor's other Soho *establishments*, when he's too busy to do it himself.' She grinned wickedly. 'Mind you, that's only if she's not throwing one of the special parties the governor gets her to put on. That's her real business and she has the privilege of running that from her own flat.'

'Flat?' Patty interrupted. 'More like a bloody palace.'

Ginny was confused. 'What, she throws parties? As a business?'

'She having me on?' Yvette asked the other two. 'It's

223

this business she's in, dopey-drawers: getting drunks drunker and then charging 'em over the odds for a bit of how's your father. Although some of her little talents are a bit more, er, specialised.'

Patty tutted. 'She's on the game, just like the rest of us. Only Leila high and mighty Harvey gets paid a proper rate and don't have to use them poxy rooms upstairs like we do. Or go to some bloke's idea of a hotel that's more like a doss-house. All right, we ain't slags like that lot outside who hang around street corners. But we're all whores, when all's said and done.'

'Some of them treat us with a bit of respect.' Carmen pouted.

'Yeah, but they're never gonna take us home to meet mother, now are they?'

'Or the wife.'

'We're their bit of fun.'

'But it don't pay that bad. Better than flaming machining in a sweatshop.'

'Machining? You try to earn a living in a poxy hat shop where every time the owner goes out, her old man's trying to get his hand down your drawers.'

'If you're gonna let 'em have it, you might as well put a price on it,' Carmen said, then added without a trace of irony, 'and it ain't a bad way to earn a living.'

Yvette nodded her agreement. 'She's right, Ginny. You wanna get the governor to let you start working with the punters. You'll never make decent money walking around with that thing round your neck.' She stabbed her thumb at the cigarette tray that Ginny had dumped on the floor. 'All you'll get from that is a backache.'

Ginny shrugged. 'It seems decent money to me. Much better than I was earning in the factory.' She bowed her head. Her hopes of finding beauty, respectability and wealth suddenly seemed so childish.

'Yeah, but why not earn more?'

'I don't want to go with no one, Yvette. I'm not saying that what you do is—'

'Look, we all felt like that at one time.' Patty fumbled around with her bag and took another hand-rolled cigarette from a silver-coloured case. 'Wanna drag?'

When Ginny looked surprised at not being offered a whole cigarette, Patty grinned. 'It's kif.'

There was still no understanding in Ginny's eyes.

'Indian hemp?' Patty persevered. 'Reefer?'

The look of shocked realisation on Ginny's face had Carmen and Patty giggling helplessly.

Yvette stood up, slowly straightening her seams. 'Look, I've gotta get back to Mr Wonderful out there, but leave her alone, eh, Pat? We was all new girls once. And a little tip for you, Ginny, before I go: try a bit of Vaseline on them pretty teeth of your'n, it helps with all the smiling you have to do.'

Just at that moment the door to the dressing-room creaked open and there stood Leila, dressed in her trade mark emerald-green silk. Behind her stood Shirley, so plastered with make-up that, in the harsh overhead light of the dressing-room, she looked like a hideous parody of a pantomime dame.

Leila scowled angrily at Patty and Carmen, before turning a smiling face to Ginny. 'Darling! Just thought I'd come to see how you're getting on.'

'We were all telling her,' Yvette said matter-of-factly, as she threw her coat around her shoulders, 'she'll never make proper money selling fags and chocolates, she wants to—'

Leila's smile became brittle. 'Thank you, Yvette.' Then she linked her arm through Ginny's and steered her towards the door.

'I think, unfortunately, that they've come to the end of

a rather *tiring* day, if you know what I mean,' she whispered, slipping something into Ginny's hand. 'Now here's a little something on account. Get yourself a cab home and treat yourself to the hairdresser. Have that hair blonded up a bit. Platinum would look just right with your complexion.' She kissed the air next to Ginny's cheek. 'We'll see you tomorrow night, sweetie. Same time.'

With that, Leila ushered Ginny forward, out of the dressing-room and into the club, then spun round and glared at Yvette. 'I don't know what you think you're up to, but there is a very lonely man waiting for you over there, Yvette. Mind you, if you're too busy, I'm sure Shirley would oblige.'

Outside on the pavement, Ginny shivered in the early morning chill. Huddling back into the doorway beneath the dim light of the red bulb, she opened her hand to see what Leila had given her. Two five-pound notes!

She hurriedly stuffed them in her handbag, pulled her coat high around her ears and set off at a fast walk.

She would walk at least half-way and only then get a taxi. She was going to save her money, buy herself out of the mess she was in. She wasn't like those other girls.

'Oi! Mum!'

Nellie, her head bristling with metal curlers, opened a sleep-reddened eye.

Ted flicked on the bedside lamp, making her blink myopically in the glare, as she fumbled around for the glass holding her false teeth.

She smacked her lips noisily and propped herself up on one elbow. 'What do you want?'

'Where's Ginny?' Ted hissed.

'Aw, her. I've got some interesting things to tell you about that little whore.'

With no one of any importance to see her, Leila yawned loudly and scratched her stomach where her roll-on was cutting into her as painfully as an instrument of torture.

'Tired, dear?' Gloria sneered. 'Ain't we all.'

'Leave off, Gloria,' Leila sighed. 'It's bad enough having to cash up here, when I've already done a night's work, without you starting.'

'Aaah! Can't you manage?'

Leila was just about to tell him his fortune, when the sound of someone coming up the stairs had her jumping to her feet. 'Those stupid tarts must have left the door open. Quick, stick this under the bar.'

She shoved the cash-box towards him, grabbed a bottle off the counter, ran across the room and stood behind the door.

As a tall, powerfully built man stepped over the threshold, Leila raised the bottle above her head, ready to crown him.

Before she knew what was happening the man had grabbed her wrist and had taken it from her as easily as if he'd been picking daisies.

'It's you! You nearly gave me a heart attack.' She clutched her heaving chest. 'I wasn't expecting you in tonight.'

'You know me, full of surprises.' He grinned boyishly. 'You can go home now, Gloria.'

Gloria rolled his eyes. 'Thank fuck for that, dear. I thought I was going to be here till the sparrows started coughing. These late nights play hell with a girl's complexion.'

The man laughed easily as he threw his overcoat across the bar. 'Fancy a drink, Leila?'

'I'd love one. Thanks.' She leaned over the counter and took a bottle of the good scotch and two clean glasses from under the bar.

She handed him a triple measure. 'I started a new one on the cigarettes for you tonight.'

'Good girl.'

'I reckon I can really do something with her. She's bright, nice looking. Actually a bit sensible, if you can believe it. Like me, I suppose.'

He winked at her. 'Good.'

'She's got potential, and with Shirley looking rougher and more miserable by the day – hardly appetising – I could do with someone to take her place when we have ...' She paused and smiled seductively up at him through her expertly mascaraed lashes. '... private parties to cater for,' she breathed through pouting lips.

'How about the other girls here? None of them do?'

Leila wrinkled her nose. 'I wouldn't trust any of them, not with the special clients. They'd show us up. You know the way they speak and act when they've had half a glass of champagne.'

He ran his hand up and down her silk-clad thigh, letting it linger close to her crotch. 'I'll leave it to you, Leila girl. You never let me down.'

'And I never will.' She took his hand and clamped it over her breasts that were spilling out of the top of her dress, her skin creamy against the green of the silk.

She closed her eyes and leaned forward, hoping for the kiss that she knew she could never depend on. Leila was in love, had been for years, but she wasn't kidding herself; she knew that Billy Saunders was a man who had no loyalty to anyone but himself.

After feeling the briefest brush of his mouth against her forehead, she opened her eyes to see him reaching over the bar for the cash-box.

'Come on, Leila girl, let's get this till sorted out and see how much they've earned me tonight.'

Chapter 11

'Hurry up, Dilys,' Ginny called through the letter-box, giving it a rattle for good measure. 'I'm getting soaked out here.'

Dilys, still in her dressing-gown despite it being almost half past three in the afternoon, opened the prefab door. Seeing Ginny, she narrowed her eyes suspiciously. After the business about her wanting to mind Susan, Dilys had been very firm about her never turning up without being asked – she hadn't barred her altogether, because the silly cow could usually be depended on to bring stuff round with her no matter how broke she was. 'What're you doing round here at this time of day? Why ain't you at work?'

Ginny flashed her eyebrows and grinned happily. 'If you'll let me in and make me a cup o' tea, I'll tell you.'

Dilys stood back and Ginny stepped inside.

She took off her headscarf, shook the raindrops out on to the path and ran her fingers through her damp curls.

Dilys gasped. 'You've bleached your hair!'

'Dil, I've done a lot of things and I'm just busting to tell you all about it.'

Dilys, her lips tightly pursed as she listened to Ginny's breathlessly happy description of her new work-place, made no effort to help as Ginny filled the kettle, warmed the pot, took cups and saucers from the cupboard and generally set about tidying the mess that covered every available work surface in the compact prefab kitchen. As usual, whenever there were jobs to be done or tea to be made – no matter that it was in Dilys's house – there was an unspoken understanding that, if Ginny was there, she would be left to get on with it.

But Ginny was so carried away with telling her story that she would have happily cleaned the whole prefab inside and out; in fact, she was so excited that she didn't even notice Dilys's openly hostile glare as she chattered away about her wonderful new life.

'And when I come out in the early hours of the morning,' she beamed, carrying the tea through to the front room on a brightly painted tin tray bearing the legend *Guinness is good for you*, 'the place is either still awake or getting ready for the next day. You wouldn't believe it, Dil. I know it can be lively round here, but *Soho*. You should see it. I wasn't sure about it at first, it was a bit unfamiliar like, but now I'm getting to know people I think it's smashing. Really smashing.'

Ginny didn't stop talking while she poured the tea. 'And you don't drink this stuff there, you know,' she went on, weighing the pot in her hand. 'Well not all the time. There's this place see, in Frith Street.' Her tone became reverent and a wistful look came into her eyes, as though she were describing some exotic vision. 'The Moka Bar it's called. And they make this frothy coffee with a special machine. You should try it, Dil. It's great.'

While this newly vivacious, platinum-haired Ginny perched herself on the edge of one of the armchairs and continued to talk nineteen to the dozen, Dilys sat in the armchair opposite, sipping mechanically at her tea, not saying a word.

'So what I was thinking,' Ginny went on, 'as this is my night off, I've got a bit of time on my hands, so, if it's all right with you, as soon as Sue gets in from playing with her little friends I'll take her down Burdett Road to

231

Mandor's. I saw this beautiful little coat and hat in their window that I want her to try on. Bright-red wool it is, with little cords with brown fur bobbles on the end to tie under her chin. And you should have seen the little hat that went with it. Talk about cute. She'd look a real sweetie in it!' Ginny dipped her chin and blushed. 'Hark at me! *Sweetie*! That's what Leila calls everyone. She's the one who got me the job, the one I told you about. Mind you, I could only put a deposit on it for now. But I'll pay it off weekly, then as soon as I get myself straight, I'll pay off the rest and get it for her. It'll do her just nice when she starts school. And that'll be here before you know it.' Ginny looked at her watch. 'I hope she gets in soon. What time did you tell her to be back?'

Still Dilys didn't say a word.

Rather than provoking Dilys by pressing her about Susan – she would probably be having tea with one of her little friends – Ginny carried on talking. 'Anyway, I could get her some of them lovely little Cherub vests and matching knickers, and some of them pretty petticoats an' all. She'll like them better than them scratchy old-fashioned liberty bodices, I'll bet.'

Dilys plonked down her cup and saucer on the arm of her chair and let out a long, slow breath. 'There's nothing wrong with Susan's liberty bodices.'

'Yeah, but they're what Florrie passed down to her from her daughter's kids. I was talking about getting her some nice new things. Not going mad or nothing, 'cos like I say, I've gotta get myself straight first and I'm gonna try saving a few bob an' all. But I definitely reckon I can afford to treat her to a few bits and pieces.'

So carried away was Ginny with this new dream world she had entered, a world where Susan would be dressed up like a real little doll and would have all the toys she could ever wish for – a Fairy Cycle even! – that she didn't

232

notice the look darkening Dilys's already irritated expression into one of pure, murderous hate.

As Dilys turned her head away to avoid having to look Ginny in the face for a moment longer, her eye was caught by the matching vases on her sideboard, a gift from one of her recently acquired American 'friends'. And, as she stared at the heavily engraved glass, she thought how easy it would be to snatch up one of them and to bring it crashing down across Ginny's pretty blonded skull.

Had Ginny realised just how close she was to being crowned with a couple of pounds of cut lead crystal she would soon have shut her mouth, but it was the sound of the street door opening, as Susan let herself in with the key she wore on a string around her neck, that saved her.

As always, the moment Susan spotted Ginny she launched herself across the room, with a delighted whoop of 'Auntie Ginny!'

After a hasty brushing of her lips on her mother's cheek, Susan struggled out of her wet, oversized coat – another legacy from Florrie's grandchildren – and let the heavy, dull-brown garment drop in a heap on the floor; an action that Ginny noticed drew not the slightest reaction from Dilys.

'And where have you been, my little angel? You're soaked.'

Susan looked warily at her grim-faced mother. 'Out playing.'

'You dopey thing!' exclaimed Ginny, reaching out to ruffle the child's damp hair. 'You should have come home when it started raining. Go and fetch me something to dry you off.'

Susan ran out of the room and returned immediately

with a dingy-looking towel, clambered on to her 'auntie's' lap and gazed up adoringly at her.

'You could have fetched a clean one,' Ginny teased.

Susan managed a thin smile and snuggled closer.

'Like I was saying,' Ginny continued. 'I meant what I said about good money, Dil. Honest, I'm earning plenty. I've even given up me job at the factory.'

She leaned forward and dropped her voice to a conspiratorial whisper, mindful that Susan was sitting with her. 'D'you know, the girls earn at least a tenner a night. Their basic's quite low, but what with the commission on all the drinks that the customers have to order,' Ginny winked at Dilys behind her hand, 'by way of payment for their company, if you catch me drift; plus all these tips they get. And even their cocktail dresses are supplied by the governor. I've never met him, but apparently he likes to keep the tone of the club just right. Likes a bit of class about the place. But I'm not a fool. I know that some of the girls', she looked down at Susan and then mouthed, '*go* with the blokes. But you should see the presents they get from the fellers when they do take them upstairs for a bit of you-know-what. I'm not saying I agree with it, but like Leila says, even—'

Dilys leapt to her feet, her dressing-gown flapping open. 'You *what*! You come round here looking like a two-bob tom with your bleached hair and your nylon stockings—'

Ginny's hand went automatically, defensively, to her legs, as her bright smile closed – snap! – on her face.

'—talking filth in front of my baby!'

'Your baby?' Ginny said quietly, hugging Susan protectively. 'What, the one who was out in the rain, Gawd knows where, and had to let herself in, while you was sitting here not even dressed?'

Dilys pulled Susan away from Ginny. 'D'you really

think I'd let you buy my kid anything out of whoring money?'

Now Ginny was also on her feet, but she kept her voice low, as she didn't want to scare Susan. 'Dilys, I told you, I ain't got nothing to do with that side of things. I sell cigarettes. That's all.'

'Cigarettes, my Aunt Fanny. Pull the other one, *sweetie*, it's got sodding bells on it.' Dilys jabbed a furious finger in Ginny's face. 'I'm disgusted with you, Ginny Martin, really disgusted.'

Susan picked up her coat, stuck her thumb in her mouth and made resignedly for the haven of her bedroom and her teddy. She knew when it was best to keep out of the way.

Dilys was now in full flight; her venom at seeing Ginny looking so good and so happy, and her own dissatisfaction with the joys of motherhood, triggering off every kind of nastiness and wild accusation.

'Just look at the way you're done up,' she finished triumphantly.

Ginny blinked back the tears that threatened to spill on to her cheeks, determined not to let Dilys see how much she was hurting her, knowing that her friend's temper would subside as easily as it flared. 'I thought you'd be pleased to see me looking smart again,' she said reasonably.

'Smart! You call dressing like a brass smart? And Christ knows what you think you're up to, hanging around clubs.'

'I thought you liked clubs.' Ginny could have added: 'Well, according to Milly Barrington, your nosy neighbour, you do,' but she didn't want things to degenerate any further, certainly not with Susan in the next room.

'I ain't a bloody married woman, am I? But you are.'

A married woman? A punch-bag more like. Ginny

235

swallowed hard, as the memories of the kicks and beatings, and the humiliation, flooded her mind. She rubbed her hands over her face. She wouldn't let the memories stay there, she wouldn't let Ted have that power over her. But then, as clearly as if it were happening right in front of her eyes, Ginny saw Pearl's funeral and Ted sitting with Susan on his lap . . .

She had to stop letting these stupid ideas taunt her, or she'd make herself ill.

'Are you listening to me?' Dilys demanded.

'What?'

'I said, you should know better. And Gawd knows what Ted's poor mother's got to say about all this.'

'Nellie don't know nothing about what I'm doing.' Ginny drew her breath in sharply, as she saw the look of triumph on Dilys's face. 'But it wouldn't matter if she did,' she added hurriedly. 'You know her. She wouldn't give a toss what I'm doing so long as there's money coming in.'

'Well, I reckon you're wrong there, 'cos even Nellie's got standards.'

There was a moment's uneasy silence, as Ginny bit back the question as to what on earth Dilys knew about standards. She couldn't risk not being allowed to see Susan for a few weeks, just to score an easy point in a row that would, as usual, be forgotten as soon as Dilys grew bored with it.

Ginny had to be the appeaser. With all the dignity she could muster she fixed on a smile and said cheerfully, 'Well, if we're gonna get there before the shop shuts, me and the little 'un had better get going.'

'Better get going?' echoed Dilys incredulously. 'I'll give you better get going. You just get out of here, Ginny Martin. Go on. You go back to your Yvette and your Carmen and your Leila and all the rest of them. And don't bother coming back. I ain't having no kid of mine mixing with no whores.'

As Dilys shoved Ginny towards the street door, she seemed genuinely unaware of the irony of her words.

While Ginny was waiting at the bus-stop in the pouring rain, not caring, or even really noticing, that she was getting drenched to the skin, so angry was she with herself at not handling Dilys better, Ted was pulling his car into the kerb outside a scruffy-looking terraced house in Plaistow.

Ted hated his new car, a tiny Austin that looked as though it should have a family squashed into the back seat, complete with picnic hamper and tartan travelling rug, singing 'Ten Green Bottles' at the tops of their voices. But he had to have something to drive after he sold the MG.

It had almost physically hurt when he'd had to let his open-topped bird-puller of a car go, even though he'd made a more than good price on it. He'd always enjoyed displaying that he had money to spend, and what sort of impression did selling the MG and driving a bloody Austin give to people? That he was having hard times, that was what. And the impression was just about right: times weren't so good for Ted Martin any more.

It seemed that no matter what he tried lately, it all went wrong. Everything was so difficult, there were barriers no matter which way he turned and it was sending him round the sodding bend. In the past he'd always been able to make a living, a very good living, ducking and diving, doing a bit of this and a bit of that – he had been well on the way to becoming what he'd always wanted to be, a face to be reckoned with – but then it had all started going wrong. And Ted was convinced he knew why.

Saunders. That was all you heard nowadays. It had been bad enough when they'd had that ruck over that stupid bitch Lilly, but that was nothing like what was happening now. Since the bastard had started expanding his business into the East End it seemed like the no-good cowson was everywhere. No matter what scams and schemes Ted tried setting up, all he got was: 'No mate, not without clearing it with Saunders first.' And Ted knew exactly what Saunders's reaction would be if he did turn up with a deal.

Even the money-lending had gone wrong on him. His loans had been 'bought up', and he'd been paid off – nothing compared with what he should have earned out of it – by a pair of goons who would have terrified even the likes of Freddie Mills. They'd told him that someone else was running the debts now, and that if he knew what was good for him, he'd sling his hook like a good little boy and keep his head down and his nose clean.

The trouble with arseholes like Saunders was they were powerful enough to do exactly what they felt like and to hold a grudge for a very long time. They didn't have to be beholden to anyone, but they still knew they had to show that they held all the cards, all the power, in their hands, or someone else was standing there, ready to step right into their shoes.

Jamming his trilby on his head, Ted shut the car door with an angry slam. Poxy rain! He could happily have murdered Saunders. He was earning a fortune and what was Ted doing? He was back to having birds doing tup-penny ha'penny hoisting for him; lifting bits and pieces to sell off in pubs for fucking peanuts. Pubs that weren't even on his own manor. Not that he had a manor any more.

And it was all Saunders's fault.

He smacked at the street door with the flat of his hand.

The silly whore had better be in. He didn't have a penny to bless himself with and he was getting bloody soaked.

'Are you telling me this is all you've got?' Ted snorted heavily, as though he had been running, but his panting was more to do with anger than exertion. He held up the striped hand-towels with a scowl of disbelief. 'You're a lazy bastard, Irene.'

'*Me* a lazy bastard?' Irene, a girl of barely nineteen, stuck her fists into her waist and threw back her head. 'If what I've nicked ain't good enough for you, then do something about it. You take the bloody risks. I've had enough of this lark anyway, and I've had enough of you thinking you can stay here whenever you fancy it. Well, you've got a shock coming, mate, 'cos I'm getting out of here. The place has been bought up by some businessman. He's paid me and all the other tenants in the street to move out. So I'm going. I've got plans.'

'What did you say?'

'You heard.'

As she continued to talk, telling him exactly what she thought of him and what she was going to do about it, Ted rose slowly to his feet.

Young Irene no longer had her prettily dimpled chin stuck arrogantly in the air, she had it tucked down close to her chest, as she cowered against the wall with her arms folded over her head, trying to protect herself.

A few hours later, Ginny was sitting alone in the front room of Bailey Street, listening to the wireless she had bought for Nellie's birthday, with the paper, unread, in her lap. She felt really miserable and instead of making the most of her first night off from the club, she was dreading spending the rest of the evening alone.

It wasn't really the row – Dilys always had been one

for making dramatic gestures – it was something else and it wasn' so easy to deal with. Ginny hadn't realised just how lonely she had become before she had met Leila.

Knowing she was going to be with the girls each evening had given her something to look forward to. Hearing their constant chatter, their joking around, sharing in their laughter, was like a bright light shining into her life. And even if their jokes were sometimes a bit close to the knuckle, at least there was no pretence with them.

Not like Dilys and her sudden moral conversion.

Ginny sighed loudly. All her adult life she had had to give in or make allowances for someone or other. And it got her down at times, but she knew that she would soon be round the prefab, knocking on the door, smiling like a fool as though nothing had happened, hoping that Dilys either wanted something off her, or was in a more reasonable mood, so that she would at least let her in and allow her to apologise. And, if she wanted to see Susan, that's what Ginny knew she would have to do.

She looked up at the clock. It was only ten to eight – although it felt more like midnight – and she didn't know what to do with herself. She had finished all the clearing up and there wasn't a single handkerchief left unironed. There wasn't even anybody to talk to, not even Nellie and her moaning, as she'd taken herself off to Florrie's to play cards and to put the world to rights.

Ginny sighed again. Things were in a bad way when she found herself wishing she had Nellie for company.

She was as bored as hell, but she was damned if she was going up to bed.

She'd make a cup of tea. That's what she'd do. There was nothing else to bloody do . . .

'Hello, gorgeous. Enough left in the pot for me?'

Ginny spun round and let out a little gasp of surprise, nearly dropping the teapot. 'Ted! I didn't hear you come in.'

He winked lazily and lifted his foot, displaying a heavily buckled, crêpe-soled, black suede shoe. 'Brothel creepers. Silent but deadly. Got 'em off this bloke in a pub. Latest thing from the States, they are. You see, they'll all be wearing 'em soon.' He laughed easily as he pulled a chair out from under the kitchen table and straddled it as though he were riding a horse. 'Swapped 'em for a set of poxy hand-towels, if you can believe it. Told him they was best Turkish quality, as found in all the big hotels up West. What a mug!'

Ginny joined in with his laughter. He was in a good mood and he hadn't been drinking. *This* was the Ted she had fallen for: the one who made her smile, made her feel good about herself. The one she loved. It was over a month since she'd even set eyes on him and that had only been for a few minutes when he'd come to collect some clean clothes in the middle of the night; and she had missed him. Well, she had missed this particular Ted.

As she looked at his handsome, smiling face, while he sat there at the table as though he had just finished his supper and was telling her little stories about his day, her old optimism bubbled up around her like water from a spring. With her earning decent money, maybe she could help him start a different sort of life, just as she had done. One they could share. A proper life. With children . . .

'Are you gonna stand there gawping at me with your gob open?' he asked, reaching out his hand to her. 'Or are you gonna give us a kiss?'

Almost before Ginny realised what was happening, Ted had bent her back over the table, had pulled her skirt up over her thighs, her knickers down to her ankles and was pushing himself into her.

It was all over very quickly. Within minutes Ted was back on his chair and the only sign of anything having happened between them was a rip in Ginny's stocking and a flush covering her face and throat.

'You're looking good,' he said, running his fingers through his thick, dark quiff. 'All this austerity shit everyone's going on about obviously ain't affecting you.' He sniffed noisily. 'How about a drink then?'

Ginny, torn between feelings of near elation that her husband obviously still desired her and an absurd shyness after their moment of what she refused to acknowledge was a brief, brutal intimacy for Ted's purely physical relief, averted her eyes from his easy, direct gaze and turned to the kettle on the stove. 'I'll make a fresh pot,' she said in a girlish whisper.

'No. I mean a proper drink. Ain't Mum got no whisky?'

Ginny turned off the tap. 'Since you ain't been bringing her stuff home, she don't really keep anything in the house no more.'

Ted frowned. 'What d'you mean by that?'

'Nothing,' Ginny hurriedly assured him. 'I just meant that I think she drank it 'cos it was there.'

'Leave off. She used to knock the stuff back like it was water.'

'No, really. I reckon the only reason she goes down the Albert is for a bit of company. It's a terrible thing being lonely.' Ginny thought guiltily of how easily she had got into the routine of leaving Nellie alone each evening. 'To be honest, Ted, I feel a bit sorry for her.'

Ted snorted and shook his head. 'You always have to see the bloody good side of everyone, don't you? She drinks like a fish and you feel sorry for her.'

Ginny hoped he'd meant it as a compliment. Checking her hair in the glass by the sink, she grabbed her bag from the door handle and smiled broadly. 'Tell you what, I'll nip over the Albert and get us a bottle.'

Bob, the landlord of the Albert, folded his arms across his big barrel chest and whistled appreciatively. 'Ain't seen you for a while, darling, but just look at your hair and everything. You're looking a right little cracker. Here, come and have a butcher's at this little lady, Martha,' he called to his wife who was through in the other bar, serving. He leaned across the counter and winked. 'Tell us your secret before the old woman comes through and I'll see if it works on her.'

Ginny glowed with pleasure. 'I'm happy, Bob, that's all.'

'Are you, babe? Good. You deserve it. And I tell you what, I know you always had a lovely head of hair on you, but you look like a film star with it all blonded up like that. I'll have to get Martha to do hers that colour.'

'Do my what, what colour, you cheeky bugger?' Martha asked, giving Bob a flick with her glass cloth.

Not bothering to wait for her husband's answer, which Martha knew was bound to be saucy, she turned her attention to Ginny. 'Hello, love. Well just look at you all prettied up. You're a real sight for sore eyes.'

'Ta, Martha.' Ginny couldn't stop grinning.

'Come looking for Nellie, have you?' She turned to her husband. 'Don't think she's been in tonight, has she Bob?'

Ginny shook her head. 'No, she's round Florrie's. I was after some scotch actually. You ain't got a spare one to sell us, have you?'

While Bob went out the back to fetch the whisky, she chatted to Martha, who was as surprised as Bob had been by the transformation of Ginny from down-trodden drudge back to the vibrant young woman she had once been.

As Bob rang the one pound and fifteen shillings into the till, and Ginny practically skipped out of the pub, Martha stood next him with a worried frown clouding her face.

'What's that look for?' Bob asked. 'I know I only charged her—'

'I didn't expect you to make a mark-up on her, you great daft sod,' Martha said affectionately. 'I just hope she knows what she's doing, that's all.'

'What you on about?'

'Think about it, Bob. Nellie's out round Florrie's and that scotch ain't for Ginny, now is it? That conniving bastard, Ted bloody Martin, must be sniffing round again.'

Ginny poured Ted a generous measure and sat opposite him at the table, nervously nibbling her bottom lip. 'Ted, there's something I wanna tell you.'

He took a big gulp from his glass, swallowed, then drew in a sharp breath, stretching his lips tight across his teeth. 'Yeah?'

'It's about me job.' She paused, trying to gauge how he would react, whether his mood had suddenly changed in the way she knew from experience that it could. 'See, it's like this, I don't work at the factory no more.'

'I know, Mum told me.'

'But—'

Ted tossed back the rest of the scotch and held out his glass for a refill. 'She might be a wicked old fucker at times, but she ain't stupid.'

She unscrewed the cap and, with a shaking hand, poured the drink. 'So you know where I'm working?'

He nodded.

'Do you mind?' Another pause, then, in a rush, it all came out. 'Because if you do, I'd give it up like a shot. I'd give it up tomorrow. 'Cos I really want us to try and get our lives sorted out, Ted. And I'd do anything for the chance to make a go of it. Anything.'

For a moment Ted said nothing, he just gulped at his drink and looked fixedly at her, then he burst into loud, coarse laughter, tossing back his head as though she had just told him the funniest joke he had every heard.

Ginny stared back at him in uncomprehending bewilderment.

'Why would I care where you work?' he finally managed to ask, as his laughter subsided. 'Unless you wasn't earning much, o' course.'

'But—'

'But *what*?' His face creased into a contemptuous sneer. 'The only reason I'm here is 'cos I need some dough.'

'No.' She dropped her chin. 'You're just saying—'

He reached out and grabbed her face, sinking his fingers deep into her cheeks and jerking her head up so that she had to look at him.

Despite the pain, Ginny knew she mustn't let out the smallest whimper or let a single tear drop on to her cheek.

'Let me tell you, once and for all, you dozy cow, what the real world's about.'

Ginny didn't want to listen, didn't want to hear any of it, but she had little choice. She sat there, gripped by the cruelty of his hand and his words as he gave her a variously censored and exaggerated version of the life he lead when he wasn't with her. Censored to hide what he considered his failures and exaggerated to brag about his self-perceived successes. It was only as he got on to more recent times that his tone changed from one of sneering bravado to barely suppressed anger.

'So,' he murmured, finally releasing his grip on her and reaching for the bottle which was now almost half empty, 'there's been this silly tart what's been going out hoisting for me. But she's another fucking useless cow.' He was talking to Ginny as though she was some bloke in a pub he was complaining to about his missus not ironing his shirts the way he liked them. 'Know what she had the cheek to tell me tonight? She's going off with some posh old bastard – one of the prats what get a thrill from buying bent gear off us. Makes 'em feel like they're bastard gangsters. And her flat's been bought by some property bloke. I ain't even got that no more.'

Ginny, no longer even noticing the throbbing pain in her cheeks, couldn't stop herself from asking the question: 'Why did you have a woman stealing for you?'

Ted slowly raised one of his dark, sculpted eyebrows. 'I ain't been able to work, have I. I needed money.'

'You could have come to me.'

Ted shook his head in wonder at her stupidity. 'I have, ain't I? But anyway, I ain't talking about needing a couple o' bob. I'm talking proper money.' His voice was beginning to slur and he seemed to be having trouble focusing on her face. 'I nearly had it an' all. I had a blag all set up. Sweet as a nut. We was gonna turn over a bank in the Mile End Road. Had all the tools organised and everything. Sawn-off jobs that couldn't be traced. Right pukka.' He smacked the side of his fist on the table, making Ginny flinch. 'Then some bastard grassed us up. We had to call off the job and now we've all gotta keep our heads down.'

He poured himself another drink, spilling most of it on the table. 'Now I ain't got a pot.'

'They're always going on about needing workers in the papers and on the wireless lately,' she said warily, as she screwed the lid back on the bottle for him. 'You could always try and get a regular sort of job.'

'What, like you? In some knocking shop?'

Ginny winced at the injustice of his words. She hadn't done anything wrong. All she was doing was trying to pay off some bills, make ends meet, keep his mother in food and earn a bit extra for some of the things that other people took for granted, that *she* had once taken for granted. Admittedly she was enjoying the job, but there was no getting away from the fact that she was working bloody long hours, which was a damned sight more than either Ted or Nellie had ever done.

Ted was staring into the middle distance. 'You know what it is, don't you?' he asked, his drunken speculation losing Ginny completely. 'It's since that bastard's had it in for me. If I ever get the chance to get my hands round that whoreson's throat . . .'

'Who? Who's got it in for you?'

'Him. The one who's been haunting me.'

'I don't understand.'

'The arsehole's ruined my business, ruined my life and *you* don't understand?'

Ginny looked blank.

'The bastard who grassed me to the law, you silly bitch.'

'What, over the bank job?'

He hesitated for a moment, as Ginny's words worked their way into his mind. 'Yeah,' he said with a nod. 'You're probably right. The same bloke. The one who stopped all the dockers trading with me, the one who—'

Now Ginny had tuned in to the corkscrew logic of his thinking, it was all she could do to stop herself laughing. 'You ain't talking about that feller from all that time back, surely? The one who had the police round here. I can't even remember his name it was so long ago.'

'Can't even remember his name?'

The low menace in his voice had Ginny wishing she had kept her mouth shut.

And as all his hatred and bile spewed out – as he slammed the truth about him and Dilys at her, and about Susan being his, and how he thought Ginny was just about the stupidest bitch he had ever laid eyes on, let alone fucked – Ginny wished she had never been born.

'Why Ted?' she whispered into her chest. 'Why?'

'Why not?'

She couldn't think of an answer.

'Be honest with yourself for once, instead of floating around like a bleed'n' idiot with your head in the clouds. You must have known.' He laughed cruelly. 'I mean, every other bugger seems to.'

Ted set about refilling his glass. 'You got any money?'

Ginny handed him her purse, turned her back on him and walked slowly from the room.

Upstairs, she packed her belongings into the suitcase that had once held packets of silk stockings, French perfume and chocolates. Things of which Dilys had no doubt had more than her share. Ginny vowed to herself that she too would have those things. But she would buy them for herself.

She'd been a mug for long enough. What did she have to lose?

Less than an hour later, Ginny walked into the club just as Carmen was fixing the cigarette tray around her neck.

'Innit your night off?'

'Yeah, it is,' Ginny said, striding past her without a glance. 'I've come in to see Leila.'

By the time Leila arrived, the club was about to close and the girls were almost bursting with curiosity.

What was going on? Why was Ginny sitting out the back with a face like a fiddle, bruises on her cheeks, a suitcase by her side and no explanation? That's what they wanted to know. But as they rushed to follow Leila into the dressing-room to find out, they were disappointed.

'Do me a tiny favour, girls,' she purred over her shoulder, 'get back to your customers and leave me alone with Ginny for a few moments.'

There was a general mutter of frustration.

'Please,' said Leila, her smile still in place, but her voice and eyes hardening.

The girls obeyed and Leila lowered herself elegantly on to one of the shabby little chairs. 'Now, what's all this about? Gloria said—'

'I want to do what they do,' Ginny interrupted her.

'Hostessing?' Leila suppressed a much broader smile. She'd been right about her all along. She could always tell, no matter what Shirley said.

Ginny nodded. 'I want to earn more money.'

'You'll certainly be able to do that.'

'And there's something else. I need somewhere to stay.'

'That shouldn't be a problem.' Leila draped her emerald-silk-clad arm around Ginny's trembling shoulder, her mind working overtime as she considered which of Saunders's properties might have a bedsit that wouldn't frighten her off completely. Ginny had something about her that men went for and Leila wasn't about to miss the opportunity of pleasing the governor by getting her to cash in on it.

'We'll find you somewhere. But you mustn't expect too much, you know, sweetie. Not at such short notice.'

'That's all right,' Ginny said flatly. 'I ain't used to much.'

Chapter 12

1952

Carmen sashayed into the dressing-room, a half-smoked cigarette dangling from her lips, her big brown eyes narrowed against the smoke. Apart from her hair, which was smoothed round big, fat rollers in an attempt to straighten its tight natural curl, she was made-up and dressed, ready for the evening's work ahead.

She tipped her head towards Ginny, who was sitting in the far corner of the dressing-room by the sink putting on her make-up. Rather than sharing one of the big communal looking-glasses that were propped up on the junk-covered tables, Ginny was doing her best to use a small handbag mirror.

'What's up with her?' Carmen asked Yvette.

Yvette flashed her eyes, shook her head and flapped her hand, in a pantomime signal for her not to ask, but Carmen was never one for subtlety.

'What's up with you then, Ginny girl?' she asked, flicking her cigarette into an already full ashtray. 'Penny for those dirty thoughts of yours.'

Ginny raised her eyes slowly; beneath them were dark mauve smudges like fading bruises, but they weren't marks of violence, they were marks of exhaustion and lack of sleep. 'Sorry, Carmen? What did you say?'

Carmen tutted amiably. 'I said, penny for them. You're miles away again.'

Ginny lowered her chin and returned to painting her face. 'I'm all right.'

Yvette glared at Carmen; she of all people should have

known what it was like to feel troubled, to want to hide away in a corner and be left alone.

Patty, who up until now hadn't said anything – she had been far too preoccupied constructing a fat, overspilling reefer – suddenly chipped in, in her increasingly London-tinged Irish brogue: 'It's about time you moved out of that room of your'n, Ginny. That dump's enough to get anyone down. And I should know. Didn't I stay there myself for a couple o' weeks? I nearly went barmy. And you've been there for what . . .? It must be getting on for eight months now.' She paused to lick the paper and to light the expertly rolled joint. 'That's what'll be upsetting you, living in that rat hole.' She paused and flashed a knowing look around the room. 'Or you've got yourself into a bit of debt maybe?'

Carmen took the cigarette from Patty and inhaled deeply. 'Well, it's either that.' She laughed. 'Or the fact that Elizabeth Taylor has gone and snapped up Michael Wilding. You've lost your chance there, darling.'

Ginny said nothing, but Patty wrinkled her nose and made a gagging sound. 'Michael Wilding? No thanks.'

Carmen handed back the cigarette. 'Not your type, eh, Patty.' Playfully, she flicked a clump of lipstick-stained cotton wool at Ginny's back. 'Hark at Miss Fussy Drawers, Gin. Making out he's not her type and we all know she'd go with Laurel and Hardy, the bloody pair of them at once, if they paid her well enough. She'd go with anyone.'

Patty leaned towards Carmen and hissed angrily, 'D'you mind. Unlike some people, I know where to draw the line.'

'Aw yeah?'

'Yeah. And I definitely wouldn't go with some of the old rough I've seen Ginny go with.'

'Shut up,' snapped Yvette; she could kill Carmen and Patty at times, they acted just like a pair of kids.

'What?' Patty was a picture of injured innocence. 'What have I done?'

'It's all right,' Ginny said, standing up, her mouth and eyes set hard behind her bright mask of cosmetics. 'Patty's right, I do go with blokes that most of you would run a mile from. But why should I worry about being fussy? What have I got to lose?'

She didn't wait for their reply.

It was barely half past one and Ginny was already leading her third customer up to one of the mercifully ill-lit rooms above the club. If the lights had been any brighter, the irrefutably sordid nature of the poky little cubby-holes, with their lumpy beds, and their faded and stained linen, would have been all too horribly apparent to anyone but the very drunkest or badly sighted of the customers that the girls took upstairs.

The customers were actually referred to as 'friends' within their hearing – what the girls called them in the privacy of the dressing-room would have appalled them. The girls' descriptions varied: according to how the customers had behaved; how far over the set rate their 'tip' had been; and – most importantly – how quickly they had managed to get it all over with. But customers is what they undoubtedly were, and the point in getting them upstairs and back down again as quickly as possible wasn't only because the girls found them distasteful, but so that they could get on with buying more rounds of the ludicrously over-priced drinks and gifts from the cigarette tray, or be sent off into the night, with reassuring murmurings about their virility and their ability to drive a woman to the heights of ecstasy, so that the girls could get on with targeting their next likely punter.

The girls earned less per trick if they took them upstairs rather than back to the flats they rented from the governor, but then they missed out on the commission from the extras and could only guarantee the one 'friend' for the night, so it was worth staying on the club premises. Plus, not only was working a foreigner – doing business on your own behalf without the governor's knowledge – strictly prohibited, but most of the girls felt safer using the upstairs, as, like the door from the street, they were watched over by an ever-changing series of minders. These were huge gorillas of men, who stood, arms folded, guarding the door to the narrow staircase that led to the rooms high up in the roof.

The minders safeguarded the girls and their customers from several potential hazards, ensuring that the men enjoyed their purchase for the evening in something like privacy and also ensuring that the club didn't attract too much attention. For while the downstairs operated quite legitimately as a licensed drinking club, upstairs was another matter and was completely illegal.

The first of the potential spoilers of the punters' fun – and the club's profit – was the local police. But because they were happy with their regular pay-off, they usually only bothered to mount the occasional, fairly half-hearted early-evening raid – at a time when no one of any importance was likely to be on the premises – more as a public demonstration of keeping the peace, than part of any genuine crusade to close what they all knew was a fully operational brothel.

Then there were the young thugs who, after watching one too many George Raft films, fancied themselves as budding gangsters and would see if extorting protection money was as easy as it looked at the pictures. They were something of a joke and were swotted away as easily as an annoying insect at a picnic.

There was, of course, the genuine article to be reckoned with: the real hard men. But they weren't a day-to-day concern. For the most part, everyone had their own patch in Soho – the English, the Greeks, the Irish, the Italians, the Chinese – and they tended to live in a sort of peaceful co-existence, where everyone knew their place in the pecking order of the criminal underworld. There was the occasional outbreak of a territorial skirmish, when one of the local firms or families decided to chance its arm and see if it could expand into someone else's manor. But those disputes were usually quickly, and often bloodily, resolved, satisfying everyone's sense of fair play and of honour. Lately, however, with the increasing numbers of Maltese arriving on the scene, there were worrying signs that the newcomers didn't intend to play by quite the same rules as the old firms.

But for now, the intruders who caused the most trouble for the club were the sightseers – who would never have set foot in the place had they even begun to suspect the charges; the do-gooders and the moralists – who wanted to clean up the area and save the girls and the customers from themselves and eternal damnation; and the wives.

The wives were a whole new breed of nuisance, who seemed permanently on the look-out for co-respondents to cite in the increasingly fashionable divorce courts. There, they were almost guaranteed deals designed to break their errant husbands, both in spirit and in pocket. Most men caught that way could only reminisce that that sort of thing would never have happened before the war when women knew their place.

The minder on the door tonight was Terry, a man with a neck wider than his head and fists like boiled hams. Usually silently inscrutable, he frowned as Ginny tottered past him on her high-heeled shoes, dragging a sweating, over-weight old man who looked barely conscious behind her.

'You all right?' Terry growled, his great bald head creasing like an ill-fitting overcoat. It took a lot to shock a man like him, but this pretty little blonde was going at it like some rough old street tom. Anyone could see she could make a much cushier living if she wanted to. There'd be plenty of blokes more than willing to have a doll like her to keep to himself – him included if he had the dough. But it was as though she just didn't care. And the old geezer she had in tow this time, well, it was enough to make Terry want to fetch up his tea.

Ginny stopped in her tracks and turned to face him. 'Why shouldn't I be all right?'

Terry shrugged and, returning the professional blankness to his gaze, opened the door and let Ginny and her 'friend' through to the upstairs.

As he stood stolidly on guard, Terry usually left the door slightly ajar so that he could hear the girls and the mug punters performing – he considered it one of his perks. But this time he made sure the door was shut tight. It made him shudder even to think of what was going on in there.

Less than two minutes later Ginny pushed past Terry with her hand over her mouth. Her hair wild and dishevelled, her lipstick smeared all over her face, her dress unbuttoned and hanging off her shoulders. And there was sick all down her front. Terry couldn't be sure if the vomit was hers or the customer's. Both maybe.

The next night, the other girls had already gone through to the club to size up the first of the customers, but Ginny was still in the dressing-room, sitting alone, looking at her painted mask of a face in one of the big shared

255

mirrors. She couldn't bring herself even to stand up, let alone shift herself out into the club to face yet another parade of men.

She traced a finger round her deep-carmine-tinted lips, then round the scarlet rouge highlighting her cheeks, and finally round the bold black lines defining her eyes. It was as though she was looking at a stranger; someone she knew nothing about. Someone she didn't recognise in any way at all. Someone her mum and dad would have been ashamed of.

She thought about what had become of Violet Varney . . .

Sticking her whole hand into the big jar of vanishing cream that the girls used to clean their faces, Ginny scooped out a great gobbet of the stuff. Ignoring the stray hairs and bits of cotton wool sticking out of it, she closed her eyes and plastered it all over her face. She would wipe it clean of every trace of paint and colour and walk out of the club. She didn't know what she would do then, but that didn't matter, she just knew she couldn't do this any more. Patty had been right about her debts, but she would find a way to pay back every penny. She would—

'Not ready yet?' someone cooed from behind her.

Ginny's eyes flashed open. Peering into the glass through the thick grease smeared over her lashes, she saw the reflection of Leila standing in the doorway with Shirley just behind her.

Leila's presence had Ginny's resolve collapsing into stammering guilt. 'I was just doing my face.' The part of her that had learned to please and appease people, regardless of her own feelings or wishes, could still instantaneously demolish any decision she had made, as surely as a bulldozer could clear a bomb-site.

'Don't get worked up, sweetie. I only want a little

word.' Leila turned to Shirley. 'How about waiting for me at the bar?' It was an order not a question.

'But, Leila—' Shirley began, not wanting to miss whatever it was that was about to take place.

'There are customers waiting,' Leila said evenly.

Shirley flared her top lip at Ginny's reflection, then flounced out. That little cow was just asking for her comeuppance and it looked as though it was about to happen. Shirley prided herself on having a nose for other people's misery and she could smell tragedy coming off Ginny as strongly as if someone had spilt a whole bottle of the stuff all over her. She was only disappointed that she wasn't able to witness it personally.

Leila, checking that Shirley had closed the door properly, said casually, 'You don't like doing this, do you?'

Ginny felt panic flood through her. Only a moment ago she had wanted to walk out of the club and never look back, but now it came to it, the question of what else she could do suddenly seemed a lot more important, the issue a lot more threatening. And where would she go? Even her rooms were tied to the job. And then there was the money . . .

'What makes you say that?' she asked, hurriedly wiping the cleanser from her face with a pad of rough cotton wool.

'No need to sound so worried. I'm not after getting you sacked.' Leila, raising her tight green shantung skirt above her knees, lowered herself on to the least unpleasant-looking of the chairs. 'Now, come on,' she encouraged Ginny, 'you can be honest with me, you know that.'

Ginny let the cream-covered pad drop from her hand and began speaking. At first she spoke to Leila, but soon it was as though Leila wasn't there and Ginny was speaking to herself.

She stared into the mirror, but she didn't see her smeared and make-up-streaked face, what she saw was her life spinning and reeling in front of her in a malevolent kaleidoscope of scenes and moments – like watching a film that was running at the wrong speed and in the wrong order.

'I'm doing something I don't understand. That I don't like. And I've got to leave. I know that. And I know all the other girls all say the same. The difference is, I mean it. But the trouble is, who'd want me when I've been leading a life like this? Where would I go? It was bad enough before. But now . . .'

A self-mocking smile lifted Ginny's lips, but her eyes remained unmoved.

'The girls talk about going to Australia, Canada, South Africa. Anywhere to get away and start a new life where no one knows about what they did. Somewhere they can become other people, turn themselves into someone else. Find a place where they don't ever have to . . .' Ginny sighed deeply. 'Where they just don't have to. That's all.'

She picked up a packet of cigarettes that was lying on the table and lit one. 'All those magic places they talk about where there's no more working until the early hours, no more fog, or cold, or bomb-sites. It all sounds like something out of a fairy story. But I knew someone once, she sent her kids to Southern Rhodesia. It was a woman from our street. I don't know how she did it. She didn't even know where the place was. It was in Africa somewhere I think. And it broke her heart, but she thought it was for the best. And at least she had her children and tried to do her best for them.'

Ginny took a long draw on her cigarette. She frowned as though trying to work out something important.

'There's something else I'm worried about. Someone who needs looking after,' she said eventually. 'What with all this polio about, I'll bet she's not even had the vaccination yet. Dilys would never think to get it done.'

Leila watched her for a moment, then said, 'Why don't you just remind this Dilys whoever she is? I'm sure she won't mind. But I wouldn't worry if I were you, it's only children they're worried about, isn't it?'

Ginny seemed flustered to hear another voice. She rubbed her hand roughly over her face, dragging the remnants of her mascara down over her cheeks. 'It's not for her,' she said absently. 'It's for her little girl. I used to mind her now and again.'

Leila said nothing; she was used to the girls having complicated lives. And Ginny having a child she 'used to mind' sounded to Leila like just another of the many ways the girls had of talking about their kids. They either wanted to keep their existence secret for some reason, or had somehow lost contact with them – whether by design, against their will, or even, most incredibly to her, just by carelessness. Leila sometimes thought she took better care of her crocodile handbags than some of the girls did of themselves and their offspring. But then she had never actually raised a child.

'And when you see what can happen to people.' Ginny was speaking again. 'It really makes you think.'

She stubbed out her cigarette and turned her head so that she was looking at Leila face to face. 'It's like when Pauline started drinking the real stuff in the club, instead of just tonic. She went downhill so quickly. It was tragic.'

Leila put on her professional, bright-but-sympathetic smile and leaned forward so that she could touch Ginny gently on the arm. 'You were very kind to Pauline when she had her operation,' she said, delicately skirting the use of the word abortion.

Ginny shrugged. 'I got rid of a baby myself once.'

Leila didn't show any sign of surprise. She just continued to touch her arm. 'A lot of girls make mistakes, Ginny.'

'No. It wasn't a mistake. Well, not in the way you think. Getting rid of it was the mistake.'

A single fat tear rolled on to Ginny's cheek and plopped on to her lap. She sniffed loudly and fumbled around clumsily with the Craven A packet on the table, trying and failing to get one out of the box. Leila took out her mother-of-pearl case and lighter, lit two gold-tipped black cigarettes and gave one to Ginny.

'But I was in such a state, you see,' Ginny explained to herself as much as to Leila. 'When there's hardship, people just can't manage. But they do what they think's best. Like poor Violet Varney.'

Leila didn't ask who Violet Varney might be, she just let Ginny continue.

'It's not fair. You see some of the big spenders coming into the club and you think, if I'd had just a little bit of the money they've got . . .' Her hand shook as she put the cigarette to her mouth. 'Yvette said that that bloke in here the other night, the one with the funny clothes, was a maharajah, all the way from India.'

'He was.'

'But I'll bet even he's got his own story. That he's either lonely, or miserable in some way. But hard times are easier to cope with when you've got a few bob. That's why I came here in the first place, to earn the money to get a better life for myself. A life I thought I deserved. Now look at me.'

A loud crack of thunder made Ginny jump.

'Just raining again,' soothed Leila in her warm, purring voice.

'Even this weather's getting me down,' Ginny sobbed, unable to hold back the flood of tears any longer.

'That's what I thought.' Leila handed her her lace-trimmed handkerchief. 'And that's why I want to put a proposition to you.'

Ginny shuddered as though someone was walking over her grave. 'How d'you mean?' she sniffed.

Leila twisted one long, slim leg elegantly around the other. 'I admire the way you dance with the customers, Ginny. And the way you speak when you're with them. You sound very classy. It impresses them.'

Ginny laughed mirthlessly. 'After nearly a year at this lark you learn how to act a part if you don't learn anything else. But I'd hardly call it classy.'

'No, I mean it. You have a way with you and you really can dance, you know.'

'I used to go dancing with my friend once upon a time. And even with my husband.' She shook her head in self-pity.

'You certainly know how to use your body.'

'You have to in this line of work.' Ginny's voice was thick with tears. She blew her nose loudly into Leila's delicate little hankie and flicked a cynical eyebrow.

'That's why I want to know if you'd like a part in the new show we're bringing in here.'

Ginny frowned briefly at the 'we' – nobody at the club was really sure why, but the governor never seemed to be around, while Leila appeared to have taken responsibility for all of the business side at Frith Street. There were rumours, of course: that he was inside, or that he was too busy with a whole lot of new interests, but nobody knew for sure. Whatever the reason, Ginny hadn't set eyes on him since she'd been there – well, not to her knowledge. In the dimly lit club, one man was very much like another.

'We have to keep up with the competition, you see.'

'What competition's that?' Ginny had lost track.

'The other clubs and theatres. The governor's keen we

should make the place look classy, so don't worry, it wouldn't involve you in anything nasty or unpleasant.'

Leila had actually mentioned the governor, but Ginny was too busy laughing, genuinely amused this time, to follow it up. 'Nothing nasty or unpleasant? After what I've been doing?'

Leila's tone hardened. 'You told me once you had dreams.'

'Yeah, so much for them. Look what's become of me.'

'Well I'm giving you a chance to make some of your dreams come true, a chance to be something special. A star in an artistic tableau.'

'What, standing naked in front of a room full of dirty old men, you mean?'

'Better than what happened last night, sweetie.'

Ginny hurriedly looked away.

'Terry told me.'

Ginny felt the tears pricking her eyes. She was so ashamed.

'Say yes, Ginny. For me. It'll be the best thing that's ever happened to you. I promise'.

'You have to keep *still* remember, Yvette. I told you, if you go wrong, just watch Ginny.'

Leila rolled her eyes and smacked her forehead with the flat of her hand. She must have told Yvette to stop quivering and wiggling about at least a hundred times during the past fortnight of rehearsals, and now here they were, in the middle of the final dress run through, due to open in a couple of hours and the girl still hadn't got it. She might be a gorgeous, redheaded beauty, but she certainly wasn't blessed with brains.

Leila tried again. '*Static* tableaux, sweetie, *static*. That's what it means. Remember? Staying still so we don't all get arrested? Now stop waggling those pretty little titties of yours all over the place and get on with it. You're meant to be a divine goddess offering herself up to Zeus, not a cheap chorus girl trying to pull a punter in the front row.'

Yvette narrowed her extravagantly made-up eyes and strode to the front of the stage that had been especially constructed at the end of the club, next to the dais where the three-piece band were positioned ready to play.

'I have never looked like a cheap chorus girl in my life!' she roared, the pink ostrich plumes on her head and the narrow, sequined straps that made up the rest of her goddess costume fluttering and glittering as she jabbed her finger at Leila. Then, grabbing her naked breasts in her hands, Yvette stuck her chin in the air and declared, 'And these titties are certainly not little!'

She spun round and glared at the drummer who had dared to mutter something about her bra size to the pianist. 'And you can shut your gob an' all, you fat old bugger. Just 'cos you've got bigger tits than I have!'

The drummer, who *was* a bit on the heavy side but didn't like to be reminded of the fact, threw down his sticks in protest. He knew it was a rather pathetic gesture, but he also knew it wasn't worth starting a row with Yvette; he'd seen her – under cover of the confusion of a police raid – floor a punter with a single left hook, just because she had taken exception to the way the man had smiled reassuringly at her. And she didn't look very happy now. In fact, Yvette looked ready to rip someone's head off.

Leila bit her lip, not knowing whether the sound that was bursting to come out of her mouth was a laugh at the absurdity of the situation, or a scream of despair over the possibility that she might have to cancel the opening night of a show that she had had advertised all over the West End. The governor would go mad.

The pianist, who was either bolder or less sensible than the drummer, grinned broadly at Yvette who still had her hands clasped to her bosom. 'Need any help holding them things, Yve? Not too heavy for you, are they?'

'That's it!' Yvette was steaming. She pulled off her head-dress and flung it to the floor. 'I've had enough. I'm off home. And don't expect me back.'

'But, sweetie,' Leila pleaded, 'if you walk out, the show can't go on.'

'Let Ginny do it by herself.'

'But it's all planned around the two of you. You know that. All the scenes are—'

'Tough.'

'Let me have a word?' Ginny asked, stepping forward. Leila raised her hands in surrender. 'Sure, go ahead.'

Ginny picked up Yvette's feathers, took her gently by the arm and tried to lead her to the side of the stage.

Yvette pulled free and folded her arms firmly across her bosom. 'What?'

'Look, Yve, I know you've been here longer than me and you've seen girls come and go. In fact, I bet you've seen it all. But, please, listen to me for just a minute?'

Yvette shrugged carelessly. 'Go on.'

'I never in all my wildest dreams expected to wind up like this.' She raised her hand to silence Yvette who was about to interrupt. 'Please, I'm not judging anyone. I just meant that I was an ordinary little housewife whose life somehow went out of control. When I first came here, you were kind to me. You made me feel at home after my first night's work. And even though it was obvious I thought I was different from the rest of you, you knew I was gonna wind up doing what I've been doing the moment you saw me. Just like Leila did. And once I started . . .' She shook her head. 'Look, Yve, this is a chance for me to *stop* doing it. A chance for both of us. And remember it's us she picked, not the others.'

Yvette shrugged again. 'So?'

'Well, for a start, even though I'm nervous as hell, the money she's offering is bloody good and I couldn't half do with a few extra quid. Plus, if the choice is between earning my living flashing me knockers at the mugs out there, or letting them have it away with me night after night, then it's obvious the choice I'm gonna make. So how about you, Yve?'

'I don't take much notice of them to tell you the truth. I let me mind go blank. Just let them get on with it and wait till they finish.'

'Liar.' Ginny touched her gently on the cheek. 'Please, Yve. I can't go on brassing. I need this chance. And Leila said you can still do business as well, if you want. And the tips we'll get if we dance with them afterwards, can you imagine?'

Yvette sighed wearily. 'All right, but I'm telling you, if she tells me to stand still once more, I'm gonna chin the bitch.'

Ginny squeezed her hand. 'Thanks, Yve, really. You won't regret it, I promise.'

Plastering on a broad smile, Yvette took a deep breath, turned to face Leila, threw her arms into a dramatic pose and said sweetly. 'Is this better?'

'Much better, darling,' beamed Leila. 'The punters are going to love you.'

And the punters did. When the curtains closed after the final stirring scene – two shy maidens caught in the act of bathing by a river – the audience went wild.

And, to Leila's relief, the other girls liked it too. She had been afraid there might be some jealousy, or worse, that one of the screaming cat fights that had broken out in the past over something as insignificant as a bottle of nail polish would erupt, but it all had worked out really well. Not only were the customers put in just the right frame of mind for going upstairs, but during the show they were so busy goggling at the stage that they were even more generous than usual – saying yes to almost any request for yet more drinks, or gifts from the cigarette girl.

Leila grabbed the only bottle of genuine champagne in the club, that she had told Gloria to cool for her behind the bar, and took it through to the dressing-room.

'You were wonderful! The governor's going to be thrilled with us.'

Yvette was about to question the 'us' when she spotted the champagne. 'I'm so pleased,' she said pleasantly.

Leila popped the cork with a theatrical flourish and poured three glasses. 'And you, Ginny? Are you pleased?'

Ginny, glowing with the adrenalin rush of performing in front of an appreciative audience, threw her arms round Leila and kissed her. 'I'm not only pleased, Leila. I can't tell you. I loved it. It was like being someone else. Like being a film star.'

Leila picked up one of the glasses and raised it in salute. 'I'm absolutely thrilled, Ginny. Thrilled to bits. And just wait till you hear what you're going to do next!'

Chapter 13

As Ginny sat at the mirror, fixing a sparkling rhinestone tiara in her hair, Leila bobbed down behind her and looked over Ginny's shoulder at their reflections.

'It's wonderful out there, darling,' she raved. 'Just wonderful. The club is simply full to bursting.' She took a box of Passing Clouds from her bag and offered the pink packet to Ginny.

Without a word, Ginny took one and waited for Leila to light it for her – at one time, such an exotic item as a deliberately flattened cigarette would have fascinated Ginny, but now it didn't merit the lifting of an eyebrow.

'How many of those *gentlemen* out there', Leila continued in a happy, encouraging trill, 'do you suppose have come up to the West End *supposedly* to buy Christmas presents for little wifey and the kiddiewinks, but have actually come here to see you instead?'

Ginny drew on her cigarette and shrugged. She couldn't give a bugger about lying husbands or their phoney Christmas shopping trips, all that interested her was trying to figure out why on earth she had ever let Leila talk her into doing this. The static tableaux were one thing – they were easy, just standing there like a statue, posing under the coloured lights, looking unseeingly into the middle distance as though you were a bit missing, while the band played a suitably cod-classical accompaniment. As Yvette always gleefully reminded her when they were counting their wages at the end of the week, it was actually *more* than easy, it was all a bit of a doddle, especially compared to hostessing. Admittedly they were stark naked up there on the stage – well as good as – but Ginny found it oddly soothing, pretending, as she stared at some imaginary vista, cloaked by the velvet darkness of the club, that she was all alone, that she was someone else, even somewhere else.

But this . . .

Ginny stared into the mirror at the exaggerated greasepaint mask she painted on nightly; the mask that the real Ginny hid behind as she posed in front of the punters. But a lot of good a bit of slap plastered across her chops would do her tonight.

Leila and her big ideas. Where did she think they were, the sodding Windmill or the bloody Moulin Rouge?

Ginny groaned and dipped her chin to her chest. Knowing that with the new act she was actually expected to look directly at the punters; to flirt with them with her eyes; to smile coyly but provocatively at them, as she wiggled, and strutted, and . . .

'Something wrong, sweetie?'

Ginny lifted her head and looked hard at the still beaming Leila. She had a way of sounding so innocent, so plausible, but there were times when Ginny could have sworn it was all an act. Times like now, for instance, when Ginny was so nervous she could barely stop trembling, yet Leila was yattering away as though it was something to look forward to, a real treat. But she must have known how Ginny was feeling. Just as she knew that she, Leila, was holding the trump card. Because, when it came down to it, it was this or hostessing. And if Ginny didn't want to do either, how else would she pay off her rent arrears? And rent arrears were certainly what she had.

Like all the other girls, Ginny was still living in a bedsit owned by the governor and had been only too pleased to accept Leila's kind offer of the occasional opportunity to put off paying for it for a week or two. Also like the other girls, Ginny had soon found herself with substantial debts.

She knew now that she shouldn't have delayed paying, but at the time it had seemed like a godsend. The trouble was, her money just seemed to go nowhere. After she'd sent her weekly envelopes – stuffed with half her wages between them – one to Dilys for her and Susan, and the other to Nellie, there was barely enough to live on, let alone to pay her bills. She had, once or twice, determined not to send them anything – Nellie and Dilys were probably both laughing at her anyway, while she ran up bigger and bigger debts – but just the thought of little Susan in that big old brown hand-me-down coat, and the guilt she felt at the state Nellie would probably be in without her help, had her sending off the envelopes by the next post.

She supposed it would have been different if Dilys had been a better mother, or if Nellie had had someone else she could depend on. But what was the point of supposing? All Ginny could hope was that Susan actually saw some of the money she sent to the prefab and that Nellie got hers before Ted had the chance to nick it.

If he was still around.

Ted. There was another worry. Had he thought to send his little daughter a birthday card last month? Ginny really hoped so.

Even though it still felt as though she was being slapped in the face just to think of Susan being Ted's child, Ginny couldn't stop caring about her. She loved her. It was as simple as that.

Ginny'd sent her a pretty lacy card and a baby doll in a cellophane-wrapped box, although she had no way of knowing if Dilys would even let Susan see it. Maybe Dilys had pretended that the gift was from her; knowing Dilys, she probably had. But, whatever happened, Ginny could only hope that Susan had had something on her birthday. And that she was happy.

Ginny shook her head, trying to clear the images from her mind of the smiling child she missed so much, took another drag on her cigarette, then ground it out with slow deliberation.

For the moment, she had more immediate things to concern her. 'Look, Leila,' she asked, twisting round to face the stylishly suited woman, 'are you honestly one hundred per cent sure about this? Are you positive I won't get in no trouble?'

Leila touched a gloved fingertip to Ginny's chin. 'I promise with all my heart. As long as you don't show anything actually moving, it's all completely legal. And let's face it, if *you* get in trouble, we all get in trouble.'

She had a way of making her words sound like a reassurance, but they could so easily have been interpreted as a threat.

Five minutes later, with Leila blowing her a final kiss of good luck from the wings, Ginny stood, quivering with fear, waiting for her cue.

And there it was: the band striking up the opening bars of the slow, sensual rumba she had rehearsed endlessly with them during the past nerve-racking weeks.

The curtains drew back to show Ginny, centre stage, lit by a single pink spotlight, with everything but her high-heel-shod legs hidden by two enormous pink feather fans.

As she took her first voluptuous steps to the left and let one of the fans drop a tantalising fraction, showing the merest hint of the creamy slope of the top of her breast, a loud cheer of approval went up and suddenly Ginny was no longer scared. Everything was going to be all right.

No, it was better than all right, it was wonderful.

Ginny was in a cocoon of soft feathers and sumptuous pink light, and lusciously flamboyant rhythms washed over her, urging her body to thrust and sway with the music. It was like being in a dream where there were no rent arrears, no worries and, best of all, no Ted Martin to hurt her.

As she gyrated behind, peeped over, and smiled coquettishly around, her provocatively swirling and dipping fans, she knew that the audience loved her.

Actually, not all of the audience was watching her. Carmen for one was too busy trying to get Patty's attention to care about what Ginny was up to.

When Patty failed to respond to Carmen's agitated waving and flapping, she reached across her punter – who was totally mesmerised by Ginny's bumps and grinds – and tapped her urgently on the arm.

'What?' Patty mouthed, angry at Carmen's interruption; she'd been enjoying a bit of peace, even letting her eyes close for a moment, while her punter goggled at the stage, his mouth half open like a drooling puppy.

'Look who's in tonight,' Carmen hissed, jerking her head towards the bar.

Patty lazily checked out the occupants of the tall bar-stools. Now her mark wasn't the only one with his mouth open.

She twisted back to Carmen. 'It's the governor!' she squeaked. 'So he *ain't* inside.' She dabbed at her hair to make sure it was tidy – although it would have taken a gale-force wind to have damaged Patty's teased and lacquered creation – and sat up straight, hitching her dress further up her thighs.

'Tits up and all, Carmen!' she giggled, sticking out her chest and adjusting her circle-stitched bra with a determined two-handed grab. 'You never know, he might take a shine to one of us and whisk us off into the night in that big fancy car of his.'

But despite Patty's and Carmen's best efforts, the governor was oblivious of their attractions; all he was interested in was Ginny's performance up on the stage.

As he sipped his drink and listened to Leila telling him about all the hard work she had put in rehearsing the fan dancer and the band so that the evening would be a success, he didn't take his gaze off Ginny for a single moment.

At the end of the number, the curtain dropped and the audience went wild. Their whoops, cheers and applause were so rapturous that even the resolutely morose Gloria, standing in his usually joy-free domain behind the bar, couldn't help but grin.

While Ginny further teased her audience by peeking around the edge of the curtain and flashing just a glimpse of her naked thigh – supposedly to acknowledge the appreciation, but actually because she was so high on the rush of performing that she didn't want it to end – the governor rose from his bar-stool and flicked a glance towards Johnno, his minder whom he had left over by the doorway.

Moving surprisingly swiftly for someone of his size, the huge man was almost immediately by his side, carrying his boss's Crombie and trilby hat with as much care as if he were a handmaiden offering up a delicate casket of precious jewels.

'Very impressive, Leila', the governor said, shrugging down into his overcoat. 'Very impressive indeed. As good as you said.'

'I'm glad you approve,' Leila said, smiling broadly in

an effort to cover her disappointment that he seemed to be preparing to leave without her. 'You're off now, are you?'

He nodded. 'Business before pleasure, you know me, girl.'

With that, he treated Leila to a friendly wink and left the club flanked by Johnno, his oversized bodyguard.

Shirley, who had spent the whole of Ginny's act with her eyes fixed firmly on Leila and the governor, was convinced she'd just witnessed something worth temporarily abandoning her punter for. And anyway, there was no risk of him going off with someone else, not tonight; there wasn't a spare girl left in the whole place. The titillation up on the stage had put them all very much in the mood and eager hands had grabbed for the nearest bit of female flesh to pull down on to their laps.

Shirley whispered something suitably lewd into her punter's ear – just to make sure she kept his interest – then sidled up to Leila, who was hovering by the bar staring into her glass of tonic water, trying to summon the enthusiasm to go and congratulate Ginny on the success of her solo début.

'It's enough to make a girl totally jealous, if you ask me, Leila,' Shirley rasped, her voice harsh with sly nastiness and insinuation. 'The way all the men in the place couldn't take their eyes off her. It was bad enough when she was just doing the tableaux with Yvette. But that fan dance. Well . . .'

Shirley paused, waiting for Leila's response. There was none, so Shirley continued dripping her poison. 'I don't think I've ever seen the governor so captivated by a girl before.'

Leila turned to Shirley and said very slowly and deliberately. 'I'd watch my mouth, if I were you Shirley.

Because no one likes a stirrer, especially a sad old stirrer who is coming very close to being a has-been.'

With that, Leila finished her drink, smiled sweetly at Gloria as she handed him her empty glass and swept off to the dressing-room to see Ginny.

Shirley was left standing at the bar, with Gloria staring at her with his usual mixture of undisguised contempt and camp disapproval.

'Don't say a fucking word, you skinny-arsed old queen,' hissed Shirley.

'A few days' time and it'll be Christmas. Can you believe it? I can't. Before we know where we are it'll be Easter again.' Carmen peered over the top of the late edition of the *Evening Standard* that she had been flicking through absent-mindedly, while she waited for the other girls to finish getting ready. 'What plans have you got for Christmas then, Gin?' she asked. 'Gonna give your feathers a few days off?'

Ginny said nothing.

'You must be due a break. You've been up on that stage every night for weeks, flapping them fans about *and* still doing the tableaux with Yvette. You must be knackered.'

Ginny, not wanting to become involved in any conversation that had anything to do with Christmas – and especially not one that was about families and Christmas – bent forward and started fiddling with the silver-sequined garter on her thigh.

'Well?' Carmen persisted.

'I don't know yet,' Ginny muttered.

Carmen, not sure she'd heard properly, but still sounding scandalised, had another stab at sorting out what Ginny actually meant. The fact that Ginny had never talked to Carmen about her family – and Carmen being a curious type at the best of times and bluntly nosy at the worst – naturally made her want to know more. And this seemed like the perfect opportunity. 'You don't what, Gin?'

Ginny sat up and snapped, 'I *said* I don't know yet.'

'Don't know?' Carmen was now clearly outraged and there was going to be no stopping her from saying so. 'But it's the twentieth of bloody December, girl. How can you not know? My mum would have me by the throat and be shaking me like a pepper-pot if I dared even think I didn't know what I'd be doing on Christmas day.'

Patty grinned. 'Sure don't we all know what you'll be doing at Christmas, Carmen? The same as every year. You'll be there with your mum, sitting in that big old church in Brixton, with your best hat perched on top o' your head, singing away like a beautiful brown skylark.'

Carmen rolled her eyes and groaned. 'Don't remind me, Pat. All Mum's sisters have invited themselves over to hers this year as well. Imagine it, all my aunties, all there snooping on me.'

She tossed the newspaper to the floor, stood up, stuck her fists into her waist and launched into an imitation of her Caribbean relatives. 'Why you not married yet, Carmen girl? I had ten kids by the time I was your age. There no nice boys where you work? No doctors?'

That last bit caught Yvette's attention. 'What you on about? Doctors?'

'Well, you don't think they know what I do for a living do you, Yve?' Carmen laughed self-mockingly. 'They all think I'm working at St Thomas's. A nurse on the night shift. You should hear the lies I tell.' She puffed out her cheeks and shrugged resignedly. 'But if I want to keep breathing, I've got no choice but to lie.'

'Least you haven't got to go all the way to bloody County Clare to see your family.' Patty sighed dramatically, handed Carmen the cigarette she had just finished rolling and flopped down on to one of the chairs. 'It'll be murder. And I bet I've told them more lies than you've told your lot. I'm working in an office, if you don't mind. Me!' She accepted the cigarette from Carmen and took a long drag, before handing it back to her. 'Still, I miss my little brothers and sisters. It'll be good to see them again. And it'll be cheaper than staying at home.'

'Broke again?' Carmen asked.

'What do you think?'

'But you've got no plans yet,' Yvette said, turning to Ginny.

'I'll probably be spending the day worrying if I can afford to put another shilling in the gas meter,' Ginny replied quietly.

'You're never still sending all your dough to that old cow of a mother-in-law of yours, are you?' Yvette exploded at full, shocked volume.

Ginny didn't answer, but it was obvious to Yvette, just from her expression, that Ginny was indeed still keeping Nellie.

'Now I understand why you've been so broke,' she went on. 'I wondered why you'd been holding on to your rent so often. I mean, it's not as though you've got kids to worry about. Not like some of us.'

Ginny had become close to Yvette in the eighteen months that she'd been working at the club, and enjoyed her company and her friendship, but she sometimes wished that her friend was a bit more subtle. *And* that she'd never mentioned Nellie to her. Yvette meant well, but it made Ginny feel vulnerable, having someone knowing things about her that, on reflection, she would really rather have kept private. She was only glad that she'd never blabbed about Susan.

Susan. The thought of what she might be doing on

Christmas morning had Ginny swallowing hard, gulping back the threat of tears. She knew from last year what hell it was, being all alone with too much time to think. Not having any money suddenly didn't seem so important . . .

'Here's someone who's not going to have to worry about having a spend-up over Christmas,' said Carmen, picking up the paper again and flipping it in half. 'Listen to this.'

She began reading out one of the news stories in a slow, halting monotone. 'Yesterday, in London's West End, three postmen were forced into an alley off Shaftesbury Avenue and attacked by armed thieves. The robbers got away with the van carrying registered mail worth over £200,000.'

'Two hundred grand!' Yvette gasped.

'And just around the corner!' Patty grabbed the paper from Carmen. 'Was anyone hurt? Fancy a terrible thing like that happening so close.'

A terrible thing. It was that all right. Patty's words made Ginny think about Ted and how he'd been so angry when they'd had to call off the armed robbery he'd been planning. From the way he'd reacted to being grassed it was more like he'd been stopped from doing an honest day's work, rather than prevented from committing a violent crime.

Ginny tugged at a loose platinum curl. How had he started thinking that way – that hurting people, stealing from them, was a reasonable thing to do? Surely he hadn't always been so callous. He couldn't have been. But was it possible for someone to change so much? Maybe he was desperate; but that was just finding an excuse. No matter how desperate or broke she was, Ginny knew she could never do anything to hurt anyone else.

Doing things that hurt herself, however ... That was a different matter.

Ginny's increasingly disturbing thoughts were interrupted by one of the girls – a pale-skinned brunette, who had been sitting on the floor studiously painting her toenails. 'It's true what they're saying in the papers, you know,' she said, her words coming out in short grunting breaths as she bent forward to reach her smallest toe.

'What's that then, Betty?' asked Carmen.

'They've got to do something. 'Cos Britain's ...' She paused. 'Hang on, how did they put it? *In the grip of a crime wave*. That's it. And it's really frightening.'

'Crime wave!' Carmen exploded. 'Are you having a joke, Bet? Most of our bloody customers are criminals. How else d'you think they can afford these bloody prices?'

'But I bet our customers don't all carry guns,' Betty replied sulkily, feeling that she'd made a fool of herself.

'Guns? Whatever are you talking about?' Leila stepped into the room looking a picture of shocked innocence, but from her tone it was clear that guns were now a closed subject.

Carmen hurriedly stubbed out her cigarette and slipped the butt into her handbag – Leila had already taken her to one side and explained very clearly the governor's views on girls using dope or alcohol while they were working and Carmen wasn't about to be caught out again.

If Leila noticed Carmen's sleight of hand she didn't make it obvious, instead she smiled coolly and clapped her hands like a headmistress calling her pupils to order. 'Don't look so miserable, sweeties. Show those teeth. Come on now, off you go. Mustn't keep them waiting.'

The girls jumped to their feet and began flapping around, hurriedly putting final touches to make-up and hair, straightening seams and slipping into elbow-length gloves. Leila turning up so early was a bit of a shock, as she didn't usually show till closing time and they were already nearly fifteen minutes behind their official schedule. Gloria must have been grassing on them again – getting on the telephone to Leila and telling tales on them like some runty little school sneak.

'By the way,' Leila purred, as the first of the girls reached the door, 'after you've all done your family duty on Christmas day, there's a party at my place.'

Patty groaned dismally.

'There's no need for that, Patty. There won't be any punters. It's strictly pleasure this time. A little treat to thank you for your hard work during the past year.' Leila didn't add that putting on a party for the hostesses was her rather sad alternative to an otherwise lonely Christmas night. 'So how about a thank you instead?'

'I wasn't complaining, Leila. It's just that I've promised my mum I'll go home to Ireland for a few days.'

Leila pinched Patty's cheek almost affectionately. 'Never mind. Another time, eh?'

Soon the girls had all drifted out into the club, and Leila and Ginny were left alone in the dressing-room.

If Ginny hadn't had been waiting to go on stage for her first number, she'd have joined them like a shot. Leila's unexpectedly early visit was making her feel nervous. 'Is anything wrong, Leila?'

Leila's smile barely stretched her lips. 'Of course not,' she reassured her.

'You don't wanna change the act again, or nothing?'

Leila shook her head. 'Don't be silly. It's a real success. Why would we want to change it?'

Ginny wasn't satisfied. 'So what's wrong? You don't usually come round before closing. Not unless something's up.'

'I just came in to see how you're getting on, that's all. And to tell you how pleased we are with the way the show's been going.'

Ginny frowned. Why would *we* want to change it? How pleased *we* are. What was this all about?

'So,' Leila continued, 'you're happy and we're happy. Good.'

Ginny relaxed a bit, but then, after a moment's thought, she continued. 'If you don't mind me saying, there is one thing I'*d* like to change.'

'Yes?'

'The money.' She took a deep breath. 'I could do with a bit more.'

'Could you?' Leila asked coolly. She wasn't sure if she liked the direction the conversation was taking, nor where it might lead.

'I want you to understand, I'm not being greedy. I've just gotta try and get myself out of all this debt. And most of the other girls are in the same boat.'

'Really?' Leila's lips compressed into thin, tight lines.

Ginny nibbled at the inside of her cheek. Had she said the wrong thing? It was so hard to know what was going through Leila's mind. Well, it was too late now.

'I know the fan dance has fetched in a lot of new punters.' Ginny tried a little laugh. 'I mean, this place must be a real gold-mine now.'

Leila blinked slowly. 'And is that your business?'

'Don't get me wrong, Leila, I wouldn't be saying anything, but like I say, it's not only me. I'm having a bad enough time, but some of the girls are in real trouble. They've been dumped by their blokes, left to bring up their kids all by themselves.' She had to make Leila see. 'How can they work if they're worried all the time? I reckon if they were treated right – paid more, I mean – it would be good for everyone.'

'You do, do you?'

Ginny nodded half-heartedly. Why had she started this? 'Well, I reckon if I had a club—'

'You? A club?' Leila snorted. 'You can't even open a second-rate spieler without the right sort of support. Money has to be paid. A lot of money. Money that would make your little debts seem quite ridiculous.'

'Look, Leila, I think you've got me wrong, I wasn't exactly serious—'

'It's probably just as well, seeing as you obviously don't know the first thing about it. Try and start up something without permission from the local firm, then you'd soon learn.'

Shirley appeared in the dressing-room doorway, smirking like a cat who'd just cornered a tasty-looking mouse. 'And you'd know, wouldn't you, Leila?'

'Shirley!' Leila fumbled around with her cigarette case and lighter, wondering how long Shirley had been standing there listening. 'I was just about to explain to Ginny that she should think herself lucky that she's working for a boss who actually understands the business side of things.'

'I hope you mean me,' said an amused male voice, from somewhere behind Shirley.

Shirley spun round. It was the governor. What was he doing here?

Ginny hastily snatched up her wrapper and pulled it round her – suddenly embarrassed about showing off her near-naked body – while Leila sprang to her feet, looking as though she'd been caught with her hand in the till.

The governor eased Shirley out of the way, stepped inside the dressing-room and lowered himself into one of the flimsy chairs more suited to a chorus girl's physique than to a man of his size.

'I was listening to what you was saying,' he said, lighting a cigar.

'I was only—' Leila began.

'Not you. Her.' He lifted his chin towards Ginny. 'Come out to the bar and have a drink with me.'

'But I've got to go on and do my fan dance,' Ginny stammered.

'I meant *afterwards*. Christ, I don't wanna stop you showing off that body of your'n and causing no riots, now do I, blondie?'

It was the first time Ginny had ever met the governor and she wanted to make a good impression on him; after all, he had the power to make or break her as far as the club was concerned – even more so than Leila. So, after finishing her set, Ginny rushed off the stage and began rummaging frantically through the clothes rail for an outfit likely to impress him.

She eventually decided on an almost modest, black moiré, ballerina-length cocktail dress with a broad patent belt to circle her narrow waist, and a plunging, sweetheart neckline – the feature that had earned it its place in the dressing-room wardrobe – that showed her breasts off to perfection.

By the time she eventually joined the governor at the bar, Ginny was panting like a highly strung thoroughbred straining at the starting line.

'Billy Saunders,' he introduced himself, rising to his feet and holding out a hand in friendly greeting.

Warily, Ginny smiled up at him and shook his hand – had she known of the connection between her husband and this big, attractive man, she would have been a lot more than wary, she would have been terrified.

'What can I get you?' asked Saunders.

'Am I allowed a proper drink?' Ginny asked quietly,

feeling that she needed something more than the usual tonic water to steady her nerves.

'When you're with me you're allowed whatever you fancy, blondie. But full marks for asking first. Shows you're using your loaf, that you ain't stupid.'

'Thanks. I'll have a Babycham then, please. And my name's Ginny, by the way.'

'And I'll have a glass of champagne.'

Ginny twisted round to see who had spoken; it was Leila, sitting stony-faced on the stool behind her.

'Don't mind if I join you, do you, Billy?' she asked.

Saunders laughed. 'Frightened you might miss something, Leila?'

'Don't be unpleasant, Billy,' she replied, forcing herself to show her teeth. 'I just thought you might enjoy the company, that's all.'

'You should know my routine by now, Leila. It's not company I'm after; I'm here on business. But I've got nothing to say that you can't hear.'

'Shall I go, then, Mr Saunders?' Ginny asked, not understanding what was going on.

'No, blondie, the business I had in mind is to do with you.'

'So, you reckon Yvette could do the dancing then? That she's up to it?'

Ginny nodded miserably. She had misunderstood Leila when she had said they were happy with the show – she'd never mentioned that they were happy with Ginny's part in it. Only the show. She was such a fool. Now here was Saunders taking her job away from her and she was helping him do it. 'Yvette could do it if she practises.'

'Good.' Saunders sniffed and tapped the ash from his cigar. 'And you'll be free to run the new club for me.'

Ginny turned round to look at Leila to wish her well – even if her own luck had just disappeared down the chute, she didn't wish Leila any ill will. But Leila wasn't sitting there any longer, she was disappearing into the dressing-room with Shirley close on her heels.

'I meant *you*, blondie.' Saunders grinned.

'Me?'

'Yeah. You're from the East End, ain't you?'

She nodded dumbly.

'I've been keeping an eye on you. The blokes like you. And you're bright. Bright as a button. But there's no old toffee with you, not like with some clever girls. And no slyness. That's rare in a bird.'

Ginny was too stunned to know whether he was paying her a compliment or insulting her.

'I've been developing me interests down your way for a few years now. I've already got one or two places up and running. All with women in charge. It was an idea I had and it seems to be working. It keeps the atmosphere calmer for some reason. Classier too.'

Ginny opened her mouth but Saunders raised his hands to silence her. 'Don't worry. You'd be the front, but there'd be plenty of back-up. Like Gloria's got muscle in this place and Leila to sort out the cash side for him.'

He paused to blow a plume of smoke in the air. 'Gloria's a right old Soho queen. Been knocking about this area for years. Knows everyone and anyone. But in the East End . . .' Saunders shrugged his massive shoulders. 'He'd be lost. Now this place I've got in mind for you . . .' He winked and grinned at her, showing even white teeth. 'You'll fit in just nice.'

Ginny knocked back the rest of her Babycham in a single swallow and slapped her glass down on the bar. 'Can I have another one d'you think, Mr Saunders?' she gasped through the bubbles. 'But before you say yes, I think you should know something. I reckon you must have heard what I said to Leila, back in the dressing-room. But I didn't mean I *really* wanted to run a club. I was sort of explaining . . .' She threw up her hands and shook her head. 'I just ain't up to a job like that.'

Saunders, obviously amused, grinned even more broadly. 'We'll see, blondie. We'll see.'

Back in the dressing-room, Leila was pretending to do one of her spot inventories of the clothes rail – the dresses had a habit of going missing and reappearing on the second-hand stall in Berwick Street market – but all she really wanted was to be left alone.

Shirley either didn't understand, or she didn't care. She was hovering over Leila like a hawk eyeing a vole. 'Didn't I tell you to keep a watch out for her, Leila. You know what the governor's like when he gets set on a girl.'

'Shirley—'

'But maybe you should be relieved rather than upset.'

Leila spun round to face her. 'Why would I be either of those things, Shirley?'

'Well, maybe Ginny in a manager's job rather than fan dancing would be a good thing. The governor would see her differently.' Shirley smiled slyly. 'Plus he wouldn't see quite so much of her, if you get my meaning.'

'I don't think I do get your meaning actually, Shirley, but maybe you can get mine. Things have become very slack lately. Girls are smoking dope and drinking while they're meant to be working.'

She leaned very close to Shirley and sniffed, her face showing her obvious distaste. 'Is that booze I can smell on your breath again, Shirley? Because if it is, I'd be very careful if I were you. It would be terrible, you losing your job at your age, now wouldn't it?'

Chapter 14

'Not the last one to leave *again*?' Gloria sighed melodramatically, wagged his finger angrily at Ginny, then switched off the overhead light in the dressing-room, plunging the place into semi-darkness. All that was left illuminating the cramped little room was an intermittent flashing from the red neon sign advertising the club across the street and a feeble glow from a string of fairy lights draped round the scrawny little Christmas tree that the girls – in a moment of seasonal sentimentality – had set up beside the cracked sink.

'Well?' Gloria demanded.

Instead of saying anything, Ginny just flopped down on to one of the rickety chairs and let her arms dangle carelessly by her sides.

'Come on, this isn't good enough. Will you please move yourself? Now.' Gloria flapped his hands about, as he lisped at her in his affected, slightly northern singsong of a voice. 'For Gawd's sake, girl, shift, will you?'

When Ginny showed no sign of moving, he minced across the room towards her, flicking disapprovingly at the shadowy, discarded heaps of clothing and shoes that formed a scented and stained obstacle course across his path.

'Well?' Gloria persisted, leaning over her, his fists stuck into his waist. 'Are you going home or what?'

With her eyes still directed at the floor, Ginny exhaled wearily and said in a tiny, pained whisper, 'D'you know, Gloria, I sometimes feel like this *is* my home.'

'This dump? Home?' Clearly horrified that anyone could even entertain such a ghastly thought, Gloria snapped upright and clenched his hands protectively across his skinny chest, as if warding off the contagion that might just cause him to start thinking the same way.

'It's like a palace compared to the pigsty of a room I'm meant to live in,' she said. 'And it's not so lonely.'

'What the hell are you going on about?'

'Even when this place is almost empty, I still get the feeling that there's a bit of life going on out there. Somewhere.'

'I really do not know what you're talking about, but I reckon you must be going a bit soft in the old head department, dearie.'

Lethargically, Ginny raised her eyes to meet his, although in the strange half-light she couldn't quite make out his features. 'Yes you do. You know exactly what I mean, Gloria.' She stabbed her thumb absent-mindedly over her shoulder in the direction of the window. 'There's the stall holders setting up before they go into the coffee shop for their breakfast; the milkman rattling around with his crates; the early papers being sorted out for the stands. People laughing and talking. It's a real little community out there. One people really belong to. Feel part of.'

'Not at nearly half past bloody three on a Christmas morning they don't, darling.'

Gloria might have sounded his usual dismissive self, but from the security of the shadows he was frowning with concern as he watched Ginny's troubled face glowing first red, then disappearing, then glowing red again, in the on-off light of the neon sign. He wouldn't have admitted it to anyone, but he felt genuinely moved by the anguish he heard in her voice. She was a sad one, all right, and an odd one too, there was no denying it.

While it was obvious to Gloria how most of the girls had wound up working the clubs – sometimes it was what they had been brought up to expect they would do; or they had run away from some man; or they'd been tempted by what they thought would be easy money; or any one of a hundred other all too inevitable reasons – Ginny ... He could never make up his mind which of the categories she fitted into – if she fitted any of them at all. Despite the way she drove men wild when she got up on that stage, swooping her fans and shaking herself about, Ginny was, at other times, very reserved, keeping herself to herself and just getting on with her job. She spoke to Yvette sometimes, but Gloria would never lower himself to ask that little madam what Ginny had to say about herself; it would have affected his authority and Lord knows he had little enough of that, what with the girls running around as if they owned the place.

Still, whatever he felt, or thought, or wondered, Gloria didn't intend letting Ginny cotton on to the fact that he was in the least bit concerned about her. She might just use it against him one day. Experience had shown him, very early on, that people were like that. You let them see a soft side and they pounced on you. They chewed you up and then spat you out. His long days and nights in Soho had taught him to be self-protective, and presenting himself to the world as a sour, spiteful old queen, rather than the rather contented old one that he actually was, was as good a protection as any.

'Come on, Ginny,' he whined impatiently, stamping his patent-clad foot, 'I've got to lock up. So stop being such a stroppy tart and get yourself shifted.'

Before Ginny had the chance to open her mouth in reply, a hand reached round the door and flicked on the lamp in the corner.

Feeling he might faint, Gloria covered his eyes, gasped

like a dying cod fish and flattened himself against the wall, uttering a silent prayer.

Ginny was more curious than scared. Shading her eyes from the light, she squinted across the room and made out the unmistakable silhouette of the governor filling the doorway.

'All right, Gloria?' Saunders enquired affably, as he threw his hat on to one of the tables, then folded his arms across his muscular chest and leaned against the door jamb.

'I said, are you all right?' Saunders repeated, clearly amused by Gloria's camp exhibition of fluttering and swooning.

'Never better, Mr Saunders,' he trilled, 'I'm just finishing off in here, then I'm off home. I told Ginny, didn't I? Five minutes, then we're off, I said. Both of us. Out of this place. Gone. And, aw yeah' – he paused to catch his breath, patting himself delicately on his chest – 'a very merry Christmas to you.'

Then, with a simpering approximation of a smile spreading unnaturally across his narrow lips, Gloria scuttled over to the door and waited politely for the governor to let him pass.

Saunders did so, and Gloria slipped out to the bar and began busying himself counting the bottles in a crate that just happened to be close to the dressing-room door.

Ginny stood up, ready to follow Gloria out of the room, but Saunders had positioned himself back against the doorpost, blocking her exit.

'I was waiting outside for you in the motor,' he said. 'I wondered where you'd got to when all the others left just now. Thought maybe you hadn't been in tonight for some reason.'

Ginny shrugged, unnerved by the directness of his gaze and unsure what she should say. 'I was in tonight,' she began hesitantly, 'but I stayed behind because I had a little bit of tidying up to do in here.'

She immediately realised how ridiculous she sounded. Not only was it obvious she was in tonight – she was bloody well standing there, wasn't she? – but seeing as they were surrounded by what looked like the tragic remains of a direct bomb hit on a make-up, clothing and fag-end factory, the idea that she was doing 'a little bit of tidying up' was an even more stupid thing to say.

Saunders laughed, a loud, booming sound that had Gloria straining his ears and moving as near as he dared to the still open dressing-room door – what the hell was going on in there?

'I think it's gonna need a bit more than a tidy up,' he heard Saunders say.

This time, Ginny too saw the funny side of what she'd said. 'Maybe a flame thrower might be the answer.'

Saunders laughed again and touched Ginny lightly on the shoulder, easing her down on to one of the chairs.

It had been a long time since a man had touched her so gently. She'd forgotten how it could feel . . .

She watched as he shifted his hat carefully to one side, perched himself on the edge of the debris-covered table and held out his hands in a sweeping gesture of what might have been pleasure, or could have been one of control. 'It's Christmas,' he said simply, taking out a packet of Players Navy Cut from his jacket pocket. 'Cigarette?'

Ginny nodded dumbly and took one. Why had she done that? Why hadn't she just shaken her head and left?

'So,' he said, squinting at her through the smoke he'd exhaled from his first deep lungful, 'what're you doing over the holiday?'

'I'm not sure if I'm doing anything,' she said automatically, although she knew exactly what she would be doing.

She would be alone in her bedsit; a place that, despite all her efforts to make it something like a proper home, would never be anything more than a disgusting little room, full of rusting, dripping pipes and wet, peeling wallpaper, three flights up from the shared lavatory that made her gag just to think about it.

She wondered if Saunders had any idea how awful the places were that he rented to the girls. Probably not. He seemed to have people to do just about everything else for him, so why would he bother himself visiting slums?

'You're having me on,' he said, interrupting her thoughts.

'Sorry?'

'Are you trying to tell me that a beautiful girl like you hasn't got a load of parties lined up?'

Ginny's cheeks flushed and she lowered her chin, hoping he hadn't noticed. It was ridiculous. She spent her working life showing off all she had and yet a single compliment from Saunders had her blushing like a virgin. It was something about him . . .

She peered up at him through her lashes and realised what it was. He was looking at her with the self-assured, direct gaze that was the prerogative of only the genuinely confident. A confidence that could come from a man's looks, his wealth, his authority, or, as in Saunders's case, she thought, from a combination of all those things.

'I've embarrassed you, darling. I'm sorry.' He smiled easily. 'But there's no shame in having no one to go to.'

Saunders's words jolted her. She turned away sharply. It was true, she had no one. They were gone, all of them. But she didn't want him to feel that she was . . . That she was what? The sad, pathetic figure that she actually was?

'I've had plenty of offers,' she said hurriedly.

Saunders raised a querying eyebrow.

'I mean, I've been invited to something tomorrow afternoon.' She paused. 'I mean *this* afternoon. So I have got things to do. I just don't feel like going.'

'Why not?'

'I feel a bit tired,' she said lamely. She could hardly have told him the truth – that she felt so depressed, all she was fit for was hiding under her bedclothes until the whole bloody holiday was over.

They sat there smoking in silence until Saunders eventually said, 'I'm on me own an' all, you know. Not always easy at these sort of times is it, when everyone's off with their families and there's no work to do 'cos no one's about? Life's always so busy; then . . . nothing. Still, you get used to it.' He laughed mirthlessly to himself, pressing his lips tightly together, as though recalling a painful memory.

'I nearly got married once,' he went on, with as little emotion as a man wondering whether he should wear his mac or his overcoat. 'But she went off with a bloody Yank. When I was away at sea serving me sodding country if you don't mind. Never had much inclination to settle down after that.'

Ginny's head jerked up. 'I thought you were, you know, with Leila.'

Saunders laughed again. 'Hark at me going on like a bloody old woman nattering over the fence. I must have had too much of the old giggle juice tonight. Or maybe it's Christmas getting to me, eh? But as for Leila . . .'

'Yeah?'

'Look, blondie, me and Leila go back a long way, but things change. Times change.' He levered himself away from the table and turned round to face the mirror. He studied his reflection as he carefully straightened his tie – a gesture clearly indicating that the subject was closed.

'I've bought the lease on them premises for the new club,' he said, turning round and standing over her like a great dark shadow. 'And seeing as you ain't got nothing to do while this place is closed, you can come and have a shufty at it. See what you think. We'll have a bite to eat afterwards.'

Ginny shrank back into her chair. She said nothing, just shook her head.

He looked at her for a long moment, then held up his hands in a gesture of surrender. 'All right. Bad time.'

Still she said nothing.

He winked, then turned away to pick up his hat. 'I'll catch up with you later on,' he said, his back still to her. 'When you're feeling a bit more chipper.'

With that he walked over to the door, paused briefly, looked over his shoulder and said, 'I've got a good feeling about this new year. I mean, 1953, even sounds good, don't it?' He winked again. 'There's gonna be plenty of opportunities for anyone who's got the brains to see 'em. Opportunities like running a club for instance. Now that *is* a good opportunity. Especially for a woman.'

He touched the brim of his hat in salute, pulled the door shut quietly behind him and was gone.

Confused and exhausted, Ginny rose from her seat, her body as heavy as if it had been weighed down with bags of coal.

She flicked off the lamp by the door and returned the room to semi-darkness. But instead of going through to the club, she just stood there, staring at the flickering lights on the scrappy little tree, feeling as though her heart could break as easily as one of the gaudy lanterns that adorned its almost bare branches.

The sound of someone singing drifted up from the street below. It was a deep male voice that could – just could – have been Billy Saunders's, crooning the sweet opening bars of 'White Christmas'.

The sentimental lyrics were too much for Ginny. She buried her face in her hands and began to sob uncontrollably.

The door flew back on its hinges and Ginny felt arms wrap around her. She squirmed away in alarm, stumbling backwards across the litter-strewn room.

When Ginny regained her balance, she looked up and saw Gloria standing before her, his arms outstretched in a bizarre parody of a caring maiden aunt. 'Look,' he snapped petulantly, 'there's no need to look at me like that. I've come to sodding comfort you. Now, come here and tell me all about it.'

Ginny wouldn't have been more astonished if the skinny little man had just announced that he was leaving the club to go round the world with a troupe of travelling acrobats. She eyed him warily through her tears, wondering what new madness was happening to her now.

She swiped roughly at her wet cheeks with the back of her hand. 'What's going on? Why are you being nice to me?'

Gloria shook his head, pursed his lips and handed her a neatly washed and ironed handkerchief. He then held up one finger to silence her, told her to 'Hang on one minute!' in a soprano-pitched squeal and ducked back out into the club.

'I'll tell you why,' he carolled to her from the bar. 'Because, for one thing, I'm a fool to myself – and, if you ever tell *anyone* I've been nice to you, just remember, dearie, I'll scratch your eyes out.'

He reappeared in the doorway, brandishing a bottle of champagne and two glasses. 'And for another, I know that if I looked like a cross between Marilyn Monroe and Betty Grable I wouldn't be bloody well sitting by myself crying.' He pointed the bottle towards the sink and shot the cork across the room. 'I'd be wiggling me little botty all over flaming London, driving all the boys to distraction, and so would any of the other girls in this place. So, I know there must be something wrong. That's why we're gonna drink this champagne, wish ourselves a merry Christmas and forget all about the rotten bleeders who make us cry.'

Ginny sniffed inelegantly as she accepted the foaming glass he was handing her. 'Who's Marilyn Monroe?' she spluttered, choking on the heady mixture of tears and bubbles.

Gloria patted her back with slightly more force than was necessary. 'Some new, innocent-looking blonde I saw in one of the film mags the other day. Someone who can make a very good life for herself, I'm telling you. If she plays her cards right and takes the opportunities what come along for the likes of her.' He sipped daintily at his glass and smiled knowingly at her across the rim.

When Ginny said nothing, Gloria decided plain talking was the only way. 'Listen to me, little Ginny Martin. Saunders is a man with power. He's got that power because he's got a brain, and because he's scared of nothing and no one. And he's a right handsome bugger an' all, but that's another matter. Anyway, he can be a very good friend, but he can also be the very worst enemy you could ever imagine. And let's just say that he wants to be your friend, Ginny my love, and you should be very grateful. Very grateful indeed. 'Cos Mr Saunders looks after his friends.' He touched first one, then the other corner of his mouth with the tip of his little finger, as though wiping away unwanted crumbs. 'And he also looks after the friends of his friends.'

He tossed his head haughtily. 'So you see, I'm not all

heart, my girl. I know which side me bread's buttered. I look after you, and you . . . Well, you know the rest.'

Ginny lowered her eyelids, blocking out the world. She felt as though she were an insignificant ball of fluff being swept 'into a corner by a very large broom.

'Don't you dare go falling asleep on me, girl!' Gloria shrieked, misunderstanding her closed eyes. 'There's me giving you the benefit and you go and start nodding off! Get some more of this champagne down you and we'll have a toast.'

Gloria topped up their drinks and raised his glass high in the air, the flickering light making the wine dance and sparkle like cut crystal. 'To all of Mr Saunders's friends. May they never be his enemies and may all our dreams come true.'

While Gloria sat in the dressing-room comforting Ginny with his unique blend of French wine, acid-tongued advice and self-seeking opportunism, Leila and the girls were downstairs on the pavement still waiting for a cab, shivering in the sleety drizzle and the bitter wind that was whipping round the corner of Frith Street, smacking their silky clothes around their legs like sails in a north-easterly.

'We'll never get enough cabs to take us lot,' Carmen wailed, shrugging down into her jacket. 'The drivers'll all be home in their beds, getting in what kip they can before their kids wake up and climb all over 'em, waving their Christmas stockings and chucking orange peel in the hearth, and—'

'What? Acting just like real people, you mean?' Yvette interrupted her, snarling through teeth clenched as much in anger as against the cold. 'I knew we should have ordered one earlier.'

'A cab'll come along, sweeties, you just see. And we'll all share if necessary.'

'One'll never take all of us,' complained Carmen.

'Want to bet?' Leila lifted her dress above her knee and winked. 'We have our ways, remember!'

As if on cue, a cab pulled up beside them, sending a muddy spray of icy water across the kerbside.

'Hello, darlings, home time, is it?' the cabbie asked. Unlike some drivers, he didn't mind the toms, they always seemed fair to him and usually gave him a reasonable sort of a tip. The only thing he drew the line at was if they wanted to go with a punter in the back of the cab. It wasn't that he would have objected, it was more to do with being scared of losing his badge if the Old Bill caught them at it. Never mind what his wife would do to him if she ever found out he'd let one get anywhere near his motor.

Yvette sidled up to the car. She was immediately in business mode, laying a black-gloved hand on the roof and flashing a dazzlingly sensual smile at the now slack-jawed driver.

While Yvette set about bamboozling the man into believing that what he most wanted in the world was to fit seven long-legged women into the back of his cab, Shirley was tapping Leila on the shoulder and dripping a cupful of her usual venom into her ear.

'Leila?' she whispered. 'Isn't that the governor over there? Just getting into his car over by the club?'

Leila didn't respond.

'I wonder if anyone else was up there?' Shirley went on, looking about her with exaggerated curiosity. 'Let's see. Milly went home with Gracie. And Lou went off with Mags, Maureen, and Iris . . .' She paused, placing a finger tip to her lips. 'Didn't Ginny stay behind? Wasn't she—'

Before Shirley could hiss another word, Leila sprang towards the taxi. She shoved Yvette to one side, wrenched open the cab door, leapt into the back seat and slammed the door firmly behind her.

She then wound the window, opened her mouth to say something, but changed her mind. After a moment's indecision, and deliberately avoiding meeting Shirley's gaze, she stuck her head out of the window and said with determined jollity, 'I'll see you all later then, sweeties. Now drive on please, cabbie, the ladies will be making their own arrangements.'

Yvette threw up her hands in despair. 'Now we'll never bloody well get home.' She spun round to confront Shirley. 'What the hell did you say to her?'

'Only the truth, darling. Only the truth.'

As the first flakes of snow began to fall in the biting early-morning air, the rest of the girls stood in puzzled silence, trying to figure out what was going on and looking wistfully after the taxi as it disappeared around the corner into Shaftesbuury Avenue.

Just a few hours later the snow had settled in a thick blanket over most of London, but its twinkling beauty held no attraction for Dilys.

On first waking, she had momentarily been captivated by the sight of the white mantle transforming even her miserable corner of Stepney into a place of almost ethereal muffled beauty, but then she remembered that Nellie Martin had stayed the night and was having dinner with them.

Ted's mum. The bloody bad penny that always turned up.

It was now barely half past eight on Christmas morning, but instead of being able to turn over for another few hours' sleep, Dilys was on duty in the prefab kitchen, with her back to the cooker, resentfully scoring the skin of a puny leg of pork, while Nellie sat alongside her, chain-smoking, drinking tea, finding fault and moaning.

It was only the fact that Dilys knew what would be in store for her if Ted turned up and she hadn't made at least a half-way decent dinner for the old trout that was preventing her from bending the leg of pork right over Nellie's curler-bristling head. Dilys had seen Nellie in action too often, twisting the truth until Ted was ready to throttle someone with his bare hands, to take the chance of upsetting her.

'This place's freezing. Can't you turn that gas fire in there up a bit?' Nellie sniped, interrupting Dilys's day-dream that had advanced to wringing the old cow's neck with the tea-towel.

'Actually,' Dilys said, wiping her perspiring forehead on the back of her hand, 'I'm a bit warm if you don't mind, Nellie. In fact, the heat from this oven's scorching me legs so bad that I don't know how much longer I can carry on. And if I pass out, we won't have no dinner.'

Nellie puffed out her cheeks and made irritating little puttering sounds through her pursed lips. 'I wouldn't say no to a little drop of something in me tea then,' she whined. 'Something to warm me through a bit like.'

'I'm sure Ted wouldn't mind if you had a drop of his scotch,' said Dilys pointedly, as she tipped a pile of salt on to the meat and rubbed it furiously into the latticework of cuts she had made.

She would have loved to have said no to the old dragon, but the chance that she might drink herself back to sleep was an opportunity she really couldn't afford to miss. 'Why don't you help yourself?'

Reluctantly, Nellie shifted herself just enough to reach the whisky bottle that stood on the side by the stove.

'Shame you don't talk much to them brothers o' your'n no more,' she said, topping up her cup until the liquor-laced tea sploshed over the side and into the saucer. 'Them wives of their'n have been filling that house with grub for weeks now. I've been watching 'em, going back and forward with bags bulging with gear. They'll be having a lovely do back in Bailey Street. Plenty of money them boys must be bringing in. Plenty.'

Dilys sank her teeth deeper into her lower lip and slapped the joint unceremoniously into a roasting tin. She wouldn't rise to her. She wouldn't.

But even if Dilys had been fool enough to say something, there'd have been little point because Nellie wasn't in the mood to listen to anyone. She was off and in full flight. And on her favourite subject – other people's mistreatment of her, a poor old girl that no one gave a bugger about.

'And that sodding Ginny. She's another one. After how good I was to that ungrateful bitch. What does she do? How does she repay me? Sends sodding gear round for that kid o' your'n that's how. And cuts me dead. Like a knife to my heart that was. How about me? That's what I say.' Nellie glugged back a mouthful of her tea.

'Mind you,' she went on, her devious mind on overtime, 'it must have saved you a few bob, her buying all them presents for the kid. You ain't had to buy a single thing for her, have you? Not a single, solitary thing. You dunno how lucky you are.' She swallowed another whisky-fortified mouthful. 'Maybe you should have spent the dough you saved on getting a bigger bit of pork.'

Dilys's blood boiled. Nellie knew they were lucky they had anything on the table at all, seeing as her darling Ted had, as usual, 'forgotten' that he had promised to bring in all the food from some bloke he'd met. In fact, if the butcher's stall up on the Waste hadn't had this pathetic bit of meat left last night, they'd have been having a tin of corned beef for their Christmas dinner.

As if reading Dilys's thoughts, Nellie's next target was her son. 'And then there's bloody Ted,' she exclaimed, throwing up her hands. 'Fancy him going amongst the missing again. Disappearing on Christmas Eve like that. Who'd believe it of your own flesh and blood? And without leaving his old mum so much as a sodding box of hankies. Don't no one think of buying nothing for an old woman at Christmas time no more? And you know what'll happen next, don't you? That kid of your'n'll be moaning and groaning.' Nellie screwed up her face into an ugly travesty of a hurt child. 'I want my daddy. Where's my daddy?'

Nellie's cruel impersonation could not have been further from the truth. Susan, a six-year-old who was already well used to her own company and to getting herself up and dressed every day, had been outside, solemnly and industriously constructing a snowman, since she had first opened her eyes to the strange early morning winter light over an hour ago.

Satisfied with her efforts, she was now ready to go in, and was fumbling with ice-numbed fingers for the doorkey she had worn around her neck on a piece of string since she had been barely four years old.

As she trotted into the kitchen, her eyes and face lit up with pleasure; when there were other adults around, her mummy was usually nicer to her than if they were alone. 'Hello, Nanny Nellie, I didn't know you was up yet. D'you wanna see what things I got in me stocking? And I can show you me snow—'

Nellie recoiled. 'Get off! You're all wet. And I told you before. I ain't your nanny.'

'But Mummy said—'

'And *I* said . . .' boomed Nellie.

With a wisdom far beyond her age, Susan dropped her chin and said very softly, 'I'm sorry.' Then she backed away and disappeared into the front room to play with the lovely china tea-set that Father Christmas had brought her.

'Queer sort of kid,' sneered Nellie. 'Too quiet for my liking.'

She lit herself another cigarette, again without offering one to Dilys. 'What a fine bloody day this is turning out to be.'

'And a happy sodding Christmas to you an' all,' Dilys muttered, slamming the dish into the oven and whacking shut the oven door, wishing with all her heart that she was anywhere in the whole wide world except in a poxy prefab in Stepney, and with anyone in the world but her bloke's bloody mother and her bloke's sodding kid.

She would have been unhappier still, had she known what Ted had been up to.

A couple of hours before Dilys had even opened her eyes, Ted had been following a heavy, mousey-haired woman up an unlit stairway.

'You can stay all night if you want,' she giggled over her shoulder. 'As a Christmas treat like.'

'What, the old man not docking till tomorrow?' Ted asked, grabbing a handful of her plump backside.

'Get off, you cheeky sod! And anyway, I ain't married, am I?'

She pushed open a door and they stepped into a pitch-dark room.

Ted began tapping around the wall, trying to find the switch to turn on the light.

'We don't want that on,' the woman breathed. 'Let's be romantic.'

She fiddled around until she found the switch to a frilly table lamp shaped like a crinoline lady on a swing. When she turned it on, the bulb was so dim, all it illuminated was a pale, red-tinted circle around its base.

Ted squinted in the gloom. Where the hell had he fetched up this time?

When he'd picked up the woman, in the dark side-street outside the spieler where he'd been playing cards and drinking, he didn't have a clue where he was. Hackney Wick way, he reckoned, but it could have been as far away as Stoke Newington. He'd been out pub-crawling till closing time and then doing the rounds of the tatty little unlicensed drinking and gambling clubs for hours. Anything to get away from bloody Dilys and his mother, moaning on about why he hadn't brought home the stuff they reckoned he should have done, because it was sodding Christmas Eve.

But after a while the Christmas spirit had caught up even with Ted, and he had been more than happy when this friendly sort had asked him up to her place to help celebrate the season of goodwill.

'How about a little bit of music?' she suggested, swinging her fleshy hips as she crossed to the corner of the room, where an old-fashioned wooden wireless set had pride of place on a little bamboo table.

Music? What was the silly tart going on about? He hadn't come here to have a poxy dance.

She found a station playing suitably festive music – a three-part women's harmony group singing 'I saw Mummy kissing Santa Claus'.

'I love this one, don't you?' she giggled. 'But it's a bit too loud. We don't want no distractions, do we?'

She twiddled with the volume control, lowering the sound until it was a barely audible background hum, then turned round and held out her arms to Ted. 'How about a kiss for me then, Santa?'

Ted moved towards her. This was more like it. But even though he was half plastered, Ted's instinct for trouble and self-preservation was still operating on full power. He stopped dead in his tracks.

'What's that noise?' he asked, visions of angry husbands, punched noses and pain filling his mind.

'It's only me little sister,' the woman said hurriedly. 'I wasn't planning on working tonight, not as it's Christmas like, so I said I'd mind her.'

Ted let the bit about 'working tonight' pass – he wasn't stupid, he'd realised straight away she was a tom and had already decided she wasn't going to be paid anyway – but he was more interested in the idea of a little sister.

'How old's she then, this little sister?'

'What?' The woman wasn't sure if he meant what she thought he did.

'Much younger than you, is she?' Ted leered. 'I get on well with young 'uns.'

He did mean what she'd thought.

'Leave off, she's just a kid.'

'Come on, it'll be a real Christmas party with the three of us.'

'Mum?' he heard a voice, thick with sleep, call from the doorway. 'Can I hear a man talking? What's going on?'

Ted grabbed hold of the woman's arm, his fingers digging into her flesh. 'What's she mean, *Mum*? You said she was your sister.'

With his other hand, Ted reached behind him and found the switch to the overhead light. 'Jesus!' he fumed. 'How old are you?'

'She's forty-nine,' the girl wailed, shielding her eyes with her arm against the sudden glare.

'Forty-nine?' Slowly, Ted shook his head. As he looked at the woman, his face contorted with revulsion, twisting into a mask of sickened contempt – not only at the woman but at himself for sinking so low. He saw in her all the women he hated. All the women who had caused his life to fail. All the women he wanted to get rid of. 'You're old enough to be my fucking mother!'

'Look, just get out,' the woman said, reaching out to snap off the light and returning the room to darkness – her irrational need to hide her raddled looks from the man who was not only insulting her, but was really hurting her arm, overcoming even her fear of him.

'You filthy, dirty whore.'

In a flash of explosive hatred, the madness inside Ted was unleashed.

With his teeth clenched as though they'd been bolted together, Ted pounced on the woman with the ferocity of a wildcat bringing down an antelope.

Try as she might, there was nothing the young girl could do to stop him, as he rained punches, slaps and kicks across her mother's twisting and writhing body.

When the girl returned to the room, still barefoot and in her night-dress, covered in snow and trembling with terror and the icy cold, with the only neighbour she had managed to awaken during the early hours of Christmas morning, she turned on the light and stared.

The shell of what had once been her mother lay in a bloody heap on the floor. An ugly, abandoned rag doll.

The young girl started screaming, screaming as though she would never stop.

Chapter 15

2 June 1953

Dilys was cheesed off.

As she sat at her dressing-table, her mouth set in a stern, straight line, her arms folded rigidly across her chest, staring gloomily into the mirror, she listened to the annoying cut-glass drawl of the radio commentator wittering on and on about: the huge crowds! the enthusiasm! the fun! and (considering the damp weather!) the general, all-round, bloody good time that every other bugger in the whole sodding world but her seemed to be having.

Hoo-bleeding-ray.

She hoped they choked on it.

Dilys had briefly entertained a vague hope that Ted would turn up at the last minute and announce that he was whisking her off to some exciting do or other that he'd got tickets for. But she hadn't seen hide nor hair of him for days – surprise – so that was off the menu.

It just wasn't fair; even Susan – a six-year-old – was out enjoying herself. All right, she'd only gone to the Coronation party in Bailey Street, but she was still out. Like every other bugger in the whole pissing country, according to laughing boy on the wireless.

And what was *she* doing? She was sitting here, with no one to answer to, free as a ruddy bird, but nowhere to bleeding well go.

She picked up her hairbrush and aimed it at the radio set. She missed.

It wasn't as though her brothers and their smarmy,

perfect little home-making wives hadn't invited her along to the Bailey Street party with Susan. They had. And Dilys had sort of said that she might be going. But when it came to it, she hadn't even bothered getting herself done up when she'd gone round there to drop Susan off a couple of hours ago. She just couldn't bear the thought of spending the whole day with that pair of self-satisfied bitches. She knew exactly what it would be like: bloody purgatory.

They would talk non-stop about how, after their father-in-law – *her* dad, mind – had died, they'd got *her* brothers to divide the old place in Bailey Street into two 'dear little flats', and how they now had plans to turn them into 'little palaces'.

Palaces! What was so bad about number 11 staying the way it was? That's what Dilys wanted to know. Maybe it had got a bit run down since her mum had got herself killed in that stupid accident, but the way that pair of dopey tarts carried on about having to rip out this, and panel over that, and cover every bloody surface in 'contemporary' bleeding fabrics and sheets of flipping Fablon, it made Dilys want to smack them round their smug, simpering faces.

Housework and home-making, it was all they ever talked about. And what was worse was the *way* they talked about it. They acted as though Dilys was a bit dim and needed helpful hints on the right way to run a home. As if she didn't have better things to do than sodding polishing and ironing.

She probably wouldn't have minded quite so much if they had been older than her, but both her sisters-in-law were only in their early twenties, a good five or six years younger than she was, yet they carried on like old women. Always fussing about in their frilly aprons, cooking and cleaning, and smiling and twittering away like a right pair of old trouts.

In fact, they reminded her of how Ginny used to be, back in her sainthood days. Killing themselves just to 'keep things nice'. It made Dilys shudder. Whatever her Micky and Sid had seen in them she couldn't begin to imagine.

At least Ginny had come to her senses and cleared off, once she'd got rid of the kid she was carrying. Dilys certainly didn't have the same hopes for her sisters-in-law. She could just see them once they started breeding. The thought was almost too horrible to contemplate.

There they'd be with their big, shiny, Silver Cross prams, suffocating under piles of hand-knitted, pearl-buttoned matinée jackets, struggling to get past the push-chairs and the rocking horses in the passage of number 11, a beaming baby covered in ribbons and lace under one arm and a bucket full of perfect, snowy white nappies under the other.

They were so stupid, they'd probably revel in the whole horrible business of motherhood and they'd make it a good excuse to spend even more of her brothers' wage packets. Not that they didn't already drain them every week as it was – the boys never had any money for her these days. Or time.

Dilys never saw them unless she went round there. And that wasn't very often, because having to watch those two witches keeping the boys just where they wanted them turned her guts.

Dilys propped her chin on her fists and puffed unhappily as she studied the faint lines that were beginning to form around her eyes and mouth, and the slight, but definitely visible, mauve smudges beneath her eyes. That's all bloody motherhood had done for her. Made her look old before her time.

Not for the first time, Dilys wished with all her heart that it had been her and not Ginny who'd gone to see Jeannie Thompson with her best yellow soap and her douching tubes. Getting herself knocked up by Ted had seemed such a good idea at the time. Where had it all gone wrong, she wondered? And, come to think of it, where had sodding Ted Martin gone an' all?

Dilys arched her back, so that she could reach into her pocket for her cigarettes.

Only two left? Wonderful! Now she was running out of fags on top of everything else. That was all she bloody well needed.

And there was hardly any milk.

She'd bet her sisters-in-law would never let themselves run short of fags. They'd never run short of anything. Not them.

She could just visualise the two polished and doilied sideboards, one in each of the flats in number eleven, and knew, as sure as night followed day, that there'd be a dinky little wineglass on each one, full of cigarettes for any 'guests' who happened to pop in from the street party, so that they could help themselves while they were sipping a drop of port or a gin and orange. And there'd be more milk in their cupboards than in a flaming dairy.

And a dairy was where they belonged, because that's what they were, a pair of right rotten cows.

Dilys's lip curled in contempt, as she flicked her spent match on to the dressing-table. She'd done the right thing staying away.

Then again, maybe she should just nip round there for a little while. It couldn't hurt just to show her face. And she could help herself to some of their fags, have a few drinks, something to eat maybe, and still be out of there all within the hour.

But, tempting as it was to see what she could mump

off them, there was no getting away from the fact that she bloody hated those two women.

With her resentment bubbling up to seething level, Dilys was now sure she had made the right decision about not going to Bailey Street. Fags or not, she had no intention of being within a mile of that pair if she could help it.

They could stick it. She'd find somewhere where she could have a laugh. Somewhere with a bit of life, where she'd be welcomed and appreciated, and not treated like the poor relation. Somewhere like the places Ted used to take her.

Bloody Ted.

She ground out her cigarette in the pickle jar lid on her dressing-table, snatched up her compact and began furiously powdering her cheeks.

She'd show Ted Martin she didn't need him to have a good time. She'd put on her war-paint and show the whole bleed'n' lot of them.

While Dilys was still dithering as to whether she should go for the Crushed Coral or the Peach Parfait lipstick, the Coronation do at Leila's flat was already well under way.

As with the one she'd put on for the girls at Christmas, Leila had ulterior motives for throwing a party for them. Again, she didn't want to be alone when everyone else would be celebrating, and doing business was out of the question. Men were expected to be at home with their families on such a special day, not out clubbing in the West End.

Inviting the girls round to the flat also presented Leila with an opportunity she couldn't resist. Having made damned sure that Ginny was coming this time – no excuses accepted – Leila was going to have another go at persuading her that taking the manageress's job in Billy's new club would be the best thing that could happen. And not only for Ginny.

During the past few months, Leila had become increasingly fixated on getting her to hang up her feathers and to leave the stage. The combination of Billy's – *her* Billy's – obvious admiration for Ginny's undeniable assets and Shirley's spiteful insinuations had convinced Leila that she had to get her working in a more sober role. She'd thought about trying to get her sacked, but she knew that was a non-starter – Ginny's act had become too much of a success and Billy had started seeing her almost as a talisman. Getting her promoted was the only way.

The trouble was, Leila wasn't having much success in persuading Ginny. She was reluctant even to consider the job.

That was why Leila was trying this new tack: she was going to give Ginny a taste of the good life and, when she compared the squalor of the sordid room in which she was living with the luxury of Leila's Mayfair flat, it might just get her thinking.

So the Coronation party had been planned, but Leila's scheme had almost fallen at the first fence.

The girls, like the majority of ordinary people in Britain, had initially been indifferent to the idea of even bothering to mark the event and were more interested in the possibility of just having the day off.

Who gave a toss about a church service with a load of toffs parading about in robes and silk stockings, was a typical comment. Especially when the average person in the street was busy coping with the day-to-day worries of overcrowded housing, the growing threat of their menfolk being shipped off to Korea and the ceaseless, grinding aggravation of the despised rationing system – *eight years* after the war had ended!

In fact, rather than being keen to throw parties to celebrate the crowning of one of their 'betters', the general mood was more conducive to throwing bricks.

But then something happened: the excitement began to gather, slowly at first, like a snowball, then it suddenly seemed that soon no one wanted to be left out of the merry-making.

In no time at all it was as though everyone had wanted to have a party all along. Community collections were swiftly organised to fund the festivities, tasks were, as always, delegated and commemorative plates, mugs and dishes were ordered. Some families were even able to boast that they'd bought a television set in honour of the big day. Although 'bought' was probably the wrong word as, unlike the little walnut number in Leila's sitting-room, most sets had been acquired with the spurious blessings of the never-never man.

Buying a television had actually been Leila's trump card in attracting the girls to her party, and it now had pride of place in the plushly carpeted room, where the girls were gathered, oohing and aahing in wonder and criticising the hairdos and hats of the female guests attending the ceremony.

Leila, as usual, was acting totally blasé. She left it to the others to behave as if they were a bunch of convent girls who'd been let out for the first time without the nuns, while she hovered at a discreetly refined distance.

'I can't get over it. It's so clear.' Ginny shook her head in amazement as she stared, transfixed, at the bulging glass of the nine-inch screen, not even put off by the fact that it was dwarfed by its massive wooden cabinet.

The picture itself wasn't actually up to much, it was grainy and flickery – nothing like the Technicolor wonders to be seen at the cinema – but as Ginny stood behind the enormous silk brocade sofa, peering over

Carmen's head at the grey and off-white moment of history being enacted in the cathedral before her, she was in no position to make rational judgements. Her critical faculties had been blown apart by her first sight of the eye-boggling marvel of Leila's sitting-room.

With her feet sinking into the soft wool rugs, Ginny felt like an actress in a glamorous motion picture about sophisticated couples leading their gorgeously urbane lives in Paris and Manhattan. It was so like a film set, in fact, that Ginny wouldn't have been at all surprised if Gene Kelly or Fred Astaire had come breezing into the room to whisk her away for a quick foxtrot across the parquet flooring in the hallway.

'Let me take that for you,' said Leila, easing Ginny's coat off her shoulders.

'What d'you think of the television then, Gin,' asked Carmen without taking her eyes from the set.

'It's just like you're there,' Ginny said, as she watched the tiny figures processing along the aisle.

'I know one or two people who *are* there, sweetie,' Leila whispered into her ear.

Ginny twisted round to face her. 'You don't mean . . .?' she breathed.

Leila put her finger to her lips and nodded.

'I feel like I'm dreaming.' Ginny turned her head so that she could take a full sweep of the room. 'Honestly, Leila, I've never seen such a lovely place in all my life. It's even better than that hotel you took me to that time.'

'You're very kind.' Leila smiled graciously and took Ginny's coat outside to hang it up.

'You should see the kitchen,' Carmen muttered from the sofa, her mouth stuffed full of canapés from one of the trays of food dotted around the room on the ivory and glass side tables. 'I saw it when I come here at Christmas. It's out of this world. There's all tiles on the walls, and a fridge and a food-mixing thing, and . . .' She shrugged. 'Everything.'

She tapped the arm of the sofa. 'Come on, Gin, park yourself next to me. Make yourself comfortable.'

Ginny couldn't bring herself to do it; perching on the pale beige arm was unthinkable. 'I'll be fine down here,' she said, lowering herself on to a squashy tan leather pouffe, tooled with patterns in red and gold.

Carmen, her gaze still fixed on the screen, held out one of the trays of food.

Ginny took a little square of melba toast spread with cream cheese and topped with a curl of smoked salmon.

'D'you reckon she'd let me have a look round later, Carmen?'

'Course she will. She gave Patty the full tour just before you arrived. She missed out at Christmas, like you. You ask her. Go on.'

When Leila returned, Ginny did exactly that and Leila happily obliged.

As they stepped into the hall – a wide oval, decorated in tastefully understated regency strips and with a classically inspired painting covering the whole of the high ceiling – Leila explained that two of the rooms in the flat were locked. They were what she called her workroom, and the maid's room – the maid's room! – but, if Ginny was interested, she was welcome to see everything else.

Leila had pitched it just right. Ginny was more than interested. She followed Leila around, her eyes taking in one wonder after another, walking as carefully and respectfully as if she were in a church, or the sort of art gallery where you knew without asking that the price of a single picture would be more than a lifetime's wages. And, with its sumptuous furnishings, its luxurious decoration and its up-to-the-minute gadgetry – there was even a telephone in the main bedroom! – it was actually more like an art gallery than anywhere Ginny had ever set foot in before.

That someone could live surrounded by such elegance and beauty was a revelation to Ginny. There were rooms everywhere and, to Ginny, every one of them was magnificent. It was all so bright and airy, and even though there were things – exquisite things – everywhere, there was still so much space and light, real room to breathe. And not a damp patch, or a rusting, dripping pipe in sight.

The thing that surprised Ginny most of all was that Shirley had her own room in the flat, with a full bedroom suite where she could keep her clothes and shoes and things. It wasn't that Shirley sometimes stayed overnight, Dilys had often bunked in with Ginny when she had been living at home with her mum and dad before she had married Ted – that's what friends did – but it was having a place that was big enough to keep a whole room for a friend, just in case she wanted to stay.

While Ginny stared about her in slack-jawed rapture, Leila chatted away, pointing out her favourite 'little pieces', as she called them: things of which she was particularly fond, or that had an amusing story behind them. Mostly they were gifts from men, but not one, Ginny noted, seemed to be a gift from Mr Saunders. Well, not that Leila mentioned. 'You like my little flat then, Ginny?' she asked as they came back to the hall.

'I think it's the most smashing place I've ever laid eyes on,' Ginny said, meaning every word, as she stared in awe, yet again, up at the painted ceiling. 'Gloria said you had a nice home, but this is . . . Well, it's . . .'

Leila noted that Gloria had been opening his big mouth. What was he after? But she'd worry about that later. Now she had to focus on Ginny. 'You could have a place like this yourself one day.'

'How?' Ginny asked with a little laugh, tearing her gaze away from the artist's vision of nymphs and goddesses. 'Rob a bank?'

'I'm serious. If you take this club manager's job, you'll be earning very good money, Ginny. Very good.'

Ginny's face clouded over. Not again. She'd been feeling so down it was all she could do to find the energy to turn up to do the show each night; how could anyone think she had what it took to do something as difficult as running a club? In fact, she had seriously thought that if it wasn't for the debts, and the weekly envelopes she sent to Susan and Nellie, she could have just given it all up and . . . That was the problem. And what?

She wouldn't even have a roof over her head. Not even a slum roof.

'Well, Ginny?'

'I can't.'

'Look at me, Ginny. And just listen to those girls in there.'

Ginny did as she was told and listened to the drunken chorus of laughter coming from the sitting-room.

'It's you Billy singled out for this job. Not them. And why? Because you're bright, you're able, you're from the area, and,' Leila added, suddenly distracted by a loose thread on her emerald-green sleeve, 'you look good. And let's face it, Billy's not asking you to run the Astor Club for him, now is he. It's only an East End drinking spot.'

They said nothing for a few moments, just stood there while the girls' giggles built to a crescendo of tipsy hilarity.

Leila took a deep breath and pulled her final rabbit from the hat. 'I've been very good to you, Ginny. And very patient. And I think you owe me a favour.'

Ginny couldn't look at her; she didn't want to hear what she was sure was coming next.

'As the governor's right-hand assistant, I was told to persuade you to take this job, Ginny,' she began, setting the foundation of her lie. 'And if you don't do this for me, I'm going to get the blame. I could lose everything I've worked for: my position in the business, my reputation, this flat. Do you want to be responsible for all those things happening to me?' Leila touched the back of her hand theatrically to her forehead.

'But Leila—'

'And I thought you were my friend.'

Ginny ran her fingers distractedly through her hair, as a fat tear brimmed over and plopped on to her cheek. 'I don't know why Mr Saunders thinks I can do it.'

Leila stretched her lips in a taut smile. 'Because he's got faith in you. He was only saying so the other day.' She then added with reckless impatience: 'In fact, it sometimes feels as though he speaks of nothing else *but* you.'

'But, Leila—'

'Look, I've put it to you straight, Ginny. You know the position now.'

'I'm sorry, I didn't mean to get you in trouble. I'm really sorry.' She shook her head at her own wickedness and sniffed loudly. 'All right if I use the—'

'The powder room? Of course. You go and get those tears mopped up.' Apart from an almost imperceptible fluttering of a nerve just below her left eye, Leila looked completely composed, but she could have smacked Ginny's face. What was wrong with her? Anyone else in her position would have jumped at a chance like this. Leila took a deep breath. She mustn't lose control. 'I'll be in the kitchen.'

While Leila and Ginny had been in the hall, Shirley was

pressed against the sitting-room door straining to hear their conversation. Now she'd heard Ginny go off to the lavatory, she dashed into the kitchen to find out the state of play from Leila.

'I wondered where you'd got to,' Shirley lied, as she hitched up the skin-tight skirt of her blue satin sheath dress and clambered unsteadily on to one of the spindly legged stools at the breakfast bar.

Leila could smell the gin on Shirley's breath from ten feet away.

'I was giving Ginny the guided tour,' she said wearily, taking a tray of ice from the refrigerator, cracking it against the stainless steel draining board and tipping it into a bowl.

'Hope you didn't let little Miss Butter-Wouldn't-Melt look in the workroom when you were showing her round,' Shirley snorted. 'You'd have scared the life out of her if she'd seen all the gear. Especially those new harnesses and whips you had delivered.'

Leila closed her eyes for a long moment. In a business where keeping your mouth shut was the first rule, Shirley's drinking was becoming a real problem. But she couldn't deal with her now.

'I like the girl,' she said lightly. 'And I was showing her my flat. Not interviewing her for a job.'

'Lucky you weren't, because let's face it, we're none of us getting any younger, are we? And having the likes of her working here, well, we wouldn't get a look in, would we?'

Leila poured herself a small gin, topped the tall glass with tonic almost to the brim and dropped in a single ice cube.

'Don't I get a drink?' Shirley asked petulantly.

'I think you've had enough.'

'Touchy!' Shirley grinned smugly. 'D'you know, she's

really getting to you, Leila. You want to get her off that stage in Frith Street before she really gets you going. You can't fool me, I know what it's all about: every time she flashes those tits of hers you never know who's going to be standing at the back of the club watching, and wanting her, do you? It must be driving you mad. But I can't say I blame you. I've seen the way Billy looks at her. And while I can't understand the attraction myself, whatever it is, she's got it. You want to get her all covered up in a frock, with her legs hidden behind a cash desk, as soon as you like.' Shirley laughed coarsely. 'And a pair of glasses wouldn't come amiss.'

Leila kept her back to Shirley, not trusting herself to face her. 'Have you finished?' she asked through gritted teeth.

'Don't blame me for the way she's making you feel, Leila. I mean, we all hate getting older. Even she must. I know she doesn't look it, but I reckon she must be, what? Late twenties? Maybe even a bit older. But she looks good. Very good. And you, Leila, you must be what? How old are you now?'

Leila spun round. 'That's it, Shirley. And this time I mean it. This is your last chance. Either you stop drinking and running off at the mouth, or I'm going to have to sack you.'

Shirley blinked. Sack? This wasn't going the way she'd intended at all. She had meant to carry on planting the idea that Leila should get rid of Ginny, not her.

'How could you sack me? Who'd help you out here with the private parties? None of the other girls have got half the brains or class I've got. None of them.'

'Brains? Class? I know you've been drinking, Shirley, but I didn't realise you'd completely lost your marbles.' Leila shook her head in disdain and turned away from her. She hated losing her temper, it was so undignified, but Shirley was really goading her. 'When did you last look at yourself?'

'This is all her fault. I told you, she's getting to you. You've got to stop her.'

Leila bent over the sink, trying to steady her breathing, her chest rising and falling as though she'd just completed the hundred-yard dash.

Shirley was relentless. 'And I don't know why you should pick on me anyway. How about Carmen and Patty smoking dope every night? You don't do anything about them.'

'They've stopped.' Leila's voice was unsteady, but quiet.

'Have they?'

Leila twisted round to face her again. 'Do you know, Shirley, you are really pushing your luck. I've told you before, there are very few things I hate more than a stirrer. But a big-mouthed, drunken stirrer is one of them. So just go in the other room, out of my sight, and keep that big mouth of yours shut for a while, because I'm going to be considering your future very carefully.'

Shirley did as she was told. Not because she thought she was in the wrong, but because she wanted to go in the other room anyway – she needed another drink. She scrambled gracelessly down from the stool, her skirt still tucked up around her thighs, and barged her way out of the kitchen.

As she flung the door back on its hinges, she almost knocked Ginny off her feet.

'Is Shirley all right?' Ginny asked, steadying herself against the wall and reaching out to stop the door slamming at the same time.

'Just a bit over-excited. Not everyday we have a coronation, is it?' Leila held up her glass. 'Drink?'

'I've already got one in the other room, thanks.'

Leila did her best to smile. But it wasn't easy. She really couldn't figure Ginny out at all. Any of the other girls would have accepted another drink without a second thought. Why should they worry about wasting other people's booze? But here was Ginny – an exotic dancer – acting as politely as if she were at a vicarage tea-party. It was like at the club, whenever men showed interest in her. There she was, up on the stage, stark naked apart from a few pink feathers, flirting and pouting with the best of them, but as soon as any of the punters made an approach – and there were always plenty – she shrank into herself and fled. Even though she'd brassed all that while.

Sexy without a sex life. It was a mystery to Leila. What did she want, a man with slippers and a pipe, reading the Sunday papers while she cooked the roast? She was such a complete contradiction. Every time Leila thought she had a handle on the girl, she immediately slipped out of her grasp, like a fish struggling to return to the river.

To make it worse, Leila couldn't even bring herself to dislike her. Not really. She was always so reasonable. So nice. So – apparently – genuine. Even if it was an act, and Leila knew all about acting, God alone knew how she managed to keep it up while working in the club every night. It was unnerving.

Much as Leila hated to admit that Shirley was right about anything, she was spot on about Ginny. She had to do something about her.

But what could she do? She'd tried her last trick and failed. She had to think. Had to be clear.

Playing for time, Leila offered Ginny a cigarette.

'Thanks.' Ginny bent forward to accept the light. 'Leila?'

'Mmmm?'

'I was thinking when I was in your, you know, your powder room, just now. And I've decided I'm fed up living in that hovel.'

Leila sighed inwardly. More complaints about the room. If she heard one more word about the slot-meter gas fire giving out less heat than a forty-watt bulb she'd scream. Ginny didn't have a clue, that was her trouble. If she did, she'd count herself lucky that the rent collectors – Saunder's real ones, that is, the hard men with the coshes – didn't visit her the way they did some of the other tenants. And she'd take the sodding job like a shot.

'It was very short notice, Ginny.'

'I know. And I didn't mean to be ungrateful, but I want something better out of life.' She paused. 'And I really didn't mean to get you in no bother.'

Leila closed her eyes. 'I don't suppose you did,' she said flatly.

'So d'you honestly think I could do it? And d'you really promise it would be more money?'

Leila's eyes flicked open again. 'Sorry?'

'Run the club. D'you really think I could do it?'

'Of course you can do it, sweetie!'

'But I never meant—'

'Look, just give it a go. What have you got to lose?'

Leila stood in the doorway of the sitting-room, a chilled bottle of champagne in each hand, trilling a loud, 'Da-daaaa!' like a conjurer's assistant – she had, after all, just pulled off a successful illusion. But her intended big entrance fell flat on its face. The historic events were still flickering away on the screen in the corner, but the sound had been turned down and nobody was paying any attention to it. Instead, they were all slumped back in their seats, with faces like kites.

'What on earth's going on?' Leila asked, scanning the

room for Shirley, who, no doubt, had been spreading more of her poison. 'It's more like a funeral than a party.'

But Shirley was sitting perfectly quietly at the far end of the room nursing another large drink.

Carmen peered over the back of the sofa. 'We were just talking, Leila,' she said, flapping her hand in the direction of the television. 'Seeing all this going on: all the fuss there's been in the papers and on the newsreels. It makes you sick when you think about them girls what have been mullered and how hardly anything's been said about them.'

'D'you know what makes me sick?' Patty chipped in. 'If he'd been doing in nice little housewives, or shop girls, it'd be all over the papers and everyone'd be demanding something was done about it. But they don't give a fuck about us working girls.'

'Patty!' Leila's face was like stone. She didn't allow the girls to use such language. 'I think you've said enough.'

'I'm sorry, Leila, but it's like we don't count for nothing. I get so wild thinking about the way we get treated.'

Leila took a deep breath and pinned on a smile. 'Well, I'm doing the treating today. So let's all get fresh glasses and have a toast, because we girls now have a reason to celebrate. Ginny, would you, please?'

Ginny went around the room with the tray of champagne goblets Leila had given her to bring in from the kitchen.

A once more serene vision in emerald green, Leila stepped into the centre of the room, leading Ginny by the hand. 'Not only are we drinking to this new Elizabethan Age, and to the success of Hillary and Sherpa Tensing—'

'Whoever he is when he's at home,' said Patty gloomily.

323

'Thank you, Patty,' Leila replied graciously. 'But we now have cause for a more personal celebration.'

Having finished handing round the glasses, Ginny stood by Leila's side.

'I know you've all heard the talk about Ginny being offered a manager's job. Well, I'd like you to be the first to know that it's true and, what's more, she's decided to take it.'

'I said I'd discuss it with Mr Saunders,' Ginny whispered under her breath, nervously twisting the stem of her glass between her fingers.

'It's the same thing, darling,' Leila whispered back, while flashing one of her most dazzling smiles. 'Now, let's drink to the future. I'm sure it's going to be wonderful for us all!'

Everyone in the room raised their glass. Everyone, that is, except Shirley.

She sat alone at the far end of the room, the smell of booze that she carried with her now nothing compared to the hatred that was oozing from her very pores. Leila had it in for her and it was all Ginny's fault. Shirley'd known she'd be trouble the first time she'd set eyes on her.

The girls crowded round with kisses and congratulations. It was fine by them if Ginny got promoted. They certainly wouldn't have wanted the responsibility of running a club, but there might be a few bob for them somewhere in this new deal. And maybe a little nightly spot taking over the fan dancing wouldn't be such a hardship either.

Shirley watched Ginny and Leila smiling at the girls as though they were a pair of princesses acknowledging the dues of their sycophantic courtiers. And she hated the pair of them.

*

324

Afraid that Ginny might get stroppy, or nervous, and change her mind about the job, Leila was on the telephone first thing in the morning, organising a get-together between Ginny and Billy Saunders. It was arranged that they would meet on the corner of Bethnal Green Road and Club Row at one o'clock the next day and Saunders would take her to see the building.

Ginny *was* nervous, but she still turned up; in fact, she arrived nearly half an hour early. She'd dressed in a simple navy costume she'd borrowed from Yvette – the plunging neckline hidden by a matching chiffon scarf; styled her platinum curls into a discreet French pleat; and topped off her outfit with a neat pill-box hat – courtesy of Carmen's going-to-church-with-her-mum wardrobe – that had a cute little spotted veil that stopped just above her mouth. She looked more like a guest at a society wedding than a fan dancer going to meet a night-club owner in the East End. The effect was intentional.

Even though Saunders had seen her performing, part of Ginny wanted to give a good impression, to look business-like and refined; to show that there was more to her than blonde hair and a body. But another part of her said she must be stark, raving barmy, and that she should get on the first bus back to Bailey Street and throw herself on the mercy of Ted and Nellie.

Ted and Nellie. The thought of those two brought her back to her senses immediately and to the reality of her situation. She couldn't let Leila get in trouble, just because she was a coward. She had to do this.

So she waited and, as she stood there smoking one cigarette after another, she went through all the advice she had been given by Gloria, her surprise champion, about what she should and shouldn't do. Gloria was right, she knew that, this was a real chance and she mustn't mess it up.

When Saunders eventually arrived at a few minutes past one, in his big, chauffeur-driven car, it had started to rain. But Ginny didn't mind, she had her umbrella, and anyway, she had other things on her mind more important than a summer shower. She had been practising what she was going to say and she knew she had to get it out before she lost her nerve completely.

Before Saunders had a chance to say hello, she took a deep breath and she was off, counting the points on her navy-gloved fingers.

'So I get a rent-free flat. Not a room. And it won't be shared. And it'll be near the job. I won't have fares or nothing to pay—'

Saunders grinned. 'Blimey, you been practising?'

Ginny fiddled with her umbrella, anything to avoid his gaze. 'I just want to get things straight. To know where I stand.'

'Good. Me too. So let's get under that umbrella of your'n and go and have a look at this gaff. And I can tell you all about it.'

Saunders told the driver to stay with the car and held out his arm to Ginny.

She paused for a moment before taking it, then allowed him to lead her through the still bomb-damaged and debris-littered streets. They walked past soot-blackened, semi-collapsed buildings with boarded-up windows and doors, deeper into a part of the East End that even hardened locals thought twice about venturing into without good reason. It was an area that had so far been neglected in the efforts to return London to its pre-war greatness; City offices and middle-class housing obviously coming first in the order of things.

As they walked, Saunders spoke. 'Well, there'll be no rent to pay. The flat's got about four rooms altogether. I think that's right. And it's all yours. So there'll be no sharing. Unless you decide otherwise, of course. And, as it's right over the shop, I don't reckon it could be no nearer.'

Ginny felt herself relax. It was strange; Saunders was a big, handsome, forbidding man, but on the few occasions she had spoken to him, he always gave her that rare feeling that she had known him for years. It was a feeling she enjoyed, it made her comfortable, put her at her ease. Sensations which Ginny had experienced all too rarely.

Suddenly Saunders stopped. They were at the top of a little unnamed alley off Virginia Road, just at the back of where the old Columbia Market stood.

'Any other questions?' he asked.

'Yeah. The big one really. Why me? I know you said you like women running the places, but there's lots of others—'

'Look, Leila said you're kosher. You've got a brain, you learn quick and you don't ask stupid questions. And', he looked her up and down, 'you look good. With or without your clothes. Now, anything else?'

She shook her head; her face burning behind her veil.

'Right. So that's that. But now I've got a question.' He gave her a cigarette. 'Like I said, Leila reckons you're kosher, but is there anything I should know? Anything that could cause me problems?'

'What sort of thing?'

'Let's just say that you'd know if there *was* anything I should be worried about.'

Ginny shrugged. 'Well, in that case, no.'

'Good.' Her jerked his head towards the alley. 'It's down here.'

Gingerly, she followed him along the rubbish-strewn cobbles.

'Here we are.'

She held her umbrella to one side to get a good look. 'This?' she gasped, staring up at the decrepit four-storey Georgian building.

'Granted it needs a bit of work.'

Saunders pulled open the rusting iron gate – a new-looking padlock dangled from one of the railings as though someone had just unlocked it – took the flight of wide stone steps two at a time, shoved open the solid wooden door and stood aside so that Ginny could go in ahead of him.

Surprisingly, there were electric lights blazing everywhere.

Ginny stood her umbrella against the door jamb and stepped inside. She saw a spacious entrance hall, with a wide central staircase and heavily panelled doors leading off both sides. And it was absolutely filthy, derelict almost.

Disappointment flooded through her. She'd thought this was a chance to better herself at last, but she couldn't work here. She was going to have to let Leila down after all.

'What d'you think?'

She looked about her, considering what to say. 'You got this lease before Christmas? What, six months ago?'

'That's right.'

'And you ain't thought about making any changes?' Unless this is your idea of decoration, she thought to herself, as she pictured the squalid tenement where she lived.

Saunders rubbed his hand over his chin. 'You know what it's like. I've been busy. I've been setting up over Virginia Water way. Very exclusive it is. Tell you what, you'll have to come over there one day and have a butcher's.' He grinned wickedly. 'You'd have a right laugh watching all them stockbroker types. They love mixing with the stars, don't they. And with the villains. Then they get a thrill reading all about it next day in the Sunday papers, knowing they've been there. And they can lie to their mates on the golf course that they know Diana Dors and that.'

'I don't know if I could live with this wallpaper,' she said, carefully avoiding responding to his invitation. It was probably one of those suggestions made out of politeness rather than a genuine offer, and she didn't want to make herself look any more stupid than she did already. Fancy her thinking that anyone would want her to run even a half-way decent sort of place. 'Mind you,' she sighed to herself, 'it'd take my mind off the floor. My feet are sticking to it like it's been covered with glue.'

Something darted across the filthy black-and-white tiles.

Ginny grabbed Saunders's arm. 'What the hell was that?'

'Er . . . A cat?'

She pulled herself together and stepped away from him. 'Funny-looking cat.'

'Look, I don't intend leaving it like this, do I? I've already got blokes in here looking the place over for me.'

The sudden irritation in his voice immediately had Ginny on guard. He was a big, powerful man and she was alone with him.

'Mr Saunders, I didn't mean—'

'Well, it is a dump,' he said flexing his shoulders. 'And the name's Billy.'

'It's not a dump exactly—'

'Look, I'll be honest with you, blondie. I ain't done nothing yet, 'cos I was waiting for you to do it up how you fancied. Give it the woman's touch, like. That's why I had 'em come in and set up all these lights, so you could see what you reckoned.'

She frowned in bewilderment. 'You've been waiting for *me*?'

'Yeah.'

'But how did you know I'd take the job?'

He grinned. 'How could you resist me?'

She hurriedly turned her head and peered at the wall as though she were studying it. He wanted to see what she reckoned? Was she going mad? 'I reckon, it's . . . er, got, you know, plenty of, what's is name, potential,' she stammered.

'I hope so, darling.'

'And . . .' she blustered, 'yeah. I'll bet it's got a great big cellar.'

'I think it has.'

'Well,' she went on, her words now coming out at a nervous gallop, 'we could have a lovely room down there. A cellar club. Right continental that'd be. Just like you see at the pictures.' Ginny strode over to one of the grimy but elegantly proportioned Georgian windows and stared wildly at the faded tapestry pelmet dangling drunkenly from a tarnished brass rod. 'I could be like Calamity Jane. You know when she put them little curtains in that shabby old log cabin to make it all pretty, and—'

'I'm sorry. You've lost me, darling.'

That stopped her burbling. She spun round. 'What, you haven't seen it?' She saw the blank look on his face. 'It's a film.'

'I don't get no time for films.'

'So you've never heard "Whipcrackaway" or "Secret Love"?'

He shook his head.

'You do know Doris Day?'

He thought for a moment. 'Don't think I've had the pleasure.'

'She's American.'

'I don't get the time to meet everyone what comes in the clubs.'

'You must know her.' Ginny, stunned that anyone could even claim not to know about Doris Day, started singing, 'Once, I had a secret love. The way that dreamers often do . . .' and immediately wished she hadn't. She couldn't imagine what had come over her. 'Now d'you know her?' she asked sheepishly.

'Sorry.'

Just as Ginny was beginning to think that she'd ruined everything by showing she really was mad, and that she might as well go over to the window and throw herself out on to the spiked railings below, one of the doors opened and two men joined them in the entrance hall.

'Afternoon, guv,' one of them said.

'Where's George?' Saunders asked.

'In the music room, for a change.'

Saunders shook his head as though that was just the answer he had hoped not to hear. He went over to another of the doors, banged on it with his fist and hollered, 'Georgie, get out here. You spend more time in that lav than a flaming plumber.'

The door opened and a short, thin man appeared. He had a newspaper tucked under his arm and was concentrating on buttoning his trouser fly.

'Yes, Mr Saunders?' he said, looking up. When he saw Ginny he cringed and covered his front with the newspaper. 'Didn't know there were ladies present.'

'This, believe it or not, is our architect.' Saunders rolled his eyes. 'I was just telling Miss Martin here how, with her help, we're going to transform this place into something special. And I want you to tell her about the structural plans you've drawn up.'

'How d'you do,' Ginny said with a smile. She was

going to add that it was Mrs, not Miss, Martin, but for some reason changed her mind.

By the end of September, the club had indeed been transformed. Staff had been engaged, bars had been stocked and in the cellar there was now a gaming room boasting the most modern of equipment. All that was left to do was for Ginny to move into the flat and the place would be ready to open.

There had been a moment, when Saunders had explained that the gambling would be what he called 'a bit on the informal side', when Ginny had paused to wonder exactly what she was getting herself into, but Leila had turned up to reassure her that all the clubs had gambling. And as they were only talking about a few hands of Kaluki and *chemin de fer*, and one simple little roulette wheel, there was nothing to worry about.

That conversation had been over a week ago and, although Leila seemed a bit strange – sort of distracted for some reason – Ginny had been persuaded. Now she had other things on her mind. If she was about to move in, she was going to make sure that her flat above the club was really as spotless as it looked. She had had enough of living in a slum and the image of the 'cat' running across the black-and-white tiles three floors below was still too vivid to be ignored. So she'd kitted herself out in a pair of slacks and a shirt, tucked her hair up into a scarf and was concentrating on giving the freshly laid lino a final going over with a bucket of Izal-laced hot water.

The sound of someone opening her new front door startled her. She looked over her shoulder, scrubbing brush still in hand, to see Saunders in the doorway, obviously amused by the sight of Ginny on her hands and knees, covered in suds.

'Leila said you was a hard grafter. But I'm well impressed. Didn't they do it out right for you?'

'Yeah, but I just wanted to make sure it was really clean.'

Saunders pushed himself away from the door frame and walked in, his nostrils twitching at the disinfectant. 'I've brought a few things round for you.'

Ginny stood up, brushing a stray curl from her forehead with the back of her hand. 'But you've already done so much. There's the kitchen . . .' she jerked her thumb over her shoulder towards the newly decorated room with its fitted Formica-covered cupboards and work tops. 'And all the wallpapering and the lino . . .'

Saunders shrugged and smiled. 'You can't get by without some decent furniture or a bit of carpet.' He stuck his head out on to the landing and called down the stairs. 'Up here, Jim.'

A man and a young lad came puffing up the stairs, carrying a double bed between them.

'Miss Martin'll tell you where to put it,' Saunders said, flattening himself against the wall so that they could get into the flat. 'And you can take all the old gear back down to the truck.'

Ginny's excitement grew as she watched the old stuff disappear and the 'few things' that Saunders had bought begin to fill the flat.

There was a wardrobe, a kidney-shaped dressing-table and a velvet-upholstered headboard with tassels to go with the bed; a light oak dining-table and six chairs, with a matching bookcase – Saunders said he figured Ginny was the type who probably read a bit – occasional tables with splayed spindly metal legs with balls for feet; an equally modern three-piece suite in the latest 'contemporary' style; brightly coloured rugs with vibrant, abstract patterns all over them; standard lamps and bedside lights; and even one of the very latest wood and gilt cocktail cabinets.

'Go on then,' he said to the now dumbfounded Ginny. 'Open it.'

She lifted the mirror-lined lid and gasped as it began to play a tune. 'It's playing "Secret Love"!'

'Thought that'd tickle you,' he said. 'Better than that old Utility gear you had up here?'

'I don't know what—' she began, but was interrupted by Jim staggering backwards into the room clutching one end of a television set.

'Where d'you want this, Miss Martin?' his young helper puffed from behind the other end.

Stunned by this final addition to her good fortune, Ginny could only point to the corner of the room, the place where Leila had hers.

With the television in place, Saunders slipped Jim and the lad some money and told them they could go.

As Jim closed the door behind them, with a muttered 'All the best in your new home, Miss Martin', Saunders turned to her and smiled. 'And that goes for me an' all, Miss Martin,' he said, bending forward and kissing her on the cheek. 'I know we're gonna have a very profitable future together, you and me, 'cos I trust you, Ginny. D'you know that? There's no edge to you. What you see is what you get.'

He grinned, looking like an oversized, handsome schoolboy. 'And let's face it, I've seen quite a lot of you, one way or another.'

Ginny blushed.

'That gets me, d'you know that?' He shook his head in amusement. 'You've been up on that stage, flashing it all about, yet you still blush. I love it. You can't lie if you blush. Shows you're an honest bird. And there ain't too many of them about.'

Chapter 16

Ginny stepped into the middle of the big room that took up the whole of the second floor of the now completely refurbished building and did a neat little pirouette. 'What d'you think then, Flora? Will I do for opening night?'

Flora, a heavily built, completely bald-headed Scotsman in his mid-fifties, put the glass he'd been polishing down on the bar and smiled admiringly. 'You look just the business, Miss Martin. Just the business. Black's always very tasteful.'

She smoothed down the skirt of the figure-hugging barathea dress and walked slowly across to him. Leaning on the serpentine maple-wood bar top, she asked, 'You don't think these shoes are a bit much?'

Flora craned his neck to get a good look over the counter. 'They're perfect,' he said, scrutinising the black patent four-inch stilettos that Ginny had bought on nervous impulse just that afternoon. 'Very stylish.'

'I couldn't agree more.' Billy Saunders handed his overcoat and hat to his minder and strolled across to them. 'You look just right, girl. A million dollars.'

Saunders sat on one of the high stools with his back to the bar and surveyed the room. 'Just like this place. Georgie was very impressed with your ideas you know, Ginny. That spot-lighting over the dance floor ... Great idea. And d'you know what else? He reckons it was the way you talked to that bloke they sent round that got us the full late-night supper licence. You've done a good job, girl. A real good job.'

Ginny lowered her chin to avoid meeting his eyes. Even though she'd done her very best, had worked her socks off to make it all work, she still found it hard, after the years of being abused by Ted, to accept compliments of any kind without a certain amount of foreboding. Always, a nagging little voice in her head had her flinching as it told her to wait for the raised fist that would surely follow what had to be the mockery of false praise.

If her eyes had been raised, however, she would have seen wordless signals being exchanged between Saunders and Flora; signals that might have given her different pause for thought.

Ginny had taken Flora on as her chief barman on Gloria's recommendation, but what she didn't know was that although he was indeed a friend of Gloria's – a very close friend, as it happened, whom he'd met in a notorious Turkish baths in Jermyn Street – it was Saunders who had told Gloria to recommend him to Ginny. Saunders's intention was that she employed someone who knew how to mix a cocktail without using a pennyworth more bitters than was absolutely necessary, but also that that someone had no doubts as to his loyalties. And Flora, like Gloria, owed Saunders enough favours to be sure that there was no doubt as to where his allegiance should lie.

It wasn't that Saunders was overly suspicious, but he had spent a lot of money opening the club and he wanted someone on the inside who would keep an eye out for Ginny – as well as on her – to make sure she was up to running the place, superficially at least. Furthermore, Saunders wanted someone who'd keep an eye on everyone else who worked there.

For while Ginny believed she had been given a free

hand with the club, Saunders was still a businessman and intended to be very much in control of the place.

There was the booze, the gambling, the girls, not to mention the band and the cabaret, and all the cleaners, moppers and washers-up in the kitchens. All of them had the potential for fiddling and conniving. Saunders had seen every stroke known to man being pulled in his time – in fact, he had pulled more than a few himself – and someone as powerful as he just wouldn't tolerate the liberty of having some two-bob hoodlum getting away with making anything out of him on the side; even a single brass farthing would have hurt.

Ginny looked at her watch. 'Quarter past eight. Only fifteen minutes to go.'

She turned to Saunders, nibbling her lip. 'D'you think many people are gonna turn up, Billy? I mean, this is Shoreditch. Who's going—'

'Many people gonna turn up?' Saunders interrupted her with a grin. 'You listen to me, darling. Tonight's little party is gonna be the biggest do of the year. After what I've told them about you, how could they resist? They've been fighting to get an invite to this opening bash. You mark my words, girl, Ginny's is gonna be a real success.'

'Ginny's,' she breathed, looking about her as though she could hardly believe she was there. 'Having a whole club named after me. It's such a big responsibility. Let's just hope you're right.'

And he was. By nine o'clock the club was heaving and the tills were ringing like church bells on Easter Sunday. Every inch of the building, barring the fourth floor where Ginny had her private apartment, had been transformed into profit-making space.

A stage had been built, with a separate area sectioned off for a three-piece band, big enough to take the cabaret turns without wasting too much floor area; there were tables for diners to eat fancy suppers at equally fancy prices; an 'intimate' little dance floor – again small enough not to waste space – and plenty of room left where the customers could knock back over-priced drinks into the early hours, while they watched the shows with a pretty girl on their knee, or went down to the discreet room in the cellar for a hand or two of cards, or a few spins of the wheel.

Saunders was sitting in one of the booths on the second floor, watching Ginny working the big main room, meeting and greeting her customers, when Leila made her entry in a shimmer of emerald-green chiffon.

'All right, girl?' Saunders called, beckoning to her.

As Leila eased herself into the booth beside him, Saunders gestured to Flora to have some drinks sent over.

'Just thought I'd pop in to wish Ginny well,' Leila smiled, allowing her fox furs to drop from her shoulders. 'Tell me, how's the little sweetheart managing?'

'You can see for yourself, girl. First class,' he said, acknowledging the arrival of their drinks by leaning back to give the young waiter room to set down the glasses. 'I've gotta hand it to you,' he went on. 'You put me on to a good 'un. Look at her. She's working this room like a real pro.'

'I'm glad you approve, Billy.' Leila sipped her drink, studying him surreptitiously across the rim of her glass, wondering how much of what she had on her mind she dared actually say. Deciding she had nothing much to lose, Leila began hesitantly: 'I hear you've no girls working here.'

Billy frowned. 'No girls? What're you talking about, woman? This place is packed with pretty girls. All hand-picked by Ginny.'

Leila hesitated, using the ritual of lighting a cigarette

338

to give herself a bit of thinking time. 'Yes . . .' she said slowly, '. . . but what I meant was', she leaned forward and said softly, 'the girls are saying there's no *upstairs*.'

Saunders grinned. 'What? There's no toms working here you mean?'

She sat back primly in her seat. 'Exactly.'

'Well, I have to say I wasn't bonkers about the idea at first, and I still ain't, to tell you the truth. I mean, I don't have to tell you, Leila, it's a very nice little earner. One of the best there is, if you run it right. But Ginny was mad keen to make a go of the business without the whoring. Said she wanted to keep it refined like.'

Leila said nothing, she just sat there with the bitter taste of bile rising in her throat, knowing and hating the fact that Billy would never give her such leeway – wouldn't even give her a club to run, because she'd made herself sodding indispensable. He thought she already had *enough to do* . . . She sucked hard on her cigarette. Now here was Ginny – the dowdy little frump *she* had dragged out of her mean little life – deciding that working girls weren't fit to do business in her *precious fucking club*. Working girls like *her*.

She continued to nod and even managed a smile as Billy carried on talking, but inside, Leila was trembling, furious at being driven even to thinking such foul language. And what was worse was that it was all her own fault. Why hadn't she just left her in the gutter where she belonged?

'And so she persuaded me to let her run it without the toms, just for a month's trial like,' he explained. 'Then I'll have a look at her profits, and if she's doing okay I'll let her carry on a bit longer.'

He laughed loudly, as though suddenly getting the punch line of a joke. 'Fancy me having a club with no whores. It ain't natural, is it, girl? Still, I reckon I can trust her to have a go. And you know how important trusting someone is to me. It's what I like, trust. Always have done.'

He took a swallow of his drink and lifted his chin to indicate Ginny who was standing by one of the tables. 'Just look at her operating.'

Leila looked. Ginny was smiling down at a customer with a hideously raïsed chiv scar right across his already ugly mug, but from her expression, anyone would have thought him the most handsome man in the room.

'Just clock the way them blokes on the next table are looking at her. She's really got something, but it's like she don't even realise it. When she used to stand up on that stage . . .' He shook his head in wonder. 'I'm telling you, there's just something about her. And you'd never believe she'd ever worked as a tom, would you? She looks too good, if you know what I mean. She ain't got that hard sort of look about her.'

Leila couldn't find the words inside her to reply, so she just nodded, staring at Ginny, the apparent receptacle of all feminine virtue, as she left the customer's table and turned towards them.

Leila could have spat: Saunders was waving to her to join them.

Ginny, smiling with delight at seeing Leila, waved back and made her way over to them, accepting more praise and congratulations with every step she took on her four-inch spiked heels.

Flushed with admiration and compliments, Ginny finally arrived at the booth. Saunders stood up, took her hand in his and pressed it to his lips. 'You're doing good, girl, very good.'

Ginny, beaming with pleasure, bent forward and kissed Leila on the cheek. 'I'm so pleased you could come.'

All Leila could offer by way of a greeting was a weak stretching of her lips across her teeth into something approximating a smile.

Ginny sat down next to Saunders with a satisfied sigh. 'D'you know, Leila,' she said, 'I don't think I've ever been so happy. And I want you to know how grateful I am, because it's you I've got to thank for all this. If it wasn't for you I'd ... Well, never mind all that, I just wanna say thanks.'

In her head, Leila responded to Ginny's gratitude by telling her that the trouble with dreams coming true was that they usually – no, *inevitably* – turned into nightmares. That, unfortunately, was the cruel way of the world, as she would find out all too soon. But she actually said nothing; she just carried on flashing her tight-lipped smile and gripping the stem of her glass as though it were trying to escape.

Before Ginny had the chance to settle into her seat, Saunders was on his feet again. 'You'll have to excuse me, Leila, but I'd better go and say hello to some of these people.' He finished off his drink and checked the knot of his tie. 'And you, Ginny, you'd better come an' all, they'll want to say they've met the governor.' He held out his hand to her. 'Come on.'

Ginny shrugged with mock helplessness at Leila, as she allowed Saunders to lead her away.

Leila lit yet another cigarette. She didn't particularly want it, but nor did she want to be seen sitting alone doing nothing, or worse, to sit there watching Billy and Ginny parading around the room laughing and joking like an over-excited courting couple out on a first date.

'Penny for them?' someone asked her – or rather slurred at her in a drunken drawl – as Leila tossed her lighter back into her bag.

Leila looked up. It was Shirley. Her hair was tousled, her cheeks flushed and her eyes bloodshot and puffy.

'Shirley! What the hell are you doing here?' Leila demanded, making sure, despite her anger, that she kept her voice low; Leila was nothing if not professional. 'You know it's Sally's night off. I told you. You were to stay at the flat and take the calls.'

'Didn't want to miss the party, did I?' Shirley mumbled. 'Glad I didn't. S'lovely party.' She smirked lazily. 'And I've been watching Billy. Real gentleman. Treating her like a proper lady. Kissing her hand like that. Nice.'

'You're drunk.'

'And you're jealous.' Shirley grinned, flashing one of her badly pencilled eyebrows and clutching the side of the table to steady herself. 'Like I said before, it's your fault. You've let her . . .' She paused to gather her thoughts, to find the right words. 'Get away with it. That's what you've done. I told you all along.'

'Shirley—'

'And do you know what?' Shirley dropped inelegantly on to the bench seat in the booth so that she was facing Leila. 'The whisper is, she's not letting the girls here do any business. Well,' she wagged her finger in Leila's face, 'I reckon that's crap. I don't believe it. She's doing a foreigner. Letting them all work without telling Billy. I guarantee it. She'll be raking it in. And he won't even care. She's got him bamboozled. Miss Innocent Bloody—'

'Shirley. I think you've said enough. If you knew how ridiculous you sounded.'

'Ridiculous? Me? You're the one who's letting her get away with all this. You and Billy had something special. Now look at him. The way he's looking at her. Hanging around her like a dog after a bitch on heat. It's so obvious, it's staring you right in the bloody face.' She slapped the

342

table with the flat of her hand, knocking Leila's drink flying. The young waiter was immediately there, mopping up.

Shirley giggled girlishly until he left, then, after another struggle to recollect her train of thought, she continued her drunken monologue. 'Anyone can see she's letting him have it to keep him sweet. But you've got to hand it to her, she's not got a bad price for it. A whole fucking club.'

Leila sprang to her feet and wrenched Shirley from the bench, signalling with her eyes to the ever-vigilant Flora that she needed help.

'That is it, Shirley,' Leila whispered into her ear as she and Flora escorted her off the premises. 'That's the final straw. You are out.'

'Who is it? Is that you, Flora?' Ginny squinted at her watch through sleep-blurred eyes. Half past ten. She groaned wearily. She hadn't got to bed until five o'clock.

The knocking continued.

'Hold on.'

She pulled on her wrapper and dragged herself through the flat to the front door.

'Billy. I wasn't expecting—'

'Never mind who you was expecting.' He scowled at her. 'What did I tell you?'

'Listen. D'you know what time I—'

'No. You listen. I told you. Use that spyhole. And always put the chain on. You never know who might be about.'

Pleased with his concern, but embarrassed by her own foolishness – Billy had warned her over and over again about security – Ginny stood there like a child being chastised by a displeased parent. It wouldn't have been

343

so bad if she'd been dressed properly and had done her hair. She must look a real sight.

'Well? Can I come in?'

Ginny stepped aside. 'Sorry. Of course. Come in.'

'Get your clothes on. I've got something to show you.'

'Can I just make some tea first?'

'No. Go and get dressed.'

Ginny nodded. 'All right.' She went back into the bedroom, shut the door and started to sort herself out. What should she put on? A dress? Slacks? A skirt and blouse? A skirt. Yes. But which—

'How many sugars?' she heard him call from the kitchen.

Ginny mugged at herself in the dressing-table mirror. Billy Saunders was in the kitchen. Making her a cup of tea ... 'Er none thanks,' she called back. 'Just a splash of milk.'

Whatever next?

'It's just a little something. To say thank you. You've done a good job.'

'Where is it?' She stood on the steps of the club, glancing up and down the alleyway, completely at a loss to know what she was supposed to be looking at.

'There.'

'What? The car?'

'Yeah.' Saunders handed her a key hanging from a silver fob engraved with her name.

She twisted round to look at him. 'For me? Really?'

'Don't get too excited,' he said, leading her down the steps to where the car was parked at the kerb. 'It's only a little Anglia.'

'I know.' Ginny touched a tentative finger to the shiny turquoise bonnet. 'It's the new one. I've seen it in all the magazines.'

344

'Can you drive?'

She thought of the times Ted had made her drive them home when he'd been too drunk even to hold the steering wheel. 'A bit.'

'Well, get in, and we'll soon have you racing about like Fangio.'

'Fangio?' she gasped, as she slipped into the driver's seat, her skirt riding up high around her legs. 'I feel more like Kay Kendall. You know, in *Genevieve*.' She laughed happily, running her hands round and round the steering wheel. 'Sorry, I forgot. You don't know much about the flicks do you?'

'I could, if the right person wanted to teach me.' He reached across the few inches that separated them and let his hand rest on her thigh.

Ginny felt his heat like a brand on her flesh. She had begun to long for that touch, but didn't want to make a fool of herself by misinterpreting its intention. 'I thought this was meant to be a business arrangement.' Her voice sounded odd. Sort of breathless.

Billy laughed easily and held up his hands in a gesture of surrender. 'Fair enough. I ain't never had to force meself on a bird yet.'

Ginny swallowed hard. He'd called her that before. In the same sort of tone. Was that all she was to him? Just some bird?

What else could she expect, taking off her clothes and going with all those men? And she a married woman. Even if she had let Billy believe she was single.

'You're a strange one, Ginny, d'you know that?' He half turned his body so that he was leaning back against the car door, folded his arms and studied her through narrowed eyes.

To avoid his gaze, and to hide her flushed cheeks, Ginny stared out of the window. Did he see her any differently from the way Ted had done? A bit of decoration to be used when he felt like it.

Ted.

Ginny was surprised to realise she hadn't really thought about him for weeks. The timid little thing who used to jump like a scared rabbit every time she heard a sudden noise, fearing it might be him, was gradually fading away. She no longer looked nervously over her shoulder at every single shadow, scared out of her wits that he might be standing there, asking for a bed for the night, because Nellie had locked the door on him. Or because Dilys was fed up with his womanising and – as she could now get by very nicely without him what with the extra money Ginny was sending for her and Susan – she'd thrown him out on his ear.

'Want a fag?'

Ginny looked round, as though she was surprised to see Saunders sitting there.

'Sorry. I was miles away.'

'I could see.'

As he lit her cigarette, Ginny was still thinking about Susan and Ted: how she still missed Susan with all her heart, but how all she felt for Ted was contempt. Then Billy's hand brushed against hers and the confused feelings of desire and a still lingering self-doubt flooded through her again.

'You okay?' Saunders asked. 'I ain't upset you, have I?'

She shook her head. 'No, I'm fine.'

And it was more or less true. She wasn't completely fine, maybe, but almost.

She didn't have Ted hanging around her neck, and she was actually having fun for a change, the sort of fun that made her feel like a woman again. She'd missed that feeling.

It was as though the excitement of the past weeks had

begun to waken her from a long sleep, just as London itself was waking. She was leaving the drab blacks and greys of the bomb-sites behind and was embracing a world of brilliant Technicolor, a new way of life, where there was plenty for everyone and people were smiling again. Just as they did in the films.

And in the films, didn't the hero always win the girl?

Ginny took a deep breath, slowly raised her head and looked directly into Billy's eyes. If he really did think of her as just another bird, she was about to make a very big mistake.

'You know what you said about not having to force yourself on me, Billy?'

'Look, I didn't mean—'

'It's all right, I just want you to know that I don't intend putting up a fight.'

Billy grinned happily as he reached across and opened the car door for her. 'Well in that case, we'd better go back inside then, hadn't we? There ain't much room in these little motors for what I've got in mind.'

It was a Saturday afternoon in October and the autumn chill was really beginning to set in, but as Ginny walked along the wide London street, all she noticed was the beauty of the afternoon sun shining through the golden leaves of the plane trees. There was a spring in her step and she felt glad to be alive, as she headed for the private hotel, just around the corner from Claridge's, where she was meeting Leila for afternoon tea.

Not only was the club showing a healthy profit after being open for only a month – without her having to open any rooms 'upstairs' – but, what was more, she was in love.

As Ginny paused at the hotel reception, Leila, who was already seated at their table, watched as she handed

347

over a pile of bags and parcels, all bearing the names of exclusive shops, for safe keeping.

'Bond Street, eh, sweetie?' Leila said, as Ginny joined her. 'You've learned well.'

'It's only what you taught me, Leila.' Ginny kissed Leila's offered cheek and sat down opposite her, moving the red-shaded lamp and the extravagant flower display to one side so they could see one another.

'A few months ago, you wouldn't have dared touch that vase in case someone told you off.'

Ginny rolled her eyes. 'I wasn't that bad.'

'Weren't you?'

A formally dressed waiter appeared by their side.

'Would you order, Leila?'

Leila did so.

Once the waiter was out of earshot, Ginny leaned across the table and whispered, 'I still struggle with the way I talk sometimes, but I'm getting better.'

She took a gold case from her handbag and offered Leila a cigarette. 'It is all down to you, Leila. Honestly. You gave me the confidence to do things. It's like when Billy told me to treat myself to something.' She jerked her thumb over her shoulder towards the reception desk. 'I didn't argue, I just gave them shops a right caning.'

Leila took a deep lungful of smoke.

'And I reckon it's down to you that I'm finding Ginny's so easy to run an' all. Hard work. But there's plenty of people helping me. You know, it still tickles me, having the place called after me.' She smiled happily. 'I miss Soho, of course, and the girls, but I'm really happy being in charge.'

Leila smiled back at her. Much as she would have liked to knock Ginny down to size, telling her that she was no more running the place than the meanest lavatory cleaner, Leila would never break Billy's trust. It wasn't only loyalty that made her keep her mouth shut, she knew a side of Saunders that Ginny probably hadn't even imagined. 'I'm pleased for you, darling,' she said. 'Now, tell me all about it.'

As the waiter set their lavish tea before them, Ginny launched into an excited description of her life at the club, any shyness about her speech completely forgotten.

'You should see the sort of people we get, Leila. Really surprising. I mean, it's in the middle of the East End, but I'm playing hostess to all sorts of customers. They're from "right across the social spectrum", Billy says.'

As she poured tea into the delicate china cups, Leila had to stop herself from yelling out loud: *Billy says*, what do you know about what Billy says?

'They're out slumming, if you ask me. But wherever they come from, I'll tell you this, all the customers have got money, whether they've earned it from some posh job in the City, been born to it, or robbed it from a bank. Mind you, from some of the things you hear them saying, I don't know that there's a lot of difference between some of the so-called honest ones and the crooks.'

Ginny took a gulp of tea and a bite from one of the tiny crustless sandwiches. 'You'd have been proud of me the other night, Leila. I'm not the soft touch I used to be.'

'I can see that,' she answered quietly.

'See, when I realised one of the girls was working a spinner—'

Leila's eyebrows shot up. 'A spinner?'

'Fixing the roulette wheel.'

'I know what it means, I'm just surprised that you're familiar with the term.'

'I'm familiar with all sorts now, Leila.'

'I'll bet you are.'

'Well, I told Billy straight away and he chucked her

349

right out and the bloke she was working with. Right out of the door they went.'

While Ginny continued with her tales about running the club, Leila sat listening with increasing bewilderment at just how in control Ginny seemed to be.

'It's from what I saw in Frith Street, I suppose,' Ginny went on. 'That's how I know how to attract the customers. That "artistic" stuff we used to do in the tableaux, that's all old hat. People want something modern, contemporary. You should see the girl I've got doing a routine to "Diamonds Are A Girl's Best Friend". Billy said it makes my fan dance look like an evening with the Girl Guides!'

'Is Billy at the club very often?'

'Yeah. Most of the time.'

'Really?'

'Mmmmm. He seems impressed with what I'm doing.'

Leila busied herself pouring more tea. No wonder she hadn't seen him for nearly a month.

'I nearly forgot.' Ginny took another swallow of tea. 'He asked me to say hello. Said he hadn't seen much of you lately.'

Leila shook her head, making the feather trim on her hat shimmer in the lamplight. 'Not for a week or two.'

'How about Shirley? Any word on her?'

'She could be on the streets for all I know.' Leila did her best to smile brightly, although the effort was nearly killing her. What she really wanted to do was scream at Ginny that she was a stupid little tart who was getting involved way over her head, and if she had any sense she'd get back where she came from and get her bloody claws out of Billy Saunders.

But Leila had never been one to display her emotions.

Ginny emptied her cup and picked up the teapot for a refill. It was empty.

'Shall I order some more?' Leila asked, a study in graciousness.

Ginny wrinkled her nose and looked at her watch. 'No thanks, Leila. It's nearly half four already.'

'You're going?'

'Yeah. I don't like being away from the club for too long.' She pulled on her gloves and grinned happily. 'I take my responsibilities very seriously, you know. I want Billy to feel he can trust me.'

'But when I told the girls from Frith Street we were meeting up they said they'd see us in the Three Grey-hounds in Greek Street.' Leila paused, checking the desperation that was creeping into her tone. 'So we can all have a natter and a drink together.'

'Sorry, Leila. Better not. But don't let me stop you going to have one with them.' Ginny stood up, took a large white five-pound note from her purse and put it on the table. 'And treat the girls for me, eh?'

With that, Ginny pecked Leila on the cheek and left, pausing in the doorway to look over her shoulder and waggle her fingers in a gesture of farewell, then she wiggled her way out to reception on her now customary stiletto heels to collect her shopping.

Leila didn't need to look round to check, she just knew that every man in the room had his gaze fixed on Ginny's backside.

Later that evening, as Ginny was putting the final touches to her hair, Dilys was standing in her bedroom in Stepney looking at her watch for the tenth time in so many minutes.

'That's it,' she snapped, throwing up her hands. 'Half past seven. I'm off. I've waited long enough for you, Ted bloody Martin. In fact, I've given you more chances than I've got lipsticks and that's saying something.'

351

She pulled her coat from where she'd chucked it over the back of her chair the night before, slipped it round her shoulders and ducked down for a final glimpse in the dressing-table mirror.

As she looked in the glass, she saw the reflection of Susan standing behind her in the doorway.

'What d'you want?' Dilys asked, wiping away a smudge of lipstick from the corner of her mouth with the tip of her little finger.

Susan gnawed the skin around her thumb-nail, unsure how much she dared say, but her empty stomach overcame her fear. 'I'm hungry,' she said quietly.

'I told you, there's stuff in the maid-saver.'

'There's not, Mum. I looked.'

Dilys sighed wearily, twisted round and snatched her handbag off the bed. 'Here,' she said, rummaging in her bag. 'Go and get yourself a bag of chips. And don't leave the lights burning when you go to bed. I ain't made of money.'

With that, Dilys threw some coppers on to the eiderdown and flounced out of the room without so much as a goodbye, let alone a good-night kiss, for her little girl.

While Dilys was out doing her now familiar Saturday night round of pubs, looking for men willing to treat her – not a difficult task as she had vamping down to a fine art – Shirley was sitting on her foul-smelling bed in the little room in Berwick Street she was renting from the most unpleasant Greek woman she had met in her entire life, wondering what on earth she was going to do next.

When Leila had first thrown her out, Shirley had found the room straight away and things hadn't seemed too bad. She had only ever had to deal with the landlady's husband and he had been a right mug; not worrying if she was late with the rent and even occasionally letting her off an entire week at a time, so long as she gave him a free seeing to now and again. But then he had gone back to Crete on some sort of family business, and Shirley had been left dealing with his monster of a wife.

As soon as the woman had realised that Shirley didn't work in the market, as her husband had claimed, but was on the game and using the room as her 'lumber', she had put up the rent, demanded a share of Shirley's weekly takings and now, worst of all, was insisting that Shirley should be *nice*, as she put it, to her elderly father as he was missing his wife who was back home in Crete.

When the landlady had said what she expected her to do if she wanted to keep a roof over her head, and for absolutely no money, Shirley had laughed, thinking she was having a joke. But the woman had just stared at her with her sunken, piggy little eyes and cursed at her in Greek.

Shirley cursed back in English. She wouldn't take that sort of crap from a runty little middle-aged woman.

But runty or not, the landlady had meant business and had cracked Shirley – smack! – right round the side of the head with a pair of brass knuckles that Shirley hadn't even suspected she was wearing.

Shirley stumbled backwards across the room, clutching her ear as blood dripped between her fingers.

She had only gone round there to pay the rent and the woman had come up with this bloody nightmare of an idea. It wasn't as though Shirley had never done an old man before, she had, plenty of times, but at least there had always been money involved. And this one looked as though he was on his last legs. His face was all yellow and shrivelled with age, and his wrists were so thin they looked as though they might snap at any minute. It would be like going with a corpse.

As Shirley pressed herself against the wall, staring at

him, as he sat dwarfed by the carver chair in the woman's kitchen, she knew she wasn't going to go through with it. It wasn't just the thought that the effort of getting him on to the bed would probably be more excitement than he could take – let alone what the act itself would do to him – it was the thought that the woman would be taking her for a mug, and before Shirley knew what she was doing, she'd have all the old cow's uncles and cousins queuing up for a free go as well.

So, here she was in her room, with a half-empty bottle of gin and the few clothes that Leila had let her keep stuffed into a brown paper carrier, knowing that she had had enough, that this wasn't the life she deserved. But what next?

She couldn't think straight. All that filled her head – apart from the pain from the blow and a raging hangover – was the knowledge that this was Ginny's fault. She hated the bitch. Hated her more than that Greek cow downstairs and her disgusting father; more than Leila for throwing her out; more than anything in the whole fucking world.

Slowly a smile began to form on Shirley's lips.

Ginny had caused her all this trouble, so it was only fair that she should get some too. Shirley would get her own back. She would get revenge.

Her smile broadened.

All the girls knew that *Miss* Martin was actually a married woman who had an old man tucked away somewhere. Just as they all knew that for some reason she never wanted him mentioned.

Shirley would go and find Ginny's husband.

And Ted was surprisingly easy to find. All Shirley had had to do was nip round to Frith Street, blow all but her last ten shillings on a nice little treat for Carmen and offer it to her in exchange for a favour.

Carmen, stupid as ever when promised some free dope, had immediately agreed to find out from Yvette where Ginny used to live and her husband's name.

Ginny hadn't been wrong when she'd worried that she'd told Yvette just a little too much, because although, unlike Shirley, she had no malice in her, Yvette did lack an ability to think things through.

A couple of hours later Carmen turned up in the Moka Bar with the information and Shirley handed over what she claimed was a really potent strain of gear she had bought from Italian Tony in Brewer Street.

Shirley had then only to visit a few pubs and buy a couple of drinks, to find herself steaming along the right track in the direction of a dismal boozers' pub near the Rotherhithe tunnel.

'Hello. Ted is it? Ted Martin?'

At the sound of a woman's voice, and a cultured sort of a voice at that, Ted looked up.

Shirley could see he was obviously half cut, but she was more interested in how good-looking he was. From the amount of drink that Carmen had reported he was supposed to put away each night, Shirley had expected someone looking more like the landlady's shrivelled old dad than this handsome, slightly stockier version of James Mason.

She smiled seductively. This was going to be more fun than she'd hoped.

'Who wants to know.'

'I'm Shirley. A friend of your wife's. Now how about buying me a drink and I'll tell you some things that might well be of interest.'

'If you're gonna tell me she's working as a hostess, I

know. I know all about her whoring. And I don't care. All women are the same.'

Shirley noted he didn't seem to know anything about the club. It wouldn't hurt to keep back a little information. You never knew when you might need a bargaining tool.

This time, as she smiled she leaned forward, making sure that he could get a good look down her dress. 'All women aren't the same, Ted,' she purred.

'No. I can see that. And I like the look of what I see an' all, darling.'

'And I like the look of you too.' She leaned closer and breathed into his ear. 'I'm not wearing any knickers. Fancy coming outside?'

She let Ted lead her from the warm fug of the bar out into the cold night air, and round the corner to where the railway arches formed a dark, dank maze behind the pub.

Without saying a word, Ted slammed her against the dripping wall, shoved up her skirt, tore open his fly and thrust straight into her.

'Like it a bit rough, do you?' Shirley giggled.

Chapter 17

1954

'Sorry to bother you, guv, but I reckon you ought to give your eyes a chance on this one.' Flora straightened up from his subservient pose over Saunders's table and looked warily about him.

Saunders nodded his apologies to the two men and women at his table and stood up. 'This had better be good, Flora.'

'It's ...' He hesitated. 'You'd better see for yourself.' Flora lead his boss over to one of the tall, small-paned windows at the far end of the room. 'Take a butcher's out there.'

Saunders lifted the fine lace curtain and squinted out into the darkness. Down below, in the dim glow of the wrought-iron street lamp, he saw the unmistakable outline of two squad cars and a matching pair of Black Marias blocking the end of the alley. Their lights were off and there was no sign of anyone inside them, not even the drivers.

Saunders snorted, shaking his head contemptuously. 'Hurry-up wagons? Are they sure?'

'Johnno gave me the whisper they were out there,' Flora said under his breath. 'I thought you'd better know.'

'Yeah, all right, Flora, get back to the bar, eh? I'll see to this.'

Flora backed away from his boss's side. He was immediately replaced by Ginny. Having seen the unprecedented spectacle of Flora leaving his precious bar to

357

the mercies of his two underlings, she too wanted to see what was so fascinating in the street below.

'It's the law,' she gasped, leaping back from the window, with the net draped limply over her head.

Saunders flicked the curtain from Ginny's hair, took her firmly by the shoulders and steered her back towards the bar. 'Keep it down, girl, we don't want no one panicking, or we'll have the customers getting upset.'

'But—'

'But nothing. It's only the Old Bill sprinkling a bit of frightening powder around the place.'

'But you said the police had—'

'You just ignore it. Carry on as usual. I'll nip down in a minute and see to 'em.'

'How—'

'Look, I've already straightened their governor out. He's getting more than a fair wage off me.' He shrugged. 'But they'll be after a few quid for themselves. It's the way the world turns, innit? A bit of bunce and everyone's happy.'

Ginny reluctantly allowed him to help her up on to one of the bar-stools. 'So why are they—'

Again he interrupted her. 'They're just flexing their muscles. Right, Flora?'

'He's right, Miss Martin.' Flora, now comfortably back in his rightful place, had relaxed. He nodded calmly. 'They like to put on a bit of a show, don't they. They'll be lurking out there until someone goes down and gives them a nice little drink, then they'll stick it in their bin and disappear like nothing's happened. Then go and bother someone else.'

Saunders lowered his head and kissed Ginny gently on the forehead.

She smiled up at him. It wasn't often he made any

358

public show of affection, but that kiss – maybe it was just a peck – he'd given her right there, in front of everyone.

He chucked her playfully under the chin and was just about to signal to Johnno to join him, when an almighty crash, followed by the sound of wood shattering and splintering, reverberated up from the hall below.

Saunders twisted away from Ginny as though an electric charge had pulsed through his body. 'What the fuck was that?' he yelled, barrelling across to the double doors that opened on to the main staircase.

As he flew down to the entrance hall, four minders tight on his tail, the whole club was erupting around him.

Someone in one of the downstairs rooms shouted, 'It's a raid!' and it was as though someone had fired a starting pistol. Men in evening dress were scrambling over tables, sending chairs and glasses flying, not caring whom they knocked out of their way as they raced towards the emergency doors and the fire escape at the back of the building. Police raids were all very well when you heard of one of your pals in the City being arrested in an illegal casino or a bawdy house, but they weren't the sort of thing you wanted to happen to you. And the girls were just as frenzied, screaming and scrapping as they chased after the men, not from fear of being left behind to the mercy of the law, but of losing out on their promised tips for the evening.

Reaching the bottom of the stairs, Saunders saw a young-looking plain-clothes man he'd never seen before, calmly stepping over the wreckage of what had once been a painstakingly restored Georgian front door. He was flanked by six more mature uniformed men – all of whom Saunders knew very well.

As Saunders stood there, panting from the exertion, trying to understand what was going on, his bewildered gaze passed from one officer to the next. The older men's faces were glowing as red as the sunset on the hand-painted mural that covered the wall behind them, but the younger man, apparently in charge of the operation, seemed entirely, and arrogantly, unmoved by the situation.

Saunders took another look at the shattered wood-work, *his* shattered woodwork, snatched up one of the heavy, mahogany hall chairs and lunged with it at the plain-clothes man. If his minders hadn't stepped in to restrain him, Saunders might well have found himself on a charge of attempted murder; this particular policeman happened to be a stickler for the letter of the law.

'Temper, temper, sir,' said the young officer, seemingly unmoved by the situation.

'Who the hell d'you think you are?' Saunders snarled, his anger giving him the strength to shake himself free from his minders' vice-like grip. 'Fabian of the fucking Yard?'

'Detective Sergeant Chisholm, actually.'

'Billy?' Ginny asked from half-way down the stairs. 'What's going on?'

Without taking his eyes off him, Saunders barked out his orders at Ginny, while stabbing his finger into the face of the now smiling DS Chisholm. 'Get upstairs, Ginny. Now. And get Millson on the blower. This *little boy* has got some explaining to do.'

Within half an hour, Saunders was sitting at a table with Detective Inspector Douglas Millson in the second-floor bar of the club.

Apart from the minders and Flora, who were all down-stairs doing their best to patch up the front door, and

Ginny, who was behind the bar pouring the drinks, the place was now empty.

'I couldn't believe it, Doug, I'm telling you. That wet-behind-the-ears little bastard was actually threatening me. Saying he was gonna send the zombies round with the kiddie wagon. The silly bleeder was even going on about white slavery. White slavery?'

Ginny put two triple scotches on the table. 'Zombies?' she asked quietly.

'WPCs,' Millson explained with a weary sigh. 'They go out looking for under-age tarts. Then they round 'em up and send 'em off to the kids' home.' He spread his hands in bewilderment. 'What's wrong with the bloke? I know you don't have no shit like that in here.' He grimaced as he realised what he'd said and bobbed his head in apology in Ginny's direction. 'Excuse my French.'

Saunders tossed back his drink as though it were buttermilk. 'Everyone knows this place is kosher. Except for the spieler downstairs, of course. And everyone gets more than his fair cut outta that.' He shook his head. 'I don't understand. What's his problem? I mean, she won't even tolerate me showing a few blue films in a private room. Will you, girl? That's how straight this place is.' He held up his glass for Ginny to refill it. 'I'm telling you, Doug, what with this and with all these other blokes causing trouble, I'm gonna get out of this lark as soon as I can. But in the meantime, just get him off my back, will you?'

Douglas Millson raised his glass and winked. 'As good as done, Billy. As good as done.'

The next morning Saunders woke up early.

As had become almost his routine, he hadn't bothered to go home to his own flat, but had stayed the night in

Ginny's bed. 'I've made us a cup o' tea,' he said, clanking the spoon in the saucer so that she'd wake up.

Ginny levered herself up on to her elbows, squinting against the bright April sunshine that was flooding the room with its golden light. 'What time is it?'

'Nearly nine.'

'Billy!' She flopped back on the pillows.

He sat down on the edge of the bed. 'Come on, drink this and you'll feel better.'

She dragged herself up into a sitting position and leaned back against the padded velvet headboard. With her eyes tightly closed, she held out her hand for the cup.

'Spit it out. What's worrying you?' she said, after she'd taken a mouthful of tea. 'Is it that business last night that's getting you all worked up?'

'You know me too well, Ginny,' he said, touching her tangled blonde curls. 'But it's not just that.'

Her eyes flicked open. 'So, what is it?'

'It's the whole business of security. How could that have happened last night? I'm paying through the nose and then some little runt—'

'Calm down, Billy, you sorted it all out with Millson, didn't you?'

'Yeah, but that ain't the half of it. There's more of them Maltese moving into Shoreditch every day. Coming over here on them assisted passages, and—'

'I'm sorry, Billy, but I won't listen to you talking like that.' Ginny slapped her cup down on to the bedside table, not caring that she spilled the tea in the saucer. 'I've made myself clear with all the staff and I want you to be clear too. I won't have no colour bar in this club. I treat people the way I find them.'

'And so do I. But we ain't talking about some Maltese geezer coming in for a few drinks and a bit of a cuddle with one of the girls. We're talking about gangs of 'em. All trying to muscle in on other people's territory. On *my* territory.'

'How d'you mean?'

'Millson put me straight last night. They're setting up a nice little network for 'emselves round these parts. A bit of gambling here. A drinking club there. Whores all over the place. They're getting more and more confident. Too confident. And I don't like it. It's attracting too much attention. That's why that young copper was round here sticking his beak in. He wants to earn himself a few points, get a chance of promotion under his belt, so he come where the action is.'

'But surely—'

'But, nothing. It's all getting silly. Out of control. This turf's gonna be carved up like bleed'n' allotments the way this mob's carrying on. At least around Soho you know where you are with the likes of Albert Dimes and Jack Spot. But these little bastards . . .'

Saunders stood up and began pacing around the room. 'I'm glad I listened to you about not running toms from this gaff. You was right about that. Even if it was for the wrong reason. At least that's one bit of aggravation I ain't got to worry about: Maltese ponces fighting me over territory.'

He pulled on the navy silk dressing-gown that Ginny had bought him – a gift that was as much a wordless confirmation that she wanted him to stay with her, as it was an actual Christmas present – and lit himself a cigarette.

'This is all getting to be too much bother.' He walked over to the window and stared down at the alley below, inhaling deeply on his cigarette. 'After the war, even *during* the bloody war, it used to be so easy. All the competition you had was the tuppenny-ha'penny spivs running their black-market scams out of the docks and maybe keeping a few pathetic old toms they could scare into working for them. They acted like tough men, but they was never no real trouble. They still ain't, their sort. You only have to shout boo! and they're running away with their tails between their legs. But these new blokes. Some of 'em sound right nutters.'

Ginny swung her legs from under the covers and went to stand next to him. 'So you meant it then, Billy, what you said to Millson yesterday.'

He turned round to face her. 'Meant what, babe?'

'That you wanna get out of this business.'

'Yeah, I meant it all right. I've been doing a lot of thinking, figuring ways of getting out of the clubs.' Saunders stretched his arms wide. 'Look at me, I'm forty-five years old. I don't wanna spend the rest of me life living off tithes from poxy little dice games, worrying about bar staff fiddling the tills and whether some Maltese slag's gonna chuck a petrol bomb through me window 'cos he fancies taking me clubs over.'

Ginny frowned. 'So what do you want to do?'

'I'm gonna expand the property side.'

Ginny sat down on the dressing-table stool and stared into her lap. 'I see,' she said quietly, then considered for a moment before continuing. 'Look, Billy, I know this is just a business to you, and you probably think I'm a right naive so-and-so at times, but this is the way I earn my living now. So if you are gonna close the club, could you give me a bit of notice, so's I can sort something out for myself?'

Saunders stubbed out his cigarette and pulled her to him. 'That's what I like about you. You're a good girl caught up in a rotten world. But you're decent. There's no edge to you. You say what you think. Not like the rest of them.' He stroked her hair off her face and smiled tenderly down at her. 'I'll make sure you're looked after, Ginny. Whatever happens, you're my girl now.'

She reached up and took his face in her hands and kissed him softly on the mouth.

He twisted round, threw himself on to the bed and pulled her down on top of him.

'I reckon I could eat a bit of breakfast after that,' Billy grinned, slapping Ginny playfully on her backside. He rolled away from her and grabbed his discarded dressing-gown from the floor. 'Get me energy back.'

'What d'you fancy?' Ginny asked, pulling the covers up to her chin and flapping her lashes at him.

'You can get that idea right out of your head!' He pulled the covers off her again and tossed them on to the floor, leaving her lying there naked. 'Mind you,' he said slowly, 'on second thoughts . . .'

He had just thrown his dressing-gown back on the floor, when a loud bashing started on the repaired front door.

'What the bloody hell . . .' He looked at the bedside clock. 'Half ten. Why don't Flora get it?' He dragged his dressing-gown back on.

'You'd better get something on and all, Gin,' he said over his shoulder as he strode out to the flat door. 'Who knows who it'll be this time?'

'Flora! You there?' he hollered down the stairs.

'Yes, guv,' Ginny heard him shout back.

'Then why ain't you getting it?'

'I am, I'm going.'

'If you need me, gimme a shout. I'm just gonna get me strides on.'

Before Saunders had the chance even to locate his trousers, let alone put them on, Flora, puffing like a steam engine, was calling to him from the flat doorway. 'Sorry, guv, I couldn't stop her. It's that Shirley Truman, she says she's gotta see you. I told her—'

Shirley didn't give Flora the chance to explain what he had told her. She shoved him out of the way and stumbled into the flat, rushing angrily from room to room until she found Ginny and Saunders.

They stared at the wild-haired, scruffy-looking, middle-aged woman who stood before them, hardly able to believe that it was Shirley. She had never been exactly beautiful, but she had always been elegantly dressed and well-presented, even when she'd had a few. That had been her big attraction for the type of punters who got a thrill from doing something naughty with a girl who could play it a bit on the posh side.

'Shirley,' Ginny said, when she'd managed to get over the shock, 'it's not even opening time.'

'Don't you start preaching to me,' sneered Shirley. She staggered sideways, hitting her shin hard against the dressing-table. 'Shit!'

Overcoming her disgust, Ginny held out her hand to steady her. 'We were just going to have some coffee. Come through to the kitchen and join us.'

'Come and join us?' Shirley threw back her head and laughed wildly. 'You've got a bit above yourself haven't you, *Miss* Martin?'

'Can I do anything?' Flora called from the flat door, scared that he was going to be blamed for letting Shirley up the stairs, but even more scared that he might be expected to deal with the drunken woman who had just knocked the wind right out of him.

'No, you're all right, Flora.' Saunders called back. 'We can manage.'

'You won't blame me for being pissed when you know what I've been through these last few months.' With a shaking hand, Shirley put down her coffee cup, sniffed loudly and pulled open her blouse, showing the small red scars dotted all over her torso. 'Cigarette burns,' she said, tucking her blouse back in. 'There're more, all over me. And I got this, this morning.' She turned her head to one side and lifted her hair away from her face.

In the bright spring sunshine slanting through the window, Ginny saw a row of raw, ugly gashes pitting Shirley's cheek.

Shirley brushed her hair forward with her fingers to cover the marks again. 'Know how that happened?'

Ginny shook her head.

'Fish hooks.'

'What?'

'Bastards who want to act the big man,' Saunders broke in, 'to keep a girl in order. They sew them on to their sleeves. And then a gentle stroke across a girl's cheek . . . Well, you figure out the rest.'

Ginny covered her mouth with her hands. 'That's *disgusting*.'

'Too right, it's disgusting,' Saunders agreed. 'You can't imagine the sort of slag who'd do that, can you?'

Ginny poured more coffee into Shirley's cup. 'But why did you stay with him?'

'Why did you?'

'Sorry?'

'You honestly don't know who I'm talking about, do you?' Shirley turned to Saunders. 'So I don't suppose you do either.' She helped herself to one of Saunders's cigarettes. 'I've been seeing her husband.'

Ginny shook her head. 'No.'

'Oh yes, Ginny. And d'you know what? If I hadn't been bringing in plenty of wages brassing for him, I reckon I'd be dead by now. Because he likes things rough, your husband. And I've just about had enough of it.'

Shirley leaned back and blew a plume of smoke into the air. 'Is that why he never topped you, Ginny, because you were earning him plenty?'

'Would someone mind telling me—'

A sly smile lit up Shirley's face. 'Silly me, I forgot. You didn't know she was married, did you, Billy? I wonder what else you don't know about little Miss Perfect.'

Ginny stood up and grabbed Shirley by the arm. 'Look, Shirley, I wanna talk to Billy. Go downstairs and Flora will make sure you get some breakfast to sober you up. And tell him to give you a tenner out of the till an' all.'

Billy shook his head. 'No. You leave her. She can get something to eat in a minute. I've got a few questions I wanna—'

'Don't listen to her, Billy. Please. It's over. It's been over for years. Why drag up old—'

'Oh yes? It's over, is it?' Shirley leaned across the table and stared into Ginny's face, as she sat there like a rabbit trapped in a car's headlights. 'That's not the way he tells it. He said he threw you out, that you begged him to have you back. But he wouldn't because you were such a trollop.' She chuckled horribly, a low, guttural sound in the back of her throat. 'He's a right one, you know, Billy. Women go mad for him, even though he uses them. Been pimping for years, he has. Pimped for you, did he, Ginny? Were you already on the game when you met Leila and me? I bet you were. I always knew there was something about you. Something not quite true to form. *Did* he pimp for you? Or did he get you to do it for free for his friends? He likes that sometimes. Likes to watch. Bit funny, isn't he, your husband? Mind you, I bet he loves your little Miss Innocent act. That sort of thing would really get him going.'

She took another leisurely drag on her cigarette. 'When did you last see him? Recently, was it?'

Saunders stood up, not caring that his dressing-gown was flapping open. 'Get out, Shirley.'

Shirley looked at him and laughed. 'There's one born every minute, they say, and you must be one of them. Mind you,' she said, lowering her eyes until her gaze rested on his groin, 'I can see what Ginny sees in you.'

'I'm gonna get dressed,' he said quietly, 'and when I come out of that bedroom, you'd better be gone, Shirley. Or you'll be sorry.' He looked at Ginny and went to say something, but changed his mind.

He pressed his lips together, shook his head and strode over to the bedroom door. 'I'm getting out of here,' he said, without turning round, 'and I don't wanna hear another word from you, Ginny. Not another single word.'

Ginny ran to him, but he slammed the bedroom door in her face. 'If there's one thing I can't stand,' he shouted, 'it's being taken for a fucking mug.'

'Let me in, Billy, please,' she sobbed.

'Leave it, Ginny. Just leave it. Keep your old toffee for the punters.'

Ginny slid down the door and collapsed on to the carpet in a crumpled heap.

'You know when they say that things are "nothing personal"?' Shirley asked, as she hauled herself to her feet. 'Well, this was completely personal. From the day I met you you've made my life a misery, now I hope you're as miserable as I am. Cheerio, Ginny. I won't wish you good luck.'

'Thanks for coming, Leila.' Ginny stepped back and let her into the flat. 'I know we've not spoken for a while, but I—'

'It's okay. No need to be embarrassed, sweetie, it's easy enough to lose touch when you're busy.'

Leila followed Ginny into the sitting-room, pulling off

her gloves and tucking them into her handbag. 'It's such a wonderful evening,' she said, walking over to the window and looking out. 'Nearly half past seven and it's still so warm. Summer's really here at last.'

She turned and faced Ginny, her professional smile lifting her lips, but not reaching her eyes. 'And this is a lovely flat.'

'I know I should have asked you over before,' Ginny began. 'I feel terrible. You've not even been back to the club since opening night, have you?'

Leila laughed mirthlessly. 'What a night that was.'

Ginny gestured for her to sit down on one of the armchairs that stood either side of the tiled fireplace. 'That was the night you told Shirley to get out, wasn't it?'

Leila shook her head. 'Don't remind me. It's been eight months and I've not heard a word. She might have sent a note of apology. No class, some people.' She took out her cigarettes and offered one to Ginny. 'Still, all that's water under the bridge. Let's get down to present-day business. Nice as it is to see you, Ginny, why the sudden invitation?'

Ginny reached across and lit Leila's cigarette with the heavy chromium table lighter that stood on the coffee table between them. 'You heard about me and Billy breaking up?'

'I heard.'

'Did Billy tell you?'

Leila thought for a moment. 'Yes.'

'So you've seen him?'

Leila lifted her hands. 'Now and again.'

'How is he?'

'Is that why you asked me over. To find out how he is?'

'Sort of.' Ginny shrugged. 'So, how is he?'

Leila didn't reply immediately; she took her time tapping the end of her cigarette into one of the pair of tall chromium ashtrays that matched the table lighter. 'Look, why don't you just tell me what's on your mind, Ginny? Where all this is leading.'

Ginny stood up. 'Would you like some coffee? Tea? Something stronger?'

'A gin and tonic would be nice.'

Ginny dipped her chin. 'This isn't easy for me, Leila,' she said, going over to the cocktail cabinet.

'I can tell.'

As Ginny opened the lid, and the twinkling music box rendition of 'Secret Love' began to play, tears blurred her eyes. She swiped at them with the back of her hand and got on with pouring the drinks.

'I wanted to find out if it really was over between me and Billy,' she said, setting the glasses down on the table.

Leila shifted uncomfortably. 'Why ask me?'

It was as though Ginny hadn't heard her question. 'You know, Leila,' she went on, staring down into her, 'I really thought Billy cared about me. But then Shirley turned up.'

Leila frowned. Shirley?

'She said these terrible things about me. Made Billy think I'd been putting on an act. That I'd been having him over. That I was . . .' Ginny sniffed miserably. 'Never mind what she made him think. Maybe she's right in some ways. But I don't understand how . . .' She rubbed her hands over her face and took a deep breath. 'How one minute, he could act as though he really wanted to be with me, then to turn against me like that. I've tried talking to him, to explain. But he won't see me, won't even speak on the phone. He's not been near the place for over two months.' She raised her head and looked at Leila. 'That's why I had to talk to you. To see if there was a way I could get in touch with him. To pass a message on. Anything. You've always been close. He'd listen to you.'

Leila said nothing; she just sipped her drink.

'Leila, please, tell me, has Billy got someone else? Is that why you're not saying anything?'

Leila opened her eyes wide and sighed loudly. 'You might as well know, Ginny. Me and Billy. We're sort of together again.'

'You and Billy?'

'Like I say, it's just sort of. And I expect there are probably one or two others in the picture. Because, let's face it, he's not exactly the faithful type, now is he?'

'He was when we were together.'

Leila smiled stiffly. 'Was he, darling? Are you sure?'

Ginny didn't answer. 'Is he happy?'

'He doesn't really say.' Leila picked up her bag and stood up. 'Look, I don't want to be rude, but I must go, I've got an appointment at nine and it's not polite keeping people waiting, now is it.'

'Will you tell him I was asking after him? And I'd love to, you know, hear how he is.'

'Of course I will.'

'Thanks for coming, Leila. Thanks for everything,' Ginny said quietly. 'Especially for being so honest.'

'Any time, sweetie. Any time.'

As Leila stepped out into the early June sunshine, she drew in a deep lungful of air. Now Ginny was out of the picture, maybe she really did have a chance of getting back with Billy again. She just hoped he never got to hear about the little white lie she'd told that they already were.

It was true then, he really didn't want her any more. Ginny lay on her bed, staring up at the ceiling, tears

372

spilling down her cheeks and running into her ears. She'd waited a whole fortnight for him to call, but she'd heard nothing.

And she'd loved him so much – she still loved him – but he had chosen to believe a drunken tart, hadn't even given her the chance to explain.

She rolled on to her side and stared at the wall. It was all her fault, she should never have . . .

Never have what? Let someone into her life again? Let herself become involved? Lie?

No, none of those things. Even lying wasn't as stupid as letting herself believe she could ever be happy again.

But it was no good going over it all again – that was all she had done for two long weeks. It was too late for that now. This was the way Billy wanted things and she had no choice. All she could do was get on with her life.

But how could she carry on without the man she loved?

She buried her face in the pillow and sobbed herself to sleep like an abandoned child.

An hour later, Ginny was wrenched awake by the telephone ringing on her bedside table.

She was alert immediately and snatched up the receiver. 'Billy?'

'No, Miss Martin, it's Flora. Just to let you know we've been open a wee while now and the customers are asking for you.'

'Okay, Flora, I'll be down.'

Ginny dragged herself from her bed, had a bath, did her hair, put on her make-up and her slinkiest black satin sheath dress and, less than an hour after Flora had phoned, she was walking into the second-floor bar with her chin in the air and her eyes as dry as if they had never seen a tear.

'You look magnificent, Miss Martin,' Flora cooed. 'The best I've seen you look in weeks.'

'Thanks,' she said flatly. 'Is Simon Parker in tonight?'

Flora wrapped his pudgy fingers round his chin. 'Parker?'

'The journalist.'

'Aw, him. The very nice-looking blond?'

'That's the one.'

'His name's Simon, is it?' Flora flapped his glass cloth in the general direction of the stage. 'He's up the other end. I've been watching him hanging on to every word that big-mouthed git, Welsh Davey, has been spouting. One of the waiters – young Alan – was earwigging earlier. He said Welsh Davey was going on about how there's not a bank vault in the whole country that he can't blow. And he said the reporter was lapping it up. Probably thinks there's a story in it.' Flora leaned across the bar and said in low-voiced confidence, 'But I hope he doesn't write it; it's all rubbish.'

'Everyone knows Welsh Davey's a liar, Flora.'

'I don't think that young newspaper feller does. From the look of him, he thinks Davey's the source of all flaming wisdom.'

Ginny did her best to produce a thin smile. 'I'll sort him out. If anyone wants me, I'll be over at Mr Parker's table.'

'I envy you, Miss Martin.' Flora rolled his eyes heavenwards. 'I only wish I could say the same.'

Ginny tapped Simon Parker on the shoulder. 'Still interested in talking to the "lady club boss"?'

Parker stood up, a delighted smile lighting up his boyishly handsome face. 'You've changed your mind. You're going to let me do your story.'

She shook her head. 'No, I just want to talk to you.'

374

She turned to stare into Welsh Davey's shifty eyes. 'There's someone over at the bar been asking for you, Davey. Said something about ... What was it? Some banking business or something? Or maybe it was about a load of old toffee. Or maybe it was just about settling up your bar bill.'

Welsh Davey finished his drink, stood up and treated Ginny to a sarcastic smirk. 'Very funny,' he said, before leaving her alone with the reporter.

'What was that about?' Simon asked.

'Just a private joke.'

'You're not laughing.'

'I don't really feel much like laughing at the moment.'

'What's wrong?'

'It's a long story. Some other time, eh?'

'Okay. So what was it you wanted to talk about?'

Ginny ran her fingers through her hair, stared down at her feet, then finally blurted out, 'I've got a bit of free time and I was wondering if that offer of a date was still on.'

Chapter 18

Ginny threw the full-skirted floral-print dress, and its matching net petticoats, on to the bed. They landed on top of the pile of clothes she had already discarded as being totally unsuitable for a day out in the country. 'Whatever d'you think you're up to?' she asked herself as she opened her wardrobe yet again. 'You've got nothing in common with the likes of Simon Parker. You're only doing this because—'

Her voice trailed off, as her attention was suddenly caught by a squash of unopened parcels and bags that had been shoved right to the back of the top shelf. She didn't need to think what they were, she knew exactly: they were the spoils of her last shopping spree, the things she had bought the day before Billy had walked out on her. She gnawed anxiously at her bottom lip as she felt her eyes begin to sting.

Blinking back the tears, Ginny reached up and pulled down the bags.

She went through them, one by one, having a struggle to remember where she'd bought what, but always remembering exactly why she'd bought every single thing. Each item would have been fully approved of by Billy. Either because they were fashionable, or because they were what he called classy looking. And, inevitably, each had been more expensive than anything she would have chosen – had she not been trying to please him.

From amongst the hoard, Ginny dug out a pair of cavalry-twill slacks, which she couldn't even recall trying on, let alone buying, and a pale-blue angora twin set that she remembered all too well. She could just see the assistant holding the cardigan up to her: cooing and smiling, saying how lovely she would look in it, assuring her how the colour would set off the blue of her eyes and how it would complement her blonde hair.

What a load of shit. She knew the moment she walked out of any one of those snooty shops that all the assistants would be talking about her behind her back, speculating on how she had so much to spend. And they probably wouldn't be far wrong.

Ginny stared into the dressing-table mirror and sighed, brushing the soft, fluffy sweater against her cheek. She might as well look the part for a day out, even if she didn't feel like it.

By ten thirty, Ginny was ready and on her way downstairs to meet Simon Parker; just as they had agreed over a week ago. As she went to open the front door, she hesitated and peered through the side lights. There was nothing surprising to see, only Simon, standing next to a sleek, dark-green car, checking his watch.

Ginny covered her face with her hands. For Christ's sake, what was she doing? She should have telephoned the newspaper office yesterday evening – as she had almost done at least a dozen times – and told him she couldn't go out with him after all. Anyone could tell him she was far too busy. She had responsibilities, a club to run. All sorts of things to do with her time.

But she hadn't called him. Instead, here she was, acting as though she'd nothing better to do than go running off to the country with the first handsome man who'd asked her for a date since Billy had left her.

She was behaving like an adolescent kid. And all because she'd been hurt again. But that was no excuse.

She was a grown woman. She should be used to pain by now.

She would find Flora and get him to make up some story – that wasn't exactly adult of her, but she saw no need to be rude to Simon. It wasn't his fault she was an idiot. Flora could go out and tell him she was ill or something. She stepped back from the door and turned on her heel to go and find him.

She didn't have to go far; Flora was coming down the stairs towards her. 'Look at you!' he trilled, slapping the side of his face with the stubby fingers on one hand and thrusting a wicker hamper at her with the other. 'Ava Gardner in a blonde wig. No. No, wait.' He put his head on one side. 'It's not Ava Gardner, is it? Wait, it's coming to me. I know! You're Grace Kelly's double! That's what you are. All you need's a row of pearls and you could pass for her twin sister.'

Ginny waited for him to finish, then held up the basket. 'What's this?'

'I got the kitchen to knock you up a few bits for the journey. A nice wee picnic. Some ham, sausage rolls, a few pies, a bit of salad stuff, and I've set aside a couple of bottles of something special to wash it all down. I've even had a Thermos of coffee made up, in case it turns nippy later on.'

'It was a kind thought, Flora, thank you. But I'm not going.'

'Oh yes, you are, Miss Martin.' Flora backed away from the hamper she was trying to return to him. 'As if I'd let you throw away the chance of spending the day in the country with that gorgeous hunk of manhood. Have you seen him? He's been waiting outside for you since ten o'clock, poor lamb. Now come on, it's just what you need, a day out. Something to bring a bit of sunshine into your life and to put the roses back into those pretty cheeks of yours.'

'The sun isn't shining, Flora,' she said lifelessly.

'What a sourpuss! You see, you'll have a lovely day. And don't tell me you don't deserve it. You've been working that hard lately.'

Flora guided Ginny forward and, with all the skill of a collie herding a recalcitrant sheep, pulled open the door, eased her outside and down the steps to where Simon was standing, smiling fit to burst.

'And don't let me see either of you *near* this place till six o'clock at the earliest,' he said, taking the hamper from Ginny and handing it to Simon. 'Now go on, have a lovely day, and I don't want a single crust left in that basket when you get back.'

Ginny climbed into the car without a word, while Flora took Simon inside to collect the bottles and flask.

'You will try and keep her out for a good few hours, won't you?' Flora said with a sad shake of his head, as he loaded Simon up with the drinks. 'Honestly, she's been that overworked, it's about time she had a little bit of a treat. You'll have to get her to relax, if you know what I mean.' He winked extravagantly. 'I know she'd be very grateful, so it'll certainly be worth the effort.'

Flora stood and waved until the car had pulled out of the alley, then he went back inside the club and picked up the telephone. 'Gloria? It's me, I've—' He tutted irritably. 'It's Flora, you silly tart, who'd you think it is, Liberace and his magic flaming fingers? Anyway, I've got rid of the ice maiden at last, thank God, so the poker game's on. Any more of her moaning and I'd be slitting my sodding throat. What?' He listened impatiently. 'Yes, of course I've fixed it all up this end. We've got the whole place to ourselves for a good seven hours. You let everyone know, and by the time they get here Casino Floriana will be open for business.'

After they had left the East End far behind and the broad South London streets had narrowed into the hilly, winding lanes of Kent, the sun made an appearance from behind the bank of clouds that was at last breaking up in the soft, late-morning breeze.

Without taking his eyes from the road, Simon handed Ginny a pair of diamanté-studded, butterfly-wing sunglasses. 'Try these for size.'

'I'm all right, thanks,' she said, balancing them on the polished walnut dashboard in front of her.

'I thought they'd make you smile.'

'Look, Simon, I don't mean to be miserable, but I don't feel much like smiling. Okay?'

'Do you know that apart from the dismal-sounding hello that you just about managed to bark at me earlier, those are the first words you've uttered since you got in the car?'

'I'm sorry.'

'You haven't even mentioned what you think of the motor,' he said, reaching out of the window and giving the car roof an affectionate pat.

'It's very nice.'

'*Nice*? This is more than nice. This, Ginny, is a Jaguar. It was meant to impress you.' He flicked his eyes sideways and flashed her his cheeky boyish grin. 'My father's Jaguar, admittedly, but it's still a Jag. I keep telling him he's too old to drive it and he should give it to me. But he won't listen. What do you think? Should he give it to me? He can certainly afford to.'

'It's up to him.'

'I suppose it is.'

They drove on in a silence broken only by Simon's

shouted 'thank you' to a roadside AA man who saluted them, and his occasional strange pronouncements on interesting features he spotted in the passing landscape. Then, without warning, he stopped the car in a layby next to a five-bar gate.

'Look, Ginny, I could talk for a living if I had to, but even I can't spin out a phoney commentary on oast-houses and hop gardens and cherry orchards for more than an hour. It's wearing me ragged. You're going to have to help me a bit. Even if it's only to note what a good-looking sort of a devil you think I am.'

Ginny stared down at her hands. 'Okay. Where are we going?' she asked eventually.

Simon looked about him. 'We're sort of here, really. I thought we might get out and enjoy the fresh air. There's a river over there. What do you think?'

'Fine,' she said flatly.

'And if we're lucky, we might see the eclipse. This is a special day, you know, Ginny. One for the old headlines.' He pointed at the windscreen, as though composing the front page of a newspaper. *'Wednesday, 30 June 1954. Solar eclipse over Britain. Ginny Martin amazed!'* He put his head on one side. 'Well? Will you be amazed? Are you looking forward to witnessing this extraordinary event?'

'I did see something about it.'

'Did you? Where?' he asked, trying to encourage her. 'In my paper, I hope.'

'No. On the television.'

'I've been thinking about getting one of those. Do you think I should?'

'If you want one.'

Simon nodded briskly. 'Right, tell you what, let's have that picnic.'

Simon ferried the picnic hamper, Thermos flask and

381

bottles, a fringed tartan travelling rug and a black leather case that he tucked carefully under his arm, to the far side of the field. There, he set out the rug on the river bank, in the shade of a massive chestnut tree. He then went back to the Jaguar for Ginny, who had shown no interest in even getting out of the car, never mind any enthusiasm for a nature ramble through a wheat field.

Gently, Simon pushed her down on to the rug. 'You have a choice,' he said, filling two glasses with deep-red wine. 'While we dine on these fine morsels, so kindly supplied by Flora, you can either listen to me telling you all about myself – how I'm going to get the biggest series of scoops ever known in Fleet Street and how my great success will mean that they'll have to make me an editor before I'm thirty-five. *Or* I'll play you my clarinet.' He held up the black leather case. 'And that will show you why, instead of editing *The Times*, I might become the best jazz clarinettist who's ever been born this side of New Orleans.' He pulled a face. 'Although, even I have to admit I just *might* need a tiny bit more practice on the old licorice stick before that happens. But with my good looks, maybe they won't notice the duff notes.'

'You really reckon yourself, don't you?' Ginny said, wondering why she'd let Flora bamboozle her into this.

He looked up from ferreting through the hamper. 'Me?' He sounded shocked.

'Yeah. You.' She could have added, *just like almost every other man I've ever met in my life*, but she didn't have the energy for a row. Instead she took a gulp of her drink.

'Well, I know I used to get upset when I was a child and the other kids at school called me big-head,' he said, topping up Ginny's glass. 'But d'you know what my mother always said?'

'Surprise me.'

382

'She'd say, don't let them upset you, son. You just go down to the fruit and vegetable shop and get me fourteen pounds of potatoes in your cap.'

Ginny stared at him blankly. 'Very funny.'

'If I'm such a comedian, then how come you look so sad?' He found a pork pie in the basket and took a large bite, giving her the chance to say something, but all she did was sip fitfully at her drink.

'Is it something I've said, Ginny? It wasn't meant to be like this, you know. We were meant to have a lovely day. And you were meant to—'

'Simon, I'm sorry,' she broke in. 'It's not you. It's just that ... I've not had much to be happy about lately.'

He aimed the half-eaten pork pie into the middle of the river, sending up a gentle plop into the still midday air. 'But you've got so much. You've got the club, and you're—'

'I know. I'm luckier than most people. In lots of ways. But that doesn't mean ... Aw, I don't know.'

Simon pulled up a blade of grass and sucked it between his teeth. 'Tell me about your dreams, Ginny,' he said in a mock Viennese accent.

'How do you know I've got dreams?'

'We all have dreams,' he said continuing his bad impersonation of Dr Freud. 'Whether it's buying a television. Owning a car like my father's. Or being the editor of a Fleet Street newspaper.' He rolled on to his stomach and touched her on the tip of her nose with the grass. 'I bet I can guess one of your dreams,' he went on in his own voice, scratching his chin thoughtfully and staring at her through narrowed eyes. 'I know. You dream of having a plush flat in Eaton Square and a pair of matching French poodles trotting by your side when you go promenading in the afternoon sunshine.'

'You're wrong.'

'How? Come on. Tell me.'

'You're not really interested.'

He sat up, refilled her glass to the brim once again and laid his hand on his heart. 'I am absolutely riveted.'

Ginny, feeling heady from the combination of drink and her choice of clothes in the sultry June heat, leaned back against the tree-trunk and closed her eyes. 'There's this bus. The number 15. It goes along the Barking Road, up through Aldgate, along to Bank, then the Strand, then Oxford Street—'

'So, I was right,' he crowed triumphantly. 'East End to West End.'

'No.' She opened her eyes and looked at him stretched out on the rug next to her. 'What I imagine is staying on the bus, and it takes me right out into the countryside. You know, like going on a Green Line. And I go to a place, well, it's like this, really. Lovely fields and a river. But then I go round this corner and there's a massive, great big house. Just like Tara in *Gone With the Wind* . . .' She swallowed the rest of her wine and held out her glass for more. 'Hark at me, going on, you must think I'm a right fool. Trouble is, you're too easy to talk to.'

'It's my job, getting people to feel at ease and talk. But I don't think you're a fool, I think you're wonderful. Hey! You nearly smiled then.'

He reached out and touched her cheek. 'There, I knew you could do it.'

He pulled himself up so that he was kneeling in front of her. 'You really are wonderful, you know, Ginny. Truly beautiful.'

Slowly he folded his arms around her, touched his mouth to hers and pulled her down on to the rug. 'You must be so hot in those things,' he breathed into her ear.

Within moments, as a skylark trilled high above them and the moon continued on its inevitable journey that would plunge the brilliance of the glorious summer's day into darkness, Ginny lay naked beneath Simon's urgently thrusting body.

It was nearly a quarter to seven; too early, really, to leave for Piccadilly, but Dilys didn't want to hang around in case Ted turned up and spoilt her plans. And anyway, it'd be no hardship waiting a while for Chuck, he was more than worth it.

She pulled up her skirt to check her suspenders and, as she smoothed her stocking-tops she eyed her thighs appreciatively. 'You're amazing, Dilys girl, d'you know that?' she said out loud to herself. 'Look at them legs. No one would ever believe you was a mother – thank Gawd.'

She straightened up and hollered towards the open bedroom door, 'Susan. Get that letter from behind the clock.'

Susan did as she was told, then hovered uncertainly in the doorway. Her mother's room was strictly off limits, unless she had been specifically told otherwise.

'Bring it here then,' Dilys snapped impatiently. 'I ain't got bloody rubber arms.'

Susan stepped cautiously into the room, knowing from experience that she was more likely to get a swipe round the ear than a thank you for her efforts.

Dilys ripped open the envelope and pulled out the contents: two sheets of folded paper and two five-pound notes.

Kissing the money before stuffing it into her handbag, Dilys tossed the rest on to the bed without a second glance. 'If Ted turns up,' she said, as she took a final glimpse in the mirror, 'tell him I've had to go round to see your Uncle Sid about buying you some new shoes 'cos I'm broke again. If he gives you anything, put it on the mantelpiece.'

Then, without another word, Dilys left her child alone in the prefab and went outside to run the gauntlet of her neighbours – Milly Barrington and her troop of apron-wearing harpies.

'There'll be murders if he comes home and catches her going out looking like that,' offered one of the chorus, in a voice pitched deliberately loud enough for Dilys to hear.

'Leave off,' Milly corrected her at the same volume. 'What would he care if she went out in her drawers? He's never there.'

'Probably got some other old bag tucked away,' chipped in one of the others. 'His sort have always got their feet under someone's table.'

'I've heard he still lives with his mum,' Milly said with a sneer. 'Fancy, a man of his age! Over Grove Road way somewhere, they reckon. Near the Roman.'

'With his mum!'

'That's what I heard.' Milly craned her neck to watch, as Dilys dodged across the street in front of a motor bike and side-car that had to swerve to avoid her. 'You know I'd lay money that kid's not his,' she shouted by way of a final parting shot as Dilys disappeared round the corner to find a cab – with ten pounds spare cash in her pocket she could afford such luxuries.

As she watched her mother from the prefab window, Susan heard Milly Barrington shouting that Ted wasn't her father and knew she was wrong. Her mum was always going on at her about it and saying how it was her fault that Ted hung around the place all the time.

Susan didn't really mind Ted. He wasn't like most of her little friends' dads, but when he was there he was quite nice to her and even brought her presents sometimes, ones that he made sure her mum let her keep. But for now, Susan was more interested in her aunt than her father.

Having dodged back into her mum's room, Susan retrieved the envelope and paper from the bed and settled herself down on the half-moon rug in the front room, where she was slowly working her way through the latest letter from her 'Auntie' Ginny.

She smiled happily to herself as she read the kind, loving words and wished, as always, that she could see her auntie again – or at least know a place where she could write back to her. It would have been hard, writing a whole letter, but Susan would have tried her very best.

There was something that Milly Barrington *had* been right about: Dilys really had no need to worry about Ted turning up. Although he wasn't at his mother's.

In fact, Ted hadn't seen Nellie for weeks; he was too scared he'd be spotted by Dilys's brothers to venture anywhere near Bailey Street. Dilys had been spinning the boys some sort of a line about how hard done by she and Susan were and the last time he'd gone to see his mum they'd threatened to knock nine kinds of bells out of him until he'd handed over every last penny he had on him to buy new summer dresses for the kid, *and* a pair of shoes for sodding Dilys.

He'd had one good hiding off them – when the silly cow had finally admitted that he was the kid's father – and he certainly didn't fancy another. They were a right handy pair of buggers. He'd tried talking his way out of it, explaining that he'd already given Dilys money for the self-same things only the week before, that the kid had dresses coming out of her flaming earholes and that Dilys had enough shoes to open a stall, but they wouldn't listen to him. They'd just kept on and on about what an arsehole he was. If it hadn't been for their big-gobbed wives dragging them indoors – because they hadn't wanted to be shown up by their husbands indulging in something as common as a street fight – Ted would probably have come off even worse than he had.

But, all that aside, Ted was the first to admit he didn't exactly look after Dilys – she didn't deserve looking after – but he always made sure the kid wanted for nothing. Well, most of the time he did.

Anyway, rather than risk another beating, Ted kept well away from that pair of nutters, dividing his time between ducking and diving in any pub where he thought he could pull a scam and with Shirley in her pigsty of a room in Soho.

That particular evening, Ted had just left the Three Greyhounds in Greek Street, after selling a slow-talking yokel type – up in London on business for the day – a camera he had earlier 'found' in the nearby Coach and Horses. He was now letting himself into Shirley's room, more than pleased to be fifty bob richer for absolutely no effort whatsoever. But his smile soon faded when he saw Shirley lounging on the bed flicking listlessly through a magazine.

'Why ain't you out working?'

'I'm tired,' she answered, flipping over the page.

'Pissed again, you mean.'

'And where would I get the money to spend on booze? You steal every single penny I earn.' She tossed the magazine aside and leapt to her feet. 'We don't all run—' She shut her mouth as though it were a spring-loaded trap. Christ! She'd nearly let the cat out of the bag about Ginny's.

'We don't all run what?'

'Nothing.'

Ted swung back his fist and smashed it into her stomach. 'That'll teach you to be lippy.'

Doubled over with pain and gasping to catch her breath, something in Shirley snapped. Sod it, why not? She'd tell the rotten bastard. And maybe it'd get him off her back.

'You think you're so clever, hitting and punching, and doing poxy little deals, but you haven't got a clue.' Still winded, she grasped hold of the bed head to steady herself. 'You don't even know about your own wife.'

'What about her?'

'She's earning a fortune, that's what. You're sleeping in this rat hole and she's running a club.'

'She's what?'

'You heard.'

Ted eyed her suspiciously, he trusted no one, but especially not toms. She was talking shit as usual. Fantasising. Like they all did. 'Why didn't you tell me before?'

Shirley shook her head and laughed wildly. 'If you can believe it, just for a while – a very short while, mind – I actually didn't want you leaving me to go back to her. Then, when I couldn't give a damn who you were with, it was too late. If you'd have found out I'd known, but hadn't told you, you'd have gone raving mad.'

He was right, she was making it up. She was rambling like a lunatic. 'Where is it then, this club?'

'How would I know?' Shirley lied. 'You'll have to ask around.'

'So how come you know about it?'

'I bumped into one of the girls. From the club. She told me,' she improvised, then added hurriedly, 'but I didn't bother with the address. I mean, I'm hardly going to go round and visit her, now am I?'

Ted was torn. Should he waste precious time beating Shirley until her teeth rattled, or should he set off straight away to find his wife instead? He could certainly do with a few quid, and if Ginny *was* running a club she must be worth a fortune. And he'd be entitled to his share. He was her husband, after all.

But then again, Shirley was really getting on his nerves . . .

Simon pulled the car into the kerb outside the club. 'Before you get out, Ginny, there's something—'

'Look, Simon, I thought I made myself clear, I need time to think. I don't wanna talk, all right?' Talk? She couldn't even look at him, she was so angry with herself at what she'd let him do. Maybe it was revenge, a way of getting back at Billy Saunders for leaving her. But whatever the reason, she'd let it happen and wished with all her heart that she hadn't, because, much as it hurt, she was still in love with Billy.

'Please, Ginny—'

'I'll talk to you later.' She grabbed hold of the door handle, but Simon stopped her getting out.

'I've gotta open the club.'

'Ginny, please, I know I don't know the form about these things, but I'd like to give you a little present.'

'Don't, Simon. Please.'

'I want to.'

With his free hand, he reached inside his sports jacket and took out his wallet. 'What's the rate?' he asked.

'I don't understand.'

'When Welsh Davey told me about you and the girls, he never mentioned how much—'

'He what!' Ginny stared at him. 'Everybody knows what a bloody liar that bastard is.' She shook her head in disbelief. 'I never had you down as an idiot, Simon.'

'I'm sorry, Ginny. I didn't—'

'Leave it, Simon. Do us both a favour.'

'But I swear—'

'I mean it, Simon. Please. Just leave it.'

'Does this mean you won't see me again?'

'Just go.'

She grabbed hold of the car doorhandle, but again he stopped her. 'No, I won't. Not like this. I've been clumsy and stupid, and I've insulted you. Promise me you'll see me again, Ginny. Please.'

'Simon—'

'But I've got to see you. And it isn't just about what happened back there. I told you, Ginny. I think you're the most wonderful . . .' He looked away as his eyes filled with tears. 'Please,' he begged. 'Give me another chance.'

A shudder racked through Ginny's body. She had to get away. 'Call me in a few days.'

As Ginny climbed up the steps of the club, she too began to cry. Was this what it had finally come to? Was it true what they said? No matter how you told yourself you'd got out of it, it was still obvious to everyone what you really were. Once a brass, always a brass.

She shoved open the door and let the hamper fall from her hand on to the tiled floor.

If whoring was all she was fit for she might as well do it right this time. Not like she did in Frith Street. She'd put a proper price on herself. Simon seemed a decent enough bloke and it looked like he had a few quid. Maybe when Billy got rid of the clubs, Simon could be her solution. He could give her a decent life; the kind of life she'd dreamed of . . .

What was the point in kidding herself? Dreams always came to nothing. Just like every other even half-way reasonable thing that ever happened to her, Simon would be snatched away, and she'd be left alone and lonely.

But then again, what did she have to lose? Certainly

not her self-respect; that had been lost long ago – on the day she had been stupid enough to get involved with Ted Martin.

Chapter 19

Ted was sitting in the prefab, staring unseeingly into the middle distance, drumming his fingers tunelessly against the side of his chair. He'd kill her when she came in. He'd fucking kill her.

At the sound of a key in the front door he leapt to his feet. As Dilys stepped inside he grabbed her by the arm. She tried to shake free of him, but he held her fast.

'I've been waiting for you for three days.' Ted spat the words at her through his teeth, his lips hardly moving. 'Where the fuck have you been?'

'Not that it's anything to do with you, but I've been out.'

'Out?' he asked incredulously. 'But it's Saturday. You ain't been here since Wednesday. How can you be *out* for three days?'

Dilys raised a cynical eyebrow. 'I'd have thought that was a question you of all people could answer.'

'That kid in there,' he went on, his face right up close to hers, 'she could've been dead. And d'you know something else? Her bed was that disgusting I had to go and get her new sheets. *New sheets*.'

Dilys laughed scornfully. 'Why're you so worried about her all of a sudden? What, turned into some sort of wonderful father, have you? Funny though, you waiting till she's seven and a half years old before you come over all concerned.'

'You bitch.'

'Look, let's forget all the old fanny, Ted. What're you after?'

Ted wanted to hit her, to knock the smug look right off her face, but he had to play it clever, there was something he wanted even more – information. He let her go. 'I wanna know where Ginny is.'

Dilys laughed again. 'So, you've heard at last, have you? I wondered how long it'd take.'

Her mocking tone was too much for Ted; he raised his hand ready to knock the laughter out of her. But instead of cringing in fear as she usually did, Dilys turned her back on him and walked casually to the door.

She stopped, looked over her shoulder at him and said very calmly, 'I wouldn't do that if I was you, Ted.' Then she yelled in a terrified voice, 'Chuck! Quick! Help me!'

Almost before Ted had a chance to realise what was going on, he had been pushed backwards into the sitting-room and was pinned up against the wall, with a hand gripped so tightly round his throat that he could barely breathe.

'Has he upset you, honey?' asked his captor in a deceptively gentle American accent, as he stared menacingly into Ted's face.

'No, Chuck. You're all right. A coward like him could never hurt me. He just frightened me, that's all.'

Dilys stepped forward and looked Ted directly in the eye. 'Let me introduce you to my fiancé, Mr Chuck O'Grady. Handsome, ain't he? And don't you just love his uniform? He's in the American Air Force, ain't you, Chuck? And d'you know what, Ted, he's got mates what're even bigger'n him.' She giggled girlishly and squeezed Chuck's massive arm. 'Can you believe it?'

'What shall I do with him, sweetpea?'

Ted's eyes bulged.

'I reckon you should let him go, then we can get going

and all. I did intend sorting out a few things first, but seeing as Ted's here now, I think we can leave it to him.'

Slowly Chuck released his grip and Ted started coughing and spluttering, and clasping at his throat.

Dilys ignored the display; she just turned on her heel, took Chuck's arm and walked with him out to the front door.

Ted wasn't going to let her get away with it. He levered himself away from the wall and, finding the breath from somewhere, bellowed after them, 'She's got a kid in here, you know.'

Dilys patted Chuck's arm. 'Ignore him, love, he's barmy. Believe it or not, he's my best friend's husband. It's his little girl I told you about, the one I was minding, remember?'

Chuck nodded. 'Poor kid. Do they still neglect her?'

'Yeah. And just 'cos I have her sometimes, to give her a treat like, he thinks he can hang about the place an' all. Bloody cheek, innit?' Dilys paused on the doorstep and looked back into the prefab. 'Don't expect me back, Ted,' she shouted.

Ted was out to the door in a flash. 'But how about Ginny? How about Susan?'

Dilys smiled sweetly at her fiancé and kissed him on the end of his nose. 'You go over to the cab and wait for me, Chuck. I'll be one minute.'

'Are you sure you'll be okay?'

'I'll be fine; go on.'

She waited for Chuck to get inside the taxi, gave him a reassuring wave, then spun round to face Ted. 'As for Ginny, you can go and ask any one of them old toms she knocks around with. I'm sure they'll be only too pleased to help you out if you bung 'em a few bob. And as for Susan, I was gonna take her round your mum's and leave her there, that's why I come back here. I reckoned I ought to do something with her. But she's your bloody kid an' all. So if you're so worried, you sort her out.'

She turned away, stuck her chin in the air and began walking over to the taxi, but she hesitated. 'By the way, Ted,' she said, peering haughtily over her shoulder at him, 'I've told the council I don't need the prefab no more, 'cos I'm going to live with Chuck. We're getting married, see. This afternoon, as a matter of fact. Romantic, ain't it? So don't think you can kip here, will you?'

She took a single step, then stopped again. 'Aw, and another thing, that money you had hidden in the back of the maid-saver, don't bother looking for it. I've got it, 'cos I reckon you owe me, Ted Martin.'

'*I know, Mum, I know.*' Ted ran his fingers distractedly through his Brylcreemed hair. 'But I only need you to let us sleep here for a few days, just till I get something proper sorted out.'

Susan didn't know why her dad was bothering. She had taken one look at Nellie, who was standing in the kitchen of number 18 Bailey Street with her arms folded belligerently across her aproned chest as though she were guarding the place from invaders, and had known she wasn't wanted here, just as she didn't seem to be wanted anywhere. And she was tired and hungry. But then she was nearly always tired and hungry.

'Why can't she stay over the road with her uncles and them two stuck-up tarts?'

''Cos Dilys has rowed with them and they don't wanna know,' he improvised, covering up the fact he wouldn't dare go anywhere near the Chivers brothers – well, not without a sawn-off shotgun in one hand and a pickaxe handle in the other, he wouldn't. 'Mum, please. Do us this one favour. Like I say, this bit of business tonight, I won't be no time at all.'

'Leave off, Ted,' snorted Nellie. 'As if I can trust you to go out on a Saturday night and only be gone a few hours. I've heard all that old toffee before, remember. No time at all you say, then you disappear for days on end.'

'Mum, believe me. I promise on my baby's life I'll be back here before you know it. And I'll see you all right for your trouble. You know that.'

Softening slightly at the idea of being paid, Nellie jerked her head sideways at the stove. 'Well, I ain't doing no cooking or nothing. If you want grub you can go and get some pie and mash if they're still open, or some fish and taters.'

'You're a diamond, Mum, thanks.' Ted pulled out one of his mother's kitchen chairs and pushed Susan down on to it. 'You sit there and I'll go and get something for us all to eat.'

Nellie glared spitefully at Susan as they both listened to Ted running down the passage. 'And you can bring me in a quart of light ale from the Albert while you're at it,' she hollered after him.

Ted was in so much of a rush to get out again that he didn't even stop to wash his hands and face after he had eaten, and he still had grease from the cod and chips around his mouth when he stormed into Shirley's room.

'Look, Shirley, I've had enough old shit today to last me a lifetime, so just save all the crap for the punters. This is me you're talking to, not some ham bone up from the country. I need to know where that club is. Now are you gonna tell me, or—'

'Or what?' Shirley blew a slow stream of smoke into the air above her head, propped her cigarette on the mantelpiece and carried on ironing her dress on the makeshift board she had propped across her sink.

'Don't try and be clever with me, Shirley, I'm warning you. I ain't very happy at the minute, so you just tell me where I can find Ginny—'

'I'll tell you something, Ted,' she butted in again, 'that Maltese bloke's been round here looking for you.'

'How d'you mean, looking for me?'

'That so-called fixed fight you told him to put that big stake on – remember?' She flipped the dress over so that she could iron the back. 'It turned out it wasn't fixed at all. It went against you, Ted. And let's just say your Maltese friend isn't very happy. He wants money off you, he said. A lot of money. And he wants it soon.' She picked up her cigarette and took another puff.

'Did you tell him where he could find me?'

'As if I'd do that.'

Ted spun her round and jabbed his finger into her face. 'You'd better not have, Shirley, but you better *had* tell me where that club is.' He smacked the cigarette out of her hand. 'Now!'

'Why should I do anything to help you?'

'Because if you don't, I'm gonna rip that wrinkled old head o' your'n right off your fucking shoulders.'

Shirley tried backing away from him, but there wasn't anywhere to escape to in the cramped, sordid little room. 'All right, Ted, I was only joking. You know me, always having a laugh. The club's in Shoreditch. In fact, I've got one of her cards right here in my purse.'

Ginny took a deep breath, then made her way downstairs to the main bar. It was only four days since Simon had taken her to the country. Only four days since they'd . . . Well, since they'd *done it*. And she had been stupid enough to call him and invite him to her big, jolly, full-of-fun end-of-rationing party. And here she was, going down to meet him, or rather to face him. She must be mad. But it had seemed like a good idea. After all, Simon was going to be her saviour when Billy sold the clubs.

She sighed loudly to herself. She could only give it a try. Maybe he'd turn out to be different from the others.

Maybe.

It was barely half past nine and the club was already full, with most of the customers crowded into the second-floor bar, craning their necks to get a view of the big attraction on the stage.

Ginny had had a real brazier set up, right in the centre and, as had been stated on the invitations, all the guests were being encouraged to burn their now useless ration books in a celebration of the good times to come. And the biggest joke of the evening – one that had everyone laughing every time they heard it – was that no one in the club had ever had to worry abut rationing anyway. But what the hell, any excuse for a party!

Someone touched Ginny on the arm and she turned round, flashing her full professional smile.

It was Simon. 'Hello, Ginny,' he said warily. 'I'm really glad you asked me to come along tonight.'

Ginny nodded. 'It'll make a good story, won't it? I hope you've brought a photographer.'

'I didn't mean that. I meant I'm glad we're talking.'

Ginny kept up the smile. 'So am I.'

'And are *we* talking?' asked a woman's voice.

Ginny turned round again. This time she was met with the unmistakable sight of Leila, clad in her trade mark emerald green. She had her head on one side and was holding out her arms in a gesture of reconciliation.

'Simon, would you go and tell Flora to take a bottle of champagne over to my booth?'

'How many glasses?' he asked cagily.

'Just two for now. For me and Leila. But get yourself a drink and give us ten minutes alone, then come and join us, eh?'

'I'm surprised Billy's not here at a big do like this, sweetie. All these contacts to be made and faces to acknowledge.'

Ginny busied herself pouring the drinks, deliberately avoiding Leila's gaze. 'He never comes round when the club's open any more. He does turn up some nights, to go over the takings and the books and things. But only when he's checked with Flora that he's not going to bump into me.'

'I've not seem much of him lately either.' Leila was smiling, but the quaver in her voice betrayed her. 'I thought he might pop in here this evening. He must be celebrating somewhere. Everyone is.'

'D'you know, I wondered the self-same thing,' said Ginny raising her glass to Leila. 'If he might show up here, I mean. But according to Johnno, he went over to see how Belle's getting on at the Old Compton Street club.'

Leila nodded. 'Belle's place. Right. So that's who he's seeing now.'

Neither of them knew what else to say. Ginny tried to ease the silence by offering Leila a cigarette, but it didn't help much, especially as they were surrounded by laughter.

It was with relief that Ginny spotted Yvette standing in the doorway, scanning the room. 'Yvette!' she called, beckoning to her. 'What a lovely surprise! Look, Leila's here as well.'

But as Yvette fought her way across to them, Ginny could see from her face that the surprise wasn't going to be quite as lovely as she'd thought.

'Whatever's wrong?' Ginny helped her into the booth and waved for one of the waiters to come over, but Simon, who had been hovering around waiting for the ten minutes to be up, beat him to it. 'Get us a large brandy, will you, Simon?'

'I can't believe it,' Yvette sniffed, her hand trembling as she tried to light a cigarette.

Ginny took it from her. 'Here, let me.'

'Take a deep breath, sweetie,' Leila said, stroking her hand.

'I've been everywhere looking for you, Leila. I didn't know what to do. I just got in a cab and went round all the clubs.'

Simon appeared with the brandy.

'Come on, Yve,' Ginny soothed her, 'drink this.'

She half emptied the glass in a single gulp, not even noticing the burning in her throat. 'Shirley's been murdered.'

'She's what?' Ginny gasped.

Yvette stared down at the table top. 'She was smashed over the head. Earlier tonight some time. In that poxy little room of her'n in Dean Street. The girl across the landing found her. She saw all this blood. It was on the stairs, when she was going down to start working for the night.' Yvette swallowed more of the brandy. 'They reckon the bastard done her in with her own iron.'

'Who? Who did it?' Leila could hardly speak.

Yvette swiped at her tears with the back of her hand, rubbing tracks of mascara down her cheeks. 'There's all sorts of rumours going round. But it couldn't have been a thief, like some of them are saying. The poor cow didn't have a pot to piss in, everyone knew that.'

Leila hastily looked away.

'I tried to tell the law when they turned up it must have been a punter.' Yvette buried her face in her hands and sobbed. 'Not that they're bothered. Once they saw she was a working girl, they didn't wanna know. But I tried, Gin, I tried telling 'em. She was so broke she was going with anyone. She must have picked up some nutcase, and . . .' Yvette shook her head. She couldn't go on.

Ginny stood up again. She went to the bar and spoke to Flora. 'Get rid of everyone, please. Quick as you can. I'll explain later.'

Within minutes, Yvette and Leila had been put into the back of a taxi instructed to take them to Leila's flat, and the club – apart from Ginny, Flora and three of the minders who'd stayed behind to deal with any late-comers – was cleared.

Over two hours later, Ginny was still sitting up at the bar, drinking her way to the bottom of a pot of tea that Flora had fetched from the kitchens. She couldn't bear the thought of going up to bed; there were too many bad thoughts spinning and churning around in her mind.

'I'm telling you, she'll let me in,' she and Flora heard someone shouting from downstairs.

'Ginny. It's me, Simon. Tell these chaps it's okay.'

'Excuse me, Flora.' Ginny set her cup in her saucer and climbed down from the bar-stool. 'I'll only be a minute.'

At the bottom of the stairs, Ginny saw Simon struggling with one of the minders. 'The party's over, Simon. Go home.'

'Look, Ginny, I know you must be angry, me running out like that, but my first reaction was to get the story. To get the scoop.'

'Simon, I don't wanna row with you, but—'

'Can't I come upstairs for a while? To talk?' He smiled winningly. 'I'll even play my clarinet for you if you like.

That'll make you laugh. I've got it out in the car. I'll go and—'

'Simon. Stop. Please.'

'Ginny, if I don't take chances like this. If I don't make my name and become a rich and famous editor' – his smile graduated to his cheeky grin – 'how can I ever buy you your Tara?'

'Simon. Not now.' Ginny turned and went back upstairs, leaving the minders to see him out.

It was almost half past two in the early hours of Sunday morning and Ted was downstairs in the kitchen of number 18, listening to the sound of Nellie snoring up above him. He was wondering how, at nearly thirty-five years old, he had come to this. He was living back home with his mum, but scared to be seen out in the street; stuck with a kid to look after; no money to speak of, but with a wife who was running a club and probably had plenty; knowing there was some Maltese arsehole after his blood; and enough tea inside him to float a sodding battleship.

He was just deciding whether he should go out into the yard again, to check whether the bonfire he'd started had at last reduced his gore-stained clothes to unrecognisable ashes, or whether he should make himself another cup of tea first, when he heard what was for him the familiar sound of a jemmy working away at the woodwork round the front door.

Shit! Dilys's brothers must have spotted him. And presumably they were hoping to give him a surprise.

Ted switched off the lights and crept upstairs to where Susan was sleeping in the front room. He lifted the corner of the curtain and peered down.

But it wasn't Sid and Micky; it was the Maltese bastard and two of his trained gorillas.

That big-mouthed whore, Shirley, must have blabbed after all.

Ted clapped his hand over his sleeping child's mouth. Her eyes flicked open in alarm. 'It's all right, it's only me,' he whispered into her ear. 'We've gotta go. Get your coat on as quick and quiet as you can and follow me on tiptoe down to the backyard. All right?'

Susan nodded in wide-eyed silence.

As they clambered over the back wall, Ted could hear Nellie screaming blue murder and the unmistakable sound of her enamel chamber pot finding its mark, as the Maltese apparently found his mother's bedroom.

'Ain't you gonna ask me in?'

'Ted, it's three o'clock in the morning. You turn up here when I ain't seen you for—'

'Don't clubs stay open till late no more, then?'

'Not tonight,' said Ginny, wishing she's never insisted that Flora and the minders took the rest of the night off. 'I've had some bad news.' She didn't bother wasting her breath telling him what had happened to Shirley, he probably wouldn't even care, knowing the way he'd treated the poor cow, or worse, he'd say she'd had it coming to her. That's what everyone seemed to say when a tom got murdered.

Ginny was just about to slam the door in his face when Ted played his blinder. 'At least let the little 'un in for a minute, Gin. To have a drink or something.'

'What little 'un?'

Ted jabbed his thumb over his shoulder at the waiting cab. 'Susan. My little Susan.'

Ginny pulled her dressing-gown round her and ran barefoot down the steps to the taxi. She wrenched open the door and held out her arms to the pale-faced child.

'Oi, before you take her, that'll be fifty-two and six, if you don't mind.'

Even Susan, huddled in the corner of the back seat of the taxi like a scared rabbit, couldn't distract Ginny from the shock of the fare. *'How much?'*

'Don't blame me, darling. It's that bloke o' your'n. He's a bit strange if you ask me. Had me driving all round the back doubles, going round in circles and back again, like he was on a treasure trail or something.' He leaned towards her. 'Not trying to give someone the slip or nothing, is he?'

Ginny sighed resignedly. Ted Martin was back.

'I've settled her down in the spare room, she's whacked out.'

'Lovely. And thanks, Gin, I always said you was one in a million.'

'Save it, Ted, I don't fall for that old madam no more. Now, how did you know where to find me?'

'I heard on the grapevine, didn't I, babe.'

'You do know you wouldn't have even got a foot through that door if it wasn't for Susan?'

'I know,' he said honestly – that having been the only reason he had brought the child with him in the first place. He knew she was Ginny's weak spot.

'What I don't understand is why she's with you.'

'Gin, you wouldn't believe it, darling. Dilys just walked out and left the poor little thing to look after herself. Can you imagine? She's been begging scraps from neighbours. Laying in a filthy rotten bed. You wouldn't believe the half of it.'

'But I've been sending money to Dilys regular, so she could buy stuff for Susan.'

'Have you? That was kind.' That conniving bitch, Dilys, had never mentioned no money to him.

'And to Nellie. Why didn't she make sure—'

'Me mother's dead.'

'Nellie's dead?'

Ted rolled his eyes towards heaven. 'Yeah, Gawd rest her soul. That's why we came here. I wouldn't let that kid stay in that prefab a minute longer and there was no one else I could turn to.'

'Where are you living then?'

He didn't hesitate. 'A poxy little bedsitter in Notting Hill Gate.'

'Notting Hill? If these are more of your rotten lies, Ted Martin, I'll —'

'I swear on my mother's . . . On my life. That's why we're here. Susan can't stay over there with me. It's terrible, Gin. Honest, you should see it. There's all these fights between the local yobbos and them West Indian gangs.' Ted was getting into his stride and was rather pleased with his imaginative choice of fictitious address. 'How could I take her over there? Poor little kid. Plus she needs a woman's touch. You know, she's nearly eight now. A proper little lady.'

'There's no need for all your old flannel, Ted. Susan can stay here while you sort yourself out.'

'I don't reckon I should leave her though, Gin. She'll be scared without her dad. It's bad enough losing her mum like this. And what with her old granny going an' all . . .'

Ginny sighed wearily. 'All right, Ted, save it. You can stay. But just for a few nights. And I really mean it.'

'I knew I could depend on you, babe.' He reached out and touched her shoulder.

'Aw no,' she said, pulling her dressing-gown tight to her throat. 'Don't even think about it.'

'But, darling—'

'And don't you darling me neither. D'you think I'm

stupid? What d'you want me to do? Stand here like a punch-bag, waiting till the mood takes you, then let you take swings at me all night?'

'But d'you think I'd have bothered hitting you, if I hadn't cared about you?'

'*Do what?*'

'And if you hadn't cared about me, you wouldn't have married me, now would you?'

'You live in a sodding dream world.'

'Anyway, I've changed.' He held out his arms. 'Look at me. Here I am with me little kiddie—'

'Bollocks, Ted, I've heard it all before. And I saw what you did to Shirley.'

He was suddenly alert. How could she know? 'What're you talking about?'

'What you did to her face with them fish hooks. That was disgusting.'

She didn't know. Thank Christ for that.

'And if you wanna stay, you can sleep in the sitting-room. I'll fetch you some blankets and a pillow.'

'You're still a tight-arsed bitch,' he muttered.

'What was that?'

'Nothing. Well, actually, I did say something. I said, I really have changed. You just see if I ain't.'

A whole week went by before Simon dared show his face at the club again; now it was Saturday morning and he had thought of a way to try and make amends, or at least to try and get himself back into Ginny's good books. He was surprised by how important her approval was to him, but he couldn't make up his mind whether it was the thought of getting a brilliant story about the lady club boss – that he could probably syndicate worldwide if he played it right – or whether he had actually fallen for her. It wouldn't be the first time he'd fallen so quickly for someone. But there was something special about Ginny . . .

'I don't know that it's a good idea,' said Flora, when Simon asked if he could go up to see her.

'It's okay,' he replied, running up the stairs. 'It's a surprise.'

'It'll be that all right, dearie,' Flora said, shaking his head at the terrible waste when you had such a good-looking hunk preferring the ladies.

Simon was only half-way up the stairs, but was already calling out to her. 'Ginny. It's only me. Simon. Flora let me in. Hurry up and get your coat on. We're going out for the day.' He reached the top of the stairs. 'To the beach,' he went on, pushing open the door and walking into the flat. 'I'm going to cheer you up if it's—'

He stopped dead in his tracks. There was a man, sitting on the sofa in his trousers and vest, with his heavily greased dark hair sticking up all over the place, as if he had been sleeping. He was eating toast.

'Hello,' Simon said politely. 'Who are you?'

'I think I should be asking you that, mate. But for your information, I'm Ginny's old man. Now piss off out of it.'

Simon left, slamming the door behind him.

'Ted,' Ginny called from the bathroom. 'Who was that?'

'No one.'

A fortnight passed and Ted was still camping out in Ginny's sitting-room. She wasn't surprised, really. Nor was she surprised that Ted's claim that he had changed had been just another of his lies. Nothing about Ted had changed at all.

Not only did she discover from Susan that Nellie was very much alive and still living in Bailey Street, but she found out from Flora that Ted was at his old game of stealing money from her. Flora had actually caught him with his hand in the till and he'd still tried to wriggle out of it. Ginny had done her best to keep calm, for Susan's sake, and she had managed quite well, but then late one night, after the club had closed and Ginny was sitting in her booth entering different versions of the night's takings in the two sets of ledgers, one of the girls came stumbling into the bar. She looked a complete mess and was crying hysterically.

'So he's been taking money off you?'

The girl was still weeping uncontrollably and Ginny was having trouble making sense of her story. 'He made me,' she gulped.

'Made you what?'

'Said if I didn't go with the customers . . .' She shook her head wildly. 'I didn't want to. He made me. I can't keep quiet no more.'

'Try and tell me.'

'I know he's your husband, Miss Martin, but . . .' She staggered to her feet and pulled open her blouse.

Ginny's hand flew to her mouth. The girl's chest was criss-crossed with bloody knife slashes.

Ginny left the girl sobbing in the booth, while she instructed Flora to telephone a doctor she knew who had gambling debts with her big enough to ensure that he would do her a favour and keep his mouth shut. Then she took Johnno, the minder she trusted most of all – even unsupervised with the takings – upstairs with her and told Ted to get out.

Ted didn't need to be told twice, not with Johnno there. But he was determined to be as spiteful and awkward as he could get away with. 'Susan,' he shouted. 'Get up. We're leaving.'

Ginny shook her head. 'You bastard.'

The door to the spare room opened and Susan came

out, wearing one of the nighties that Ginny had bought her. She was hollow-eyed with sleep and fear. 'I don't wanna go,' she whispered, her bottom lip trembling with the effort of holding back her tears.

'You're not going anywhere, dolly face. Come on, come and give us a cuddle, you'll be all right with your Auntie Gin. Daddy's the one who's gotta go away for a little while. He's just going downstairs with Johnno, aren't you, Ted? So go and give him a kiss and he can get off.'

Susan kissed Ted's unshaven cheek, then fled back to Ginny's side. She watched warily as Johnno and her dad left the flat.

Ginny took her back to her bed and tucked her in with her teddy bear. 'If you want me, I'll just be in the other room sorting out a couple of things. All right?'

Susan nodded.

Ginny kissed her on the cheek, turned on the squirrel-shaped night light that stood on the bedside table – another of the many things she had bought for Susan during the past weeks – and sat with her until her eyes finally closed.

Then she went back into the sitting-room, bundled up the blankets off the sofa and threw them in the kitchen ready for the laundry. At least the place didn't have to look like a refugee camp any longer, nor did it have to stink of Ted Martin.

She had no fear that he'd be back, he was too much of a coward for that, but he was such a spiteful bastard, he might just try and get Susan away from her. And she couldn't bear that. She'd have to work something out; find a way to keep her safe. She couldn't let her go again. She just couldn't.

She went over to the cocktail cabinet to pour herself a drink, but, remembering the music box rendition of 'Secret Love', she stopped. She didn't want Susan being disturbed again, the poor little thing had been through more than enough already.

Ginny dropped wearily on to the sofa. But, exhausted as she was, she vowed she wouldn't go to sleep until she had worked out a way to keep the child she loved.

She felt as though her head was ready to split with the effort of going round and round the same useless ideas, then, quite suddenly, it came to her. Ted had let slip that Dilys had married some American soldier, whom she'd kidded about Susan not being hers. If she got in touch with her somehow – it couldn't be that difficult – Dilys would have no choice. Her name – the only name, the father being *unknown* – would be on the birth certificate. If Dilys wanted to keep up her little pretence she would have to give Ginny guardianship, or she would spill the beans so fast, Dilys wouldn't know what had hit her.

She'd done it. She'd found a way. Now Susan could stay with her for ever.

Chapter 20

April 1955

It had been another long day. Ginny had originally intended to get herself into a routine of getting up to see Susan off to school, then having another couple of hours' sleep, but once she was up it seemed slatternly to go back to bed, especially with the bright spring mornings. Feeling a bit tired was nothing, compared with the happiness, love and pride she felt as she looked down at the peacefully sleeping child, barely recognisable as the pale-faced waif who had turned up at the club in the early hours of the morning over nine months before.

The morning after Johnno had thrown Ted out, Ginny had gone to Bailey Street to see Dilys's brothers, Sid and Micky, full of foreboding at what they would have to say about her suggestion that Susan should stay with her at the club. It had been quite a while since she'd seen them, but when Ted had stayed, he'd told her plenty about the women they'd married and they sounded terrifying.

But she had had no need to worry. They – or rather the wives – had seemed only too pleased that they weren't about to have a seven-year-old cuckoo forced into their cosy little nests and soon persuaded their husbands that Ginny caring for Susan would be best all round for everyone. Then Ginny had crossed the street and popped in to see Nellie. It was an odd sensation going into number 11 again after all that time, but it had to be done. She had to warn Nellie that if her son came anywhere near Ginny's club she would have the law on him.

Nellie had been her usual aggressive self, but Ginny had remained calm and just told her to remind Ted that she had enough high-ranking policemen amongst her customers to make his life very uncomfortable. And if Nellie forgot to give Ginny's message to her son, she might just find that her weekly envelope started getting forgotten as well.

She had then spoken to a solicitor – another regular at Ginny's – and had asked him about tracing Dilys.

With all that organised, and Susan enrolled in the local school, the only worry Ginny had was what she would do if Billy Saunders did eventually get rid of the clubs. She would need to find a new job and a new home, and now there were two of them it wouldn't be quite so easy.

Nor would it be easy meeting up with Billy Saunders again. She'd heard the odd word of gossip about him, but she hadn't set eyes on him in a long time. She couldn't, though, put it off any longer, she really would have to find out what he intended doing about his businesses.

She'd make a cup of tea, have a glance through the paper and get herself off to bed. Then, in the morning, after she'd got Susan off to school, she'd organise a meeting with Billy to get things settled once and for all.

She'd only intended a quick flick through the news while she drank her tea, but when she read the headline – *Ruth Ellis charged with murder* – and saw that the story had been written by Simon Parker, Ginny put her untouched tea down on the side table and read every word.

To begin with, she had been half smiling with embarrassment at her own foolishness, remembering how she had actually considered Simon as her potential saviour, but by the time she had finished any trace of amusement had vanished.

Simon was a good sort of bloke and she hoped he was doing well, but had he been the most wonderful man in the world, Ginny still wouldn't have been able to do what it seemed that Ruth Ellis had done.

Ginny studied the photograph of her in the paper. It showed a woman, not particularly exceptional, but attractive, with hair dyed as blonde as her own; and she wondered whatever had made her do it. What had made her put a man before her children? What had made her decide that that man, any man, was so important?

She folded the paper and picked up her tea. It was stone cold. How long had she been sitting there? She looked at her watch.

Ten to four?

Johnno should have been round to pick up the takings nearly an hour ago. Where the hell had he got to? It wasn't like him to let her down.

She yawned loudly. She might as well make a fresh cup of tea while she was waiting.

She had just set the water to boil when she heard the welcome sound of footsteps on the stairs. 'Come in, Johnno,' she called from the kitchen, getting out another cup. 'You must have heard me put the kettle—'

Her words froze on her lips and the cup fell from her hand and went spinning across the tiled floor. Standing in the kitchen doorway was Ted, looking and stinking like a meths drinker who'd just been thrown off a bench on the Embankment.

He lifted his food and stamped on the spinning cup, shattering it into a myriad pieces.

'How did you get in?'

Ted winked and stumbled into the room. 'Fire escape and a bit of force, darling,' he slurred. 'You wanna get that checked. You never know who might find their way up your stairs.'

'What d'you want?'

'I've decided,' he said, waving his arms wildly about him. 'If you ain't gonna give me a fair share of this gaff, then you ain't gonna have the kid. I'm taking her with me.'

'If you go anywhere near that child,' she said, putting herself determinedly between Ted and the door, 'I swear I'll—'

She put up her arms to protect herself, but she was too late. Ted caught her a sharp crack to the side of her face, splitting open her cheek like a gaping mouth. She screwed up her eyes in pain, but didn't utter a sound.

Don't let her wake up. Please, don't let her wake up, Ginny prayed in her head.

He pulled back his fist for a second shot, but lost his balance and staggered backwards, then, trying to steady himself, tripped forward and crashed into the table.

Ginny's mind was racing in spite of the blow. If she could get him downstairs, away from the flat, away from Susan, Johnno would be here soon.

'Look Ted, I'm sorry. I'm being selfish, you are her father after all. And it's not fair, me keeping her all to myself. Tell you what, let's go down and discuss it over a drink.'

Unable to resist the offer of another drink, Ted followed her out of the flat and down the stairs.

The second-floor bar was in darkness. Ginny turned on the red-shaded lamp in her booth. 'Make yourself comfortable, Ted, and I'll fetch a bottle over. Scotch all right?'

Ted's angry sneer distorted his once handsome face into a brutal mask of hatred. 'Here's you living like Lady fucking Docker, while I'm on me uppers.'

Ginny swallowed hard, willing Johnno to hurry up. 'I won't be a minute.'

She flicked the switch that illuminated the bar, found a bottle of whisky, then hesitated over whether to take one or two glasses. Ted was just as capable of belting her for not wanting to drink with him as for having some of the scotch that he could have drunk.

She decided on two and put them on a tray with a jug of water. If he wanted her to drink she would at least keep a clear head by watering it down. She had to keep control until Johnno arrived.

'Here you are.'

'What's that noise?' Ted frowned. 'It's someone letting themselves in. You'd better not have no bloke shacked up here with you.' He made as if to stand up.

'No, Ted, of course I haven't. I'm your wife.'

There was the sound of the door being closed.

'Well who is it?'

'It'll be the bloke come to do the bottling up for me.'

'At this time of the morning?'

'He works nights. Does a double shift.' Christ she was talking crap. She just hoped he was drunk enough not to notice. Anything to give Johnno time to get up the stairs.

'Go and get rid of him.'

'Okay. But you stay here.'

Ginny fled from the room, terrified that Ted would go back up to the flat.

'Johnno,' she whispered as she ran down the pitch-dark stairs. 'Please. Keep your voice down. Please. It's import—'

Suddenly she felt a pair of large arms grab hold of her. It was all she could do not to scream.

'What's up?' a man's voice asked.

'Billy?' she gasped. 'Is that you?'

'Yeah. What we whispering for?'

'I didn't expect—'

416

'Johnno's old woman's gone into labour and he's having to mind the other kids and—'

'That don't matter—'

'I left it late so's you'd be in bed. He should have phoned, but he probably—'

'Look, Billy, please, you've gotta help me.'

Ginny stood behind Billy as he turned on the main overhead lights that lit up the whole second floor for the cleaners.

Ted shielded his eyes. 'What the fuck are you up to, you stupid tart. Turn them lights off.'

Billy stared in disbelief. 'Ted Martin? *Ted Martin*? One of the stupid little two-bob snakes what's been trying to have one over on me over the years? *He's* your old man? This piece of—' He turned to look at Ginny. 'What's happened to your face?'

'Billy? Billy Saunders?' Ted was on his feet, barrelling across the room straight for him. 'You bastard!'

'Billy, mind out!' Ginny yelled, pushing him sideways.

The chair that Ted had thrown at Billy's head missed him and hit Ginny instead, sending her tumbling backwards towards the stairs. She grabbed hold of the banister and fell, screaming in agony as her arm was nearly jerked from its socket.

Billy ran to help her.

'No. I'm all right,' she gasped. 'Just stop him getting upstairs. Please, there's a kid up there. Don't let him hurt her.'

Ted was already half-way up the stairs to the flat. Billy lunged at him at full stretch and just managed to get hold of the back of his jacket. He pulled him backwards and the pair of them fell in a heap on to the landing. By the time Ginny got to them they were up on their feet again, punching and kicking at each other like savages.

Ginny wanted to get past, to get up to Susan, but she was too scared to go near them, they were completely out of control.

Suddenly, Billy was staggering backwards holding his arm and blood was pouring down his sleeve.

'Billy?'

'Mind, Gin, the bastard's got a knife.'

Ted started laughing, then turned round to run up the stairs.

She wasn't sure where she got the courage from, but Ginny launched herself at Ted and started smacking him round the back of the head. 'Keep away from her,' she sobbed. 'Keep away.'

Ted laughed louder and turned round, shaking her like an Alsatian trying to rid itself of a troublesome terrier. 'Piss off.'

Ginny, her eyes wide with fury, sank her teeth deep into his hand. He dropped the knife and she snatched it up and stuck it straight into the side of his neck.

The next thing Ginny knew, she was standing looking down at Ted, who was stretched out on the landing with his head twisted round like a broken doll and his eyes staring up at the ceiling.

Billy took her by the shoulders, rolled Ted out of the way with his foot and eased her towards the stairs. 'Go up to the flat. I'll be up in a minute.'

As soon as he saw her close the flat door behind her, Billy ran back down to the second floor and grabbed the telephone from behind the bar. 'Yeah, Johnno, I know it's hard, but I need you here. I need someone I can trust.' He pulled out his cigarette case. 'I need you to clear something up for me. Right away.' He flicked his lighter and inhaled deeply. 'Yeah. That's right. It's some rubbish. I want it out of Ginny's way. It's not too bulky but you might wanna bring one of the chaps with you. Someone we both like, if you see what I mean. I'll get straight on the blower to Leila. She'll get someone round yours to mind the kids.'

As Johnno put the phone down he rubbed his hands over his unshaven face. This was all he needed. He'd promised Chrissie faithfully he'd stay with the kids while she was in the hospital. And after all the rucks they'd had lately she'd said this was his last chance. He was just about fed up being at everyone's beck and call. He earned good money but he never had the chance to bloody spend any of it. And if Chrissie knew that her nippers had been minded by one of Leila's toms she'd kill him stone dead. But he couldn't say no to Billy. He'd just have to get it done as quick as he could and get back home before the kids woke up and saw that it wasn't their daddy who was looking after them.

'Are you all right, girl?'

Ginny nodded, her hand was trembling so badly she could hardly hold her cigarette.

'I'll make you a cup o' tea, yeah?'

'But how about—'

'Don't worry. Someone's sorting it out.'

Billy went into the kitchen and made the tea. When he brought it through to the sitting-room Ginny's shoulders were heaving as she wept silently into her hands. He put the tray down and knelt beside her. 'Don't cry, girl, it's gonna be all right.'

As she dropped her hands to look at him, Billy winced at the sight of the bloody gash across her cheek. 'That slag did that, didn't he?'

She turned her head away. 'What am I gonna do, Bill? This is all such a mess. There's a little girl asleep in there and—'

'Who is she, this kid?'

419

'Her mother was the person I used to think was my best friend. She's not around any more, so I took her in.'

'How about the father?'

She lifted her chin and looked into his eyes. 'I just killed him.'

The next evening Ginny was in too much of a state to go downstairs to the club, but Billy insisted they should open as usual, keep everything as normal as possible – he would see to things, make sure everything was all right, while she got some rest. There were a few eyebrows raised amongst the staff when Billy emerged from the flat upstairs, but they all knew better than to ask any awkward questions.

It was nearly half past nine and Ginny, her nerves twanging like badly tuned harp strings, had just been in to check on Susan yet again, when there was an urgent knocking on the flat door.

As she carefully closed Susan's door, Ginny's stomach was turning back flips and she ran through all the possibilities of who it might be. She had to remember what Billy had said about keeping up a calm appearance. She managed to call lightly, 'Okay, I'm coming,' and walked unsteadily out to the door that she had double-locked and chained for the first time since she had moved in.

She didn't know whether to be relieved or even more worried when she saw that her visitor was Leila. What did she want? They'd not said a word to one another since the night Shirley had been killed.

'I'd like to talk to you, Ginny,' Leila said very formally. 'May I come in?'

Ginny stepped back and ushered her through into the sitting-room. 'Course. But I'd appreciate you keeping your voice down. As I'm sure you've heard, I've got a little girl living with me now.'

Leila draped herself across the sofa and allowed her fox furs to fall from her shoulders. 'That's not the only thing I've heard.'

'No?' Ginny automatically covered the gash on her face with her hand. Surely Leila hadn't found out about last night. Her other hand shook as she offered Leila the cigarette box from the coffee table.

Leila took her time lighting and inhaling, then with her eyes fixed on Ginny's she said, 'You know what people are like. How they talk.'

Ginny said nothing.

'Billy stayed here last night, didn't he?'

Was that it? Was that all she knew? 'He's downstairs now, if that's what you mean,' said Ginny warily. 'I didn't feel too well today and he said he'd keep an eye on things.'

'I can see from that cut on your face that something's wrong.'

'That's nothing to do with Billy.'

'I didn't think it was.' Leila pinned on her professional smile. 'And it's no concern of mine. But you don't have to lie to me, Ginny. And before you ask, no he doesn't know I'm up here, I slipped past him. Regular little spy, aren't I?'

'Leila, I don't know—'

'Look, darling, it's no secret that Billy and I haven't exactly been what they call an item for quite a while now. But when he's just messing around with different girls – Belle one week, Sylvia another – I know I still have a chance.' She tapped the ashes from her cigarette and studied the little grey mound in the chromium ashtray as though it were an item of great fascination, then she raised her eyes and laughed mirthlessly. 'I'm having a bit of trouble saying this, sweetie. Bit embarrassing, if you know what I mean. You see, until you came along I was always the one Billy came back to. The trouble is, he likes you, Ginny, he likes you a lot.'

Ginny's head was thumping. She really didn't need this. Not now. She stood up. 'Leila. Please, I—'

'Just hear me out.' Now Leila was on her feet too. 'All I want to say is, it's up to you what happens next. You're the one with all the cards. But if you don't really want him, then please tell him, Ginny.' Leila looked away. 'You can't imagine how much I hate being reduced to this.'

'Sit down, Leila,' Ginny said wearily. 'I'll get us a drink.'

She went over to the cocktail cabinet and lifted the lid; the mechanical opening bars of 'Secret Love' came plinking out, as loud in Ginny's head as a round of church bells. 'Bugger! I forgot.' She snapped down the lid and paused, listening for any sound of Susan stirring. 'I'll go in the kitchen and get us—'

'I'd rather you stayed here,' said a man's voice.

Ginny and Leila both twisted round to see a youngish man standing behind the sofa.

Shit! She must have forgotten to lock the door when she'd let Leila in.

'Remember me?' he asked.

She shook her head.

'Try,' he persisted.

She really didn't remember him and she was too pre-occupied with trying to remember all the other things that Billy had told her she should do – apart from locking the door and not letting anyone into the flat – to bother playing guessing games with some punter who'd somehow found his way upstairs. She just knew he was about to beg her for a loan so he could play *just one more game* of chemmy, or to have an extension on his bar tab. She'd heard it all before.

'Look, if you—' she began, but then she saw the two

422

policemen blocking the doorway behind him and a sick-ening realisation flooded over her.

Of course she remembered him. He was a copper. He was Detective Sergeant Chisholm, the cocky young plain-clothes officer who'd raided the club; the one who had threatened all sorts – until Billy had got Doug Millson round to sort him out.

'Leila,' she said calmly, 'would you mind going down and telling Billy, please.'

Leila went to stand up, but Chisholm shook his head. 'You'd only be wasting your time, Miss Harvey,' he said, using Leila's name as though they were old acquaint-ances. 'Saunders knows I'm up here. Two DCs are keeping him company downstairs and I don't think he should be disturbed. He wanted to have a word with DI Millson on the phone. But I told him, like I told you, he'd only be wasting his time.' He sighed contentedly. 'There's no wriggling out of it this time you see, Mrs Martin. We've got everything we need. It's as simple as that.'

Ginny's mouth was so dry she could barely speak. 'What d'you want?' she croaked.

'Well, I'm not here for a cut of the gambling, or for free drinks, or even a free fuck for that matter. I leave that sort of thing to my older colleagues. I'm here to tell you that the body of Ted Martin, your husband, was found washed up in the tide on the Essex marshes earlier today. And from the rocks in his pockets it seemed that someone was trying to conceal it. Not very well, as it happened. Rather a rushed job I'd say. Or maybe an amateur's attempt.'

Leila's eyes widened just a fraction, but she didn't utter a word.

'We found something else in his pocket,' Chisholm continued, digging inside his jacket and pulling out a clear cellophane envelope. 'This.'

Ginny wouldn't look at it, whatever it was. She shook her head. 'I've been separated from my husband for years.'

Chisholm took a step forward. 'I've just noticed your face, Mrs Martin. 'How did you get that injury?'

'I fell.'

'Your husband had quite a reputation for smacking women around, didn't he?'

'Did he? I don't know. I've not seen him for I can't remember how long. And—'

'Do you recognise this, Mrs Martin?'

Chisholm held up the clear packet so that she had no choice but to look at it.

'What ' Ginny swallowed hard. 'What is it?'

'It's a business card. It was found tucked inside the torn lining of his jacket pocket. It's a bit soggy from the river water, of course, but it's quite obvious what it is if you look. It's your card, Mrs Martin.'

Ginny dropped down on to the sofa next to Leila, the taste of bile bitter in her throat.

'I think we'd better continue this conversation down at the station, don't you, Mrs Martin.'

'But there's a little girl—'

'Don't worry, Ginny,' Leila said. 'I'll look after her.'

'Oh dear, oh dear, Chisholm, you have been a bit previous, haven't you?'

Chisholm was standing – standing! – stony-faced in front of DI Millson's desk, while Millson, and Saunders, and Saunders's fancy, over-priced West End brief sat looking at him as though he was something they'd just stepped in.

'You've held Mrs Martin in custody all night, haven't you?'

'Yes, sir. I—'

'Keep your trap shut, Chisholm. If you listened a bit more you might learn something.'

Chisholm's jaw was rigid with anger. How dare that bent bastard Millson tell him what to do?

'Mr Saunders here has been, let us say, keeping company with Mrs Martin and she had not been out of his sight for three whole days. Gentleman that he is, Mr Saunders would like this to be kept quiet, of course, to protect the lady's reputation.'

Billy Saunders grinned happily at the now puce-faced Chisholm. 'If you wanna do a proper bit of detective work, son,' he beamed, 'I can help you. Would you like that?'

Chisholm managed a brief nod. He wanted to smash the bastard's face in.

'You take yourself down the docks. Anyone'll do. The Royal, the Albert ... And talk to some of them fellers down there. The ones in the bonded warehouses all knew Ted Martin. They're the ones who reckon their stock keeps "disappearing". They were business associates of his, you might say. I wonder if he owed any of them any money? You could ask 'em, couldn't you? But you'll have to watch yourself, son, they're hard men down there.'

Saunders leaned back in his seat and pulled his cigarettes out of his pocket. 'Tell you what, when you've finished down there, you can try talking to some of the girls round Soho. Ask them about him. They'll be able to tell you all about his nasty little ways and what a no-good slag he was. There must be plenty of toms and their ponces who had the right needle with that piece o' shit.'

Chisholm stared determinedly in front of him. 'Can I go now, sir?'

Saunders knew full well he was talking to Millson, but he couldn't resist. 'Course you can, son,' Saunders said.

'And mind how you go. Some of them brasses can be right hard nuts.'

As Chisholm left Millson's office, Saunders's laughter followed him like a bad smell.

'Don't you say a single word,' Chisholm barked at an open-mouthed WPC who just happened to be walking past.

Within ten minutes, Billy had shown his appreciation to Millson with a bundle of used notes, had paid his brief for his very expensive time – which hadn't actually been required, but Saunders always liked to be prepared – and was now helping a deathly pale Ginny into the back of a cab.

He told the driver where to take them and slid the glass screen shut. 'Are you all right, girl?'

She shook her head and stared down at the floor. 'I can't take any more of this, Billy. I can't. I just don't know what to do. I wanted to tell them it was me. But I was so scared for Susan, I—'

Billy folded his arms around her and she buried her head in his shoulder.

'Ssssh, girl, don't get all upset, I'm here now and I'm gonna look after you.'

Chapter 21

July 1957

Ginny leaned back in the blue-and-white-striped deck-chair, stretched out her bare, tanned legs and pressed her toes into the soft, cool grass. Maybe, when your life was so good, it wasn't right to ask for more, but it wasn't as though she was asking for herself. And it wasn't as though she was asking for that much – just for Dilys to mention Susan in her letters. Then at least Ginny could show them to her. That would be something, some sort of contact with her mother. But no; not a word in any of them about anything other than how wonderfully Dilys was doing in America. It was as though her daughter had never existed.

Ginny sighed and let the single sheet of airmail paper, and the two brightly coloured snapshots showing Dilys and a tall, handsome man holding a baby in his arms, fall into her lap. She would put this latest one with all the rest and maybe, when Susan was older, she would let her see them and try to help her understand.

In the meantime she would write back to Dilys asking her, yet again, please to jot down just a few extra lines for Susan. Anything would do.

Perhaps it was silly bothering, especially as Susan was so happy. She knew she was wanted, treasured and loved. That she was Ginny's very special girl.

But was that enough? Ginny sighed again. Love was powerful all right, but could it ever take away the pain of rejection completely? She could only hope so.

'Mrs Saunders.'

At the sound of the woman's voice Ginny looked up,

squinting into the bright sunlight at the neatly uniformed maid standing a respectful distance to the side of her chair.

'Have I got to collect Susan already, Janette?' Ginny asked with a concerned frown. She put her watch to her ear to check it was still working.

'No, ma'am, that's not for over an hour. And Mrs Taylor said she'd be dropping her off, if you remember.'

Ginny relaxed. 'Of course.'

'You have a visitor.'

Janette's formality drove Ginny mad. 'Who is it?'

Instead of acting with her usual efficient primness, the maid pursed her lips and waggled her head with displeasure.

'Is something wrong?'

'She wouldn't say who she was, Mrs Saunders. Said it was to be a surprise. I didn't know what to do.'

Ginny smiled thinly. It would be one of the local worthies after a donation for some charity or other, thinking she was being a real wag by aggravating the staff. She still hadn't got used to the way of things in her new neighbourhood; in fact, it was like living in a foreign country at times.

'It's okay, Janette. Don't worry. Just bring her out, please.'

As the maid returned across the sweeping lawns with the surprise visitor in tow, Ginny leapt to her feet. 'Leila!' she yelled, running towards her with outstretched arms.

'Sweetie, you recognised me!'

'How could I fail to, with that bloody emerald-green frock coming across the grass?'

Ginny saw the shocked expression on Janette's face but she didn't care. 'It was like you was in flipping camouflage, girl!'

*

Ginny filled Leila's cup, sat back in her deckchair and took in a deep lungful of flower-scented air. 'I might not be Grace Kelly, like Flora used to reckon, but sitting here drinking tea in the garden with my old mate, well, this'll do me.'

'Less of the old thank you, Ginny – but we're still friends, are we?'

Ginny smiled and tutted loudly. 'Of course we are.'

Leila avoided her gaze, picking at an imaginary thread on her skirt. 'And you're happy are you?'

'Yeah, I reckon I am.'

Leila lifted her chin and Ginny winked at her across the rim of her cup. 'D'you know, Leila, there were plenty of times when I never believed that poor little Ginny Martin would ever make it. But just look at me now, eh?' She cocked her head on one side. 'And how about you? How are you doing? 'Cos pleased as I am to see you, I'm dying to know why you've turned up out of the blue like this.'

Leila didn't answer her question; she took her time breathing out a long plume of lavender smoke, then said: 'Strange, isn't it? Who knows what'll become of any of us? What'll happen in our lives. The twists and turns.'

'Well, you know what they say, Leila.' Ginny held her hands to her heart, stared dramatically towards the horizon and gasped in her best southern belle's drawl, 'Tomorrow is another day.'

Leila clapped her thigh. 'God! I remember that. It's from that old film.' She flapped her hand. 'Don't tell me. You used to drive us all crazy going on about it. And that woman in it. The one with all the dreams . . .'

Slightly shamefaced, Ginny grinned. '*Gone With the Wind*. Scarlett O'Hara. And they were *my* dreams too, if you don't mind.'

Leila shook her head and smiled, remembering. 'That brings back some memories.'

'I still dream, you know. When I'm sleeping, I mean. All about this place I knew a long, long time ago.'

'What place was that?'

'The street where I used to live. I see the rooms in that house as plain as day. It's a strange feeling. And all the neighbours, I see them too. There were some really decent people there once, back in the old days. And some right old cows.'

'You get those everywhere.' Leila laughed.

'It's all been knocked down now. Nothing left but a big patch of bare earth. Slum clearance, they reckon.' She paused. 'You know, it never seemed like a slum. Not back then. Still, things have to change, I suppose. And now they're talking about putting up one of them big blocks of flats. Well, that's what I heard.'

'And is Billy still in the property business?' Leila asked casually, suddenly fascinated, apparently, by the ash on the end of her cigarette.

'Yeah. And he's doing very well.'

She nodded. 'So I can see. This place is fantastic.'

'Not bad, is it?' Ginny looked about her, taking in the solidly respectable seven-bedroomed red-brick house, set in its four landscaped acres. 'And very well thought of he is nowadays. Works with this bloke. Peter. And talking about slums, that's what they do. They buy up slum property; terrible old places, all over London. Then, when the tenants move out, Billy's firm does them up.'

Leila's eyebrow rose very slightly. She knew all about the slum landlords and their scams: acquiring occupied properties on the cheap, then terrorising the tenants until they got out. In fact, she'd put on enough private parties for them during the last few years to be able to write a book about them and their influential friends. But she said nothing. She'd never been able to figure out whether Ginny really didn't know what was going on half the time, or whether she just chose not to see what was right in front of her.

Well, it wasn't any of Leila's business. Not any more.

She closed her eyes for a brief moment, then, flashing her lips-only smile she said, 'This really is a glorious garden, Ginny. And I'd love to see around the house.'

'You're on, girl, but the guided tour'll cost you half a crown.'

'I'll pay willingly, darling, and I'll bet it's every bit as wonderful as . . . What was Scarlett's place called again?'

'Tara,' Ginny replied without a second's hesitation.

'That's it. Tara. I should have remembered.' She tapped her chin with an exquisitely manicured fingertip. 'Well, Ginny, my love, it looks as though you've got your Tara at last.'

'And it's just right for a family.'

Leila stared at Ginny's flat stomach and frowned. 'You mean you're . . .'

Ginny shook her head – more to dispel the visions of Jeannie Thompson and her best yellow soap than by way of an answer. 'No, I'm not pregnant,' she said evenly. 'I'd like to be, but it just hasn't happened. Anyway, I've got my daughter. We adopted Susan.'

'Susan? Not that lovely little girl you were caring for?'

'That's my Susan. You'll be able to see her later, when she gets home from her riding lesson.'

'You're a lucky woman, Ginny.' Leila's voice caught as she spoke.

'I know. And when you think how things could have turned out. When you think of Shirley and some of the others.' She took a moment to top up their cups. 'Poor Shirley, eh?'

Leila showed no sign of what her thoughts were about

Shirley, she just took a dainty sip of her tea. 'So, where's Billy?' she asked as matter-of-factly as she could.

'Out wheeling and dealing as usual. Entertaining some bloke. A politician, if you must know! They'll be in some club somewhere I suppose.'

This time Leila raised both eyebrows and made sure that Ginny saw her questioning expression.

'Don't look at me like that. It's probably some very respectable gentlemen's club for all I know. But to be honest, I don't have anything to do with the business side of things any more. I've got all I want right here.'

'I think you have.'

'Tell me, Leila. It's something I've always wondered. Why did you help me out that time? Looking after Susan when the law took me away.'

Leila hesitated before she spoke, then, staring down into her cup, she said: 'I had a child myself once. A little girl. She must be, what, twenty-two. Almost twenty-three.' She held up her hand. 'And before you say anything, I was a child myself when I had her.'

They laughed uneasily, as old wounds opened for both of them.

'The trouble is, she's ashamed of me. Won't even see me.' Leila raised her head and looked at Ginny. 'She was adopted. By a very nice couple. Friends of the doctor who delivered her. Actually, he was the same doctor who made me pregnant in the first place.' She pinned her smile back on. 'Aren't some men absolute shits?'

'I'm so sorry, Leila. I didn't know.'

'Don't worry, no one does. I don't even know why I brought it up.' She gave Ginny a cigarette and lit it for her. 'And anyway,' she went on, screwing up her eyes against the smoke as she lit one for herself, 'that was then. At the time it was all I could do to get by from day to day. You know, just clinging to the wreckage and hoping for the best. But things got easier. Over the years.' She laughed carelessly. 'Well, when I saw your face as that little creep said he was taking you down to the police station, I had to stay with her, didn't I? How could I have done otherwise?'

'But you were so upset with me.' She considered before adding: 'You know, about Billy. You could have got one of the others to stay over.'

'Ginny,' Leila said, her chin jutting, 'there was a child involved. I'm not a monster.'

'I'm sorry, I never ...' Ginny looked at her, at her expertly made-up face and her elegantly dressed hair. It was like talking to a lovely mask. 'There's so much we don't know about one another. I'm really glad you came today and that we're talking like this at last. Tell me, Leila, how are you? How are you really?'

'Rather well, actually. I've found myself a decent chap at last.'

'You haven't!'

'Thank you!'

'I didn't mean—'

'How about some more of that lovely tea?' Leila said a little too brightly. 'Pour me some, will you?' She held out her cup. 'He's a reporter actually. His name's Simon.'

Ginny nearly dropped the teapot. 'Not Simon Parker?'

'The very one.' She allowed a genuine, if self-deprecating, smile to curve her lips. 'That's one of the reasons I came to see you, I suppose. To brag.'

'So what were the other reasons?'

'Only one. To come and see you.' Leila should have said: to come and see if you and Billy really look like staying together before I finally throw in my lot with Simon. But she didn't.

'Come on, how did you and Simon get together?'

'When Billy was selling up and he gave me the pick of the clubs—'

'Did he? I didn't know that,' Ginny broke in, then added hastily: 'But like I said, I don't have anything to do with the businesses now.'

With a shameful kind of pleasure Leila noted the edge that had crept into Ginny's voice. 'I suppose he thought he owed me something for all those years. I was very loyal.' She gave a little shrug. 'Well, I chose Ginny's. But don't even think of asking why, I'd be much too embarrassed to answer.'

'Leila—'

'Don't worry, water under the bridge, and before you ask, no it isn't called Ginny's any more. It's called Leila's. Far more classy.' She chuckled lazily. 'Anyway, Simon turned up one night. He was looking for you, but he found me instead. We got talking and I asked him if he still wanted a story. He did. And did I have a story to tell.'

'You didn't tell him everything?'

Leila looked horrified. 'Edited highlights, darling! Edited highlights! But it still took months to get through it all and he was absolutely riveted. He treated events like ... like ... let me see ... I know, like Johnno being killed, as if they were crossword clues.' She stared directly into Ginny's eyes. 'Do you know he simply refused to believe it was a hit-and-run accident?'

'I often wondered if that was anything to do with the Maltese gangs,' Ginny said quietly.

Leila leaned back in her deckchair. 'He never came up with that theory,' she said with a shake of her head. 'But it's possible, I suppose. Although Simon always thought Johnno was being paid off by someone close to home. For some mistake he'd made. Maybe—'

'Whatever it was,' Ginny cut in, 'I know it was really sad, happening just two days after his wife had her baby.'

Leila did her professional smile again. 'Perhaps he'll get to the bottom of it one day.'

'Isn't he too busy playing that clarinet of his?'

'Don't!'

'Is he just as bad?'

'Let's just say he'll never be a Benny Goodman.'

They laughed, slightly more easily this time, and sat for a while in almost companionable silence.

'He decided not to publish my story in the end.'

'Why not?'

'He fell in love with me instead. Wanted to keep me all to himself. That's why he proposed.'

'Leila!'

'I know.' She took a long draw on her cigarette. 'I didn't really take him seriously for a while. Plus I suppose there were things I had to be sure about.' She paused as though she were thinking something through. 'It took me a while, but I eventually said yes to him. Last weekend, actually.' She held out her left hand and flashed a large, square-cut diamond solitaire.

'So that's an *engagement* ring?'

'It is. Can you imagine, darling? Me, about to become a respectable married woman, marrying a man who is about to be made editor of the *Evening News*?'

'Leila, that's wonderful.'

'It's a start. But he's still got his eye on *The Times*, of course.'

'No, I meant about you getting married.'

'It is a bit of a turn-up, isn't it? And do you know, I've decided that on the big day I'm actually taking off the emerald green for once and I'm going to—'

The droning of a low-flying aeroplane drowned out the rest of Leila's words.

'Bloody row,' Ginny shouted, shielding her eyes against the sun, as she sought out the culprit. 'Who'd's he think ...' But then her tone changed from one of protest to one of amazement. 'Well, will you look at that?'

Ginny pointed at the clear blue summer sky, where the plane was now flying up and away in a wide swoop, high above their heads. Behind it snapped a long white banner, whipping and flapping in its trail. The inscription on it read: *You never had it so good, love Mac X.*

Ginny clapped her hands with delight. 'I reckon he's right there, you know, Leila.' She grinned, raising her teacup by way of a toast. 'We really haven't had it so good, have we? All our dreams really have come true.'

Leila looked at Ginny and was about to say something, but changed her mind. Instead, she too lifted her cup in salute and smiled. 'Let's hope so, sweetie, let's hope so ...'